KING'S WAR

THE KINSMAN CHRONICLES

King's Folly
Darkness Reigns: Part One
The Heir War: Part Two
The End of All Things: Part Three

King's Blood
Kingdom at Sea: Part Four
Maelstrom: Part Five
Voices of Blood: Part Six

King's War
The Reluctant King: Part Seven
A Deliverer Comes: Part Eight
Warriors of the Veil: Part Nine

KING'S WAR

JILL WILLIAMSON

BETHANYHOUSE
a division of Baker Publishing Group
Minneapolis, Minnesota

© 2018 by Jill Williamson

Published by Bethany House Publishers
11400 Hampshire Avenue South
Bloomington, Minnesota 55438
www.bethanyhouse.com

Bethany House Publishers is a division of
Baker Publishing Group, Grand Rapids, Michigan

Printed in the United States of America

ISBN 978-0-7642-1832-3 (trade paper)
ISBN 978-0-7642-3140-7 (cloth)

Library of Congress Control Number: 2017961590

This is a work of fiction. Names, characters, incidents, and dialogues are products of the author's imagination and are not to be construed as real. Any resemblance to actual events or persons, living or dead, is entirely coincidental.

Cover design by LOOK Design Studio

Author is represented by MacGregor Literary, Inc.

18   19   20   21   22   23   24   7   6   5   4   3   2   1

KEY PLAYERS

ARMANIA

House Hadar

Trevn-Rosâr Hadar, king of Armania
+ **Hawley**, Trevn's onesent
+ **Ottee**, Trevn's honor man
+ **Sir Cadoc Wyser**, Trevn's High Shield
+ **Rzasa**, Trevn's backman
+ **Nietz**, a guard
+ **Bonds**, a guard
+ **Jhorn**, Master of Requests
+ **Grayson**, a spy

Mielle-Rosârah, Trevn's wife
+ **Tonis**, Mielle's onesent
+ **Pia**, Mielle's High Shield
+ **Bero**, a guard
+ **Abree**, Mielle's honor maiden

Onika [ON-ik-ah], the True Prophet, a blind woman
+ **Kempe** [KEM-pay], Onika's personal maid
+ **Rustian**, Onika's dune cat

Zeroah Barta-Hadar, the dowager queen
+ **Doth**, Zeroah's guard
+ **Ephec**, Zeroah's guard

Brelenah-Rosârah, the dowager queen mother
+ **Hrettah-Sârah Hadar**, Trevn's half sister
+ **Rashah-Sârah Hadar**, Trevn's half sister
+ **Enetta**, Hrettah and Rashah's nurse

Inolah-Sârah Orsona-Hadar, Trevn's half sister, mother of Emperor Ulrik and Prince Ferro
+ **Princess Vallah Orsona**, Inolah's daughter, Emperor Ulrik's sister
+ **Princess Tinyah Orsona**, Inolah's daughter, Emperor Ulrik's sister
+ **Sir Doran**, Inolah's High Shield
+ **Kreah**, Tinyah's nursemaid

Other Armanians

Oli Agoros, Duke of Canden
+ **Kipp**, Oli's honor man

Danek Faluk, Duke of Highcliff
+ **Zura**, Danek's wife
  ○ **Hinckdan Faluk**, Earl of Dacre, a spy, a seer

Barek Hadar, Duke of Odarka
+ **Arzah**, Barek's wife
  ○ **Lady Brisa**, daughter of Barek and Arzah
  ○ **Lady Trista**, daughter of Barek and Arzah

Joret Vohan, Earl of Idez
+ **Cabena**, Joret's wife
  ○ **Sir Ransen**, son of Joret and Cabena
  ○ **Enko**, son of Joret and Cabena
  ○ **Madara**, daughter of Joret and Cabena
    ○ **Rennik**, son of Madara and Jarmyn Koll

Tace Edekk, Duke of Raine
+ **Gitla**, Tace's wife
  ○ **Lady Imara**, daughter of Tace and Gitla
    ○ **Lander Leevy**, husband of Lady Imara
+ **Captain Korvoh**, captain of Tace's private army
+ **Natod**, Tace's onesent

Gunrik Koll, Earl of Blackpool
+ **Sabin**, Gunrik's wife
  ○ **Sir Jarmyn**, son of Gunrik and Sabin
    ○ **Dendrelle**, Sir Jarmyn's wife, Tace and Gitla Edekk's daughter

Finbar Wallington, Duke of Everton, brother of Mahat, father of Finnel Wallington
+ **Gia**, Finbar's wife
  ○ **Hirth**, son of Finbar and Gia

Allain Ortropp, a nobleman

Rayim Veralla, captain of the King's Guard
+ **Sir Keshton**, Rayim's son, an officer in the army
+ **Zanre**, Rayim's son, swordplay drillmaster

Father Burl Mathal, medial priest of the Arman church

Admiral Aldair Livina, admiral of the king's fleet

Norgam Bussie, captain of the *Seffynaw*

Novan Heln, a guard

Irlond Hearn, sheriff

Collak Ensley, general of the Armanian army

Rowan Winstone, marshal in the Armanian army

The Omatta Clan

Rand, leader of the Omatta
Meelo, Rand's son

Zahara, Rand's daughter

BARTHIA

Barthel Rogedoth (also known as **Prince Mergest III**), self-titled king

+ **Timmons**, Barthel's onesent
+ **Dendron**, a great shadir, bonded to Barthel Rogedoth
  ∘ **Paliki**, a slight shadir in Dendron's swarm

Agmado Harton/Harton Sonber, Barthel's general, a mantic

+ **Yobatha**, a common shadir, bonded to Harton

Captain Orbay, captain of Barthel's guard

Laviel-Rosârah, former queen of Armania, Barthel's daughter

+ **Iamos**, a common shadir, bonded to Laviel

Sârah Jemesha, Trevn's aunt, Oli and Eudora's mother

+ **Zeteo Agoros**, Jemesha's husband, Oli and Eudora's father, former Armanian general
  ∘ **Sir Briden**, captain of Zeteo's army

+ **Eudora Agoros**, daughter of Jemesha and Zeteo, Oli's sister, Barthel's wife

+ **Daliza**, a slight shadir, bonded to Jemesha

Filkin Yohthehreth, Rôb prophet, a mantic

+ **Mikray,** a common shadir, bonded to Filkin

Zithel Lau, Rôb priest, a mantic

+ **Shama**, a slight shadir, bonded to Zithel

Zenobia, a mantic

+ **Kabada**, a common shadir, bonded to Zenobia

Mattenelle, called Nellie, a mantic

+ **Hwuum**, a slight shadir, bonded to Mattenelle

Lilou Caridod, a malleant

Mahat Wallington, a malleant, brother to Finbar Wallington

Burk, a soldier

SARIKAR

House Pitney

Princess Saria Pitney, daughter of the late King Loran

+ **Sir Menel**, Saria's guardsman
+ **Sir Oris**, Saria's guardsman

Princess Nolia, Saria's aunt, sister of the late King Loran

+ **Finnel Wallington**, Nolia's husband, son of Finbar and Gia Wallington
  ∘ **Sir Malder**, Finnel's High Shield

General Norcott, general of Sarikar

Wolbair, a prophet of Arman

RUREKAU

House Orsona

Emperor Ulrik Orsona, emperor of Rurekau

- **Sir Iamot**, Ulrik's High Shield
- **Taleeb**, Ulrik's onesent
+ **Jazlyn**, Ulrik's wife, empress of Rurekau, former High Queen of Tenma
  - **Qoatch** [KO-ach], Jazlyn's eunuch slav, a seer
  - **Niklee**, an acolyte
+ **Prince Jael (Adir)**, son of Ulrik and Jazlyn

+ **Princess Jahleeah (Noyah)**, daughter of Ulrik and Jazlyn
  - **Zinetha**, nursemaid to Ulrik and Jazlyn's children

Prince Ferro Orsona, Ulrik's younger brother

Thallah-Rosârah Orsona, former queen of Armania, Trevn's mother, Ulrik's great-aunt

General Balat, head of the Igote guard

Kakeeo, Rurekan sheriff

MAGOSIA

Ruling Clan

Charlon, Magosian Chieftess

+ **Shanek**, Charlon's son
+ **Rurek (Gozan)**, a great shadir, bonded to Charlon
  - **Masi**, a common shadir in Gozan's swarm
+ **Sir Kalenek Veroth**, protector of Shanek, number One of Charlon's Five Men
+ **Kateen**, First of Charlon's Five Maidens
+ **Astaa**, Second of Charlon's Five Maidens

+ **Roya**, Third of Charlon's Five Maidens
+ **Rone**, number Two of Charlon's Five Men
+ **Nuel**, number Three of Charlon's Five Men
+ **Vald**, number Four of Charlon's Five Men
+ **Gullik**, number Five of Charlon's Five Men

Amala, Kalenek's ward, Mielle's little sister

NATIVE CLANS

Ahj-Yeke Giants

Bolad mi Aru, headman of Ahj-Yeke

Uul-Yeke Giants

Ulagan, Bolad's nephew

Jiir-Yeke Giants

Abaqa mi Niseh, headman of Jiir-Yeke   **Duu Ovdog**, a kholoi priest

Puru

Muna, a matriarch   **Conaw**, Muna's grandson

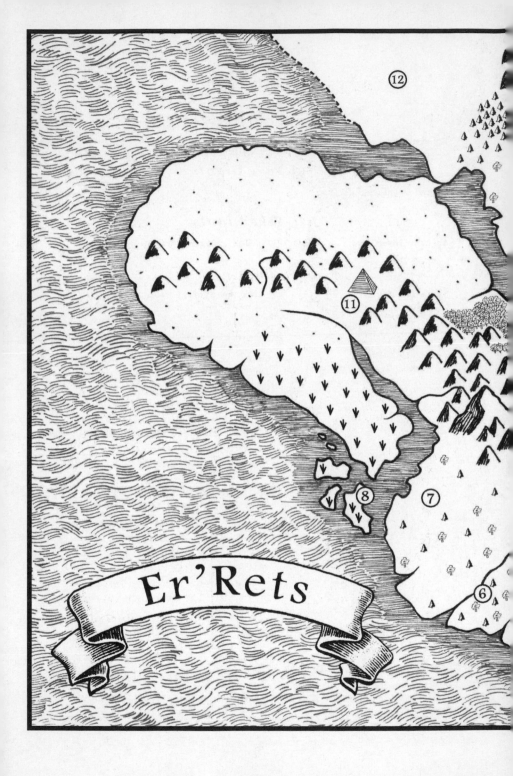

Er'Rets

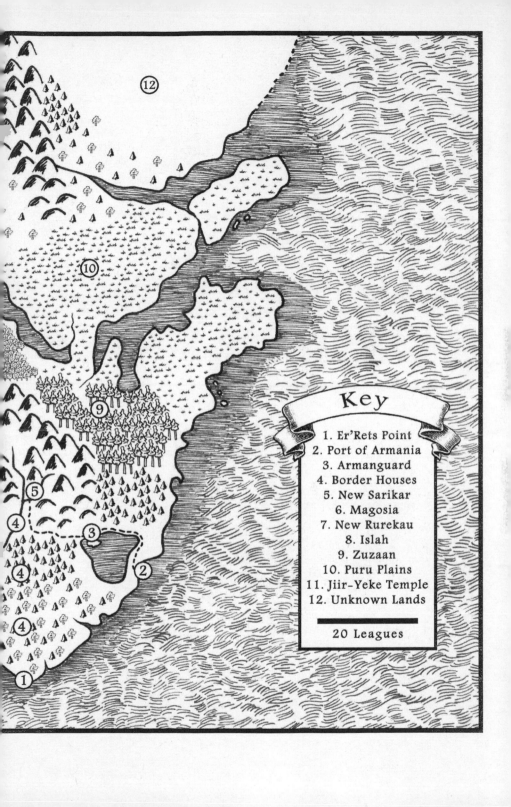

Key

1. Er'Rets Point
2. Port of Armania
3. Armanguard
4. Border Houses
5. New Sarikar
6. Magosia
7. New Rurekau
8. Islah
9. Zuzaan
10. Puru Plains
11. Jiir-Yeke Temple
12. Unknown Lands

20 Leagues

PART SEVEN

THE RELUCTANT KING

Trevn

The kings were dead.

The ambush, led by Fonu Edekk, had nearly destroyed the veteran armies of Armania and Sarikar and had taken out both kings, leaving Trevn to defend his people from the threat of takeover.

He had no idea how to do that.

As the *Seffynaw* anchored off the eastern coast of Er'Rets, he stood with Mielle at the starboard rail of the quarterdeck and observed the caravan that had assembled on the yellowed plains. It seemed like Barek Hadar had brought every wagon in Armanguard to safely transport Trevn and his party back to the castle stronghold.

"That's a lot of wagons," Mielle said, fingering the seashell on the cord around her neck. "I'm nervous."

Trevn felt it. The soul-binding allowed them to share each other's emotions, and right now Mielle's apprehension was distracting him from making plans. "Nervous about wagons?" he asked, taking hold of her chilled hand.

"About needing so many." She met his gaze. "You have always been a prince—been carted around in fancy carriages—but I know nothing about being a princess, let alone a queen."

Sweet Mouse. Trevn lifted their joined hands and kissed the back of hers. The trip south had given Trevn plenty of time to consider his new role in the realm of Armania. For years Wilek had trained for the position, while Trevn had been climbing buildings and drawing maps. Still, his life had given him plenty of perspective, while Mielle's sole experience had been her short stint as Zeroah's honor maiden.

She didn't want to fail him.

"Father Tomek used to say that leadership is about taking responsibility, not making excuses," he told her.

She frowned and looked back to the procession of wagons. "That sounds wise."

"He *was* wise," Trevn said, wishing he were here now. Wilek too. Though if Wilek were here, Trevn wouldn't be in this position. Wouldn't be king of Armania.

Cadoc approached and bowed to Trevn. "We're ready, Your Highness."

Trevn nodded and steered his wife toward the boat fall. The sounds of their footsteps on the wooden deck combined with those of his ever-growing retinue and became a jumbled sound with no rhythm. Some two dozen people were already waiting in the longboat. Nietz, Rzasa, and Bonds sat on the back bench, talking and laughing, with Maleen looking on. Cadoc's parents sat beside Kempe, who was speaking to Grayson and Ottee about the tides. Then came Princess Saria and her guards. The next bench had been left open for Trevn, Mielle, and Cadoc. Trevn helped Mielle in, and Cadoc's father rose to receive her. Trevn vaulted himself over the railing and settled beside Mielle. He grasped her hand and squeezed.

She was trembling.

"It will be all right," he voiced, sending all of his comfort with his thoughts.

She returned his warm feelings, but Trevn knew better. The magic of the soul-binding between them made it possible to trick each other, but Trevn's false comfort would not relieve Mielle's anxiety.

The sailors still on board started cranking the pulleys, and the longboat lowered into the water. Trevn took a deep breath of chilled air and exhaled slowly.

Why had this happened?

Such a question had no answer, he knew. One choice had led to another and another. Choices Trevn himself might have made had he been in Wilek's boots. After all they had been through—surviving the destruction of their homeland, the harrowing journey across the Northsea, and a myriad of attacks by traitors—it seemed a grossly unfair end to such a man as Wilek Hadar. Why had Arman let him die? Brave, intelligent, strong, and willing to fight for truth and goodness and righteousness, Trevn's brother had been the perfect man to rule Armania.

Trevn hadn't even been able to return in time for the burial—the first in more than two hundred years for the realm of Armania, which usually practiced shipping their dead. Trevn had given permission for rosârahs Zeroah and

Brelenah to take charge of the ceremony. The women had given his brother a traditional funeral of an Armanite believer and buried Wilek in a tomb they had commissioned beneath Castle Armanguard.

"I'm sorry, Trevn," Mielle voiced. *"I've pulled you in again, haven't I?"* She had, but he would not admit it. *"I am perfectly well."*

He shook his head clear and forced his thoughts back to his top concerns: determine the size of his army, build defensive outposts, and, once Hinck succeeded in his mission to sabotage Rogedoth's evenroot supply, plan an attack.

"I feel your mind spinning," Mielle voiced. *"Arman will guide us, as I'm sure you know. Plus, we're alive and healthy. We're safe. And the sun is out."*

He glanced her way and found her smiling. *"I couldn't do this without you."*

"Of course you could. Trevn, you can do anything you set your mind to. It's a little annoying, actually."

His heart swelled with affection, and he leaned in and kissed his wife.

She turned her head away. *"Trevn . . . people are watching."*

He sat back, discouraged that his new position would interfere with his relationship with Mielle. They'd been married less than a week when they'd been separated, and Trevn had spent the last year trying to get her back. In that time he'd been captured by giants, rescued Princess Saria, located the root child Grayson, and now Trevn was king. *"Get used to it, Mouse. From now on, people will always be watching."*

He was thankful for the soul-binding, which allowed Trevn and Mielle to speak to each other's minds when they were close, and the mind-speak magic, which enabled Trevn to initiate similar conversations over distances. It gave them a small amount of privacy they might not otherwise have.

The longboat slipped across the water to a low bank where several King's Guards helped Trevn and Mielle ashore. His own men—Cadoc, Maleen, Nietz, Bonds, and Rzasa—quickly replaced the King's Guards and ushered Trevn and Mielle up a steep hill. The grass had yellowed since Trevn had left. The seasons were changing. Winter would return soon.

At the top of the hill they backtracked until they reached the wagons. Grayson, Ottee, Saria and her guards, Kempe, Cadoc's parents, and the rest of Trevn's party followed behind.

Trevn approached the plain carriage in the center of the procession. It had been parked directly behind the fancy decoy with gold-leaf trim. The door to the plain carriage was already opened, and Barek Hadar, the Duke of Odarka, stood waiting.

The duke had a flat face and a receding hairline, though his gray hair had been worked into slender coils that hung thick to his shoulders. Relief washed over Trevn at the sight of a man he could trust to help him navigate all that he was about to encounter. Not only was Barek a longtime member of the Wisean Council, he had helped Trevn during the Five Woes and was Father Tomek's son. Trevn saw a hint of his old mentor in the man's eyes. See? Mielle had no cause to worry. All would be well.

The duke bowed. "Your Highness, welcome back."

It should be a welcome time of celebration, but the loss of Wilek and so many others overshadowed any achievements.

"Thank you for coming to meet us, Your Grace." Trevn helped Mielle into the carriage, then climbed in beside her. Cadoc entered last and sat opposite them.

Mielle's apprehension thrummed through Trevn. "What is it?" he asked.

"I feel strange being parted from Madames Wyser and Stockton."

The two women had been her companions for many months. "Did you see the number of guards here to escort us?" Trevn said. "They'll be all right."

"I'm simply used to traveling with them." Her eyes shifted to Barek Hadar, who settled onto the bench seat beside Cadoc, directly across from Mielle.

"We are ready to depart," the duke told a guard outside.

"Yes, lord." The guard shut the carriage door and walked away. "Move out!"

"No problems on the journey back?" the duke asked Trevn.

"None," Trevn said. The carriage jolted and began to roll over the uneven terrain.

"We need to increase your guard," the duke said. "No offense, Sir Cadoc, but one shield is not enough to protect a king."

"I agree, Your Grace," Cadoc said, "which is why we have already increased Sâr Trevn's security detail to four."

"He is *Rosâr Trevn* now," the duke said. "Even though he has not been crowned, the title is his. And surely you don't mean those grimy sailors? They are not even soldiers."

His tone not only stung, his words shocked Trevn. While he did not know Barek Hadar well, he hadn't expected him to be so pompous. "Those sailors fight as good as any soldier. I chose them myself and trust each with my life—better, with Mielle's life."

"If you say so," the duke said. "Make one of them your backman, then, and I'll see if I can find a few more. You should have a squadron of ten at all times."

Ten men following him everywhere. How had Wilek remained sane?

They were rumbling over the yellowed grass at a good clip now, but the ride to Castle Armanguard would still take about an hour.

"You must also have a onesent," Barek said. "Onesent to a king is a grand responsibility. Not just anyone can be trusted with so much power and sensitive information. I fear young Ottee is not up to the task."

That much was true. Ottee had already become frantic over the prospect. "The obvious choice is Master Schwyl, who served your father."

"No," Trevn said. "That man is as corrupt as my father had been. Still no sign of Dendrick?"

"Miss Onika believes he was killed when she was taken captive."

Immense sorrow rushed through the soul-binding. "How terrified she must be," Mielle said.

"Has she discovered her location or who is holding her captive?" Trevn asked.

"She has not, Your Highness. Both Empress Inolah and the Duke of Canden have been voicing with her, but they have been unable to discern her whereabouts."

Trevn's first thought was to send Grayson to find her, but if she was injured or being poorly treated, well . . . Grayson might look Trevn's age or older, but he was really only a boy. Trevn would have to consult Master Jhorn before sending his son on such a mission.

"Have they learned anything helpful?" Mielle asked.

"We do know that her captors speak Kinsman," Barek said. "It seems they were some of Randmuir Khal's pirates who joined up with Fonu Edekk before he left the giant village of Zuzaan."

"Is she certain they are loyal to Rogedoth?" Trevn asked. "Hinck has heard nothing about the prophetess being captured and doesn't believe Rogedoth knows."

"She overheard her captors talking about their plans to take her to King Barthel in exchange for favor or bounty."

"He's no king," Trevn snapped. The duke's use of the title gave the traitorous usurper respect he didn't deserve. "Might we pay the bounty instead?"

"Duke Canden believes the men are afraid to come to Armanguard after fighting against us in the Battle of Sarikar."

"They should be afraid," Trevn said. They were partly responsible for Wilek's death, and Trevn intended to see someone brought to Justness in that matter.

The carriage crested a hill and Lake Arman came into view. The worn trail stretched out before them, drawing a faint line through the landscape until it reached the lake. There it curved along the shore, working its way around the body of water. Large swaths of the land along the east coast of the lake had been cultivated. Dozens of Kinsman people, most dressed in black, dotted the fields, working the harvest. Too many had died in the battle that had claimed his brother. That these people who had endured so much could still get out of bed each day and carry on with life impressed Trevn. Armanians were survivors.

"There have been three claims to the throne of Armania besides your own," the duke said. "King Barthel, of course, and one from Emperor Ulrik submitted by Taleeb, his onesent, on behalf of the Rurekan council. They believe the succession should pass through Inolah as King Echad's firstborn."

"The Rurekan council has no say in Armanian matters," Trevn said, annoyed. "They know we've never followed the right of first blood. Besides, Wilek named me his Heir the day our father died. The matter is not open to contestation."

"Your mother fully supports you, of course," the duke said.

Trevn did not doubt that for a moment. It had been his mother's lifelong dream to see him crowned king of Armania.

"She has asked your permission to come to Armanguard."

Trevn's father had banished her from the realm due to her treasonous involvement with the Lahavôtesh cult. Trevn didn't think he could handle his new role if his mother was here, causing trouble. "Who is the third claimant to the throne?"

"It comes from Magosia. Ridiculous as it sounds, Chieftess Charlon claims to be warden over Sâr Janek's son. Says she can prove the child's heritage."

Already she was trying to use the babe? No wonder Wilek had been worried. "He is baseborn, but she is not lying about his heritage," Trevn said.

The duke's jaw twitched. "How is it you know this?"

Trevn ignored the man's offended tone. "The child cannot be much more than a year old. Does she really expect us to hand over our realm to a babe?"

"She claims he is a child of prophecy. Says he has magical powers that enabled him to grow faster than normal."

Trevn grimaced. "I suppose that's possible. He is special, in the same way Grayson, son of Jhorn, was born special. The gray speckled skin. A root child."

The duke sighed, leaned back against the carriage wall, and folded his arms. "Your Highness, you must not keep such things from me. If I am to advise you, I need all the facts."

Trevn stiffened at the duke's condescending tone. He had not expected the man would lecture him.

Mielle's love gusted over him so suddenly he turned to look at her.

"Just helping you keep your temper," she said, smiling.

He pulled her hand into his lap. "I did not ask for advice about Janek's son, Your Grace. Wilek swore me to secrecy in regard to the child, and I would ask the same from you until we know if this threat is real or not."

"You just confessed that the child has magic. Sounds like a real threat to me."

"We shall see," Trevn said.

The duke cleared his throat. "Well, the legitimate line of ascension is only five names long before it extends to distant Sarikarian cousins. It wouldn't take much effort to wipe out the entire Hadar line."

The carriage swept into a deep stand of trees, and Trevn glanced out the window at the naked branches, marveling how quickly the leaves had turned shades of orange, red, and yellow, then fallen to the ground. Soon it would snow again.

"Who is in the line of ascension?" Mielle asked.

"Oli and Hinck," Trevn said.

"Emperor Ulrik is technically first," the duke said, "then his son Adir and his brother Ferro. Then Oli Agoros and finally Hinckdan Faluk."

"Why do Rurekans rank above Armanians?" Mielle asked.

"Because they are Inolah's children," Trevn said, "and she was my father's firstborn. But as I've said, Armania does not follow the right of first blood, so none of that matters."

"It matters because you have yet to be crowned and to name your successor," the duke said. "Since you have no brothers or children, there is no obvious choice for your Heir. That has people digging deep into the line of succession for other options."

Mielle's annoyance flared. "Even though Rosâr Wilek named Trevn his Heir?"

"Transfer of power is always a tenuous time," the duke said.

If Trevn was going to keep trouble at bay, he would have to deal with this quickly. "Schedule my coronation ceremony as soon as you are able. Mielle will be crowned beside me—on that I will not negotiate. As to my Heir, I will write a directive bypassing my nephews and any children they have or might have."

"I am not so sure we should write out Emperor Ulrik altogether," the duke said. "He has experience ruling a nation."

"Very little," Trevn said. "And his values do not align with mine or Wilek's. After all you and your father did to get an Armanite on the throne, I'm surprised you would even consider a follower of Sheresh."

"I certainly don't want that at all," Barek said. "I do feel, however, that stability is the most important factor at present. Oli was raised much like Sâr Janek and was a member of the Lahavôtesh, so—"

"Which he betrayed to help Wilek," Trevn said.

"Still, his faith is questionable. And Hinckdan Faluk—"

"Converted when Arman saved his life," Trevn said.

"Yes, but many think him a traitor from his behavior aboard the *Seffynaw*. Besides, there is little hope of introducing a new faith to the general populace with King Barthel threatening to overthrow us."

"Barthel Rogedoth is *not* a king, Your Grace! You will stop calling him such." The duke blinked. "Forgive me, Your Highness. I meant no offense."

"As to the succession," Trevn said, pausing in an effort to calm himself, "that puts Oli and Hinck as First and Second Arm."

"Until you have an heir of your own." The duke looked out the window and swallowed. "May I suggest you work on that right away?"

Mielle squeezed Trevn's hand, and her amusement wound through him.

"You may *suggest* it. . . ." Trevn squeezed back. "So, Oli will become First Arm, but if Hinck is to act as Second Arm, he cannot remain a spy. He is currently looking for a way to sabotage Barthel Rogedoth's evenroot supply. Once he succeeds, we must find a way to bring him home." Trevn motioned to the duke's scroll, pleased how naturally the task of ruling was coming to him so far. "Write that down."

The duke sighed heavily and scratched his nub of charcoal over the parchment. "Very well, Your Highness. You must also make a new appointment to the Wisean Council."

To replace Rystan, who had died far too young. "Joret Vohan," Trevn said. "If he is willing." The other nobles all had ties to Rogedoth, but the Earl of Idez had always supported Wilek.

"Poor Zeroah," Mielle said. "She has lost everyone who mattered to her. How is she?"

"She has been in confinement," the duke said. "I hope seeing you both will cheer her."

The carriage passed out of the forested area and the castle came back into view, still several miles off and seeming to float on the surface of the lake like a ship. The fortress looked small from here, especially compared to what Castle Everton had been back in the Five Realms.

"Another thing, Your Highness. You must start holding court."

"No." Trevn felt strongly about this. "Wilek did not hold court, and I see no reason to do so either."

"There is a very good reason," Barek said. "The nobles feel unimportant."

"They are no better than any commoner, in my opinion," Trevn said.

"That is untrue, Your Highness. Nobles have more power than commoners—they can influence the people to serve you or not. You need their support—their soldiers, their laborers. The kingdom is confused and somewhat divided after Rosâr Wilek's short rule. He hadn't enough time to develop stability in the realm. Holding court is a quick way to let your nobility know they matter, and if they know they matter, they will extend that feeling to the people."

"I cannot stomach bootlicking," Trevn said. "And the people have always liked me."

"I could go in your place," Mielle said.

"No, Mouse," Trevn said. "I would not wish that upon my worst enemy."

"I agree it can be ridiculous nonsense," Mielle said, "but I *can* do it. Do you think it would help if I held court in Trevn's stead, Master Barek?"

"It's 'Your Grace' when speaking to a duke, Mielle," Trevn said. "A prime reason why you are not ready to hold court."

"The queen can be taught," Barek said. "She will need to learn such things, anyway. She could be a help to you, though some will not attend a court of the queen when it is the king's ear they want."

Trevn frowned at Mielle, not liking any of this. "If you took Zeroah or Inolah with you—at least at first . . ."

"If they are willing," Mielle said. "It might be too much for Zeroah, in her grieving."

"You ask Inolah and I will ask Zeroah," Trevn said. "If one of them will accompany you, I will permit it."

He felt annoyance simmer within Mielle, who looked out the window. Why would she be upset when he had given in?

"Are you angry?" he asked her.

"No."

"I can feel it, Mouse."

"If I am a Mouse, what are you? A cat?"

"What?"

She shot him a quick, glossy-eyed glare, then resumed looking out the window. *"Can I look forward to begging for your consent any time I want to do something?"*

Now Trevn's own annoyance mingled with Mielle's, quickly enhancing the emotion. "That's not fair," he said aloud.

Cadoc frowned at Trevn, looking puzzled.

"Beg your pardon, Your Highness?" Barek asked.

Trevn's cheeks heated. "Sorry."

"No need to apologize," Barek said. "If you are displeased, I would like to know why, so that—"

"I was voicing Mielle," Trevn said.

"Ah." Barek looked between them and fought a smile.

His reaction only fueled Trevn's displeasure. "Something amuse you, Your Grace?"

"No, Your Highness." He sobered and grew suddenly interested in his scroll again.

A sudden lightness flooded Trevn's heart, and a giggle pulled his attention to Mielle, who was holding her hand over her mouth, eyes still moist but now sparkling as they held his gaze.

He pulled her hand away and tucked it behind his back. *"Now you're laughing too?"* he voiced.

"I'm sorry," she said, leaning close. *"But he sure jumps to please you."*

"At least somebody does."

She elbowed him. *"Don't be a nuisance. I know you're simply trying to keep me safe."*

He kissed her cheek. *"So you forgive me?"*

"I will always forgive you." She pressed her mouth to his, her emotions quickly consuming him. He leaned into her, happy to indulge in a moment of reprieve.

A faint awkwardness pressed against Trevn's senses. Mielle pulled away, rested her head on his shoulder, and closed her eyes. Trevn sat back and realized that the source of the awkwardness was coming from Cadoc and Barek, who were each looking out the windows.

This amused Trevn, and he sat back and looked out his own window. They passed through grassy plains, hilly in parts, with sparse trees of average height—none so magnificent as the trees in the giants' forest. The procession passed by two settlements of the nomadic Puru people. They had followed the herd south for the summer and, if last year was any indication, would be starting north again soon.

"How safe is Armanguard?" Trevn asked. "I know we lost many in the battle. Are we vulnerable?"

"Castle Armanguard is currently well fortified," Barek said, "as is the surrounding settlement. Rosâr Wilek took only half his army so that we would be protected. With those who survived the Battle of Sarikar, we have just over twenty-four hundred soldiers. General Zeteo Agoros, as you know, has joined his wife in supporting Rogedoth, so you will need to appoint a new general. Under-General Collak Ensley has been temporarily filling the position, and I think he would make a fine—"

"Why not promote Captain Veralla to general?" Trevn asked.

"He has never served in the army, Your Highness, but in the Queen's Guard, and then unofficially as Rosâr Wilek's captain of the King's Guard after Captain Alpress's death. Under the circumstances, appointing him to any new position would be unwise."

"Has Captain Veralla's condition changed?" Trevn asked, alarmed. "I thought the physician released him."

"You misunderstand me, Your Highness. The captain is in fine health, but he is in the dungeon awaiting his trial for deficiency. Novan Heln faces the same charge."

This Trevn found absurd. "Since when is it a crime to lose a war?"

"It is a crime to fail to defend and protect the king. Both took oaths to do so, and both violated them when they allowed Rosâr Wilek to die."

"The council brought forth these charges?" Trevn asked.

"That was not necessary, Your Highness. It is tradition. They will hang, once you sign the order."

A pang struck Trevn's heart. "Absolutely not," he said. "They are well-trained, experienced men. We need them."

"You said you wanted Justness for your brother's death," Barek said.

"For those responsible for luring us into a trap. Barthel Rogedoth and whoever was working with Fonu Edekk. Not Wilek's closest friends."

"But they are failures," Barek said. "The other soldiers will not follow anyone so accursed."

"Superstitions are the makings of nonsense, Your Grace," Trevn said. "You have read the Book of Arman. I am surprised you would entertain such folly."

"The lesser penalty is to have their sword hand chopped off, but the king's death is worth more, don't you think?"

"I think you are not hearing me," Trevn said. "Wilek would be mortified to hear us contemplating the execution of his two closest companions for nothing more than obeying his orders. It will not be done, and that is final. I want both men released immediately."

Trevn felt Mielle's pride course through him. The duke, however, looked to be fighting an outburst.

"I am glad to see you found your confidence on the journey home," the duke said. "But I must caution you in making rash decisions without consulting your elders. Just because you are the king of Armania, don't think that means you can change decades of tradition to your liking. There will be consequences to every choice you make, so choose carefully."

Mielle's anger burned into Trevn, and he had to fight to keep himself from being swept along. His mind-speak magic enabled him to sense that the duke's words had been kindly meant, but they only increased the pressure looming over Trevn. He'd never considered that he and Barek Hadar would differ on so many issues, but the duke's little speech had reminded him that this man was not Father Tomek. Trevn couldn't rely on assumptions in regard to any man's character. He would need to quickly figure out dozens of agendas, because everyone would be watching him, criticizing his every move, waiting for him to make mistakes. He could not afford even one misstep. The wrong choice could ruin them all.

OLi

Oli knew without asking that the empress was on the roof. His voicing ability had developed into a sixth sense when it came to locating other gifted people. He only need let his mind quest, then seek out her uniqueness. It was difficult to explain how he did this since it happened rather instinctively. He followed the circling stairwell to the roof, and as he passed through the doorway, a gust of cool wind lifted away the stuffy castle air. Inolah stood at the parapet looking southeast.

"Anything yet?" he asked.

She glanced over her shoulder, then calmly resumed her original posture. "No."

"Why not voice Barek for an update?"

"Voicing is an amazing magic, Your Grace, but sometimes I simply want to use my eyes and ears and practice patience like a normal person."

Oli stopped beside her and set his hands on the stone crenellation. One hand of flesh and blood, another carved of wood, now scuffed and worn. He well understood the desire for normalcy and knew how little she liked this new magic. "That is why I came up here, rather than voice you."

"Is something wrong?"

"Again she did not come. I waited half an hour."

Inolah's shoulders curled inward and she sighed softly. "She is suffering. We all are."

Sorrow crawled up Oli's throat then, threatening to consume him. He forced it down. Rosârah Zeroah could hide away as long as she needed to, but he could not. There was far too much to be done at present. "What can I do if she won't come?"

"I'm sure you have other tasks, Your Grace," Inolah said. "Work with the boys?"

"Teaching her to shield was the last thing he asked of me."

"And you will do it, when she is ready."

"We are talking of Zeroah Barta-Hadar. She might never be ready."

"She might look frail, but she has bones of bronze. I promise she will surprise you."

Oli doubted that. He had known the newly widowed queen since she was a child. She had always been predictably Sarikarian—temperate and pious. She might have bones of bronze, but she had a disposition to match. She was not a woman to give way once her mind was set, and like Inolah, she disliked the voicing magic.

"I am far more concerned about my youngest brother," Inolah said. "I don't know Trevn at all. They say he is a troublemaker. That he plays more than he works. I did not see that in his behavior aboard the *Seffynaw*. He proved the opposite of every rumor. Still I wonder . . . can he handle this burden?"

Oli did not think so, but he would never speak such things aloud. "It is unfortunate he trained for the priesthood. We could use a military man at present."

She cocked an eyebrow his way. "Like you?"

Warmth spread through his chest. "That is not what I meant. I have no desire to rule."

"Neither does Trevn, I daresay. Barek is afraid someone will kill him and is determined to increase his guard. He says Rosâr Wilek should not have had only one guard with him when he died."

"Even with five dozen guardsmen, one cannot predict what will happen in the heat of battle. Rosâr Wilek made his choice to try to rescue Miss Onika. It was a noble and righteous decision, and I will not fault him for it."

Inolah looked back out over the lake. "A lot of good it did anyone."

"She is alive," Oli said. "That is something."

"They never planned to kill her," Inolah said. "Had Wilek let her be, he might be alive now."

It was true; he might. But Oli did not expect a woman to understand decisions made in the chaos of battle.

"Have you communicated with Miss Onika lately?" Inolah asked.

"Not since yesterday, but I can sense her awareness."

Inolah huffed. "I think you imagine that you can sense a person's awareness."

"I knew you were on the roof, didn't I?"

"You could have found me by making inquiries."

"I made no inquiries. I sensed your awareness, just as I sense hers."

"Where is she, then, Your Grace? Use your magic, if you can. Because if we
cannot find her, my brother died for nothing."

Oli closed his eyes and sought out the pale prophetess. His mind's eye traveled thorough the castle at breakneck speed, in and out of rooms and down
the spiral staircase, then suddenly jumped to a camp in a forested area. The
mismatched tents gave the appearance of a refugee camp, but the circular
formation suggested a military operation. Oli drew near one tent in particular.
It was smaller than many of the others and located on the outskirts of camp.

He passed through the green canvas of the tent and found himself looking
down on the interior from above. A woman lay on a pallet. She had pale skin
and nearly white hair. Miss Onika. She appeared to be sleeping.

"I see her," he said, keeping his eyes closed. "She is in a tent in a military
camp."

"She has told us that much," Inolah said.

Oli tried to back away and instantly found himself on the castle roof again.
He blew out a frustrated sigh and opened his eyes. "If I had better control
and could keep my mind from jumping, I might be able to trace my way to
the location of the—"

"There," Inolah said, pointing across the lake to the east. "Armania's new
king comes."

Oli followed her gaze to the procession, which, from this distance, looked
like a line of beetles. Uneasiness filled his stomach. If Trevn Hadar were able
to rule himself with some consistent level of decorum, Oli might have faith
in the young man commanding their realm, but the firebrand of Castle Everton had never been known for practicality or restraint. Still, Rosâr Wilek had
believed in his little brother enough to make him his Heir. That had to count
for something.

Didn't it?

Trevn

With the castle isolated on its island, nearly impregnable and accessible only by water, commoners could not congregate outside the castle gate as they had done in Everton. The bargemen were not permitted to take just anyone across. So the people gathered at the pier gates, even though their chances of seeing any royalty were usually quite slim.

Today was an exception, however, and when the procession stopped inside the gates and Trevn climbed out of the carriage, the crowd grew rowdy, yelling out his name.

"Rosâr Trevn will help us!"

"He's a good sort."

"The people's king, he'll be!"

Trevn reached out for them with his mind and sensed a hodgepodge of emotions, the strongest of which were eagerness, excitement, and overwhelming concern.

He helped Mielle down from the carriage. It seemed colder here, near the water, and he pulled her cloak closed in front. "I'm going to speak with the people," he said. "Would you like to come?"

"Absolutely," she said.

"Today might not be the best day," Barek said. "The crowds have been rude and uncivilized of late."

"Then I shall find out why," Trevn said, leading Mielle toward the gate. He had always been a favorite of the people for the very reason that he consistently made time to talk with them. After being gone so long, he would not pass them by without a word.

Cadoc whistled, and Nietz, Rzasa, and Bonds came running. The four men spaced themselves out around Trevn and Mielle and escorted them to the gate that separated the road from the pier.

As they neared, the crowd got even louder. Trevn tried to make out the words. *Hungry . . . Dead . . . Stolen . . .* Something about a tree . . . a missing child . . .

"Hush now!" Cadoc yelled, waving his hands. "His Highness wants to hear you, but you must speak in turn."

The crowd quieted, and one man's voice rose from the back. "Outlaws stole five of my sheep."

"Took eight from me!" yelled another.

"Stole laundry right off my lines."

"Emptied my cellar!"

A woman in front, hands clutching the bars, said, "My child was taken, but I think it was giants. Will you help me find him? He's just a boy."

"What is his name?" Trevn asked.

"Hedry. He is six years old."

"My Alpert was taken too!" a man yelled.

"We will look for your children," Trevn said. "Mielle, please learn their names, ages, and descriptions."

Mielle stepped close to the woman at the gate.

"We don't have enough food for winter," another man yelled. "Our lord takes our crops and leaves none for us who grew them."

"He means the Duke of Raine," another man said. "Conscripted my boys into his army."

"Took my son too!"

Tace Edekk, Fonu's father. "I will speak with him," Trevn said, not at all looking forward to it. "And I will not let anyone starve."

"How you going to feed us all?" A man's voice. "Food goes into Castle Armanguard, but it don't come out."

Trevn didn't have an answer. "You who work the fields, do you take no share for yourselves?"

"That's against the rules," a woman said. "Our lords pay us our share, but lately there hasn't been enough."

"Not enough to feed the workers?" Trevn couldn't believe it. "What lord do you serve?"

"Lord Blackpool."

"I will speak with the earl and find a solution," Trevn said.

"My sons were killed in Rosâr Wilek's war!" a man shouted.

"Mine too. Died on a fool's errand."

"Died for a trick."

"Died for nothing!"

Trevn choked up at the grief he felt in these voices. "Your men died for our freedom," he said. "As did Rosâr Wilek. They are all of them heroes."

This quieted the crowd.

"I will see to your concerns," Trevn said, then led Mielle away from the gate and onto the barge. They stopped at the rail beside Cadoc's parents. The bargemen pushed off the pier, and the craft began to carry them across the lake toward the castle.

Barek Hadar had seated himself beside Princess Saria on the bench that ran around the bow. Mielle released Trevn's arm and walked straight up to the duke.

"Why do you ignore them?" she asked, gesturing back to the people at the gate.

"Commoners always protest," Barek said. "It's been that way for decades."

Trevn followed his wife. "Who from the castle hears their complaints?" he asked.

"None that I'm aware of," Barek said. "Rosâr Wilek talked of reinstating the Rosâr's Bench but never had the time. Nor do you have time at present, Your Highness, so I suggest you put it out of your mind for now."

"I will do no such thing," Trevn said. "Make a list of worthy men I can consider for the title Master of Requests and submit it to me for approval. This person will take down each and every complaint the people have and give a daily report to me."

"To us," Mielle said, taking Trevn's arm. "I would very much like to help."

Trevn gave his wife a single nod of agreement. "There were several complaints about missing boys, and some accused the Duke of Raine of taking them for his army," he said. "Those are usually paid positions, are they not?"

"The duke pays his army, yes, and he cannot conscript underage boys without their parents' permission."

"Look into it," Trevn said. "The people also mentioned some outlaws."

"Food and animals have been stolen from several farms, but the sheriff believes the thieves are not outlaws but men sent by one of the lords to cause dissent against the throne."

As if the throne didn't have trouble enough. "Sent by Lord Edekk?" Trevn guessed.

"Could be."

Trevn felt overwhelmed and took a seat on the other side of Princess Saria. Mielle sat beside him and wrapped her arm around his waist, settling her head against his shoulder. Her warmth felt nice in the chilled air, but Trevn's thoughts were too scattered to relax. He had always been able to pick and choose which problems had interested him, but now every little thing would be laid at his feet. He wasn't sure how to manage it all.

"Trouble on your first day?" Saria asked.

"A king always has problems of some kind," Trevn said.

"You think *you* have problems?" she said. "I'm going to have to find myself a husband very quickly since you got yourself out of our betrothal."

Trevn felt Mielle stiffen beside him, and he sent joyous thoughts her way. He had continually made it clear that Saria Pitney was like a sister to him and their betrothal had been a sham Wilek had devised to appease King Loran.

"Will you stay here long?" Mielle asked.

"Just the night," Saria said. "I must return before my ragtag council gives rule of my realm to someone unworthy. Women can't rule in Sarikar, and since all the royal males were killed, they are quite desperate. But I can't let them give the throne to just any man, nor will I marry just any man."

"I could ask Hinck to marry you," Trevn said, winking.

Saria rolled her eyes. "Oh, do go on, Trevn. To have a husband who would put spiders in my bed, jelly in my soap dish, and call me Sorry Odd all day? I confess it has always been my dearest wish."

Trevn chuckled. "Yes, well, I do believe your Stink Man has given up *most* of his pranking ways."

"Did he ever tell you about our little romance?" Saria asked.

Trevn balked. "You and Hinck? When?"

"When you went to King Echad's wedding to Lady Ojeda. Kanzer invited him to Faynor to hunt."

Trevn couldn't believe it. "He never even hinted that something had happened."

Saria shrugged. "It wasn't anything worth telling, I suppose. The trip was short, and once we returned to Pixford, life went back to its routine and Hinck went back to teasing me. Rosârah Mielle, let me tell you about the time I entered my bedchamber to find three pigs running wild. They had numbers one, three, and four painted in charcoal on their sides. I spent three days looking for pig number two."

"Until I had mercy and told her Hinck had never brought in a second pig," Trevn said.

Mielle laughed, and Trevn and Saria joined in.

"That was my life with two spoiled boys growing up in my home," Saria said.

Trevn smiled at the fond memories, saddened at the knowledge that he would never visit Brixmead again, but as they neared the castle entrance, a nostalgic sense of home pleased him. That anything felt like home at this point in his life seemed hopeful. Trevn thought of the grieving commoners out working the fields. If they could endure in the wake of such loss and hardship, then he—despite the growing adversity surrounding him—must also find the courage to carry on.

They reached the pier on the other side and climbed out of the barge. As they walked under the castle gatehouse and through the outer bailey, Trevn noted the busyness of a castle preparing for winter. Several coopers were hard at work assembling barrels for storage. Carts of hay, fruit, nuts, wheat, and jugs of milk were being transported inside, either for storage in the cellar or to the kitchen for making cheese. A crowd around the butcher area was assisting with the slaughtering of livestock.

By the time they entered the inner bailey, a crowd had formed in two lines, parted by the guards leading the procession. Everyone was talking, and Trevn sensed frustration and annoyance above all other emotions. These soldiers were in the way of hardworking people with much to do. He again noted how many were dressed in black mourning clothes. Too many had died.

A child's voice cut through the din. "There he is! It's Sâr Trevn. And Miss Mielle too."

Trevn felt the crowd's mood shift into a barrage of conflicting emotions: relief, hope, frustration, though curiosity rose above all else as wandering stares sought him out.

Those who saw him surged forward, calling his name. The soldiers pushed back, fighting to maintain the path to the castle doors. Mielle clutched Trevn's arm and he pulled her through the narrow space, desiring only to get her safely inside before they both were trampled.

They passed through the arched doorway. Now inside the stone walls, the noise instantly dampened, but it was not much warmer. A reception awaited at the foot of the spiral staircase, the entire crowd dressed in blacks. Trevn first saw his sister Inolah standing with her daughter Vallah and holding baby Tinyah. Beside Vallah stood Jhorn—the double amputee who had raised Grayson—holding himself up on his canes, then Oli Agoros and Danek Faluk. To their left, Rosârah Brelenah and Trevn's younger sisters Hrettah and Rashah. Many other nobles and various servants were present as well.

The crowd bobbed unevenly as men bowed and women curtsied. No one rushed to embrace him. Even Rashah stood dutifully in place.

"Jhorn!" Grayson, who'd been traveling with the larger retinue this entire time, pushed past Trevn and ran to the legless man. He dropped to his knees and the two embraced.

Trevn, as the king of Armania, received no such greeting. He disliked the level of decorum everyone was exhibiting toward him, but protocol demanded a formal respect and honor toward the crown, and he might as well get used to it.

Oli Agoros stepped forward and bowed swiftly. "Welcome back to Castle Armanguard, Your Highness," he said.

Trevn took a deep breath. "Good midday, everyone. I am glad to be home."

Rosârah Brelenah emerged second and curtsied deeply before Trevn and Mielle. Inolah and Wilek's mother had always been a stunning woman, but grief seemed to have aged her, adding new creases on her forehead and around her eyes. "Your Highness, we were so pleased to hear that you found your bride safe and were able to bring her home," she said.

"As was I," Trevn replied.

"And Princess Saria too," she added. "Welcome to Armanguard, my dear. I am so sorry for your great losses."

Saria curtsied. "Thank you, rosârah."

Rosârah Brelenah stepped close to Trevn. "If it pleases you, sir," she said softly, "I offer you my onesent, Master Hawley. He has been with me since I came of age. He is very capable, wise, and above all, completely trustworthy."

A surge of relief ran through Trevn at one problem solved. Rosârah Brelenah was one of the few people he trusted without question, and he had always liked Master Hawley. Ottee would be grateful as well. The boy could continue on as Trevn's honor man without needing to worry about carrying the administrative burdens of an entire realm.

"Are you sure you can part with him, madam?" Trevn asked the former queen.

"I will miss his company dearly, but anything that will make your transition easier is far more important."

Trevn reached into her mind. *"No one is forcing you to give him up?"*

"Not at all. I want to help."

"Very well," Trevn said. "I thank you, rosârah. I know what a sacrifice this must be, for both of you. Please have Master Hawley report to my office directly after morning bells tomorrow. And, rosârah, I am deeply sorry for your loss."

"My son's death was a great loss for us all," Brelenah said.

A moment of silence stretched out, and Trevn found himself looking at the floor as he fought off yet another surge of sorrow.

"Where is Rosârah Zeroah?" Mielle asked.

"In her chambers," Brelenah said. "She is not feeling well this morning."

Mielle turned to Trevn. "I must go to Zeroah."

He nodded. "Cadoc, send Nietz and Rzasa with my wife. She is to be protected at all times. Kempe goes with her as well."

The arrangements were quickly made. As Mielle and her entourage ascended the stairs, Trevn reminded himself to appoint a separate guard for his wife. Perhaps Captain Veralla would have some ideas.

"Has Rosârah Zeroah been ill this whole time?" he asked, curious if the woman still suffered effects of the poison that had been inflicted upon her.

"I think it more grief than illness, sir," Rosârah Brelenah said. "However, I have not pressured her to join us, as the Duke of Canden is concerned she might be a window through which the enemy could spy, due to her inability to shield her mind. She is the only gifted person we know of who never learned."

Trevn met the duke's gaze. "Is this true?"

"She has refused to come to a single mind-speak lesson," Oli said, coming to stand beside Trevn. "Rosâr Wilek felt it imperative that she learn."

"I agree she must," Trevn said. "I will see that she complies as soon as possible, Your Grace. Perhaps Mielle can convince her."

"I hope that will help, Your Highness," Oli said.

"Are you hungry, sir?" Barek asked Trevn.

"Not really, but I would like to—"

"Trevn!" Hinck's voice burst into Trevn's mind. *"Rogedoth is about to set sail for the mainland on his quest to conquer the father realms."*

"Sir . . . ?" Barek asked.

"A moment, Your Grace," Trevn said. "The Earl of Dacre is voicing me with an urgent message." Trevn took a seat on a bench on the outer wall and leaned back against the cool stone.

"When does he leave, Hinck?"

"He plans to set sail in the morning. I've been eavesdropping on Lady Mattenelle, who is in a meeting with his acolytes now. He just announced his plans to ready all nine of his ships to depart tomorrow after breakfast."

"He has nine ships?" Trevn asked. *"And enough people to fill them?"*

"He has ten ships, actually, but one is beached for repairs and he is leaving it behind. Only two of his ships are even close to the size of the Seffynaw, *though. The others are much smaller. His compelled Puru army is over fifteen hundred strong, and he also has three hundred of his own men."*

"That is still fewer than we have," Trevn said.

"And you have some time to prepare," Hinck said. *"He is setting sail for the coast nearest Rurekau. He plans to go there first and work his way toward you."*

"I will let Ulrik . . ." Trevn sighed, remembering that both his Rurekan nephews were bedridden, having been poisoned. *"I will let my mother know at once. You were not summoned to this meeting?"*

"It's been weeks since I've been summoned even to breakfast," Hinck said.

"Confirmation that he suspects you still."

"Yes, but I'm not the only one. He told Rosârah Laviel she must rule the isle and care for Eudora while he is away. He is leaving some of the Puru behind to defend her, should she need aid. He promised to send for them once he has taken Armanguard. Rosârah Laviel is quite put out at being left behind."

Fear for Hinck overwhelmed Trevn. *"The mission to destroy Rogedoth's evenroot—it's too risky, Hinck. Especially now with Rogedoth leaving."*

"Too late, Your Indecisiveness. I've been at it for the past hour. My arms are cramped, my trousers soaked, but I've refilled nearly all his bottles with water."

Triumph at Hinck's cleverness overshadowed his worry for a moment. *"How many are left?"*

"Only eleven. I had hoped to be done by now, but there were more bottles than I had expected—thirty-six total."

So many. Hinck had just saved all their lives. *"Perhaps you should stop now,"* Trevn said. *"If Rogedoth is leaving, he will likely take his evenroot with him. Are you certain you're safe?"*

"Fairly," Hinck said. *"He is still in his meeting at the moment."*

"Fairly does not ensure strong enough odds for me, Hinck. You are the Second Arm of Armania now. I need you alive. In fact, I need you here."

"Second Arm, bah. I well remember how you behaved as Second Arm, and it was rarely to obey your father."

"Hinck—"

"Trev, please. Let me finish. Without his evenroot, he is only an old man."

A glorious notion. *"Only eleven bottles left?"*

"Nine now."

Praise Arman, this was magnificent news. *"What about dry root? And plants? Does he have any other stores?"*

"There is a large store of evenroot tubers in the village cellar, but it is all the new root from the field he harvested this summer. None of it is magical. He very well might have more powder or liquid kept elsewhere, but I have no idea how to find out. I only learned about these bottles because Nellie saw them on the . . ."

His friend's silence concerned him. *"Hinck?"*

"Someone's coming."

"Get out of there!"

"I can't!"

Trevn closed his eyes and looked out through Hinck's. A small, dark room came into focus. Waist-high racks filled with dark bottles lined the walls. Hinck was in the process of carrying a bucket of water behind the door. The dirt floor was soaked, pockmarked in places and filled with puddles of liquid.

The door swung in, and Hinck barely managed to slip behind it with his bucket. A woman entered, dressed in an elaborate green gown, her straight black hair unmistakable.

Rosârah Laviel.

"The meeting must have ended," Hinck voiced. *"I should have waited to tell you about Rogedoth so I could keep a closer watch on Nellie. Laviel will kill me. I know it."*

"Relax, Hinck. Remain still." Though Trevn's own anxiety for his friend was making him tremble.

Rosârah Laviel glanced at the floor, lifted her skirts off the wetness, then stepped carefully forward. Trevn could feel the fear buoy inside Hinck's chest as he leaned forward, eager to slip around the opened door and run to safety.

"Wait," Trevn voiced. *"Not yet."*

Rosârah Laviel picked up two bottles from the bottom row of one of the racks. Holding one in each hand, down at her side, she turned and jumped, eyes locked on Hinck, who was still holding an open bottle in his hand.

Rosârah Laviel lifted her chin. "I will not speak of this if you will not."

Hinck nodded once and slipped out the door, leaving his bucket behind. He strode down a short hallway and out into the light of day. He fell against the outer wall of the building and released a trembling breath. *"Sands! I thought I was dead!"*

"Don't just stand there," Trevn said. *"She might discover what you've done. Get yourself somewhere safe!"*

Hinck ran, and Trevn drew back into his own mind again. He opened his eyes and found Barek Hadar standing over his bench.

"Is everything all right, Your Highness?" he asked.

"I hope so," Trevn said. *"Hinck? Will the rosârah question you?"*

"If I had only been there to steal a bottle, perhaps not, but those bottles she took . . . They were filled with water, Trev. What will happen when she drinks some?"

"You'd better not be there to find out," Trevn said. *"I want you off that island. Today."*

Hinck

Hinck made it to the reed house he shared with Lady Mattenelle before he realized he was still clutching a bottle of root juice—one he had yet to empty. He'd so tightly fisted the cork in his hand, it had left a red indentation. He pushed the cork back into the bottle and stashed it in the bottom cabinet of his sideboard.

Then he fell onto his longchair to recover.

Sheer madness. Out of control, madness.

But Rogedoth was leaving the island, and Trevn had ordered Hinck back. Finally.

If only Hinck could manage to escape before Rogedoth discovered that someone had tampered with his evenroot. Surely once Laviel found out the root juice was only water, she would tell her father about seeing Hinck in the storeroom. He would have to go back and get rid of the water bucket he left there. Hinck had no idea how he could possibly get away to Armanguard, but the mere thought of going back to his old life filled him with such hope he could barely breathe.

The door opened and Hinck jumped to his feet, certain it was Laviel and a squadron of guards come to arrest him. When his gaze met that of Lady Mattenelle, he felt foolish. Her shadir, Hwuum, followed her inside.

"Oh, Lord Dacre," she said, weepily. "I have ill news." She ran to him and threw her arms around his neck.

Hinck instinctively caught hold of her. "What happened?"

"The king is leaving, after all this time." She sniffled. "He has ordered servants to pack all his belongings, even his throne. He does not plan to return."

Hinck tried to look surprised, as if he hadn't been eavesdropping on Nellie all morning. "We knew this was coming," he said, taking note that Hwuum had floated over to the darkest corner of the room. "Why are you sad? This is what we've been training for. Besides, I thought you hated the rain."

She fingered the laces on his shirt. "I hate the snow just as much, and that is what will be coming to the mainland soon enough. But that's not why I am sad. The king has ordered me to go along, and you . . . you are to remain behind."

"Oh. I see." Relief coursed through him. As long as Hinck got rid of that water bucket—unless Laviel took from that bottle of root juice today—Rogedoth would likely be at sea when he discovered Hinck's betrayal.

He might just live through this nightmare.

Lady Mattenelle pushed away from him. "I see you are pleased to finally be rid of me."

Her injured tone brought him to his senses. "Not you, Nellie. It is distance from Rogedoth that relieves me. Are you certain he will let me live?"

"Undoubtedly. He is leaving behind a garrison for Rosârah Laviel, and you are to continue training new archers."

Hinck poured on his best acting skills, doing his best to look shocked. "He is leaving his daughter behind?"

"She is to wait until the king marches on Armanguard, then she is to set sail with Eudora so that his queen will be present when the final battle ends."

Hinck still couldn't fathom why. "Rosârah Laviel is so powerful, though. Wouldn't she be an asset in battle?"

"Oh, she would, but I'm not certain he plans to fight anytime soon."

What? Hinck should have waited to voice Trevn. Clearly he'd missed something important. "I thought he was going to attack?"

"He is traveling to Rurekau first, but not to fight."

"Then why go?"

"He didn't say, but my guess is to try to make allies." She released him and sat down on the bed. "It is strange that he is leaving Laviel behind. I think the king is punishing her for some reason I cannot see."

Now, that could be. Laviel and Jemesha had been plotting against Rogedoth for quite some time. If Rogedoth had found out, Hinck was surprised the man was letting her live. Though he likely saw his daughter as his only heir, since Eudora had yet to produce a child.

"Well?" Nellie said. "Don't you have anything to say?"

Hinck opened his mouth and found he didn't.

"I'm leaving!" she cried. "Won't you miss me at all?"

"Of course I will," he said automatically, then realized that he meant it. "You are my only friend here. I'm sure I will go quite mad without you."

That brought forth a smile that faded as soon as it had appeared. "I am undone! First Oli abandons me. Then the Woes destroy our homes. Then Janek is killed. I am forced to leave Pia. Fonu and Kamran die too. And now I am to be parted from you, who holds my heart. The gods are unnecessarily cruel." She fell back on the bed, one arm draped over her brow. "Will I never be happy again?"

Hinck didn't know what to say. Though Nellie often drove him mad with her incessant drama and manipulation, he would miss her. She had taken care of him when he was injured and sick, stood by him when no one else would, kept secret his being a spy, and on top of that, pampered him as if he were a prince. But he hadn't time to indulge her hysterics, so he set out to do the one thing he knew she hated. Treat her like the helpless female everyone thought she was.

"You deserve every happiness, lady, and I shall pray for that very thing." He sat down beside her and pulled her up, tucking his arm around her. "Promise me you will take care during the battles and stay out of the path of arrows? I do hope the king will assign you a protector."

She threw off his arm. "I don't need a protector when I have Hwuum at my side."

Hinck glanced at the shadir, who was pretending to sleep in the corner. Hwuum was merely a slight, but he was clever and somewhat deranged at times. "Yes, but if Hwuum is powering a spell, he might not be able to see every arrow the enemy directs your way."

I see everything, fool human, the creature said.

Nellie's eyebrows sank and her lips twisted into a pout. "And I can shield myself well enough, lord. Surely you have not forgotten the maelstrom?"

"Yes, but that was only water. Arrows are another matter entirely. And if the king is going to Rurekau, he might face the Tennish priestess, who is a powerful sorceress. If her army doesn't harm you, her magic might."

He is a fool to doubt your strength, Hwuum said.

"You are, you know." She shoved Hinck and stood. "Fetch my trunk from under the bed. I need to pack my things."

Hinck got up and pulled out her trunk. He set it in the middle of the room, then made himself useful to Nellie, fetching whatever she indicated and folding it inside. As she prattled on about her former mantic exploits and Hinck packed, he thought over his own plight. He must find a way to Armanguard. Rogedoth was taking all but the beached ship, which would be abandoned with no one capable left behind to finish the work. There were plenty of native canoes with small sails and windward outrigging, but Hinck wasn't confident enough to manage one for any real distance. He needed an experienced sailor, but all of the natives had been compelled. They would not be able to join him, even if they wanted to.

The pale captain in the dungeon house came to mind. Nellie had told Hinck about the ship Randmuir Khal had pirated for Rogedoth. The king had tried to get the pale captain to lead them to his island home, but the maelstrom had kept them from it. Rogedoth had finally given up and followed the Armanians until he'd reached these islands off the western coast of what Rosâr Wilek had named Er'Rets.

Surely a ship captain might know how to fix the beached vessel, and if not, he likely knew how to sail a canoe. Hinck had no doubt the man would want to escape.

"Is the king taking the prisoners in the dungeon house with him?" Hinck asked as he wrestled a fat red gown into her trunk.

"I heard him specifically ask Rosârah Laviel to bring them directly to Armanguard," Nellie said.

Well now. Could this be Arman's blessing? Hinck would have to wait until the morning to obey Trevn's command to leave, but hopefully the pale ship captain would be just the man to help Hinck get home again.

The next morning Hinck stood on the shore, watching as Rogedoth boarded his ship. The tiny fleet was still being loaded. Hinck considered waiting until they had set sail—once Rogedoth departed, Hinck would have freedom to explore without consequence. But so eager was he to leave this place, he figured he might as well try to speak to the pale captain now.

Hinck had no plan, really. He made his way to the dungeon house, a windowless mud structure hidden in the spindly trees some twenty paces from Rogedoth's reed fortress. It was no bigger than a shed, really, and completely out of place in a village consisting entirely of airy reed dwellings.

A lone guard stood watch outside a narrow door. Hinck checked the Veil carefully, but saw no shadir at present. Their absence gave him the last boost of confidence he needed.

"Open this door," he said, trying to look authoritative.

Hinck had devised several excuses to give, should the guard question his motive to go inside, but to his delight, the guard obeyed and uttered a fast, "Yes, sir. Right away."

Hinck stepped inside and balked at the stench. The guard closed the door behind him, and the sudden darkness sent a jolt of panic through him. At first he thought there was no light at all inside, but after a few terrified heartbeats, he spotted a thin shaft at the top of each of the four walls that let in slivers of pale light. Though not nearly enough.

He pushed back against the door. "Hold this ajar," he told the guard. "I cannot see my own nose in here."

The guard complied. Hinck took a deep breath, then plunged back in.

Even with the open door it took a moment for his eyes to adjust. A short corridor ran straight ahead along the outer wall. Three adjacent walls divided the small room into four stall-like cells that each opened to the corridor. They had no doors. The first stall was empty. The second housed an old woman, who lay sleeping on the floor, her legs in irons attached to the wall behind her. The third stall was also empty, and the fourth held a pale man, who looked to be near the age of Hinck's father. He was sitting against the wall, resting his arms on his knees, and staring at several flies crawling about on the dirt floor between his feet. Irons were clapped around his ankles as well. He glanced at Hinck, then went back to staring at the flies.

"Do you speak Kinsman?" Hinck asked, keeping his voice low so the guard could not overhear.

The man did not move.

"I would like to help you. If you'll agree to help me." Hinck took notice of the man's extremely long fingernails. "There is a beached ship in need of repairs," he said. "Do you know about repairs?"

A fly took flight and circled the man. It stopped to take a short walk along his arm, then flew on.

"What is your name?" Could the man be deaf? "My name is Hinckdan."

"Danek's boy?"

Hinck jumped. That had been the woman's voice. He walked back to the second cell and found the old crone sitting up now, legs extended straight before her. The tattered dress she wore did little to cover them.

"You know my father?" Hinck asked.

"In a different life." Her voice was soft and low-pitched for a woman, somewhat nasal.

"Who are you?" Hinck asked.

"A slave who has been locked away for a very long time."

"How long?" Hinck asked.

The woman did not answer. The stretch of silence gave Hinck time to glance at the door. The guard had left and propped the door open with a rock. Panic gusted over Hinck at the thought of the man going to report him.

Hinck started for the exit, but the woman's answer stopped him.

"That depends. How old is Laviel Nafni?"

What a strange thing to say. Hinck took his best guess. "She is in her mid-forties, I think."

"What do you want with the pale man?"

Hinck was not about to let this woman change the subject. "Tell me who you are."

"You would not believe the slave. No one will."

Sands alive . . . "Tell me your name, woman!" Hinck snapped.

"Islah," she said. "The slave was once called Islah Pitney."

Hinck stared, dumbfounded by a name that had come from before his time. "You are Rogedoth's *wife*?"

"Mergest's *first* wife, for the slave heard the lord recently married another."

"But you are dead!"

She chuckled, a bitter and hopeless sound that made Hinck's skin crawl.

"But why would anyone—?"

"Lord Dacre."

The voice in his head belonged to Rosârah Laviel. She had never voiced him before, and that she happened to do so while Hinck stood talking with her supposedly dead mother struck him with terror. He'd been caught. He should have waited until Rogedoth had sailed away.

"Yes, lady?" he answered, wincing.

"Come to the throne house immediately."

Five Woes . . . Just when he was about to finally escape . . . *"Yes, lady."*

The connection vanished. Hinck blinked and refocused on the dungeon, his mind flashing memories of the horrors Laviel had inflicted upon himself and others.

"You have a shadir with you?" Islah was staring at him with narrowed eyes.

"No." But the fact that she had asked such a question made him wonder if she was a mantic like her husband. "Rosârah Laviel, your daughter, has summoned me. I must go, madam."

She rose onto her knees. "It's because he is a ship captain, isn't it? That's why you want to speak with Bahlay. If you're planning an escape, the slave wants to go with you."

Bahlay? "You know the pale's name?"

"If you want him to talk, you will need the slave's help," the woman said.

Hinck sighed, conflicted. "I will think about it," he said, walking toward the opened door. No matter what, he could not keep Rosârah Laviel waiting.

Hinck entered the throne house with much trepidation. Ever since he'd watched Rosârah Laviel kill Sir Jayron and survived her ripping at his own face, he found it difficult to stand confident in her presence. He imagined the worst possible scenario for her summons: She'd caught him in Rogedoth's storeroom. She must have seen the bucket before he'd managed to clean it up or discovered the two bottles she'd taken were filled with water. Or perhaps she knew he'd been in the dungeon house, talking to her not-at-all-dead mother. Whichever it was, surely she would kill him this time.

He approached the throne and bowed low, giving her all the deference he could muster.

"How do you fare this day, lord?" she asked.

The friendly greeting lessened his fears, but only a bit. He rose and noticed there was only one shadir in the room. Iamos, who had taken the form of an elderly healing woman.

"I am well, my queen," Hinck said.

"You must be heartbroken over the impending departure of your beloved lady," Laviel said.

Oh, she meant Nellie. "I am trying not to think about it at the moment," he said, feigning the look of a tragically wounded man. "I am confident our king will find swift victory. Then we shall all travel to Armanguard, and Nellie and I will be reunited."

Laviel raised one of her thin eyebrows. "Is that what you think is going to happen?"

Woes! These people drove him mad with their subterfuge. "Is it not?"

"I applaud your loyalty to my father, Lord Dacre, but I must be bluntly honest. He still does not trust you."

"But I nearly died for him."

"Do not take offense. He does not trust me either, which is why he is leaving me behind." She smiled, but there was no joy in the expression. "I was impressed by how far you were willing to go to prove yourself faithful. Drinking that entire bottle of root juice . . . it was obedient, brave, and utterly beautiful. I was wrong to suspect you—to accuse you. And since that moment I have ever been looking for a way to make up for the part I played in the situation."

This felt wrong—all of it. Rosârah Laviel had never apologized to anyone, had she? "That is not necessary, Your Highness," Hinck said. "We survived a harrowing ordeal in our exodus across the sea. It is understandable that there would be confusion in the wake of such a calamity."

She smiled again, but this time it looked sincere. "I so admire how you extend grace even to those who have affronted you. I think you would make a fair king, Lord Dacre."

Hinck's cheeks tingled, and he scrambled to try to guess what she might be up to.

"My father is a fool," Laviel went on. "He has wasted my entire life for his ambition—my son died for it! And now he plans to wander over to Rurekau to waste more time building unnecessary alliances. Well, I have had my fill of his method of taking over a nation. And I intend to act. Will you help me?"

Help her do what? "Forgive me, Your Highness. I guess I don't understand what you want of me."

"I am rambling a bit, aren't I? And putting you in a tough spot. I apologize. Let me ask you this: Do you still admire Lady Eudora?"

Hinck tensed even more at that name. "The queen is a remarkable woman."

"She tells me you loved her once."

Heat flared up Hinck's neck, and he tried to guess what the rosârah might be getting at. "I did love the lady when I was younger."

"Ah, first love." She sighed and traced her index finger over the arm of her chair. "It never really fades, do you know that?"

Hinck begged to differ. He felt nothing but disgust and shame and sadness when he thought of Eudora Agoros.

"You and Lady Eudora will marry," Laviel said.

Marry? "But the lady is already married, Your Highness, and polyandry is against the law."

She waved her hand at Hinck. "Once she is widowed, of course. I have no doubt my father will die. Or perhaps I could find a priest willing to annul their union. She was forced into it, you know."

Hinck did not know and could not fathom how he had gotten into this position.

"There is time to decide how we will work it all out," Laviel said. "If my father behaves as I know he will, he won't attack Armanguard for months yet. He fears failing. I intend to arrive first. If the realm were not so backward, Eudora might claim the throne as queen on her own, but since women cannot inherit in the father realms, it would be easier if she had a husband who was legally in the line of succession. Like you. The two of you would make a strong blood claim to the throne, and yours would be a welcome face in the wake of Rosâr Trevn's death."

Heat flashed over Hinck. "Trevn is dead?"

She shrugged. "Not yet. My father intends to kill him at some point, though if I attack first, I will be forced to do the same. Deposing him is too light an act for one as strong-willed as Trevn Hadar, I'm sure you know."

"Yes, of course."

"If we can take Armanguard and set you and Eudora on the throne, we will hold the advantage when my father finally arrives. Then I will kill him and we will all finally be free of his endless manipulations."

What could he say in reply to such insanity? "I do not think the people of Armanguard would accept me as their king," Hinck said. "I am a traitor to House Hadar. Dozens of people saw me hold Rosârah Zeroah captive aboard the *Seffynaw*."

Laviel waved her hand. "Most of those people were killed in the Battle of Sarikar. It will not be difficult to persuade support, especially when the commoners see how handsome a couple you and Lady Eudora make—much better than that commoner drick Trevn calls a wife. My father spent years compelling loyalty for Rosâr Echad. I and my shadir can do the same for you."

Hinck could hardly believe the woman was serious. "What does Queen Eudora say? And her parents?"

"Father is leaving us all behind, you know, and in doing so, he has set in motion his own demise. Sârah Jemesha and General Agoros side with me, of course, and have for some time. In the beginning, my father promised them that Lady Eudora would marry Janek and they would rule Armania. Taking Eudora for himself was a grievous insult to the entire Agoros family. Not to mention naming that boy Harton his general when he'd promised General Agoros the position." She sighed and folded her hands on her lap. "So? What say you, Lord Dacre? Will you join us?"

Hinck held her gaze but desperately wanted to look elsewhere. He had no way of knowing if she were only testing him, nor could he know how she would react to any answer he might give.

She frowned, slowly. "I see I have astonished you. Forgive me, lord. Go and take some time to get used to my plan. And do not alert my father of our conversation, or I will be forced to tell him this was your idea and kill you."

And there was the ruthless woman Hinck knew. "Thank you for your offer, Your Highness," he said carefully. "You have given me much to think about." He bowed low and departed, shields strong around his mind, yet still feeling as though she was inside his head this moment, learning everything he'd been fighting to keep secret for so long.

When he finally passed outside, he relaxed slightly, thankful to be out of her presence. Just when he thought he might finally escape this place. The woman fully intended to kill her own father. She was mad.

Did she know her mother still lived?

Hinck went straight to his house, consoled by the fact that Rogedoth's ships would soon set sail. Once he was inside with the door secure, he lay down on the bed and voiced the day's happenings to Trevn. First he told him all about Lady Islah Pitney being alive, then about Laviel's scheme to put him on the throne of Armania.

"But this is wonderful news," Trevn said.

"I beg your pardon, Your Psychoticness. How is any of this wonderful?"

"They are divided against each other. If Laviel, Jemesha, and Eudora will not fight alongside Rogedoth, who will? How many mantics does he have?"

Hinck did a quick count. *"Yohthehreth, Lau, Zenobia, Nellie, Harton, and himself. Six total. Plus several malleants, Lilou Caridod among them."*

"And what of General Agoros? And you mentioned Mahat Wallington is with Rogedoth's group as well."

"Yes, both will remain here, but they are only malleants."

"We must pray that Rogedoth will deplete his evenroot long before he reaches Armanguard. As for Laviel's plan, take time before answering, and once you do, stall the wedding as long as possible. Fight against an annulment."

Hinck pounded his fist against his leg. *"You don't actually mean for me to go along with this? Are you insane?"*

"I don't see any way out of it. Furthermore, I think it would be of great value to our cause."

"But—"

"This is your plan, Hinck."

"What do you mean?"

"It's your childhood wish granted at last."

"That's not funny, Trevn. That wish died when Eudora used me as a fool, and it died a second death when I began eavesdropping on her mind. She is not a nice person."

"I'm only teasing," Trevn said. "Tell Lady Islah you will bring her along when you escape, and she will help you secure the help of Bahlay Nesos in finding some way off the island. I would love to talk with her. Until then, do what you can to stall, but do not forget that Eudora is already married. If they do force you to wed, unless Rogedoth is dead, she would be breaking the law, not you, and I will annul such a union without question."

That appeased Hinck a little and he rubbed his face, still overwhelmed by the situation. "Laviel plans to kill you, Trev. What if she succeeds? You can't stand against her magic."

"Use those superb playacting skills of yours, Hinck. Urge Laviel to use magic as much as possible so that when she reaches Armanguard, she will have little left."

"So that she discovers her two spare bottles of root juice are nothing but water and decides to take out her wrath on me? That's not much of a plan."

"When you speak with Lady Islah, question her about Rogedoth's intentions. If you can learn something more . . . if she knows what his plans are . . . if she'll confide in you . . . if she's against him . . ."

"That's far more ifs than I like in my strategies, Trev."

"There is no cause for panic yet. Give me some time to figure out an alternative. I promise I shall try."

"Try quickly. Laviel could compel me to marry Eudora today!"

"If you get desperate, tell her you discovered Bahlay Nesos in the dungeon and offer to take charge of overseeing repairs on the beached ship. That should keep you too busy to bother with a wedding. And be sure to take a good long time to repair that ship. While all that is going on, talk with Lady Islah and find out what she knows about Rogedoth's plans. Can you do this, Hinck?"

"Do I have a choice?"

"You always have a choice. Sometimes it's just a difficult one."

Hinck sighed, weary. *"I will do as you propose."*

"Thank you, Hinck. Oh, and speaking of proposals, enjoy your marriage while it lasts."

Trevn ended the conversation before Hinck could reply. Hinck growled and threw a pillow across the room, sulking at his circumstances. He found consolation in one thing: It would not be long now. No matter what, he would soon be going home.

GRAYSON

B ut why can't I go too?" Grayson asked Jhorn.

Danno had just left for the practice field, to join the other young men training as soldiers and backmen, but Jhorn had made Grayson stay behind in the chambers the three of them shared in Castle Armanguard.

"The king needs you close," Jhorn said.

"He can voice me anytime, and I can pop to him in an instant. I want to practice swords."

"You are not learning to fight, Grayson. Not today, at least."

"You don't want me to. Even after the pirates made me practice, you're still trying to protect me."

"This is not about you, Grayson. Danno needs a path for his life. It cannot be the same as yours. I must go or I will be late to hear the people's requests."

Master of Requests. That was all Jhorn cared about now that the king had given him the position. Grayson wanted to do important things too. "I could come and help."

"I need no help to listen to people's woes." Jhorn picked up his walking sticks and vaulted himself toward the door. "But when I return, I want to talk with you about something important."

That sounded hopeful, at least. "What am I to do until you get back?"

"Practice making light."

The request made Grayson squirm. Making light with his hands was part of his magic. Jhorn said it was important that he practice all of his abilities, but Grayson didn't like the light. Didn't trust it.

"If you will not, there are plenty of other things you can do," Jhorn said.

"Relax. Sleep. Eat your fill in the great hall. Go outdoors while it is still sunny. These are all glorious blessings. Enjoy them while you can. Trouble will come soon enough."

"Can I go visit Onika, at least?" Grayson hadn't seen her since the thieves had rowed him away in the stolen dinghy in Everton Harbor. She wouldn't recognize him now.

Jhorn grimaced. "That's part of what I want to discuss with you later. Promise me you'll wait to visit Onika until after we talk?"

Grayson sighed and nodded. He was nervous about seeing Onika, anyway. So much had changed since he had been separated from her. Like Jhorn, she now had an official position for House Hadar, while everyone was still treating Grayson like a child.

Jhorn left. Grayson did go to the great hall to eat, and after that he popped up to the roof and walked along the parapet edge. There were some shadir there, floating in a group. He ignored them. He soon grew bored and popped down to one of the barges that was bringing across a load of chickens. His sudden arrival spooked the birds and made the bargemen yell. He popped back to his chambers, worried that the bargemen had recognized him and would complain, but it wasn't long before boredom took him down to the practice field to see what Danno might be doing.

Over the past few months, Grayson had greatly improved his popping skills. He now could pop to people he knew as well as places. The king had been particularly excited about this.

Grayson exited in the Veil, where he would be hidden, and watched from a distance as Danno practiced with the other soldiers—boys, really, aged between ten and fourteen. They were lined up, all moving together, doing the same drill. They each held a wooden sword, which they lifted out in front, held it as the drillmaster counted to three, then moved it above their heads and held it again.

There were far more shadir down here—must have been thirty-some. They liked pain, and some of the boys were getting struck with the wasters. Three ugly slights instantly drifted toward Grayson, but he ignored them.

"Your sword is crooked," he voiced to Danno.

Danno's arm wavered, straightening his blade. *"It's not as easy as it might look."*

"I *could do it,*" Grayson said.

"Maybe. But you would get in trouble because you would never be able to follow instructions for so many hours at a time."

He had a point. *"How does holding a sword in the air help you know how to use it?"*

"Master Zanre says it strengthens our arms and our ability to direct the sword where we want it to go."

Grayson grunted, not wanting to admit his interest. He popped closer to inspect this Master Zanre. He was a very tall man with thick muscles, thicker eyebrows, and a flat nose. The sides of his head just above his ears were shaved, and what remained of his hair was very long and braided into dozens of ropes that were bound in three places down his back.

Grayson continued to watch Danno and voice unsolicited advice, which his friend did not always appreciate. Even this eventually grew tiring, so he popped to the great hall, where Empress Inolah and the Duke of Canden taught school when meals weren't being served. There were no shadir here, which pleased Grayson.

Last night at dinner, the young princesses Rashah and Vallah and their friend Lady Trista had befriended Grayson, impressed by his ability to pop around. He had enjoyed entertaining them and was delighted when he learned they could use the mind-speak magic.

Knowing Empress Inolah would not welcome his intrusion in her class, he exited in the Veil and moved to stand over Princess Rashah's shoulder. She was working mathematic sums. She was seven years old and a giggler.

"Four and four makes nine," Grayson voiced, hoping to make her laugh.

She gasped and spun around, her wild curls bouncing, *"Where are you?"*

He popped to the front of the class, right behind where Empress Inolah was helping Lotte, one of the orphan girls. *"I'm up front."*

As soon as Rashah faced forward, Grayson pushed out of the Veil, so she could see him, then went right back in, invisible again.

Rashah giggled.

A knock came to Grayson. *"Vallah Orsona."*

Grayson lowered his shields. *"Yes?"*

"You're going to get us in trouble." Vallah was only eight but acted like an adult.

Grayson popped to Vallah's side and darted in and out of the Veil long enough to knock the stylus out of her hand.

"Oh!" she said.

Empress Inolah straightened, her eyes fixed on her daughter. "Is there a problem?"

"I dropped my stylus."

"Then pick it up and get back to sums."

"Yes, Mother." Vallah bent down and reached for her stylus, but Grayson popped into the physical realm long enough to swat it under the desk.

Vallah's groan of frustration was drowned out by another knock. *"Trista Hadar."*

Grayson opened his mind to Trista and popped over beside her, staying hidden in the Veil. At twelve, Trista was closest to Grayson's true age. *"You finished all your sums, I see,"* he said, studying her tablet.

"Guess what I'm thinking?" And she raised her shields so quickly, Grayson had no time to listen.

He tried to push inside her mind, but Trista was very good at shields. He made an absurd guess, hoping to vex her. *"You wish you were seated beside Porvil?"* Grayson looked over at the orphaned boy who had a tendency to follow Lady Trista everywhere. He was fourteen years old and almost as tall as Grayson.

Trista's mouth gaped in shock. *"Never! Porvil is a bully. No, I wish Danno were here, suffering with the rest of us. Go tell him I miss him."*

Grayson didn't like that Lady Trista was so obsessed with Danno after only briefly meeting him last night. *"Tell him yourself."*

"I don't want him to know I miss him," Trista said. *"I want you to tell him so he'll think about me and wonder if it's true."*

Grayson didn't understand girls. *"I'll tell him that's what you told me to say."*

A third knock came then—*"Inolah Orsona-Hadar"*—and Grayson knew he'd been caught.

The empress was scowling, arms crossed. Princess Vallah stood beside her, mimicking her mother.

"Vallah," Trista voiced to Grayson. *"Such a babbling mouth."*

Grayson popped back to the practice field before answering that last knock. *"Yes, Empress?"*

"Are you in my classroom?"

"No, I'm down at the practice field watching Danno learn to fight. He's using a wooden sword as long as his leg. Do you need me?"

"I need you to stay out of this classroom while my students are working."

"I can do that, Empress."

"I certainly hope so." And she ended the conversation.

Grayson sighed and looked for Danno. The young soldiers-in-training had been divided into several groups. Some were doing drills, some sparring, while others waited their turn. Some were running with their wooden sword and shield out and ready. Grayson didn't see Danno anywhere and decided to scare him. Instead of voicing to see where he was, he concentrated on his friend and popped to his location in the physical realm.

And got hit in the arm by a wooden sword.

Grayson cried out, stumbled back a few steps, and tripped over a discarded shield. He fell onto his backside in the dry dirt, sending up a cloud of dust.

"Halt!" The tall drillmaster loomed over Grayson. "Who are you and what are you doing on my practice field?"

Embarrassed, Grayson shifted into the Veil where no one could see him, though he was still sitting on the ground. He rubbed his arm and glared up at Danno, who had apparently been sparring against his instructor. An orange shadir flew around Grayson, cackling.

"Who was that and where did he go?" the drillmaster asked.

"He is Grayson, son of Jhorn, sir," Danno said. "He has special abilities that allow him to become invisible."

"Why did you tell him that?" Grayson voiced his friend as two more shadir arrived.

"You expect me to lie for you?" Danno asked. *"Master Zanre is my superior, and I'm not going to let you get me in trouble. I am learning to be a soldier, and you don't belong down here."*

Angry, Grayson popped back to his room in the castle. Jhorn had still not returned, so he fell onto his bed, annoyed. He'd thought his days of being seen as just a troublesome child were over. He'd been the god-man for the giants and the Deliverer for the Puru people. Important. Now he was back to being a pest. At least no shadir had followed him.

Wanting to feel better about himself, he popped to where Conaw was—into the Veil this time, not wanting to live through anything so embarrassing as jumping into the middle of a sparring match. A visit to his friend's camp would surely make him feel better.

When Grayson returned to his chambers in Armanguard, Jhorn was waiting.

"Where have you been?" Jhorn asked. "You smell like a campfire."

"I went to visit Conaw."

"After you caused trouble in Empress Inolah's school and on the practice field?" Jhorn fixed Grayson with a disappointed look. "The king wants you in that very school tomorrow as a student."

"School!" Grayson cried. "I'm to study sums?"

"You are to study whatever the duke and empress deem fitting. If you are not on a special assignment, you are to be in the school."

"But I . . ." Grayson felt miserable to have to say it. "I don't look like a child."

"Yet you still behave like one," Jhorn said. "Sit down." He removed the red cushion he wore on his back, dropped it on the floor beside Grayson's bed, and settled on top of it. "It's time I tell you about your mother and how you came to be born."

Grayson's stomach flipped in anticipation. Months ago, Trevn had implied that Grayson had royal blood in his veins since only royalty had the ability to mind-speak. Now he would find out whether or not that was true.

"How much do you know about Barthel Rogedoth's past?" Jhorn asked.

"He is a banished Sarikarian prince and the father of Queen Laviel," Grayson said, wondering with trepidation if the evil queen might be his mother. "King Trevn told me how Master Rogedoth gave away his daughters to be raised by a noble family because he hoped one of them might marry the king. And one did, but probably only because she had magic to help her."

"Well, this story is about Rosârah Laviel's younger sister, Darlis. Twelve years ago, when Barthel Rogedoth was high priest of the Rôb church, Darlis Nafni was a noblewoman, unmarried despite two engagements that had both ended with her fiancés' deaths. Her elder sister Laviel was the second wife of King Echad and had borne him two children. Morek had been lost in Rosâr Echad's Great Sacrifice, but Sâr Janek was a beloved prince. I was a soldier, twenty-eight years old, who had conveniently managed to avoid the war by being in the employ of Barthel Rogedoth, the high priest. I served as one of his many guards, and he often sent us to Nafni House.

"Darlis was a spoiled, reckless woman. She was jealous of her sister's position as queen. There were no Armanian princes available for Darlis to marry, and the Nafni family, while noble and well connected, had too distant a royal heritage to draw interest from foreign princes. Besides that, Darlis was not a tempting woman. Don't mistake me, she was lovely to look upon, but she had an unstable mind and was known to abuse her servants and discharge them without notice."

Jhorn was talking about the woman in the past. "Is she dead?"

"Yes, she is," Jhorn said.

The hope in Grayson's heart shriveled. "Was she my mother?"

"Yes. She died bringing you into the world."

He shivered. "Because I'm a root child."

"Yes."

Tears flooded Grayson's eyes. He had killed his own mother. Ever since Trevn had said that Grayson likely had royal blood, he'd hoped his mother might somehow still be alive. It had been silly to hope, but the truth felt like a big rock crushing his chest.

"I know you, boy, so don't go blaming yourself," Jhorn said, patting Grayson's knee. "This wasn't your fault, and you'll hear my full story before you go casting blame in the wrong places."

Grayson sniffled. "Yes, sir."

"Now, Father Rogedoth, as he was called back then, used to send us guards to Nafni House when there was trouble between Darlis and one of her guests or servants. On one such occasion, we arrived to find her in a fight with Finbar Wallington, Ander Nafni's nephew and only male heir."

"The Duke of Everton?"

"Yes, that's his title now, and the very title Darlis so coveted. She seemed to think it should be hers and fancied herself worthy of being a duchess if she could not be a queen. Finbar apparently had made it very clear that his uncle—Ander Nafni, her adopted father—had chosen him to inherit the title upon his death, and she would have to deal with that. Insults were thrown. Things got quite nasty."

"Why did she want the title so bad?" Grayson asked.

"She had always come second as the younger sister, and now that Laviel was a queen, Darlis was mad with jealousy. Back to the fight with Finbar Wallington—Darlis began throwing things at the man. Anything within reach. Plates, paintings, vases, sculptures came flying at the young nobleman. Master Finbar had the unfortunate position of standing before an inner wall with Darlis blocking his exit. There were three of us guards called by Father Rogedoth to intervene. I was the highest-ranking soldier, so I sent my two workfellows to subdue Darlis, while I escorted Master Finbar out.

"I returned to find Darlis struggling with the guards, screaming obscenities as to how she would have them all killed. I sent them away. Then, for some reason, I helped her sit and sent her servant for a drink and a blanket.

She calmed and started talking, venting her frustrations on me. Not yelling, like she had at the other soldiers, but confessing, pouring out her heart. She told me how Finbar had once sworn to marry her so they might be Duke and Duchess of Everton together, but he had changed his mind when he met Lady Gia in Brixmead. Darlis felt rejected—all her life rejected, though it seemed to me as if she sabotaged her own happiness on a regular basis."

"Why do you think he chose Lady Gia over her?"

"Who's to say? Darlis was often cruel. Demanding and heartless too. It all stemmed from her insecurities but was still hard to tolerate. Well, the next day, Father Rogedoth called me into his office and told me I had been reassigned as a personal guard to Darlis. It was technically a demotion, but the high priest tripled my salary and all but begged me to accept. So tired was he of seeking out anyone willing to work for Darlis, and she had asked for me by name. Father Rogedoth was determined to convince me."

An idea dawned slowly in Grayson, crawling up his arms like a chill. He shook it off, wanting to be patient and wait for Jhorn to finish his story.

"I accepted the position," Jhorn said. "While Darlis was a miserable creature, her sorrow intrigued me and I felt I could cheer her. But there was a darkness in her that I had never sensed before. I often caught her talking to herself, and drinking from a flask. I thought she was addicted to spirits."

"It was root juice."

Jhorn nodded, almost sadly. "It was. Though I didn't realize that until much, much later. When she grew affectionate toward me, I reminded her that the high priest paid my salary and that I would not betray him.

"I worked for her about three months before I was called before Father Rogedoth yet again. I was worried that my rejection had annoyed Lady Darlis and felt certain he was going to discharge me. But no. This time he made me an indecent proposal on behalf of his daughter."

Grayson's cheeks burned. He not only understood, but this further convinced him that the inkling growing inside him might be right.

"Father Rogedoth did not simply ask me to carry on with Darlis Nafni," Jhorn said. "He was very specific. If I accepted his proposal, he would double my already tripled salary, but I must do anything she asked of me—no questions, no refusals. Either would be cause for dismissal.

"It wasn't a hard decision for me. I was a lonely bachelor who had no time for romance, and Darlis was beautiful. Her drunkenness and mumbling to herself often made me nervous, but I wasn't afraid of her like the other soldiers were. I agreed, and so began our relationship.

"I quickly discovered she was a mantic witch. I'll spare you the strangeness of that time and move ahead to when I overheard her speaking with the high priest one night in her study when she thought I was asleep. She called the man her father, and not in a priestly way. I came to learn—in bits and pieces—that Barthel Rogedoth was not only Darlis's birth father, he was Laviel's birth father as well. They spoke of Darlis's plans to have a child by me. That startled me because I'd never heard her so much as mention wanting to be a mother. They spoke of other times she had failed to conceive, and she told Father Rogedoth that she was certain I was the one."

Grayson could stand it no longer. "You're my real father?"

Tears glistened in Jhorn's eyes. "Yes, my boy. I am."

Grayson popped to Jhorn's side and embraced the man.

Jhorn chuckled at first, catching hold of Grayson tightly, as if he might fall over if he didn't hang on, but soon deep sobs shook him. Shook Jhorn, Grayson's father. Grayson started to cry as well. "Why didn't you say?"

Jhorn pulled back. Tears had rolled down his cheeks and soaked into his thick beard. "I was afraid," he said, taking a deep breath. "I hadn't planned to keep you."

"Why not?"

"Let me finish the story, yes?"

Grayson sat cross-legged on the floor beside his father and nodded.

Jhorn removed a handkerchief from his pocket and dabbed his eyes and cheeks. "As I said, I was eavesdropping on Darlis and Father Rogedoth. Their conspiratorial tone put me on edge. They didn't want just any child. They were trying to use mantics to conceive a root child. The stuff of myths and legends. They felt such a child would grow faster than other children and become a sorcerer beyond compare. They hoped to use this child to take the throne of Armania, then conquer Sarikar. I remember thinking I should run away—get free of them—but I had always hoped to have children someday, so the idea of being a father sat well with me. And I also rather liked that Darlis had chosen me.

"Over the next few months, life proceeded as normal. Darlis used many spells to help her conceive a child, but as far as I knew, we were unsuccessful. Then one day Father Rogedoth summoned me to his office and told me I was being sent to the war. I quickly guessed at how I had been used. Darlis was pregnant, and they had never intended for me to be part of the child's life. I took a risk, told the high priest that I couldn't leave, as Darlis and I were expecting a child. He quickly put me in my place. Darlis was expecting, yes, but she did not want a husband. I had served my purpose and was no longer needed. The war effort was looking for more men, and Father Rogedoth had signed me up. I was to leave the next day."

"Why wouldn't she let you stay?"

"Darlis wanted to be in control of everything. If I had stayed, she would have had to share that control with me. No, she had used me to get what she wanted. You."

Grayson felt conflicted. He liked the idea of his mother having wanted him so badly, but he did not like that she had sent Jhorn away.

"I fought with Father Rogedoth," Jhorn said. "Told him what I thought of his and his daughter's plans—that, yes, I knew he was her father. He reminded me that I had been well paid and had agreed to ask no questions and make no demands. He threatened me with death if I told anyone about Laviel or Darlis's parentage. There was nothing I could do. I was escorted to the military camp by six armed soldiers. When I thought that my child might never know me, I fell into a despair so deep I could see nothing but darkness. Such anger served me well on the battlefield. You know my story there, except that I never told you how I came to find you."

"You said I was wandering alone."

"A half-truth. You know the story of how I hurt my legs in battle. Because my captain cared about my welfare, he had me sent to Raine—to the home of Tace Edekk, Master Fonu's father. He was a young man then, married with three children. With Raine on the border of Magonia, the king had claimed his home to be used as a wartime hospital. As you know, they took my legs. I wanted to die, but Arman kept me alive. I cursed the God for that, but while I wanted to hate him, I found I could not. And as I was praying one morning, praying out of delirium and pain, confused why the God had let me suffer so, I heard a child's voice. I opened my eyes and saw you, toddling between the cots in the hospital. You had speckled gray skin and a thick head of black hair. A moment later a frantic nurse ran into the ward, calling the name *Merek*, and though you looked about two years old when you couldn't have been more than six months, I knew instantly that you were my son."

Grayson wanted to say something, but he was too shocked.

"I remembered Darlis and Father Rogedoth talking of how fast a root child might grow and knew they must have worked some mantic spell upon you. I asked my nurse a few questions and discovered that Darlis had died giving birth. I knew then that I had to live and to get you away from your grandfather so that he couldn't use you for his evil plans. It wasn't easy, but I eventually did just that. I took us to the cabin in Magonia, and we lived there happily for years until Dun got captured at the border and I went to find him."

"Raine was very far from Everton," Grayson said. "Why was I there?"

"After Darlis died, Rogedoth couldn't very well claim you, so he sent you to be raised by Tace and Gitla Edekk."

Grayson couldn't believe it. Had Master Fonu known they could have been raised as brothers when he'd been trying to capture Grayson? "I still don't understand why you didn't tell me I was your son."

"What kind of a father could a legless cripple be? I could barely get around on my own. I'd had to enlist the help of a nurse to get you out of Armania, but I couldn't force her to stay. I planned to deliver you to Ebro. I had a friend there who had agreed to take you in. It wasn't the best environment, though, and once I got us to that little cabin in Magonia, time went on, and we did okay, just the two of us. I kept meaning to take you to Ebro but found I couldn't. And once I'd told neighbors my lie, it stuck."

"That I was an orphan."

"That you were the child of a friend who'd been killed in the war. That you'd come to live with me. Then Onika came, then Dunmore, and when people started to assume that the crippled veteran took in orphans, I didn't correct them. I figured you'd be safer lumped in with such a group, and the others needed a place to live."

"Didn't you want to be my father?"

"I've always been your father, Grayson. In every way that matters."

Grayson guessed that was true.

"When we got the message that Dun had been arrested . . . If I had known that was the last time I would see you before the Five Woes began, I would have told you all this then. But when you came for me with Sir Kalenek, I was too afraid word might reach Rogedoth. And if you knew, you might not be able to keep it a secret."

Grayson smirked. "I've never been good at secrets."

"You kept secret your magic until Onika's prophecy came to life."

Mostly he had.

"I imagine it feels good to finally be yourself," Jhorn said. "Not to have to bottle up your abilities anymore."

"Sometimes. But Danno hasn't treated me the same ever since. Nobody does, really."

"Nor should they. You are special, Grayson."

All his life he had wanted to be special, but this was the wrong kind of attention. "I still don't know how I'm supposed to do half the things Onika said." Grayson had always thought he would marry Onika when he grew up and that she would help him do all those special things.

"Prophecies are often vague," Jhorn said. "There are three I know of, though Onika occasionally spoke of others. I have the three written down if you would like to hear them."

Grayson's heart swelled with hope. "I want to hear them," he said.

Jhorn pulled a small scroll from a pocket in his tunic and unrolled it. He cleared his throat and read: "'Minions of Gâzar, beware the remnant of Arman, led by his Deliverer.' That's the first one."

Grayson's cheeks tingled at the word *Deliverer*. "It's very short."

"Think it through. What does it mean to you?"

Grayson repeated the words to himself. "The remnant are those of us who survived the journey across the sea, right?"

"Onika thought so. Think you could lead them?"

Grayson shook his head.

Jhorn laughed. "Don't give up so soon, my boy. Here is the second prophecy: 'Servants of the Lowerworld, tremble, for Arman will send against you his servants of the light. Led by their Deliverer, they will stand against your evil kings and send you back to Gâzar's realm.'"

Again the word *Deliverer*. "That sounds kind of like the one about shadir ruling kings," he said. "I remembered that one when I saw the great shadir with King Barthel."

"Here is the third," Jhorn said. "'With an overwhelming army the Deliverer will come. He will make an end of the enemy; he will pursue his foes into the arms of darkness.'"

Grayson sighed, thinking over the words. "What do you think they mean?"

"That you have a rough path ahead."

Grayson figured that much, but it was nice to hear Jhorn admit it too. "Do you think I can do it?"

"I think the prophecy is clear. You won't fail. Arman will be with you."

63

Grayson was glad of that, but it sure sounded scary.

"Something is bothering you," Jhorn said.

Grayson winced. "They all talked about the Deliverer."

"That's what Onika sometimes called you. Does it bother you?"

"Not exactly. Isn't the Deliverer the person the Magonians have been waiting for?"

"They believe they are awaiting a Deliverer, yes, but their prophecies are incorrect."

Grayson squirmed, wishing he could talk about something else for a while, but he should be honest with Jhorn—his father. That made him smile briefly. "When I first met Muna, a Puru clan chief, she called me 'Massi' because of my skin. It means gray in her language. She called Danno 'Komo,' which means brown."

"Simple enough," Jhorn said.

"They name their people by how they look or act. They give new names all the time. Not all of the names stick, but . . . well, after I started helping Puru people escape from the Ahj-Yeke mines under Zuzaan, Muna started calling me 'Masaoo.'"

"And what does that mean?"

Grayson finally met Jhorn's gaze. "Deliverer."

Jhorn's face lit up. "You see? It's already begun. Not so scary, was it?"

Grayson shrugged. "I guess not."

Jhorn exhaled a deep sigh. "Some things in life are scary, because life is sometimes hard. I've one more thing I need to tell you, Grayson, and this is one of those hard things. It also comes with a request from the king."

Grayson perked up. He longed to do something to help the king—as long as it wasn't going to school. "What is it?"

"It's about Onika," Jhorn said. "She needs your help."

QⵙATCH

Qoatch had been in the kitchen, helping himself to a midday meal, when word of Empress Jazlyn's return reached him. He gathered a tray of her favorite refreshments, ordered two servants to bring a hot bath, then hurried upstairs. He reached her apartment moments before Jazlyn arrived and handed Jahleeah off to Zinetha, the nurse. The appearance of Jazlyn's older body still caught him off guard.

"Draw me a bath at once," she commanded, her voice crackly. "I fear I brought half the road home on my gown." She trudged into her sitting room and lowered herself onto a longchair, leaned back, and sighed. "Those Magosians live like animals, sleeping on the ground—they have no furniture at all. My back is terribly sore. And their clothing . . ." She narrowed her eyes. "What is it? You look like you have something to tell me."

Her servants were still hauling her things inside. Good. Qoatch needed an audience if they were to succeed in this subterfuge. He only hoped Jazlyn was not too tired to catch on and play well to these witnesses. "I have dire news, lady. A mysterious illness has left Emperor Ulrik and Prince Ferro bedridden."

Jazlyn sat up at once. "What kind of illness?"

"I know not. The physicians are puzzled."

She stood and hobbled toward the door. "I must see my husband at once."

"I don't think that is a good idea, Your Highness," Qoatch said, stepping in her path. "The physician has ordered their quarantine until the cause of the illness can be discerned."

"How dreadful. There must be some way I can communicate with my husband. Might I write him a letter?"

Qoatch should not have worried. Jazlyn had always been a professional deceiver. "Forgive me, Great Lady, for being unclear. The emperor and prince are not only bedridden, they are unconscious. It is as if they have fallen asleep and will not awake."

Jazlyn began to pace. "Could this be the same poison that took the life of the Armanian princeling?"

What a clever thing to say. "I think not, Great Lady."

"It could be poison, though? Someone could be trying to kill my husband?"

"It is a possibility."

"I demand to speak with the physician at once."

"Yes, lady, I will summon him."

Qoatch started for the door, but it opened before he could reach it. Rosârah Thallah squeezed by one of Jazlyn's Tennish Protectors and pushed inside. In the corridor behind her, a group of Igote guards pressed against the Protectors, but Jazlyn's men did not let them pass.

"You!" the stubby queen yelled. "You are under arrest, Empress." She bustled toward Jazlyn, shaking her finger. Her behavior was odd enough, but what grabbed Qoatch's attention was the flickering orange-and-yellow shadir coiled around her neck like a scarf of tiny flames.

"Great Lady . . ." Qoatch said, shocked to see a shadir after so long without them nearby.

"Arrested for what?" Jazlyn asked the Armanian queen.

"Kidnapping the princess and poisoning the emperor and his brother," Thallah said.

"As you can see, the princess is in the arms of her nurse." Jazlyn motioned to Zinetha, who was now standing at the window with the babe. "As to the state of my husband and his brother, how dare you insinuate I had anything to do with it. I only just learned of their illness."

"The way of the guilty is devious!" Thallah yelled. "I will not be swayed. You bade your man poison them while you were away."

Jazlyn gestured to Qoatch. "Was my eunuch caught in the act?"

"No."

"Was he seen around the emperor or Prince Ferro?"

"No."

"Qoatch, did you feed poison to my husband and his brother?"

"I did not, Great Lady," he said, and it wasn't even a lie. He had poisoned them with incense.

The shadir around Rosârah Thallah's neck shifted and turned its eyes onto Qoatch. Had the Armanian queen bonded with this shadir? Or was it merely drawn to her rage and fear?

"I might not have proof," Thallah said, "but I know the truth. A false witness will not go unpunished."

"You have no grounds to barge into my chambers and accuse me of attempting murder," Jazlyn said. "You should know how rumors abound in the midst of catastrophes."

"Surely you're not going to accuse *me* of poisoning my great-nephews?" Thallah asked.

"I accuse you of nothing, but I did hear some guards at the gatehouse say you orchestrated the death of the Armanian king to put your son on the throne."

The chubby queen gasped. "That is ridiculous! My son has never desired to rule."

"You see my point about rumors, then," Jazlyn said.

Thallah sputtered. "You have been trying to take control of Rurekau since you first boarded the *Baretam* in Jeruka, so the emperor told me."

"More gossip you cannot prove. Why don't you go back to Armania, now that your son is king?"

"You would like that, wouldn't you?"

"Be gone, woman, and do not come back," Jazlyn said.

"I know you did this," Thallah said. "I know it!"

"Remove this woman, Qoatch," Jazlyn said.

"Yes, Great Lady." The door was still open. Qoatch walked toward Rosârah Thallah, who allowed herself to be herded into the hallway.

"Go ahead and hide behind your Protectors, Empress," the queen spat, "but know that I consider this apartment your prison cell. You will not set foot outside that door without my permission. When you left this place and poisoned your husband and his brother, you put the rule of Rurekau into my hands. Until they recover, I rule this nation, not you."

The fiery shadir slipped off her neck and into the room moments before Thallah slammed the door. The creature drifted along the wall, hovering near the floor as if hoping not to be seen.

"The nerve of that woman!" Jazlyn strode through the sitting room and into her bedchamber. "Qoatch, fetch a pen and parchment," she said, her voice muffled by the walls between them. "I must write to the Chieftess of

Magosia and implore her assistance in this matter. Rosârah Thallah has no right to keep me prisoner— threatening me as if I would harm my husband."

She returned to the doorway and met Qoatch's gaze, expectant, holding the door open. Qoatch quickly grabbed the inkwell and several sheets of parchment off the desk. Once he had passed into the empress's bedchamber, she slammed the door and came nose to nose with him.

"Great Lady," Qoatch began, "Rosârah Thallah brought a—"

"Why are they still living?" Jazlyn whispered.

Qoatch's gaze panned over the walls, searching for any variance in the stone. "I had hoped the dead sleep would appear as an illness and keep away suspicion. That way, should you return without magic, I could administer the antidote and nothing would have changed."

"Clearly your plans failed to keep suspicions off me. Do not think of administering an antidote. Instead, I want you to prepare more of the same for Rosârah Thallah."

"Forgive me, Great Lady, but I have no more torterus fangs. And I must warn you, the rosârah had a shadir with her just now. She left it behind in the sitting room. I do not see it at the moment, but I am certain it must be here to spy. It is one I've never seen before."

Jazlyn's eyes grew round in their deep sockets. "Do you think she has ahvenrood?"

"I don't know. I have never seen her with a shadir. It could be operating on its own, or spying for another master. It did not speak."

"I must know if she is a mantic. Find out." Jazlyn pulled open the door. "We will finish the letter later," she announced for the benefit of Zinetha and the servants hauling in buckets of steaming bathwater. "I cannot concentrate until I learn how Ulrik fares. Have the physician brought to my chambers at once. I want to hear his side of this mysterious illness."

"Yes, Great Lady." Qoatch bowed and left her bedchamber. He quickly glanced around the room but no longer saw the shadir. He exited the apartment and passed by the dozen Tennish Protectors posted outside the door. Igote soldiers were stationed on either end of the corridor. Qoatch turned left, taking the shortest route to the royal wing of the castle. He counted seventeen Igote blocking the left end. No one spoke to him as he passed, but he suspected that if Jazlyn had accompanied him, there would have been a fight.

Qoatch was not permitted to enter the emperor's bedchambers and was turned away at Prince Ferro's room as well. It took a great deal of questioning the right people, but he finally learned the name of the physician—Master Nelkin—and found him in a small chamber near the kitchens, where he had set up a workspace cluttered with mortars and pestles, vials, a variety of dried herbs, mushrooms, insects, and some fresh greens hanging from a line in the corner.

Master Nelkin was a young man about Qoatch's age. He had one lazy eye and a bucktoothed, gaping mouth. From Qoatch's guess, the man had been using this workspace to find a cure for the dead sleep.

Qoatch would give him no help there.

"Greetings," he said. "I am Qoatch, servant of Empress Jazlyn. She has just now returned from a trip to Magosia and heard the news of her husband and his brother. She is understandably distraught and requests your presence in her apartment so that she can make inquiries as to her husband's welfare."

Master Nelkin fixed his good eye on Qoatch. "I'm afraid I cannot do that, Master Qoatch. The council has ordered me not to speak with the empress."

Thallah's doing, likely. "Have you similar orders in regards to me?"

The man grinned, displaying his buckteeth. "No, actually. How can I be of service to you, sir?"

"What can you tell me about this illness?"

"That it is no illness at all. If it were an illness, more people would have been affected. That only the emperor and his brother fell ill at the same time is not only convenient, it is suspicious."

"That is sound logic," Qoatch said. "Will you be able to find a cure?"

"An antidote, Master Qoatch. A cure is a general term for a remedy for a disease. An antidote refers to an agent that counters the effect of a harmful substance that has been ingested into the body by various means."

"I see," Qoatch said. "An antidote, then?"

"I am doing my best, but without knowing what poisoned them, it is difficult. The moment I first saw the emperor, I administered a mustard emetic, which induced vomiting but overall did not help. Their condition resembles a dead sleep, brought on by torterus venom."

"But there are no torterus here," Qoatch said.

"No, but someone could have brought the powder from our homeland. Both the emperor and his brother have exhibited muscle twitching and slowed, shallow breathing, but I found no evidence of poison in any of the food trays found in their apartments, no punctures on either body, and no trace of the powder on their hands or beds or in their clothing. It is very strange."

"Why not give them an antidote for torterus venom, just in case?"

"The antidote is quite dangerous. It can cause hallucinations, depression, addiction, and in some cases, death. Proper dosage is vital, and I cannot know for certain how much each patient consumed or how much antivenom I should administer. On the other hand, to do nothing . . . Well, they will both of them die eventually, likely within a week or two."

Master Nelkin was an intelligent man. Qoatch wondered who had trained him. "The empress will be grieved to hear how dire the situation is," he said. "I wish there were some way I could help."

"Pray and make offerings. I will continue to experiment, and should the council decree it, I will take my best guess about administering an antidote to torterus fangs. But the truth is, both the emperor and his brother are at the mercy of the gods."

⊙ПĪКΛ

For many years Onika had seen light. Bright, colorful, ever-changing, and often distracting light. At the moment, she saw only a dark brown canvas sprayed in purple spots that shifted, as if trying and failing to come into focus. Now the dots were green. Now blue with flecks of yellow and orange, and it seemed as if some of the blue was threatening to break through the brown canvas and outshine everything else, but for some reason it could not.

Onika had never experienced darkness—pitch blackness—even in the dead of night. She had always wanted to—but not this darkness that had so consumed her soul.

Bring light, O Holy God, and vanquish the darkness surrounding me. My ragged soul is withered to a shadow. How long must I endure? I beg you grant me the mercy of sleep, that I might close off the memories and forget.

But sleep did not come, and her memories continued to betray her. Again and again she relived the horrors of that day. Cries of death from kindly servants. Screams of terror and anguish from Tulay and Yoana. The jeers of the men. Villains, all of them. Rough hands that grabbed her. Smothering fear. So many voices. So much pain.

She'd told them to stop. Again and again. But they would not. Finally, desperation gave way to defiance, and Onika had reached into the nearest mind and commanded it to stop.

Her attacker had collapsed. Shouts of disgust rang out. Accusations of

71

murder and witchcraft followed by a different kind of violence with fists and kicks and ugly curses, as if *she* had done something to harm *them*. Fear laced deep in the men's voices kept a question at the forefront of her mind. What *had* she done?

Then young Master Burk had arrived, yelling censure to anyone who dared harm a prophet of the gods. His clammy hands had pulled her to her feet and led her away, his reedy voice warning the men that anyone who dared touch her again could expect the same as what happened to Aloz.

Onika had no idea what she'd done to Aloz or who that even was. She had made no curse—not even a prayer at that moment—but she *had* reached into someone's mind. Perhaps the man Aloz had heard her? Sensed her emotions and become convicted? If so, why then did the men claim he had died?

Master Burk had led her away from the turmoil, helped her inside a transport of some kind. Tied her hands and bade her sit. Told her the bonds were for her own safety and that he would take care of her.

She knew better than to believe that. He was no better than the others.

Master Dendrick had been in the transport already—the rebels had wanted him for his knowledge of Armania's politics. He had tried to calm Onika, but she remembered little of the words he'd spoken.

How long she had sat in that wagon, she did not know. At some point Master Dendrick had nudged her shoulder and whispered those glorious words: "Help is here, Miss Onika. We are saved."

Onika knew a fleeting moment of joy that her Rescuer had come at last, but the moment she'd heard Rosâr Wilek's cultured voice instead of Sir Kalenek's rough one, that joy had vanished. Despair had nearly made her collapse, for she knew two things in an instant: She would not escape for long, and Rosâr Wilek and Master Dendrick would not survive.

She had tried to speak. To warn the men. But what could she say? She hadn't seen the future. Arman had not spoken to this directly. She simply felt certain from everything put together.

She simply knew.

The rest had happened very fast. Master Dendrick had pulled her along by the arm as branches snagged her skirt and scratched her ankles. She'd smelled a horse. Master Dendrick had lifted her onto the animal, but before he'd been able to join her, someone had attacked. A loud crack rang out, and Master Dendrick had yelled, "Heeya!"

The horse had taken flight. Onika had wrapped her arms around the animal's neck and done all she could to hold on. The animal had not gotten far before something struck Onika's head and knocked her to the ground.

She'd lain still, gasping for breath, knowing she must hurry but unable to move. Men had descended upon her, one mocking her for not knowing when to duck under the branch of a—

Stop it! Onika must stop this madness. She had again allowed the memories to whisk her to the past, where death reigned supreme. She had forgotten to focus on praise. On goodness. On joy. She begged Arman for forgiveness, then for sleep, though she knew that even when exhaustion finally consumed her, the memories would be waiting in her nightmares.

She could not escape. She could never escape.

How could such evil be overcome? How would she ever find the light again? She knew it was there, but darkness had trapped her under a boulder she could not lift.

And where was her Rescuer? Why hadn't Sir Kalenek come? She had seen that he would free her. When would he—?

A gust of cold and the sound of rumpling fabric lodged a pebble of fear in her throat.

Someone was inside her tent.

She closed her eyes. If the intruder thought she was sleeping, maybe he would go away.

Footsteps scuffed the dirt floor, drew near. Toes nudged her mat. Knees cracked as they bent down. Hot, putrid breath at her ear followed by words in a familiar, arrogant voice. "Time to get up, prophetess."

Master Burk. He had made himself her protector, stood sentry outside her tent each day, claiming that protecting the prophet of the gods would give the soldiers luck on their journey, asserted that only he was safe to touch her since he had stepped in and saved the gods' anointed.

His superiors had believed him, the fools.

A clammy hand grabbed her arm, shook it. "Get up, woman. They want to tear down your tent."

Onika rolled to her side and pushed to her knees. Like a cloak reeking of an unbathed man, Master Burk stayed with her, helping her stand, pulling her forward. From his winding steps, she guessed he was maneuvering her around several obstacles. The sound shifted. Canvas walls that muffled the sounds of nature fell away, and Onika's senses were overwhelmed by chilled air, the smell of pine and horses, the sounds of men and birds.

73

As Master Burk had every day for the past week or more, he took her to the wagon, bound her hands, and reminded her that his kindness was not without cost.

"You owe me for protecting you, don't forget," he said in his cocksure manner. "I'll come to you tonight."

He had said those words every day since the night of the battle, yet he had not come. She sensed he was afraid of her—of whatever she'd done to the man called Aloz—but Master Burk's fear would not stop him forever. Arman had revealed that much long ago.

Master Burk left her alone in the wagon. She sat listening to the sounds of the men breaking camp, barks of laughter from souls still whole, distant birdsong, the wind rustling leaves. She knew from Dendrick that the south was not a large section of land. So why was the journey to meet Barthel Rogedoth taking so long?

The wagon jolted softly and a rolling purr met her ears. Rustian. He circled her, rubbing his fur against her body, then climbed into her lap and settled down.

All these days the dune cat had kept her sane. He was the small glow of Arman's goodness, and she held him close as long as she was able. Eventually the men would come and chase him away, leaving Onika again alone in the darkness.

"Move out!" someone yelled, and the wagon rolled forward.

That night after the men had set up camp again, she was lying on her mat, trying to sleep, when her bedroll shifted.

"Onika?"

She startled, shocked that she had not heard this man coming. A voice she did not recognize.

"Who is there?" she asked.

"It's Grayson," the man said. "I know I sound different than I used to, but it's me."

Tears flooded her eyes at the deepness of that voice—what he must have suffered. "Oh, Grayson!" She sat up, reached for him. "How did you get here?" Perhaps her rescue had finally come.

"I popped here." Cold hands gripped her fingers. The bedroll tugged as he sat beside her. "Back when we were at sea, I learned how to travel through the

Veil," he said. "I could go from one place to another in the blink of an eye! Sir Kalenek came and gave me your message, about holding onto my secret, and when we landed here and I met the giants in the forest, I knew it was time to stop hiding what I could do."

Praise you, Holy God, for keeping him safe. She trailed her fingers up his thick sleeve to prickly cheeks. "You are shaving?"

He turned his head. "Sir Cadoc taught me," he mumbled. "Said it made me look less like a barbarian slav."

She chuckled. "I am glad you have friends looking after you. You have changed so much."

"Just on the outside," he said.

"You should not stay long," Onika said. "I've heard these men talking. They were charged with capturing you and would still like to succeed."

"These were Master Fonu's men," Grayson said. "I'm not scared of them. I'm too fast."

"But should a mantic join them . . ."

"Did you know Jhorn is my father?"

She heard the pride in his voice. "I suspected as much, though he never said. Something about your personalities felt similar. You have the same determination. Did he tell you this?"

"Yes." And Grayson shared the whole story, which led into a second story about Grayson rescuing the Sarikarian princess and many Puru people from the giants' mines.

"You are falling into your role as a hero," she said. "I am proud of you."

Movement behind Onika made Grayson twitch, but at the thick purr that followed, he laughed. "Hello, Rustian. Did you miss me?" He moved away, and a chill ran over Onika.

"It's been a long time," she said. "Why did you come now?"

"I didn't know you were a prisoner until Jhorn told me. Rosâr Trevn wanted me to find you so I could lead a rescue party here."

Oh how she wanted to flee with him, but that was not Arman's will. "No, Grayson."

"Why would you say that? I can lead you out of this tent and far away from here."

"You don't even know where we are yet, do you?"

"I will figure it out."

"The nights are very cold," Onika said. "We would freeze out there."

"I can steal us some warm clothes."

"And how will I find my way back to Armanguard? Rustian does not know the way."

"I'll walk with you," Grayson said.

Sweet, precious boy. "That would take far too long. Even with your help and Rustian's, I cannot move very fast. As soon as these men realized I escaped, they would come looking for me. They have horses. They would catch us."

"No one can catch me. And I could probably steal us some horses."

She felt for his hand, found it, and squeezed. "I appreciate your wanting to help, Grayson, but I must wait for Sir Kalenek. Arman showed me long ago that he is my Rescuer."

"But he already rescued you. This time I want to help."

She shook her head. "Sir Kalenek will come for me again."

"But the king said I must."

"I will explain to Rosâr Trevn. We must trust the God's plan. Now, tell me what you have been doing in that big castle."

Grayson stayed very late, filling Onika's ears with story after story of his exploits. How his presence lifted her spirits and reminded her of the bigger plan at work. She chose to wait for morning to voice Rosâr Trevn about his rescue plans, but his voice woke her before Master Burk could.

"Miss Onika? Do you hear me?"

She opened her eyes to spiraling orange flecks on a sea of mauve light. She made herself sit up before answering, hoping the position would help her more quickly gather her wits. *"I hear you, sir."* To call the boy "sir" felt strange, but he had been made king. Onika's service must defer to Arman's chosen.

"Grayson tells me he found you and can lead a rescue party to your location. Yet you have refused?"

It did sound rather foolish when put like that. *"I do not claim to know the mind of Arman, Your Highness, but he has revealed some things to me that I know with certainty. And I have known since long before I met him that Sir Kalenek will be the one to free me from this place."*

A long stretch of silence passed before the king spoke again. *"Miss Onika, Sir Kalenek fled the* Seffynaw *after killing my brother. He lives in Magosia now."*

"Yes, Rosâr Wilek sent him to watch over Sâr Janek's child. But he will come."

"Have you spoken to him? Told him what happened to you?"

It had never occurred to Onika to use Arman's voicing magic to speak with Sir Kalenek. Well, why not? Rosâr Trevn spoke to non-gifted minds all the time. *"I have never tried to, but I will."*

"I must warn you, Wilek told me that Sir Kalenek is not himself. The Chieftess has placed several compulsions upon him to keep him loyal. He sometimes struggles against her magic to have coherent conversations."

Poor Sir Kalenek! He so hated magic. How must he feel to be bound by it? *"I will let you know what happens,"* she said.

"Miss Onika, getting you back safely is my top priority, but I also seek to arrest your captors. Those men are enemies of Armania who are responsible for my brother's death."

"Do not waste your time and resources on this matter," Onika said. *"You must trust me, and your enemy's judgment, to Arman."*

"How certain are you about all this? It could be that Sir Kalenek is meant to rescue you from another place in another time."

Onika had wondered that, but this was one of those things that she simply knew, just as she had known the Five Realms would fall into the sea, that Sir Kalenek would find her in Magonia, and that she and Grayson would be parted. *"I sense that my waiting for Sir Kalenek will be of mutual benefit. If you send others for me, Sir Kalenek will be lost. I must wait for him to save him. Should the God say differently, Your Highness, I will tell you at once."*

"Very well. Take care, prophetess." He closed off the conversation so abruptly that Onika felt cold. She hadn't realized there had been any warmth in her connection to Rosâr Trevn until he had relinquished it. How strange.

She reached out with her mind, feeling for Sir Kalenek the same way she felt for Rosâr Trevn or the Duke of Canden. She did not find him at first, and wondered if she even knew how to accomplish what the young king had suggested. The task kept reality at bay, however, so she kept trying. After some time, she came to feel something familiar, like a tangible memory calling her close. She followed the sensation until she recognized Sir Kalenek's smell of leather, mossy sweat, and the orea oil he used to clean his hair. She also smelled soil and something foreign and feminine.

"Sir Kalenek? It is Onika. Can you hear me?"

She felt him jolt at the sound of her voice. A hesitation. *"I hear you."*

"I am being held captive by evil men. Can you help me?"

"Who is this?"

"Onika."

Confusion clouded his mind. He seemed . . . stuck, as if searching for a memory that was just barely out of reach.

"I don't know that name," he said finally.

Despair fell heavily. *"We traveled together out of Magonia, through Rurekau, where we boarded the ship* Baretam. *Then we journeyed around the Five Realms and came aboard the Armanian ship* Seffynaw, *which carried us across the sea until you left to watch over Sâr Janek's child."*

"How do you know this?"

"Because we are friends. A magic spell has made you forget."

"I don't . . ." He breathed deeply and seemed to be fighting something within himself. *"Do you go by any other name?"*

What a strange request. *"I am Onika, daughter of Jhorn. Some call me Arman's prophetess, the king's prophet, or the True Prophet."*

A rush of wistfulness passed between them. *"I know you."*

"Of course you do. You are my Rescuer. And I need your help. I am the captive of men who formerly served Fonu Edekk. They are taking me to Barthel Rogedoth in hopes of earning a ransom."

"Villains, all of them," Sir Kalenek said.

"Yes! Can you help me?"

"I cannot leave."

"Because the Chieftess has compelled you. Rosâr Trevn told me as much."

Sir Kalenek recoiled and confusion bled through their connection. *"Rosâr Trevn?"*

"Sir Kalenek! You are needed in Shanek's tent this instant." A woman's voice. The source of that foreign, feminine smell.

A surge of obedience rose up to compel Sir Kalenek's movements. Onika sensed his annoyance, though he was quick to obey.

Onika tried again. *"Sir Kalenek?"*

He jumped. *"Yes? Who is this?"*

"Onika still."

"I know no one by that name."

Frustration made her throat tighten, and she took a deep breath, trying to calm herself. *"The True Prophetess of Arman?"*

A jolt of emotion pierced his heart, and she heard him mumble, *"Prophetess . . . prophetess . . ."*

Onika's heart sank. For some reason, the Magosian Chieftess's compulsion had made Sir Kalenek forget who Onika was. Why? And however would she convince her Rescuer to come and find a woman he did not remember?

Throughout the day as they traveled, Onika tried several more times to converse with Sir Kalenek, determined to break through to her Rescuer, but each attempt ended in his confusion and her dismay. That night as she lay on her mat, a commotion of men's voices outside her tent led Onika to believe that something was happening in the camp. She strained to hear but could make no sense of anything until two men spoke directly outside.

"What is your name?"

"Burk."

"Is that a given name or a surname?"

"I got only one name, Your Highness," Master Burk said. "I've been Burk long as I can remember."

"The captain said you stepped in to help the prophetess."

"I meant no disrespect, sir, but when I saw what she did to Aloz, I figured we'd be smart to leave her be."

"And you posted yourself outside her door."

"Only because I worried that some of the men wanted to kill her, and Master Fonu had said she was important to you, sir."

"That she is, Master Burk. You've done very well."

"Thank you, Your Highness. I'm honored to help, sir. Anything you need."

"Right now I need to see the prophetess—confirm she is who you claim she is. She could be a Puru impostor."

"She's no impostor, sir. I met her back in Magonia and traveled with her to Rurekau. She's the prophetess, all right."

"Remain outside while I speak with her."

"Yes, sir."

Fabric rustled, a gust of cold air passed by, then footsteps brushed over packed dirt.

Onika knew the fear overwhelming her at present was illogical. Barthel Rogedoth did not come to attack her like the other men, but he did represent the evil descending upon Arman's people.

Holy Arman, I am your servant. I know you see me now. Protect me from this man's machinations, and give me wisdom and words that might convict him to serve you instead.

"I never really had any doubts that you were here, prophetess," Barthel Rogedoth said. "My shadir have been watching you closely. When I first heard Wilek Hadar speak of you, I thought he was telling tales. A female prophet? Ridiculous. But when your predictions came true, I realized I had been naïve to dismiss you so quickly. I apologize for the cruelty you suffered at the hands of Fonu's men. I assure you that you are safe now that I am here."

Onika did not believe that for a moment.

"You probably think me a pagan, but I want you to know I fear all the gods, though Barthos, whose namesake I am, has always been my master."

"Did you not name yourself Barthel once you could no longer use the name Mergest Pitney?" Onika asked.

A moment of silence passed. "The point, my dear, is that I know Arman, your god, well. He and I have had many conversations, and on his altar I have sacrificed much."

"What have you sacrificed to Arman? Not your pride. Not your ambition."

"Arman has never asked that of me."

"Then your Arman is an impostor, for he asks those things of us all. If you had truly followed Arman, your father never would have disowned you and you would have had rule of Sarikar over your brother. Yet you chose to defy Arman and your father, and so you will reap what you have sown."

"Do not spout my life back to me as if you have lived it," he snapped. "I know what really happened, and you do not. Barthos has promised me supreme rule of Armania."

"That is not his promise to make," Onika said. "And stop calling him Barthos. You and I both know that you are really speaking of Dendron, the great shadir you worship."

A stretch of silence, then, "How do you know that name?"

"I know all that Arman gives me to know," Onika said.

"You tell Arman this, woman. Tell him that I will worship him, make sacrifices and burnt offerings, and praise his name before all my people if he will help me defeat every foe that comes against me. If he will promise me that, I will worship him now and forever."

Onika felt Arman's wrath rise up within her. His presence brought intense heat and his words poured forth, "Hear the word of the God. This is what Arman says: 'I set you up to be ruler over my people in Sarikar, but you did not behave like your father, who kept my commands and followed me with all his heart, doing what was right in my eyes. You have done more evil than all who lived before you. You have made for yourself other gods, worshiped idols, tortured innocents, and made sacrifices to demons; you have aroused my anger and turned your back on me.

"'Because of this, I am going to bring disaster on the name you gave yourself. With the measure you use to enslave others, it will be measured to you. I will strike you and your flock, so that you will be like the chaff of wheat after threshing. Birds will feed on you and the flesh of those who die alongside you. Arman has spoken!'"

For the space of a dozen heartbeats, there was silence but for Onika's labored breathing, slowly decreasing to normal.

"I gave you a chance," Barthel Rogedoth said at last, "though Dendron warned me not to. It is his desire that I make you a sacrifice at the next full moon to honor Gâzar, to bolster the courage of my men, and to send a message to Rosâr Trevn. So when you are fed to the god who is loyal to *me*, don't you forget that I gave you every opportunity to live and you chose death."

Footsteps stomped away. The curtain over the doorway whipped and fluttered, bringing again a flurry of cold. And Onika was left alone.

Never alone. She might have forgotten for a time, as trauma and pain and loss had gripped her in talons of fear, but she knew the truth again as if learning it for the very first time.

She was not alone. Arman was with her. And with that knowledge came the warmth of hope, welling inside her heart, and a glimpse of light. This world belonged to Arman, as did every world, and he was and always would be victor over all.

Trevn

Trevn awoke to the clatter of Ottee setting a breakfast tray on the sideboard and asked, "What did you bring me?"

"Fried ham and boiled eggs and some local berries," Ottee said. "They're overly ripe but still sweet. Hope you don't mind me bringing the tray right in, but Hawley said you must get up and to remind you about your plans to visit the Duke of Raine."

Trevn's heart sank at the prospect. He sat up, his muscles screaming, and instantly knew without looking that Mielle was not in bed beside him. "Where is the queen?"

"Up early and off to visit Rosârah Zeroah."

Of course. She had missed her friend. Trevn was glad they could spend time together again. The coronation had spooked her. She needed normalcy after that ostentatious event. Trevn hadn't much cared for it either, nor did he like wearing a crown all day.

He got out of bed and pulled on a robe, hoping to diminish the chill. His legs and arms ached so. He'd been practicing swordplay—at the insistence of both Cadoc and Barek. It had been too long since he'd done anything active. He had not served as a sailor on his quest to find Mielle, and it had left him somewhat out of shape.

He ate his breakfast in the comfort of his sitting room, where a roaring fire already crackled in the hearth. There had been few trees back in Armania, where they had burned coal for warmth. Here they made fires of split logs that snapped and hissed as flames devoured them.

Hawley and Rosârah Brelenah both insisted his apartment wasn't proper for a married couple. It had only one bedchamber, one wardrobe, and one sitting room. Trevn and Mielle didn't mind. Neither could stomach sleeping in the royal rooms where Sir Kamran had poisoned Wilek, Zeroah, and Chadek. Those rooms stood empty still, as Zeroah remained in the apartment she and Wilek had moved into after the poisoning. Trevn had no desire to push Zeroah out, nor was he ready to look upon his brother's belongings or decide what to do with them. Besides, he preferred having Mielle close, especially since he rarely saw her during the day.

Since Trevn had returned, he spent his time in meeting after meeting, every one of which existed to pour information into his ears. If the fate of their realm didn't depend so fully upon his actions, he would have long ago claimed boredom and passed off the responsibilities to someone else. The shrewd preparation Barek Hadar had shown in the carriage ride from the ship had served as a warning that kept Trevn on high alert. Many expected him to not just fail, but to fail spectacularly.

He would not allow that to happen.

So when he wasn't sitting in a meeting, he was planning ways to defend against a mantic attack. Master Jhorn maintained there was little that could be done, but Trevn had read scroll after scroll from the Centenary War and had learned a few things. He'd also read Wilek's journals and consulted his maps. If Rogedoth came at them on foot from New Rurekau, he'd have to pass by New Sarikar and would likely attack there first. Unless he came by sea.

A knock on the door preceded Father Mathal. "Good morning, Your Highness," the man said. "Shall we read together from Arman's holy book?"

Trevn grunted. The former medial priest of the Rôb church had converted to Armanite with Wilek, but the man rubbed Trevn the wrong way. Master Hawley said a king must have a priest, however, so Trevn tolerated him.

Mathal read a portion from the second chapter, in which Sarik's wife was taken up to Shamayim. "Take comfort from these words, Your Highness," he said when finished. "I know Rosâr Wilek is looking down on us from Shamayim, and I'm sure he is proud of how well you are handling yourself."

A twinge of annoyance made Trevn shift in his chair. "Just because Arman took Sarik's wife to Shamayim does not mean she looks down upon those still living. Furthermore, it does not mean Arman takes all his children to Shamayim in the same way."

"I only mean that—"

"I know what you meant, Father, but your statement has no textual basis.

You are a priest, and when you bend truths to please men, know that you do more damage than good."

"I am sorry, Your Highness."

"Read more, Father, and allow only Arman's word and voice to shape your thinking. Dismissed."

The priest left, and Trevn finished eating. He let Ottee help him dress—choosing the thinnest crown in the bunch Hawley had brought to his dressing room—then exited his apartment into a wall of people outside. He fought to keep a neutral expression as Cadoc, Nietz, and Rzasa pushed the crowd back. Their continual presence annoyed him. He longed to open his door and find the landing empty.

"Make way," Cadoc yelled. "Against the wall or railing, please, so we can pass."

Nietz was not so polite. "Get back, all of you! Out of the way!"

Among the dozens congregated around the circular landing, Trevn saw three Athosian priests, who had been begging to share their concerns over his conversion to the Armanite faith; several entertainers—jugglers, minstrels, bards, and players—including Keson Orrey and his daughter Fairelle, a musical duo Trevn's father had once employed; and a handful of concubines, who seemed to think him lonely and in need of companionship in spite of the fact that he and his wife shared a bedchamber. He was frankly surprised to see the concubines still here, since he'd twice witnessed Mielle sending them away.

The guards managed to escort Trevn and Hawley through the crowd to the spiral stairs.

"I want those people dispersed," Trevn said to Hawley as they started down. "There must be another place they could assemble."

"The circular shape of the keep makes it difficult to set up boundaries, Your Highness," Hawley said. "Push them far enough away and they end up back where they started."

"Then post guards at the bottom of the stairs and keep people from coming up," Trevn said.

"Very well, sir," Hawley said, "but that won't keep those living in the castle away, and you will still have to pass the people at some point."

Then Trevn would simply have to outsmart them. Create a route only he knew about. There had been a series of secret passages in Castle Everton. Why not add some here? One or two private corridors and staircases would be just the thing to allow him to move around the castle without being seen when he deemed it necessary.

Which would be often.

They reached the ground floor and walked out into the chill morning. The barge carried them across the lake, where five horses were saddled and waiting with Marshal Winstone and a contingent of mounted soldiers.

Barek had wanted Trevn to summon Tace Edekk to a meeting in the castle, but Trevn felt it would be better to drop by unannounced and catch the man off guard.

The Duke of Raine had chosen for his manor a section of land in the forested foothills north of Armanguard. Trevn and his party had barely entered the woods when soldiers appeared on the road ahead, blocking their way.

Trevn sensed no hostility in the men. "They are merely curious," he said. "Nietz, ride ahead and announce my intentions to meet with the duke."

Nietz spurred his horse out from the pack. As Trevn watched him go, movement in the trees to the right of the road caught his eye. More soldiers.

"There are men in the woods on our right," Trevn voiced Cadoc.

"I see them," Cadoc said. "On our left as well."

"So much for the element of surprise," Trevn said.

"My guess is, the duke doesn't like surprises," Cadoc said.

Nietz returned. "They'll escort us to the manor. Said they patrol the forest for giants."

"We've had no report from the duke about trouble with giants," Trevn said.

"Apparently his men can handle such problems themselves," Cadoc said.

Trevn didn't see how. The soldiers escorted Trevn's party another two leagues into the foothills before they finally came upon a log palisade in a clearing. There was no moat, but Trevn could see a second, taller palisade beyond the first. He suspected Lord Edekk's fortress was nearly impenetrable, even by giants.

"Looks like the duke has giants of his own," Nietz said.

A man on foot pushed through the horses clustered at the gatehouse and approached Trevn and his guards. He was broad, a few hands taller than Trevn, and wore so many warrior twists in his hair that his head resembled a bush. A deep scar creased his left cheek, making a pale line through his thick, short black beard.

Trevn recognized the man as the captain of Lord Edekk's army. "Captain Korvoh."

Korvoh gave Trevn a jerky bow. "Your Highness, welcome to Nawhar, House Edekk's northern fortress."

"He has a second one?" Trevn asked.

"The duke built a house in town, yes, though he spends little time there."

"Hawley," Trevn voiced, *"remind me to have someone visit Lord Edekk's house in town."*

His onesent nodded subtly in response.

"Nawhar Manor is not overly large, Your Highness," Korvoh said. "It would be best if you left some of your men outside."

"They all come with me inside the palisade walls, though I will take only my personal guards into the building."

Korvoh inclined his head. "I'll have the gate opened." He set off through the horses, making his way back toward the gatehouse.

"I want everyone alert and watching for anything suspicious," Trevn said to Nietz. "I want to know what the duke is doing here. See if you can speak to any of the boys about new recruits to his army."

Nietz nodded.

The gate, which was also made of log stakes, swung open, and Trevn's men rode slowly inside a cramped bailey. The manor house stood three levels high and had been built of horizontal logs. Nietz and Rzasa dismounted, and a group of barn boys swarmed the horses. Korvoh was standing in an open archway with a tall, slender man dressed all in black, and a servant. Trevn immediately recognized the stern expression on Tace Edekk's lined face.

Trevn dismounted and a boy immediately claimed his horse. Cadoc was by his side before he could step away from the animal, and they walked together toward the duke.

"You have a nice place here, lord," Trevn said.

The duke bowed. "Thank you, Your Highness. I did not expect the honor of such a visit. I confess I am ill prepared to house so many men."

"We are not staying," Trevn said.

"Please come inside where it is warm," the duke said. "We had snow three days ago, but it melted as soon as it touched the ground. I fear winter is not far off."

Trevn and his men followed the duke, Korvoh, and the servant inside. They traipsed down a narrow hallway that smelled strongly of evergreen trees, and up a split turn staircase walled in hewn planks. A hallway on the second level led them to a bright sitting room, where a wall of windows overlooked a garden in back of the manor. The room was elaborately furnished, and a warm fire crackled in an ornate hearth that took up over half the wall.

Trevn walked straight for the windows, curious how the duke had managed such extravagance. "Where did you get the glass?" he asked. Castle Armanguard had nothing so large.

"Took them from the cabin in my great ship," Edekk said. "I hated to do it. Don't sail much now, though, so I boarded up the holes in the ship and put the windows here. Might as well enjoy them."

"That's quite clever, Your Grace," Trevn said. "The garden is nice, as well."

"My wife must have a garden. She is out there now, I believe, torturing some poor plant. She wraps them in fabric each night to save them from the frost. Foolish if you ask me, but she seems convinced it will help them survive the winter."

"It is not a garden that grows food," Trevn said, glancing down the rows of flowers and vines. "Where are your fields?"

"Don't have any," Edekk said. "I buy or trade what I need from other lords."

How interesting. "You used to make the most of your wealth through importing and exporting across the border. What are you doing now for income?"

"Making wine, mostly, which I confess has always been a hobby of mine. I also make and sell furniture to the other lords. I have access to lots of trees, as you can see, and employ several gifted woodsmiths."

Furniture would bring in little, as there would be few who could afford it on a regular basis, but wine would be very profitable. "I did not realize grapes grew in Er'Rets."

"My wine is not made of grapes, Your Highness, but cranberries. It's slightly more acidic in flavor but has a delicate sweetness I enjoy. And my wife finds it doesn't induce headaches like grape wines. Would you like to try some?"

"I would, yes," Trevn said, curious if the man was being honest.

"Natod, bring some wine for the king. And put five crates on a wagon for him to take back to the castle."

The serving man who had entered with them departed quickly.

"My condolences on the death of your son," Trevn said. He probably should have said it sooner, but Fonu Edekk had been a traitor and was responsible for Wilek's death. Trevn found it difficult to extend too much respect to the man's father.

Lord Edekk's eye twitched. "Ah, yes. I thank you." He stroked his jaw. "And you as well, Your Highness." He motioned to Trevn's blacks. "Ghastly thing, losing someone like that."

"Yes, it is," Trevn said.

The duke stepped forward, then rocked back, as if uncertain what he should do with himself. He finally motioned to an array of chairs upholstered in gold silk. "Won't you sit?"

Trevn chose the chair that gave him a view of both the windows and the entrance to the room. Cadoc and Hawley stood behind him, while Rzasa and Bonds posted themselves at the door. Trevn wondered how Nietz was faring on his mission to question the barn boys.

Lord Edekk lowered himself onto a chair on Trevn's right. He sat on the very edge, as if ready to rise in a flash, if necessary. Though the man's expression looked calm enough, he exuded anxiety. Trevn liked that he had surprised him and looked forward to the coming interrogation. He said nothing yet, though. Dragging things out would likely increase the duke's apprehension to the point he might let something slip.

The wine arrived, and the duke popped to his feet as the same servant, Natod, set a tray on a low table between the circle of chairs. Trevn sat patiently, watching with interest as the duke hovered over his man.

The next half hour passed in awkward conversation as they sipped from glasses of cranberry wine, which was surprisingly good and like nothing Trevn had ever tasted. Dry, but tart and fruity. Trevn asked questions about the design and construction of Nawhar Manor, enjoying the wine and how his casual visit seemed to increasingly annoy the duke.

"It's not every day a man gets a visit from his king, Your Highness," the duke said. "Dare I hope you are here to offer me a position on the Wisean Council?"

He had a lot of nerve. "No, Your Grace. That position has been assigned to Lord Idez."

"Ah." The duke's eye twitched and he finished off his goblet of wine. "Then I cannot guess as to the reason for this unexpected honor."

"There have been some complaints," Trevn said, pausing for effect, "about your methods in recruiting for your personal army."

The duke's brow sank. "How strange. I am not currently recruiting, nor have I since coming to this land."

Would he dare lie about such a thing? "That does not match the reports coming from my Master of Requests. He has received several complaints of this very nature. Do you have that number, Master Hawley?" Trevn looked over his shoulder at his onesent.

"Seventeen, sir," Hawley said.

"Seventeen complaints. All the same," Trevn said to the duke. "Any idea why so many would invent such longtales?"

"I cannot say, Your Highness. It might help if I could hear the full allegations."

"It is being said that you take boys into your army without their parents' consent," Trevn said.

"Ridiculous. I have never taken boys into my army. They are too young to be of use."

Truth.

The word pressed faintly upon Trevn's mind, and he instantly fortified his shields. "How odd that so many would claim such a thing, then. Any idea why?"

"None," the duke said. "Except . . ."

"Yes?" Trevn prodded.

"Mett Lycor. He was an old friend of Fonu's. Since my son was killed, he went rogue—knows he'll be executed if I get my hands on him. I've heard rumors he has gathered a group of men to do mercenary work, though I have conflicting reports that he and his band are nothing more than thieves."

Truth.

Again the word whispered against Trevn's mind like a nagging memory. He realized with a sudden jolt that he had experienced this before. The day he'd been compelled to ask Mielle to marry him. There was a mantic in Nawhar Manor, and Trevn had no wish to linger.

He set down his wine glass and stood. "It seems I have an outlaw to apprehend, then. I'll waste no more of your time."

The duke stood and followed Trevn to the door. "You are welcome to stay for dinner, Your Highness. Or if you'd like to go hunting, there are many fine stags in Nawhar Forest."

"Thank you, but I must return to Armanguard. I will send word when Master Lycor is apprehended. Thank you for the wine."

"It is my honor, Your Highness."

Trevn left. Once he and his men were alone on the road out of the forest, he questioned Nietz about what he had learned from the barn boys.

"None would say a word against the duke," Nietz said, "and none have seen any new boys in the manor. A few did say that giants come to Nawhar Manor every few weeks."

"To attack?"

"No, sir. To visit with the duke. It seems he has befriended some, though the boys didn't know which tribe of giants—didn't even know there were different tribes."

Befriended giants. "I felt magic in that sitting room," Trevn said. "I don't know whether Lord Edekk, Korvoh, or that servant was the wielder, but someone was trying to compel me to believe the duke's story, which tells me part of it, at least, was false."

"But which part?" Cadoc asked.

Trevn had no idea. "That is what I intend to find out."

MIELLE

W ell?" Mielle pranced out from behind her changing screen and struck a pose for Zeroah, who was sitting on the bed. "What do you think?" The flowing blue silk skirt swept around her ankles like water. "It's so very soft and light."

"It's lovely, especially that rich royal blue against your light brown skin. And the way it . . ." Her voice broke, and she began to cry.

"Oh, Zeroah!" Mielle rushed to the bed and sat beside her friend, pulling her into an embrace. "What is wrong? Did I say something?"

"It's nothing you did. I simply miss Wilek."

"I'm so sorry."

Zeroah sighed deeply. "Most days I wake and forget he is gone. I think, 'What shall I do today? Perhaps Wilek and I will go for a walk in the fields.' Then I remember." She dabbed her eyes. "People are always staring at me. I am the most pitiful creature in Armanguard, and there is nowhere to hide."

"Let me show you something fun." Mielle jumped off the bed, took Zeroah by the hand, and pulled her to her feet. She walked to the sideboard and pressed an indentation in the wall just beside it. The hidden door clicked open.

Zeroah gasped. "A secret door?"

Mielle nodded, beaming. "Trevn commissioned two secret passageways. They won't be finished for another few weeks, but isn't it fun? This one exits into the king's office, and there will be a second passage from the council chambers that comes out behind the curtain on the dais platform in the great hall. You are welcome to use them if you wish. It will make life so much easier for all of us. And hopefully those wretched concubines will finally go away."

Zeroah wrinkled her nose. "They are still there?"

"Every day! No matter how many times I've banished them, the awful creatures."

"That is unfair, Mielle," Zeroah said. "They are Arman's beloved too. I wonder if there are men looking for wives. Perhaps if you found the women a match, they would stop coming here."

Mielle considered that. "Now, there's a clever idea. Perhaps the Duke of Canden would take them all off my hands."

"I did not mean anyone who lives in the castle," Zeroah said. "You would be wisest to send them out of your home. You might ask Lady Pia's advice."

Lady Pia, whom Trevn had assigned as Mielle's shield. The woman followed her everywhere and was at this moment standing guard outside the door. "I feel like a beast in her presence. Even with her scarred face, she is still so lovely." Mielle walked to the bed and fell backward, sighing dramatically. "Trevn hired me a staff, you know. I now have two guards, a onesent, and an honor maiden. Sometimes all of this is simply too much and I wish myself back in the north, where I could look for the Puru children who were traded to those horrible giants."

"It is awful to even think about," Zeroah said. "I pray Arman's protection over the poor dears."

"Trevn says it's not our concern, but I cannot fathom how he can justify doing nothing."

"He is king now," Zeroah said, her voice small as she sat on the edge of the bed. "It is a great responsibility, Mielle."

Oh tuhsh. "I don't mean to make light of that . . ." She was tired of so much awkwardness. To this day, neither of them had said a word about their reversed stations. Never in Mielle's wildest dreams had she imagined such a thing could happen.

She wished it hadn't. Zeroah made a much better queen. Ten times so.

"We have persevered through so many setbacks," Mielle said. "Will we survive this one too?"

Zeroah looked down on Mielle. "What do you mean?"

Mielle pushed herself up until she and Zeroah were sitting face-to-face. "Do not pretend you cannot feel the strain between us. Words fail me continually. Me! The girl who prattles on nonstop. I hear the maids gossiping, saying that you will leave Armanguard and go live with Princess Saria in New Sarikar. Will you, Zeroah? Is that your intent?"

"I *have* thought about it, but I do not know Saria well or any of my cousins. I am closer to you and Rosârah Brelenah than anyone in my own realm."

Hope kindled in Mielle's stomach, and she clutched the shell on the soul-binding pendant she wore. "Please say you'll stay. I don't think I can do this without you."

Zeroah took hold of Mielle's hand. "Of course you could, but do not worry. I will stay."

"Oh, thank you!" Mielle hugged Zeroah, tears misting her eyes. She finally let go and wiped her eyes with her fingers. "I so covet your help, but I worry that every question I ask you is like a knife in your heart."

"Do not be silly."

"I am not! I was your honor maiden. You confided in me your deepest secrets and fears. You were born to be queen, Zeroah. You trained your whole life for it. That I must take your place grieves me deeply. It is horribly unfair and utterly ridiculous. What do I know of anything? I can't even remember the name of Trevn's former nursemaid, let alone all the dukes and earls and their wives and children."

"His nurse was named Liso," Zeroah said.

"See? You should be queen. You know so much more than I do."

"I *was* queen, and I did the best job I could with the time I had. Now the title has fallen to you, whether or not you wish it. Arman gave us to each other, Mielle, knowing what we would need. I will help you just as you helped me. Trust in that."

Mielle sniffled. "Thank you, dearest friend."

They hugged again, and when Zeroah finally released her, Mielle broached the topic that was most on her mind.

"The Duke of Odarka says we must hold court. He believes I might be a help in such a place. What do you think?"

Zeroah grimaced. "I do detest court, but I agree it would be beneficial to Trevn's reign. It is common knowledge that he has always disdained the nobility. Holding court would give the nobles a chance to see him behaving like a king and to speak with him."

"He refuses to go. He doesn't want me to go either, unless I take Empress Inolah along. Or you."

Zeroah drew in a deep breath. "What about the ball? I thought that would be your first foray into dealing with the peerage."

"Yes, well, Trevn said I must wait to plan the ball until he knows what is happening with some threat from Rosârah Laviel."

"A threat? Is it dangerous?"

Mielle sighed. "He would not give details, which is something else I hate about being queen. Trevn used to tell me everything—now he has so many secrets."

"Much of what he deals with every day is trivial. He likely doesn't want to bore you. Where would he hold court? The castle keep is too small. It does not even have a worthy throne room."

"I suppose we could use the great hall, though that seems rather dull. Outside, perhaps? In the bailey?"

Zeroah shook her head. "That won't do. Nobles do not like to spend time where commoners forge blades and behead chickens. You need a place segregated specifically for this purpose, in the same way Rosârah Brelenah once held court in the garden colonnade."

"What about the roof?" Mielle suggested. "That would be similar to how Rosâr Echad held court on the stern deck of the *Seffynaw*."

"It's not a bad idea, though some will complain of having to climb so many stairs." Zeroah pursed her lips until her brows suddenly rose. "What about one of the barges? I believe there are four, though two are rarely used. You might commission one to be outfitted for parties. You could tent it to provide shade. Bring out blankets and chairs, a throne for yourself and the empress, should she join you. You would need a secondary plan, though, since it's been getting colder. Winter will be here soon enough. Until then it might work nicely. What do you think?"

"I think you are brilliant! I never would have thought of such a thing. Oh, Zeroah, you are so good at this. I'm to be a laughingstock, aren't I?"

"Not with an empress and two former queens as your advisors. We three shall not forsake you. I only hope you will not become too busy for my friendship."

"How could I ever?"

"When the *Rafayah* was lost, everyone worried over Rosâr Trevn, myself included, but you cannot imagine my sorrow at losing you. Arman gave me Wilek, and though things were awkward at first, we grew very close. And now that Arman has taken Wilek away, he mercifully returned you to me. Is not he a thoughtful provider? After Wilek died, had I not had the hope from Trevn of your return, I might not have survived."

"Zeroah! You mustn't say such things."

"Just as I once insisted from you, Mielle, I will always speak the truth. You can count on me for that. Now, let us go to the school, for I know you are eager to see your orphans again."

Lady Pia and Bero, Mielle's second guard, escorted Mielle and Zeroah to the great hall so she could observe the school. A quick count totaled only thirteen children present today, orphans and nobles combined. Zeroah said that nobles learning alongside orphans was normally unheard of, and there were some nobility who refused to allow their children to be taught here. Mielle thought it was grand, though she couldn't help notice the highborn children sat together in the front tables, while the orphans sat in the rear.

"Were the children assigned places to sit?" she asked.

"No," Zeroah said. "When the school first met here, the children were scattered through the great hall. The noble children were sitting at their family tables, the orphans were in the back, and the princesses sat in the front row at the same table." She smiled. "The Duke of Canden forced them all into the front six tables, but they still clustered into groups."

It made sense, Mielle supposed. The children would want to sit near friends and, like it or not, their friends tended to be in the same social class.

Empress Inolah stood at the front of the left-side row of tables, where all the girls had been seated. There were far fewer boys today; the Duke of Canden was absent as well.

"Where are all the boys, I wonder?" Mielle asked.

"On the roof for swordplay lessons," Zeroah said. "The boys adore the Duke of Canden. It is good of him to take the time to teach them so many things, don't you think? They will be vastly ahead when they are old enough to train with the soldiers."

The front row was filled with little boys, and one older boy sat in the back, alone. He was dressed shabbily and must be one of the orphans. "Why does that boy remain here?"

"That is Porvil. I don't know why he did not go along. He always has before."

"Let's ask him," Mielle said, eager to speak with one of the orphans. "You two may wait here," she added to her guards.

Mielle and Zeroah walked to where the boy sat staring at his tablet and not writing.

"Hello," Mielle said. "What are you working on?"

He looked her up and down, then glanced at Zeroah. His eyes widened and he stood up and bowed, remaining bent like the bracket of a table.

"Please stand," Mielle said. "I want to speak with you."

The boy straightened, but his gaze remained prominently on Zeroah. He was nearly as tall as Mielle and had a round face and sullen eyes.

"Master Porvil, this is Rosârah Mielle," Zeroah said, "Rosâr Trevn's wife."

Porvil grew a bit pale. "*Two* queens?"

Mielle laughed. "I suppose we are, aren't we? Why did you not go to the roof with the other boys?"

"The duke dislikes me." Porvil glanced at his hands. "Because I'm an orphan."

Fire shot through Mielle's chest. Surely that could not be true. The duke taught dozens of orphaned children each day.

Trevn's concern quested toward her. *"I am well, Trevn. Sorry to frighten you."*

Porvil went on. "No matter what happens here, the duke blames me. The little boys talk and make mischief with Master Grayson, and the duke scolds me, makes me apologize, and I'm punished for the rest of the week. And that's not the worst of it."

Mielle could not believe this. Why would the duke hold such a prejudice against this young man?

"Is there a problem, Porvil?" Empress Inolah approached. She folded her arms and gave Porvil a raised eyebrow.

"No, Empress." Porvil sat back on the bench, picked up his stylus, and pulled his wax tablet toward him.

"It is wonderful that Duke Canden takes the elder boys to the roof," Empress Inolah said, "but I often struggle to give enough attention to his other students while he is away."

"Why doesn't he find himself an assistant to teach the boys while he is gone?" Mielle asked, still watching Porvil, who was now dutifully writing on his tablet. "He should not abandon you with everyone."

"Oh, we had assistants in here before, but the rosâr has had to call them away on other errands. I'm sure they will return when they can. I wonder if you ladies might be willing to read with some of the younger boys who have finished their assignments?"

"I would love to!" Mielle said.

"And I," Zeroah added.

"Wonderful. Let me introduce you to some of the children." She walked toward the front row of boys. Mielle and Zeroah followed, but Mielle glanced back at Porvil. The young man looked so forlorn. She would find him later and hear the rest of his story. She had made it her mission to make sure every orphan in Armanguard was provided for, but she could do little to fight against the prejudice of others. If the Duke of Canden had treated Porvil unfairly, he would regret it.

That midday, Mielle sat in her apartment with Abree, sewing dressing gowns for some of the young orphan girls and thinking of Porvil, the boy who had accused Duke Canden of wrongdoing. When she had looked for the young man after class, he had already gone. Bero was dispatched to fetch him but returned to say that Porvil had left the castle. Mielle had no idea why he would go into the city. According to Empress Inolah, Porvil had been apprenticed in the kitchens, but Bero said the cook had not sent him on an errand.

A knock sounded on the door. Lady Pia opened it, revealing Grayson. The usual crowd lingered behind him on the landing.

"Grayson, come in," Mielle said. "I'm surprised you did not voice me and appear here when you received my summons."

"Jhorn says it's rude to do so when it's not an emergency, and since Master Tonis didn't say it was an emergency, I figured walking to the door was probably best."

"You were very kind to take such precaution. Please, sit down. Lady Abree, would you wait outside with Lady Pia and Master Bero? We will not be long."

Abree nodded, and she and the guards let themselves out. Grayson sat on the edge of the longchair Abree had vacated and folded his hands in his lap, looking uncomfortable.

Mielle smiled warmly and did her best to set him at ease. "I am glad you came," she said. "We spent so much time together aboard the *Seffynaw* on our way back, but now that we have returned to Armanguard, I rarely see you."

"Jhorn keeps me busy. And the king too."

But not busy enough, if Trevn's stories of Grayson's exploits were to be believed. "I do hope you are not overloaded, for I had hoped to ask you a favor."

Grayson leaned forward. "I'm happy to do anything for my queen."

"I am glad to hear that," Mielle said. "I cannot stop thinking of the orphaned Puru children who were given to the Jiir-Yeke giants. I want to know what happened to them and what the giants do with the people they take."

"But we know that already. Conaw said they sacrifice them."

Mielle shuddered at those ugly words. "Yes, but to what? Or to whom? And how soon?"

"I asked Muna about it once," Grayson said. "She says it's the Jiir-Yeke's way of keeping peace, though she doesn't support it. She said a guilty heart finds no peace."

"She sounds very wise."

"She is. She also said there's one person who might know for certain how the sacrifices began." And Grayson told Mielle all about someone called Tuwa, the eldest matriarch of all the Puru tribes, who lived in a place called the elder village. "Tuwa is in charge of remembering the history of her people. If anyone knows why the Jiir-Yeke make sacrifices, it would be her."

"Could you find this elder village?" Mielle asked.

"Maybe. Muna said Tuwa lives in the north with those who no longer follow the herds. Once a month, each Puru tribe takes a tribute to her village to thank her and the other elders for their years of remembering. The elders survive on their tributes. Next time Muna's tribe goes, maybe I could go too?"

"That would be perfect," Mielle said. "If we could discover the motivation of the giants, we might find a way to stop them. But I also want to know what happened to the children they took away. Are they all dead? Or is there any chance of rescuing them?"

"I could try to find out," Grayson said. "I could go where you last saw them, then track them from there."

"That sounds dangerous." Trevn would not like it if Mielle put Grayson in danger.

"It wouldn't be, not if I went through the Veil where no one could see me."

Hope welled in Mielle's chest at the very idea of finding those children. "Only if you are certain it is safe."

"I am positive, Your Highness. Nothing will happen to me. I promise."

"Very well. Find out what you can about the children, and look for the elder village too. The more we find out about all of this, the better chance we have at setting it to right."

Grayson departed, and Abree and the guards returned. Abree settled back into her chair and picked up her sewing.

"How many gowns will we sew, Your Highness?" Abree asked.

"As many as needed," Mielle said, picking up on a hint of annoyance. Abree reminded Mielle of her sister Amala, but while her honor maiden might hint at displeasure, she never outright complained.

"I was nobly born, you know," Mielle told the girl. "My parents died when I was little. My sister Liviana had married Sir Kalenek, and they took in Amala and me. And after Liviana died, Kal kept us. It would have been easier for him to put us out. But he kept us. One person caring is all it takes sometimes, to change an orphan's whole life."

Not that it had done much for Amala.

"I think that's lovely, Your Highness," Abree said.

"Yes, well, I can only help the children I know of." And Arman had specifically laid those Puru orphans on her heart. Too many nights she had awakened with them on her mind. Such vulnerable dears, and she could do nothing but pray they would live long enough for Grayson to find them. Only then could she do anything to help.

"Barek Hadar loves the idea of holding court on the barge," Mielle told Trevn that night as they lay in bed.

He was silent for a moment, then his deep voice came from the dark. "That does not surprise me."

Tension grew between them. "Why are you angry?"

"I'm not."

"You're lying. I can feel it."

"I'm not angry at *you*. It's about something else."

Mielle pushed up onto one elbow, though she could not see her husband in the dark. "No, it's not, Trevn. You were fine until I brought this up."

"I don't want to hold court. I've told you this. And I've told Barek over and over."

"But I thought you were frustrated that the nobles don't like you."

"I am. But I'm not going to bribe them to like me either."

Mielle tried to force her feelings of hope and desire toward him, wanting him to sense how important this was to her. "Zeroah and I already worked out the invitations. 'You are cordially invited to join Rosâr Trevn and his queen for a water party.' Doesn't that sound fun?"

"Indeed," Trevn said, "if I were inviting friends rather than perfect strangers who despise me."

"Barek said, *'No offense, my dear, but no one will come for you alone.'* Zeroah said that simply wasn't true. She agreed that few of the men would care to see me, but she thinks the ladies would surely come. She says everyone is curious what kind of queen I will be."

"And what kind of favors they might be able to garner from you," Trevn said.

Irritation spiked through Mielle. "They can ask all they want, but I will agree to nothing without asking you first. Zeroah said we mustn't discount the noblewomen—that they have influence over their husbands, but also over the people who work for them."

"Servants have ears, you mean?"

"Well, yes. And, Trevn, I agree that it would be best if you did come, at least for the first time."

"I cannot believe you are still pressing me." Now Trevn was irritated, and their combined emotions made Mielle twice as angry and sent her heart racing.

"Don't get so upset," she said.

"Mielle, I have an endless list of tasks before me. This is one I've already crossed off my list. Please do not put it back on."

"But Barek and Zeroah think—"

"I heard you. I did. But I don't care what they think. I don't want any part of it."

"But, Trevn, I don't think it would be all that bad."

"Rubbish and nonsense, is what it is."

"If you'd only listen."

"Talk if you like. I will not change my mind."

"Well, that is rude."

He sighed heavily. "Mielle, I have made a decision, and my feelings on the matter have not changed."

"Well, mine have, and you should care enough about me to at least hear why." Tears laced her voice, and she felt Trevn soften.

"Fine. Tell me why."

"Thank you." Her words lifted the tension between them a little, but it was still a taut line. "The whole point of holding court is to give your nobles a place where they feel they can be heard by you. I am happy to be the one who listens, but the duke believes that none of the men will come if they know you're not going to be there."

"So?"

"Well, we need the men to come! They make the decisions that affect the people who live near them. You said your army is disjointed. You need loyal soldiers who will follow you to war if the worst comes. Well, Hinck has already told you it's coming. So, like it or not, you need the support of those noblemen so that they will bring you fighting men. If only their wives attend court and hear your cause, then each woman is left to try to convince her husband, and you can see from present circumstances how well that goes."

He chuckled, rose up, and took her chin between his fingers. "You did well enough." He kissed her soundly on the mouth. "I can't promise to come, Mielle, but I will ask Hawley to see where he might make room in my schedule."

She wrapped her arm around his side. "Oh, thank you, Trevn! I knew you would be persuaded once you heard the logic."

"I only hope not to regret letting you talk me into it," he said, pulling her close.

"You won't. I promise!"

"Don't make promises you have no control over, Mouse," he said, kissing the top of her head. "Those nobles all have minds and agendas of their own."

The next morning when Mielle first glanced out a window, the ground was covered in a thick blanket of snow, and the lake looked frozen. She ran to Trevn's office with Lady Pia at her heels, passed Cadoc at the door, and entered without knocking. Her husband was not alone. Barek Hadar and Hawley were sitting on the other side of his desk.

"Did you see?" she asked. "I shall have to cancel court!"

Barek stood and bowed to her. "Did we see what, Your Highness?"

"It has snowed! Not only that, the lake is frozen. I don't think we could move the barges if we tried."

Trevn stood and walked around his desk. "Frozen lake? This I must see." He opened the door and walked out.

Mielle followed, as did Cadoc, Barek, Hawley, Lady Pia, and two of Trevn's King's Guards. The nearest window was in the council chambers a few doors down, but instead, Trevn took the stairs to the roof.

When they stepped outside, an icy wind whipped around them and Mielle gasped. She could see her breath on the frigid air. "It's freezing out here!"

Trevn took one step, slipped, and barely managed to catch his balance. "It's icy too. Looks like winter has arrived."

Cadoc took hold of Trevn's elbow and led him carefully toward the parapet. Bonds appeared beside Mielle and offered his arm. Mielle took hold, and the King's Guard led her after Trevn. She reached his side and looked down on the lake. It wasn't completely frozen after all. Just around the edges near the shore. Men below were beating at the ice with poles, trying to free the barges.

"Only part of the river froze last year," Trevn said, "unless we found it after it had thawed some. I do hope this winter will not be colder than anything we experienced last year."

"What about court?" Mielle asked.

He grinned at her. "I suppose we'll have to postpone it until spring."

"Trevn!" Mielle folded her arms. "Zeroah, Tonis, and I have already done too much work to cancel."

Trevn's brown eyes lit on hers. "In one day?"

She would not give in to his teasing. "There must be a room in the castle we could use."

"You know very well there is not," Trevn said. "I do hope the crops didn't freeze. If so, we could be looking at a food shortage."

"Many farmers had already harvested," Hawley said, "but not all of them."

Trevn walked back toward the castle entrance. "We must pen letters to all the farmers to inquire after their crops. If too many were lost, we will have to make up for it with hunting and foraging."

Mielle watched Trevn go, scowling. Her husband had a million concerns and more piling up each day, but her best hope for helping solve one of those was packed in ice. What could she do now?

ϘOATCH

Qoatch collected two dozen clay pots of various sizes from the work shed near the emperor's garden. He filled them with fresh soil and transported them to Jazlyn's apartment. The Great Lady had asked him to multiply the ahvenrood plant Chieftess Charlon had given her. His goal was to divide it into as many cuttings as possible.

The plant was not overly large. Qoatch took great care in each cut, making sure to leave enough stem. It hadn't rained in weeks, and his biggest concern was that the cuttings might dry out before they could grow roots of their own. He left Jazlyn's apartment in search of fabric to tent over the pots in an effort to create a humid environment. After that, there would be nothing to do but wait and see.

He was in the tailor's workroom, trying to decide between two lengths of linen, when muted screams caught his attention. He ran out into the corridor, found it empty, and followed it to the inner courtyard, where people were scattering like ants after a dropped boot.

Qoatch grabbed the arm of a serving woman and tugged her to a stop. "What is happening?"

"Giants, sir. They've breached the bailey."

Qoatch must warn Jazlyn. Giants had made dozens of attacks against the outlying settlements, but never against the stronghold. Why now? He couldn't imagine that anything had been done to provoke such an assault.

Qoatch sprinted to Jazlyn's apartment, surprised to find that the Igote guards had left. Her loyal Protectors remained, circled around his Great Lady, who stood in the open front door, barking orders like an army general.

"... you other four, with me and Niklee. No one is to leave this apartment for any reason, and no one but Niklee, Qoatch, or myself is to enter. Niklee, come." She pushed out of the group and started down the corridor, approaching Qoatch with Niklee and four Protectors at her heels.

"Qoatch, where have you been?" Jazlyn asked. "Giants are attacking and we must see that Prince Ferro is moved into hiding."

Qoatch's steps slowed, and when she reached him, he reversed direction to walk alongside her. "I don't understand, Great Lady. What of Princess Jahleeah and Prince Jael?"

"Safe inside the apartment with Zinetha. Prince Ferro is my concern now."

But this made no sense. Why save a boy she had wanted dead? "And the emperor?"

"Rosârah Thallah will not permit me anywhere near my husband," she said, "but I might have a chance at helping the prince."

"His attendants have likely done so already," Qoatch said. "My concern is to get you safely hidden before the giants infiltrate the castle."

She lowered her voice to a whisper. "If I hide and we live through this attack, but the emperor and his brother are killed, the people will hate me forever and many will believe Thallah's accusations against me. New Rurekau will be lost to me. It will be impossible to rule as regent when the people want me dead. But if I were to save Prince Ferro's life ..."

It might change the way the Rurekan people felt about her. And Ferro was young enough that Jazlyn could serve as regent for many years. Qoatch had almost discarded the antidote for the dead sleep. He was glad he had not followed through. "I will see that Prince Ferro is moved to safety, Great Lady, but I urge you to return with your Protectors to your apartment."

"I will not. I must be seen."

Qoatch didn't like it. He was unarmed—should have run inside the apartment to grab his sword. Too late now.

They crossed the courtyard that stretched before the great hall, then entered the royal wing. Shaved-headed Igote soldiers clogged up the hallway outside the doors to Emperor Ulrik's chambers. Prince Ferro's rooms were around the corner on the other side of the soldiers. Unfortunately, this was the only way to reach them.

"Come," Jazlyn said. She pushed open the nearest door and went inside. Qoatch and Niklee followed.

It looked to be a high-ranking servant's chambers, likely belonging to Ulrik's onesent, Taleeb, though no one was present now. Jazlyn waved the Protectors inside and out of sight, then stood watching from the open doorway as the Igote passed by in the corridor. The litter came into view, carried by four Igote with Rosârah Thallah leading the way. That same fiery orange shadir was coiled around her throat.

"Quickly now!" Thallah said. "We must get the emperor into the cellar. The giants are too tall to go down there."

When the corridor cleared, Jazlyn waved her party out. Qoatch stayed at her side as she tottered around the corner and entered the first room she came to.

Prince Ferro's room.

A maid hovered at the boy's bedside—the same maid who had given Qoatch Prince Ferro's box of childhood toys the day he had planted the poisonous incense. "He's ready," she said, picking up a belt with sheathed sword and a fat satchel. "I've put some extra clothing in his bag in case he remains in hiding a long while, and this sword was a gift from his father. I think he would want it."

The woman apparently couldn't tell Igote guards from Protectors.

"Pick him up, Qoatch," Jazlyn said.

Qoatch hesitated only a moment, then quickly obeyed his Great Lady. So malnourished was the boy, he weighed little more than one of the twins. Shame washed over Qoatch at the knowledge that he was responsible for the young prince's condition.

"Don't you have a litter?" the maid asked.

"They're using it for my husband," Jazlyn said, "and there is no time to wait for their return. We must go now. Quickly, Qoatch." She nodded to the door. "We must get him to safety. You will come with us," she said to the maid. "Niklee, help carry the prince's things."

"Yes, Great Lady." Niklee took the satchel from the maid.

The Protectors held open the door, and Qoatch carried the boy out into the corridor. Jazlyn hurried ahead, leading the way.

They reached the courtyard just as Rosârah Thallah and her Igote guards entered from the opposite side, returning from wherever they'd taken the emperor. The shadir around Thallah's neck unwound itself and floated into the air above her head.

"The orange slight is with the queen," Qoatch mumbled to his Great Lady.

The two groups came to a standstill in front of the doors to the great hall. The short, fat Armanian queen and Empress Jazlyn's thin, elderly form looked almost comical as they faced each other, as if ready for battle.

Thallah's eyes narrowed to slits. "How dare you lay hands on the prince!"

"We are taking him to safety," Jazlyn said.

"That is not your responsibility."

"I am Empress Jazlyn of New Rurekau. Do not stand in my way."

"Anyone tormented by the guilt of murder will seek refuge in the grave."

"Does my husband know you are a mantic?" Jazlyn asked. "We all know how he feels about such things."

Thallah's startled expression gave her away. "How dare you imply . . . I don't owe you any . . . Hand over Prince Ferro this instant!"

"I will do no such thing," Jazlyn said.

Something banged in the distance. Qoatch shifted slightly and peered down the corridor that led straight to the stronghold's main entrance. The doors were closed for now, blocked with several crossbars. Another bang shook them. Then another.

As the pounding continued, Thallah began to fidget and pace. "I do not wish to see our soldiers kill each other unnecessarily, Empress. Is that what you want?"

"My only desire is to get the prince to safety before the giants break down the doors. Use your magic to stop the giants. Cast a protection spell over all the entrances."

"You speak nonsense, Empress," Thallah said. "I told you I have no magic."

Jazlyn's wrinkled face pulled into a smile. "Even if you hadn't given yourself away with your reaction moments ago, my eunuch is a seer, Your Highness. He tells me your shadir is with you now—orange and looks like fire. Let him help us, rosârah. Tell us the name of the one who can save us."

Thallah's eyes grew wild. "He is called Cherem. He has been my companion for many years, but I have never been proficient in rune magic."

"Do not be confused by archaic Magonian rituals," Jazlyn said. "If you are bonded, then he is yours to command. You need only make your request. That you live is in his best interest. Have you taken ahvenrood recently?"

"Not in several days, but I have some with me." Thallah withdrew a small glass vial from her ample cleavage and held it up.

Greed lit Jazlyn's eyes as she looked upon that white powder. "Take it and order him to protect us."

A crack turned everyone's heads toward the doors, where the banging continued. The blade of an axe rent through one side, knocking out a single plank. Heavy blows resounded and increased in ferocity. It wouldn't be long now.

Thallah Hadar hasn't the courage to perform magic.

Qoatch met the dark eyes of the shadir. "Cherem says the queen doesn't have the courage," he said.

"It's not about courage!" Thallah cried. "I cannot create magic. I am nothing more than a malleant."

"Then give the root to me," Jazlyn said, walking toward the Armanian queen, "and I will save us."

Thallah took a step back. "You can't have him! He's mine."

"I only wish to save the people of Rurekau. Save my husband and his brother. Save my children. If you will not do that, then at least order your men to step aside and let my eunuch get the prince to safety."

"I will not take orders from you!" Thallah screamed.

Wood splintered. Down the corridor, Qoatch could see a giant's arm push through the broken planks and fumble with the crossbars barricading the door.

"Don't let them get me!" Thallah shrieked, pushing her way behind the Igote. "Cherem, keep me safe!"

The fiery shadir merely smiled and swam around the queen's waist.

"Protectors!" Jazlyn said. "Into formation. Push through. And you—" She clutched the sleeve of one Protector and whispered into his ear. He nodded.

Oh, Great Lady. Qoatch hoped she would take care and do nothing foolish.

The Protectors arranged themselves into a V around Jazlyn, Qoatch, Niklee, and the maid, then marched forward, pushing through the Igote, none of which tried to stop them. All were staring down the corridor at the doors that would soon be no more.

Just as the Protectors' formation passed the queen and her Igote, the Protector Jazlyn had whispered to lunged at Thallah and grabbed her wrists. Jazlyn flew at them and snatched the vial from the queen's hand.

"No!" Thallah screamed. "Don't take him from me!"

But Jazlyn had already choked down the root. "I gave you every chance to save us, but you refused." Her gaze roved the courtyard until it latched onto the shadir. "Cherem." She curtsied deeply to the creature. "*Ata yakhol bara hay ecâr rakas yahda shelno nehfesh.*"

The shadir perked up, swelled in size—not much, but Qoatch knew Jazlyn had succeeded in making the creature her own.

"*Athawn yahfeh,*" she said, then began to change physically, shifting back into the great beauty Qoatch had always known before Gozan had ended the spell. A small smile turned his lips and he shook his head. Jazlyn was entirely too predictable.

"Great Lady, take care," he warned. "This shadir is not Gozan. Its power will not last as long before you will need to purge and take more root."

"Do not worry over me, Qoatch," Jazlyn said, her voice silky smooth again.

One last peal of cracking wood and the doors were ripped off their hinges. A line of giants spilled into the castle, making a hailstorm of footsteps that quickly drew nearer.

"Our enemy comes," Jazlyn said. *"Pasas."* Everyone vanished, becoming invisible just as the first giants lumbered into the courtyard.

The giant in the lead shouted, a confused wrinkle in his brow. He stopped, and the giant behind him skidded to a halt.

"Get the prince to safety!" Jazlyn yelled. "Protectors and Igote, you will fight beside me. I have given us the advantage. We must not fail."

Shouts of agreement rose up along with the scrape of steel as the men drew their swords. Qoatch handed off Prince Ferro to Niklee, then took the boy's belt and sword from the maid.

The lead giant urged his companions forward, and the invaders lumbered into the courtyard, foreheads scrunched and gazes roving. They took tentative steps forward and spoke to one another in their native tongue. They were pale-skinned, though most had painted stripes of mud on their cheeks and foreheads. Their hair and beards were long and braided with bits of leather and bone.

"Qoatch, beside me," Jazlyn said, stepping back into the opened doors of the great hall as the lead giant walked over the place where she had been standing and sniffed.

"I am with you, Great Lady." He followed her inside the hall and drew the blade from Ferro's belt. The sword was at least two hands shorter than his own, but it would have to do. He threw down the belt and raised the blade.

Two giants entered the great hall. Jazlyn whispered a few ancient words, and the giants floated off the floor, shouting.

As Qoatch slowly walked backward, his foot knocked against a chair. The nearest giant swung his club above his head and smashed the chair in pieces, breaking a hole into the floor as well.

Qoatch jumped aside and—as the giant tugged his club from the jagged floorboards—slashed his blade across the giant's forearms.

The giant howled and yanked his club free from the floor. He yelled in his foreign tongue and swung his club before him like a flag. Qoatch ducked back to keep out of the way.

Of the half dozen giants inside the great hall, all but one, who was trying to tug his floating companion back to the floor, mimicked the behavior of Qoatch's opponent. They had caught on to the fact that the enemy was invisible and knocked their clubs into tables and chairs or slammed them against the floor and walls, leaving jagged holes and shaking the room.

Jazlyn sent benches and chairs flying, using the objects to strike the giants in the face or under the chin. The giants fought back by pulverizing the furniture. Splinters of wood exploded all around Qoatch. A sliver the size of his index finger stuck him in the thigh. He ripped it out, and a trickle of blood oozed from the wound.

One of the giants spun toward Qoatch, nostrils flaring and eyes roving as if hoping to see some hint of where his opponent might be standing. Qoatch used the point of his sword to shove a chair, and as the giant slowly swung his club up above his head, Qoatch darted behind him. The giant brought down his club with great force, and Qoatch slashed Ferro's sword across the back of his legs. The giant howled, sank to his knees, and Qoatch chopped the short blade through his opponent's neck, beheading him.

On they fought. Qoatch killing giants, and Jazlyn throwing furniture or making giants float. Several were drifting through the air, one pinwheeling his arms and legs; the others were unable to move. All floated slowly toward the ceiling.

Qoatch went after those he could reach, slitting their throats. Once he had slain all the immobilized giants, he realized Jazlyn had left the great hall. He jogged out into the courtyard, following the trail of floating giants, which led him to the castle entrance. The remaining giants were fleeing through the bailey, headed toward the drawbridge.

They froze suddenly, bodies stiff, then toppled off the sides of the drawbridge and into the water. "Great Lady?" Qoatch called out, wondering where she was. "Do you need to purge?"

"Cherem says a swarm roves just outside the gate. Another mantic has come." Jazlyn's voice came from his right, near the gatehouse.

Qoatch looked past the drawbridge to the wooden gate, surprised to see several dozen shadir advancing toward them. At first glance, most appeared to be slights, until he recognized Mikray, who took on the appearance of a slender, tattooed man. He had last seen the common giving orders during the takeover of Emperor Ulrik's former flagship *Baretam*.

"I recognize one of the shadir," Qoatch said. "This swarm belongs to

Dendron, who serves the man who calls himself King Barthel, though I see no sign of Dendron himself."

"Strange that he arrives just as giants are attacking," Jazlyn said.

"We come in peace!" a man yelled in Kinsman, his voice deep and grating.

"We shall see about that," Jazlyn mumbled.

The gate opened, and three people entered, walking abreast of one another. Two women and an elderly man dressed in white and gold robes. Around them, the swarm of shadir flitted about, confident and joyful.

Qoatch searched for Dendron the great but did not see him. These humans were clearly mantics. Behind them, on the other side of the moat, a long procession could be seen approaching the now-opened gate.

"Identify yourselves!" Jazlyn called.

Qoatch moved toward her voice, eager to be close in case she had need of him.

The elderly man stepped forward, frowning as his gaze roamed what must appear to be an empty bailey. "I am Filkin Yohthehreth," he said, "prophet of King Barthel. This is Lady Zenobia and Lady Mattenelle, my comrades." His lined face was thin and sensitive, with large black eyes and a sullen mouth. "We come on behalf of our king, who wishes to meet the emperor and empress of New Rurekau."

"I am the empress," Jazlyn said, "but perhaps you could come back some other time. We are busy at the moment, as you can see."

"I see nothing but dead giants," the man said. "Where are you?"

Jazlyn chose that moment to reveal herself and everyone else. One of the women on the drawbridge took a step back as Jazlyn, Qoatch, and some two dozen Igote suddenly appeared as if from nowhere.

Jazlyn's eyes were bright but her ashen face concerned Qoatch. She needed to purge. "I am Empress Jazlyn, former Priestess and High Queen of Tenma," she said. "Like yourself, I do not fight with swords."

"I hope you did not mind our assistance in attacking those giants," Yohthehreth said.

"Not at all," Jazlyn said, "though it was unnecessary."

"May I call my king to greet you, Your Eminence?" Yohthehreth asked.

"Your king has come at a precarious time," Jazlyn said. "We have just defended our fortress against giant invaders. I must dig a pit in the field to hold the captives for questioning, then set our fortress to rights again. As you can see, there is much work to be done."

"With your permission, Empress, might we assist you?" Yohthehreth asked. "We are quite capable of healing the wounded and repairing the damage done."

"I would not deny such service," Jazlyn said.

Yohthehreth spoke to the women standing beside him, then set off across the drawbridge and exited through the gate, his white robes billowing behind. The women advanced, setting to work by casting spells to repair the damage.

"They do not seem bent on attack," Jazlyn said. "Shall I trust them?"

Qoatch watched them warily. "I remain unconvinced that the arrival of King Barthel and the giants' attack are coincidental," he said, "but you are weary and need purging, so their assistance will help you greatly. Besides, King Barthel's fight is with Armania, so while he might try to impress us, lie to us, or attempt to use us, I see no reason why he would harm us."

"Keep watch," she said, her eyes following the female mantics, "and direct these women. I am taking Cherem to Rosârah Thallah's chambers to seek out any more root she might have hidden. It is best to search now, while the coward is still hiding in the cellar."

"Take some guards along," Qoatch said.

"Most certainly." She smiled, and her beauty struck him with a sense of nostalgia.

"It is good to see you reclaim your former glory," Qoatch said.

"Do not get sentimental, Qoatch. I need you sharp."

Jazlyn departed, and Qoatch kept a close watch on the mantics as he supervised the restoration of the castle.

Yohthehreth returned with a group of men. Two more male mantics—one strong and handsome, the other round and middle-aged—wore white and gold robes. They made their way through the bailey with their shadir, healing Igote and Protectors, moving giants outside the stronghold, and repairing damage.

Also among the group were four guards dressed in red uniforms and a second elderly man. The man was taller than Yohthehreth and wore fine robes of green velvet and gold. A narrow circle of gold sat atop his head. He had tight skin for one so aged, pulled thinly over bony, small features. His receding gray hair hung in a fat braid that draped over one shoulder and stretched down to his knees. Halfway down, the braid darkened to black.

One of the women introduced him to Qoatch. "May I present King Barthel Rogedoth of Islah," she said. "He has come to pay his respects to Emperor Ulrik and his bride."

"The empress is busy at present," Qoatch said. "I am sure she will greet you as soon as she is able. If you would like to wait inside, I can take you to a spare bedchamber where you can rest until the empress is ready to receive you."

The king grunted, obviously displeased to be kept waiting. "I suppose that will do."

Qoatch called forth a servant to escort the king and his guards inside to a spare room, while he remained outside with the king's mantics. Just as all had been set to rights, Jazlyn returned, looking bright and refreshed—glorious, truly. She must have found more root in Rosârah Thallah's chambers.

Jazlyn stopped in the center of the bailey, and when she spoke, she used magic to magnify her voice. "Hear me well, for I have news."

The work ceased as all eyes turned to regard the empress.

"Prince Ferro has recovered," she said, smiling. "He is awake, though still very ill. I give praise to the goddess Tenma for restoring my magic so that I could grant the boy his life."

"What of the emperor?" an Igote guard asked.

Jazlyn's eyes instantly glistened with tears. "I know not. Rosârah Thallah took him to the cellar, and I've not had a moment to try to break past the defenses she has set up against me. Qoatch, send a servant to the cellar with word of Prince Ferro's recovery and the arrival of our guests. I set our cooks to work preparing a feast that I am sure the rosârah will not want to miss."

Qoatch bowed. "Yes, Great Lady." And he set off to obey.

Two hours later, when the castle was fully repaired and all had freshened up, dinner was served in the great hall. Jazlyn had taken the seat of honor and placed King Barthel at her right hand. Qoatch stood behind her, keeping a close watch on the great shadir the king had brought with him.

Dendron, or so he was called, looked like a stubby tree with skin like dirt, arms like branches, clothing of leaves, and a waterfall of hair that dissipated before hitting the floor. He stood no taller than an average woman and glided along in a puddle of soft mist. Though he appeared unassuming at first glance, such detail in his appearance, right down to his pale, stone eyes, was proof of his immense power.

He held an air of great importance, as if he considered himself above the physical gratification that obsessed the lives of most shadir. He stood against the back wall like the rest of the servants and did not speak—at least not aloud. Qoatch had no doubt that this creature considered himself superior to everyone in the room. No wonder Gozan had always avoided him.

Jazlyn and King Barthel were speculating over the giants' motives—the king had *claimed* to have had no part in the attack, though Qoatch knew Jazlyn did not believe him. She wanted rule of Rurekau, however, and could not afford to make an enemy of this man, though she would not make herself submissive to him either.

Rosârah Thallah came running into the great hall. "Your Highness!" The Armanian queen bustled up the center aisle, skirts hiked up and revealing thick ankles. Her footsteps pattered over the wood floor that no longer showed any signs of the morning's destruction.

King Barthel's face broke into a wide smile. "Rosârah Thallah, there you are. I looked for you in the restoration, but it seems you had other responsibilities."

That King Barthel had expected to see Rosârah Thallah bothered Qoatch. Both had the ability to mind-speak, so the rosârah had likely known the king would visit.

The Armanian queen reached the front, stopped, and swept into a shaky curtsy. "I gave the empress the last of my evenroot," she said, panting. "So that she could fight the giants."

"How generous," the king said. "Empress, are you in need of root?"

"I have a little," Jazlyn said, watching him warily. "But the bulk of my supply was taken from me during the voyage across the sea."

"A grievous loss," King Barthel said. "I could spare some of my own if you would be interested in discussing a trade."

Jazlyn's eyes lit with interest. Using it earlier that day had brought about a relapse in both desire and dependency. She craved the return of the power she once wielded, and Qoatch knew that she would ally with this man if she saw a way to do so without giving up her freedom.

"Ahvenrood in exchange for what?" she asked. "I hope you do not intend to conquer us."

"Goodness, no, Empress. I seek allies to my cause, and Rosârah Thallah suggested Rurekau might be willing."

So they *had* spoken ahead of time. Qoatch wished he could communicate with his Great Lady as King Barthel and Rosârah Thallah were likely doing this very moment.

Jazlyn regarded Rosârah Thallah, who still stood awkwardly on the floor below the high table. "I find that a strange recommendation. Coming from you, Your Highness."

"How so, *Empress*?" Thallah asked.

"King Barthel, you are an enemy to Armania, with whom we are already allied, and the realm of which Rosârah Thallah's son has just become king. Why would a mother put herself against her own son?"

Thallah's cheek twitched and she glared at Jazlyn. "My son is young and foolish. He no longer heeds my counsel, but I adore him and will do all I can to spare his life."

"Interesting," Jazlyn said. "And what is your cause, King Barthel?"

"I want only what is due me—what is due us all. For too long men and women have ruled unfairly, forcing their morals upon their people. I seek only a world where everyone is free to do as they please. Worship who you like. Marry who you like. A man's—or woman's—business is their own, as it should be. King Echad believed that, but his sons . . . no offense to you, rosârah, but they believe otherwise."

"Oh, to my own shame I know it," Thallah said. "You are so wise, Your Highness."

This man spun words well and had clearly won Rosârah Thallah's allegiance.

"You have gallantly stated your motivation, Your Highness," Jazlyn said, "but not your end goal. What do you want to achieve?"

"It is not a matter of wanting, Empress. I *will* depose King Trevn and Queen Saria and rule both realms as one—as is my right."

"Why not Rurekau as well?" Jazlyn asked.

"I have no legitimate claim over Rurekau, Empress, nor do I seek one. I am of Sarikarian blood, and rule of that realm is clearly due me. My grandson, Janek, should have ruled Armania, but he was murdered. That realm has since fallen into disarray, and I seek only to bring stability to the lost remnant of the Five Realms."

"I finally understand," Jazlyn said. "But yours is a war we want no part of. New Rurekau will not battle beside you, nor will we fight beside Armania or Sarikar. We will stay out of this war entirely. But if we learn anything that might aid in your cause, we will pass on the information. How much ahvenrood is that worth to you?"

"Your offer is understandable, Your Eminence, though not what I hoped for," the king said. "For such a treaty I would give you a bottle of evenroot juice."

Jazlyn narrowed her eyes. "What size bottle and what concentration?"

"A standard. Full strength."

She lifted her chin. "For the support I've offered, I want two bottles."

"I will give you one now, and a second when Chieftess Charlon of Magosia becomes my ally."

"What has the Chieftess to do with me?" Jazlyn asked.

"I need your help in winning her support."

"I will try, but I cannot promise to win her. If she refuses, I will keep my first bottle of root juice and you and I will have peace between us."

The king inclined his head. "Very well. I ask only that you try, Empress."

"Then I accept," Jazlyn said, turning to look over her shoulder at the servants. "Boy, bring some wine so we might celebrate this union."

The boy scurried away.

"What do you know of Magosia and Chieftess Charlon?" the king asked.

"We signed a treaty of peace between us," Jazlyn said. "You should know that right now. I will not betray her, so never ask me to."

"I have no intention of doing so."

"Good," Jazlyn said. "The Chieftess is strong in magic. I could not see into the Veil when I was there, but I could feel the hum of shadir in the air. She no doubt leads a swarm of several hundred."

"Did you catch the name of her shadir?" he asked.

"She lied about that. Said it was called Mitsar."

"Small one?" The king chuckled, as did the shadir in the Veil who surrounded them.

"Her shadir helped her kill Magon and Mreegan so that she was able to take power," Jazlyn said.

The king's eyes widened. "Chieftess Charlon killed a great?"

And behind him, in the Veil, Dendron vanished.

Jazlyn nodded. "Some of her women witnessed the event. She terrifies her people. All but Sir Kalenek, who guards her son, a root child fathered by your grandson Janek Hadar."

The king stiffened. "The child lived?"

"He lives still," Jazlyn said. "The Chieftess claims he is under two years of age, but he looks to be nearly a man. He is . . . different. Having grown abnormally fast has put him at a disadvantage."

"I must meet him," King Barthel said. "Might we invite the Chieftess to join us here? I could send out a messenger shadir to her today."

"Why here, Your Highness?" Jazlyn asked. "We don't have much room, as you can see, and you must be eager to take your army east toward Sarikar."

"Not just yet, Empress. While I am here, there is one more nation I seek an alliance with."

"Who is that?" Jazlyn asked.

"The giants."

Jazlyn narrowed her eyes. "The giants you *helped us* defeat?"

"No, actually," the king said. "Those giants looked to me like the Ahj-Yeke, from the forests northeast of the mountains. I seek an alliance with the giants who live to the northwest of here. They have a magic that has made the other giant tribes and the Puru people fear them. I hope to find out how that magic works and use it to aid my cause."

"And what do these northern giants call themselves?" Jazlyn asked.

"Jiir-Yeke," the king said. "The bird makers."

CHARLON

"Did you see that?" Charlon twisted to regard the real, flesh-and-blood Sir Kalenek. He sat on the ground behind her. Beside the cold campfire. Mashing root into a stone bowl.

He glanced at the illusions of himself. Then quickly went back to his work. "Can't you practice duplicating someone else?"

Charlon turned back to the two illusions of Sir Kalenek standing before her. Both were dark and brooding. Except for red eyes. "I prefer you to any other. Though I wish I could master the eyes. Can you tell them apart?"

Sir Kalenek sighed and again looked up from his work. "They are different somehow?"

"I've used only one gowzal to make them. The Kalenek on the right is a mask. The one on the left is an illusion. Powered by the magic in the first gowzal."

Sir Kalenek grunted. "They look identical."

Charlon pointed to the mask of Sir Kalenek. Commanded the gowzal inside. "*Râbab.*" She felt the power strain. A third Sir Kalenek flickered into sight. Stood on the other side of the mask. The illusion warped, fizzled. Maintaining a second illusion proved too much for the single gowzal. It screeched through the mask of Sir Kalenek's mouth. Collapsed into a pool of mud.

Both illusions vanished instantly.

"Thank you," Sir Kalenek said.

Charlon did not appreciate his sarcasm. "I cannot hold two illusions of the same mask," she said. "And I have no idea how to transform the eyes."

"Use the right magic words?" Sir Kalenek suggested.

Such ignorance angered Charlon. As if he hadn't seen. Seen her try such a thing weeks ago. She needed her son. At least he would appreciate all she had accomplished. "Where is Shanek? I summoned him over an hour ago."

"Haven't you noticed? He no longer responds to a summons."

Dismay crept into her heart. She hadn't noticed. "Why not?"

"Because he finds every person dull in comparison to his new companion, and Shanek DanSâr will always choose what he enjoys best."

"He must practice."

"He has his own magic, Charlon. He does not care to learn yours."

She spun around. Located the great shadir, who stood watch from the Veil. "Do you know where he is, Rurek?"

He is in Miss Amala's tent.

Charlon ground her teeth. Hated that Sir Kalenek had been right again. "Tell Shanek to come instantly. Or I will not teach him to use the birds."

Very well. Rurek vanished.

Charlon regarded the three remaining shadir in the tent—Nwari, Caph, and Okda—all slights that had possessed the gowzals. The birds had hopped close to Sir Kalenek, who often exuded enough anger to thrill the creatures. Charlon had selected these three from Magon's swarm. Wanted to build trust with those who were not Rurek's minions. They seemed to like living inside the birds. Rurek had said Dominion was the greatest prize for a shadir. Apparently it needn't be Dominion of a human.

Since none were paying attention and Rurek was gone, Charlon quickly moved three more jars of magical ahvenrood powder. Out of her trunk and into the bottom of an empty basket. She covered them with a pile of burlap. Sacks Sir Kalenek used to pack root tubers from the field. As per their plan, Sir Kalenek would bury Charlon's old root in the field. When next he went down to harvest more of the new root with Shanek. As long as the boy saw no shadir nearby. Only Sir Kalenek, Shanek, and Charlon knew. Knew where it was being hidden. A few more trips. And all would be stashed away.

Kateen and Astaa had already come begging for more. Claimed they'd run out. Charlon had told them she had no more to give. She was glad Mreegan's newt had died in the winter cold. Now no one would be able to find what she'd hidden.

Her mantic maidens were grieving. The loss of their way of life fell hard. Rightly so. Charlon found it difficult to do many things by hand. Things she had relied upon magic for. But it was more important to save the magical ahvenrood. Once she was with child, she wouldn't be able to take any. But it would be waiting. When her child was born. Ready to help her take the crown of Armania for Shanek.

Charlon sat upon her throne and admired Sir Kalenek's muscled arms. Arms pounding ahvenrood tubers to mush. She grew fonder of the man with each passing day. It gnawed at her that his affection for her was compelled. She longed to matter to him. Without magic.

Rurek appeared then. Brought with him a chill that made her shiver. *Shanek says he will come soon.*

Anger flashed over Charlon. Her son lacked respect. "Rurek tells me Shanek says he will come," Charlon said aloud for Sir Kalenek's benefit. "Likely after I remind him twice more."

"Ah, the blitheness of youth," Sir Kalenek said, smiling.

"Do you approve of their friendship?"

"Would it matter either way?"

"You could say something to her."

"Amala has not listened to me for years," Sir Kalenek said. "She is not about to start now."

"I don't like them together." Shanek should remain single. So he could marry a princess once he took the throne.

"Get used to it," Sir Kalenek said. "She sees him as her hero."

For killing Sir Kamran. "And he will not part with her near worship of him."

"It is not worship, Charlon. She respects and admires his abilities while everyone else in Magosia sees him as a monstrosity. Can you blame the boy for loving her? She is the only person who is not afraid of him. Even you and I are wary."

Because he was so unpredictable. Had his own dark magic none of them understood. Had killed twice. Charlon quavered and rubbed her arms. Just thinking about the power that boy had within made her nervous.

"You are cold," Kalenek said. "About time I lit the fire, I suppose."

"No," she said, perking up. "Allow me." She enjoyed practicing this new trick. She pointed to one of the gowzals. "*Sabab bay êsh.*"

The bird collapsed. Turned into green light. Revealed hardly any of the black mud. The slights within the gowzals were getting better at this. Faster.

Once the creature had fully transformed, Charlon pointed. To the ash wood within the circle of stones. "*Yaqad chatab.*"

The green orb sailed across the tent. Landed in the fire pit. Yellow flames flared up and the green glow faded. The gowzal screeched. A black muddy blob slithered over the rocks. Pooled on the dirt floor. Slowly transformed back into feathers and fur.

"Now *that* I find impressive," Sir Kalenek said. "That's similar to what Shanek can do, though he doesn't need the gowzals."

Charlon found Shanek's magic eerily similar to the new magic. She rather enjoyed its power. Though the limitations were frustrating. She could make masks of anyone. Without the need of hair, blood, or bone. Yet she could not disguise herself. Unless, perhaps, she took a shadir within. And that she would not do.

She could create masks of substances. Turn the gowzal into fire or a spear or a gust of black smoke. These types of masks performed the physical characteristics of their object. Fire burned. Spears stabbed. Smoke obscured or blew things about. Masks of humans stood or sat still. She could make them move. Though she could not make them speak or match their eyes. Eyes that always remained red.

She could also conjure illusions of a source mask. As she had just done with Sir Kalenek. Illusions had no substance. They were transparent like shadir in the Veil. Charlon could not cast compulsions or soul-bindings or move objects. Still, the possibilities offered plenty of hope.

She would remain in power here. She had taught the magic to no one but Shanek. Sir Kalenek had watched all along, of course. But he had no ambition to wield. For that Charlon was grateful. They all simply had to get used to this new way of life.

Shanek walked into the red tent on foot. This was a surprise. The boy usually appeared out of thin air. Movement behind him revealed his motives. He'd brought Miss Amala along.

"Do you need something, Shanek?" Charlon asked.

"I'm to learn birds," he said. It often made her skin crawl how much he resembled Sâr Janek. But for that strange, dapple-gray skin.

"You, yes," Charlon said. "But I did not invite Miss Amala."

"Amala wants to learn," Shanek said, taking hold of the girl's hand.

Fire kindled inside Charlon. She fought to conceal her rage. Shanek never responded well to anger. "I haven't even shown this new skill to my maidens. Why would I teach this girl?"

"I want it," Shanek said.

Fool boy. "I need time to consider this," Charlon said. "Leave us for today, Miss Amala. I will give you my answer soon."

Shanek's brow wrinkled. "What do I do?" he whispered.

"Accept her decision, of course," Amala whispered back, drawing him into a hug. "For now."

Of all the insolent . . . Sir Kalenek had been right. Shanek would never give up this girl. Charlon would have to get rid of her. Before her influence over Shanek superseded her own.

It might have done that already.

Amala kissed Shanek's cheek and, thankfully, left. Though the boy stood stupidly staring after her.

"Let us begin," Charlon said. "Turn one of the gowzals into a mask of Miss Amala." He should like that well enough.

The lesson moved swiftly. Shanek easily performed every task Charlon set forth. He needed no gowzal to aid him. Somehow he could do the magic on his own. The gowzals obeyed him without question. His mask of Amala was perfect. Charlon bid him make an illusion as well. He made six. All with brown eyes and Amala's voice.

Charlon hated the incompetence she felt each time Shanek bested her skill. He seemed ignorant of his superiority. Once he fully understood what was happening, he would grow arrogant. Possibly uncontrollable. She dreaded what would happen then.

Charlon ended the lesson. Sir Kalenek took away the boy and the basket of hidden ahvenrood. Charlon must distract Rurek. Keep him from following them. From knowing where she was hiding her supply.

"What do you think of Shanek?" she asked the great.

His powers continue to surprise me.

"They resemble the new magic. Perhaps there is some connection. If so, would that mean I might someday do all he does?"

An intriguing idea, Rurek said. *I will think on it.*

Masi, a shadir that served as one of Rurek's commanders, appeared before Charlon's throne. *A common has arrived from Rurekau and wishes to speak with the Chieftess, master,* Masi said. *She is called Yobatha.*

"The goddess of pleasure?" Charlon asked.

It could be a trick, Rurek said. *Let me disguise myself and speak with her first.*

"No," Charlon said. "I fear no common with you at my side. Bring Yobatha here, Masi."

Rurek scowled but nodded to Masi, who vanished. *It is against my better judgment to allow this, Chieftess,* he said, transforming into the vaporous form of the slight he called Chelo.

It increasingly annoyed Charlon how Rurek contradicted her. "Your concern is noted."

Rurek drifted beneath Charlon's ironthorn throne. Why did he insist on hiding his existence? Could he be less powerful than he claimed? Had he not bonded with Charlon in secret, would Magon have been able to defeat him?

Masi returned then with a shapely female who walked like a human. Hips swayed with each step. Gauzy robes of purple and red wrapped her body tightly. Her eyes were bright mossy green. She brought with her the smell of spices and incense. She had bronzed skin, amber eyes, and caramel hair so thick and luxurious Charlon yearned to touch it.

Goddess of pleasure, indeed.

Charlon did her best to look unaffected. "What do you want?"

My master King Barthel is visiting the nation of Rurekau and requests your presence.

"If he wants to speak with me, he knows where I live, apparently. He is welcome to pay me a visit."

Forgive me, powerful Chieftess of Magosia, Yobatha said, *but my king and the empress of Rurekau are currently strategizing together. They would like to include you, as they value your wisdom and skill, but by the time they are ready to travel again, their plans will be finalized.*

"So I must drop everything and travel to Rurekau, or I am left out of this alliance? I am not accustomed to being treated so rudely."

I am only a messenger, honorable Chieftess, Yobatha said. *My master arrived in New Rurekau today, and Empress Jazlyn told him that he would be wise to consider you a friend.*

"That much is true," Charlon said, appeased by Jazlyn's praise. "How long do I have to decide?"

My king would like you to come within the week.

"Impossible," Charlon said. "I have duties here. They require my full attention. I might be able to come next week."

My king would be honored to meet you whenever you are able, Chieftess.

"But he might be finished planning if I don't come soon?"

Yobatha bowed her head. *That is correct.*

"I must consider this carefully," Charlon said. "I will send a shadir with my answer. Dismissed."

Yobatha bowed again, then walked out of the tent.

Her sensuality annoyed Charlon. "Why does she bother to walk about? She could simply appear wherever she likes."

It is part of her mystique, Masi said. *The goddess of pleasure must move slowly so that she can be watched.*

Charlon was not impressed. "What say you, Rurek? Shall I go?"

I must caution you, Chieftess. The shadir who has bonded with King Barthel is a great.

"Like you?"

Yes. And while we both wield large armies, Dendron still possesses a vast amount of ahvenrood and mantics loyal to his cause who have each bonded with commons. There are many shadir of mighty name in his swarm, with mantics who have been loyal for years. As we are, we could not stand against them.

"You think they wish to subdue us?"

I think they want an alliance against Armania. King Barthel is blood-related to Shanek, so I am certain he will want to meet him. And when he sees what the boy can do . . .

"Yobatha did not mention Shanek," Charlon said, suddenly suspicious.

I only seek to caution you, Chieftess. I do not trust Barthel Rogedoth or his great. And it would be best if he didn't know that you have bonded with a great yourself.

"Wouldn't that be a warning to him? That I too am strong?"

Dendron would see it first as a mystery to be solved—which great serves you? We shadir have ancient history, you see. If he discovers my name, he will know me. And then he will see me as a challenge to be won into submission or destroyed.

"Just knowing you exist would cause a war? Is that what you are saying?"

It is a concern, yes.

"Can you disguise yourself?"

I can try, but shadir can sense strength in each other. It would be difficult to hide my power.

This was easily enough solved. "You must remain here, then."

I will not let you go to them alone.

"I will not be alone. I am not a fool, Rurek."

Nor am I, which is why I will go with you.

"Will you never do as I tell you?"

He began to grow. Swelled in height until his head touched the ceiling of the tent. Shook it. *You do realize I don't need your permission.*

She was not intimidated by his theatrics. "You would disobey me?" Charlon asked.

Rurek smile wickedly. *Perhaps you forgot how Magon left Mreegan to bond with you. Shadir choose whom to bond with, human. We have the power you seek. Without us, you are nothing.*

Devious creatures, all of them. How had Charlon ever thought them divine? She doubted her slights would ever leave her. But she had no trust for Rurek. And she did not want him bonding with another. "What do you recommend I do?"

Take Masi as your shadir. He is a common and quite powerful. I will go within a gowzal. The act of Dominion will dampen my splendor.

"Fine," Charlon said. "I must not be left out of whatever King Barthel is plotting with the empress. Shanek is meant to be king of Armania—no one else. I must do what I can. To see that he fulfills his destiny."

That evening, Charlon made plans for her trip. As she instructed Astaa in what clothing she wanted packed, Sir Kalenek entered the red tent.

"You're taking Amala to New Rurekau?" he asked. "Why?"

Charlon looked up from where she sat on her ironthorn throne. "I need a fifth maiden."

"I know what you're doing." He came to stand before the throne, arms crossed. "Keeping them apart will not change the way they feel about each other. You risk losing him. Manipulation is not love."

Always Sir Kalenek could see through her. "I carry the burden of ruling Magosia and training Shanek for his destiny."

"Then you should teach him to stand on his own two feet. You and I will not always be here to hold his hand. Life is hard, and he must learn to live it on his own."

"Miss Amala is your ward, Sir Kalenek. If you forbid it, I will revoke my offer."

His lips curved, but it was not so much a smile as a rebuke. "I learned the hard way with Amala that I cannot control her. She will do what she will do. I must love her no matter what."

"All that I do is out of my love for Shanek."

"No, you fear losing control. And you will drive him away if you keep this up."

Miss Amala arrived then, and Kalenek dismissed himself. Charlon pushed aside his lectures. What did he know of ruling a realm? Charlon must do whatever necessary. To separate this young woman from her son.

"King Barthel has asked me to visit him in New Rurekau, and I have decided to go," Charlon told Miss Amala. "You will accompany me."

The young woman nodded. "I would be honored, Chieftess."

"There is one more thing," she said. "I do not trust Barthel Rogedoth or Empress Jazlyn. I need you to be my ears as well as my eyes. In order to see into the Veil, you must take a spoonful of ahvenrood each day. I will administer the root myself. You will purge to Nwari. He is an orange slight that looks like a wisp of smoke. He will be waiting for you."

Miss Amala's eyes became like two round stones. "I am honored to serve you, Chieftess."

"Barthel Rogedoth has titled himself king. Set his sights on the throne of Armania. But that is Shanek's birthright. So we must be on our guard. He will seek to learn about Shanek's special gifts. And we will reveal nothing. Do you understand? Shanek's future depends upon our discretion."

"I would never do anything that might hurt Prince Shanek."

"I know you would not. It is why I chose you."

"I will not fail you," Amala said.

"Dismissed," Charlon said.

The girl curtsied deeply, then scurried away, no doubt to tell Shanek all that had taken place.

Charlon was uncertain she had done right. Asking Miss Amala to take ahvenrood. To come on the trip. But of her options, the girl was—at present anyway—the best choice to act as a second set of eyes. Charlon did not trust Roya or Astaa. Which was why she was taking them along. To watch them closely. Surely this many safeguards would protect her realm. From those seeking to take it.

TREVN

Trevn sat dutifully in his chair before a tall mirrorglass so that Ottee could tend to his hair while he listened to Master Jhorn's report. Hawley sat at a desk in the corner, taking notes.

"I have finally gotten word from Lord Blackpool's steward," Master Jhorn said.

"He has returned, has he?" Trevn had tried to pay the earl a visit to investigate the people's claims that he was not giving them their share of the harvests, but the earl had been on an extended hunting trip. "And what does he say?"

"He claims innocence, of course," Master Jhorn said, "and demands to know which commoners have accused him."

"I did not get their names," Trevn said.

"I'm sure they would not want their names reported for fear he might abuse them further," Jhorn said.

"You think he is maltreating his workers?"

"I do," Master Jhorn said. "I've received several more documented reports of the same nature. I was thinking you might send me there when the next harvest comes in."

"That would only raise his ire at House Hadar," Hawley said.

Trevn sighed. He wanted to punish those who deserved it, but it was not easy. "For now, any people who come to you hungry are to be given a week's provisions and the opportunity to work elsewhere, so long as you can find them a position."

"I will do my best, sir," Jhorn said.

"And we must continue to monitor both Lord Edekk and Lord Blackpool in hopes of catching them in the act of subversion. Now, is that all?"

"Yes, Your Highness."

"Continue with the excellent work, Master Jhorn. You are dismissed."

Jhorn left, and while Ottee finished off Trevn's hair, Trevn studied his reflection in the mirrorglass. He brushed his palms over his cheeks, annoyed that the scruff had remained just that. Why wouldn't it grow faster? A beard would go a long way in making him look older, which might ease the doubts the nobles harbored toward him.

The royal rebel, or firebrand of Castle Everton, had never let such vanity bother him before. His old nicknames had been badges of honor: proof that his Renegade ways had been noticed. He must not allow the nobles to bother him so.

Ottee stepped away from Trevn. "Do you approve, sir?"

"Thank you, Ottee." He looked well enough, though he grew tired of this mourning ensemble. "Would you see to it that my other black tunic is mended?"

"The tailor is working on it," Ottee said. "He should be done today."

"Perfect." Trevn stood, but before he managed one step, his mother began voicing him.

"Trevn? This is your mother. King Barthel Rogedoth has come to Rurekau. Answer me at once."

While Trevn had no desire to speak with his mother, any information on Rogedoth far outweighed the grudge he held against her.

"My mother is voicing me," he said to Hawley. "Ottee, go tell the Duke of Odarka I will be late for our meeting."

"Yes, Your Highness." The boy scurried out of the room.

Trevn sat back in his chair and answered his mother. *"Has Rogedoth attacked?"*

"Trevn! Thank the gods. You cannot know how much your silence tries me."

"Mother, has Rogedoth invaded Rurekau?"

"Not at all. He came seeking an alliance and offered assistance during a giant raid. Now he and the empress are becoming fast friends. Ulrik is still unconscious, but Ferro has recovered, so the—"

"Ferro is awake? Have you told Inolah?"

"No. You were the first person I wanted to speak with. Empress Jazlyn and I

have been at odds as to who should rule as regent. She thinks she should rule, but I don't trust her. She is taking evenroot again, and I just know she had her eunuch poison my great-nephews. If I could prove it, I could arrest her, but—"

"Rogedoth, Mother. Has he made threats? Have the Rurekans promised him anything?"

"He is too powerful to ignore, so I have simply tried to keep the peace. The empress, however . . . She and King Barthel have started talking with the giants."

"Which giants? The ones who attacked you?"

"Does it matter?"

Trevn had not forgotten his time in the Ahj-Yeke mines. *"It matters a great deal."*

"Well, they all look alike to me," Mother said.

A raid sounded like the behavior of the Ahj-Yeke giants, but New Rurekau was closest to the Uul-Yeke, who Ulagan claimed were peaceful. *"Could Rogedoth have sent the giants to attack so he could pretend to offer aid to Rurekau?"*

"What a thing to suggest! Why would he do that?"

"Perpetrating an attack would help him win an alliance, which he now has. Besides—"

"King Barthel and the empress have invited Chieftess Charlon to visit. What can I do?"

Trevn sighed as he struggled to keep up with his mother's changing subjects. *"Stay out of their way, but continue to tell me everything. Has Rogedoth shared his plans?"*

"He wants rule of Armania and Sarikar."

"I know that. What is he talking to the giants about? I must know . . . and also to which group he speaks."

"You are right to fear him. He is powerful."

"I don't fear him, Mother. I will find a way to stop him, but I would appreciate your help in discovering—"

"Oh, Trevn! How you try my patience. I should come to Armanguard where I can have some influence over you."

"If you think I will endure more of your nagging criticisms when you are under my roof, you are mistaken. Inform me the moment you learn anything more of Rogedoth's plans. Good morning, Mother."

Trevn withdrew from the conversation and raised his shields. His mother raged against them, but he'd become quite adept at tuning out her voice completely. He opened his eyes and found Hawley and Ottee watching him warily.

"Bad news, Your Highness?" Hawley asked.

"That remains to be seen. Hawley, it is time I assembled a war council. Will you help me make a list of names to invite?"

"Certainly, Your Highness." Hawley fetched his tablet from the sideboard. "Should I reschedule the Duke of Canden? He is waiting to speak with you about Rosârah Zeroah's mind-speak education."

"No, send him in."

As Hawley exited the apartment to fetch the duke, Trevn thought over the situation in New Rurekau. He felt sick just thinking about his mother licking Rogedoth's boots, calling him king. Trevn would never bow to that traitor. Ever. And he would do everything he could to keep Armania safe from Barthel Rogedoth's ambition.

Two hours later, Trevn sat in his office reading Wilek's journal and the entries written just prior to his leaving for the Battle of Sarikar.

Hawley entered the room. "Your war council is assembled," he said.

Trevn released the scroll, letting it roll up. "Did Captain Veralla and Novan Heln come?" he asked.

"Yes, Your Highness. Everyone you invited is waiting in the council chambers."

"Excellent." Trevn had met individually with Captain Veralla and Novan Heln after his return. He had offered to appoint Captain Veralla as general over the army and named Novan Heln as one of his shields. The men had been grateful to receive a pardon and to get out of the dungeon, but both were reluctant to continue on in any kind of position of authority. They considered themselves failures, unworthy of further service to the crown. This annoyed Trevn, who was determined to have his way.

Trevn exited his office and stopped at the small crowd that had gathered outside his door. There were nowhere near as many people as before, now that Hawley had forbidden any commoners above the first floor, but the few nobles and servants that lingered were enough to block the way.

"Step back against the walls!" Nietz yelled.

The crowd obeyed at once, and Trevn strode past. It wouldn't be long now and he would have his private passageways completed. He couldn't wait.

They rounded the landing until they reached the council chambers, and Cadoc and Nietz whisked Trevn inside. He instantly smelled the fresh wine in the goblets on the table. The room was filled with soft talk. Trevn walked to his seat on the far end of the long, narrow table, hopeful he'd get more accomplished in this meeting than he tended to with the Wisean Five.

Most had noticed his entry, stood, and bowed—Inolah curtsied—but some were too busy talking.

Trevn said a quick prayer for wisdom and pounded his fist on the tabletop. "Let us begin this meeting."

All went silent. The few who hadn't bowed jumped to their feet and did so, eyes fixed on Trevn. He glanced around the table. On his right stood all five members of his Wisean Council—Barek Hadar, Danek Faluk, Oli Agoros, Inolah Orsona, and Joret Vohan, his newest member. Also present were Admiral Livina, Captain Bussie, and Captain Stockton; Captain Veralla, Under-General Collak Ensley, Marshal Rowan Winstone, and Sheriff Irlond Hearn; Master Jhorn; Novan Heln; and Cadoc, Nietz, and Hawley, who had entered with Trevn.

"Please, be seated." Trevn remained standing while everyone settled back into their chairs. "You have all been briefed on the current situations we are facing, but I thought we might be more productive together. As you know, Rogedoth the Pretender left his island fortress for New Rurekau. I've just heard from my mother that he has arrived and made an alliance with Empress Jazlyn. He seeks to ally with at least one of the giant tribes. He has also invited Chieftess Charlon of Magosia to join in their discussions. And, as the council has discussed before, Rosârah Laviel is making plans to take Armanguard for herself. She has not yet left the island, as she has no means of transportation."

"Can't she use her magic to fix the broken ship?" Barek asked.

"She would need someone with knowledge of ships to help her cast the right spell," Oli said. "My guess is Rogedoth took all of those people with him."

"Except for Bahlay Nesos," Trevn said, then told the story of Maleen's father. "Hinckdan Faluk managed to sabotage much of Rogedoth's root juice before the Pretender set sail, but we don't know how much is left and who might have access to it."

"That he managed to destroy any is excellent," Jhorn said, "but my guess is Rogedoth still has enough to kill us all. I like that his daughter is parting ways with him, but it's not enough. We still don't stand a chance against that kind of magic, no matter who gets here first."

"I agree," Captain Veralla said. "Especially not if giants join them."

"I thought the giants were on our side," Sheriff Hearn said.

"There are three tribes of giants," Trevn said. "The Uul-Yeke have allied with us. Their assistance in the Battle of Sarikar was the only thing that kept it from being a full-on slaughter. The Ahj-Yeke have caused no trouble since that day, and Ulagan tells me they would rather stay out of our conflict altogether. His uncle is wary of the root magic Fonu Edekk used to compel his people."

"The giants are indeed formidable," Jhorn said, "but it's the magic that worries me. There is no way to fight it."

"Why is Rogedoth stalling, then?" Novan asked.

All heads turned, eyes focused on Novan Heln, former backman to Wilek.

"Why do you think he is stalling?" Trevn asked.

"Well, Master Jhorn says we cannot defeat him and that he likely has enough root to defeat us. Then why hasn't he? We've been here almost a year, and he has remained on his island, compelling natives into a dismal army. That doesn't seem like the behavior of an all-powerful sorcerer."

"He's right," Marshal Winstone said. "Had the man attacked Armanguard during Master Fonu's siege on Sarikar, he could have wiped us out. We wouldn't have had any means of standing against that magic. So why didn't he?"

"Doesn't matter," Under-General Ensley said. "It's in the past."

"No, it *does* matter," Trevn said, intrigued by the question. "If Rogedoth is afraid of something, hesitant for some reason, or has any kind of weakness at all, I want to know so we can exploit whatever it is."

"How could we possibly learn that?" Under-General Ensley asked.

"His wife?" Novan suggested. "Could Lord Dacre get information out of Lady Eudora?"

"Not if she's compelled," Oli said, "and Hinckdan said she was."

Islah. Trevn had told only Hawley, Cadoc, and Mielle about Hinck's discovery of Rogedoth's first wife, and only Mielle had believed it possible. Now seemed the perfect time to open that jar of flies. "Perhaps his first wife would help us," he said.

The room fell silent.

Admiral Livina was the first to speak. "Islah Pitney died over thirty years ago."

"Apparently she did not," Trevn said. "Hinck discovered her in the prison with Maleen's father. For some reason, Rogedoth faked her death and has kept her locked away all these years."

"That's awful," Inolah said.

"It's impossible," Barek said.

"I don't believe it either," Livina said. "Why would he have done that?"

"Hinck hasn't figured it out yet," Trevn said, "but if anyone knows Rogedoth's weakness, it would be her."

"Can Hinckdan free her?" Oli asked.

"I imagine so. Right now, he is focused on leaving the island, but Rosârah Laviel's presence complicates things."

"What about General Agoros?" Under-General Ensley asked.

"Rogedoth has left him and his wife behind with Rosârah Laviel," Trevn said.

"I would normally not fear a compelled army of natives," Under-General Ensley said, "but with him at the head . . ."

"I'm not ready to worry about an attack yet," Trevn said. "I want Hinck and Islah Pitney here in Armanguard. Captain Bussie, how soon could you get the *Seffynaw* to the islands to rescue them?"

"Six or seven days is my guess, depending on the wind," the captain said. "Though I've never sailed those waters."

"They're calm that far south," Captain Stockton said. "I'd agree that a week is a fair estimate to reach the islands."

"If no one has started work yet on repairing that ship," Captain Bussie said, "tell the earl to keep it that way and I'll have time to reach him."

"I want you to leave as soon as possible," Trevn said. "Now, say we rescue Hinck and abandon Rosârah Laviel on the island, and say we discover Rogedoth's weakness from Lady Islah. If magic weren't an issue, how does our army look?"

"We've got just over twenty-four hundred trained men," Captain Veralla said.

"But they won't fight for you, Captain Veralla," Under-General Ensley said. The words had not been cruel or spiteful. Merely matter-of-fact. Yet Trevn felt the emotions in the room tense, his own included.

"They will fight for their king," Trevn said, "and if I appoint Captain Veralla to lead them, then they will obey their orders or be court-martialed."

"Forgive me, Your Highness," Marshal Winstone said, "but threats don't inspire loyalty, and men who aren't loyal to their superior don't put all that much effort into obedience, fighting, or winning, for that matter."

"Do you agree with the under-general's opinion that the men will not fight for Captain Veralla?" Trevn asked the marshal.

"Not only that, sir, but I believe Captain Veralla should be executed," Marshal Winstone said, dark eyes fixed on the captain. "Both of them should be, and I mean no offense by it." He changed his stare to Novan.

"The majority of the fighting men agree," Under-General Ensley said. "It is tradition."

Trevn sucked in a slow breath through his nose. "My father was a puppet ruling a country steeped in superstition. I realize that much of Armania still believes in such nonsense, but I will not throw away perfectly good and loyal men because that is what always has been done. What will it take to change the attitudes of the men?"

"Men fight for a man they believe in," Under-General Ensley said.

"And I suppose they believe in you?" Trevn asked.

"They will obey my command," Ensley said, "but it will not be the same as Rosâr Wilek. He spent hours on the practice field every day since he was four. And once he came of age, he trained and fought beside his men. They loved him."

Trevn understood. "And I am a scholar who hides behind tablets and scrolls."

"That schooling will likely help you with the nobles," Oli said, "but this is different. In Rosâr Echad's situation, the men were loyal to his uncle, Prince Wodek, and later his son, Sâr Wilek. And since they were loyal to the king, the king had his army."

"Do the soldiers want Rogedoth as their king?" Trevn asked, incredulous at the idea.

"The men know little about him or you," Under-General Ensley said. "They are grieving Rosâr Wilek. And your pardon of both Captain Veralla and Master Heln has been seen as an insult to the rosâr's memory, no matter what kind of fancy logic you might have used to spare them."

Trevn's mind raced as he sought a solution that might appease everyone. He would not throw away Captain Veralla or Novan Heln, yet two thousand plus men-at-arms needed a leader they could respect. His first instinct was to promote Oli Agoros, who had been primed since birth for the position of general, but without his arm . . . "Would they fight for Duke Canden?"

Across the table, Oli stiffened, and Trevn sensed his panic.

"They might," Under-General Ensley said. "He's one of them, at least."

"I *was* one of them," Oli said. "Your Highness, I've been practicing with the shield, learning to fight despite my lost arm, but I'm just not the soldier I used to be. Putting your trust in me as a warrior would be a mistake. Besides, the matter of my father's current allegiance might taint me as well."

Because General Agoros had sided with Rogedoth.

"Why don't *you* train with them, Rosâr Trevn?" Captain Veralla suggested.

"Me?" Trevn tried to picture himself at the head of a charging army.

"If you could win them, there would be no one better," Veralla said.

"Except that they would see through his actions and know he only hopes to win them over," Ensley said.

"So?" Veralla said. "Yes, they'll mock him at first and curse him behind his back, but if he holds up under their taunting—if you can measure up, Your Highness—there is no better man to lead an army than their king."

"He did this already aboard the *Seffynaw*," Cadoc said.

That was just what Trevn had been thinking.

"Come, Sir Cadoc," Ensley said. "A sailor and a soldier are different breeds, and while there have been rumors of what our king did aboard the *Seffynaw*, that vessel was one of several hundred ships. Few of our fighting men witnessed it."

"I can't make up for my years training as a priest," Trevn said, "but I've been working with the sword every day since my return, and I'm more than willing to practice with the men, though my best might not impress them."

"That would be an excellent start, Your Highness," Veralla said.

"Don't know when you'll find time to sleep," Inolah said.

"I'll sleep once we win peace for Armania," Trevn said.

"Spoken like a true general," Oli said.

Trevn warmed to Oli's praise. "Very well. Cadoc, Nietz, Captain Veralla, and Master Heln, I charge the four of you with getting me ready to take the practice field."

"Do you still have your warrior tail?" Cadoc asked.

"Yes," Trevn said slowly, thinking of the drawer he had shoved it in.

"What warrior tail?" Ensley asked.

"The rosâr killed a man in an assassination attempt on Rosâr Wilek back on Bakurah Island," Cadoc said.

"Wear it, Your Highness," Ensley said. "Marshal Winstone and I will spread the story. It will help."

Trevn nodded, reluctant to gloat over the life he'd taken, yet resigned to his task of winning the army. "Under-General Ensley, for the time being, you will continue as acting general, but I will not rescind the pardons I gave Captain Veralla and Master Heln. No two men meant more to my brother, and he would not wish them harm. Master Heln is hereby assigned to my security detail, and Captain Veralla will become captain of my King's Guard. He will work with Duke Canden to train new men to fight."

"A fine plan, Your Highness," Admiral Livina said, though Trevn could sense that not all the men agreed.

He felt as if the meeting had been going on for hours, and they'd only discussed a small portion of his agenda. He moved on to how the castle fared defensively and other strategies to safeguard the lands they had claimed thus far, how to best use the garrison to protect the castle, possible defense strategies for each route an enemy might use to attack, and how to produce weapons of iron since bronze was scarce in the mountains they'd mined thus far.

"We will have these meetings once a week until the threat is over," Trevn said, when the discussion began to repeat itself. "Dismissed."

Trevn left the council room feeling apprehensive, even after what he had to deem a somewhat successful meeting. Winning the army seemed a terribly daunting task. He had no desire to wear the braid of the soldier he'd killed and pretend to be some grand warrior, but considering the threat facing them, winning the army was imperative if they were going to defend Armania from the many threats that faced them.

⊙Lİ

Oli sat on a longchair in the training room Rosâr Wilek had long ago designated for mind-speak education. For today's lesson, he had directed a servant to arrange four longchairs in a tight circle. The rest had been stacked along the back wall.

Empress Inolah had been the first to arrive, bringing with her one of her daughter Vallah's companions, a girl named Kaye.

"Thank you for coming, Empress," Oli said, standing to greet her. "I know that you are leaving soon for New Rurekau, so I appreciate your taking the time."

"Anything to help the dowager queen," Inolah said. "How is she coming along?"

"Well enough," Oli said. "She can shield now, but I want her to practice voicing a variety of different people."

The girl Kaye shifted her gaze to the empress. "Forgive me, but I cannot use the voices."

"That is precisely why I asked you to come, miss," Oli said. "Sometimes we need to practice our ability on non-gifted individuals."

A rap at the door preceded two guardsmen and Rosârah Zeroah. Oli hadn't seen the dowager queen in almost a week. She was still rail thin with somewhat sunken cheeks and eyes, but she no longer appeared skeletal. The return of Rosârah Mielle seemed to have done her some good. Minibraids had been twisted into a crown of bantu knots on the top of her head, while the rest hung loose down her back. She looked very nice.

"Please wait in the hallway," she said to the guards, then approached Oli. "Forgive me, Your Grace. I did not mean to be late."

Oli bowed and motioned toward the chairs. "You are right on time. Please join us."

As Zeroah neared the longchairs, Oli was careful to position her on his left, where he could touch her without having to bring attention to his missing arm. Inolah sat on his right. Kaye across from him and on Zeroah's left.

"Rosârah Zeroah, you claim that you cannot listen in on a non-gifted mind," he said, crossing his ankles. "It is my goal that you learn how to do just that. I would like you to try to hear Miss Kaye's thoughts."

"What shall I think about?" the girl asked.

"Imagine yourself doing some activity you enjoy, or remember a time you did that activity," Oli said. "Something like that should work well enough. You may close your eyes, if you feel more comfortable."

The young girl leaned back in the longchair and closed her eyes. Oli did the same. He reached for the girl's mind and found her thoughts occupied with eating a massive slice of cake. He tried not to chuckle at Kaye's delight.

Beside him, Zeroah sighed heavily. "I cannot even sense Miss Kaye's mind."

That much had happened just as Oli had expected. "Let us try this another way, Your Highness. It is important to the king, since you are so close with his wife, that you become proficient with the mind-speak magic and are able to instigate your own connections without my help. For now, I will leave my shields down. Reach into my thoughts. Once I sense you there, I will speak to Miss Kaye, and I want you to try to hear our conversation."

"I am happy to try, Your Grace," she said, "but what if I cannot hear you? Rosâr Trevn says you are difficult to read, even with your shields down."

"I do have a proficiency in shielding, which is why I would like you to try several tactics in the following order. First, simply try on your own. If you cannot reach me, use this." He pulled his old leather ball from his pocket and handed it to her.

She wrinkled her nose slightly as she took it into her slender fingers. "What is it?"

"Bit of leather stuffed with feathers. A toy from my childhood."

"You must have played with it daily."

"I still do," he said, grinning. "Since the ball belongs to me, holding it should forge a connection between our minds. You'll need to concentrate, of course, but it should make things easier."

Her golden eyes met his. "Is this how Rosâr Trevn first found Master Grayson?"

"That's right," Oli said. "And if those two things do not work"—he held out his hand—"touch, skin to skin, increases the ability for two minds to connect."

She looked at his hand but did not take hold. "But I'm to try the others first?"

"If you please. If you are successful, you should be able to hear Miss Kaye's thoughts through me. Miss Kaye, continue with your original line of thought, please."

Zeroah set the ball on the chair beside her, then closed her eyes. Oli connected with Kaye, but he left his eyes open, curious whether or not the queen would need to make use of the ball. He waited patiently, keeping his shields down and his senses open, straining to detect even the faintest brush against his mind.

Zeroah lifted her hand and took hold of the ball. Oli sensed her mind then but quickly realized it was his magic, not hers. He pulled back and concentrated on keeping his shields down and his gift in his own head.

Several seconds passed by, then Zeroah's slender fingers slid over his forearm, sending a tingle up his arm. Her mind brushed up against his. She brought with her a heaviness—love masked in duty and prayer for those around her. Mielle. Trevn. The people of Armania.

And himself. The Duke of Canden, Oli Agoros.

Concern rose up within her. *"Your Grace? I can feel you in my mind."*

"Yes, you have done it, lady. Masking your presence will take practice, but this is a start. Do you sense Miss Kaye at all?"

"You believe yourself worthless. Why?"

Horrified, Oli closed his eyes and tried to push her out, and when he could not, he tried to bury that deepest part of himself, but she had already wound her way inside. A memory flashed by, and Oli knew that Zeroah could see it as if she'd been there all along, watching.

He was a child, eight years old, awakened in the dark, pre-dawning hours by a kick to the back. He'd been lying on the ground, curled into a ball behind a cat's claw bush.

"You lazy flop! You fell asleep and let them pass. They attacked and stole half our horses. What have you to say for your actions, boy, eh?" A hand fisted his hair and pulled. "On your feet. A man stands in the presence of his betters."

Oli the boy straightened to attention and fought the urge to massage his scalp. "I'm sorry, Father."

"Sorry? The yeetta will probably cross the border and kill a hundred in-nocent farmers—women and children, dead, because you couldn't keep your eyes open. And all you have to say is '*Sorry*'?"

Young Oli fought back tears. His eyes ached with fatigue, but his heart was pounding so fast it reminded him of a galloping horse. "I failed you, Father."

"Indeed you did, and the king as well. You will go to the pole as any other soldier would for such inadequacy. Sir Briden, take him." Father shoved Oli into the arms of his captain.

The adult Oli fought, struggling to push the memory away. It was common for such negative thoughts to snag him in their grip, but to have a witness . . . How humiliating!

Despite his resolve, the memory flashed by in bits and pieces. The flog-ging. His mother's indifference toward what had taken place. The two days he'd spent in the infirmary. His own guilt at having failed so horribly, and his determination to make it up, to prove to his father that he was worthy.

He saw Zeroah, then, standing in the infirmary—inside his memory, some-how. She sat down on the edge of his bed, where he lay on his stomach. She stroked his hair and took hold of his small, child-sized hand.

"Do not be afraid," she said.

"My father is angry," the boy said. "I failed him."

"He should not have asked a boy to do a man's job."

"Father says I must become a man sooner than others. I must prove to everyone that I am royal, even though my name is not. I must impress the king."

"No, sweet boy. You must play and enjoy your childhood while you can."

The boy frowned. "I'm not allowed to play. Only when Janek asks me."

Adult Oli girded himself and concentrated, pushing against Zeroah's hold with all his strength.

He came back to the present with a sharp intake of air. His eyes flashed open. Inolah was standing over him, crouched and peering into his face.

"You were yelling," the empress said. "Are you well?"

Well? No, he was not well. His entire body was shaking and his cheeks were wet with tears. Zeroah had witnessed one of the most demeaning and hor-rible moments of his life. While a small part of him wanted to know how she had done it, he was too embarrassed to speak at present. He glanced quickly at the queen, met her golden eyes long enough to know she was well, then pushed to his feet.

"The lesson is over for today," he whispered, then strode from the room on unsteady legs.

Out in the corridor, he set his hand against the wall and breathed deeply, trying to catch his breath, to calm himself. Zeroah's guards eyed him. Oli pulled a handkerchief from his pocket and dried his cheeks. Crying like a babe? How humiliating!

"Your Grace?"

His spine stiffened at the sound of Zeroah's voice. He wanted to flee but instead tucked away his handkerchief and turned to face her. "Yes, lady?"

She stood in the opened doorway of the classroom, her brows crinkled above golden eyes that penetrated his very soul. "Forgive me." A little shake of the head. "I didn't mean to invade your privacy."

What she had done . . . while it had been far too personal and downright terrifying, it was nothing short of remarkable. "How did you do that?"

"I was trying to do as you said—to enter your mind, and when I finally succeeded and listened for Miss Kaye . . . I was distracted by the pain."

Pain he had hidden from everyone for years. It was fascinating, really. He should explore her ability further, but his pride swept away the idea before he could speak it aloud.

"Will you forgive me?" she asked again.

That he had yet to answer shamed him. Where were his manners? "Of course," he managed.

She clasped her hands. Her eyelashes fluttered and her nose wrinkled slightly. "And you'll come back and continue the lesson?"

Movement behind him made him reach for his sword, but it was only Zeroah's guards, drawing near. He forced himself to answer. "Yes. I will join you in a moment."

She grabbed a handful of her skirt and glided back to the classroom. It wasn't until she disappeared around the doorframe that he realized he'd been watching her every move.

Did he fear her? Gods help him. He must not allow a woman to intimidate him. He must teach her how to use her gift, then learn more about her unique power—preferably without having to make himself vulnerable again.

Two more hours in close proximity to Rosârah Zeroah did not ease his discomfort around the woman. They did make progress, however. Zeroah was able to connect to Miss Kaye's mind through Oli's connection. And though it took several tries, she also succeeded in hearing Miss Kaye's thoughts on her own by holding the girl's shoe.

Oli was just about to dismiss everyone when Rosârah Mielle barged into the classroom and walked right into the center of their circled longchairs. Hands on her hips, she glared down upon Oli. She was nearly as tall as he was and thickset. She wore her hair in minibraids, but hers hung loose. A slightly wild look for a queen.

"Is it true you struck Porvil in front of the other boys?" she asked.

Oli sat up and swung his feet to the floor. "Your Highness, you are interrupting my class."

"Answer the question, Your Grace. This is an order from your queen."

His cheeks tingled at her disrespect. "No, I did not strike him. Is that what he told you?"

She folded her arms. "He said you would deny it. He said you treat him differently because he is orphaned."

Why would the boy lie? "That's absurd."

"I won't have anyone abusing children in this castle."

Oli fought back his growing rage. "Forgive me, lady, but the young man in question is not of trustworthy character."

"Porvil is a known troublemaker," Inolah added, coming to stand beside the queen.

"I expected you would defend the duke, Empress, having worked with him, but answer me this: Have you ever gone up to the roof while he is teaching the boys to be soldiers?"

"I have not," Inolah said. "I always remain with the girls."

"Then you cannot know what goes on up there, can you?" Rosârah Mielle asked.

"Swordplay and exercises, as always," Oli said.

"And perhaps going harder on some children than others?" Rosârah Mielle asked.

"I'm sorry, Your Highness," Oli said. "I didn't realize you had so much experience in teaching young men to fight. Have you a better method that I should know about?"

"Don't you dare mock me," she said. "I came here to defend a young man who has accused you of wrongdoing. What say you to this?"

Oli took a deep breath. "I deny any wrongdoing. Porvil, on the other hand

. . . When he first arrived, he caused fights daily, but he has improved a great deal in the past few months, or so I thought."

"Because the Duke of Canden beats him?" the queen asked.

"I have *never* beaten a child, Your Highness, and I take exception to being accused now on the sole testimony of a known troublemaker. Ask any of the boys and I guarantee they will tell you the same."

"You claim he was never struck with your sword, then?" Rosârah Mielle asked.

That stopped Oli. "These boys are learning swordplay, Your Highness. All of them have been struck with the wooden practice swords as they spar with each other."

She narrowed her eyes. "And do they spar with *you*?"

"Sometimes with me, yes."

"But you have never struck Porvil with your blade?"

"Not on purpose."

"So it *is* true!"

"Accidents happen in training, Your Highness. With Sir Kalenek as your warden, I'm sure you must know that."

"Why would the boy lie?"

Oli could only guess. "He has been challenging my authority for weeks. Testing the boundaries of our class. Where he finds no boundaries, he continues to push. It is a cry for attention."

"Then give him the attention he needs."

"To coddle a boy like Porvil is to create a useless man," Oli said. "I will not do it."

"You should not be teaching children, Your Grace," Rosârah Mielle snapped. "And I will tell my husband as much. Come, Zeroah. We will leave the duke to his guilt. No doubt the king will summon him come morning."

Zeroah stood and smoothed out her skirt. "Will we have our class again tomorrow, Your Grace?"

"If you wish it," Oli said. And if the queen didn't have him in the dungeon or worse.

"Zeroah!" Rosârah Mielle had reached the door and stood, holding it open.

The dowager queen glanced at her friend, then returned her golden gaze to Oli. "I will see you tomorrow, then. Good midday, Your Grace, Miss Kaye, and, Empress, my prayers go with you on your journey to see your son. May you find him healthy and strong."

"Thank you, Your Highness," Inolah said.

The rosârahs departed, leaving Oli feeling as if he had barely survived an attack on his life. An attack set in motion by an orphan boy with a penchant for twisting the truth, whom Oli would need to speak with very shortly.

Fewer people seemed to be taking advantage of first sleep in Er'Rets since it stayed light much later, so Oli no longer felt the need to rest like he had back in the Five Realms. He also had far more work to do than he'd ever had in Janek's retinue, and he'd spent the hours of first sleep with Master Grayson on the roof, working through basic swordplay exercises.

The young man looked a shambles, as usual. He was gangling—needed to eat a great deal more. His clothes were always wrinkled past the point of bothering with an iron, and his hair . . . He wore it like King Trevn used to, wrapped in a puff at the back of his head like he cared naught what he looked like.

Grayson was eager and a quick learner, though he relied too heavily on his ability to move through the Veil. Oli had forbidden him to use his magic until he had mastered the weapon, but he easily saw how the young man's ability could someday make him an invincible opponent.

Oli kept that opinion to himself, of course. Grayson had the tendency to take any form of flattery or praise as authorization to behave recklessly.

Oli finally dismissed him, changed for dinner, then went down to the great hall. As First Arm, Oli had received an open invitation from Rosâr Trevn to sit at the high table, but since only the queens and princesses had arrived thus far, Oli decided to sit elsewhere rather than go near Rosârah Mielle and her wrathful, unsupported allegations.

That Porvil had manipulated the queen was bad enough—he had laughed when Oli had confronted him, claiming he'd been playing a prank on the queen—he'd be lucky if the queen didn't send him to the pole. But of course she wouldn't. The daft woman had believed his story over both Oli *and* Inolah . . . He could not fathom why.

Oli took a seat at Barek Hadar's table, which was currently empty. His mother's cousin was likely still in a meeting. Vivia, a caramel-skinned serving girl with loops of thick, amber braids, arrived almost instantly, holding a pitcher of ale in one hand and a bottle of wine and an empty goblet twisted among the fingers of the other.

Eyes sparkling as always, she said, "Wine, I presume, Your Grace?"

"Yes."

She set down the ale and took the goblet in her free hand. Poured his wine. He admired her slim waist, the low neckline of her dress, and how her braids fell over her shoulders. Vivia was his favorite of all the maids. She had a way of making him forget, not only his pain but his deformity as well.

She set the goblet before him, then brushed her fingertips over his hand, almost by accident. "Shall I come visit tonight?"

The words were less than a whisper, though Oli's ears tingled at the notion that someone might have overheard. "I would not turn you away," he said.

Vivia twisted her full lips into a knowing smile as she gathered up the ale and wine. "As you like, Your Grace. I'll bring you back a platter."

He watched her walk along the table opposite his, and just as she disappeared through a side door, his gaze caught that of another woman looking his way. Rosârah Zeroah, watching him with a puzzled expression from where she sat beside Rosârah Mielle on the dais.

His cheeks burned, and he lowered his gaze, instantly annoyed at his reaction. Why should he care what the dowager queen thought of him?

"Good evening, Oli." A glance over Oli's shoulder revealed Barek, standing behind him. A welcome distraction from Zeroah's reproving stare.

Barek pulled out the chair on Oli's left and sat just as Vivia reappeared with a platter of food. This time Oli made sure not to look at her.

"No sign of our new king?" Barek asked as Vivia again departed.

"Only his bride and her ladies." Oli helped himself to a wedge of cheese from the platter.

Barek grunted. "What I wouldn't give to have seen him wed a lady of quality."

"Do you mean Princess Saria or your own daughter?"

Barek turned his rich, tawny brown eyes Oli's way—Father Tomek's eyes, though Barek's held none of the depth and respectful censure that used to make Oli's knees quiver.

Barek changed the subject rather than rise to Oli's bait. "You are a military man," he said. "What do you think of the boy's recruitment plans?"

Oli finished his bite of cheese before responding. "We have to recruit from somewhere."

"If he would have married Saria, he would have what is left of the Sarikarian army."

"He has them already through the alliance," Oli said.

"But they are lost without a king. I can't imagine they would come, even if we called them."

"I think they would. Saria is very capable, plus she still has General Norcott to help her."

"And we have Captain Veralla."

This time Oli grunted.

"Pardoned after losing the king. It's absurd," Barek said. "And so many important occupations assigned to foreigners, pirates, and nobodies."

"He is young," Oli said. "To him it makes the most sense to appoint his friends."

"If only my father were here to talk some sense into him. They greatly admired each other. All I'm trying to say is, I know the young man to be smarter than his actions. Too much pressure, I suppose."

Oli didn't think so. Rosâr Trevn had his own mind and did things his own way. "The harder you push, the harder he pushes back. Perhaps if you praise his efforts, he will dismiss them and get around to trying things your way."

Barek chuckled. "He does seem to take the opposite side of anything I propose. When I first spoke to him, the boy was terrified. You should have heard his voice."

"He seems to have found his courage. It's a shame he hasn't more experienced, trustworthy friends."

"You distrust Captain Veralla?" Barek asked.

"Not him, no. He is the only one I do trust. The rest of them . . . those sailors, the pales, that mountain giant he speaks of, Zahara the pirate, and the queen, especially."

"The queen's taken a disliking to you, has she?"

"Oh, she means well, of course, but she has as much common sense as a puppy. She seems to care only for what is cute and helpless."

"Don't you fall into that category, Oli? I hear what the women say about you. Even my daughter admires you." He raised an eyebrow. Oli glared at the accusation that he was in any way helpless, and Barek chuckled. "I take that as a no."

"Rosârah Mielle accused me of beating one of my students. Believes I'm still a mantic too, so say some of the maids. And a skirt-chaser. As long as I'm a member of the Wisean Council, I will do what I can to help this realm. But my personal life is my own business."

"And if you were not a council member . . . ?"

Oli turned to face the older man. "Do you know something I don't?"

"Not at all. I only wondered if you had any ambition beyond serving the throne."

Barek's words infuriated Oli. He had no stomach for political machinations. "I serve the throne out of respect for Rosâr Wilek and to combat the evil that Barthel Rogedoth wields with shadir. My only hope in succeeding in those tasks is to keep the throne of Armania stable. The object is to help Rosâr Trevn succeed. If the throne comes to me, I have failed. We all will have failed. So pray that does not happen. Pray that Rosâr Trevn rules until he is gray and half blind and must be pushed around in a rollchair like his father. Pray that he has sired a dozen heirs to rank between the throne and me. That is my only ambition. Anything else is unforgivable."

Trevn

Trevn stood at the head of the table in the council chambers and surveyed the faces of those present. There were four of the Wisean Five, minus Inolah, who had departed for New Rurekau to see her recovering son. Also present were Hawley, Master Jhorn, Cadoc, Nietz, and Captain Veralla, whom Trevn had invited for a particular purpose.

"I call to order this meeting of the Wisean Council." He did not sit down, but brought up his first topic from where he stood before Barek could seize the opportunity to take over. "First and foremost, as my sister the empress does not plan to return soon, I have made a new appointment to the council. Captain Veralla will serve as our fifth member. That decided, I am officially promoting Collak Ensley to General of the army."

Instantly the emotions in the room darkened, the most hostile coming from Barek Hadar, of course.

"But Veralla is not of noble birth," Barek said.

"It's true," Danek Faluk said. "The council has always been made up of nobility."

"I care not," Trevn said. "Captain Veralla is a wise and decorated soldier. He knows more about this realm than some of you, I daresay."

"I thought you planned to give the position to the Earl of Dacre," Oli said.

"I considered it," Trevn said, "but while Hinckdan is trying to get back to us, he is not here yet. This council needs a new member now."

"The nobles will not like it," Barek said.

"What you mean, Your Grace, is that a handful of argumentative nobles will not like it," Trevn said. "But as I cannot trust that particular handful, I had no noble options to fill the seat."

"But what about the captain's failure to protect the king?" Barek asked.

"That we have already put behind us," Trevn said. "Now, I'm concerned about how the snow has affected the crops and our people. Master Hawley?"

"Reports from the nobles are mixed, Your Highness," Hawley said. "Some had already harvested most, if not all of their crops. The biggest concerns lie with Lord Blackpool and Lord Idez."

Trevn turned his attention to Joret Vohan, Earl of Idez, whom he'd appointed to replace young Rystan Barta. "Lord?"

The man was slender with over two dozen gray warrior braids and a bronze tooth. He was dressed in black to mourn the loss of his son, Greth, who died in the battle that took Wilek. "The wheat was lost, Your Highness," Lord Idez said. "All of it."

Trevn's heart sank at the gravity of that news. "We survived at sea without wheat. What was Lord Blackpool growing?"

"Turnips and clover," Hawley said. "He also raises sheep."

"They'll go hungry without food for winter," Captain Veralla said.

"Master Jhorn, gather a group of commoners looking for work," Trevn said. "Send them west until they find grassy hills to make silage. How do the people fare in this cold?"

"Most have shelter," Jhorn said. "And there are plenty of trees to make firewood, but food is going to be scarce for some, especially if this early winter sticks. The people either need jobs so they can earn money or they need land to work, with the hope of providing their own food."

"They could hunt," Captain Veralla said. "Give the people free reign to scavenge and hunt wherever they please and that will go a long way."

"The nobles won't like it if commoners come onto their land to hunt," Barek said.

"No land has yet been assigned," Oli said, raising an eyebrow toward Trevn. "Isn't that right?"

"It is," Trevn said carefully, sensing enthusiasm rising within Barek Hadar. "So, Master Jhorn, employ commoners for silage and hunting. And make it known that anyone can hunt and scavenge wherever they like."

The Master of Requests nodded and scrawled something down on the parchment before him.

"And what do I tell the nobility when they complain?" Barek asked. "When will you hear their concerns?"

Trevn had put off the subject long enough. "I will hear them now. From all of you," he added so that it was clear he wanted to hear from more than Barek.

"You must give land to the titled," Barek said. "It would go a long way toward appeasing them, especially if you allow commoners to hunt and scavenge wherever they please."

"The nobility hates your youth," Lord Idez said. "They call you the Sapling King and King Lackbeard."

"Yes, I've heard their names for me," Trevn said, trying not to sound annoyed.

"They know you have always disdained them," Danek said, "so they never liked you much to begin with, beyond the hope that you might marry one of their daughters, which is no longer a possibility."

"Unless you take another wife," Barek said.

"No," Trevn said. "I won't do that."

"But your common wife is a big concern, Your Highness," Barek argued. "The nobles feel that one of them should have married into the Hadar family. Wilek married a Sarikarian, Janek is dead, and you are the only one left. The nobility feel cheated out of a chance for one of them to join with the royal line."

"It's true," Master Jhorn said, "disgusting, though it is. Most of the nobles hate your queen."

"But they don't even know her!" Trevn said.

"Permission to speak plainly, Your Highness?" Oli asked.

"Please do," Trevn said, bracing himself.

"The queen seems drawn to seeking out and righting injustice. This is wonderful, but she sometimes jumps to conclusions without conducting an investigation. To the nobles and to those who have served House Hadar for many years, she has the tendency to make herself a meddlesome distraction. Take the school, for instance."

Trevn set his jaw. "My wife loves children."

"She can spend every other waking moment with the children, if she so wishes, but she must learn that not all orphans are darlings. Some lie. And yet she is quick to believe every word."

Trevn raised his eyebrows. Before he could formulate a reply, Oli went on.

"I mean no ill will, Your Highness. But if your wife does not take more care with where she goes and whom she offends and accuses, she could cause your reign more trouble than good."

Trevn wanted to rage and defend Mielle, but Oli was right and he knew it. "I will speak with the queen."

The press of conflicting emotions made Trevn pull back the use of his gift. Rather than sit through the awkward silence, he went on. "I know a majority of the nobles do not like me. *Besides* assigning land and titles," he said with a look to Barek, "what can I do to change that?" He'd never cared if anyone favored him as a prince, but being king was different. As much as he hated to admit it, he needed the nobles' support.

"It's nothing personal," Captain Veralla said. "They hate that they cannot buy your loyalty. They hate that you are monogamous. Wilek had this problem as well. Taking concubines and extra wives is one way of giving noble families a voice in the politics of the kingdom. Their daughters would have your ear. Your denying the nobles this avenue is merely another way they feel cheated out of gaining any power over you."

Of all the ridiculous . . . "Why should anyone have power over me?"

"*Influence* is more the word, I'd say," Danek said.

"And if they cannot gain influence or land from you," Barek said, "history shows that they will rise up and take it, whether they attack the castle directly, indirectly, or pillage each other."

"They would attack their own people?" Trevn asked.

"Some might," Lord Idez said. "A simple fight over a missing flock of sheep could quickly escalate into a war between two households."

"Unless you give your nobles a permanent means of making a living," Barek said, "many will see war as their only hope of increasing their wealth and influence."

"Will holding court appease them?" Trevn asked.

"It would be a start," Lord Idez said.

Trevn took a deep breath, annoyed that he was already capitulating. "I will revisit the idea of holding court. The other matters I hope will improve over time. Now, the ore pit mines have brought in plenty of raw material, but the snow will likely end the process until spring. How many weapons can we produce with what we have already mined? And will it be enough should we be attacked?"

The meeting went on and in the end lasted just over two hours. Trevn, though exhausted, could not rest as he wanted to. Instead, he ate a quick meal, then had Ottee dress him in armor. He had been practicing swordplay on the castle roof for a few weeks now. The soreness in his body had finally begun to fade, and Cadoc thought he was finally ready to make a showing on the practice field without being completely humiliated.

Trevn was eager for some new opponents. He had never enjoyed sparring with Cadoc. The man was shorter than he was and nearly twice as wide—all muscle. Getting pummeled continually by someone like that did not help a man's confidence, especially when he couldn't even grow a beard. Cadoc and Nietz were of a similar build, but Trevn did not mind sparring against Nietz. That might be because the former first mate was not as adept in swordplay as he was with his fists.

Novan was Trevn's favorite to duel. They were similar in height and build, though Trevn was a trifle thinner. The man was quick, though, and always left Trevn with new bruises each time they fought.

Once Trevn was dressed, he set out for the practice field with Cadoc, Nietz, and Rzasa. They passed through the castle and out into the frigid air without drawing too much attention, but the moment the foursome stepped off the barge, people began to stare. By the time they reached the field, a distant crowd trailed along behind them.

"I expected to be seen," Trevn murmured to Cadoc, "but by soldiers, not a bunch of oglers."

"Want me to dismiss them?" Cadoc asked.

"No, no." He would simply ignore them.

"Are you ready, Your Highness?" Cadoc asked.

"As much as I can be." Trevn's breath puffed out before him as if he were smoking a pipe. It would be nice to get warm, at least. He lifted his waster and crouched into position. "Which one of you is going to fight me first?"

"Rzasa can," Cadoc said. "Better that you warm up on someone you have a chance of besting."

"Thanks for the vote of confidence," Rzasa said.

"It's your youth I am referring to, boy, not your skill. That you and the king are close in age gives him a fighting chance."

"Now I'm the one to be insulted," Trevn said. "Let's have a little more affirming talk from you or silence, Cadoc, if you don't mind."

Cadoc said nothing, and Trevn chuckled. "So that's how it's going to be, is it? I see I shall have to prove all of you wrong." He lunged forward, jabbed his waster at Rzasa, and the two began to spar unsteadily on the slippery snow.

Wishing and a cocky attitude did not make up for Trevn's lack of experience with a blade. He made simple mistakes and wondered if perhaps he had been practicing too much.

Rzasa stumbled. His boot slid in the snow, and Trevn was able to knock away his blade. He'd gotten lucky, and from the amused emotions surging around him, the onlookers knew it.

A soldier stepped forward and bowed. "If you are looking for sparring partners, Your Highness, I would be honored."

Trevn instantly recognized Hirth Wallington. The man was about twenty-four and, in his younger days, had run with Janek's crowd. His uncle, Mahat, had joined Rogedoth's traitors and thus abandoned his family to the care of Hirth's father, the Duke of Everton.

"All right, then," Trevn said, sizing up the man. He was no taller than Trevn but much stronger. If Trevn could devise a way to trip him and get him on his back—

Sands! He needed to stop thinking like Nietz. Biting and breaking fingers would not win him an army.

Hirth stood across from Trevn, unmoving. Did he expect Trevn to make the first strike? Very well. Trevn swung the blade. Hirth twisted easily and raised his flat against the blow, halting Trevn's stroke in midair. He spun away and brought his blade in a circle over Trevn's weapon and toward his other side.

Trevn barely had time to parry before Hirth's waster chopped against his left side. Hirth continued on his offensive, going slowly and methodically.

Just as slowly, but with no real skill, Trevn somehow managed to block each swing of Hirth's sword and counter every step, though it took great effort to do so and to keep from falling in the slick snow. His lack of skill frustrated him to the extreme, as did Hirth's faint yet amused smirk and the swell of his confident emotions.

Hirth slowly drove Trevn back toward the racks. Humiliation burned Trevn's cheeks, making him doubly hotter under the heavy armor, even in the winter cold. Trevn ducked a swing of the sword, turned, and parried, but Hirth's blade knocked Trevn's flying.

An involuntary cry escaped Trevn, which drew a handful of chuckles from the crowd. He bit back an oath as he stood before Hirth, weaponless.

The young soldier stepped back and bowed overly deep, oozing a thrill of delight over his stench of sweat. "I will wait for you to retrieve your waster, Your Highness."

"Thank you," Trevn said. He moved slowly, trying to catch his breath. Out of desperation, he reached for Hirth's thoughts.

. . . out of shape he must be if his muscles are crying. We have a king who cannot even hold his own against me, and I am not nearly as strong as Sir Jarmyn or Sir Keshton. If I crush him now, the army will never follow him. They will follow Jarmyn. And whatever prize Jarmyn sets for them, they will rally toward.

Trevn set his jaw, shocked at how this soldier saw him. How desperately he wished to have heard a different reaction, but could he really blame the man for thinking the obvious? Trevn was inferior to Wilek in just about every way except climbing trees, sailing, drawing maps, and perhaps brawling. What good were such talents when one had a kingdom to rule?

He picked up his sword, still concentrating on Hirth's thoughts, and sank into guard position, but this time, as Hirth grinned and darted toward him, Trevn kept a hold on the soldier's mind. He willed grace and kindness into the man. Respect for his sovereign. Fear for the power his king wielded—not with a sword, but with a word. Trevn could bring pain upon Hirth. He had yet to send anyone to face the pole, but there was a first time for everything, and if Hirth saw fit to disgrace his king, then Trevn just might have to disgrace the soldier right back.

He might not.

But he might.

They were only thoughts, and Trevn didn't know why he felt the need to fall upon such childish games, but the intimidation worked. Hirth eased up, and Trevn was able to match him strike for strike until he finally slipped his waster past Hirth's guard and the end of the wooden blade tapped his opponent's breastplate.

Murmuring rose above the scattered applause. Trevn quested into the crowd and found the audience puzzled. They knew Hirth had let up, but they didn't know why.

Trevn knew. But did Hirth? He again reached for the man's thoughts.

. . . will berate me. But I'm not sorry. I did what I felt was right. He is the king, after all, and deserves respect. Doesn't he?

Hirth seemed just as puzzled as the audience. None knew that Trevn had used his magic—that their king had cheated.

Was it cheating? To use every tool in one's arsenal? Trevn wasn't exactly sure how he had manipulated Hirth's thoughts, but the man no longer disdained him. He wasn't exactly for him either, but wasn't this an improvement?

Hirth bowed, this time without the mockery of his previous two. "Thank you for the contest, Your Highness."

Trevn nodded. "You fight well, Master Hirth. I am proud to know there are men such as you in my army."

Hirth met his eyes, bowed again, then walked toward a cluster of soldiers who were watching him with disdain.

Rzasa appeared at Trevn's side. "Will you go again, Your Highness?"

Trevn handed him his waster. "Not today." He needed to end on a victory, and he knew very well that he would lose any other match at this point. Nor was he ready to use his mind-speak magic in such a way again right now.

The more he thought on it, the worse he felt. Hirth had no idea that his king had reshaped his thoughts. It seemed to Trevn a moral breach. He had no doubt that if Wilek had known what he'd done, he would have scolded him. Surely Arman would not approve either.

Trevn walked off the field, adding the weight of the onlookers' stares to the weight of his own guilt. Cadoc, Nietz, and Rzasa left with him.

"Not exactly what you had in mind, was it, Your Highness?" Cadoc asked.

"No, but I kept my sword pointed in the right direction. That, at least, must make you proud."

"Why'd he suddenly ease up?" Nietz asked. "Another few seconds and he could have had you."

"What makes you think he eased up?" Rzasa asked. "Maybe he got tired."

"I think he realized he was about to best his king and thought the better of it," Cadoc said.

"Did you hear his friends mocking him for being a bootlicker?" Rzasa asked.

"That's just men being men," Cadoc said.

Trevn felt sick. He would have to improve. That was the only answer. But he knew as well as anyone that these men had been practicing swordplay all their lives while Trevn had been poring over prophecies, religious texts, and histories. Arman would have to provide a way.

Trevn ambled back to the barges, his men keeping pace while he caught his breath. About halfway back, Hinck's words startled him. *I have news.*

"Wait, don't tell me," Trevn voiced. *"You're married!"*

"No, thankfully. But I've finally managed to get back to the dungeon house, and Lady Islah is gone. Rogedoth must have taken her with him after all."

Trevn groaned. *"This is terrible! How will we discover his secrets now?"*

"That is why I am seeking your counsel. I had presumed this was obvious."

"Well, I don't know what to do."

"Neither do I. Except . . . What about that boy Grayson? Didn't you say he can all but fly?"

An intriguing idea. *"It's his magic. He moves by thinking himself from one place to the next. If anyone could find her, it would be him."*

"Once again, the lowly Hinckdan has solved a problem for the mighty king of Armania."

"Would you prefer the job?"

"I have enough difficulties here, thank you just the same. But Grayson is welcome to take this one off my list."

"Grayson has lived only ten years. How can I ask so much of him? Plus, this woman is his grandmother. Furthermore, I can't imagine Jhorn would grant me permission."

"Perhaps you need me to be king after all. This is why Barek wants you to wear that crown. It's so heavy, you can't possibly forget it's on your head because it'll throw out your back. You decide things now, Trev. Use your position to let the boy's father know you need him."

"I'll ask Jhorn, but I'm not going to force Grayson to do something he doesn't want to do or that Jhorn disapproves of."

"Either way, this problem is no longer mine."

"Oh the joys of being king."

"Still, assuming Grayson will find Lady Islah, that turned out not to be such bad news after all, which is good, because I have still more to share."

Trevn winced. *"What else?"*

"Laviel remembered Bahlay and, with his help, has been using magic to fix the ship. They've been at it all day, and from the look of things, might finish by tomorrow. How close is the Seffynaw?*"*

A thrill of fear ran up Trevn's spine. He'd have to voice Bussie, but he knew the answer. *"Not close enough. They've been gone only three days."*

He sensed Hinck's helplessness and understood. If Laviel reached Armanguard and attacked, they would fall. They had no way to defend against her magic. The strategies Trevn had found in the ancient scrolls had been desperate, though he supposed he was just that.

"I'll inform the war council," Trevn said. *"We'll come up with a defensive plan. But I'm going to need you to do all you can to stop her."*

"How?"

"The ancient scrolls told several stories of mantics being taken out from afar by bowmen."

"You want me to kill the queen?"

It was the best way. *"She's a traitor setting out to attack us. If you can stop her before she reaches us, you will save many lives. I'm sorry, Hinck."*

"Not as sorry as you'll be if I fail you."

Back in Trevn's apartment, once Ottee had helped remove his armor, Trevn sent the boy to fetch him a snack, wanting a private moment with Sir Cadoc. Ottee scurried from the room, closing the door softly behind him.

"I cheated, Cadoc," Trevn said. "On the practice field. I got into Hirth Wallington's head and somehow influenced his thoughts. Reminded him that he should respect his king."

Cadoc fixed Trevn with his familiar expression of concern. "You used your mind-speaking magic?"

"Not to speak directly. It's difficult to explain, as I'd never done it before." Trevn looked away, embarrassed to have to admit this to a man he greatly respected. "It seems I put thoughts into his head, reminders that, in the end, caused him to ease up—changed the way he felt about me as a person."

"I don't understand how that is possible."

"How is any of this magic possible?" Trevn asked, raising his voice. He felt Mielle's concern and took a breath to calm himself. "Arman's ways are mysterious, Cadoc, but I don't think he intends for me to use my magic like that. I crossed a line. Wilek would not have approved."

"Nor do I," Cadoc said.

Now that was just irritating. "Trust you for that."

"Neither do you approve or you wouldn't be telling me now," Cadoc said.

"There must be something I can do to learn swordplay faster."

"You can stop overthinking everything."

"Novan said I need to concentrate on my opponent."

"You're not Novan. All that overthinking slows you down. Just let yourself react to what comes at you, just as you did when you killed that traitor on Bakurah Island."

"You weren't even there. How do you know what I—?"

"Wilek told me. And Sir Kalenek. And Harton before he went bad. And if you must use your voicing magic, why not use it to read your opponent's intentions and be one step ahead? I'd think that a much fairer use of your ability and one that would serve you well in a battle with your enemy too."

Now there was an idea Trevn could put to good use. "How did you get to be so wise, Cadoc?"

His shield grinned. "By making a thousand mistakes, Your Highness. The same will be true for you."

Trevn grunted. "Oh good. Something to look forward to."

The night bells had come and gone by the time Trevn finally left his office that night and returned to his apartment. He found Lady Pia sitting on the longchair beside the fire. Cadoc walked to the hearth, picked up the poker, and stirred the coals, which spat orange sparks up toward the dark chimney.

"Is she asleep?" Trevn asked Lady Pia.

"I think so. Went to bed about an hour ago."

"Good night, Lady Pia, Sir Cadoc." Trevn let himself into his bedchamber. It was so dark he had to feel his way to the bed. He drew back the covers and sat on the soft mattress. He pulled off his boots, his vest, and shirt, then lay down and tugged the blankets over him. The bed felt cold and his back ached. He stretched his arms over his head, sore from his bout with Hirth.

"Where were you all day?" Mielle asked.

"I thought you were asleep."

"I've been waiting up."

"You didn't have to do that."

"I wanted to."

The words implied that she cared for him, but all he sensed through their soul-binding was annoyance and distrust. Her shields were up as well, and he could not hear her thoughts. "I had a busy day." And he told her all he had done from his very first meeting to the very last.

A pang of concern for Hinck momentarily overshadowed all other emotion, but when it faded, Mielle's negative feelings were still present.

"What is bothering you?" he asked.

"Porvil did not come to class today."

Trevn tried to keep any emotion at bay, knowing she would feel it. "Duke Canden says the boy admitted to having lied, and I sensed no deceit in the duke."

"You and your gift. Your senses didn't keep you from leading your men into a trap in Zuzaan, did it?"

"That's not fair. I was new to the ability, then, and barely understood it. And you didn't let me finish. I also checked with Inolah. She says Oli has never laid a hand on any of the boys and that Porvil is a bit of a scoundrel, if a child could be called one. She said if he gets struck with waster swords, it's not because anyone is overly cruel. It's because he never practices."

Silence met his ears.

"Mielle?"

"You're saying the boy beguiled me in an attempt to get the Duke of Canden in trouble, and I fell for his trick?"

"So it seems."

"Oh, Trevn. How can I enter that school again? And the duke! I must apologize."

"The duke has much on his mind, and further discussion on this matter will only annoy him. As to Porvil, leave his antics to Duke Canden."

The bed and blankets shifted, opening up a space between them and sending a gust of heat toward Trevn's still-cold side of the bed. "I don't like this," she said. "It feels very much like Trevn Hadar, the Curious, has died, and Rosâr Trevn, the Head, has taken his place. And I have no part of Rosâr Trevn's life."

The words shocked. "That's not true."

"Isn't it? I'm not permitted in your very important meetings. You don't want my help even to choose your clothes. You promised we would have adventures together, but they are for you alone."

It could not be easy for her. There was one thing he knew would please her greatly. "We will hold court in the great hall. It is not ideal, but with winter upon us, it is the only option. Will you take charge of the event?"

Hope swelled between them, and he felt her shields lower. "Oh, Trevn, truly?" *"And you'll come?"*

"I will."

All anger vanished in a gust of unbridled joy. She drew close and her lips found his. Trevn praised Arman that they had again made peace. Marriage had turned out to be much more difficult than Trevn had ever imagined, but in times of peace and companionship, it was the best experience of his life.

GRAYS⊙N

Two soldiers held open the door to the king's office so that Jhorn could vault himself inside on his canes. The king wanted to see Grayson, for some reason, and he followed on foot, feeling nervous. The king usually voiced Grayson when he wanted something. All this formality . . . it felt like bad news was coming.

Onika. Grayson sucked in a sharp breath as he approached the king, who stood in front of his fancy desk. Could something have happened to her? He suddenly wanted to reach for her mind to make sure she was well, but King Trevn spoke before he got the chance.

"Please sit down." The king gestured to the chairs before him.

Jhorn swung up onto one seat, and Grayson lowered himself carefully onto the other.

"Thank you for coming," the king said. "I have news for you and a request. The two are intertwined, and I completely understand if I am asking too much."

"You have a task for me?" Grayson asked.

"Yes, I do."

Grayson sighed, relieved that no one was hurt or in danger. "I will help, Your Highness."

The king smiled. "Thank you, Master Grayson. I would first like you to hear what I have to say. I believe it is just the opportunity we need, both to right a wrong done long ago and to stop Rogedoth in his attack against this realm."

Barthel Rogedoth. Grayson realized with a jolt that their enemy was his grandfather.

"You may or may not know," the king said, "that the Earl of Dacre, Hinckdan

159

Faluk, has been serving as a spy. He infiltrated the cult known as Lahavôtesh and made himself a part of Rogedoth's inner circle."

Grayson had never heard of Hinckdan Faluk, but his mission sounded awfully scary.

"Hinck discovered a woman in Rogedoth's prison who identified herself as Islah Pitney," the king said. "This is a woman who all the Five Realms thought died decades ago from an illness, before even I was born. She is Rogedoth's wife—his first wife, I should say—and the birth mother to Rosârah Laviel and to Darlis Nafni who, Jhorn has informed me, was your mother."

Grayson's arms tingled. "She is my grandmother?"

"She is. She seemed lucid to Hinck, though her husband has kept her incarcerated for the past thirty-five years, so I can only imagine how that might affect a person."

Grayson didn't know the word *incarcerated*. "You want me to talk to her?"

"I would like to know why he has locked her away for so long. More importantly, I am looking for his weakness. I know some about mantics from the archives and from your father, who saw such tactics used in the Centenary War, but I cannot understand why Rogedoth hesitates in attacking us. I am thankful he has not done so, but I want to know why. Each day brings us closer to a war, and I must do all I can to try to learn his secrets and discern his weaknesses. This may be our only chance. And who would know him better than Lady Islah Pitney?"

Locked away for thirty-five years. "I want to help her," Grayson said. "I want to meet her."

"It could be dangerous," Jhorn said.

Grayson realized that his father hadn't tried to stop him. "You don't mind if I go?"

"You are your own man now," Jhorn said. "Younger than most, but much as I'd like to, I can't treat you like a child anymore."

Grayson's heart felt so full he thought it might burst from his chest. "I will find her."

"Thank you, Grayson," the king said. "Now, I've studied Miss Onika's prophecies about you, and they reminded me of some other prophecies I studied as a boy. I searched through the archives until I found them. Will you have a look?" He motioned to the sideboard, where he had laid out a tablet and anchored open three scrolls.

Grayson stood and approached the sideboard. The words were in foreign languages, but he could read them all as if they were Kinsman. He expected more words about the Deliverer, but these prophecies were not about Grayson—at least not directly. He read the first aloud.

"'The Deceiver will be deceived. He will break from his true family and be led astray by those he considers friends. He will stir up against Arman's remnant an army who care only for their own pleasure and have no delight in the truth.'"

"Any ideas who the Deceiver might be?" the king asked.

Grayson's mind spun as he inserted one name after another into the prophecy to test the words. Barthel Rogedoth had led his friends astray, not the other way around. Master Fonu almost fit, but Grayson hadn't heard anything about him stirring up the shadir against the remnant. Empress Jazlyn had not been led astray by friends. Perhaps Chieftess Charlon?

"The Magosian Chieftess?" Grayson asked. "I don't know much about her."

"Could be," the king said. "Read the first scroll."

Grayson turned his eyes to the loopy handwriting, which was harder to read than the etched tablet. "'Whatever the Deceiver plots against Arman, the Deliverer will bring to an end.'" Grayson looked at the king. "That makes it sound like I will have to face him."

"That was my interpretation as well," the king said. "Read the next scroll."

"'The Deceiver has built himself an army. He has heaped up evil like dust and divided his minions amongst the rulers of darkness.'"

"Only Rogedoth has built an army," Jhorn said from his chair.

"Unless the army hasn't been built yet," King Trevn said. "Read the last one."

"'Arman has given a command concerning you, Deceiver. "Your descendants will not bear your name. I will destroy the carved images and cast idols that are in the temple of your gods. I will prepare your grave, for you will be cut down by your own family."'" This one puzzled Grayson more than all the others. "I'm related to Master Rogedoth. Do you think I'll have to kill him?"

"Perhaps, if he is the Deceiver."

"What about Lady Islah?" Jhorn asked. "She could be the mastermind behind all of Rogedoth's actions."

"That's an interesting theory," the king said. "I myself was thinking of Shanek DanSâr. Chieftess Charlon believes him to be a Deliverer, but I think the old Magonian prophecies were misinterpreted. You are the true Deliverer, which makes Shanek something else."

"The Deceiver, perhaps?" Jhorn asked.

"Perhaps," the king said. "Remember, these are prophecies, and while I believe they came from true prophets, men are fallible, prophets and scribes alike. We must treat them as warnings, but not as holy writ."

Grayson didn't like the idea of cutting down anyone, especially not someone he was related to. "I don't use a sword very well," he said.

"The Duke of Canden tells me you are learning quickly," King Trevn said. "But I wouldn't worry too much about this just yet. We have a lot of investigating to do. In the meantime, I would encourage you to talk with your father about what it means to take a life. Swordplay is all competition and romantic notions until you are forced to drive your blade into another person."

Grayson had seen death on the pirate ships, so he understood the gravity of the situation. "Yes, sir."

"You must go carefully as you seek out Lady Islah," the king said. "Despite her captivity, she might support her husband still. I suggest you approach her on the pretense of getting to know her and learning about your mother. Asking her to tell you about Darlis might be the best way to earn her trust. Take your time. Relax. Go slowly."

The king was worried that Grayson would get overly excited. It was something he had been trying to work on. "I will be careful, sir. I won't fail you. I promise."

CHARLⓞN

I t took three days to reach Castle Rurekau. Charlon brought along five overtaken gowzals in addition to Masi and a small swarm of commons and slights. She wanted to appear strong—but not too strong. Rurek, therefore, had taken Dominion inside one of the gowzals. One that rode perched upon her shoulder as they entered the inner bailey of the fortress. Approached the arched entrance.

Empress Jazlyn and King Barthel stood waiting. Side by side. United. A massive horde of shadir filled the Veil around the pair. Caterwauling and crowing. Well fed. Strong.

Why would the empress partner with this man? Charlon silently asked Rurek.

Meet her eyes and know your answer.

Charlon slowed to a stop before the empress. Smoky gray eyes spoke clearly enough. *He has purchased her loyalty with ahvenrood.*

So it seems, Rurek said. *We are at a disadvantage, not knowing what they have already discussed. You must find out what they want from you without offending them.*

These two had summoned Charlon as if she were a commoner. She owed them no courtesy.

"I am honored to see you again, Chieftess Charlon of Magosia," Jazlyn said, curtsying. "Allow me to introduce my guest, King Barthel, heir to the realms of Sarikar and Armania."

Charlon bristled at such a declaration. "My son is heir to Armania," she said.

That is no way to make friends, Rurek said.

163

But King Barthel bowed deeply. "The empress misspoke, Chieftess. I am heir to Sarikar alone, and seek only to act as regent in Armania until your son comes of age. I have no doubt that Sâr Shanek is worthy of his inheritance."

"He is, indeed." But only Charlon would be Shanek's regent.

"It is an honor to finally make your acquaintance," the king added. "I have heard much of the woman who killed a great shadir. I do hope you will tell us the tale."

They would have none of her secrets. "I am weary," she said. "We were told you would house us. Is there someplace I might rest? For a short while?"

"Of course, you must be exhausted," the empress said. "I hate traveling myself. Qoatch will lead you to your rooms." She waved forward a handsome young man. "We have planned a ball in your honor after first sleep. Qoatch will return for you then. I hope you will be rested enough to attend."

A ball? Charlon knew nothing of such things. In all her time wearing Lady Zeroah's mask, she hadn't needed to attend even one formal dance. "Magosians are not accustomed to such formalities," she said.

"You will be sitting with me and the king at the high table," the empress said. "It will be entertaining enough to watch, I promise you. And of course you are under no obligation to participate."

You could at least try to be agreeable, Rurek said.

"I'm sure I will be rested. By then," Charlon said.

The manservant ushered Charlon to the second level of the fortress. That she had no need to grovel and beg for ahvenrood pleased her. The substance held no temptation at present. She hadn't taken any in weeks. Much to Rurek's annoyance. She had been using the little stored within. To maintain her contact with the great and to see the Veil. She didn't dare take more. Hoped to be with child soon. If she had need to defend herself, the new magic would serve her well enough.

Charlon bathed. Tried to rest. But she could not sleep. The solid roof loomed overhead. Threatening to fall in and crush her. She missed the softness of her tent. The familiarity. She finally rose and dressed for dinner. Left her bedchamber. She found Miss Amala in the front room. Hugging her knees on the longchair. Weeping and looking quite green.

"What has happened?" Charlon asked.

The girl sniffled. Wiped a finger under her nose. "Forgive me, Chieftess. I did not mean to startle you."

"Answer my question."

"I had an unpleasant conversation; that is all. I am well, truly."

"With whom did you have this conversation?"

Miss Amala frowned. Shook her head slightly. Tears welled afresh. Frustration rose. "I demand you tell me this instant!"

"I saw Master Harton. He—" She took a deep breath. Began to sob.

Charlon tensed at that name. The name of her brother who had sold her. To a brothel. So young.

Who is Master Harton? Rurek asked from where he was perched atop the gowzal cage.

Perhaps this was how Charlon might reveal her new magic. She would kill Harton. *Someone who must die,* she said to Rurek as she sat beside the girl. "Tell me what was said."

Miss Amala hung her head. The girl's shame brought back memories. Charlon's many compulsions had hidden her own dark past. She wanted it to stay hidden.

"He said that he and Sir Kamran used me to escape the *Seffynaw,*" Miss Amala said. "That neither of them cared a whit about me, but only paid me compliments to trick me into helping them. He said I was a drab, silly girl who was too stupid to know when I was being made a pawn, and that it's my fault Sir Kamran is dead. He threatened to tell Lady Zenobia as much. She was Sir Kamran's mother and is one of King Barthel's mantics." A fat tear rolled down her bronzed cheek, but when she next spoke, her voice grew fierce. Bitter. "That they both used me ill is bad enough, but that Master Harton would blame me for Sir Kamran's death . . . as if Sir Kamran were some sort of casualty. That man deserved death and more for his many crimes."

"Harton has always been a monster," Charlon said. "Listen well, Miss Amala. No man can ever be trusted fully. No woman either, for that matter. Trust no one in this life—and you have a chance at survival."

"Not even you?" Miss Amala asked.

Charlon leveled a stare at the young woman. "Especially not me."

Miss Amala sniffed. The pallor in her cheeks had faded.

Discomfort made Charlon stand. Such sentimental moments unnerved her. "I must prepare. Once Harton knows I am here, he will certainly try to kill me."

"Oh, but he wouldn't!" Miss Amala said. "King Barthel invited you here as his guest. He needs you, and Master Harton has no choice but to be loyal to the man who feeds his addiction."

Charlon chuckled. "You learn quickly, Miss Amala. But I know my brother better than anyone. Harton might pretend to serve masters when it suits his purposes. But he is his only master. He knows I will come for him. So I must attack before he does."

You would kill your own brother? Rurek said from the gowzal cage.

Yes, Charlon said. *And you will help me.*

That night Charlon dined at the high table. Looking out over the open great hall. Empress Jazlyn sat center front. King Barthel on her right. Beside the king sat Rosârah Thallah. Then the king's various retainers, Harton and Lady Zenobia included. Charlon had been seated on the empress's left. Astaa, Roya, and Amala beside her. Dinner had come and gone. Many were dancing now. Roya and Amala included. Charlon had brought Rurek. Hidden in the gowzal perched on her shoulder.

Long enough, Charlon had glared. Glared at Harton as he danced with one woman after another. Now that he was eating, she could ignore him with ease. A mixed group now danced on the floor below. Some formally. Some as the music moved them. Rurekans, Barthians, and Magosians. Noble and common. Shadir clouded the air. Spinning and looping among the dancing bodies like insects.

Do you see the king's great shadir? Charlon asked Rurek.

No, he said. *There are some powerful commons here, but no sign of Dendron.*

She regarded the giants. Dressed in fur, leather, and feathers. Standing in groups of three to five. Along the outer walls. Hovering over the food-laden tables. Why were they here? Hadn't they recently attacked this fortress?

"How did you make peace with the giants? So soon after their attack?" Charlon asked the empress.

"The giants you see here are from a different tribe than those who attacked us," came Jazlyn's answer. "The raiders sought slaves to work their mines. These giants seek to know us better."

"I did not know there were different tribes," Charlon said.

"The Five Realms supported dozens of different peoples," Jazlyn said. "Why should the new land be any less diverse?"

"Who is that dancing with Miss Amala?" King Barthel asked.

Charlon followed the king's gaze. Stiffened. The young man's back was to their table. But Charlon recognized Shanek in an instant. He was here. Dancing with the girl.

Masi, tell Shanek to leave at once, Charlon said as she wrestled away her shock. Tried to pretend nothing was amiss. "One of my tribe, it looks like." She chuckled. "See how poorly Magosians perform the dances of the father realms?"

"They are doing remarkably well compared to others," the king said. "You must have someone in your tribe who knows the dances of the father realms."

"Perhaps Sir Kalenek taught them," the empress suggested.

How dare she mention Sir Kalenek's name? Charlon shot the empress a dark glare. But the damage had been done.

King Barthel leaned toward Charlon. "Rosâr Wilek's former shield?"

"Yes," Charlon said, offhandedly, pleased to see Masi appear near the dancing couple. "Sir Kalenek is in my service now. A more loyal man I could not purchase. Isn't that right, Astaa?"

"Indeed, Chieftess," Astaa said. "Sir Kalenek needs no magic to be formidable."

"He is your great-grandson's protector," Empress Jazlyn added.

The woman's loose tongue continued to annoy.

"Is he?" the king said, narrowing his eyes. "I wish you would have brought Sâr Shanek along. I so desire to meet him."

"Someone had to rule in my stead," Charlon said. "Who better than my own son?"

"Rule? He couldn't be more than two years old," Rosârah Thallah said.

"He is a root child, Your Highness," Jazlyn said. "So he has grown much faster than the years he has lived. My own Jahleeah is already a full hand taller than her brother, without the aid of extra ahvenrood that Prince Shanek was given."

"Fascinating," King Barthel said, taking a sip from his goblet.

Masi appeared on Charlon's left. *Prince Shanek does not wish to leave.*

Shanek and Miss Amala neared the end of the line. Her son turned the girl in a half circle. To lead her back. Face exposed for all to see. Charlon cringed.

Empress Jazlyn gasped. "Why . . . that is Prince Shanek," she said. "I did not recognize him from behind."

"Nor did I," Charlon lied.

"Why, he is nearly a man!" Rosârah Thallah said.

"So he likes to think," Charlon said.

"You said he did not come with you," King Barthel said. "Did he hide himself in the procession?"

"He did not hide himself," Charlon said. "Nor did he travel with me. He has a fervent attraction for my fifth maiden. He must have come on his own."

The king chuckled. "Very like a young man to travel so far for a female, though I do hope his desertion of his post did not leave Magosia vulnerable."

"Sir Kalenek and my other maidens are more than capable. Of ruling the realm for a few days." Charlon tried to keep her voice calm. Indifferent. But within, she raged. How could Shanek betray her like this? And Miss Amala should be here on the platform. Ready to help in the attack against Harton. What fools!

"You will introduce us now, I hope?" King Barthel asked.

"Astaa," Charlon said, "go to Prince Shanek. I wish to see him and Miss Amala at once."

"Certainly, Chieftess." Astaa stood and departed.

"They do seem very fond of each other," King Barthel said, watching the pair dance through the sequence.

"He is very handsome," one of the king's women said.

"He looks like Sâr Janek," Rosârah Thallah said.

"I think so too," cooed another of the king's women.

Charlon seethed. Kept her eyes on Astaa. Watched her weave her way around the dancers. Close in on Shanek and Amala.

Her son's presence had distracted her. She must push the conversation elsewhere. "This giant tribe is peaceful?" she asked, eyes on Shanek.

"The Jiir-Yeke have caused us no harm," Empress Jazlyn said.

On the dance floor, Astaa tapped Shanek on the shoulder. He turned. Drew back from the maiden. Then vanished. Taking Amala with him.

Gasps abounded from the high table. Charlon stared wildly at the empty space. How? How had he done it?

"Extraordinary!" the king said. "Did he make them invisible?"

"So it would seem." Though Charlon knew better. Shanek had traveled away. And while he had done so many times, she had never before seen him carry anyone. When had he developed this ability? And why had he kept it from her?

"Look there!" the empress said, pointing to the opposite corner of the room.

Shanek and Amala were dancing in the new space. As if nothing were amiss. Chagrin overwhelmed Charlon. Fools. Both of them. That Shanek could ever rule a nation was laughable.

"He traveled in an instant," King Barthel said, his voice laced with wonder. "I knew root children could move through the Veil, but I had no idea they could take another with them."

Charlon feigned boredom. As if all Magosians could move in such a way. But the king's interest in Shanek terrified her. After all she'd done to keep him hidden. He had dangled himself in front of the very people. The people who would seek to exploit him.

Astaa set off toward Shanek's new location. Charlon wished the woman would hurry.

"It's incredible," the empress said. "Oh, I do hope Princess Jahleeah will be so gifted."

"I daresay he could abduct anyone," the king said.

Charlon could not let such a comment pass. "As I told you, Prince Shanek and Miss Amala have a special friendship. I doubt even he understands how his ability works."

"But he could try, couldn't he?" the king asked.

"Oh, he must!" Jazlyn said. "To have such a gift and not explore its potential would be a terrible waste."

"Why would Prince Shanek wish to abduct anyone?" Charlon asked. "My son is not a spy or mercenary. Nor is he a novelty to be played with."

"I mean no disrespect, Chieftess," the king said, "but if your son could be trained, he could abduct Rosâr Trevn and bring him here. To deprive our enemy of their regent would make the goal of conquest much easier."

"Abduct Trevn, but not harm him," Rosârah Thallah said.

King Barthel inclined his head to the portly queen. "Of course, Your Highness."

Charlon did not like it. "You say 'our enemy.' As if your nation and mine are one and the same," she said. "But Magosia has no treaty with you."

Astaa reached Shanek again. This time when he disappeared, he left Amala behind.

"It seems my son has had enough dancing," Charlon said. "I'm sorry I will not be able to introduce you after all."

"Another time," the king said. "I did not mean to push my aspirations onto you, Chieftess, but I hope you can see what an asset such an ability would mean to all of us—Sâr Shanek, most of all."

Again he implied that Charlon had already joined his cause. She had not—and would not. Shanek was meant to be king of Armania. And she would be his regent. Not Barthel Rogedoth. "I will not risk my only heir," Charlon said. "He is poor in combat. A trained swordsman might kill him."

"I would never put the young man in harm's way, Chieftess," the king said. "We must think of whom he might bring to us instead. Until that is decided, he should be trained to fight."

Charlon fumed. That this man felt he could order her . . . "I will consider your ideas, Your Highness. But I decide what Shanek will and won't do."

"Most certainly, Chieftess," the king said. "I meant no offense."

A tense silence descended upon the high table. What could she do? Nothing. Nothing but continue with her plans to reveal her power and kill Harton. When King Barthel and the empress saw what she was capable of, they would cease trying to manipulate her and her son.

But where had Amala gone? Charlon did not see the girl. Fine. She would do this herself. Once she killed her brother, King Barthel would see. That she needed no man.

"Have you sworn fealty to this man as your king?" she asked Empress Jazlyn.

"I have not, nor will I ever," Jazlyn said.

"I see." Charlon fixed her gaze on the man. "Well, King Barthel? We are both of us here. Speak, mighty king. Tell us what you want to say to us together. So we can both return to the important business of ruling our nations."

"Very well, Chieftess. What I want is simple. The three of us must unite against Armania and Sarikar."

"I have no fight with Sarikar," Charlon said. "But Armania is my son's to rule." She did not want the king to think she was against him. She relaxed her tone and her words. For now. "I am sorry he behaved so poorly tonight. Had he known you were in the room . . . I'm sure he would have been eager to meet you."

"Why do you feel so strongly that he should rule Armania?" Empress Jazlyn asked.

"He is the son of Sâr Janek. Ranked before Sâr Trevn."

Rosârah Thallah grunted.

"But illegitimate," Jazlyn said. "And therefore he has no rank in Armania's eyes."

"Even if his being baseborn were not an issue," King Barthel said, "Armania does not practice the right of first blood. The current king names his successor, and Rosâr Wilek named Sâr Trevn. You must have another reason Prince Shanek should inherit."

"It had been prophesied," Charlon said. "The Deliverer will unite the mother and father realms. Shanek is flesh of Armania and Magosia. He is our Deliverer. Come to bring unity. Ruling is his destiny."

"But that's wonderful," the king said. "Don't you see? I am of the father realms. I can teach the boy many things about Armania. I can groom him to rule. And as I have no heir, I can make him heir of Sarikar."

170

Two nations for Shanek? Charlon did not trust the man. "You have experience with root children?"

His hesitation was enough. "Not I," he said. "My great shadir, on the other hand . . ."

"Your offer is generous, King Barthel. But I have a great shadir of my own. We two will suffice to prepare Shanek for his calling."

King Barthel narrowed his eyes. "I can see from your eyes that you aren't using root at present."

"From your eyes I would say the same," Charlon said.

"Yes . . ." the king said, "but Chieftess, if you have run out, I can help you get more."

The nerve of this man. Believed himself so important. "You think I bluff about my power?"

A shrug. "You brought less than two dozen shadir with you, none of them great."

"Nor do I see your shadir Dendron."

"You know Dendron?"

"I know many things, King Barthel. You may have bought the empress's favor with your bribes. But let me make this very clear. That will not work for me."

"He has not bribed me," Jazlyn said.

"Rurekau would never ally with this man, Empress," Charlon said. "Your doing so tells me that you are either afraid of him—or greedy for power."

"I would rather be on his side than against him!" Jazlyn snapped. "Is that what you will be, I wonder?"

"Would that void our treaty?" Charlon asked.

"I suppose that would depend upon the circumstances."

"I have yet to see proof that this man is stronger than me. Or that he can offer something I don't already have. I have no reason to ally with him."

"What if he were to attack you? Could you stand against him, I wonder?"

"Most certainly. And without the crutch of ahvenrood."

"Ladies," King Barthel said. "Let us talk as friends."

Jazlyn appraised Charlon. "One cannot do magic without ahvenrood."

"I can."

"She's lying," Harton said. "I know my sister well."

Finally. Her brother had finally spoken. A thrill pulsed within. Now Charlon would get her revenge. She glared his way. "You know nothing about me, Harton."

"I know everything," her brother said. "She has always been a spoiled child, Empress. Find out what she wants, and you will win her."

"I want revenge." Charlon pushed back her chair. Stood. "Against the one who betrayed this child. *Bara* gowzal *tselem ba olel* Charlon."

The spell took root. A tether of ice grew between Charlon's soul and Rurek's. His gowzal host left her shoulder. Fluttered down the table. Perched on Harton's trencher. Collapsed into a pool of mud.

The ladies exclaimed. Chairs pushed back. Eyes fixed in horror. Harton's as well.

The mud began to change.

Every head turned to stare. Even on the dance floor, people stopped to watch.

The mud swelled. Took form. A little girl appeared. Sitting on her knees on the tabletop. Small with a bush of spiral curls. Wore a knee-length white linen dress. Her gaze scanned those at the table. Locked with Harton's. Her red eyes widened. Grew cold and wild. She crawled forward. Slid off the table. Stood beside Harton's chair.

Charlon's brother looked pale as he stared at the girl. "What is this? An illusion?" He swiped his hand out, but rather than passing through, it whacked the child's arm.

"Oh," the crowd cried. That any man would strike a child.

The gowzal within shrieked. The unnatural sound came from the girl's mouth.

The crowd drew back. Hundreds of eyes filled with fear.

"You cannot imagine how many times, brother. Times I have killed you in my dreams." Charlon walked slowly behind the king and his ladies. Approaching Harton.

"You always did think too highly of yourself," he said. "It is a mask, then? One that cannot even speak? *This* is your great power?" He chuckled.

The women beside him laughed too.

Soon they would never laugh at Charlon again. "I will give you one chance to live."

"You wish to duel?" Harton asked, eyes merry with the game. "I don't think you realize how strong I've become under King Barthel's tutelage."

"One chance, brother, or you will die."

Rosârah Thallah pushed to her feet. "There will be no killing at this table!"

"Sit down, rosârah," King Barthel said.

Harton swallowed. Throat bobbed. He cast a worried look to his master. His king who had just abandoned him to Charlon's pleasure.

"Give a heartfelt apology," she said. "Not to me." She gestured at the child. "To her."

"For what?" Harton asked, eyes narrowed. "It was her turn to suffer. I did what I had to and do not—"

"You did what you wanted!" Charlon yelled. "What most benefitted you."

"So what if I did? Our father died a pauper so that you and our mother could eat sugared berries and wear cloth-of-gold shoes. She took everything from us. From me. It was my turn to take. And her turn to suffer."

"She was already dead!"

"Hurting you was the best I could do to punish her."

Something niggled in Charlon's mind. A memory that fizzled away against the compulsion. She smiled, safe at last from the horrors of the past. "Apologize to the child, Harton," she said. "Apologize and I will forgive you."

"I will never apologize!" He lifted his hand toward Charlon. The child stepped in his way, red eyes blazing.

"*Kabash môwth!*" Harton yelled, just as Charlon said, "*Harag.*"

In the mystery of this new magic, Harton's shadir abandoned him. Green light shot from the girl's eyes. Seared two holes in Harton's chest. He screamed. Stumbled back. Tripped over his chair. Landed on his knees on the platform. Groped at his tunic.

"Help me!" he cried to King Barthel, then collapsed. His head passed out of sight. Beneath the edge of the tablecloth.

Charlon walked toward him. Stopped beside the mask of her child self. Together they looked down. On her brother's body.

"All choices have consequences, brother," she said. "I hope your brief success as a soldier was worth it."

His breathing ceased. He was dead.

Vindication. Freedom. Great satisfaction.

King Barthel snapped his fingers. "Zenobia, heal him."

Charlon's attention fixed on the mantic woman, who threw herself on the floor at Harton's side. Began to mumble a spell. Sir Kamran's mother.

"No," Charlon said, lifting her hand. "*Atha . . .*" Her voice trailed away. Muted. Clogged by an oppressive force. A green mist that had appeared over Harton like a shield. Charlon knew a moment of terror as she came against magic mightier than her own.

Dendron is here, Rurek said in Charlon's mind.

King Barthel's great. *How does it exude so much power?*

By the many mantics who serve it and the ahvenrood they ingest. If you would take more, you would have such power too. What a battle we would have then.

"Forgive me, Chieftess, but I cannot allow you to relieve me of a loyal mantic," King Barthel said. "I have so few left. I need every one for my attack against Armania."

Charlon turned toward the man. He had said Armania, not Sarikar.

"I will allow you to speak if you promise to behave," he said.

Charlon nodded, desperate to be free, though she mustered up her most hateful scowl. Submitting to this man—to any man—had not been part of her plan.

She felt her throat clear. "My claim to Harton Sonber was made long before yours," she said.

"When Rosâr Trevn is defeated and Armania is in our hands, you may kill him," King Barthel said. "Until then, he is useful to me."

Empress Jazlyn looked upon Charlon with a respectful awe. "How is your magic powered, if not by ahvenrood?" she asked.

"I did not come to share the secrets of Magosia," Charlon said. "You invited me here to talk of treaties. Yet you harbored an enemy of Magosia in your ranks. One who tried to kill me. Do you seek a war with me?"

"Not at all," the king said. "I had heard that you and Master Harton were siblings, but I did not realize there was discord. Forgive me for bringing him to dinner. I will not allow him in your presence again."

This appeased Charlon somewhat. "All my life people have been trying to kill me," she said. "Staying one step ahead of my enemy. That is what keeps me alive."

"Fair enough," King Barthel said. "The empress and I will not press you about your magic, which is most impressive. Our invitation to join our alliance remains. What say you, Chieftess Charlon of Magosia, shadir-slayer and wielder of powers unexplained. Will you stand with us?"

"I will not stand against you," Charlon said, well aware that Harton's foot had just moved. "For now, that will have to be enough."

"You fool!" Charlon yelled, pacing in front of the chair on which Miss Amala cowered. "Do you know what you have done?"

"I'm sorry," the girl cried, her cheeks wet with tears. "I told him he should go, but he wouldn't listen."

"King Barthel saw how he moved. How he carried you. And now he wants my son as his slave! This is a terrible mess that I must try to clean up before we leave this—"

A knock on the door.

"Answer it," Charlon said.

The girl jumped up. Scurried toward the door.

Rosârah Thallah lumbered inside. "May I speak with you privately?" she asked.

What could *she* want? "Certainly," Charlon said, on edge.

The Armanian queen plodded over to the empty longchair beside Charlon's and fell onto it. The wood creaked under her weight. She glanced at Amala.

"Leave us," Charlon said.

Amala darted from the room and closed the door behind her.

Fool girl had better run. "You have something to say, Your Highness?" Charlon asked.

"I need your assistance, Chieftess."

Charlon grew wary. "In what manner?"

"Mantics." She bowed her head. Studied her fingers. "As you know, Emperor Ulrik and his brother were ill. The empress healed Prince Ferro, but not Ulrik. She has said she will, yet keeps putting it off. It's because she seeks to rule this realm herself. And I cannot let that happen. She knows nothing of Rurekan ideals. She cares nothing for our people. She seeks only power and glory for herself."

Charlon did not doubt it. "I would rather not get involved in such a matter."

"It is much more than that. Any day now Ulrik might die. And if she takes power, I have no doubt she will set out to rule everyone, yourself included. She already seeks to learn the secrets of your new magic. Do you think she will fail?"

Such a future boded poorly. "She is not the kind of woman who fails," Charlon said.

"In the end, you will be counted among the wise, Chieftess. If you were to use your magic to create a duplicate of the emperor, then take his real body with you, I could fake his death here. And you could heal him once you return to your realm."

Charlon did not follow. "How does faking his death help anyone?"

"If you heal him now with King Barthel here, he and Empress Jazlyn will find another way to kill him. Death is the only way to save Ulrik and this realm from their devious plans."

"I thought you were on King Barthel's side."

"I am on my own side, Chieftess, as are you."

"Yes, but why ask me? We both want our sons to rule Armania. Does not that make us enemies?"

The woman kneaded her chubby fingers. "It is true that I would like to see Trevn remain king all his life, but he cannot stand against magic. King Barthel will see that Sâr Shanek sits on the throne, I know it. For my loyalty, he has promised to let Trevn live, but he has made no such promise to my great-nephew—nor will he, for Empress Jazlyn's sake. Ulrik is a dear boy. I cannot bear to see his life cut short because of that conniving woman."

Charlon could respect the queen's position. Besides, Empress Jazlyn had taken too many liberties with all that she had shared with King Barthel that night. The woman deserved to be thwarted in some way. "If I help you, I will never admit it. If word gets out that the emperor is in Magosia, I will say he hid himself in our caravan. Without my knowledge. And if anyone is to take credit for healing him—for faking his death—it must be you."

"No one would believe that," Thallah said. "I have always been a malleant."

"Do what you must," Charlon said, "to make your story believable. Leave me out of it. And you have a deal."

The rosârah nodded. "It will be done."

"Then take me to the emperor." Charlon stood. Very much looked forward to Empress Jazlyn's reaction. When she learned that her husband had made a full recovery.

QꙨATCH

hieftess Charlon's swift departure had left the empress in a sour mood. Seeing the woman's power had unsettled even Qoatch. It was dangerous to try to fight a magic one did not understand, and while the Chieftess seemed to pose no threat at the moment and had somewhat agreed to support them, her assertion that her son should rule Armania and her antagonism toward King Barthel made her a volatile ally.

Nor could King Barthel be trusted. He claimed to have had nothing to do with the giants' attack on New Rurekau, but that was a lie. Cherem had learned the truth from some of Rogedoth's shadir, who had been bragging about their clever king. Jazlyn, who desperately wanted as much ahvenrood as she could get, had reluctantly decided to humor the man. She was worried that the Chieftess's attack on the mantic Harton might have given King Barthel cause to renege on his promise of a second bottle of root juice, yet when the man entered the great hall at breakfast the next morning with his procession of mantics, servants, and shadir, he was carrying a bottle identical to the first he'd given the empress.

He climbed the platform, handed the bottle to Qoatch, and bowed deeply to Jazlyn. "Good morning, Empress," he said. "Thank you for your help in convincing Chieftess Charlon to join our cause. She was much harder to win than I anticipated."

"I am uncertain we won her at all," Jazlyn said. "But her caution is to be admired. What she has accomplished on her own for Magosia—it is no small feat."

"She is a most impressive woman," the king said, pulling out the chair beside Jazlyn. He sat, and his women all took their places on his right, as usual.

Jazlyn waved Qoatch over. He carried the bottle of root juice reverently and handed it to his Great Lady.

She worked the cork free, held the mouth of the bottle close, and breathed in. A frown of displeasure. She took a small drink and frowned deeper, her brows low over her eyes. She handed the bottle back to Qoatch.

"You think me a fool?" Jazlyn said to the king. "This is nothing but water."

King Barthel chuckled. "Well, that would be a poor trick now, wouldn't it?"

"Taste it," Jazlyn said. "Confirm this treachery for yourself."

King Barthel snatched the bottle away. He took a swig and his face twisted into a mask of rage. "I have been betrayed!" He whirled about and glared at the ladies seated beside him.

"You?" Jazlyn asked. "I am the one without the ahvenrood."

"You shall have what was promised you," the king said, "as long as I have it to give."

"And if you don't?"

"Then we have a much bigger problem than one stolen bottle."

"That is the only problem that concerns me," Jazlyn said.

"What does it mean?" Lady Mattenelle asked.

The king thrust the bottle at Lady Zenobia. "That one of my mantics has betrayed me," he said. "Someone must have refilled their bottle from my store and replaced it with water."

"None of us would dare," Lady Zenobia said. "Nor would we have need. You have always provided for us."

"None of *you* would dare. But those I left behind, I left for good reason." King Barthel stood and stalked away, descending the steps at the end of the platform.

Lady Zenobia stood and pressed her hands against the tabletop. "Where are you going?"

"To check my stores," the king said. "I must know how much has been tampered with."

A motion from Lady Zenobia, and the women and servants hurried after their king. Jazlyn followed, so Qoatch went as well. The group made it as far as the courtyard and were weaving through a scattered crowd of commoners and servants working there, when Rosârah Thallah scuttled out from the stairwell, screaming.

"He's dead! Gods have mercy on his soul, Ulrik is dead!" She lumbered to a halt before the king, who had stopped and was watching her with interest. Rosârah Thallah pointed a finger at Jazlyn. "You did this, witch. You could have healed him this past week, but you did not. You reclaimed your beauty but had no time for healing your husband. That is proof of your allegiance to none but yourself."

The people in the courtyard murmured their agreement.

Someone yelled, "You let him die, Empress. After all he did for you."

In two heartbeats, Jazlyn's startled expression darkened to anger. "You dare imply he sacrificed for *me*? He kept me captive for months aboard his ship. He made me his prisoner here until I had no choice but to marry. Me! A Tennish priestess."

The servants drew back, creating an empty space around the empress.

"I knew you hated him," Thallah said, folding her stubby arms. "Admit you poisoned the emperor and his brother."

"I admit no such thing," Jazlyn said.

"Did not you just confess to all how much you disdained your husband?" the rosârah asked.

"No matter how we felt about each other, Ulrik's death is a grievous loss to Rurekau and to our children, who now must grow up without a father."

Rosârah Thallah sputtered. "Grievous loss, indeed. Everyone knows you care nothing for the family unit of the father realms. Spare us your lying tongue, Empress. We have seen the truth of you, and your words will not change our minds."

Several emotions passed over Jazlyn's face, as if she were struggling with what to say. She took hold of her long skirt, swept in a half circle, and dropped to her knees before King Barthel. "Your Highness! My shadir does not have enough power to bring back the dead, but surely you, with the assistance of your great, Dendron, could restore life to the emperor." She grabbed the hem of the king's cloak. "Please say you will save my husband."

A stillness followed. Everyone in the courtyard stared at the empress. A horse whinnied in the distant bailey, the only sound beyond Rosârah Thallah's labored breath.

"Someone has tampered with my evenroot," the king finally said. "I must find out how much damage has been done. If someone has sabotaged my supply . . . Do you understand what that would mean? And healing the dead—no, I must see to my root first, before I make any promises. Forgive me." The king turned away and departed the castle, his retinue in his wake.

Rosârah Thallah glared after the king. Qoatch hurried forward and helped his Great Lady stand.

"Perhaps it was only one bottle," Jazlyn said, eyes pleading as she looked on the witnesses present. "When he discovers all is well, he will come back."

"He will not come back," Rosârah Thallah said. "It is in his best interest that Rurekau have no emperor."

"You imply he wanted Ulrik to die?" Jazlyn asked.

"We are much easier to use with no ruler."

"Our emperor might be dead, rosârah," Jazlyn said, "but Rurekau is not without leadership. I am here, as is the council. I will call a meeting to appoint a regent to rule until Prince Jael comes of age. Then—"

"You will do no such thing!" Rosârah Thallah yelled. "Prince Ferro was Ulrik's heir. His mother is on her way here to preside over the council. You have no place there."

Jazlyn's eyes smoldered as she stared down upon the pudgy Armanian queen. "You move to cut me out of any leadership? Is that your goal?"

"You are well aware that it always has been."

"Very well." Jazlyn shook her head and raised her voice. "Let Empress Inolah and the council decide how to move forward. Until she arrives, I shall care for Prince Ferro. But if the council exiles me completely, do not hold me responsible the next time giants come and you seek my protection." She grabbed hold of her skirt and set off, back into the castle. Qoatch hurried after her, at a loss as to what they would do now.

Back in Jazlyn's apartment, she commanded everyone to leave until only Qoatch remained behind.

"King Barthel is not the man I thought he was," Jazlyn said. "It is one thing that he cleverly compelled the giants to attack us in order to trap us into accepting an alliance. But if his evenroot has been so easily tampered with, he and his shadir are careless fools. His power is going to diminish quickly, and when it does, this place will not be safe. Empress Inolah will return, and she and Rosârah Thallah will keep me from having any authority. The council will choose Prince Ferro to rule over Jael, I'm certain. But they will also seek to take my son from me. That I healed Prince Ferro and begged King Barthel to restore Ulrik's life are the only things that might keep them from taking my life."

"You were wise to do both, Great Lady," Qoatch said.

"Little good my wisdom will do me now. You and I both know that the supply of original root brought to this land was already diminishing swiftly. Once it is gone, so will all our magic be."

"Except for Chieftess Charlon's new magic," Qoatch said.

"Yes." Jazlyn paced before Qoatch. "The Chieftess found a way to do magic apart from ahvenrood. I must learn her secret."

"You could send Cherem to watch her in the Veil," Qoatch said.

"One from her swarm might sense he did not belong, and I do not want her angry with me unless I can get what I want first. No, let me try to befriend the girl."

"What girl?"

"The one called Amala. She has the affection of Chieftess Charlon's son. If I can win Miss Amala's loyalty, the son will follow. And then I will be in a place to ask them to teach me what they know."

"How will you earn the girl's loyalty?" Qoatch asked.

"Offer her more power at my side than what Chieftess Charlon gives her," Jazlyn said. "I must mend things with King Barthel, though. He will be angry that I put him on the spot to save my reputation, and I cannot afford to anger him, even if he has misrepresented his strength. Go to him and offer your services in his time of need. Tell him you are a seer and are willing to help him question and watch Dendron's swarm, to see if any are hiding information as to who might have tampered with his ahvenrood supply. In the meantime, I will send Cherem to extend an invitation to Miss Amala."

"Yes, Great Lady."

Qoatch acted swiftly, relieved that Jazlyn had rallied with a plan. He went to King Barthel, who immediately set him to work questioning shadir, a task Qoatch disdained, as the creatures were mischievous and rarely told the truth. This also put him in the vicinity of Dendron, who made his skin crawl. The great shadir certainly had none of the hideousness of Gozan's likeness, but he gave off a deep and dark sense of power that made Qoatch want to flee. Thankfully the great did not show himself often.

King Barthel made no official report as to the status of his ahvenrood stores, nor could any of his retinue be persuaded to share details, but the man's melancholy mood told Qoatch that he had lost something of great value. He made no new offer of a bottle of root to Jazlyn. Annoyed as she was by it, she did not press him, but continued with her own plans.

The funeral of Emperor Ulrik Orsona proceeded with three times as much pomp as his coronation had. His brother Ferro was still too frail to attend, and Jazlyn set guards over her apartment to ensure Rosârah Thallah did not try to take the boy into custody while Jazlyn was preoccupied.

When the ceremony ended, Jazlyn's guards escorted her back to her apartment. Zinetha met them at the door.

"Forgive me, Great Lady," she said, curtsying. "I don't know how they got past the guards without my seeing them enter. I've been right here all morning, and I can't understand it!"

Jazlyn pushed past her lady and stopped in the sitting area, staring at the two people waiting there: Miss Amala Allard and Prince Shanek.

Miss Amala stood and curtsied. "Hello, Empress," she said. "May I introduce Prince Shanek DanSâr of Magosia."

The young man jumped to his feet, beaming from ear to ear. "I am happy to visit, Empress."

Jazlyn glanced at Qoatch, and he read the humor in her eyes at the prince's clumsy manners, though she kept it from her face. "It is a great pleasure to meet you both," she said, curtsying. "Won't you sit? I will have Qoatch bring us some refreshments while we talk."

Qoatch departed, but just before he pulled the door closed, he heard his Great Lady say, "Tell me all about yourselves. What are your hopes and dreams? And what can I do to help you achieve them?"

Qoatch grinned as he made his way toward the kitchens. When his Great Lady set her mind to achieving a goal, there were none who could stop her. He only hoped that she would be able to stand against Chieftess Charlon's power if the woman found out what she had done.

MIELLE

I want minstrels *and* the band," Mielle said, as she and rosârahs Zeroah and Brelenah ascended the circular stairs. "That way we can alternate between dancing and being entertained."

"I like that," Brelenah said, cuddling one of her dogs in her arms. "Though you know how much I am entertained by watching people dance. There are some days I desperately miss holding court. I will do all I can to ensure a large turnout for Rosâr Trevn."

"I as well," Zeroah said.

"Thank you both, for all your help," Mielle said. "I would be lost without you."

"You are doing very well," Zeroah said.

"Thank you," Mielle said. "And how are you?"

"I am focusing on learning my mind-speak skill," Zeroah said. "Wilek wanted it for me, so it feels like something I can give him, even now. The Duke of Canden is convinced I have some rare skill, though I think he is mistaken. He has told the king about it, though, and now I must practice more than ever."

"Trevn said nothing to me about it," Mielle said, annoyed that he wouldn't think to share something involving her dearest friend.

"What is the skill?" Brelenah asked.

"He thinks I can pull forth memories from the mind of another. I did it once by accident but have yet to accomplish it a second time. It is quite vexing."

As they reached the fourth floor and circled to climb to the fifth, a chorus of giggling girls caught Mielle's attention. A male voice spoke over the laughter,

183

startling Mielle by its contrast. "Whose room is that?" she asked, pointing to the open door two down from where they stood.

"Princess Rashah's," Brelenah said, brow furrowed as she started toward the open door.

The three women arrived together. There were eight girls in the room, clustered onto the bed or in chairs that had been turned away from the fireplace toward the center of the room. Mielle recognized all of them from the school.

A man appeared in the middle of the room, standing on his head. The girls burst into laughter, and the dog in Brelenah's arms leapt to the floor, barking at the man, who suddenly vanished. The girls' heads twisted around, eyes seeking out every corner of the room, though Princess Vallah's gaze had fixed upon the eldest queen.

"There he is!" Rashah yelled, grinning and pointing at the wardrobe on the opposite wall, where the man lay on his side, his head propped up on one fist.

Grayson.

Brelenah's little dog went wild, climbing over legs and furniture, trying to reach Grayson.

"What is the meaning of this?" Rosârah Brelenah yelled.

The girls silenced, and most of them stood and curtsied. Grayson disappeared.

"Anyone who does not bear the surname Hadar or Orsona is to leave this room immediately," the eldest queen said.

At once, five girls ran toward the door. Mielle stepped aside to let them pass. All kept their eyes fixed on the floor but the last, who glanced at Mielle with wide brown eyes before passing out of sight.

"Master Grayson, you had best show yourself as well," Rosârah Brelenah said, loud and clear.

"I'm sure he left." This from Princess Vallah, Empress Inolah's eldest daughter.

"I have called him back," Zeroah said, smiling. "I'm getting better at voicing."

Sure enough, movement in the hallway behind Mielle turned out to be Grayson, hands tucked behind his back, head hanging pitifully. His dapple-gray skin was tinged pink at his cheeks, neck, and the tops of his ears.

"Come inside at once," Mielle said, grabbing him by the sleeve. Once Grayson was in the room again, she closed the door.

"I am responsible for the virtue and reputation of these young ladies," the eldest queen began. "It is unacceptable for any of them to have a man in their bedchamber."

"Grayson's not really a man," said Lady Trista, who was Barek Hadar's youngest girl. "He's closer to my age."

But Grayson did not look like a child. He looked every bit like a young man in his early twenties. Though he was skinny with an angular nose and pointed chin, and his round head gave him a boyish air, he had thick eyebrows, dark brown eyes, waves of chin-length black hair—most of which had escaped its tail—and a smile that could certainly break hearts if ever he grew into the notion.

"I realize you did not grow up in the castle by my rules, Lady Trista," Brelenah said, "but I have no doubt that your mother would not like to hear that you sassed me."

Trista curtsied. "No, ma'am."

Brelenah turned her wrath on Grayson. "I am sure you meant no harm, Master Grayson. Such games are fine for the roof or outdoors or even in the great hall or foyer. Public places. You see the difference?"

"Yes, ma'am."

"Your power is unprecedented. Please do not abuse it. I would hate to have to ask the king to restrict you in any way."

"I'm very sorry, Your Highness."

"I am glad to hear it. Now off you go."

"Wait," Mielle said. "I would have a word, Master Grayson. Out in the hallway."

Grayson briefly met Mielle's gaze, then turned and walked from the room. She followed him out, and he slowed, allowing her to pass by and lead him to the railing.

"Have you made any progress finding the Puru orphans?" she asked.

He hung his head. "No, ma'am."

Mielle cringed at his use of *ma'am*. She was not old enough for that title. "Did you learn anything?"

"I tracked a group of giants into the forest, but they were hunting. Then the king asked me to do something, and I haven't had time . . ."

Mielle raised her eyebrows. "Yet you have time to stand on your head to make the girls laugh?"

"I . . . I'm sorry. I'll keep looking."

"I hope so. Now, I have another question for you. There is a boy in the school named Porvil. What do you know of him?"

"No one likes him. He fancies Lady Trista a great deal, but she likes Danno, and the other day Porvil picked a fight with Danno and Danno gave him a black eye. He says mean things to pretty much everyone, but not me. I think he's afraid I'll punch him in the other eye, and maybe I would if he tried to fight me."

"Who are his friends?"

Grayson shrugged. "Doesn't have any. I've seen him following around Gilkin Trumboke, but Gil doesn't like him either."

"I know you don't have much spare time these days," Mielle said, dramatically, "but keep an eye on Porvil for me. Where does he live? Who, if anyone, is his friend? Think you can do that?"

"Sure I can, Your Highness. I'll find out what he's up to."

"I didn't say I suspected him of anything. I'm simply curious about him." And why he would so viciously lie about the Duke of Canden. "Now, if you'll excuse me, I need to finish my conversation with the dowager queens before meeting Master Jhorn."

"Why are you meeting him?" Grayson asked.

"It's not to tattle on you, though I won't be surprised if he gets wind of your mischief today. Master Jhorn is Master of Requests, and he passes on to me any matters involving women or children. I like to help people, you know."

Grayson grinned. "Me too!"

"Wonderful, now go find those Puru orphans so we can help them."

"Yes, Your Highness." And he disappeared.

Mielle shook her head. If Grayson could simply focus on one thing long enough to see it through, she was certain he would be one of the greatest heroes to have ever lived.

Onika

The camp had long ago moved to a new position, which Onika believed was somewhere outside the stronghold of New Rurekau. She had no proof, of course, except that Rosâr Trevn had said Barthel Rogedoth was in New Rurekau and she had heard men outside her tent mention having seen Empress Jazlyn's great beauty. Rogedoth had not yet returned to speak with her again, though it was still several weeks until the next full moon, so said Rosâr Trevn. At her king's suggestion, she tried to listen in on the minds around her, but she only heard fragmented thoughts about the empress or upcoming dice games. Nothing helpful.

Onika had often felt lonely in her life. Being blind did that to a person. She'd felt separated from what was happening around her, as if everyone was keeping a secret. They weren't, of course. Jhorn, Dun, and Grayson had always tried to include her.

Being captive in this place, however, brought on a new loneliness that, when coupled with the dark thoughts and nightmares of the attacks against her, left her feeling on the edge of despair. She found solace in reciting former prophecies, especially those she knew from Jhorn were words directly from the Book of Arman. She prayed, she sang or hummed, and she worshiped a God who loved her no matter what.

She also questioned. She asked "Why?" often, knowing full well that such a question did not always have an answer. She dwelled far too long on the dark memories, particularly wondering why she had been spared and Tulay and Yoana had not. They had been lovely young women, who served her with joy and kindness. Why had Onika lived? She was no better.

Then came moments of such suffocating darkness that she began to think perhaps Tulay and Yoana had been spared after all. She grew jealous, knowing that they were with Arman, healed and whole again in a place with no evil. She wondered how she might take her own life and join them there. She crawled around her tent, feeling for anything that might be used as a weapon. She never found a thing, and such searches often ended when she awoke, cold and shivering so far from her bed, or when Master Burk found her and dragged her back to her mat.

Finally came a day filled with something new. The noises of men arriving on foot—foreign men by the sound of their strange language. Onika wanted to give Rosâr Trevn an update and waited all day, listening for any hint as to the identity of these visitors. Master Burk brought her dinner, but when she asked who they were, all he would say was, "Don't you worry about that. I promise to tell you tonight."

Hours later, she lay pondering his words when a cool breeze alerted her. The swish of the drape over the entrance to her tent quickly dampened the breeze. A footstep. A creak of a knee.

Someone was inside.

"Who is there?" she asked, faking a confidence she did not feel.

"I have come to answer your question, Miss Onika."

Master Burk's voice. He was beside her, sitting or squatting. Horror welled up from the pit of her stomach. Arman had given her glimpses to prepare her, but now that this moment had finally come, she found herself terrified.

"King Barthel is meeting with some giants. When the full moon arrives, he plans to make you his sacrifice. He is inviting the giants to join him."

Onika sat up and pulled her knees to her chest. "I will not be sacrificed."

A soft chuckle. "Always so certain of everything. It's a little mad." A hand brushed her head. She flinched and turned her neck, but the hand stayed with her, caressed her hair.

"I've done a lot for you," Burk said. "I saved you from the men, and I've kept them away, kept them from killing you by weaving stories that terrified them. They think you're a witch, you know. They think you can kill with your thoughts."

"No one can do that."

"A goddess could. I've made them think that's what you are. I told them you're angry they attacked you, and if they don't stay away, you'll kill them all." His hand moved to her throat and pulled the neckline of her dress off her shoulder.

She brought up her hands to push him, but he grabbed her wrists and held them tightly. She felt his breath on her skin and began to pray.

If I have found favor in your sight, O God, protect me. Do not let this man douse the light within.

"I kept you fed and watered," he said, his mouth against her throat.

Onika held her breath and repeated her prayer, trying to think what she might do to get away.

"I take you to the privy hole." A kiss on her shoulder. "Bring you clean clothes." He released one wrist and moved, his weight shifting the mat beneath them. "Now it's your turn to give something to me." Fingers touched her forehead, traced along her hairline, threaded through her hair. She jerked her head aside, and his free hand moved down her body and pulled at her skirt.

"Stop that." She swung her fist, connected with his arm. She followed it higher until she felt his ear; then she cuffed him, as hard as she could.

He swore and grabbed her wrist again. "I never expected Arman's prophetess to be an ungrateful wench."

She tensed at his sharp tone. "Leave me be."

"You? You lay around all day. I am the one who is tired. Tired of serving you like a slave with no form of payment. You owe me much, so you can give yourself to me or I can give you to the entire camp. What will it be?"

She longed for Sir Kalenek to arrive and whisk her away to safety, but he would not come today. And for reasons she did not understand, she must pass through this shadow.

Shelter me, Holy One. Let me not be afraid. My enemy attacks, but you are my redeemer. You make beauty from terror, joy from pain, laughter from tears. Focus my mind on the good you promised that such hope might carry me though this darkness.

"When you pass through deep waters, I will be with you; your troubles will not overwhelm you."

Arman's warmth reminded her that her God was with her. He saw her fear. She was not alone.

She felt Master Burk's hot breath on her face and grimaced. His lips touched hers. She cried out, slapped his head, and kicked her feet. He crushed his mouth over hers. The stubble on his face was sharp and needled her, scratched like sandpaper as he dragged his cheek along hers and again kissed her neck.

"Stop." She tried to scoot back. "Don't do this."

But he did not listen. Hands snaked around her waist and pulled her body against his. He twisted her in his arms and suddenly she fell. Her back hit the straw mat and his weight landed on top of her, pinning her down.

She screamed and pushed at his chest, trying to keep him back, to put obstacles between them. Her memory returned to the last time men had attacked her. She had somehow stopped the one called Aloz. She had been desperate. She had pushed him away with her mind.

Onika focused on Master Burk's thoughts, felt his presence there, his dark intentions. She shoved with all the strength of her voicing magic.

They flew.

Off the mat and up through the canvas ceiling. Onika stopped struggling and gasped, awed by the sights around her.

She could see.

They were sailing through a dusky sky, over the tops of trees capped in white. She released her attacker and willed her motion to stop. Watched as Master Burk floated away, arms and legs pinwheeling. His head whipped around until his wild eyes met hers.

"You *are* a witch!" he yelled across the distance. "Is this what you did to Aloz?"

No.

Perhaps.

Onika didn't know. If she had pushed Aloz to this place, she had not come with him. Not like she had with Master Burk.

She could no longer see him. Where had he gone? What was this place? Had the both of them died? Onika couldn't have. There was to be more to her life, she had seen it, shadowed though it was.

She took a moment to marvel at the land around her. So much beauty! It had been far too long since she'd lost her sight. Snow covered everything, like a sheet of thick cotton. A vast stretch of flat land separated a lake or pond from a forest where trees coated in layers of snow bobbed and swayed in the wind, sending flurries of white dust from their branches. The sky above was a riot of purpled clouds against a fiercely orange sky.

Sunset. She'd never thought she'd see one again.

She let herself float along, taking in the stunning prospect until the sun set fully and darkness fell over the land.

What now?

Arman, what has happened? I do not understand.

"WHEN JUSTICE IS DONE, IT IS A JOY TO THE RIGHTEOUS BUT TERROR TO EVILDOERS."

Yes, she did feel joy. And Master Burk, wherever he'd gone, must surely be terrified.

Something moved up ahead. Onika flew toward it, cautiously. She did not know if Master Burk could harm her in this place, but until she was certain, she would take care.

It was not Master Burk. It was not human at all. It looked very much like a mouse—a large mouse—yet it was yellowish green and transparent, as if it was made of fog. She followed it at a distance, curious.

As she neared, she saw dozens of the strange creatures in many different shapes, sizes, and colors. Some flew fast, painting the air in rainbows of color. Others remained still, alone or in small groups, talking to one another. Nearest her she regarded a two-headed orange-and-black snake having a conversation with some kind of silver fish with a face like a man.

A cackle. "Look! A deader lost."

The voice brought with it a chill and a sense of foreboding. Onika turned toward a red rabbit with tail feathers like a rooster.

"What you doing here, girlie?" the rabbit asked. "Can't you tell which way to go?"

"Feels like a pure to me," said what looked like a bushel of dead grass, yellowed and wilted. "Best keep your distance."

"She looks scared," said one head of the two-headed snake as the second head hissed.

Onika floated backward, wanting to get away from these strange creatures, but a group of them surged forward, taunting and cackling. Some floated around her, bringing with them a frigid breeze. One flew right through her.

She shrieked and glided away, but the creatures gave chase.

"In my Name you have the power to banish shadir. Speak with authority and they will flee from you."

The heat of Arman's voice felt warmer here—like heat from a fire, as if he were nearby. Peace filled Onika, and she found it suddenly easy to ignore the creatures.

Shadir. She should have known. And Arman said she could send them away.

She turned back to face her pursuers. "You who torment me, in the name of Arman, I command you be gone to the depths from which you came and never return to this land again. Now go!"

A chorus of screams pierced the air. Onika clapped her hands over her ears as the group of shadir fell toward the earth like drops of rain. The shadir who hadn't taken part in taunting her scattered to the wind. Curious, she flew after those she had banished, but just as she reached the ground, they passed into the earth and were gone.

She stopped above the thick snow and sent up a prayer. *Praise you, Arman, for you are mighty and powerful. Thank you for saving me.* She closed her eyes, then, eager to feel his presence the way she was used to—without the distraction of sight.

She grew warmer, joyful. A tingling pressure in her chest made her sing a song of praise. How mighty was the One who made everything, the One who spoke into being all that had been void. Holy and glorious and merciful and kind was he!

A sweet nectar filled her lungs, and she opened her eyes to see what smelled so lovely. She found herself in a new place. A place without snow. Inside a leafy green forest of trees so tall they stretched out of sight overhead. Bright light shone just outside the forest, as if a fire were burning the whole land. Drawn by the warmth, she drifted toward the light, eagerly longing to see the glow for herself. She passed out of the forest and over a vast meadow carpeted in mossy green grass and flowers of every color. Oddly, the sweet nectar on the air did not come from them. It smelled of hope and laughter and endless joy. She followed it, and the light turned out to be not a fire at all but a gate.

Onika's heart longed to go inside, to enter into the joy of such a place. She started toward it but found she could not move.

"THIS IS NOT YET FOR YOU, MY CHILD. YOUR DAYS ARE DETERMINED WITH LIMITS YOU CANNOT EXCEED, BUT YOUR SOUL IS NOT REQUIRED OF YOU THIS DAY. GO BACK AND DO THE WORK I HAVE SET OUT FOR YOU."

The heat of Arman's voice dizzied Onika. A high-pitched whistle drew her gaze. A great speckled brown bird was soaring toward her, bringing with it a great calm that pushed away every concern. It flew past, and somehow Onika knew to follow. The bird led her away from the glowing gates, soared over the meadow and back into the forest. The occasional flap of its massive wings brought a warm gust of wind over her face, and she eagerly anticipated the next.

The bird moved quickly, and within moments, they were descending into the darkness of night toward a snow-covered land and the torchlights of a camp set up outside a castle.

New Rurekau?

The great bird dove toward a tent near the center of camp and flew right through the roof. Onika followed, wincing slightly as she passed through the canvas. Shockingly, she felt nothing, not even a tug. She stopped inside, searched for the bird—Nesher, for it had to have been Nesher—but the bird was gone.

Her gaze fell to the bed on the floor, where a man lay on top of a woman. Both looked dead. Onika drew close and studied herself. How pale she looked against Master Burk's dark skin. No wonder everyone thought her so odd.

What should she do? If she was to remain in Er'Rets, she would need her body, wouldn't she?

The thought transported her, and instantly the world blurred into a kaleidoscope of shifting dots. Her heart sank. She was back in her body, blind again, with Master Burk's weight pressing down. Oddly, she felt him breathing still. So he was alive, but could the part of him that was still drifting find his way back?

Onika pushed Burk's body to the side until he rolled off. She sat up, heart pounding in her chest. What now? How could she escape when she could not see?

Arman? What would you have me do?

"PUT YOUR HOPE IN ME."

Onika relished Arman's warmth, which was not as hot in this realm as it had been in the Veil. She knew now that was where she had gone.

"Prophetess?" a man called.

She jumped. "Yes?"

"Is Master Burk in there?"

"I think so. I can hear him breathing, though he has not spoken in quite some time."

Canvas rustled and footsteps sounded as the man came inside. "Woman . . . What did you do?"

"Is something wrong?"

The man growled. "I'm not carrying him out of here myself. I'll be back with help, but just you leave us alone, you hear?"

"You are safe in my presence," Onika said, then added, "for now."

The man breathed out a shudder as he stalked away mumbling about witches and goddesses. He promised an offering to Cetheria if she would protect him.

Onika smiled.

For the first time in a long time, she was not afraid. Arman had given her a way to protect herself from evil men and to destroy the enemy's minions.

In fact, if she could leave her body again, perhaps she could study the camp and discover something important to pass on to Rosâr Trevn. Finally, she was taking a step toward the future she had seen so long ago. She had no ideas as to what Arman wanted her to do at present, but until he made that clear, she would make good use of her time here and her new gift by spying for Rosâr Trevn. She concentrated, and as she left her body again, everything came back into focus.

PART EIGHT

A DELIVERER COMES

Hɪⴖᴄᴋ

Hinck sat at the desk in his cabin aboard the newly repaired *Gree-nore*, carving a new bow and wondering if he could really commit murder.

Truth be told, he'd rather not kill anyone, certainly not a woman, and especially not a woman as vengeful as Rosârah Laviel. If he should fail, the scars on his face would be mere scratches compared to how she would torture him.

Master Nesos had finished the repairs on the ship three days ago. At Rosârah Laviel's command, they had set sail for Armania the next morning. If Hinck hadn't lived through it, he would have thought packing up an entire village in one day impossible. His back ached from his short stint at slave labor. Hunching over his carving was no way to loosen stiff muscles either.

His old bow worked fine, but he needed an occupation now that Nellie was gone. In all his hours on the practice range, giving poor instructions to the compelled Puru archers, his own skill had improved a great deal. He could do this. *If* he could restrain Sârah Jemesha and Eudora so that neither could heal the rosârah.

"May I come in?" a woman asked.

Hinck jumped at the sound of Eudora's voice. She was standing just inside the doorway; he hadn't even heard it open. "You already have," he said.

She closed the door and leaned against it. "I don't want to marry you."

Hinck almost laughed. "Then tell Rosârah Laviel you refuse."

"You know I can't do that."

Hinck went back to his bow. "Well then. Thanks for visiting. Come anytime."

Eudora walked to his side. "We made a good team once."

197

Hinck set down the bow and pushed back from the desk. "You used me to get revenge on Sâr Janek. For us to have been a team, you would have had to inform me of your plan in advance. Which you did not."

She folded her arms. "I didn't take you for the type to hold a grudge."

Hinck snatched up his bow and scraped off an uneven patch. "I'm not holding a grudge, but that doesn't mean I want to marry you."

"So we are agreed. We both don't want to marry the other."

"Apparently not." He wished she'd say what she had come to say. He had no desire to invade her thoughts and suffer through that self-absorbed mind of hers.

She fingered the curls of shaved wood on the desktop. "I never wanted to rule."

"You told me this long ago, yet you married Rogedoth, so perhaps you don't know yourself as well as you think you do."

"You weren't there. You didn't see what he did. How they"—her voice fell to a whisper—"forced me."

Hinck smoothed out a lump in the wood.

"I wed the Pontiff against my will," she voiced. *"Laviel compelled me to obey him."*

Her sudden switch to mind-speak made Hinck look around for shadir. He saw none.

"I don't support this enterprise," she said. *"I expect you will deny it, but I don't believe you support this either. I think you are loyal to House Hadar."*

Was she trying to trap him? *"I proved otherwise by drinking the root juice."*

"I know you, Hinckdan. Your heart is pure. Nothing but duty and honor could possibly compel you to join King Barthel in this madness."

"What do you want?" he asked aloud.

"To show you."

He lowered the bow to his lap and met her glistening amber eyes. "Show me what?"

She slid her fingers over his cheek and hooked them around the back of his neck. He shrugged his shoulder in an attempt to throw off her touch.

"Please," she whispered. *"Close your eyes and unshield your mind."*

Though he felt ridiculous, her odd behavior had piqued his interest. He lowered his shields and let his eyes fall shut.

Memories flooded his mind. Eudora and her parents entered Seacrest, found Laviel, Rogedoth, and Zithel Lau waiting in the small throne room. Laviel told Eudora she would marry Rogedoth. She and her parents protested. Tried to leave. A struggle ensued. Laviel used magic against them. General Agoros fell to the floor. Sârah Jemesha and Eudora raised their hands in defense, but before their magic could manifest, Laviel captured them in an invisible vise. Zithel Lau performed a wedding ceremony.

Her memories continued to zip through Hinck's mind. A forced consummation to match the forced ceremony. Attempt after attempt to conceive a child. Eudora continually tried to use her magic to escape, but not only did the compulsion prevent it, her shadir abandoned her to serve Rogedoth's great, leaving Eudora with no means to defend herself from the trap into which she'd fallen victim.

Eudora removed her hand, and the memories stopped.

Hinck opened his eyes, dumbfounded by the overwhelming compassion she had stirred within him. "How did you do that?" he managed to ask.

"It's part of my new magic. I learned it by accident."

Hinck hadn't heard of anyone else doing such a thing. "Why show me?"

"So you would believe me when I say I'm not one of Rogedoth's minions. Nor is my mother or father. We are his prisoners."

So it seemed from what she had shown Hinck. "I'm sorry, lady," he said, and found that the words were true. "What you have suffered is reprehensible."

Tears welled in her eyes. "Thank you for saying that. You are right that I took advantage of you once, Lord Dacre. I know now that such a thing is abominable, so I apologize and beg your forgiveness."

Hinck had never seen Lady Eudora Agoros so humbled. Words with any profound meaning failed, so he simply said, "You have it," though what he'd experienced with Eudora and what she'd suffered at the hands of Barthel Rogedoth were in no way similar.

"I had hoped you would forgive me." She smiled. "And I wonder if you might find it in your wholesome heart to help a lady in distress."

Hinck's suspicions rose. "Help you do what?"

"Help us—help me and my parents kill Rosârah Laviel."

Hinck again looked for shadir, certain that Rosârah Laviel's common, Iamos, might drift out from the wall at any moment and catch them talking treason. But they were alone.

"Are you all insane?" Despite what Eudora had shown him, he wasn't quite ready to confess that his own premeditation of murder matched hers.

"Mother says this is our only chance," Eudora said. *"We must act before Rosârah Laviel takes Castle Armanguard and compels herself a loyal army."*

"Her shadir is too powerful," Hinck said.

"Surely your shadir is stronger, lord. It healed you from the root juice."

"That was no shadir, lady. That was Arman."

Eudora's face crumpled in confusion. *"A god healed you? How is that possible?"*

"As I lay dying, the prophetess Onika voiced me. She told me to submit to Arman and he would vouch for me at the gates of Shamayim. I did, and he healed me."

She considered this. *"Then surely with the help of your god we can defeat Laviel."*

"I don't know that Arman works that way, but I will voice Miss Onika to ask her advice."

"Then might we make a plan?"

Hinck thought it over. If Eudora could be trusted, and if she and her mother refused to heal Laviel once Hinck shot her down, his plan would have a much greater chance of success than it did at present. *"If Miss Onika thinks it wise, I will consider it,"* he said.

"Oh, thank you, Lord Dacre!" She kissed his cheek, and he stiffened, annoyed.

Eudora left, and Hinck went back to his bow, the adrenaline racing through him slowly subsiding as he worked. The thought of joining with Eudora on anything made him uneasy. Was this a trick to trap him once and for all as a traitor? Was there any way he could know?

But of course there was! He climbed into bed and shadowed Eudora's mind, surprised to find her motivations sincere. He spent some time in Sârah Jemesha's mind as well, then monitored General Agoros. While the sârah had ambitions of her own about putting her son Oli on the throne instead of Eudora, and the general saw himself as king, the threesome really did intend to kill Rosârah Laviel before they reached land.

Hinck could not overcome his astonishment. He voiced Trevn and told him all that had taken place. Trevn didn't see how Eudora's involvement changed anything and agreed that Hinck should ask Miss Onika's advice. When Hinck voiced the prophetess, however, she needed time to consult Arman.

So Hinck waited. And waited.

A servant called him to the midday meal, but he sent the man away, claiming an upset stomach. Finally, as the sun began its descent toward the horizon, Miss Onika knocked.

"Yes, lady?" Hinck said, eager to hear her answer.

"Arman will always help his faithful, Hinckdan Faluk, but he is not a man who can be scheduled into our plans or a weapon to be wielded against his

own children. All creation belongs to him. Though it is never wise to trust those who consort with shadir."

"Is there no way to stand against a shadir?"

"I didn't say that," Onika said. *"Arman has recently shown me how to send shadir back to the Lowerworld."*

Hinck's heart leapt at the idea. *"Can you teach me?"*

"In time, perhaps. It must be done in the Veil."

In the Veil? *"I don't understand."*

"I have learned to enter the Veil by leaving my physical body behind. When I encounter a shadir, I can banish it in Arman's name to the Lowerworld where it can no longer harm us."

"That sounds perfect," Hinck said. *"Without her shadir, Rosârah Laviel would have no one to power her spells. How do I do it?"*

"There is no time to train you at present, so Arman has asked me to do this for you."

"How is that possible? You're not on board the Greenore."

"In the Veil, those with the mind-speak magic can travel at a thought."

Trevn had told Hinck that Grayson moved in such a way. *"Like Master Grayson?"*

"Only partly. Because Grayson is a root child, he can move corporally through the Veil and the physical realm. Those with the mind-speak magic can move only their spirits in the Veil. Therefore, my body will remain in this camp until I am rescued."

"I see. So your spirit will come to this ship?"

"That is correct."

Hinck wanted to laugh—he felt so light now that things were falling into place. Maybe he wouldn't have to kill anyone after all. *"If you can banish Laviel's shadir, I could find a way to apprehend her and take command of the ship."*

"To you, Hinckdan Faluk, this is what Holy Arman says: 'Go and attack Laviel Nafni. Destroy her and all of her evenroot. Do not harbor pity toward her. I am the Lord All-Powerful, and I delight in the obedience of my people.'"

Hinck reeled at the power of Miss Onika's voice, which had changed in tone and pulsed though his nerves with some sort of mesmerizing, tingling heat.

"Did you hear me?" she asked, voice normal again.

Hinck made the sign of the Hand over his heart. *"Yes, lady,"* he said, still shaken.

"She must not live," Miss Onika said, *"and you will be the one to kill her."*

GRAYS☉N

How could Grayson find his grandmother when he didn't even know what she looked like? He figured she must be somewhere in Rogedoth's camp, and since Onika was also there, he concentrated on the prophetess and popped through the Veil.

He'd never seen so many tents. Hundreds. Maybe a thousand. Most had flags perched on their pinnacles, red and gold with an image of Barthos's head. Would Grayson have to pop in and out of every one until he found Lady Islah?

The tents had been set up in circles, one inside the next. The large tents on the outer ring housed soldiers—many Puru, which surprised Grayson. He'd forgotten that Rogedoth had compelled so many natives. There were compelled Kinsman soldiers too, though plenty had full control of their minds and were perfectly happy to be a part of this group of traitors.

Grayson figured an important prisoner would be kept near Rogedoth, so he moved toward the center of the camp, looking for a royal tent. The closer he got to the middle, the more shadir he saw. Grayson hated shadir. If any looked closely at him, they'd see he was in the Veil—that he was different from the other humans. So he started walking instead of popping. This took much longer, and by the time he found Rogedoth's tent, the sun was low in the sky.

He didn't see any shadir at the moment, so he risked a peek through the canvas wall. There were plenty of shadir inside the tent—so many that none noticed Grayson—including the great who look like a tree. Grayson saw no humans, thankfully, so he moved on.

Directly behind the pavilion, he discovered a tiny tent that didn't fit in. A gray-haired man in a tattered red cloak was sitting on a stump of wood at the back of the royal tent. Standing guard? Grayson drifted toward the little tent and looked through the dingy brown canvas. It was too dark inside. Smelled bad too. Maybe it was for Rogedoth's dirty laundry?

He slipped inside, let his hand enter the physical realm, and concentrated on the magic that so unnerved him. He grimaced as a kernel of green light gleamed on the tip of his finger. Before his eyes could focus, a woman spoke.

"Who's there?"

Grayson's heart leapt at the idea that he might have found his grandmother. He lifted his arm above his head and focused until the kernel of light bloomed larger on his palm and brightened the inside of the tent. A center pole was all that held up the roof. At the bottom of the pole, an old woman sat on a thin mattress. A thick iron chain ran out from the end of her blankets to where it was attached to the center pole with a metal ring.

The woman had a flat nose, large lips, wrinkly dark skin, and long grayish-black hair twists that were tangled with bits of dirt and leaves. Her eyes were yellow and stared at the light as if it were dangerous and might burn her.

Grayson let the rest of his body enter the physical realm. He lowered his arm and shrank the light some. "Are you Lady Islah?"

Those yellow eyes narrowed. "You're a mantic."

"Not exactly. My name is Grayson, son of Jhorn. But the first name I ever had was Merek Nafni."

It got very quiet then. He could barely hear the woman breathing.

Grayson tried again. "I'm looking for Lady Islah. A man called Hinckdan Faluk said I might find her here."

The woman hummed. "The slave met him once. Knew his grandparents on his father's side. His mother was a friend to my Laviel for a time."

This sounded right! Grayson had found her, though she sure did talk funny. "My mother was named Darlis. She died giving birth to me."

This time the old woman scowled. "Not my Darlis. She and her baby died together."

"Is that what your husband told you?"

"Yes." She said this softly, like she was just now realizing it might have been a lie all along and that made her sad. "You're far too old to be that child."

"Your husband and my mother were playing with magic back then, trying to make someone like me. I grow faster than normal people. I can travel at a thought and make light from nothing. They call me a root child."

"Holy Arman, no," she whispered.

That sounded like a curse. "Are you scared of me?"

"No, young man. You seem kind. The slave is only disappointed. He lied to me again."

"You mean Master Rogedoth? I hear he does a lot of that," Grayson said.

"He's had a lot of practice."

A knock came in Grayson's mind—*"Trevn Hadar"*—and made him jump.

He lowered his shields like Duke Canden had taught him. *"Yes, Your Highness?"*

"I need you in my office at once. I have a task for you."

"But, sir, I've just found Lady Islah. Could I talk with her for a moment? Please?"

"That's wonderful, Grayson! Well done. Yes, talk with the lady for a bit, then come straight to my office. There is a situation I need your help with."

"Yes, Your Highness. I'll be back soon." What could have happened?

The whole time Grayson had been voicing with the king, Lady Islah had been staring. He sank cross-legged on the ground by her bed and tipped the ball of light off his hand and onto the trampled earth. It hovered there, softly blowing away bits of dead grass. "I can't stay long today," he said, "but I'm glad I found you."

"How did Mergest manage to hide you? Does he know you're here?"

"No," Grayson said. "Please don't tell him either. He lost me when I was a baby. Really, my father stole me away." And Grayson went on to tell Lady Islah Jhorn's story.

"Why are you chained to that pole?" he asked when he was finished.

She sighed. "Mergest wanted more from magic than the slave. After his father banished him, all he could think about was marrying off one of our girls to the Armanian king. If he could not rule Sarikar, he would find a way to rule Armania. He infiltrated the Chokmah Rôb priesthood but knew that no compulsion would ever convince King Echad to marry the daughter of a priest. So he devised a plan to have our girls secretly adopted by noble friends. When the girls came of age, the family would bring them to court and introduce them as their own. No one would know they were false. The only problem was the slave."

"You?"

"They were my babies! I forbade Mergest to do it. Told him it was too much. So he locked the slave away."

"And told everyone you died."

"The risk that I might tell someone the truth was too great. His plans would be ruined."

"Why not kill you?" Grayson asked, then added, "Sorry. It seems like something he would do."

She smiled. "It's a fair question, young man. I—"

The tent shook. "Who you talking to, woman?" A man's voice.

"It's Perchard with the slave's dinner," Lady Islah whispered. "You should go."

Grayson didn't want to stop talking, but King Trevn needed him. "I'll visit again."

"I'd like that. Thank you for coming to see me, Grayson."

The tent flap opened, allowing a shaft of twilight inside. Grayson put out his magical light and popped back to King Trevn's office.

The king was sitting at his desk, arms crossed as he looked at Sir Cadoc, who was standing on the other side. Grayson entered the physical realm, startling both men.

"Sorry," he said, bowing to the king.

"You have a report for me?" King Trevn asked.

"Yes, Your Highness." Grayson told the king all that had happened with Lady Islah.

"Excellent work," Trevn said. "It's clear she has more secrets to uncover. You must visit her again. Take your time as you question her. Don't push, or she'll think you've only come for information."

"I like her."

"I'm glad to hear that. She sounds like a kind woman who has suffered greatly. I wonder if she would leave if we could rescue her."

"I could ask."

"Not just yet. We must proceed slowly. Understand?"

"Yes, sir."

"Now, about this other task. Hinckdan Faluk is currently on board a ship headed this way. He needs your help with something dangerous, if you're willing."

Grayson couldn't help but smile. Two tasks in one day! "Yes, sir. Whatever you need."

TREVN

"I have spoken with Lord Dacre and Miss Onika, and we have a plan to stop Rosârah Laviel," Trevn said.

He stood at the head of the council table, trying to ignore the wave of frustration from those he'd kept waiting this morning. He'd been reading Wilek's journals lately, and while his brother had experienced some negativity from the nobles, it was nothing like the animosity Trevn dealt with every day.

He went on to explain how Hinck would attack the former queen with his bow while Lady Eudora and her parents kept the deck clear of soldiers and Master Grayson and Miss Onika fought shadir in the Veil.

The frustrated mood shifted to contempt. Trevn had expected it, but the magnitude of such disdain was hard to ignore.

Barek Hadar was, unsurprisingly, the first to speak. "*That* is your plan?"

"Not merely a plan, Your Grace," Trevn said. "It's the offensive action that will occur sometime today. Any moment, perhaps. I have already given the order."

A heavy moment of silence. "Without asking our opinion first?" Barek asked.

Trevn fought to keep hold of his own temper. "I do not need to consult the council on all matters," he said, annoyed that Barek would dare scold him in public. "A decision needed to be made. I made it."

"It's not a very good—"

Trevn lifted his hand. "If you have a better idea to stop Rosârah Laviel, Your Grace, I would love to hear it."

"I could come up with one," Barek said. "Given time."

"Feel free to think on it," Trevn said. "But while you are thinking, Lord Dacre and Miss Onika will stop the threat before it reaches us."

"It's not a bad strategy, Your Highness," Lord Idez said tentatively, though Trevn could sense the man's doubt. "But there's a lot of margin for error."

"Especially when sending an untrained assassin to kill the spider at sea." This from Oli Agoros, who was leaning back in his chair as if disgusted with the entire proceeding.

Danek Faluk shot Oli a dirty look. "My son has been working with the bow almost daily for nearly a year now. He is vastly improved."

"So Hinckdan tells you," Oli said. "But we have no one to corroborate his assertion. And furthermore, does he have any practice shooting on the water? Can he compensate for the motion of the ship over the waves?"

"If Hinckdan says he can do this, I believe him," Trevn said. "He is not a man to exaggerate."

"Nor is he a soldier," Oli said. "He has not been trained to handle an assassination."

Trevn had not expected so much hostility toward his choice of bowman—as if there had been a host to choose from. "I will hear no more against Hinckdan's qualifications. Is that clear?" He looked from face to face, and every man, with the exception of Danek Faluk and Captain Veralla, averted his gaze. Thankfully no one spoke, and Trevn continued. "Any other questions?"

"What about Barthel Rogedoth?" Captain Veralla asked.

"Miss Onika confirmed he is still camped outside New Rurekau," Trevn said. "Rosârah Laviel is acting on her own in this."

"I don't understand how the prophetess can know that. Or how she can fight shadir in the Veil," Lord Idez said.

"Does anyone?" Barek asked, lifting his hands and falling back in his chair. This Trevn was ready for. "Arman has gifted Miss Onika with a new ability." He told the council how Miss Onika had entered the Veil, and while she had been there, Arman had taught her to banish shadir. "I've assigned Master Grayson to help her."

"Did Master Grayson witness Miss Onika banish shadir?" Barek asked.

"Not that I know of," Trevn said. "He is with her now. Taking her to Laviel's ship. They will wait with Hinck until it is time to attack."

"How can you be certain Miss Onika can do what she says?" Oli asked. "She has been a captive for months. She might be delirious."

"She is not," Trevn said. "You have my word on that. I put her through a test to determine her sanity. She also prophesied that Hinck would be the one to kill Rosârah Laviel."

"That is a relief," Danek said. "Did she say whether Hinckdan would survive?"

The question sobered Trevn. "She made her prophecy directly to Hinck, so I don't know the exact words. I only know that Hinck is fully invested in the mission."

"You've been going on and on about all that you've learned in the ancient scrolls," Barek said. "Didn't you discover some other methods of defense against mantics?"

Trevn heaved a dramatic sigh, wanting to make it clear how very tiring he found his council's lack of trust. "Most generals did all they could to kill mantics from afar with bows," he said, "which is why I suggested it to Hinck. Some sent in a squadron of men to do the job, knowing that none would likely return. The Earl of Blackpool during King Nathek's reign abandoned his fortress and gave the servants instructions to poison any food served to the usurping mantics. The mantics didn't get wise to what had happened in time to heal themselves, and they all died. Then there was a young general who got it in his head that if he gave his soul to a shadir, that shadir would help him overpower the enemy. It did not. Instead it compelled the general to give himself over to the mother realms. The man did so and turned against his own. Forgive my haste in dismissing such options without consulting all of you, but I didn't think them feasible or worth the risk."

Again there was silence, though this time the men were throwing off a mix of disgruntled shame, embarrassment, or annoyance—all but Danek, who seemed all around pleased, if not a little worried for his son.

"Well then," Trevn said, "if there is nothing else, I'll release you until I hear word from Hinck. In the meantime, I ask you all to pray and make offerings to Arman on behalf of this mission. Father Mathal will be in the Temple Arman. He will also join me at the midday meal in the great hall to lead a corporate offering and prayer. I expect to see you all there. Dismissed."

Trevn didn't wait for everyone to leave. He retreated to the servants' antechamber, which had been converted to a haven, since the secret passage would soon let out there. He fell into the longchair Hawley had brought in. Mielle's concern pressed against him, and he connected his mind to hers. *"The meeting has ended,"* he voiced.

"How did it go?"

"My council has no faith in me. I see it in their eyes—worse, I sense their emotions. It's difficult to lead confidently when I feel disdain from those who are supposed to support me."

"Who disdains you?"

"I don't know. All of them, likely. Barek for certain. Oli too, I think. They disliked my plan. They don't think Hinck is qualified. They don't believe Onika can banish shadir." He sighed. *"Oli should rule. He's better suited. He's a warrior, like Wilek. Groomed to be a general. Everyone respects him."*

"Being a fighting man didn't help Wilek succeed," Mielle said.

"I can't take any more of their animosity. It's maddening."

"This task Arman has put before you is no small thing. But he put it before you. Not Oli. Not Hinckdan. Not Barek. You. So you will do your best. Renegades keep going when things get difficult. They prove everyone wrong. You're a good king, and soon enough Barek Hadar and Oli and whoever else might doubt you today will owe you an apology. Just you wait and see."

Trevn didn't know about that, but her talk had bolstered his resolve. *"You might have to give me that Renegade speech again and again until those apologies start coming."*

"I promise to. Now, can you come to the school and see what the new students have accomplished? I could give you the Renegade speech in person."

"I wish I could, but I need to make an offering for Hinck. Then Hawley is bringing more battle records to my office in hopes we might be able to find something we've missed."

"That sounds dreadfully boring."

"Desperate is more the term I'd use."

"Take heart, my love. You will not need any of those battle plans because Hinckdan will be successful and end all this worry. I will ask Zeroah to pray, though I'm sure she already is."

"You too?"

"I'm not as good at prayer as Zeroah, but I will try."

"Thank you, Mouse." Praying was just about all Trevn could do at present, and he would do it with all his heart in hopes that his will and Arman's were one and the same.

Hinck

G rayson and Miss Onika appeared in Hinck's cabin like apparitions from a dream. They had come and gone several times throughout the night and early this morning, testing their ability to travel around the ship. Grayson could move between the physical realm and the Veil, but Onika could not leave the Veil—said her body was back in Rogedoth's camp and there it must stay. Hinck hoped nothing would happen to it while her spirit was here. He could only see her because of the spell Oli had put on him. If someone had told him such magic existed even just two years back, he would have thought them mad.

At the moment, Grayson sat reclined on Hinck's longchair, feet crossed as if enjoying a leisurely rest. How could the boy be so calm? Perhaps because his part was to remain invisible in the Veil and keep watch while Hinck attempted to murder a queen.

Miss Onika stood beside the longchair, transparent like a shadir, though she was every bit herself. Also strange, in the Veil, she was not blind, and her pale eyes were currently staring at him, which he found unsettling.

"The God is with us, Hinckdan. Do not doubt it," she said.

How did she know the fears he had pushed to the back of his mind? Everything had been meticulously planned out. Hinck knew where to go and the spot where Eudora would lead Rosârah Laviel. Grayson had spoken with Bahlay Nesos—in his native tongue—and had told him that his son Maleen was alive and well in Armanguard and eager to see him again. This had won the man over, and when Grayson explained how Rosârah Laviel wanted to destroy Armanguard, Bahlay wanted to help stop her. Hinck had given Bahlay a knife in case he needed a weapon when the attack took place. With the navigator on their side, they were as ready as they could be.

Then why did Hinck feel so unsettled? He'd never killed anyone and knew that was part of what bothered him, yet there was something else he couldn't quite name. But what? Even the prophetess had told him not to doubt Arman's plan.

Eudora. She was the problem. Partnering with her felt like wearing another man's boots. After all her deceit and manipulation, how could he depend on her?

He couldn't. No wonder he felt so on edge. Their entire plan rested upon a woman he wouldn't trust to bring him a glass of wine. Which was why he'd only told her part of the plan.

"We are on deck," Eudora voiced. *"Come now."*

"On my way." Hinck took a deep breath and grabbed his bow. "It's time."

Miss Onika vanished. A second later Grayson disappeared as well.

Hinck hurried out the door of his cabin and voiced the prophetess. *"Wait for me!"*

"I will not act without you."

He ran up the stairs to the stern deck, which stood empty but for a handful of pales, swabbing the old wood.

"Go below now," Hinck commanded them. "Stay there until I tell you otherwise."

Compelled to obey, the pales were quick to comply. Hinck took position at the railing overlooking the quarterdeck and held his bow at his side where it might not be noticed. He looked down to where Bahlay was manning the whipstaff. To his left, Eudora and Laviel lingered by the quarterdeck rail. No sign of Iamos in the Veil, though Hinck did see Daliza, Princess Jemesha's slight, circling the main deck like a turquoise eel. And on the distant foredeck, five small shadir looped and darted around some Puru workers.

Movement on the stairs from the main deck. Jemesha, heading toward them.

"Why is your mother here?" Hinck voiced to Eudora. The princess had not been part of the plan.

"My parents want to help," she said.

Parents? *"What! I thought we agreed—"*

"We need them," Eudora said. *"My father is wearing his sword. If you miss—"*

"I will not miss." Hinck might not be the greatest archer to have ever lived,

but he could certainly hit a shot from twenty paces out. He glanced about for the mighty General Agoros but didn't see the man anywhere.

"Just in case, Lord Dacre." Eudora glanced his way from below. *"Don't be offended."*

But he was. More than that, he was caught off guard. She'd changed the plans without telling him. It was a sign of betrayal, and considering her past history, Hinck was reluctant to move forward at all.

He searched for Miss Onika and spotted her at the starboard railing of the quarterdeck, Grayson beside her. At first glance he would have thought them passengers, but a closer look proved them to be as translucent as the shadir in the Veil, invisible to anyone not under the influence of evenroot or its magic. Hinck hoped the shadir would not notice them.

"Miss Onika," he voiced, *"something has happened."* He told her about Eudora and her parents.

"Arman is on our side," Miss Onika said. *"Do what he has asked of you and let the rest unfold."*

She spoke so calmly, as if he were setting out to deliver a missive rather than an arrow of death. To forge ahead felt like madness, but no other choice remained. Eudora's parents already knew his plans, and he could not allow Laviel and her shadir to reach Armanguard.

"Grayson, watch Lady Eudora carefully. I don't trust her." Hinck took a deep breath. He might only have a moment to take his shot. He drew an arrow and set it to the bowstring, holding the weapon below his waist. *"I am ready, Miss Onika. Go now."*

Onika vanished. Hinck searched madly for her in the Veil and finally caught sight of her in the air above Laviel's head. He saw Iamos too, then, hovering over Rosârah Laviel, completely unaware that Miss Onika was floating behind her.

"Servant of Gâzar, hear and obey," Onika said, her voice fierce. *"In Arman's name I command you to the foot of your master's throne, never again to return to the human realm."*

Iamos spun around and hissed, but she did not look the least bit fazed. The sound drew Laviel's attention, and she looked up.

This couldn't be happening. Onika had failed, upset the shadir, and, on top of that, she'd alerted Laviel.

Hinck should shoot now, while Laviel was distracted, but with her shadir still living, she would simply heal herself, then kill them all.

"Who are you to order me?" Iamos said to Onika. The voice of the old woman was gone, replaced by something deep and dark.

"I am Onika, a servant of the One God Arman. He has given me authority over you, and I demand you release your hold on these humans and return to the depths from which you came. Now go!" Onika thrust out her hand, as if she might push away the shadir, though she wasn't close enough to touch it.

To Hinck's delight, Iamos released a ragged cry and sank toward the deck, head tipped back in agony. It was working.

"Iamos!" Laviel yelled, stepping toward the creature. "What is happening?"

The shadir slowly faded into vapor and vanished altogether moments before it passed through the wooden deck.

"Iamos, come back at once!" Staring at the deck, Laviel stood over the last place Iamos had been seen.

Hinck raised his bow, drew back the arrow, and took aim between the rosârah's shoulder blades. His heartbeat pulsed in his ears. *Arman, help me not to fail you.*

A dazzling warmth filled Hinck's chest and spread quickly down his limbs. He tried his best to account for the motion of the ship, then released the arrow. It streaked toward Laviel and stabbed through the center of her back. She stumbled forward and collapsed on her side. Eudora screamed. Sârah Jemesha sank down beside the fallen queen.

"Betrayal . . ." Laviel's voice, low yet terribly fierce. She writhed on the deck, trying to get to her feet, all the while mumbling words Hinck couldn't hear. Sârah Jemesha struggled to keep her down.

Hinck studied the angle of the arrow, how it extended through her body. It was a fatal wound. He'd succeeded, had made the shot, though nausea overwhelmed his relief. He'd killed a woman. Shot her in the back like a coward.

"That woman took a flask from the queen!" Grayson yelled.

The words confused Hinck. He examined Eudora, trying to make sense of the warning, but her hands were empty. His gaze flitted to Sârah Jemesha, who sat on her knees beside Rosârah Laviel's now still body, fumbling with the cork of a hip flask.

That couldn't happen. Hinck drew another arrow, raised his bow, and let fly. The arrow grazed the princess's hand. She cried out and dropped the flask. It rolled away. Eudora gave chase.

Not her. *"Get the flask, Grayson!"* Hinck voiced.

The boy popped to the other side of the deck and crouched, fully visible in the physical realm. The flask rolled right into his hands.

Eudora stumbled to a halt. "Who are you?"

Grayson faded away and reappeared beside Hinck, flask in hand. "I got it."

"Dump it into the sea, then find Rosârah Laviel's cabin and look for any other bottles. We must dispose of it all."

Grayson vanished.

Hinck's heart was still racing as he surveyed the scene below. Miss Onika stood with Grayson at the railing as he emptied the contents of Rosârah Laviel's flask into the sea. Bahlay stood over Princess Jemesha, knife in hand. Rosârah Laviel appeared dead. Eudora was sneering up at Hinck—obviously annoyed to have lost the vial of evenroot. But she'd changed the plan without telling him, so all was fair in his—

A footstep behind him. Hinck twisted just before something sharp pierced his side. He gasped. An arm grabbed his, pulled his body close, and shoved the weapon deeper.

"I've had quite enough of your interference, lord," General Zeteo Agoros said in his ear.

The dagger brought searing pain. Hinck lunged away, but General Agoros stayed with him, hands locked on Hinck's arm and the dagger. They staggered across the stern deck, Hinck struggling to get away, the general fighting to keep hold. Hinck reached over his shoulder to his quiver and fumbled for an arrow, thinking he might stab the general through the eye, but the man released Hinck and ripped away the quiver. It clattered to the deck. Then the general fisted the back of Hinck's tunic, heaved him up to the rail, and threw him overboard.

Horrified, Hinck flailed as he fell. He broke the surface, head first, and choked in a breath of cold seawater. Arms and legs thrashed wildly. Lungs burned. He fought the urge to open his mouth. *Please, Arman!* He kicked his feet. The surface had to be close. Every second he was underwater felt like twenty.

His head broke through and the open air wrapped him in a soft breeze, bringing a chill over his body. He heaved and choked, fighting to clear his lungs.

"The general threw me overboard!" he voiced to Onika. *"Can you help me?"*

"I'll send Grayson to lower the dinghy," she said.

It would be too late by then. The dagger was still protruding from Hinck's side. The salt water stung so badly he could barely focus enough to stay afloat.

Something glubbed in the water by his right shoulder. His first fear was of sharks until he saw something enter the water a good distance ahead.

He glanced at the retreating ship and saw General Agoros aiming the bow this way. He released an arrow, and as the shaft propelled toward Hinck, he knew a moment of terror. He just managed to lunge aside as the arrow speared the waves where he'd been swimming.

"The general is shooting arrows at me!" Hinck cried to Onika. *"Can you stop him?"*

"Grayson can."

"No! I need Grayson at the dinghy!"

But Grayson suddenly appeared on deck behind the general. He snatched a handful of arrows from the quiver the general had slung over his shoulder and vanished. Unfortunate that the boy couldn't carry Hinck the way he could carry arrows.

The general wheeled around, yelling about cowardly thieves. That, at least, amused Hinck, despite how heavily he was grinding his teeth against the throbbing in his side. He turned slowly in the strong waves, straining to see any sign of a coastline. He saw nothing but water. Even if he knew which way to swim, he doubted he'd have the strength.

Sands, he was dying, wasn't he? So close to making it back to Trevn, his parents, and Lady Pia. He should tell Trevn what happened, at least. Maybe even voice his father.

Instead, he prayed. *Arman, give me strength. I did as you asked. You didn't promise I would live, so if this is the end, I suppose I died well enough. One threat against Trevn has been stopped, so that, at least, is good. Please reunite Bahlay with his son. Help Miss Onika get back to Armanguard. Keep Trevn safe from his enemies. Protect Saria from the giants. Protect all of Armania and Sarikar. They are your people. And while many would never speak your name, just as many or more are your faithful servants.*

While Hinck continued to pray, his body grew numb and cold. He was still mumbling when a dark object appeared between each rolling wave, slowly making its way closer.

He imagined a great fish, looking for a meal. When it reached him, however, it did not swallow him whole. Hands descended from above, grabbed his tunic, and pulled him out of the water and into the arms of sleep.

✦ ✦ ✦

Hinck woke chilled, a dull ache in his side. He was lying on the bottom of a dinghy, shirtless. A rib of the boat pressed hard against his shoulder blades. He shifted to find a more comfortable position, and a tickle in his throat made him start coughing.

"Here." Someone held out a carafe.

Hinck reached for it and winced at a sharp pain in his side. The knife was gone, and strips of what looked like his favorite green tunic had been wrapped around his waist.

The person vanished, then hands were pushing at Hinck's back, helping him sit. He glanced behind him. It was Grayson. Once Hinck was sitting up, Grayson disappeared again. The dinghy rocked, and Hinck faced forward to find the root child sitting on a bench in the middle of the boat, handing Hinck the carafe.

"You thirsty?" he asked. Frizzy wisps of hair had fallen out of the thong at the back of his head and hung around his chin. He looked like a young pirate.

Hinck accepted the carafe and guzzled a long swig of water. He took in his surroundings. Bahlay Nesos was rowing. The sky was pink, purple, and orange; the sun had nearly set. Random objects had been piled around Hinck. His personal trunk from his cabin on the *Greenore*. His bow and quiver of arrows. His sword. A silver platter of tarts sat on the bench beside Grayson. A basket full of clothing was topped with rounds of bread. A collection of empty bottles on the floor, which Hinck recognized from Rogedoth's collection of evenroot.

"You hungry?" Grayson asked. "I have all kinds of food."

"How in all the Northsea did you get all this in the boat in time to fish me out of the water?" Hinck asked, his voice scratchy.

"I fetched all this after," Grayson said. "Miss Onika helped me decide what was important enough to go back for."

"If you can carry things when you move, why can't you carry people?" Hinck wished the boy could have fished him out of the water before he'd nearly drowned.

Grayson tucked his loose hair back behind one ear and frowned. "Never thought to try."

"Well, why not?"

A shrug. "What if it didn't work?"

What kind of an answer was that? "What if it did?"

Grayson merely stared.

Hinck took another long drink of water. "Why not test it with a chicken or piglet or something meant to die anyway?" he asked. "Because if you could carry people the way you carry things . . . well, that would be incredible."

Grayson's blank stare curled into a wide smile. "That's a good idea about the pig. I'll try it." And he vanished, making the dinghy rock.

Hang it all. *"Grayson, come back here at once,"* Hinck voiced. *"You can practice later. I need to talk with you now."*

The boy reappeared in the boat, jolting it again in the water. "Sorry."

Bahlay chuckled and shook his head.

Hinck knew how he felt. "Who tended to my wound?" he asked.

Grayson nodded to Bahlay. "Master Nesos knows lots of things. He was captain of the *Weema-ell.* On our voyage across the sea, Randmuir Khal of the Omatta attacked Master Nesos's ship and put all the survivors into some dinghies, including his son, Maleen. The *Seffynaw* picked them up. They're from Gallimau, which is an island chain in the Land of Shards."

"Please give him my thanks for helping me."

"*Kia ora,*" Grayson said to the pale as he pointed to Hinck's side.

Bahlay nodded and continued to row.

"Where is Miss Onika?" Hinck asked.

"She returned to her body," Grayson said. "And I already told Rosâr Trevn everything that happened, but he wants to talk to you when you wake up. It looks like Lady Eudora and her parents might be sailing on to Armanguard. They don't have any evenroot now, thanks to us, but they do have an army of five hundred compelled pales. The general was giving them a talk about how to fight when I was on board last. I think they might attack Armanguard."

"That liar!" Hinck cursed Eudora in a dozen different ways, furious that he had ever believed her a good person or pitied her at all.

"Don't feel bad," Grayson said. "The rosâr said we did a good job."

That stopped Hinck's tirade. "Yes, we did," he said, thankful and relieved to be alive. "You all did. Please tell Master Nesos I said so and that we are going to his son now."

"*Mahi pai runga te kaipuke,*" Grayson said.

Master Nesos grinned. "*Mauruuru koe hoki faaora ahau.*"

"He poured shards of blessings over your head, whatever that means."

Hinck nodded to the man, then pointed at the silver tray. "Could you hand me one of those tarts?" he asked.

Grayson delivered one, and Hinck ate it in three bites.

"Maybe one more," he said over a full mouth.

Four tarts later, Hinck finally voiced Trevn.

"Thank the God you're alive," Trevn said. *"I thought I'd lost you."*

"Apparently I'm nearly impossible to kill."

"That's just how I like my soldiers."

Soldier. Bah. *"Grayson says Eudora and her parents are headed your way."*

"Captain Bussie is on their trail," Trevn said. *"I want you to go to Er'Rets Point and heal. Grayson says you're not far from there."*

"Really?" Relief washed over Hinck that he might not be in the dinghy much longer.

"Your parents will be thrilled to hear you survived," Trevn said. *"Grayson appeared in the middle of a Wisean Council meeting to give his report, so your father heard what had happened and nearly lost his mind with worry."*

Of all the nonsensical . . . *"The boy moves fast, but his thinking is a little slow."*

"Grayson's mind is only ten years old, Hinck. Extend some grace to the boy who saved your life."

Hinck looked over at the scruffy young man, who was eating another tart. *"His magic is remarkable, though I wonder why he cannot carry people through the Veil if he can carry bottles and trunks and plates of tarts."*

"I've never thought to ask him, but that's brilliant."

"You expect any less from me?"

Trevn chuckled darkly. *"A little less pride, perhaps."*

"Arman was with me, Trev. I could feel it."

"I praise him for it. Rest up, Hinck. I want you back here as soon as you're able."

Trevn withdrew, and Hinck let his head fall back against the gunwale of the boat. Giddiness washed over him. He was free. He'd finally escaped from the enemy and was on his way back home. Not that he'd ever been to Armanguard, but for Hinck, home wasn't so much the place as it was the people.

He only hoped they'd all still be there by the time he arrived. Because when Rogedoth found out his daughter was dead, he would not be pleased.

CHARL⊙N

When Charlon reached Magosia, she bathed, reunited with Sir
Kalenek, then scolded Shanek for his risky behavior at the Rurekan ball.

"I wanted to dance with Amala," he said.

"And risk yourself? King Barthel saw you. Now he wants you for himself."

"I'm not afraid," Shanek said. "I talked to his shadir. They like him. Even
the great named Dendron said he is a fair master."

Fear stabbed like a sudden headache. "You must not trust King Barthel's
swarm."

Astaa entered the red tent.

"You have work, Mother. I'll go now." And Shanek disappeared.

Charlon growled at Shanek's insolence. "What do you want?" she yelled
at Astaa.

"I've come to inquire about Emperor Ulrik, Chieftess. What should be
done?"

Charlon had forgotten all about Emperor Ulrik. Before leaving New Rurekau, she had given the task to Astaa. To transport him within the Magosian
procession. Charlon had not known where. Had not cared. But she had promised Rosârah Thallah. Said she would heal him.

"Take me to the emperor at once," Charlon said.

"He is in Rone's tent," Astaa said as they set off down the hill. "He looks
very ill."

"He's been poisoned," Charlon said. "What did you expect?"

Astaa gave no answer and led Charlon inside Rone's tent. The darkness made it difficult to see. Charlon pulled from the remaining root within. Enhanced her eyesight. The interior of the tent brightened.

She crossed the open space and stopped before a narrow mat. She'd never met Ulrik Orsona. He lay as if dead, hands arranged over his middle. He was young, not long past adolescence. Might have been handsome once. Instead, looked wild. Body malnourished and gaunt. Golden-brown skin tinged yellow. Head and chin coated in black stubble. Charlon would have been afraid. To have met him on the streets of Bar-Vorak. When she had been in hiding.

"I will strengthen his body," she told Astaa. "You must nurse him back to health."

The second maiden nodded. Charlon inched toward the mat until her toes touched the thick, corded edge. She made eye contact with Rurek, who lingered on the other side of the emperor, eyes eager, hungry.

Take more ahvenrood, he said. *This spell requires a great deal of power.*

"I have enough." Charlon found the great shadir's strength within. Drew from it. Spoke words that would change the emperor's body. "*Râphâ zōt geveeyah. Oor, chalam.*"

She watched closely. Such healing always brought a thrill. To see the change take place. To see her power manifest.

Magic invaded the tent. Gripped her in its chill. Frost coated the black stubble on the emperor's head, chin, and eyelashes. He moaned. His arms twitched. Fell to his sides. Head arced back, throat long and pulsing.

Magic nourished depleted stores. Gauntness faded from his cheeks, arms, and legs. Muscle strengthened. Skin brightened, its sallow hue fading. Charlon's power drained. Her confident stance wilted. She would need to purge after this healing.

The chill in the tent faded away. Frost melted, leaving behind puddles of moisture. The emperor opened his eyes. Wild eyes that roved from face to face of those looking down.

Astaa clutched Charlon's arm. "You did it," she said, her voice tinged with awe.

"Had you any doubt in my abilities?"

"Of course not. I'm simply astonished each time I see you perform such feats. You amaze me, Chieftess. There is no one like you."

Astaa's words pleased Charlon. "Can you hear me, Emperor Ulrik?"

"Yes," he rasped. "Where am I?"

"In Magosia. I am Chieftess Charlon. Rosârah Thallah negotiated a trade for your healing."

His brow furrowed. "Was I ill?"

"The rosârah asks you to refrain from using your mind-speak magic to communicate with anyone but her for now. She will explain. Do you agree, or must I compel you?"

He swallowed, and his "I agree" was barely a whisper.

Charlon ordered a serving girl to bring the emperor a drink of water. While he refreshed himself, Charlon explained what she knew of his circumstances.

"You and your brother were poisoned," she said. "While there is no proof, Rosârah Thallah believes the blame lies with the empress's eunuch."

"Qoatch," Ulrik said. "I must get back to my people."

"Rosârah Thallah faked your death to save your life. By now all of Rurekau will be mourning the loss of their emperor. Rest here. Once you have regained your strength, you will be in a position to take back your realm from Empress Jazlyn."

"What about Ferro?" the emperor asked. "I can't leave him with that witch."

Charlon did not know who Ferro was. Assumed it must be the brother. "You must speak with Rosârah Thallah. I have done my part. Astaa will care for your needs." She gestured to her second maiden, then turned and walked away. She needed to purge. Before she fainted in front of this crowd.

Charlon had been ill on the journey home. Blamed the motion of the wagon. But when her dinner that night made her retch, hope crested through her in waves.

Could she have succeeded? Would she finally have a child?

Hope warred with fear. She wanted a child. But how could she survive without ahvenrood? Would the new magic be enough? How would she know what the shadir were doing? If she could not see into the Veil?

Her stomach roiled with nausea. Her bed seemed too far. She lowered herself from the throne to the floor. Stretched out on the mats there.

"Rurek?" No answer came. She mumbled the words to summon him.

He appeared beside her empty throne. *What are you doing on the floor?*

"I think I might be with child. Can you sense it?"

Be silent and let me listen.

Charlon held her breath.

Yes, I hear a second heartbeat. Congratulations, Chieftess. You have suc-ceeded.

Joy rushed through Charlon. She pushed to her knees. Sat back on her ankles. Triumphant. She was going to be a mother. This time, a birth mother as well.

Take care, her heart said. *Protect the child.*

A prickle of fear rose within. She was still burning a small amount of ah-venrood. To see into the Veil. She must purge! And take no more. Not until the baby was born.

She fell to her knees. Began the ceremony. "I feel weak, Rurek. Help me purge."

The baby is sharing your strength, the great said. *Purging is unnecessary. Take more ahvenrood and cast a spell to strengthen yourself.*

"We have been over this! I want to hold my child in my arms. To love it. See it grow. I will not die bringing it into this world."

There are ways to live through the birth with ahvenrood. I will help you.

"No! I want this child to be normal, Rurek. Take the magic from me. I beg you!"

No answer came. Charlon turned to study his face.

Promise me Dominion, he said.

Of all the insolent . . . "You dare turn my victory into an opportunity to control me?"

Dominion is not what humans make it out to be.

"You will heal me, Rurek. As you promised all along."

Healing you gives me no benefit. You expect a great shadir to give up nine months of worship and magic? Why should I?

Charlon had been right. Not to trust him. "I lied. My ahvenrood is not so depleted. I have much. Hidden away. So leave if you must. Find another human to bond with. But my maidens have no root to offer you. Empress Jazlyn has bonded with another. And going to King Barthel means facing Dendron. Dendron whom you dread. I am your best choice. Even if that means going without. For a time. Now heal me at once!"

You dare speak to me like you are in control? You can do nothing without me.

"I don't need you. My new magic gives me power. I can call other shadir to purge to. There are many who once served Magon. They will not hesitate to betray you."

I will kill any who bond with you.

222

"You dare, and I will never bond with you again."

Rurek glared. Eyes dark and angry. Might he destroy her? Right where she knelt?

Very well, little human, he said at last. *I will heal and cleanse you, but make no mistake . . . this is the last time you make demands of me.*

"Thank you, great one." Charlon bowed low. Until her head touched the mat. She had pushed her luck far, she knew. It had been a risk. But she had prevailed. Her baby would live. And once the child was safe in this world, Charlon could use the old ahvenrood again. If she wanted.

Rurek did what he promised. The magic left Charlon. Her body grew tired and sore. Her stomach ached. And a strange fear settled over her. That someone might touch her.

Hide, her heart said. *Protect within.*

All of the spells that had kept her strong—gone. She was once again frail and vulnerable. Fully human. Magic free.

But so was her child.

GOZAN

Gozan was restless. Only a few hours had passed since he had drained Charlon of her magic. He scoured the camp in search of any mantic-shadir bond that he might exploit, but all existed on reserves at the moment. His swarm would soon have no access to the Solid.

They would go mad.

Gozan couldn't last nine months without a magical bond—especially not when there was unused evenroot nearby. The newts brought from the Five Realms had died with the snow, so Gozan had no method of even manipulating someone to find the root stash. Shame gnawed at him. That a human had fooled him—had dared to deceive a great deceiver. The insult stung worse than any he had ever experienced.

Hurting Charlon was the only thing that would truly satisfy.

He was about to visit Roya's tent and trick the woman into helping him when waves of anger and betrayal drew him to one of the tents near the foot of the hill. There he found Sir Kalenek on his knees, weeping, his arms stretched out on the table he'd built. A handful of slights were circling the man, feeding off his pain. Shanek was there too, with Amala. They stood on either side.

Gozan drifted toward Sir Kalenek, wondering what had put so stalwart a knighten into such a state. The slights scattered at Gozan's approach. The man's right index finger was moving, tracing over deep grooves in the table. There were letters there, roughly carved in the wood.

REMEMBER ONIKA

Frustration filled Gozan. He had tried many times to learn to read, but shadir were incapable.

"Kal?" Amala gripped the man's shoulder. "What's wrong? Did something happen?"

The knighten combed his fingers through his beard. "Magic is a foul thing," he said. "It brings nothing but pain and destruction. Promise me you will stop using it."

"Kal, be serious," Amala said. "Magic makes me feel safe. To know how to protect myself means that no one can hurt me again."

"No!" He grabbed her arms. "People will continue to hurt one another because we are selfish creatures. We take what we want without care for how it might affect anyone else."

"Told you he's strange," Shanek said over the knighten's head.

Sir Kalenek shuddered and gazed at the table. "Onika."

"Miss Onika isn't here, Kal," Amala said. "She lives in Armanguard."

Sir Kalenek pushed to his feet and brushed his hand over the rough letters carved into the wood. "Charlon compelled me to forget her."

Amala frowned. "She can do that?"

Sir Kalenek's expression hardened. "But her spell wore off, for some reason. And I remembered."

Gozan thrilled at the words. Instantly he returned to Charlon's tent, found her sitting on her bed. He knew the lie that would stir her worst fears.

I have news, he said. *I overheard Sir Kalenek, Miss Amala, and Shanek plotting a visit to New Rurekau to see Empress Jazlyn and teach her your new magic.*

Charlon pushed to her feet. "How dare that witch manipulate my son?"

She stomped out of the tent, and Gozan followed her down the hill, already enjoying the fury that poured off Charlon like steam from a hot bath. She shoved people out of her way and barged into Sir Kalenek's tent. The knighten was standing at the table now, Shanek and Amala beside him.

"Betrayers unite, I see." Charlon propped her hands on her hips. "You think me a fool? That I wouldn't find out?"

She was glaring at Amala, whose heart began to thud within. Gozan reveled in the girl's fear, in Charlon's anger, in the silent distress exuding from Shanek and Sir Kalenek.

"*What* did you find out, Charlon?" Sir Kalenek asked, his voice laced with disgust so thick Gozan could taste it.

"That you all mean to betray me to Empress Jazlyn. You think her a more competent mantic than me? Is that it?"

"None of us know what you are talking about," Sir Kalenek said.

"I do," Shanek said. "She's talking about our visits to see Empress Jazlyn."

What was this? The boy had been to see Jazlyn? And more than once?

"Proof!" Charlon bellowed. She raised her hands and began the words of a spell. "*Gowzal darash bay ani. Gowzal ba shel ayder. Athah!*"

She had no magic in her—Gozan knew—yet she had called forth a flock of gowzals. Why?

A squawk turned his attention toward the entrance of the tent. Two gowzals glided inside and landed on the mat-covered floor. The tent shook slightly as more shadows alighted on the roof outside.

Shanek raised his voice. "Amala said you'd be angry."

"Because the empress wants my magic!" Charlon yelled. "Wants control of you!"

Shanek shook his head. "No, Mother. She only wants to be friends."

"She's a trickster," Charlon said. "She seeks to use you."

"And you don't?" Amala asked, defiance in her dark eyes.

"You stay out of this!" Charlon yelled.

Several dozen birds had fluttered inside now. Some perched on Charlon's shoulders or outstretched arms. Others walked in and gathered around her feet. It was the strangest sight Gozan had ever seen. He savored the fear that the strangeness evoked in those around her, the drama he'd created.

"I trusted you," Charlon said to Amala. "Allowed you to befriend my son. Took you to Rurekau. Gave you my ahvenrood. Yet you betrayed me."

Shanek spoke up again. "Amala didn't—"

"She seeks to take you from me!" Charlon yelled. "To make you hers. After all I did for her. *Sabab bay êsh!*"

In the space of a breath, several gowzals screeched, while four collapsed into mud and transformed into green fire that shot up onto Charlon's palms as if it belonged there, hissing and crackling. Gozan put himself in the middle of the action, eager for the pain that was surely to come.

Sir Kalenek stepped forward. "Stop this now, Charlon."

"*Azal da tsarab besar ba Amala.*" Charlon thrust her hands toward Amala. "*Daah!*"

Green fire shot out in a stream, but before it could hit Amala, Shanek moved. He appeared beside the girl, grabbed her, then carried her to the back of the tent, leaving Sir Kalenek in the fire's path. The flames struck the knighten, covering his body like bees on honey.

Everyone screamed at once, thrilling Gozan to his core.

"*Âtsar!*" Charlon yelled. "*Shamat aoto!*"

The fire snuffed out. Sir Kalenek collapsed, slathered in oozing black mud and blood. Charlon fell to her knees at the man's side. Mud became feather became wing became bird. Three birds, and pieces of a fourth that hadn't survived.

"Get away!" Charlon swatted at the gowzals. They fluttered their wings but walked off, in no hurry to go. She reached for Sir Kalenek but stopped herself, hands hovering over the man's torso. "Rurek! *Râphâ zōt chêts. Râphâ zōt serafah.*" When nothing happened, she spun around, face streaked in tears, blindly searching the tent. "Rurek, help me!"

So glorious was this moment—her horror and fear, his power over her need. *You have no magic in you, Charlon*, he said to her. *Take some ahvenrood, so I can help you.*

"I cannot!" Her eyes were wild and desperate. "You know that!" She shook her head, turned back to the knighten. "Sir Kalenek? Do you hear me?"

No answer came.

A sob from the back of the tent. Shanek passed through the Veil to stand on Sir Kalenek's other side. "I'm sorry, Father."

Amala came closer, staring at Sir Kalenek, her eyes round as eggs. "You did this," she said to Charlon. "You meant to kill me."

"You don't belong here," Charlon spat. "You ruin everything!"

"You threw the fire," Amala said. "You're the one who can't control your anger . . . who killed Kal!"

"Be silent!" Charlon stood, mumbled foreign words, and a gowzal shot up from the floor and blossomed into green fire on her palm.

Amala ran from the tent.

Charlon gave chase, and Shanek followed, leaving Gozan and Sir Kalenek alone.

Gozan drifted over the man and looked down on his burned, bloodied body, feeding off his agony. His fear. Death lingered nearby, but Gozan hoped he would fight. The longer he held on, the longer Gozan could feed off his pain.

That Charlon had controlled so many gowzals at once awed him. He hadn't realized she had become so proficient at her new magic. Such power was impressive, though obviously limited. Charlon could transform the creatures into weapons. She could destroy. But she could not heal.

"Faster!" Charlon's voice outside the tent. Footsteps drawing nearer.

The Chieftess entered with Kateen, Astaa, and Roya. The foursome gathered around Sir Kalenek, peering down upon the dying man.

"Heal him, one of you," Charlon said. "Do it now!"

"We have no ahvenrood, Chieftess," Kateen said. "You know this."

"You have reserves," Charlon said.

"Not enough," Roya said.

"One of you must have stashed away some root. Heal him now."

The maidens merely stared at their Chieftess.

Charlon screamed. "Obey me at once!"

"Forgive me, Chieftess," Astaa said, "but I haven't the power."

"None of us have," Kateen added.

Only you can save him, Gozan told Charlon. *Fetch some root from your stash and do what is right for the father of your child.*

Charlon trembled with rage, and Gozan let himself float in the flow.

"Who knows about healing?" Charlon asked the women. "Natural healing?"

Roya shrugged. "We've never had need."

Astaa took Kateen and Roya's arms and pulled them toward the exit. "But we will look."

Charlon stayed by Sir Kalenek's side until the women's footsteps faded, then she left. Gozan followed her along the path toward the red tent. At the bottom of the hill she slowed to a stop and whirled around.

"I know you're following me, Rurek." Her eyes roved the air as if she might spot him by merely trying hard enough. "I won't reveal the location of the ahvenrood. So you might as well go. Find a new human to bond. If that's what you want. You saw the magic I'm capable of. I don't need you."

Gozan fumed. In all his days, no human had ever dared send him away. He remained silent. Let her believe he wasn't here after all.

She marched up the hill and into the red tent, where she sat on her bed and picked up a small tunic Shanek had worn as a babe. She fought the sorrow that threatened to overtake her, somehow managed to hold it at bay. Perhaps the hope of her child kept her afloat. Gozan waited for her to retrieve a vial or bottle of ahvenrood from some secret place, to call another shadir—one of Magon's swarm, perhaps—or to beg forgiveness and ask him to heal Sir Kalenek. But the time went on far too long, and Gozan came to realize she would truly let the knighten die.

So Gozan returned to Sir Kalenek's tent to revel in the man's pain as long as he still drew breath, which at this point would not be long.

KALENEK

K al's eyes were too swollen to open fully. His body pulsed with heat, and any movement was excruciating. Yeetta warriors carved obsidian blades over his face and demanded military secrets he didn't know. He slipped in and out of consciousness, tormented and confused. Had he been recaptured? Where were his men? Was Charlon on their side? Is that why she'd attacked? And what about Wilek? Had he really died?

The pain kept him trapped in a place of darkness, death, and agony. Somewhere nearby, almost in the shadows, a pale face watched. A woman with hair of gold and eyes like the sky in summer. Was she a captive, like him? Kal's heart reached for her. He grasped the air around her face but could not touch her. Perhaps she was the goddess Iamos, coming from beyond the Veil to heal his body so he could stand whole before Athos's Bench to be judged.

Kal was ready. He'd been ready for a long time.

Yet death did not come.

Voices caught hold of his drifting thoughts. Someone calling his name.

"Can you hear me, Kal? It's Amala."

"He can't hear us," Shanek said. "He's dead."

"His chest is moving," Amala said. "He's not dead."

"He's not?" So much hope filled those two little words.

"Can you heal him?" Amala asked.

"My magic doesn't heal. Only breaks. I break everything!" Anguish and tears laced Shanek's voice and made Kal want to hug the boy.

"We need to help him, Shan. There has to be a way."

229

"The empress's magic can heal," he said. "She wants to know about the new magic. I could trade."

No, Shanek, Kal wanted to say, but the words were buried in his mind.

"Your mother won't like it," Amala said.

"This was her fault. My father needs me."

Arms dug beneath Kal's back and legs, pulled him roughly off the ground and onto someone's lap. The motion inflicted pain and nausea. Kal gagged and dark images overwhelmed him. A dead woman and child. A longsword beheaded a horse, and the animal fell into a mass of bloodied soldiers. A thin blade carved a line down his cheek.

A sudden jolt pushed Kal through a breeze. He felt weightless and strong. Whole. He opened his eyes to light and color, saw Shanek's face from below.

The sensation ended just as quickly, thrusting Kal back into darkness and flames that seared his skin and mind. A woman screamed. A man shouted. Footsteps trampled away. Kal's body began to tremble. He willed it to stop, but his control had finally ended.

"He's dying," the woman said. "You are too late."

"Help him!" Shanek cried. "I'll teach you Mother's magic. It's a fair trade, yeah?"

"You vow it, Shanek DanSâr?" the woman asked. "You vow to teach me?"

"Yes, Empress. I vow to teach you the new magic. Now hurry!"

Not Jazlyn! She could not be trusted. Kal opened his mouth to speak, felt the withered flesh around his lips tear and rip hairs from his beard. A sound came forth like a dying animal.

Then Jazlyn spoke. "*Cherem âthâh. Âtsar serafah. Âtsar dâm. Âtsar makobay. Râphâ zōt chêts. Pârar môwth.*"

Slivers of ice spread over Kal's skin and stung like drops of poisonous water from the Red Lakes back in Magonia. He arched his back, and again came the animal cry from deep in his breast. He thrashed his arms and legs, and they slid over a hard floor coated in icy liquid. Kal shivered and convulsed, gasping in air so cold it coated his throat in frost. His breathing slowed, which caused his lips to dry up as well.

The floor beneath Kal slid away. He circled his arms and kicked, looking for purchase. Flames danced in the blackness around him. A creature materialized, doglike with no fur. Pimply white skin like that of a plucked chicken clung to its skeletal body. It had a flat face with black eyes, nostrils, and lips. It opened its mouth to speak, but all Kal heard was a piercing scream.

Though no words were spoken, Kal could sense the creature's offer. It wanted to create a bond. It knew his pain—not the burns that had been healed, but the memories that tortured him anew each day. If Kal would bow down and swear to serve the creature, the dark memories that haunted him would vanish forever.

Never had Kal been so tempted to acquiesce. He reached out, but a face appeared between him and the creature. The pale woman with the bright blue eyes. Her name danced on the edge of his memory, yet Kal knew that the woman and the creature were of different worlds. If he gave way to the creature, he would never draw near the woman again.

"Be gone, shadir," he said. "Away from me."

And the creature left.

Kal opened his eyes to a yellow ceiling and gasped in a breath that smelled of incense and fresh bread. Several faces peered down. Shanek, Empress Jazlyn, Qoatch, and two women.

Shanek grinned. "You're okay now, Father. The empress healed you."

Kal bit back his censure. The boy had done what he felt was best. Saving a life was a step in the right direction, even if he had indebted himself to Jazlyn. "Thank you, Shanek, for your sacrifice." Kal would not thank the empress. She hadn't healed him out of the kindness of her heart.

"Why don't you carry your father back to his tent to rest?" Jazlyn suggested. "Then return here at once. I am eager to learn what you have to show me. And come alone, Your Highness. Our bargain does not need an audience."

Shanek hung his head. The boy was discouraged. He'd made a promise he shouldn't have, but he'd done it to save a life.

Kal reached out his hand. "Help me up, Shanek. I'm strong enough to stand now."

The boy took hold and pulled Kal to his feet. Before Kal could get his balance, they were weightless, passing through the in-between world where Shanek liked to roam.

They arrived in Kal's tent, standing beside the table where Amala was sitting. The stench of blood was strong, and Kal recoiled at the mess his dying body had made.

"Kal!" Amala jumped up and embraced him.

Kal squeezed her back, touched by affection she had not shown in a long while. He met Shanek's gaze as the boy watched them. "Teaching the empress Charlon's new magic will create an enemy who could destroy you," he said.

"I had to, Father," Shanek said. "To save you."

Kal released Amala and hugged the boy. "I'm proud of you, Shan. It's always good to save a life."

The boy pulled away. "I've got to go back. To the empress."

"Take me with you," Kal said. "I cannot help you from here."

"The empress doesn't want anyone else to come."

Kal snorted. "So she can draw you into her web. You agreed to teach her, Shan, but she has no right to tell you how. Remember that."

"Take me along," Amala said. "The empress likes me."

Shanek looked reluctant, worried. "I'll teach her quickly, then come back."

"Be careful, Shan," Kal said. "I have never trusted Empress Jazlyn, and Barthel Rogedoth is even worse. Stay away from him if you can. And trust nothing they say. Nothing. They have no reason to tell you the truth and every reason to convince you that their plans are best."

Shanek scratched his head and winced. "Do you think I should be king?"

"Of Armania?" *Oh, my boy, what a question to ask.* "Should the line progress to you, then yes. But a good man should never dethrone another good man without reason. Have you reason, Shanek, to take the throne from King Trevn?"

"Mother says—"

"I know what Charlon says, but what has King Trevn done that you feel is so wrong? What would you do better?"

Shanek frowned. "I don't know."

"Well, that's a start." Anyone so gullible would make a terrible king, but explaining that wasn't easy. "The bigger problem, Shanek, is that people will try to manipulate you, and you have not shown me you can stand against that. A king should be able to make up his own mind and keep others from twisting it. Don't let anyone change you."

Shanek nodded. "Yes, Father."

Kal took Shanek's face in his hands and looked into his eyes. "I love you, boy. Don't you forget it. Be good."

Shanek's demeanor softened and he smiled. "Yes, sir."

Then he disappeared.

Amala cried out and ran from the tent, sobbing. A rush of sorrow seized Kal's heart, and tears glazed his vision. A deep breath helped to dispel them. He looked around the empty tent, feeling strange. Like his old, battered self.

Kal could not leave Shanek alone and under the influence of two mantics as devious as the empress and Barthel Rogedoth. He would take a horse and ride there.

It occurred to him anew that his compulsions were gone. Charlon had refused to heal him, which was why Shanek had made a deal with the empress to save his life.

What was the Chieftess up to? She had gone through a lot of trouble to compel him and alter his memory. Why remove all those spells and leave him to die?

He took his time walking to her tent, thinking through what he would say. By the time he stepped into her open doorway, he still hadn't figured it out.

She glanced up from where she was sitting on her bed, then jumped. "Sir Kalenek, how . . . ?" She rose slowly, looking him over. "How is this possible?"

"Shanek took me to Empress Jazlyn. He had to agree to teach her your new magic, but she healed me."

"No." Charlon stepped back, her eyes cold. "He cannot do that."

"He did it to save me," Kal said.

She folded her arms. "What he has done cannot be undone."

For the first time in months, Kal noticed how very fragile Charlon seemed to be. "This is your doing," he said. "Shanek had no interest in teaching the empress your magic until you tried to kill Amala, then refused to heal me."

"That's not true! Rurek said you were planning for Shanek to teach the empress . . ." She frowned and glanced away.

"Rurek lied to you, I suspect," Kal said. "It's what shadir do. You're smart enough not to believe everything he tells you."

Charlon's features grew solemn. "I'm through with his lies. Sir Kalenek, you must talk to Shanek. He listens to you. If he's to rule Armania, he must not spend time with—"

"I never wanted to put that boy on any throne," Kal said. "You have used your magic against all of us for too long. I'm done with it, Charlon. I'm leaving Magosia."

"You can't leave!"

"I'm Shanek's Shield. I must go where he goes, and he's in Rurekau now."

"He'll come back."

"I hope so, but they'll work hard to keep him and his magic on their side. I must be a voice of reason in the chaos around him."

"What if he comes here looking for you?"

"Tell him where I went and he'll find me. Unless you plan to compel me again."

She looked away and sniffled. "I'm done with compulsions."

"Why?"

She lifted her chin. "They're too dangerous. With the new magic . . . I don't need a powerful shadir to wield gowzals."

Kal stepped toward the door, eager to leave.

"I don't want you to go," Charlon said.

"I don't care what you want."

She seemed to shrink at those words. "You don't mean that."

Oh, but he did. He left the tent.

"Kalenek, wait," she called after him.

He kept walking.

Footsteps scuffed over the snow, and Charlon appeared at his side, jogging to keep up with his long strides. She reached for him but stopped short of actually touching him. "Don't go."

"There's nothing for me here."

"Miss Amala is here."

Kal thought of his youngest ward. "Amala can take care of herself."

"What about me?" Charlon asked. "I love you."

"Woman . . ." Kal stopped and turned to face her. "You don't know what love is." He continued down the hill, feeling light and free for the first time in over a year.

"I'm pregnant."

The words shocked his heart. He forced himself to keep walking, but his steps were slower as emotion crawled slowly over him.

She again appeared at his side, striding to keep up. "Did you hear me? I carry your child."

Her statement brought a rush of memories over Kal that disgusted and shamed him. That he had ever lain with this woman made him ill. His commitment was to Shanek, no one else.

"Wait!" She ran ahead and stopped in his path. "You must stay. Help me raise the child. Like you did with Shanek."

"I'm finished with your lies, Charlon." Kal stepped around her and continued to his tent. Inside, he balked at the stench of blood. He upended his bed, pulled out the mat underneath, piled his spare clothing there, then set about gathering other supplies.

Charlon appeared in the doorway, holding the drape aside. "It's why I stopped taking ahvenrood. To protect the babe. That's why you suddenly remember. The compulsions ended with my magic. I made Rurek heal me so the babe won't turn out like . . ."

Kal whirled around. "Like Shanek?"

She wilted. "He's not normal."

It suddenly made perfect sense. "You did this on purpose. You wanted a child to replace the one you lost—and the one you'll lose when Shanek leaves."

She had the nerve to smile.

"Why me?" Kal roared. "You have an army of men eager to serve you."

"They're not like you. You're wise and brave and good with children."

He pointed at her face. "This changes nothing." He went back to packing.

"You would abandon your child?"

"I see no child," Kal said, "but Shanek is alone in Rurekau. He's my responsibility. He needs me, and I will go to him."

"But you'll come back? When the baby is born?"

Kal ducked to pick up his scabbard and sword and strapped them on.

Charlon wrung her hands. "You'll come back?"

Kal looked her up and down—really looked. She'd always been small but usually exuded power. Now she seemed downright lost. He didn't even want to think that she could be telling the truth about a babe. How would a child survive such a mother?

"Only the gods know what the future holds," he said. "Now get out."

Within the hour Kal said goodbye to Amala and departed. He didn't bid Charlon farewell. He was afraid he might harm the woman. Never in all his days had he been so humiliated. So angry. So terrified.

As he rode his horse northwest, his thoughts dwelled on Shanek, what he might be doing, and how Empress Jazlyn would try to manipulate him. He had no doubt she would. He wished he knew her agenda.

"Sir Kalenek? Can you hear me?"

A chill ran up his arms at the familiarity of the voice in his head. He reined the horse to a stop on the trail. "Yes," he whispered. *"I hear you, Miss Onika."*

"You know me? You remember?"

"I do. Chieftess Charlon had placed several compulsions upon me, one of which was to forget you. But the compulsions ended and I remembered."

A surge of joy tingled in his mind. *"Praise Arman. Where are you?"*

"Some two hours northwest of Magosia on a trail headed to New Rurekau. My ward traveled there and I must find him."

"I'm being held captive in a camp just outside of New Rurekau."

Alarm rang through Kal. "Have they hurt you?"

"Say you will come for me, Rescuer. I know that you will, for I have seen it. But to hear you say the words after so long would soothe my battered soul."

Dread grew inside as Kal took meaning from her words. Sudden memories flashed in his mind. "You've asked me for help before, haven't you?"

"You were under her spell."

Kal rubbed his face, overcome with sorrow and shame. "Forgive me, lady. I've failed you."

"Failure is part of success, Sir Kalenek. A man falls down, and he gets up again. We are sometimes hurt but not destroyed. Even in the darkest of times, our spirit is strengthened by our reliance on Arman, for he never leaves us alone."

Her words took him back to her cabin aboard the *Seffynaw*. "This is what you meant before, when you spoke of the darkness to come? Am I too late to save you from that torment?"

"Oh, Sir Kalenek. I see you! You are on horseback."

Kal looked around, confused, and scanned the surrounding plains. "You see me? How?"

"I've learned something new with my magic," she said. "I can enter the Veil."

Such words seemed impossible. "Like Grayson?"

"Not quite."

"And you can see, though you are blind?"

"It's a glimpse of my eternal self, healed and whole. Oh, Sir Kalenek, you are beautiful to look upon."

Kal tensed, his eyes rolling from side to side as he searched the land around him. "It's seems I am the blind one now, for I cannot see you."

"Now you know how I felt all this time, hearing your voice but not seeing your face. Did the Chieftess heal your scars?"

He grimaced. "That's a long story."

"And we have a long journey. Though we must move swiftly. Rogedoth is preparing for a journey of his own. I want to escape while he is gone. Move your horse onward, and while we travel together, tell me all that has happened while we have been parted."

Kal obeyed, though he felt slightly mad in doing so. He continued along the trail toward New Rurekau, but he no longer knew for certain what his future held. Were the gods so cruel as to force him to choose between rescuing Miss Onika and finding Shanek? And if the choice came before him, which would he choose?

TREVN

The *Greenore* had vanished.

Trevn sent Grayson in search of the ship, but the young man couldn't find it. This made Trevn suspicious that magic was at play. Oli had tried shadowing the minds of his sister and parents but continually found their shields solid. It bothered Trevn that General Agoros and his mantic wife and daughter were out there somewhere with a compelled army of five hundred.

He set the matter aside for now and reached for Conaw's mind. His Puru friend was still uncomfortable with the mind-speak magic but agreed it was the easiest way to communicate.

Once they exchanged the usual pleasantries, Trevn got right to the matter at hand. *"My wife is haunted by the Puru children she saw traded to the Jiir-Yeke right before we found her. She daily begs me to try and find the children and rescue them."*

"That is unwise," Conaw said. *"The trade was enough to keep the Jiir-Yeke away for two or three moons. If you freed the children, the Jiir-Yeke would attack many villages and take more than necessary. Let the past remain."*

Mielle wouldn't be pleased to hear this. *"I've tried to speak with some of the local Puru, but they've been nonresponsive, even when I involved Grayson. I know we claimed much of the land they relied on, but I'd like to make amends."*

"Give it time," Conaw said. *"The tribes are wary. Most know you freed Puru from the Ahj-Yeke mines, but this divided many villages. Puru want freedom, but they are afraid."*

"What does Muna want?" Trevn asked.

238

"Muna is firm in her plan to stand against the Yeke, but this must be done carefully."

"When you come up with a plan, we will do all we can to help you," Trevn said.

He pondered this as he went down to the practice field but could find no easy solution. His swordplay was improving, as was his ability to use his voicing magic to anticipate his opponent's next moves. He held his own against Sir Jarmyn Koll, no small feat and the first time he saw admiration in the eyes of some of the onlookers. Not from Sir Jarmyn, of course. That man held no love for Trevn, as his father, the Earl of Blackpool, was friends with Tace Edekk.

Back in their chambers Mielle kept Trevn company as Ottee helped him out of his armor.

"Has Inolah reached New Rurekau?" she asked.

"Not yet," Trevn said. "Another day, I think. I only hope she can take matters into hand there. My mother will no doubt make that difficult. Empress Jazlyn as well."

"I hope her sons can recover. I'm glad she can go to them. It makes me think of the Puru children. How could any mother give up her child?"

"Different cultures, Mielle. It'll take time to understand. Even then we might not agree."

"We must do something."

"I asked Conaw about it today, and he made it clear we should not meddle." He went on to explain Conaw's position in greater detail.

Mielle's anger rushed through Trevn. "But that's not right!"

He sent his calm. "They're not our people to decide right or wrong. If you're concerned with missing children, help Jhorn in his search for the Armanian boys taken for the army Tace Edekk claims to have no knowledge of. There's a mystery that concerns our people."

She folded her arms, sorrow spilling into him. "Both should concern us."

Ottee finished with the armor and Trevn dismissed him. "We must take care of our own first, Mielle."

She wrung her hands. "I'll ask Jhorn about the local children, but please don't ask me to forget the Puru children."

"Of course you should remember them in your prayers, but at this time, we can do nothing else for them."

She sighed. "I don't suppose I can go back to planning court?"

"Not until I find the *Greenore* and know there's no threat. Now kiss me and say a prayer for a smooth council meeting." Trevn wasn't looking forward to the panic over the missing ship.

Mielle pecked her lips against his. "Why do you dislike the nobles so much? Is it just about how they try to boss you?"

"That's part of it," Trevn said. "I dislike how they think they're better than everyone else—that their lives are worth more. I've been reading Wilek's journals, and they've made me realize how much the nobles remind me of our father. Sometimes just being around them makes me want to argue. Or run off and climb the castle walls." Something he'd yet to have a chance to try here.

This earned him a bright smile. "Well, they're *not* your father, and you are king. Perhaps you should treat them how you would have liked your father to treat you."

Trevn wrapped his arms around her waist and pulled her close, staring deeply into her eyes. He saw her need to connect. He'd been missing it too. "I'm sorry we're apart so much."

Her eyelashes fluttered. "It sometimes seems like I don't matter to you."

"You can't believe that," Trevn said. "I spent the better part of a year looking for you."

"Yes, but now that you've found me, the adventure is over. I know it's not true, but it's how I feel."

"I'm sorry, Mielle." He kissed her, allowing his soul to sink into hers for a moment. Her response made him forget his agenda, until behind them a man cleared his throat. Trevn opened one eye. Hawley. The meeting. He groaned and broke away. Kissed her one last time. "I'll try harder, Mouse."

Though he didn't know when he would ever find the time.

GRAYSON

Grayson didn't understand why he moved slower with Trista on his back. He could actually see glimpses of walls and corridors as he carried her crosswise from the roof to the council chambers on the third floor. They finally appeared in the dark room.

"You did it!" she said, her voice a tickling hum in his ear.

He did. He could carry a person through the Veil. He set Trista on her feet and brought forth a ball of light on his palm. Her eyes focused on the light and gleamed brightly. "Are you well?" he asked.

"Perfectly well," she whispered. "How are you doing that?"

He shrugged and tried to hide his smile. "It's just something I can do."

Trista thrust her fists above her head and squealed. "That was amazing!"

Grayson couldn't help it. Her excitement made him grin. He liked impressing Trista.

She grabbed his arm with both hands. "This time, take us to the kitchens where—" She gasped. "Wait, can you take us to the forest with the giant trees? Or how about the—"

The door to the antechamber opened. Sir Cadoc entered, holding a torch in one hand. Behind him came King Trevn, Queen Mielle, and Lady Pia.

"Oh," Trista said.

"What's going on here?" the king asked.

Grayson slid back from Trista and fought the urge to pop away. "We were looking for a missing chicken," he said at the same time as Trista said, "Master Grayson was just showing me this table."

Trista spun toward him, glaring, and punched his arm.

"Ow!" Grayson put his hand over the throbbing spot. "A table?" he whispered. "Why would I show you a table?"

"This is highly inappropriate," the queen said. "After what happened the last time, did neither of you listen to Rosârah Brelenah?"

Grayson stammered. "I . . . uhm . . . that's not what I . . ."

"We weren't kissing, if that's what you think," Trista said, rolling her eyes.

Grayson choked in a sharp breath and started coughing. When he managed to stop, he confessed. "We popped. And I carried her with me."

The king's eyebrows rose. "You traveled through the Veil? *Together*?"

Grayson swallowed and desperately wanted to run away. "It was an experiment."

"He practiced first with a chicken," Trista added.

King Trevn pulled out a chair at the council table. "Sit."

Trista sat, and Grayson claimed the chair beside hers.

The king folded his arms. "Tell me everything."

It wasn't a very smooth story, as Grayson and Trista continued to interrupt each other. When they both stopped talking, the queen was the first to speak.

"Could you carry the Puru children to safety, if you found them?"

"*Mielle*," the king said. "We've been over this."

The queen did not waver. "But could you?"

"I suppose," Grayson said. "I was hoping to rescue Onika. And my grandmother." He'd only been to visit Grandmother a few times. She'd told stories of what it had been like to grow up in Sarikar, but she never wanted to talk about Rogedoth. Bringing her here might change that.

The king inhaled a deep breath. "Lady Trista, you will not tell anyone about Grayson's ability to carry a person through the Veil. Until we fully understand it, we must keep it secret. Some people might not understand. They might grow afraid."

"Like some fear the voices?" the queen asked.

"Exactly like that," the king said.

"Or they might try to abuse his power," Trista said, gazing at Grayson with admiration.

"That too," the king said. "Do I have your word?"

"Yes, Your Highness." Trista stood and curtsied her agreement.

"You are dismissed," the king said.

Trista sent one last adoring gaze at Grayson, then left him alone with the king, queen, and their guards. Grayson slouched in his chair, certain that the king would be angry and punish him for putting Lady Trista's life at risk.

The king surprised him by sitting in the chair Trista had vacated. "I want Miss Onika back as much as you do, but she has made it clear she will wait for Sir Kalenek. Lady Islah, on the other hand . . . I would very much like to talk with her."

"Shall I go right away?" Grayson asked, eager to make amends.

"No." The king held up his hand. "At this moment, I need you to keep trying to find the *Greenore*. I must know what General Agoros is planning."

Grayson nodded. "Yes, sir." Though he doubted he'd find it.

"Once we know where the *Greenore* is, we can talk about rescuing Lady Islah." The king stood and walked toward the main exit. Sir Cadoc reached the door first and opened it.

"But, Trevn," the queen said, "if Grayson could find the missing Puru children, he could carry them away to safety."

The king glanced back. "We have already had this discussion, Mouse."

"We can't just leave them to die!"

The king sighed. "The *Greenore* could very well be on its way to attack Armania. Protecting our people is my only objective at present."

"But—"

The king lifted his hand and looked at Grayson. "There will be time to experiment with your new skill. I myself am eager to consider the possibilities. But for now, do not carry anyone else through the Veil until I give you leave. Is that clear?"

"Yes, Your Highness."

"Good." The king glanced at his wife, then left, taking Sir Cadoc along.

The moment the door fell closed, the queen claimed the chair the king had vacated. "Did you ever find any trace of the Puru children?"

"No, Your Highness," he said, suddenly reluctant to talk to her about it. "The king sent me to assist the Earl of Dacre with the attack on Rosârah Laviel and I . . . um . . . I've been following Porvil." Which was partly true. He had followed Porvil twice. Over a week ago.

"Did you learn anything?"

"I saw him talking to Lady Brisa Hadar."

"What were they talking about?"

"She was asking him about Sir Jarmyn. Trista said her sister fancies the man, even though he's married."

The queen glanced at Lady Pia. "Don't worry about Porvil right now. I want you to keep looking for those Puru orphans. After you find the *Greenore*,

243

of course. If you do find them, could you bring them here to me? If Trevn agreed?"

The possibilities of what Grayson could do suddenly opened wide before him. Yes, he could rescue children and his grandmother and Onika too, if she'd let him. He could even grab on to Master Rogedoth and carry him to some deserted island.

"Grayson?" the queen prodded.

He straightened. "Yes, Your Highness. I believe I could. If the king agreed."

"Oh, this is marvelous," the queen said. "Find the *Greenore* quickly. I only pray it's not too late."

QOATCH

Qoatch watched Empress Jazlyn cast a spell to transform one of the small birds into a little dog. The animal was just as full of energy as the real thing. It wiggled and wagged its tail, all the while sniffing the floor for food. It looked completely authentic. Until it crowed.

His Great Lady stood in the middle of her sitting room with Sâr Shanek, receiving another lesson in the new magic, which strangely made use of the gowzals as a medium.

"Oh, how marvelous!" Jazlyn released the spell, and the dog collapsed into a pool of black liquid.

"Our trade is over now," Shanek said.

"You're not leaving?" Jazlyn motioned to Qoatch. "How about something to eat?"

Qoatch carried the tray he'd prepared from the sideboard to the low table between the two longchairs. A gowzal fluttered to the tabletop, and Qoatch shooed it away from the food.

"I must go," Sâr Shanek said.

"Perhaps we could celebrate our friendship with a meal?" Jazlyn said. "You could bring Miss Amala for dinner and dancing and the finest entertainment New Rurekau has to offer. She would like that, wouldn't she? How about tomorrow evening?"

Shanek frowned. "Amala could see the baby?"

"Of course!" Jazlyn said. "Jahleeah would be delighted to see her again."

Shanek jerked his head in a single nod. "We will come." Then he disappeared.

Jazlyn collapsed on one of the longchairs. "Well, *that* was exhausting, and

I don't mean the magic. I see why Chieftess Charlon kept it to herself, though. Sâr Shanek taught me nothing more than parlor tricks, but I can devise much greater purposes for such power."

"You learned quickly," Qoatch said, eyes roving the Veil for spies.

"No doubt my years of training as a mantic helped me. That this magic requires no sacrifice on the part of the wielder is remarkable. Why, even you could learn this skill, Qoatch."

He had no desire to wield magic of his own and preferred to keep himself separate from shadir. "You might create an army," he said.

"Yes, and I could make them all look like you." She chuckled. "Is that what the Chieftess is doing, I wonder? Making an army? Do you think it possible?"

"So she could attack Armanguard and take the throne for her son? I suppose."

"She kept the magic to herself and Sâr Shanek. Did you hear him say that? She hasn't taught her maidens."

"With the exception of Lady Amala."

"No, *Sâr Shanek* taught Amala," Jazlyn said. "And if I recall, the Chieftess was not the kindest to the girl. Why might that be?"

"She is a threat," Qoatch said. "She has the ability to take the boy from his mother."

Jazlyn smirked. "She already has. He would do anything for the girl. Still, it's clear that Chieftess Charlon is formidable in her abilities. If she believes Sâr Shanek is meant to rule Armania, why isn't she planning her own attack?"

"Perhaps she is," Qoatch said. "Or perhaps she feels he is not ready to rule."

"He *is* gullible," Jazlyn conceded. "What to do, Qoatch? Shadir are running wild without mantics to temper their cravings. If I could harness this new magic, I could not only rebuild my swarm, it might be bigger and stronger than before. I could establish New Tenma."

"You would need a great supply of the new ahvenrood," Qoatch said.

"I have only the one plant that Chieftess Charlon gave me. How quickly has it grown?"

"Not quickly enough," Qoatch said. "King Barthel mentioned having planted a crop on the islands he came from."

She sat up straight. "Was it harvested or left for seed?"

Qoatch didn't know. "I could ask."

"No, I don't want to call attention to myself or my desire to gather new root. Should King Barthel discover my interest, he would keep me from it until he learned its value."

"Perhaps you could offer your services as a vassal," Qoatch suggested. "King Barthel left his daughter Laviel to govern his fortress on Islah, but she betrayed him to her own demise. The fortress now sits abandoned, perhaps with a store of new ahvenrood waiting to be claimed."

"What an intriguing idea. But how would I explain my interest? Someone of my stature has better things to do than run errands for a king she does not serve."

Qoatch thought for a moment. "Empress Inolah will arrive any day now to help her son transition to his role of regent."

She grimaced. "Don't remind me."

"Why not tell the king you want to get away for a time? To avoid the discomfort the empress will surely put you through. So you volunteer to govern his interests in Islah in exchange for distance from those who seek to dismiss you as a villain."

Jazlyn's eyes glittered. "I like it, Qoatch. The question is, will King Barthel agree?"

"He will if you give him something he wants," Qoatch said. "A meeting with Sâr Shanek and Miss Amala."

This brought a scowl to Jazlyn's face. "Give the man a chance to steal Sâr Shanek and Miss Amala away from me?"

"Miss Amala is quite fond of you and Princess Jahleeah," Qoatch said. "And you have never asked anything of Sâr Shanek beyond his instruction after saving Sir Kalenek's life. King Barthel may try to win the boy to his side, but if the prince is unable to see the king's motives, surely Miss Amala will."

Jazlyn seemed to consider this. "If the king finds out they can do the new magic, he'll want to learn it. Then I'll have no advantage over him."

"Then we will warn them to keep their secrets safe," Qoatch said.

Jazlyn shook her head. "I dare not leave them alone with him. You must stay behind to protect my interests here. King Barthel is still livid over the death of his daughter. Offer yourself as a seer who can watch the Veil for spies. He is paranoid and bound to accept any offer of help."

Qoatch stood before the throne in King Barthel's tent. The man wore black to mourn his daughter's death, and it made him look sinister, like a lesser version of Gozan. His female mantics and the malleant woman were here as well, sitting on mats on the ground.

Qoatch made Empress Jazlyn's proposal to travel to Islah and take care of whatever mess Rosârah Laviel might have left behind. He also offered his services to the king while Jazlyn was away, then invited the king to dine with his Great Lady, Sâr Shanek, and Miss Amala that evening.

"These are pleasing developments," King Barthel said. "I'm eager to meet Sâr Shanek and Miss Amala, and I would appreciate your assistance in dealing with those that travel the Veil. Please thank the empress for me. As to her part, I left little on Islah. The fortress is nothing more than a drafty house of sticks. The air there is humid and it rains nearly every day in the winter. It would be most unpleasant."

"The empress does not want to be gone long," Qoatch said. "She simply wishes to distance herself from New Rurekau while Empress Inolah gets settled."

"She will lose all her power here," King Barthel said, "especially if she is away."

"The empress is tired, Your Highness," Qoatch said. "The babies keep her very busy. She does not have the energy to fight for the throne, especially when her magic is waning and she knows that those who stand in her way are set against her."

"She's in an unfortunate position." The king furrowed his ridged brow and rubbed his bony fingers on the arm of his throne. "I cannot part with any of my mantics at present, nor can I offer her the evenroot I promised, as that has been destroyed. I can, however, send her with twenty of my guardsmen for added safety and to aid in packing up the area. There is likely some furniture left behind. Perhaps even some of my daughter's personal effects, though she likely moved nearly everything to the ship. The empress can communicate with me through the shadir if she has any questions. And she must bring back any compelled Puru when she returns."

"She would be happy to, I'm sure, Your Highness," Qoatch said, bowing.

Timmons entered the tent and signaled to catch the king's attention.

"Well?" the king said.

The onesent bowed. "Abaqa mi Niseh has arrived, Your Highness. He brought with him three men."

"Bring them in at once," the king said.

"Yes, Your Highness." Timmons bowed and departed.

"Zenobia, Mattenelle, Lilou," the king said, snapping his fingers. "I don't believe the giants will attack, but be on your guard all the same. Zenobia, you will translate. Qoatch, watch the Veil for any unfamiliar shadir. I'm convinced these giants must have access to some."

"Should you call forth Dendron as well, Your Highness?" Qoatch asked. "Surely a great shadir could sense more about these newcomers than I could observe."

"He is busy with other matters at present," the king said. "You will have to do."

Qoatch bowed, though he couldn't imagine what task Dendron might find more important than the arrival of giants who harbored their own mysterious magic.

Timmons returned with four of the overly large men. Each had to squeeze through the tent entrance, which shook the canvas structure again and again.

Abaqa mi Niseh stopped before the throne. The Jiir-Yeke headman wore a leather cape covered in black feathers and a crown studded with gowzal teeth and claws. His men stood side by side behind him. He grunted and hit his fist against his chest in greeting.

King Barthel inclined his head. "Abaqa mi Niseh, welcome."

The giant headman spoke, and Lady Zenobia cast a spell that enabled her to translate the guttural language of the giants.

"You brought the Puru?" she asked.

"They are here," the king said. "Do we have a bargain?"

Abaqa grunted. "As I say, it will be done."

King Barthel clasped his hands together. "Excellent! We will leave first thing in the morning. Qoatch, if the empress doesn't mind, I'd like you to accompany us to the Jiir-Yeke village."

Visit the giants? Qoatch had no desire to make such a journey.

"Your men are welcome," Abaqa said once Zenobia had translated, "but women may only participate in the sacred ritual as . . ." Lady Zenobia paled, ". . . as sacrifices."

"How strangely barbaric," King Barthel blurted, then gripped Zenobia's arm. "Don't translate that. Mikray, fetch Yohthehreth, Lau, and Harton. Tell them to be ready to leave at dawn for a journey into the mountains. Tell them to dress warm."

The shadir vanished.

"Shall we eat, Headman?" the king asked. "You must be hungry from your journey."

"We will not to eat," Abaqa said. "Take us to the people now."

"Very well. Timmons, take the headman to the Puru tents."

Zenobia translated and the giants exited with Timmons, the tent again shaking each time one squeezed out the narrow entry.

Qoatch hadn't heard of any Puru people in King Barthel's camp. What negotiation had he just witnessed?

"I must prepare for dinner with my great-grandson," King Barthel said. "It's better that the giants have no stomach. Now I won't have to split my attention. Lady Mattenelle, choose twenty soldiers to accompany me tomorrow. Qoatch, inform me at once if you'll be joining us."

"Yes, Your Highness," Qoatch said.

When the king had gone, Qoatch made his own exit and met Mattenelle in the doorway.

"Why would the king give up his soldiers to the Jiir-Yeke?" he asked.

"Not soldiers," Mattenelle said. "He traded twenty of the Puru women and children he brought from Islah as an exchange for a demonstration of their magic."

How intriguing. "What kind of magic can they wield?"

"That's why the king is going to the giant village. To find out."

That night Qoatch watched his Great Lady struggle. They had agreed he would accompany King Barthel to the giants' village. Neither could understand why the man refused to attack Armania, and while Jazlyn hated to part with Qoatch for so long, she believed he would learn much by spending time in the king's service. What preoccupied her thoughts even more at present were the risks involved in the evening's dinner.

She had warned Sâr Shanek and Miss Amala against Barthel Rogedoth, but the man had charm and magic on his side. As the guests feasted on the best food and wine New Rurekau had to offer, the king regaled the young couple with tales of his childhood as a prince in Sarikar, stories of his service as a soldier in the Centenary War, exploits of hunting cheyvah in the Echo Crack, and the history of how he and his wife started the Lahavôtesh.

King Barthel's mantics worked steadily all night, upholding spells of trust and fascination between the king and his guests, not that Barthel Rogedoth needed their help. He was an expert at manipulation, and Sâr Shanek and Miss Amala—despite the warnings Jazlyn had given them—listened raptly, their eyes only leaving the king when they reached for food or drink.

"I'm so glad you came tonight, Sâr Shanek," the king said, "and that you brought such a lovely young woman with you. I've been longing to make your acquaintance, but I feared too many would seek to keep us apart. I thank you, Empress Jazlyn, for introducing me to my great-grandson. Your kindness knows no bounds."

"My pleasure, Your Highness." Jazlyn took a sip of wine, hiding her fake smile behind her goblet.

"I'm going on a trip north," the king told the young guests. "The empress is also going away. I do hope that when we return you will come and visit again?"

Sâr Shanek glanced at Miss Amala, clearly incapable of making a decision without her input. The girl nodded eagerly as she finished off the last of her cranberry crispel.

"We will visit again," the prince said.

"Wonderful." The king raised his glass. "Let us drink to friendship."

As everyone lifted their glasses and drank, Qoatch met Jazlyn's gaze. He knew that look. She would be counting on him to monitor the situation while she was gone. It was imperative that she find the king's new ahvenrood store before the man learned of its value. Only then would she stand a chance at succeeding in her plans to break free from King Barthel and establish New Tenma.

İℿ⊙LAH

Inolah's contingent approached New Rurekau just as the midday bells were tolling. A two-level log palisade set up on a rampart of earth surrounded the city on all sides. The river had been diverted into a moat that ran along the eastern and southern walls. The rooftops that Inolah could see were all thick layers of stepped thatch. Strangely there was no snow here.

She noted with distaste the dissimilar tents assembled outside the stronghold, no doubt belonging to Barthel Rogedoth. If she discovered that he and Jazlyn had conspired to kill her sons and take control of this realm . . .

That could wait. First she must see to Ferro's safety, then do what she could to make sure that New Rurekau was firmly allied with Armania in regard to Rogedoth.

The procession stopped outside the gate, then continued over a drawbridge. It pleased Inolah to see the vast number of Rurekan soldiers here to greet her men. Surely if Rogedoth had taken over, it would have been his men here instead and they might have prohibited her entry.

Inolah glanced out her window as the carriage rolled to a stop. The crude log castle was vastly inferior both architecturally and aesthetically to the fortress Jazlyn had destroyed in Old Rurekau.

Sir Doran opened the carriage door. "We are here, Your Eminence. Rosârah Thallah comes this way."

Interfering woman. Inolah hoped she knew better than to speak of Ulrik and their deception aloud. For now, no one must know that her eldest son was alive.

Inolah took Sir Doran's hand and, with his assistance, climbed from the carriage. The streets had been laid out on a rectangular grid. Wet and warped wooden planks covered the boggy ground. Inolah treaded carefully, thankful for a chance to stand and stretch her legs. Sure enough, Rosârah Thallah was headed toward them, planks bouncing under her heavy steps.

Father's third wife seemed to have aged a great deal since Inolah had last seen her on Bakurah Island. Her hair had grown thick streaks of gray, and deep wrinkles creased her mouth and forehead.

"Empress, thank the gods." Rosârah Thallah bustled to a stop on the planks outside Inolah's carriage. "We must act quickly to protect Rurekau from the influence of mantics."

"Doesn't that include yourself?"

Thallah set her hand over her ample bosom. "I am no mantic, Empress."

"Yet you kept a shadir *and* evenroot powder."

"Had I not, the giants would have taken us all."

"How fortunate, then, that you are so deceitful."

Thallah's brows sank. "I saved your son, Empress. The least you can do is—"

Inolah raised her hand and pushed her voicing magic into the woman's mind. *"Any reference to Ulrik will be spoken silently, is that understood? I would think a woman familiar with shadir would know better than to speak where the creatures can listen."*

Thallah puffed up her cheeks and expelled a long breath. *"I'm not a fool, in spite of what Taleeb and his band of men might have told you. They simply don't like being ruled by a woman."* She glanced at the baby in Kreah's arms. "Is this the princess Tinyah? She's a precious one. Wait until you see your grandchildren, Empress. They are equally beautiful."

Inolah's heart constricted. "I long to see them," she admitted.

"That woman keeps them in her chambers," Thallah said. "Prince Ferro as well. I'm afraid she's working a compulsion so he'll want to remain with her, despite your arrival."

"I know she has not, for I have spoken with Ferro often." Inolah walked past the rosârah, toward what she assumed to be the entrance. Sir Doran followed alongside, and Kreah, holding Tinyah, kept pace on her left. "Step carefully over these boards, Kreah," Inolah said.

"Empress Jazlyn is planning a trip," Thallah said, her heavy steps clacking behind Inolah. "I don't think she should be allowed to take the prince anywhere."

"Where is she going?" Inolah asked.

"She won't say, though it's by ship."

Inolah recalled Ulrik's concern for his children. She couldn't allow the empress to take them away. She also wanted Ferro out of Jazlyn's control. Immediately. "Have a servant show my staff to my rooms. You will take me to Ferro."

Thallah passed Inolah's order to a boy, and Sir Doran quickly split the guard in half, leaving ten men to accompany Inolah. They passed through a corridor with no ceiling. A section of carved, burned woodwork along the wall was quite ornate. It seemed Ulrik had made some attempts at beautifying this overly plain structure.

Thallah led Inolah through an archway and into a wooden foyer. From there they passed down another corridor, up two flights of stairs, and halfway down a narrower hallway to a set of double doors painted in gold leaf. Where had Ulrik found gold leaf enough to waste on the apartment of his traitorous wife?

Thallah knocked, and they waited in silence. Inolah's stomach flipped. It had been over a year since she'd last looked upon her Ferro. He would be ten now. They had conversed with their mind-speak magic, but Inolah worried things might be awkward between them, especially since he thought Ulrik had died. She hated to lie, but Ferro could not keep a secret.

The door opened, revealing a Tennish serving woman. She inclined her head. "Empress."

Inolah pushed past her. "I have come for my son."

"He's just waiting in the—"

"Mama!" A boy with short, wiry black hair pushed out the door and threw his arms around Inolah's waist. He was taller. And no one had bothered to keep his head shaved during his confinement.

Her eyes blurred as tears filled them. "Oh, my Ferro! It does my heart good to see you well. How I've missed you." She pulled him close and kissed the top of his head. "Is Empress Jazlyn here?" she asked the Tennish woman, who hadn't moved from her place near the door where Sir Doran stood, holding it open.

"The empress is in a meeting with the Tennish remnant," the woman said.

How interesting. "Does she meet with them often?" Inolah asked.

"I don't know, Your Eminence," the woman said.

Inolah doubted that very much. "I am taking Ferro into my custody. Have his belongings sent to his old chamber."

The woman bowed. "It would be my honor."

Inolah took Ferro's hand and led him away from the empress's apartment.

If these people were against her, she wished they wouldn't bother being so disgustingly polite about it. It was much easier to disdain rudeness.

Thallah followed alongside. "Would you like to pay your respects to King Barthel?"

"I owe him no allegiance," Inolah said. "Rule of this realm belongs to my son, therefore Barthel Rogedoth is our guest. He should be the one to pay his respects to me."

Thallah grunted. She led Inolah back through the courtyard and down another hallway to a set of doors on the other side of the castle.

"Has the empress always roomed so far from the royal chambers?" Inolah asked.

"Her deceit was discovered before the castle was complete," Thallah said. "The emperor made her reside in the apartment he had built for special guests."

That explained the gold leaf, at least.

Rosârah Thallah stopped before yet another set of gold leaf doors. "Your chambers, Empress. These rooms were built for the emperor's wife. Ferro's apartment is around the corner."

Sir Doran opened the door, and Inolah and Ferro went inside. Inolah's staff had already arrived and were preparing the room.

"I want to see Taleeb at once," Inolah said. "And see that the council is informed of my arrival."

Thallah pursed her lips and dipped into an awkward curtsy. "Yes, Your Eminence."

"Now, Ferro," Inolah said, smiling. "Come and meet your baby sister."

To Thallah's credit, Taleeb arrived not a half hour later. She bade the man join her and Ferro before the fireplace. Once they had made themselves comfortable, she began her inquiries.

"What is happening here?" Inolah asked. "Does Jazlyn rule?"

"She claims to," Taleeb said, "yet we have given her no responsibility."

"She wants to rule her own people," Ferro said. "I heard her say so to Qoatch."

Inolah nodded to her son. "That's good to know, Ferro. And Thallah?"

"She sits on our council and tries to rule as much as anyone," Taleeb said. "Now that you are here, she will likely back off."

Inolah wasn't so sure. "What is the status of our army?"

"We were fifteen hundred strong before the last wave of giants attacked. While the empress worked her magic here in the castle, the people in the village weren't so lucky. Over two hundred were taken by the giants as slaves, and another four hundred fell in the conflict."

"Then we still have nine hundred in the army?"

"Only just, lady," Taleeb said. "They are eager to take back their family and friends, though the council feels it is folly to fight the giants."

"They do have a great tactical advantage," Inolah said.

"We heard Rosâr Trevn escaped from the giants without a fight," Taleeb said. "How did he accomplish this?"

"He escaped down an underground river with the help of Master Grayson," Inolah said. "Perhaps King Trevn would lend us use of Master Grayson to seek out our people?"

"That would be ideal, Empress."

"Tell me about Barthel Rogedoth. What are his plans?"

"I am uncertain. He has slowly become popular with the people. He gives them food."

"Our people?" Inolah asked.

Taleeb nodded. "Venison, goats, fowl, fish. I don't know where he gets it, but he has used it to win their trust. Also, our soldiers and his have been patrolling together. I fear the men have become friendly."

"Who authorized this?" Inolah asked.

"The empress and King Barthel."

Inolah should have come sooner—the moment she'd heard of Ulrik and Ferro falling ill. Their enemies had been given free rein for far too long. "Will our people choose Barthel Rogedoth over their own royal family?"

"I cannot say, lady, but it has been a sparse winter," Taleeb said. "Food is better than gold to the hungry, and men don't like being ordered to fight their comrades."

The situation was far from ideal. "It seems to me that Barthel Rogedoth came here to manipulate an alliance from a people with no leader."

"Actually, we have more leaders than we know what to do with."

"My point exactly. Ulrik had decreed Ferro would rule upon his untimely death," Inolah said. "Did that change?"

"No, but Empress Jazlyn believes Prince Adir should rule with her as regent."

"Did Ulrik write a new directive naming her regent in the case of his death?"

"He did not," Taleeb said.

"Then the matter is settled," Inolah said, thankful for that much. "Prince Ferro is too young to rule as emperor at present, so until he reaches his majority, he can act as regent under the guidance of the council, of which you will make me a member, at least until our common enemies are defeated."

"I believe the council would support that motion, Your Eminence," Taleeb said.

"Good." Inolah took Ferro's hands in hers. "We must fight to keep our realm strong, Ferro. I want to know what Empress Jazlyn does at these meetings of the Tennish people. It's impossible, I believe, that it will be what's best for Rurekau."

"He's beautiful," Inolah said, taking Prince Adir into her arms. Her first grandchild. She could not be so old, could she? Too much time, wasted.

She had asked Empress Jazlyn to meet her in the council chambers to deliver the council's verdict on the ascension. She had not expected the woman to bring Prince Adir to meet his grandmother. If Jazlyn thought this might be a means of manipulation, she was wrong, but that didn't mean Inolah wouldn't enjoy this moment.

"Does Adir look very different from his sister?" she asked.

"I have named him Jael, Empress," Jazlyn said. "And though they look alike, Jahleeah is much bigger."

Strange to hear Jazlyn call the children by different names. "I'd like to meet her."

"Certainly," Jazlyn said, "though it must be soon. I'm planning a trip and hope to leave in a day or two."

"Yes, I heard that you were preparing for a journey. Where are you going?"

"I don't see why it's any of your business, but I'm sailing to Islah. Rosârah Laviel abandoned King Barthel's fortress, and I volunteered to aid him in packing up the place."

"Such a task seems beneath you."

"Perhaps," Jazlyn said, "but with Ulrik dead and his brother being groomed to rule, I see no place here for me at present."

Inolah sensed there was more to this story, but she had never been good at reading thoughts. She considered making an attempt, but a bigger worry sidetracked her. "I'm sorry, Empress, but I cannot allow you to take away Prince Adir."

"Jael, Empress." Jazlyn's eyes flashed. "And you have no authority to say such a thing. He is *my* son." She reached for the prince.

Inolah reluctantly handed him off. "He is also the heir," she said.

"The council voted for Prince Ferro to rule, so I see no reason why Jael must stay."

"He's the heir presumptive, Empress. Should anything happen to Ferro, Prince Adir—my pardon, *Prince Jael*—will be our last hope."

"I have Protectors enough to keep him safe. And you should know that Ulrik and I signed a betrothal agreement that enables female ascension in the event that no male heirs exist."

Inolah knew Ulrik had signed a betrothal agreement, though she had not known all the particulars. "Then Princess Jahleeah will have to remain in New Rurekau as well."

"Absolutely not!" Jazlyn cried. "You cannot take both my children."

"Then let us compromise," Inolah said. "If you'll leave Prince Jael with me, I'll speak to the council about granting special permission for you to take Princess Jahleeah on your trip."

"You do realize I have magic again, don't you?" Jazlyn asked. "I could simply take my children away and compel everyone to forget they exist."

"Your children are not yours alone," Inolah said. "They belong to all of Rurekau. Was that not the case with children in Tenma? They belonged to the realm?"

Jazlyn glowered. "I will do as I please where my children are concerned."

"If you are going to behave like a traitor to the realm you married into, then you and all of your associates will be treated as such," Inolah said.

"Which means . . . ?"

"Which means I will have you all arrested. You, Qoatch, your staff, your Protectors, and every Tennish national."

"You cannot do that."

"Watch me."

"I will magic them all away."

"If you must, though I suspect it will waste a great deal of evenroot."

Jazlyn's eyes closed to slits. "If I agree to leave Jael behind, that will suit you?"

Inolah relaxed. She had won. "If it suits the council, then yes."

"It had better," Jazlyn snapped, "or I will be forced to drain my magic to place compulsions over this entire realm."

Inolah inclined her head. "Your restraint is very gracious."

Jazlyn handed the prince back to Inolah. "I will not forget this." She strode away, head held high.

Inolah snuggled Prince Adir close and watched the boy's mother exit the chamber. She had won a single battle with the Tennish mantic, but she feared she might have started a war.

KALENEK

For three days Kal traveled north through snowy fields, the distant mountain range ever in his sights. Onika acted as guide, regaling him with the story of how she had discovered her new ability. She also told him how she and Grayson had helped Hinckdan Faluk assassinate Rosârah Laviel. Kal listened in awe as she spoke of banishing shadir and acting the part of a soldier in the Veil. He didn't understand her new magic, but her presence, even if only verbal, was more comfort than he'd had in the past year.

"I so look forward to returning to Armanguard and my friends there," Onika said.

Kal grimaced at the mention of that place. He would not be welcome. In fact, he would likely be executed as a traitor. Wilek had warned him never to return.

As Kal rode north, Onika guided him though forests and around craggy rock bends, across snowy meadows and over rolling hills. Eventually he reached a moorland without snow, though the air was still bitter cold.

If felt strange to take direction from an invisible voice. Too often Kal wondered if this was all another hallucination. The gods only knew how much damage Charlon's spells had caused his mind. What if he were imagining Onika's presence? What if he'd gone mad?

As if in answer, Kal topped a final ridge and spotted a castle stronghold sitting atop the highest hill in the distance. He sighed in relief. If he'd lost his mind, how could he have imagined a voice that had brought him so directly to civilization?

"Where are we?" he asked.

"New Rurekau," Onika said. *"Barthel Rogedoth has been camped outside the stronghold these past few weeks, though he's currently journeying north."*

Was Shanek in the stronghold with Empress Jazlyn? Had he met Rogedoth yet?

"He has been holding me captive in one of his tents," Onika said, *"waiting for the full moon so he can sacrifice me to his god."*

That got Kal's attention. The moon had been growing in the sky these past few nights. *"That must be soon."*

"Three or four more days, I believe. Find someplace to wait for the cover of darkness."

Kal stopped at the next stream. He ate, rested, and refilled his water jug. Mostly, he began to worry. *"Miss Onika, I carry a sword, but that's no guarantee I can use it for long. You do recall my . . . condition?"*

"Violence causes your arm to fail you."

"Yes, and while a great deal of time has passed since that last happened, I have no reason to believe anything has changed."

"Things will only change when you make an effort to heal the wounds inside."

Heat flooded Kal's chest. *"You sound like Jhorn."*

"I wish you would have spoken to him about the war."

"Nothing he could have said would change anything. The past is set in stone."

"You cannot change the past, no, but I have seen many make peace with it."

"Through Jhorn's magical healing ways?"

"It's not magic," Onika said. *"It was years of hard work."*

That wasn't what Kal had expected to hear. *"He tried to tell me, but I wouldn't let him."*

"Jhorn knows there is little point in trying to help someone who doesn't want it."

Kal understood that well enough. How often had he tried to help Charlon? The woman had made such a companion of her pain, she couldn't part with it. *"How did he make peace?"*

"There was no one thing. As I said, he struggled for many years. But his healing started because of a merchant. He was an amputee as well, walked with one wooden peg. He sold Jhorn his first set of canes. Whenever he passed through Magonia, Jhorn would invite him to stay. One such night, when we children had been put to bed, Jhorn asked about the merchant's leg. The story was one of horrific abuse at the hands of his father. Jhorn asked how he could be so joyful, for the man smiled often.

"The merchant said he was thankful for what he had gone through. While painful, it had drawn him closer to the God, allowed him compassion to help others, and enabled him to forgive his father. This angered Jhorn, who didn't see why evil should be forgiven. The merchant had infinite patience. The longer the conversation went on, the softer Jhorn became. Soon he was telling his own story. He wanted the peace the merchant had and asked how he might obtain it.

"The merchant told Jhorn that a wound that goes untreated becomes infected and, over time, festers. A festering wound needs to be drained or it will infect the whole body.

"Jhorn saw friends die. He lost his legs. His anger was valid. As was his sorrow. The merchant advised Jhorn not to trample those feelings, but to wander through them until he made peace with them. To forgive himself for any part he played, then to seek the good that came of it.

"Again Jhorn grew angry. What good? But as he raged, truth made itself clear. Had Jhorn not lost his legs, he might never have found Grayson. He would not know Dun or me. This small realization was enough to give Jhorn the first measure of peace he'd ever had in regard to his pain. From that moment on, whenever bouts of sorrow, anger, or humiliation came upon him, he acknowledged each with truth, then sought out a reverse emotion. Joy that he could care for us, empathy for himself over the loss of his legs, and pride that he was alive and able to move and care for three children. He transformed pain into joy, curse into a gift."

Kal considered this. *"So it's trickery. He simply trains himself to think positive."*

"There's more to it than that," Onika said. *"It was a difficult road. You'll have to ask him about it. But your anger, guilt, and nightmares, your numbness . . . all are symptoms of one or more festering wounds."*

Kal couldn't deny it, and he was weary of being a victim. He wanted the freedom Jhorn had, but his past was a convoluted mess of tragedy and failure. He didn't know where to start.

At dusk he continued on. Though he could see the torchlights of New Rurekau, it still took over an hour to reach the outskirts of the city. By then, the waxing moon hung fat in the black sky, a reminder that they had little time left.

Onika led him toward a field of mismatched tents. Kal tied up his horse and crouched behind a bush on the edge of what he could now see was a military camp arranged in a circular formation. The moon was not bright enough to see well. He listened to the distant sounds of the men, talking and laughing, someone playing a lute. These soldiers appeared no different from those he'd known during the war. Why were they here? Was their allegiance to Rogedoth? Or were they simply against House Hadar?

"Which tent is yours?" he asked.

"It's near the center of camp," Onika said. *"See those two tents on the outer edge? Someone has strung a laundry line between them."*

"I see them."

"Your most direct path would be to go through there."

Kal prepared to stand but hesitated. *"Is there a guard outside your tent?"*

"There were two when I left to find you."

Kal didn't like it. *"Miss Onika, what if my arm fails?"* Positive thoughts would be of little use with a sword flying at his throat.

"Do your best, Sir Kalenek. Arman and I will assist you."

What an odd thing to say. But the woman had brought him this far; he might as well trust her fully. *"I live to serve, lady."*

Kal set out, running in a crouch toward the clothesline. He reached his destination without incident and crept along the line until he could peer between the legs of a pair of trousers. Just ahead, five soldiers sat circled around a campfire. They were Kinsman, and Kal recognized one of them from Tace Edekk's personal guard. Traitors, all of them.

"Best go the other way," Onika said.

Kal crept around the back of the tent, then decided to circle the tent beside it too. He met no one in the shadows. As he came up around the far side of the tent, he peeked back toward the campfire in time to catch the men hooting about something.

"Go!" Onika said, and Kal sprinted through the gap.

Thus he went ahead, following Onika's commands. The air smelled of cooked meat, campfire smoke, and oil from burning torches. Twice her warnings saved him from walking right in front of guards, and in a very short time Kal found himself crouched behind a pale tent, looking at a dark one she claimed was her own.

It did indeed have two guards outside the entrance. They were talking casually to one another as if confident of the easy task they'd been given.

"Is anyone in the tent with you?" Kal asked.

"No," Onika said. *"If you sneak under the canvas in back, no one will see you."*

Kal much preferred that plan. He backtracked and approached the tent from behind. He dropped to his stomach on the cold grass and rolled underneath the canvas wall. It was very dark inside as he hopped to his feet and slowly stood. The fire in the center of the tent had burned down to orange embers. His eyes adjusted. He spied a mat on the other side of the tent and took slow, careful steps around the fire pit, eyes locked on the still form under a wool blanket.

Something small moved in the darkness. A familiar hiss made Kal smile. He crouched and held out his hand. "Hello, Rustian," he whispered. "I've come to help Onika."

The dune cat approached, sniffed Kal's fingers, then pushed its head under his palm, purring heavily.

"You remember me, don't you?" Kal indulged the animal with a lengthy scratch behind its ears, then stood and continued toward the mat. Rustian ran ahead and plopped down beside the body. As Kal neared, he was able to make out Onika's unique features: nearly white hair, pale skin, the curve of her eyebrows, her slender nose, and pink lips.

"You're beautiful," he told her.

"I think the same as I look at you," she said. "Eyes see differently than hands. You were handsome when my hands first felt your face, and you are magnificent to my eyes now."

Such words. Kal swallowed to clear the lump in his throat. "Let's get you out of here."

"My body cannot move on its own while my consciousness is in the Veil. If you carry me, I will subdue the guards myself."

"I would rather you didn't. Besides, who's the Rescuer here? Me or you? Return to your body long enough to crawl under the canvas wall. That will make things easier."

"Very well." A breath later, Onika's body shifted and she opened her eyes.

"Hello," Kal said, breathless at the sight of those silvery blue orbs.

She smiled and pushed herself to a sitting position. "Rustian can lead me when we're outside," she whispered, "but you must help me out of the tent. Also, remember that in my body, I cannot see shadir. If any spot us, they will warn their masters."

The audible sound of her voice so mesmerized him, it took him a moment to register what she'd said. "Did you see any shadir when we came in?"

"A few," she said slowly. "There are normally hundreds in this camp. Most likely went north with Rogedoth."

Kal took hold of her hand and hauled them both to their feet. He led her around the fire pit toward the back of the tent. "Stand here a moment." He dropped into a crouch and peeked under the canvas. The night appeared dark and still. He saw no movement. He stood, lifting the canvas as he rose. He again found Onika's hand. "Duck and step forward."

Onika obeyed, and Kal pulled her under the wall. Once they were outside, he let the canvas fall back into place. He looked for the dune cat and found the animal at its post against Onika's right leg. Good cat.

Kal drew his sword, just in case, then took Onika's hand with his left. They circled a small tent and came face-to-face with a gray-haired soldier holding a mug.

"Intruders!" The soldier dropped the mug and drew his sword. "Throw down that weapon and kneel, hands out where I can see them."

Kal shoved Onika behind him. "Stay down!" He'd have to kill this guard before reinforcements came. He lunged forward to scare the old man, but the guard met his stroke, then lashed out with a strike of his own just as a second guard arrived on the scene.

Kal cursed his bad luck as he blocked the strike and barely managed to dodge out of the path of the second guard's sword.

Kal was rusty, and fighting two guards was always challenging. He held steady, though, until three more guards rushed into the fray. Kal managed to clip the shoulder of his first attacker. At the sound of the man's anguished cry, Kal's sword arm began to tingle.

"Onika, it's happening!" he yelled. "My arm!"

"I will fight them, Sir Kalenek, but you must carry my body."

Her comment confused him—*how* would she fight?—but he could do nothing but focus on his own circumstances. The five men came upon him with such force, they quickly pushed him back against the tent. Rustian darted in and hissed, tripping one of the men and scratching another. On the edge of Kal's vision, he saw Onika fall.

"No!" He glanced back to see who had dared strike a defenseless woman, but no one was there. His hesitation enabled the soldiers to seize him. They wrestled him to the ground. He yelled, panicked by the idea that Onika would be here for the full moon—that he had failed her.

Someone pushed a knee into his back. "I need some rope to bind him."

Kal needed to escape before they bound his hands. Before he could come up with a plan, one of his attackers collapsed to the ground beside him, eyes glassy.

What in blazes had happened to him?

Overhead, his attackers cried out in surprise. A sudden weight fell onto Kal's back.

"What's happening?" a man asked, his voice laced in terror.

Kal struggled to his knees and threw off the limp body. He regarded the two men on the ground, then the three staring at him, swords pointed his way.

"You're a mantic, aren't you?" one of them asked.

"Not me." Kal's sword was within reach, so he grabbed it and stood to face the men.

The nearest lunged at him. Kal deflected the blow. Another jabbed his blade toward Kal, and just as Kal blocked it, the man fainted away.

The last two soldiers swept back, eyes wide and searching the shadows. One collapsed, leaving the other standing over the bodies of his comrades, a look of confused shock on his face.

Kal couldn't blame him.

"See to my body, Sir Kalenek." Onika's voice was back in his head. *"This man is about to yield."*

Kal sheathed his sword and tossed Onika's limp body over his shoulder. By the time he turned around, the last soldier lay on the ground as if dead.

"I'd love to know how you accomplished that," he said.

"We will have time to talk later, Sir Kalenek."

Kal stepped carefully over the felled soldiers, then picked up speed. Rustian padded beside him, ears perked up. They had created so much commotion that they met guards at every turn, but Onika attacked each before Kal ever had need to draw his blade. A curious fear at her power prickled his arms in gooseflesh. Huge men swooned at the sight of them as if an invisible storm had blown away each life. Kal wove around their bodies, uncertain if they were dead or merely sleeping. In this manner they made their way out of the camp. They reached Kal's horse, and he pushed Onika's body up, then mounted behind her. It wasn't until he was riding hard for the trees that he remembered Shanek was in Rurekau with Empress Jazlyn—that he had been coming to help the boy. Kal couldn't go back now. Apparently he had made his choice.

Trevn

Trevn awoke, alert yet confused. Had there been a noise? His chamber was dark. He sensed no one here but Mielle, and from the steady cadence of her breathing, she was still asleep.

"Oli Agoros."

Ah. Oli must have been knocking, but why at this hour?

Trevn yawned and lowered his shields. *"Yes, Your Grace?"*

A rush of relief filled the connection between them. *"I'm sorry if I awakened you, Your Highness, but my mother just voiced me and I wanted to tell you all she said."*

Trevn's heart lurched and he pushed to sitting. *"Please do so."*

"She not only confided in me the names of several noble families who she claims are loyal to her cause, she confirmed her plan to attack Armanguard, to kill you, and to make me king of Armania. She is awaiting my response as to whether or not I will help her."

A nightmare come to life. *"Could this be some kind of trick?"* Trevn asked.

"I think not, Your Highness," Oli said.

"You have my undivided attention, Your Grace. Tell me everything."

"The *Greenore's* location is still a mystery," Trevn told the council the next morning. "Master Grayson will inform me the moment he finds them."

"Who are these traitors Sârah Jemesha named?" Barek asked.

"Tace Edekk, Gunrik Koll, Allain Ortropp, and the Wallingtons," Trevn said. Clearly some of the noble families had sided with the enemy in hopes that

Trevn might be killed and Oli promoted in his place. Trevn watched the man now, vexed that he could never sense his emotions. He well knew that if Oli Agoros wanted the throne of Armania, he could take it without much difficulty. Trevn simply had to trust that the duke was on his side.

"We cannot let those men and their armies fight alongside the rest of us," Lord Idez said.

"Why would they fight when they could stay home and let us be slaughtered?" Barek said.

"Slaughtered by a compelled Puru force of five hundred?" General Ensley said. "Do you really have so little faith in our army?"

"But Sârah Jemesha has magic," Barek added.

"Had magic," Danek said. "Master Grayson destroyed their root."

"Then how is she hiding the *Greenore*?" Marshal Winstone asked.

"She must be expending her reserves to shield their ship," Captain Veralla said.

"Either way, the traitors should be arrested," Lord Idez said.

"I won't arrest anyone or label them traitor without evidence of wrongdoing," Trevn said. "General Ensley, keep an eye on those families named and their armies. But unless you see acts of treason, let them fight."

Ensley nodded. "Yes, Your Highness."

"Oli, please inform the council what we can expect from your father." Trevn purposely used the duke's first name, hoping to remind him that they were all of them friends here.

"My father will shoot fire arrows inside the castle to smoke us out. If that fails, then he may try laying siege to Castle Armanguard."

"We mustn't let it come to that," Captain Veralla said. "Castle sieges are long, drawn-out affairs. A standoff could last months or even years. The general would cut off our food and water supply until we surrendered or starved to death."

"We have the lake," Lord Idez said. "With fish and plenty of water. Plus snow to melt in the meantime and food for several months. Longer if we evicted the commoners to safety."

"There will be no safety for our people outside these walls," Oli said. "My father's army will rape and pillage the city, burn fields to destroy crops, slaughter the herds—"

"Why would he do that if he looks to rule?" Barek asked.

"My father rules by fear alone," Oli said.

"Then we don't let him reach the castle," Trevn said. "Avoid a siege at all costs. General, can we attack first?"

"Certainly, Your Highness," General Ensley said, "but until the ship is located, we don't know which direction around the lake he'll come. Where would I assemble the men?"

"Divide them between the nearest coastlines," Captain Veralla said. "Half on the north side of the lake, half on the west. Grayson can warn us which way they're coming from, then you'll have time to move the rest."

"Won't that leave the city defenseless?" Lord Idez asked.

"The garrison will remain with me in the castle," Trevn said.

"Actually, Your Highness," General Ensley said, "you must ride out with the army. Your First Arm can lead the garrison against any who might get past our defenses."

Leave Oli Agoros the castle? Was that wise?

"If you're leading the army, General, why can't the king remain here?" Lord Idez asked.

"The army belongs to the king, not me," Ensley said. "He should lead them."

This had been the plan all along—the reason Trevn had been going to the practice field each day. To hear it said so calmly made him feel woefully inadequate. And while he trusted Oli, it would be wise to leave another trustworthy man here, just in case.

"Very well," Trevn said, "but as I have no command experience, I will defer to your tactical wisdom, General. Captain Veralla, I put you in charge of Duke Canden's security. See that my First Arm is kept safe. The moment we get word from Grayson, I will ride out and join the army."

Oli met Trevn's gaze. "Go with Arman, Your Highness."

"You as well. General Ensley, call the army to prepare for battle. We shall see who comes and who does not. Meeting adjourned."

Grayson awoke Trevn before dawn. The *Greenore* had dropped its anchor off the coast of Er'Rets, directly east from the castle, about five leagues up the coast from the Port of Armania. Trevn quickly passed along the news, then called Ottee. As the boy set about dressing Trevn for battle, Mielle became frantic. She alternated between frustration over not being able to fight, lamenting as to what might become of her if Trevn were killed, assuring him he would have victory, and fighting through bouts of gut-wrenching tears.

Through their soul-binding, the woman's emotions were making Trevn's spin. He finally kissed her goodbye and ordered Lady Pia and Bero to take her to Rosârah Brelenah so he might have some peace.

When Trevn was ready, he took the stairs to the roof, where he stood with Oli Agoros, Captain Veralla, Nietz, and Cadoc, helm in hand, looking across the partially frozen lake toward the southeast. The men's combined emotions were much more stable than his wife's had been, and Trevn was finally able to prepare himself for what was coming.

We are in need of your protection today, Arman. Help us prevail.

Trevn had been expecting war since Wilek had become king, but it was strange to be facing someone other than Rogedoth. He couldn't believe that the former general and his wife—Trevn's aunt—would not only commit treason against Armania but would betray Barthel Rogedoth after all their years of supporting his cause.

"Grayson, give me an update," he voiced.

"They're unloading the ship now," Grayson said, *"and the Puru soldiers are marching in a line toward Armanguard. Shall I stay here?"*

"Yes," said Trevn. *"I'll have Miss Onika advance with the soldiers. Keep me apprised of everything. And watch General Agoros and his wife and daughter closely."*

"Yes, Your Highness."

Grayson believed he had destroyed all the evenroot aboard the *Greenore* after Hinck had killed Rosârah Laviel, but was there truly any way to know? That Sârah Jemesha might attack with magic was Trevn's greatest fear. It was the only possibility for which he had no defense.

Trevn voiced Miss Onika next. Sir Kalenek had rescued her from Rogedoth's camp—they were on their way back. She assured him she could enter the Veil to help and that Sir Kalenek would ride on with her body. Trevn didn't know how he would deal with the man Wilek had publicly declared a traitor for having killed Janek. But that was a problem for another day. Trevn asked Miss Onika to follow the enemy's march and keep him informed as to their location.

He looked through his grow lens. Nothing. "Grayson says they are coming." He studied the western bank, where half the army was to report. Scattered groups of soldiers stood on the snowy field, looking bored. To the north he found a similar showing. "Is this all our men?"

"General Ensley said they are missing over half," Oli said, breath clouding as he spoke.

Half of two thousand? "Why so many?"

"Either not all the soldiers received the message that Armanguard is about to be attacked," Oli said, "or they did get the message and have chosen to ignore it."

Trevn stiffened, incensed by the latter possibility. "Even combined, the suspected traitors' armies are no more than five hundred. Where are the others?"

"It could be that men simply don't want to risk their lives anymore."

Both options made fury well inside Trevn's gut. "Well, perhaps this man would be pleased to send a thousand deserters to the pole."

"Maybe not all one thousand, Your Highness," Captain Veralla said. "Find out who those missing men report to. It could be that those officers are the ones who openly defied your order, not their men."

That seemed logical. "Cadoc, Nietz, let's go find out, shall we?" Trevn said, walking toward the stairs. He nodded to Captain Veralla, then looked to Oli. "Guard the castle well, Your Grace."

When Trevn stepped off the barge, he found his horse saddled and waiting, snorting steamy gusts into the frigid air. Trevn greeted Seeker, put on his helm, and mounted. The metal felt cold on his head, but his breath quickly warmed it. He rode hard with Cadoc, Nietz, Rzasa, Novan, and Bonds over the slushy snow toward what would soon become a battlefield. The sky was dark gray and cloudy. Trevn hoped it wouldn't storm.

"Grayson? Give me an update," he voiced.

"The general divided the soldiers into three units and sent them north around the top of the lake," he said. *"The first has already set out. The second is nearly gone. They're not all Puru. About twenty in each group are Kinsman."*

"Did you overhear any of the general's plans?"

"He wants to reach the castle quickly and lay siege."

"He's too late for that. Stay with him and inform me of anything you think important."

"Yes, sir."

Trevn checked in with Miss Onika and received a similar report, though she had spotted several shadir among the Puru army. She couldn't tell whether or not they were bonded to anyone in particular. It could be they were simply drawn to the possibility of bloodshed.

Trevn and his men approached a long line of foot soldiers stretched out along the top of a small hill facing southeast. They steered their mounts toward the center back, where General Ensley was positioned on a horse with Marshal Winstone and a few mounted officers. Trevn recognized Sir Keshton Veralla, Gunrik Koll, and Sir Jarmyn Koll. Interesting that Lord Blackpool and his son had come. Trevn had been certain they would have been numbered among the deserters.

"I thought we were going to meet the enemy on the plains, General," Trevn said.

"The plains would give Agoros too easy an approach, Your Highness," Ensley said. "Plus, that snow will become a miry bog in no time, so I've assembled the army across the top of this ridge. They'll form a shield wall, seven men deep with our best men in the front. The enemy will exhaust themselves in futile attacks against our defensive line."

Trevn nodded, seeing the wisdom in Ensley's plan. "How many men do we have?"

"Near fifteen hundred, Your Highness."

A few more had decided to come after all. Good. "Any idea which men have failed to report?"

"Unfortunately, no," the general said. "All of my officers and lords are accounted for. In all honesty, with only one night to spread the word, it's likely those missing didn't get the message."

That possibility lifted Trevn's spirits. He took out his grow lens and peered in the direction Ensley had indicated. The first division of General Agoros's pale army was drawing near, the line stretching out into the distance. No more than five hundred total, Hinck had said. Archers were at the front. The others seemed to be carrying pikes.

"Their archers will shoot first, I assume?" Trevn asked.

"Yes, Your Highness," Ensley said. "General Agoros will try to break our formation with his archers, then attack with his infantry to create gaps in our line. My guess is his Kinsman men will try to get past us and head toward the castle. We'll stop them, though." Ensley looked through his own grow lens. "They look fuddled. I've never seen anything like it."

Trevn peered through his lens at the nearest Puru. Many were snarling like animals; some looked to be talking to themselves. "Hinck said Rogedoth compelled them to believe we have wronged them. My guess is they will be passionate fighters."

"That's unfortunate, Your Highness," Ensley said. "And terribly sad."

"Yes," Trevn said. "I do not wish to kill these Puru."

"Retreat would bring dishonor."

"Oh, we will not retreat," Trevn said. "We'll put our hope in Arman and trust in his will."

"I usually ride up and down the line to encourage the men, Your Highness," Ensley said. "Might you like the honor instead?"

"I would." He regarded the spread of soldiers, then glanced at his personal guards. "Ride with me." He steered Seeker out to the front of the line and was heartened to see the glossy blue shields blazoned in black paint with his own sigil of five Nesher birds in flight. The shields ran out into the distance, one locked against another as far as he could see.

Trevn sat as tall as he could in his saddle and spurred his horse forward. "Soldiers of Armania!" he yelled as he rode slowly along the front line. Some heads turned toward him. "Arman is with us. The same Arman who brought the Five Woes upon our former home. The same Arman who wrought judgment upon my father and his Pontiff advisor for their sins against him. The same Arman who led us across the seas to this new land. A land he has given us to protect."

The men near him had grown silent. They were listening.

"We fight today for our wives, our children, and our families. We fight for those who have fought before us. We fight for the life Arman has provided. The life Rogedoth and other traitors continue to threaten. Our attackers today are but pawns. They serve our enemy out of force, not devotion. They will come hard against us, so protect yourselves well. Do not wither or retreat from battle but fight to the last. Defend our home with the power Arman provides. We are brave. We are courageous. We are strong. We are Armania!"

The soldiers cheered. Some lifted swords or poleaxes in the air. Trevn continued down the line, encouraging the men. He gave his speech a few more times and eventually passed around the other end of the shield wall and returned along the back side of the line.

Across the ranks, blue banners bearing Trevn's sigil whipped about in the chill wind. Though the day was bitter cold and the sky gray, the sun shone down through a patch of pale blue and gleamed against the oiled armor and polished weapons. As Trevn regarded his army, a measure of pride welled within him. These men had obeyed his call.

May we honor you this day, Arman, if such a thing is possible in war. We fight against the evil we brought here. Help us banish it for good.

Trevn and his guards finally reached General Ensley again. It seemed odd to wait for the enemy to arrive. His instinct was to send the army out now, before the enemy had a chance to fall into ranks. He voiced the question to Cadoc.

"An army has strength when it acts as one," Cadoc said.

Trevn tried to imagine what Cadoc meant, but then the left wing of the Puru, who were the only enemy division fully assembled, attacked prematurely. Their archers fired on the Armanian line, and the Puru infantry charged past the archers, following the path of the artillery.

A shout from General Ensley, and the Armanians lifted their shields.

"They're doing exactly what I was tempted to do," Trevn voiced to Cadoc.

"Yes, and it's a foolish act, as you'll see soon enough. They should hold their position and wait for the rest of their forces to arrive. Unite their whole army. Watch and see how it affects the outcome. My guess is the attack will be short."

The slope of the hill and the flat trajectory of the arrows rendered the artillery fire ineffective. Most of the arrows stuck into the snowy ground dozens of paces from the front line. The few that did manage to reach the shield wall thunked into wood as if the Puru archers were merely exercising target practice.

"Not very good aim, are they?" Trevn asked, silently thanking Hinck for his poor tutelage.

"Perhaps not," Ensley said, "or it could be the cold. It dampens taut bow-strings and makes the fingers stiff."

Brandishing their pikes like enraged animals, the charging Puru infantry slogged up the incline toward the Armanian shield wall. They jabbed at the shields and tried to stab through gaps. General Ensley gave the order to hold the position, and the shield wall remained solid, a united force that easily halted the attack. Not one Armanian soldier broke away to engage the Puru, who could find no way through the defense. Some lost patience and lobbed their pikes over the wall, but with nothing to aim at, the weapons were wasted.

It was a strange kind of assault: one side frenzied and out of control, the other calmly rooted to the ground like trees. The Puru infantry, unable to create a single gap in the shield wall, finally retreated just as the second division of Puru arrived. Seeing their comrades beaten, some of the newcomers turned and took flight. For a moment it looked as if the battle might end right then, but the Puru slowly reformed themselves into two separate divisions as the third approached the field.

"Where would General Agoros put himself?" Trevn asked General Ensley.

"In the back of the center division, I would guess."

"Miss Onika?" Trevn voiced. *"Do you see the general?"*

"I don't know what he looks like, Your Highness, though it appears that the commanders are standing in a wagon at the back of the third section of Puru."

Trevn looked through his grow lens and studied the enemy line until he spotted a wagon approaching the left side of the center division. "I believe General Agoros is there," he said, pointing to the wagon. "Can we take him out?"

"Sir Jarmyn has the best archers," Ensley said. "I'll have him send a squad around to attack from the back. If we take out the general, there will be no one to order the compelled."

"Make it happen," Trevn said, liking that idea and hoping Sir Jarmyn would prove loyal.

General Ensley sent his onesent riding away to deliver the order.

"Grayson, give me a report," Trevn voiced.

"General Agoros is yelling at some of his captains to keep the men together."

Why had the boy left the ship? *"What of Eudora and Sârah Jemesha?"* Trevn asked, still concerned about the possibility of magic.

"You told me to stay with the general."

Had he? Trevn had intended for Miss Onika to move ahead with the army and Grayson to stay with the ship, but it could be he had miscommunicated that desire.

"Last I saw Sârah Jemesha, she was standing on the main deck of the ship," Grayson said, *"watching some sailors haul a dinghy onto land."*

"Why would they do that?" Trevn asked.

"To keep the boats from freezing in the sea?" Grayson said.

Impossible this far south. *"Go back to the ship and see what my cousin and aunt are doing. Now, please."*

"Yes, sir."

The silence in Trevn's mind left him feeling vulnerable. Fool boy. Why would he not tell Trevn something so odd as men hauling ashore a dinghy? In fact—

"Oli," Trevn voiced. *"Grayson said the enemy was carrying a dinghy ashore. I'm concerned they might try to use them to come at the castle over the lake. Be on your guard."*

"I will, Your Highness," Oli said. *"How fares the battle?"*

"They failed their first attempt to break our shield wall."

"If our men stay focused, they won't ever break it," Oli voiced, just as the entire Puru army advanced as one.

The arrows came again, still too low, followed by a frenzied infantry charge. The clash lasted longer this time, or perhaps the Puru, in their compelled state, were unable to give up.

Trevn worked his fingers, still cold despite the two pairs of gloves he wore under his gauntlets. When the Puru again retreated from the unbroken shield wall, he was unsurprised and proud of his army. Until an Armanian man ran forward, waving his sword and yelling. Two followed him, and soon men poured through a sudden gap in the wall like water from a pitcher.

"No! No!" Ensley screamed. "Hold your positions!"

"Back! Get back in position!" Marshal Winstone yelled, riding toward the rift. "Reform the wall!"

But the line continued to break as the Armanians gave chase, pursuing the fleeing Puru.

"What's happening?" Trevn asked.

"Looks like a feigned retreat," Ensley said. "General Agoros is well-known for them. One of our men fell for it, broke the wall, and led a pursuit. Unfortunately those around them joined in like sheep."

Sure enough, the fleeing Puru suddenly wheeled around and brandished their spears to a surprised Armanian infantry. The two sides collided in a melee.

Trevn stared at the dark mass of the two armies locked in combat. In mere seconds men were collapsing into the snow, and what once had been a field of pristine white become mottled with bodies and blood. The sun cast spears of light across the leaden sky, which was now dropping fat snowflakes upon the scene.

"It's time, Your Highness," Ensley said, "if you still wish to ride with the cavalry."

Trevn spurred Seeker forward, his guardsmen riding on either side. He had just kicked the horse into a canter when Grayson's breathless voice burst into his mind.

"Lady Eudora is locked in her cabin aboard the ship, Your Highness, but Sârah Jemesha is in a dinghy."

"Crossing the lake?"

"Yes, sir. She had her men carry some dinghies over land and ice and put into the lake. I'm sorry, but they are approaching the castle from behind."

As Trevn had feared. He growled his frustration. If only he had thought to ask about his aunt sooner. *"How many, Grayson? And how close are they to the castle?"*

"There are thirty-two in her boat. Six boats total. I can't see how close they are to the castle because the snow is so thick."

"Go to the boathouse and see if it has been breached."

"Yes, Your Highness."

Where had they gotten additional men? *"Oli,"* Trevn voiced as his horse carried him toward the melee. *"Your mother and nearly two hundred men are coming to see you by way of the lake. Be ready to receive them."*

Then he lifted his sword and yelled, "Defend this land for Armania!"

⊙Li

That Oli's mother might have used him to give false information to the king . . . He should have known better. They all should have.

He squinted through the falling snow, straining to see out over the surface of Lake Arman. Looking through his grow lens did not help. "I see no sign of anyone," he said.

Captain Veralla stood beside him. "Could be they're still too far out."

"*Where are my mother's boats now?*" Oli voiced Grayson.

"*One moment, Your Grace, and I will check.*"

Anger pulsed through Oli's chest. "*I thought you were in my mother's boat.*"

"*The king asked me to check the boathouse,*" Grayson said.

Oli expelled his frustration in a puff of cloudy breath. "Fool boy left the boat."

"The guards are at their posts," Veralla said. "No one can breach the castle."

Oli knew that, but he also knew his mother. The woman's tenacity had no limit. "What if she has evenroot?"

"Master Grayson said he disposed of it all."

Oli highly doubted that his mother would have agreed to attack the castle without magic. His father might take such risks, but she would not.

"*They're still in the boats,*" Grayson said. "*I can't see the castle yet. Just snow and fog.*"

Good enough. For now. "*Thank you, Master Grayson. Please stay in my mother's boat.*" He remembered his rank and added, "*Unless the king has further need of you.*"

"*I will, sir.*"

Oli relayed the update to Captain Veralla.

"Then there is nothing to fear," the man said. "Why not go inside and warm yourself while you wait?"

Oli was not the type to sit while men were dying. He wished he could have gone with the king to the battlefield, but he did no good standing here in the wet snow. He turned suddenly, sending a gust of icy air up his cloak, and strode inside the castle. He followed the circular staircase down to the third floor and entered the council chambers. Danek Faluk and Lord Idez had gone to fight, so Barek Hadar was entertaining the women alone. Rosârahs Mielle and Zeroah, Lady Brisa, and three maids sat around one end of the table, talking softly to each other. Lady Pia stood near the door with Bero and Zeroah's guards.

Oli's entrance captured their attention, and Rosârah Mielle stood.

"Any sign of them?" she asked.

"Not yet. Master Grayson is in my mother's boat. He will notify me when the castle comes into view."

"The king has entered the battle," Barek said. "He voiced the queen."

From the sober mood, this must have been the topic of conversation prior to his arrival.

"I sense his fear," Rosârah Mielle said, "though he's trying not to show it."

Oli gaped at the woman, embarrassed on behalf of the king that she would say such a thing aloud. "Fear is a perfectly normal reaction," he said, "like breathing, or jumping when one is surprised. It's what a man does with his fear that makes him brave, and we know our king does not back down from a challenge. Besides, the battle rage will come over him soon enough."

"What is battle rage?" Rosârah Zeroah asked, her golden eyes fixed on his.

Oli circled the table. "It often claims a man in the midst of war, energizes him, makes him eager to kill lest he be killed himself." He took hold of the queen's chair and nodded to it.

"*Eager* to kill?" Mielle asked, sitting down. "That sounds dreadful."

"Battle rage is both horrible and a gift," Oli said. "Without it, for some, every kill becomes a moral debate. Others freeze up and fail to defend themselves. Such men are not ready for battle because they're unable to fight quickly enough, or even react to defend themselves."

The women stared at Oli with expressions of reverent horror—all but Lady Pia, who had killed as many or more than most of the soldiers would on the battlefield today.

279

A maid entered and curtsied beside Rosârah Mielle's chair. "Beg your pardon, Your Highness, but Princess Vallah is asking for you."

"Poor girl is missing her mother." The queen stood. "I'll return shortly."

"Shall I come with you?" Zeroah asked.

"No. I'll only be a moment." Mielle smiled at Oli on her way out the door. She had been almost friendly lately. He wondered what Trevn had said to inspire the change.

"Won't you sit, Your Grace?" Zeroah asked.

"I prefer to stand." The women were staring, so he went on, wanting to say something positive after his macabre speech. "We are fortunate to have this new magic," he said. "That we can communicate with the battlefield from here is an incredible asset."

"Indeed, Your Grace, you are right about that," Barek said. "A blessing, indeed."

"You seem worried, Your Grace," Zeroah said to Oli.

Lest she try to pull forth his memories, he checked his shields and found them solid. "I'm anxious to stop whatever madness my mother has planned." He paced to the opposite end of the table. "That she omitted her part in the attack tells me she knew I would not side with her—that I would tell Rosâr Trevn all she had—"

A woman's scream sounded out in the hall. *The queen.* Oli tore out of the chamber but saw no one. He ran around the circular landing, glancing into each open door he passed by.

"Your Highness?" he yelled.

No answer came.

He reached out with his mind-speak ability, sensed the rosârah's mind, and easily pushed inside. *"Your Highness, are you well?"*

Her thoughts were blank.

Gods, don't let her be dead. The king would never forgive him. Oli fisted the railing and looked down into the curving stairwell. No sign of anyone.

"She does not answer my knock," Zeroah said, coming to stand beside him.

Oli glanced back to the council chambers. Everyone had come out into the corridor.

"Where is Princess Vallah's chamber?" he asked Zeroah.

"Upstairs," she said, starting toward the landing. "On the fourth floor."

Bero raced up the stairs. By the time Oli caught up, the guard was kneeling on the floor beside a woman. Lady Pia.

"Is she dead?" Oli asked.

"No, sir," Bero said. "But something is strange."

Pia's eyes were open, staring at nothing. Oli could hear her breathing, see the rise and fall of her chest, but she did not respond.

"There's a mantic in the castle," Oli said. His mother, likely.

A series of distant screams drifted up from below. Oli flew back to the stairs. Rosârah Zeroah, who had just reached the top, turned back, but Oli lunged forward and caught her arm. "Stay with Duke Odarka while I see what's happening."

She tugged her arm away. "I will not."

"We are at the castle!" Grayson's voice burst into Oli's mind. *"I don't know how. One moment we were in the middle of the lake, the next we were coming alongside the dock. The guards were loyal to your mother, but then she changed and isn't your mother anymore."*

"You're not making any sense, boy," Oli voiced as he watched Zeroah escape down the stairs. *"What did my mother change?"*

"I think she put a mask of herself on one of her maids. Her shadir must have seen me."

"Find my mother, Grayson." The boy should be able to travel to her in a thought.

"I just did," Grayson voiced. *"She's in the great hall. She has Queen Mielle with her."*

Oli's heart sank. Mother must have come here to capture Rosârah Mielle while Father led his army against the Armanian force. How would Oli manage to—?

"Who is watching the queen?" Trevn voiced.

"I am, Your Highness." And Oli sprinted to his room on the fourth floor. If he was going to fight, he would need his shield.

TREVn

The charge slowed once it reached the melee. Thick snow flurries blinded Trevn, and he steered Seeker through the throng, cutting down any Puru he happened upon. The great cacophony of voices yelling battle cries and shouts of pain shocked Trevn. His world was usually quite silent. He tried not to think about what might be happening to Mielle in the castle. The burst of fear he'd felt from her through the soul-binding combined with the tumult of emotions around him was so intense, he shielded his mind. Oli would take care of her.

"Enemy archers firing again, Your Highness," Miss Onika voiced.

Trevn lifted his shield overhead, which cleared the snowy onslaught from his eyes. From the back of the Puru army, another volley of arrows shot toward them.

"Shields up!" he yelled, ducking behind his own and praying the arrows missed his horse.

The narrow shafts streaked out of the blizzard. One struck Trevn's shield with enough force to knock him backward. He caught hold of the pommel on his saddle and barely kept his seat. He spurred Seeker onward, eager to reach the bowmen before they could reload. Folly, he realized soon enough, as even poor archers could be quick to draw.

Again Miss Onika warned of arrows, and again Trevn called for shields. He somehow reached the line of archers and cleaved through a bow about to fire. The taut wood snapped under the force of his blade, and its wielder fled. Trevn let the man go and turned his sword to the archer on his right.

A group of Puru infantry swarmed the horses, jabbing spikes into the animals and their riders. Trevn chopped his blade over a Puru soldier's arm. As the man's hand and spear separated from the rest of him, something sharp glanced off Trevn's right shin. He whipped around, instinctively pushing out his shield. He struck a man's head and sent him sprawling into the mass of bodies.

Another Puru jabbed a pike into Seeker, causing the animal to rear. Trevn held on but his legs slipped. When Seeker returned to all fours, the force knocked Trevn off. He hit the ground on his left side and slid a few feet in the icy slush. Cold gripped his skin from thigh to waist. He scrambled to his feet and barely managed to block a pike coming at his head. The impact knocked him to his backside. He kicked his attacker's ankles with both boots. The Puru man stumbled, and Cadoc ended his life with a sword thrust to his side. Trevn's High Shield stepped on the dead man's thigh, pulled out his sword, then hauled Trevn to standing.

"Stay . . . your feet . . . Highness!"

Trevn could barely hear him over the screams and din of clashing weapons.

Cadoc shifted to block an attack on his right. Trevn put his back to Cadoc and engaged the closest Puru soldier. The snow was falling so thickly, he could hardly tell one side from the other. Only the pale faces set apart the enemy.

Trevn fought for his life, knowing full well he could be cut down. He wanted to call to Oli and ask about Mielle, but instead, he voiced Miss Onika. *"Have Sir Jarmyn's men reached General Agoros yet?"*

"I will check, Your Highness."

The two armies hacked, stabbed, and thrust at each other, clambering over the bodies of the slain. One by one the Armanians felled the poorly trained natives.

"The officers are still in the wagon," Miss Onika voiced. *"Sir Jarmyn and a large group of soldiers are riding to the north."*

"What!" Trevn dodged the thrust of a spear, then jabbed his sword into the neck of the man holding it. With a violent tug he jerked his sword free, the tang coated in red. Revulsion burst within him, but he reached for Sir Jarmyn's mind, found it, and forced himself inside. *"Sir Jarmyn, you not only defy direct orders to lead an ambush against General Agoros, you flee the battlefield like a coward? Believe that all of Armania will know of this."*

A mixture of confusion and humiliation filled Sir Jarmyn's mind. Trevn shoved away from the deserter, dodged the thrust of another spear, and found the mind of a more trustworthy man.

"Sir Keshton," he voiced, again taking his listener by surprise. *"Circle the*

melee and attack General Agoros. Take your best archers and make sure the general is defeated."

"Yes, Your Highness, right away."

Someone plowed into Trevn's back. He stumbled headfirst toward a bout between an Armanian and Puru. He stabbed his sword into the slush, pushed his weight against the pommel, and slid around, reversing his direction. He ran back toward where he'd been, tripped on something buried under the snow, and kicked up the shaft of a broken pike.

The majority of the Armanian line still stood, defending the hill. As more of the Puru attackers fell, many of their comrades fled, first in singles and pairs, then in larger groups. They always turned back, however, as their compulsion gave them no choice. Their uneven behavior quickly landed them in a rout. Many slipped or stumbled helplessly down the slope that had become slick with bloody slush. Trevn saw firsthand the value of Cadoc's warning to stay on one's feet as the Armanians assaulted the downed pale natives. Most of those who did manage to keep their feet were killed by Armanian cavalry still on horseback.

A moment of calm settled over Trevn. He blinked away sweat and melted snow from his eyes and panted, dazed to suddenly have no one to fight. His shin throbbed. A Puru man lay dead before him, his torso and legs crushed under a fallen horse.

"Your Highness!" Out of the blizzard, Cadoc slogged toward him. "Stay close. Here comes another group."

They moved together, engaging any Puru who crossed their path. Trevn parried dozens of stabs from pikes and chopped his blade over as many or more shafts. He killed one man with a lunge of his sword, another when he sliced his blade into a man's shoulder.

The cold faded, as did the sting on his shin. He no longer knew pain or feeling of any kind. He fought on, slaying men as if harvesting wheat. His actions seemed impossible for his skill or strength, and he began to move instinctually, knowing only that he must kill or be killed.

OLI

Oli's shield was not on the hook where he'd left it. He glanced at his bed, the floor underneath, in front of the sideboard, along the wall under the window, beside the—

"It this what you're looking for?"

The door to his wardrobe opened slowly, and his father stepped out, holding Oli's shield. A quick toss and it smacked on the floor in front of Oli's boots.

How could the man be here? Oli snatched up the shield, keeping his eyes on his father's. "You're not on the battlefield?"

"Sir Briden is fully capable," Father said. "And I can take the castle without an army."

Oli put together the pieces. "You're using the battle as a distraction."

"It got the king and his army out of my way, did it not?"

"As a general, you should be on the battlefield instead of sneaking into the castle like a coward and abandoning your compelled innocents to their fate."

Father's eyes lit. "You dare call me a coward?"

"Rebels might be heroes, Father, but traitors will always be cowards. Why are you in my chambers if you've come to take the castle?"

The man curled his lip. "Your mother believes you will join us. I knew better, of course, but because she wishes it, I promised I'd give you one last chance to switch your allegiance."

"I made my choice. I will not change my mind."

Father drew his sword, letting the tang scrape menacingly against its scabbard. "Then I'm afraid you must die, my son."

285

"Your Grace?" The door swung inward and Rosârah Zeroah stepped into the room. "Oh, General Agoros, I—"

"Rosârah," Oli said, "would you ask Captain Veralla to send some guards to escort my father to the dungeons?"

"Yes, of course." She turned and ran.

"That won't be necessary." Father slashed his blade through the air in a quick warning. Oli flinched but held his ground. "I will leave this engagement as acting lord of this castle," his father declared.

"Unless I kill you."

"With one arm?"

Oli unfastened his wooden arm and dropped it on the floor. Then he looped the shield's strap over his head and pushed his stump against the brace until it squeezed into the groove. He stepped back and drew his sword in his left hand.

Father grinned. "I would very much like to see how you manage this great feat." He raised his blade and stepped forward, swiping lightly. Oli stepped back and parried. Father sent another well-aimed strike. Again Oli back-stepped, parried.

Father was forcing him toward the door and jabbed his next strike deep enough it could have passed through Oli's middle. Oli whacked his shield against the blade, deflecting the blow. The force knocked him into the doorframe. He stumbled through the exit and onto the circular landing. Zeroah watched from the stairs, one hand on the rail. Her guards were ascending the steps toward her, both with swords drawn.

"It seems you shall have witnesses to your death, my son," Father said. "I'm glad of it. I wouldn't want anyone to doubt your bravery. Or your loyalty."

"You want help, Your Grace?" Doth asked.

Oli gritted his teeth. "Only in carrying away his dead body."

Father chuckled. "Always the dreamer." He lunged, Oli parried, and though it had been many years since they'd sparred, they fell into a familiar rhythm. Father pressed his attack hard, pushing Oli around the circular walkway. Oli focused on defense, hoping to tire his father. They completed the circle, and when they returned to the landing, Oli drove forward, swiped his blade in from the side, and bashed his shield into his father's chest.

Father escaped by backstepping up the stairs that led to the fifth floor. Oli struck hard with sword and shield, knocking his father back against the stairs.

Oli tried to sneak in a jab, but a twist of the wrist and Father locked the guards of their swords from his reclined position. He grimaced and thrust forward, pushing to his feet. Oli's one arm was no match for Father's two, and his father easily shoved Oli back into the open.

Oli parried and parried. The heel of his boot snagged on the edge of a carpet and he tripped. Father's blade sliced his left shoulder, and Oli stumbled back against the wall. Father pressed forward, and they locked guards again, bodies close, only Oli's shield between them.

"Bleeding already." Father tsked at the spot of blood swelling on the shoulder of Oli's shirt. "You should have let Barthos finish you off. Was this extra year of life really worth it?"

Oli yelled and shoved out his shield, managing to break free.

"What did it gain you, really?" Father asked. "You saved Sâr Wilek's life two times and still he was killed. One cannot thwart the plans of the gods."

"When I meet the gods, at least I'll have honor," Oli said. "What will you have?"

"Riches," Father said. "And favor."

They moved faster, the swords a haze between them. The sound of Zeroah's voice startled him. Was she trying to tell him something? As they circled close and her words rose above the clash of the weapons, he realized she was praying.

Her loyalty bolstered Oli, and he gave everything he had. To his great surprise, his blade suddenly slipped past Father's guard and sank into flesh. Father dropped his sword, which clattered against the marble floor. Doth ran and picked it up.

Father lifted both hands, eyes focused on the tang of Oli's sword where it was embedded in his stomach. "You proved me wrong." His words were tight, pained. "While I'm embarrassed to have underestimated you, I'm exceedingly proud that my son bested me. And with only one hand!" Father fell to his knees, dragging down Oli's arm, as he still gripped his sword.

Oli winced and pulled back. The blade slid out, the flat slick and red.

Father's forehead wrinkled. "Tell your mother I went bravely?"

Something moved on the edge of Oli's vision. Captain Veralla and two guardsmen, standing side by side with Doth, all with swords drawn.

Father collapsed, and Oli moved back, overcome.

The guards converged upon Father's body. One removed his belt and tossed it on the floor, while the other checked him for more weapons. No point in that. He was no threat now.

"Captain Veralla," Oli said, eyes fixed upon his father's body. "Is the queen still in the great hall?"

"With your mother, yes. Sârah Jemesha has sixty-some guards with her, all of them Kinsman. We've killed or taken captive just as many out in the bailey. I have eighty-five of our garrison in the hallway outside the great hall and have sent a man to call the rest inside to help."

Oli tore his gaze from his father and strode to the stairwell. "Let us end this."

"Your Grace." Zeroah fell into step beside him. "Please, don't put Mielle in the middle of a battle where she might be injured." She lowered her voice. "There's a door to a secret passageway behind the curtain that divides the high table from the serving antechamber. If you could distract your mother, I could get Mielle behind the curtain and to safety."

Oli stopped midway down one of the flights of stairs. "Why did no one tell me of this passageway?"

Zeroah blinked innocently and her lips curved in a slow smile. "Because, Your Grace," she whispered, "it's a secret."

Of all the . . . "Go through the passage and wait on the other side of the curtain. Remain hidden until I tell you otherwise. Is that clear?"

"Perfectly." She fled down the stairs.

Oli followed her. *"Grayson? Can you come to the castle for a moment?"*

"Yes, sir. Which part?"

"Meet me at the bottom of the stairs on the second floor of the keep."

Rosârah Zeroah peeled away on the third floor, and Oli continued on to the second level. There he found Grayson waiting with the garrison.

"I need you to divert my mother somehow," Oli told the young man. "She is holding Rosârah Mielle in the great hall. I'll go in and speak with her. When I tell you, I want you to distract her long enough for me to help the queen escape. Can you do this?"

"Yes, sir. Shall I come with you now or wait for your signal?"

"Come now, though keep yourself invisible."

Grayson vanished. Oli stepped up to the double doors of the great hall and peeked through the crack between them. Soldiers clad in red milled about the tables. They had moved the captives along the left wall. On the dais, Oli's mother was seated in the king's chair. She wore a red formal gown and a black cape. Rosârah Mielle stood stiffly beside her, unnaturally, with her arms against her sides and a vacant expression on her face.

Oli realized he was still holding his bloodied sword. He glanced at Captain Veralla, swallowed past the tightness in his throat. "Uh . . . might I, uh . . ."

"Certainly, Your Grace." The captain took Oli's sword and traded for his clean one.

"Thank you." Oli sheathed the fresh weapon. Shield still in place, he smoothed the front of his tunic, swept his hand back over his hair, and entered the great hall.

"Mother, good midday," he called out. He let his gaze sweep the room as if seeing everything for the first time, mentally counting the guards. Captain Veralla's report seemed accurate. "I thought you were staying on the ship."

"Oli!" Mother's face lit up. "Did your father find you?"

Oli walked slowly down the center aisle. "Is Eudora here?"

"We left her on the ship where she couldn't cause trouble."

"Eudora? Can you hear me?" Oli voiced his sister as he continued up the center aisle. "She does not answer me. Why?"

"A sleeping draught," Mother said. "Had I children who loved me, I would not have to stoop to such means. Do not doubt that I can control her when the time comes."

Oli passed the center of the great hall and meandered closer to the dais. "What have you done to Rosârah Mielle? Why does she stare so?"

"My magic holds her captive." Mother held her hands out to the side as if considering a work of art not quite complete. "Don't you like how submissive she looks? When Sâr Trevn sees how we have made his wife our captive, he will renounce the throne and swear fealty to you."

"No, Mother. He will never do that."

"Then you will kill him and all this nonsense will be over."

"I would really rather not."

"Do not worry. When he sees my power, he'll have no choice but to agree to our demands."

"What power?" Oli asked, hoping to insult her. "You may have scrounged together enough root to sneak past the garrison, but I know you. Your skill is minimal at best."

"You men have always underestimated me," Mother said, scowling. She gestured at the queen. "This is magic you see before you. I also fooled that root child. He sat right beside my mask, clueless that he was following my maid."

"I'm sorry!" Grayson voiced.

Oli had no idea where the boy had hidden himself. *"Stay on guard, Grayson, and be ready for my cue."*

Oli had almost reached the dais. As he neared the front row of tables, Cles, one of Mother's guards, stepped into his path. Oli had trained with Cles when they were younger. He had no interest in fighting the man, so he turned and walked behind the front table, heading toward the right wall and the steps that led to the dais. Cles turned as well and walked along the front side of the table, a few paces behind Oli.

"At least let the queen sit," Oli said. "To keep her stiff like that . . . It's terrible manners, Mother. I expected more from someone of your good breeding."

Mother glared at Rosârah Mielle. "This common orphan deserves no noble treatment. That she would be queen of Armania is an insult to us all. My Eudora was meant to be queen. All her life she trained for that role. She should have married Sâr Janek. They were beautiful together. Filled with grace and poise."

And deceit and selfishness and cruelty and a bit of insanity. "Janek would have been a terrible king. And Eudora never wanted to be queen. She didn't even wish to marry."

"She would have done as she was told," Mother said.

The distant clicking of approaching hobnails signaled the arrival of the rest of the garrison. Oli bounded past Cles and up the stairs to the dais, eager to make his move before the great hall became a war zone.

Cles followed like a shadow, twice as wide and three times as ugly.

Oli reached his mother and bowed. "I'm afraid I bring bad tidings."

"Now, Grayson," he voiced.

Grayson appeared behind Oli's mother, grabbed the hem of her cloak, then vanished only to reappear in front of her, still holding the cloak, which he twisted over her head.

Mother screamed, tangled in her cloak. Oli lunged around her to the queen. He crouched and grabbed her around the legs with his arm. "Hold tight, Your Highness. I'll get you out of here." He lifted her, hoping she'd fall over his shoulder, but she remained stiff from the spell.

The magic would likely wear off once it faded from Mother's system, but that could be days. Mother, who was still screaming. Grayson had somehow pulled the bottom corners of the cloak around to her back and tied them behind her. She looked as if she had a potato sack over her head. Oli carried the queen awkwardly behind the throne and toward the curtain.

Cles stepped in his way, sword drawn. "Release her, Your Grace."

"Grayson! Distract my pursuer. Rosârah Zeroah, open your secret door. I'm coming."

Grayson appeared between Oli and Cles, holding a pitcher, which he heaved forward, dousing the soldier in a stream of red wine.

Oli hobbled past Cles and into the curtain. He pushed against it, struggling to find the center opening, and might never have made it through had Grayson not pulled the curtain aside to make way. The serving antechamber had only four torches in wall sconces to offer light. Oli strained to find Zeroah in the dimness.

"Here, Your Grace."

He walked toward the sound of her voice, and together they moved the queen into the dark passage. Some five or six paces in, Zeroah dropped the queen's feet and went back to the door. She pulled it shut, and everything went black.

Zeroah's voice rose out of the blackness. "Are you well, Your Grace? Your shoulder?"

Mention of his shoulder wound brought attention to its sting. Oli had forgotten all about it. His father had stabbed him. And he had killed his father. He swallowed as emotion threatened to overtake him. "Yes, I'm fine."

"I'm thankful for that," Zeroah said. "And very sorry about your parents."

Father dead. And Mother would surely be executed. Oli did not want to think about them. "I must message the king now."

"Yes, of course."

"Your Highness?" Oli voiced to Trevn. *"Your wife is safe."*

But while he was able to sense the king's mind, he received no answer.

TREVN

One dead, then another and another. Trevn must kill or be killed. A man came at him with a spear. Trevn plunged his blade into the man's stomach, elbowed him, and jerked free his blade. When no more attacked, he searched those writhing on the ground, finishing all he could.

"Your Highness!"

Trevn spun around, sword out, ready to strike. Someone grabbed his wrist from behind and disarmed him. A second attacker wiped snow over his face. Trevn screamed and tried to throw a punch, but several men seized his limbs and pushed him to his back on the ground, holding him down. They heaped snow over his chest and throat. The cold shocked, and he struggled until he could think of nothing but cold.

"Trevn!" An icy hand slapped his face. The touch of skin on skin jolted his mind into the present. "Look at me. At my eyes."

Trevn shifted his gaze to the man half kneeling on his chest. The concern on that familiar face washed over him. "Cadoc?" His voice came out hoarse, throat sore from yelling. The stench of sweat and blood and horses filled his nostrils. The battle.

Fear rushed him and he thrashed, wanting to be on his feet, sword in hand so he could protect himself. "Get off me!" he shouted. "Let me up! I must fight!"

Cadoc slid off Trevn. "Calm, Your Highness. The fighting is over. We've won."

"Over?" Trevn pushed himself to sitting. Three paces away, a dead horse stared at him, its eyes glassy as the snow melted on their surface. That he couldn't recall what had happened unnerved him. Hair hung over his eyes and he pushed it away. He'd lost his helm. "Was I struck in the head?"

"I removed your helm, Your Highness," Cadoc said, motioning to Rzasa, who held the bronze piece under one arm. "You lost yourself to the battle rage there toward the end."

Trevn's cheeks grew suddenly warm. He felt ashamed to have lost himself when he was supposed to be leading.

Cadoc stood and extended his hand. Trevn took hold, and his High Shield hoisted him to his feet. Trevn's legs felt like custard. He had never felt so weary, even after awakening from days of sleeping draughts after his hand had been crushed.

He walked out from the cluster of guardsmen, wanting some space to work his aching legs. He surveyed the killing field, a vast bloody stain on a white plain scattered with corpses and discarded weapons. Some of the bodies jerked or heaved, resisting as death fought to take them. Some moaned, choked, gasped. Some wept.

Most lay still.

A weight pressed upon Trevn's heart as he regarded the immense loss of Puru life. It brought him no joy, knowing the natives had been pawns used by a coward. And how many Armanians were among the dead? That they might have all lived seemed impossible, though Trevn saw none at first glance and hoped against logic that all had survived.

"Oli?" He suddenly wondered about his First Arm and how his wife fared, for while he could sense her presence, he still could not hear her thoughts. When the duke didn't answer right away, fear flitted through his mind that Oli had in fact chosen to betray him.

But then, *"Yes, Your Highness?"*

Trevn berated himself for doubting the man. *"My wife?"*

"My mother put a spell on her that will likely remain until the root wears off or is purged. But the queen is safe, Your Highness, and will recover fully."

Immense relief brought tears to Trevn's eyes. He turned from his men and blinked them away. *"And the castle?"*

"Secure," Oli replied and then explained all that had taken place. They had almost been outmaneuvered, but Arman had been with them.

"How many of our garrison did we lose?"

"Thirty-one, Your Highness."

Thirty-one. *"And how many of theirs died?"*

"Of the one hundred forty-three that entered the castle, fifty-two were killed."

Such low numbers compared to what Trevn looked upon. *"Thank you, Your*

Grace." Trevn ended the connection. He felt oddly hopeful despite standing in a field of bloody snow. He watched his men carry bodies toward one of two piles: pales to his left, Kinsman to his right. At first glance he guessed the Puru had died twenty to one.

A Puru man sat on the bloody field, clutching an arrow that protruded from his stomach and mumbling in his native tongue.

"Nu naawakna-qa niina," he said, then repeated it.

"Grayson?" Trevn voiced. *"A Puru man is saying 'Nu naawakna-qa niina.' What does it mean?"*

"'I don't want to kill.'"

The words sobered Trevn to the point of shame. Had his people not landed in Er'Rets, the Puru people would never have suffered such atrocities. *Arman, forgive us, though we don't deserve it. And have mercy on the Puru victims of this war we brought to their land.*

Trevn wandered the field, mourning the loss of so many innocents. He stepped on something that jerked under his boot. He jumped back as a Kinsman man covered in snow tried to sit up. Trevn recognized him from the battle. Dark blood glistened on his torso all around where a spear had impaled his chest. Someone had broken off the end.

"Help me," he croaked.

Trevn knelt and took hold of his hand. It seemed clear that the man would die soon. "You fought well," he said. "Help is here."

"My king," he said. "I fought for you."

"I thank you. You are very brave."

Trevn sat with the man until he died. Then he wept. He was wet with blood. It had spattered and seeped and soaked him as much as the snow, though none of it seemed to be his.

"Here come some traitors, Your Highness," Cadoc said.

Trevn stood and regarded the approaching soldiers. Captain Veralla's sons, Sir Keshton and his brother Zanre, and three other Kinsman soldiers were leading four men this way. Trevn recognized one as Sir Briden.

"We captured them trying to flee around the lake," Sir Keshton said. "There was no sign of the general, I'm afraid."

"Because General Agoros was not on the battlefield today," Trevn said, eyeing Sir Briden's general's uniform. "He bade Sir Briden act as his decoy while he breached the castle. But he and his men failed. All who are not dead will be soon."

"He's a coward," Sir Keshton said. "To leave his army to fight without him."

A great deal of Kinsman soldiers had gathered round. Trevn knew what he must do, though it took effort to make himself speak. "Execute these men," he said, following the order with a deep breath. "As to the rest of you, soldiers of Armania, you are all as brave as any general. I am glad to know you and proud to have fought beside you. Thank you for risking your lives for our great realm and our great God."

The men cheered, and Trevn again had to choke back his emotions. He felt as weak as a newborn babe, completely spent both physically and mentally. He had done the best he could. Time would tell if it had made a difference in how the nobles saw him. For now, Castle Armanguard was safe, though he doubted it would be long before Barthel Rogedoth marched upon them. Trevn could only pray that they would be ready when that day came.

GRAYSON

The aftermath of the battle would take days to recover from, but one of the king's first decisions was that they could not get caught off guard again. They needed any information on what Barthel Rogedoth's plans might be, so the order was given for Grayson to rescue his grandmother.

Much had happened since his last visit. Grayson worried she wouldn't want to come. That she'd be too angry that he'd helped in the attack against her daughter.

When he arrived inside Lady Islah's tent, he could see better than last time. The sun shone down on the canvas and bathed everything in a rusty orange glow. Lady Islah sat hugging her knees to her chest and rocking. The chains that held her ankles grated against themselves.

The chains. How foolish to have forgotten. If Grayson carried her away, would she be hurt? Maybe he should go back to Armanguard and carry a locksmith here?

He might as well talk to her first. He entered the physical realm. "Hello, Grandmother."

She twitched, turned her head slightly, but continued rocking.

"Are you all right?"

She grunted. "No different than usual."

Had she not heard about her daughter's death? Well, Grayson wasn't going to tell her. "I, uh . . . I've come to rescue you. I mean, if you want to go."

She stopped moving and turned her big golden eyes his way. "Is that so?"

"Yes, ma'am. It might be risky, so I'll understand if you don't want to try."

Those eyes narrowed. "Risky how?"

"Well, you've seen how I can move about. It turns out I can carry a person with me. But I'm worried about your chains. What if they can't come with us and they . . . um, they . . ." He paused, not wanting to say "*rip off your feet.*"

"Oh dear."

Good. She seemed to understand.

She fingered the chains. "Steal the keys, then you have no worries."

Grayson perked up. "You know where the keys are?"

"On Perchard's belt."

That shouldn't be too hard. "Be right back." Grayson thought about the gray-haired man with the red cloak and popped into the Veil. He found Perchard pacing between the king's tent and Lady Islah's. A faint clinking brought Grayson's attention to a set of keys hanging off the man's belt, opposite his longsword. Grayson could take the keys easily enough, but Perchard might come into Lady Islah's tent or call for help before they could get the chains off.

A better idea came to mind. Grayson popped behind the guard, grabbed him around the waist, and carried him through the Veil to the back side of the New Rurekan castle. He released him on the riverbank and snatched the keys off his belt.

Perchard staggered back from the water's edge. "What in the Five Realms . . . ?"

Grayson popped away before the man could see him. He returned to his grandmother's tent, sank to his knees beside her, and handed her the keys.

"Where's Perchard?" she asked.

"I carried him to the Rurekan castle. We have plenty of time now."

Lady Islah chuckled. "You're a clever one, aren't you?"

They worked together and managed to unlock the chains. Lady Islah released a cry and pushed to her feet. "Oh, legs. The slave hasn't done much walking in a long while." She took hold of his arm. "I'm ready."

Grayson focused on King Trevn's office in Armanguard and felt himself shift. He jerked through the Veil and stopped just outside the tent. Grandmother was heavy! Grayson moved slower when carrying people, but no one had ever had so much weight before. And from such a skinny lady too. Scared he might lose her, he grabbed her around the waist and tried again.

The journey went very slowly, as if Grayson were leaping like a stag. He jumped over barren fields, snowy hills, and thick forests. The ground seemed to pull at him, as if wanting him to stay. He grew weary and thought about stopping to rest. King Trevn voiced him to see what was taking so long. Grayson explained as best he could, then kept on, determined to finish.

The moment they reached the council chambers in Armanguard, Grayson released his grandmother and sank cross-legged to the floor. King Trevn had been waiting, along with Jhorn, Rosârah Brelenah, Cadoc, and three more guardsmen.

Grandmother cackled. "You did it, my boy! You broke the spell of a great." She kissed the top of his head and mussed his hair. "How strong your magic must be! The slave never thought it possible to be free from Dendron."

Grayson didn't understand what Dendron had to do with anything, but he liked seeing his grandmother so joyful. "What do you mean?"

"They didn't just lock up the slave," she said. "There were compulsions binding the slave to that place. You broke all those spells!"

Was that why it had been so hard to move?

"Aunt Islah?" Rosârah Brelenah stepped forward and extended her hand.

Grandmother took in the other people in the room. Her eyes shone as she paused on the former queen. "Brelenah. How lovely you look, after all these years."

The two women embraced and started crying. Grayson never understood why women cried when they were happy. "If Grandmother is related to Rosârah Brelenah, why can't she speak with the voices?"

"Lady Islah is Rosârah Brelenah's aunt through marriage to Rogedoth," the king said, "—er, to Prince Mergest, I mean. She does not have royal blood."

Ah. That made sense, then.

"Why did he do this?" Rosârah Brelenah said, stepping back from the hug.

"You mustn't blame him alone," Grandmother said.

"But I do!" Brelenah said. "We all do!"

"Could the slave have a chair, please?" Grandmother asked. "And some water?"

Trevn motioned to one of the guards, who pulled out a chair at the table, then went to the sideboard and poured a cup of water.

Brelenah helped Grandmother sit down. "Why do you call yourself a slave, Aunt Islah?"

"It's what I was. What I am. For so long. Too long."

Brelenah took the water from the guard and gave it to Grandmother. "No longer. You are free now. And safe."

Grandmother's face crumpled, and it looked like she was going to cry again. She sniffled the tears away, though, and took a sip of water. "Well, Grayson? Where are your manners? Are you going to introduce the slave—your grandmother—to the rest of these people?"

"Yes, ma'am." Grayson did his best to make formal introductions all around, though Sir Cadoc had to supply the names of the guards.

"We believed you long dead, lady," the king said. "When Hinckdan Faluk told me he found you in Rogedoth's prison, I knew we needed to try to free you."

"For the slave's sake?" she asked. "Or so the slave can tell you all Mergest's secrets?"

The king blinked. "Um, in all honesty, madam, both."

Grandmother's face wrinkled in a huge grin. "Been a while since the slave met an honest king. Very well, young sir, the slave can tell you much about the man you call *Rogedoth*."

She proceeded to talk about the mantics who worked with her husband. There were surnames like Modim, Jervaid, Rolan, and Borid, which Grayson had never heard of, but he recognized Edekk, Wallington, Koll, Nafni, Yohthehreth, Lau, and Agoros. She talked of which mantics were the strongest, which shadir were the most powerful, and which nobles Rogedoth still spoke to. And while it seemed to Grayson that some of those she mentioned were dead—like Fonu Edekk, Kamran DanSâr, and Canbek Faluk—others were very much alive.

"He communicates with Tace Edekk still?" the king asked.

"Oh, yes. Through shadir. The duke's son is a mantic, you know. As is his servant."

"I knew Fonu was a mantic," the king said. "But which servant do you mean?"

Grandmother's eyes bulged. "You expect the slave to remember a servant's name?"

The king winced. "I hoped you might."

She sighed and glanced at the ceiling. "You know, I think he was called Natad."

"*Natod?*" the king asked.

"That's what I said. Oh, and one more thing. Lady Zenobia is his second in command. Always has been."

"Thank you," the king said. "I very much appreciate your help."

"Would you tell us your story?" Rosârah Brelenah asked. "How this all came to happen?"

"The slave—" She paused, shook her head, and started over. "*I* discovered mantics a few months before I turned fifteen. Sarikar had strict rules about such things, but I fought those rules, pushed against the boundaries, and all my wild living eventually led to my bonding with a shadir. Oh, I tell you, it was fun—at first. I married Mergest on my ageday and quickly pulled him into my world. My power was immense. Shadir came to me constantly, begging me to leave my bonded and choose them. I upgraded steadily, until one day, a great shadir came. Dendron, he was called. His glory and might went straight to my head. When I bonded with Dendron, I not only won him, I won an entire swarm."

Grayson couldn't believe it. He had expected to hear that his grandmother had been an innocent captive of Rogedoth's, not that she served Dendron.

"For many years Dendron and I did plenty of damage," Grandmother said, "until my children were born and softened my heart. I wanted to give them a home with loving parents and the chance to find their own way in the world, apart from magic. Dendron advised against such sentiments, of course. And Mergest saw our girls as assets to get revenge upon his father. He and Dendron developed a plan to marry one of the girls to King Echad. The best way to do this, they decided, was to secretly give our girls to the Nafni family to adopt as their own. This would give them a noble name so they might have opportunity to meet the king. Well, I forbade it. No one would take my girls away. Mergest and I fought about it for months, until one day, he and Dendron conspired against me. They locked me up, and when I cast spells to get free, Dendron ignored them. He preferred Mergest's ambition to my love, and so they have continued to use me all these years. So many years. Lost. Darlis lost, and now Laviel too."

"You knew about Laviel?" Grayson asked.

She nodded, and a tear rolled down one cheek. "Dendron told me."

"He still speaks with you?" King Trevn asked. "Even after Rogedoth stole him away?"

"Oh, Mergest didn't steal Dendron," Grandmother said. "The great has always been mine."

"But why didn't Dendron bond with Master Rogedoth if they liked each other so much?" Grayson asked.

"Because, dear boy, your grandfather is a malleant. He cannot wield magic at all."

Hinck

Hinck studied Castle Armanguard for the first time as the barge carried Bahlay Nesos and him across the lake. He felt like he might be in a dream. His journey here had been long, and many times he'd thought he might never make it, but now the structure seemed to float impossibly on the water in front of him. How in sands had they built such a thing?

They disembarked on the other side and were met at the gatehouse by Bahlay's son, Maleen. Hinck witnessed their joyful reunion but didn't understand a word as they chattered on in their native tongue. Longing for a few reunions of his own, Hinck left Bahlay with his son and walked through the inner bailey and into the keep. An impressive circular staircase wound up through the center of the fat tower. A maid informed him that the royal court was assembled for the midday meal in the great hall on the second floor. Hinck climbed up a level to a breezeway that circled the stairwell. Doors led off at somewhat evenly spaced intervals. Opposite the landing, a short hallway stretched to a set of double doors.

Hinck paused outside, wondering how many knew he had been a spy and how many still thought him a traitor for his actions aboard the *Seffynaw* that day so long ago, when he had appeared to be an accomplice in taking Rosârah Zeroah hostage.

He finally entered the great hall and took in the scene. Trevn and Mielle sat center front at the high table. How strange to see his closest friend not only married but king of the realm. A year ago, Trevn never would have believed such a thing possible, yet tragically, here they were. Also seated at the high table were rosârahs Brelenah and Zeroah, the sârahs, and Oli Agoros. Hinck made his way up the center aisle. Halfway there, Trevn saw him and stood.

"All hail Hinckdan Faluk," Trevn crowed, raising his goblet, "Earl of Dacre, hero of the realm, whom I now name Duke of Armanguard and my Second Arm."

A rumble rose among the crowd, and Hinck beamed at Trevn's high praise. With a shout from a table in the front right of the hall, his father came running toward him, Mother on his heels. Hinck continued on, choked up more than he wanted to admit in front of so large an audience. Father embraced him with such a force, the stitches in his side throbbed.

"My son, my son, come home at last." Father took Hinck's face between his palms and stared into his eyes. "I am so very proud of you, my boy." Then he shouted to the crowd, "My son is home!" A scattered cheer rose up. It seemed not everyone understood what was happening.

Mother kissed him over and over, her face streaked in tears. "What that woman did to your face . . ." Her thumbs brushed over his burn scars. "You still look as handsome as any prince. Doesn't he, Dan?"

"He looks like a hero come home from his very important task of saving the realm."

Trevn appeared and threw his arm around Hinck's shoulders. "Never again will I send you on such an assignment. A year and a half it's nearly been since I first asked you to infiltrate Janek's retinue."

"You really were on to something there, telling me to follow Eudora," Hinck said.

"Only by lucky accident, my friend," Trevn said.

"You kept us in the dark for far too long," Mother said. "You have no idea how much I worried that you had gone off your head."

"She made offerings to Cetheria every day those first few months you spent with Janek," Father said.

Mother took his hand. "I was terrified Rosârah Laviel would take you from me."

"Don't mention that woman's name after what he's been through," Father said.

"I am well, Father," Hinck said. "Arman was with me."

"Well said, my son." Father beamed with such admiration, Hinck began to choke up again.

"Come sit with me at the high table," Trevn said. "I want to hear the story again, this time from your mouth, not your mind. Duke Highcliff, Duchess, you're welcome to join us."

Father waved him off. "Enjoy yourself, my son. We will talk with you later."

Mother embraced him again, then Hinck followed Trevn up to the high table, where a chair had been wedged in between Trevn's throne and where Duke Canden sat.

Hinck removed his cloak and handed it to a servant, then sat down. He nodded to Duke Canden. "How fare you, Your Grace?"

"Well enough, *Your Grace*," Oli said as his gaze flickered over Hinck's scars. "Glad to see you here and whole, if not a bit worn. You've done well. How do you feel?"

"Thankful to be alive."

"I well imagine that," Oli said.

Trevn sat down and leaned back in his throne, beaming at Hinck.

Miss Mielle—Rosârah Mielle, now—leaned over her husband's lap. "Welcome home, *Duke Armanguard*," she said. "I'm so pleased to see your marvelous smile."

This made Hinck grin even wider, which he knew likely showed every tooth in his mouth. "Thank you, lady," he said. "It seems we both had a treacherous adventure."

"I not so much as you," Mielle said, her eyes flicking toward the scars on his face. "I always had an army around me, making sure I was safe."

Hinck met the golden eyes of Zeroah as she peered past Mielle and felt heat rise in his cheeks. He had voiced her a formal apology not so long ago for his part in the mutiny, but it still felt strange to see her. He nodded and said, "Hello, Rosârah."

"I too am glad to see you well, lord," she said. "Though I am grieved to hear that you were injured more than once."

"My side is a little sore," Hinck admitted, "but it is healing nicely."

"Unlike your face," Trevn said, punching his arm. "She certainly left her mark on you, didn't she?"

"Why, yes, Your Royal Rudeness, she did," Hinck said.

Trevn chuckled. "It's good to have you back, my friend."

"Waste no worry over those scars," Zeroah said. "They make you look brave."

"Oh, I agree," Mielle said. "No one will dare cross you now, and you're still quite handsome."

"Hear that, Hinck?" Trevn said. "All the ladies will be pining over you now."

Hinck flushed, wishing they would speak of something besides his scars. "Yes, well, I'll believe that when it happens."

"Recount for us all that you've been doing since arriving in Er'Rets, Your Grace," Oli said.

So Hinck told them about his life as a member of Barthel Rogedoth's trusted few. His affinity for acting made it easy to regale those at the high table with tales of the danger he had experienced as part of his mission. Princess Hrettah asked several questions, surprising Hinck by how much she'd grown. Strange how time had passed by in his absence. It seemed only yesterday that Shessy Wallington had been chasing after Trevn at the behest of Sâr Janek. Oddly enough, that very woman was sitting at a table on the floor with the other Wallingtons. Somehow Trevn and Hinck's youth had gone. Now they were both of them men. And Trevn married. And somewhat bearded.

"You must come to court," Mielle told him. "Now that things seem quiet, Trevn has permitted me to host it in the great hall. It's less than two weeks away, and I still have much to do."

"Oh, he'll come," Trevn said with a glance at Hinck. *"Arman knows I will not survive without some friends present."*

Mielle swatted Trevn's arm. "What did you say to him? I felt your sarcasm! Trevn Hadar, you'll be sorry you tease me so."

"I still think it's a waste of time," Trevn said. "Unfortunate though it sounds, the Battle of Armanguard helped my reputation with most of the nobles. I've never had so few complaints."

"Yes, only two dozen a day now, rather than ten dozen," Oli said, smirking.

"Is it really so bad?" Hinck asked.

"Oh, it's dreadful," Mielle said. "The nobles hate the *Youngling King.*"

"I prefer King Lackbeard myself," Trevn said, scratching his scruffy cheek.

As the group laughed, Hinck regarded his friend, who sat on the throne like it was any other chair. He looked weary. His eyes had a distant coldness, and he carried with him a sorrowful demeanor that Hinck had never before seen him wear. The battle, the throne, the loss of Wilek—or all three together—had brought on an incredible weight.

"The rosâr did not exaggerate about the success of the Battle of Armanguard," Oli said. "He won the loyalty of the army with how he dealt with the attack."

"Only with Duke Canden's help," Trevn said, then voiced, *"I truly had no idea what to do. If Arman had not blessed me with loyal men, I would be dead."*

Hinck gave Trevn a subtle nod of understanding, then turned his head back toward the Duke of Canden. "I'm sorry about your family," he said to Oli.

"They certainly made a mess of my good name, didn't they?"

The man had killed his own father, his mother had been executed a traitor, and he made jokes. "What became of Lady Eudora?" Hinck asked.

"In the dungeon," Oli said.

"I'm inclined to pardon her," Trevn said, "but she has so many compulsions upon her, I don't dare."

This brought a shiver over Hinck. "No offense to you, Duke Canden, but I don't trust her. What if she voices Rogedoth?"

"She cannot," Trevn said. "Unbeknownst to Lady Eudora, she's being fed a steady diet of the âleh plant, which keeps her from voicing or hearing anyone."

"Might I have some of that?" Hinck asked. "It would be handy should I find myself in need of some undisturbed rest."

"I have not voiced you since yesterday!" Trevn said.

"I know it. And I grew rather fond of the silence." Hinck winked at Mielle, who giggled.

"You're still blinking," Trevn said, shaking his head. "Pathetic. Here returns a lauded hero who cannot even wink."

Hinck's face burned as everyone had a good laugh at his expense. He decided another change of subject was in order. "Any idea of Rogedoth's plans?" he asked, wondering what the man might be forcing Nellie to do.

"He's allied with some of the giants," Trevn said, "and they've been harassing Sarikarians. Princess Saria has asked for aid, but I have no one to send her at present."

Concern for Saria rose within Hinck. "Does she need soldiers?"

"She needs everything," Trevn said. "Her father wrote her in as his Heir, and she has General Norcott on her side, but the council will not accept a female regent. Plus, there's a lot of conflict with her aunt and others scheming behind her back. I really don't know how to help her beyond sending food."

"The Sarikarians are a critical lot," Zeroah said. "It's partially why I chose to stay here. You are all my family more than they ever were. I pity Saria, though. It must be difficult to go this alone."

"I could go to her," Hinck said, hating that his childhood friend might be in trouble.

"Absolutely not," Trevn said. "You've only just returned."

"I don't have to be gone for long," Hinck said.

"I will not hear another word about it," Trevn said. "You and I both know Saria is tough as leather. She will find her way. Besides, I need you here. If it's work you want, I have several tasks for you." Trevn popped a piece of roast chicken into his mouth and continued the conversation in their minds. *"I want you to continue eavesdropping. I have reason to believe that some of my nobles are colluding against me."*

"Anything but that," Hinck voiced. *"I'm weary of shadowing thoughts. It's tediously boring and forever ruins my opinion of the people I monitor, even the good people. The things that go through a person's head . . . I tell you, it's very off-putting."*

"Then who will help me if you will not?"

"Kempe has eavesdropped for you before, hasn't she?"

"Yes, but she is not as perceptive as you are."

A serving woman ducked between them. She set a platter of food before Hinck and filled his goblet with wine. He glanced back to thank her and caught sight of Lady Pia, standing against the curtained wall with Sir Cadoc and a man Hinck thought was a sailor. His stomach sank as he took in the deep scars that slashed across her cheeks and forehead.

"Why is Lady Pia with the guards, and what happened to her face?" Hinck asked Trevn.

"I made her a guard. She's quite efficient."

A guard? Pia? *"And her face?"*

"Kamran DanSâr found out she was Wilek's spy and tortured her. I never told you this?"

"No," Hinck said, horrified that he hadn't known. *"You did not."*

"Well, there was a lot going on at the time with Kamran having poisoned Zeroah and Chadek. And I was in the north. It must have slipped my mind."

Hinck pushed back his chair and stood.

"What are you doing?" Trevn asked. "You haven't taken a bite."

"I must speak with Lady Pia." Hinck walked toward her.

Cadoc met his gaze. "Attention!" he said.

Pia and the sailor turned their backs to the wall, facing forward like soldiers.

"Lady Pia," Hinck said.

Her gaze traced the scars on his face. He fought the urge to stare at hers, knowing how it felt to have such blemishes be the focal point of every glance.

"Might we talk after dinner?" he asked.

"I am High Shield to the queen now, lord," she said. "I will be busy after dinner."

High Shield? Hinck wondered what else Trevn had neglected to tell him. He didn't like how awkward he felt standing here with Pia, as if he were speaking to a complete stranger. "Could we talk now, then? Cadoc and this man can see the queen clearly."

"Go on," Cadoc said to her.

The sailor glared at Hinck, and he recalled that this was the man who'd taught Trevn to brawl. He made a better pirate than sailor.

Lady Pia sighed, as if terribly inconvenienced, and pulled aside the curtain, which revealed an open space with tables holding pitchers and trays and servants bustling about.

"This is terribly embarrassing," she said as he followed her into the ante-chamber. "You do realize everyone in the great hall likely saw us exit together?"

"So?"

"What do you want, Lord Dacre?"

Such coldness made Hinck feel foolish. "I have thought about you ever since I left, though I can see now that I wasted my time."

Her eyelashes fluttered. "I didn't expect you would think of me—not when you could be with Nellie." A glance to his eyes. "You stayed with her, didn't you?"

"You told me to!"

She nodded, and her eyes hardened. "Because I didn't want you feeling guilty when it happened. She was good to you, wasn't she?"

He frowned, thinking it best not to answer.

Lady Pia folded her arms. "I knew she would be. She's good at her job, but even more so when she feels indebted."

Hinck suddenly understood. "It was your idea I rescue her from her cell on the *Seffynaw*?"

"I didn't think you'd survive, honestly."

"Well, I did. And I've come back. To you."

She glanced away. "You're very kind, Your Grace, but since you're still so terribly naïve, I'll make this very clear. I release you from whatever promise you think you made to me. I've moved on. So should you."

Her words stung like the scratch of an angry cat. "Moved on? With who?"

"Master Nietz. You saw him standing beside me moments ago."

Hinck couldn't believe it. "The pirate?"

A smirk. "He's one of the king's guards and a good man. He's had a hard life, like me. We understand each other's pain. He and I . . . we fit."

"And we didn't?"

She smiled then, and Hinck caught a glimpse of her former beauty. "Not in the slightest. What we had was a game. You were always above my station, and now you are a duke and the Second Arm of Armania. And I'm no longer a concubine. Find someone who fits your rank, poet. It will be easier for everyone. Now, if you'll excuse me, my duties await."

She stepped past him and her familiar smell of spices wrenched something in his heart. He reached for her hand, caught it ever-so-briefly, but she tugged it away.

Hinck stood awkwardly in the antechamber and watched her go. In all of his eavesdropping for Trevn, he'd learned that women rarely said what they meant. Had Lady Pia spoken the truth? Or was this some kind of test, and she was secretly hoping he would chase after her and fight for their love?

Did they have love? While her words had been shocking and had stung his pride, he didn't feel overly sorrowful about her rejection. Did that mean he'd never loved the woman? After all this time, had he been clinging to a lie?

How ridiculous that moments ago he had pondered in awe the passing of his childhood, yet here he stood, completely baffled over the rejection of a woman.

An idea came to him. It felt deceitful, yet at the same time necessary. To be certain he wasn't making an error, he reached for Lady Pia's mind.

So many times since learning the voicing magic he'd wanted to reach for Pia, to speak with her and ask how she fared. But he'd been afraid. Perhaps that hesitation had cost him.

He easily found her mind and drifted inside, listening for her thoughts. But she wasn't thinking. She was speaking. Whispering, actually.

"Don't worry about him," she said. "I'm shocked he even remembers me."

A man replied, "Any man who would forget you is not a man. Are you sure you feel nothing for him?"

"I told you, it was my occupation. He romanticized that it was more, but I never loved him."

"*I* love you," the man said.

Lady Pia's heart soared at those words. "And I you."

Flustered, Hinck withdrew.

Not a test, then. Pia hadn't been awaiting his return, and she really did love the pirate. But she'd lied about one thing. Hinck had sensed her thoughts and felt the nervousness of her fib.

She had loved Hinck once.

He supposed that would have to be enough.

GRAYSON

With the battle over, and Grandmother safely rescued, Grayson's time was again his own, and so he went back to spying on Porvil. He found the boy in the wine cellar, unloading crates and organizing the bottles.

Discouraged that he had nothing to tell the queen, Grayson also returned to his search for the Puru orphans. The giants he'd been tracking before were hunting in the mountains, so he ventured back to where Queen Mielle had been living with the Puru and moved south, looking for signs of life as he went.

It took three hours until he found any giants. Unfortunately, the dead deer they were hauling marked this as another hunting party. Grayson followed them for a while. When he got bored, he memorized the leader, then practiced popping away until he could do so easily. Then he returned to Armanguard and spent a few hours on the roof, playing with Lady Trista and Princess Rashah. He checked back every hour or so until he saw the giants had made camp. Grayson slept in his own bed, and when he woke the next day, he found the giants on the move again. He went back and forth, which allowed him to go to school in the great hall, practice swordplay with the Duke of Canden, and continue shadowing Porvil.

Two days passed uneventfully. Around midday on day three, the giants had reached a settlement that brought Magonia to mind. No snow. Few trees. A ground of thick reddish-brown clay and rocks. Rounded huts stretched into the distance. Those he could see from the road had pitfires outside their front doors—doors that were nothing more than a hole cut through the wall and covered with a mat of woven straw or bark. The rat birds were all over, perched on the roofs of huts, on carts, or hopping on the ground and nipping at bugs.

Grayson looked ahead to see how far the settlement might go, and a looming building stopped him on the path. Shaped like a pyramid and made of the same brown clay as the huts, it rose up in the center of the city, taller than even Castle Armanguard.

How did the center not collapse?

Grayson abandoned the hunters and popped closer to the pyramid until he was standing just outside the entrance where the ground fell away in a sharp cliff. A bridge crossed over a moat of dark, flaming liquid to an archway in the center front of the building. Rat birds had perched on the railings. Grayson shifted through the Veil to the other side of the bridge and went inside.

He looked up, surprised to find the structure hollow like a tent. Dozens of black birds had clustered on the rafters in the top point. There were four entrances, one in the center of each wall. Long stone steps descended on all four sides and met in the center at a square platform.

Grayson crept his way down. The knee-high platform sat on a dirt floor and supported a shallow stone cistern big enough for him to lie in. What could be the purpose of such a place?

He went about exploring the pyramid as families of giants came inside and took seats. Three of the exits emptied into the city. The fourth led to a clay hut, larger than those Grayson had seen on his way into the village. Inside, two giants stood over a Puru woman with orange hair, who lay on a table between them. They were feeding her some sort of black liquid from a bowl. She squirmed, her face pinched. Grayson was contemplating grabbing her and popping away when he heard a child scream.

He followed the sound to the back side of the hut, where he came upon a large pit with a roped railing. Rat birds had congregated along the wooden posts at each corner. Three giants stood at a cart holding about a dozen Puru women and children. A giant pulled a child out of the bed and dropped him into the pit. The boy yelped as he fell. Voices rose from below.

Grayson popped to the roped railing and peered into the depths. The pit was twice as deep as Grayson was tall and filled with Puru people—women and children mostly. He spotted one young man.

This must be it! Grayson had found the prisoners. Queen Mielle would be pleased. Now he must see about rescuing everyone.

He popped to the bottom of the pit and entered the physical realm. The heat surprised him. How could it be so warm here when there was snow in Armanguard?

A little boy with beige hair and skin saw him and gasped, his bright blue eyes fat and round. A girl not much taller with brown curls screamed. Some of the others glanced her way, but most were too busy trying to catch the newcomers being dropped down.

Grayson crouched in front of the little boy. "*Uma,*" he said in the Puru language.

The boy reached a pale finger toward Grayson's mottled gray hand. Amused, Grayson let the boy touch him. As soon as that tiny finger slid over his skin, the little girl pushed close and grabbed his wrist. Her face lit up in a smile that made her eyes nearly close. The boy touched Grayson again and smiled, revealing a missing front tooth.

More were watching him now. Above, the giants were rolling away the cart. The boy and girl were taking turns touching Grayson's hand when an old woman pushed between the children and yanked them away by the arms.

"I didn't see you arrive," she said in the Puru language. "You are also from Shelosh?"

"I'm from Armania," Grayson said. "Why are we in this pit?"

Another boy gestured to the pyramid. "Jiir-Yeke offering."

A chill ran over Grayson's arms. "You die?"

The young man stepped forward and glared. He had beige hair like the little boy. "We *rest*. To save our kin."

"They're lying." This from an older girl who looked about Vallah's age. "They're going to kill us."

"Hush, you!" the old woman yelled, jerking a hand toward the girl as if to slap her, but the girl ducked into the crowd. The pale-haired boy ran back to Grayson's side.

"You don't have to die," Grayson said. "I'm here to rescue you."

The old woman narrowed her eyes. "How?"

"I'll show you." He picked up the boy, concentrated on the servants' side of the curtain behind the dais in the great hall, then popped there. He appeared in front of a maid holding a tray. She screamed and dropped her load.

"Sorry!" Grayson set down the boy and knelt to help the maid pick up the food.

The boy fell to his knees, grabbed a chicken leg, and bit into it.

"You're a hazard, you know that?" the maid said.

"It was an accident." Grayson scooped two handfuls of chicken onto the tray and voiced the queen. *"Your Highness? I think I found your Puru children. I carried one to the serving antechamber in the great hall."*

"I'm on my way," she replied.

Bootsteps behind Grayson sent him to his feet. Guards from the dais, pushing through the curtain that separated the serving antechamber from the high table. Sir Cadoc, Lady Pia, Master Nietz, Bero . . . Where was the queen?

"It's okay!" Grayson said, hands held out. "It's just me."

"Appearing from out of nowhere and making me drop my tray," the maid added.

Sir Cadoc reached him first, slowed to a stop with his hands on his hips. "You're going to kill someone if you keep that up."

"He should have a room of his own to appear in and out of," the maid said. "That way he won't terrify people left and right."

"An excellent idea, miss."

Grayson winced at the sound of King Trevn's voice.

The king slipped between the guards and took in Grayson, the maid, the mess, and the boy, who was holding the drumstick, his mouth and cheeks greasy. "Who is this?" he asked.

"I don't know, sir," Grayson said. "I just this moment rescued him from a pit."

"What pit? Where?"

"In Jiir-Yeke territory. I think this is one of the orphans Queen Mielle asked me to find."

The king frowned. "She *asked* you?"

"You found them!" The queen strode toward them from the curtain.

The boy's face lit up. "Mismelle!" He ran toward the queen, still holding his chicken leg.

"The rest are in danger," Grayson said. "I must go back."

"You asked Grayson to look for the Puru orphans?" the king asked his wife.

Queen Mielle crouched down and embraced the boy. "Um . . . months ago, yes."

"And you didn't think to tell him to stop? After we talked about this? After I explained Conaw's side?"

"You said the others are in danger, Master Grayson?" the queen asked.

"They're going to be sacrificed," Grayson said, shrinking back from the king.

The queen lifted the boy onto one hip. "Then you must bring them here this instant!"

"Not here." The king stared at the queen through narrowed eyes, his face darkened. "Carry them to the council room, Master Grayson. We will take this boy and meet you there."

Grayson bowed and popped away, worried about how angry the king had seemed. He hoped he wasn't in too much trouble.

He appeared in the pit outside the pyramid, and someone tackled him. His body slapped against the soft dirt. Grayson shifted into the Veil. He righted himself and watched the young man squirm until he realized Grayson had gone.

Grayson crouched in front of the young man's face and popped back into the physical realm. "Why did you tackle me?" he asked.

The young man rose to his knees. His eyes were red and glossy. "It wasn't Tiyo's turn. What did you do with him?"

Grayson hadn't meant to scare anyone. "I took him to Armanguard," he said. "To the woman some of you know as Miss Mielle."

"Mismelle?" The little girl with the brown curls crowded close.

Other children joined in, many repeating the Puru version of the queen's name.

"Mismelle sent me to help you," Grayson said. "Who would like to go next?"

A half dozen children raised their hands, some of them hopping and shouting, "Me, me!" in the Puru tongue.

"No!" The young man scrambled to his feet. "The sleep is our calling. We must not betray our elders."

Grayson grabbed the nearest child—a girl with yellow braids—and popped to the council room in Castle Armanguard.

The little girl screamed the entire way and was still screaming when he arrived.

"Come here." Queen Mielle took her from Grayson and hugged her tightly.

The child calmed at once, but King Trevn, who was now holding the boy with the chicken leg, was glaring at Grayson with such fury that Grayson immediately returned to the pit. He grabbed the next boy from behind and transported him to the council chambers.

"—when I specifically said not to?" the king asked.

"Had Grayson told me he'd found them and asked how to proceed, I would've come to you first," the queen said.

"Somehow I doubt that," the king said.

Grayson left before the king could ask him anything. When he reappeared in the pit, the children had been lined up against one wall with the adults standing before them like guards.

"What is your name?" Grayson asked the young man.

"I am Sosovik," he said. "You must not free any more of us."

"You all want to die?" Grayson asked.

"No!" the girl with brown curls cried. "I want Mismelle."

Grayson popped into the Veil, right in front of the girl, then shifted into the physical realm, grabbed her, and carried her to Armanguard.

"—put the Puru tribes at risk," the king was saying. "The Jiir-Yeke will likely retaliate against them. Or they might decide to attack us."

"I'm sure it will all work out." The queen touched her nose to that of the little girl in her arms, and the child grinned. "The Jiir-Yeke would have killed them."

"And now they might kill us."

Grayson put down the girl and returned to the pit. This time the children were sitting on the ground in the corner while Sosovik and the women stood over them.

"Why do you want to stop me?" Grayson asked. "I'm helping you."

"If you take us away, they will kill our elders," Sosovik said. "Our parents."

"Your elders are leagues away from here," Grayson said.

"I want to go," said a girl about Vallah's age.

"Me too," said a boy sitting beside her.

"We mustn't!" said a woman. "If we leave, they'll curse our families."

"It will cause a war," the old woman added.

"And many more than us will die," Sosovik added.

"Then fight back!" Grayson said. "Whatever they're doing to you . . . it's wrong." It had to be. Didn't it?

"It is the only way," the old woman said. "They are too strong."

"I am Masaoo," Grayson said, using Muna's title of Deliverer. "I freed the Puru captives from the Ahj-Yeke mines. I can save your people too."

The old woman looked skeptical. "Where will you take us where the Jiir-Yeke cannot go?"

Grayson held out his hand to the woman. "Take hold and I will show you."

QꙨATCH

For five days Qoatch had traveled northwest with King Barthel's retinue until they reached a city of giants. The Puru prisoners had been taken away, and now the group stood inside a pyramidal temple with Abaqa mi Niseh. The interior was hollow, three or four levels high, and filled with wide steps that ran the length of each wall and down to a cistern of some kind, which sat on a square platform with raging fire pits in each corner. The steps were filled with spectators. Giant men, women, and children sat in groups, eating from baskets, talking, or staring at the cistern.

The squawk of a bird drew Qoatch's gaze up. Beams crisscrossed into the walls at the apex of the pyramid, creating perches for dozens of birds.

Abaqa led them to the bottom. A group of men sitting along one front row were chanting and beating on circular animal-skin drums. As Qoatch drew nearer, he got a better look at the cistern. It was a shallow circle, as wide as an average giant was tall. It had an outer rim of masoned rock no more than a hand's breadth deep that was covered in bird droppings. Inside, a shrouded form had been laid out as if on a funeral pyre. The red-stained rock beneath the body brought a jolt of realization over Qoatch. This was no cistern but a basin to contain blood flow.

It was an altar.

Abaqa bade them sit in the front row opposite the drummers. Here they waited. Heat from the fires warmed Qoatch's face, clouds of gnats swarmed, and the smell of boiled blood hung in the air. Twigs from evergreen trees had been placed in the fire pits and gave off a smoky, fragrant scent. In the Veil, Dendron remained at King Barthel's side, but some two dozen of his shadir flitted over the altar, curious, it seemed, and somewhat eager.

316

What would Jazlyn make of this? In the past five days Qoatch had learned much of the king's plans to take over Armania. The man had allies in that realm—including one in Castle Armanguard itself. There was even a mantic who still had evenroot. King Barthel had many plans for Shanek. He meant to use him to transport evenroot from his Armanian ally, to teach him the new magic, and to distract Rosâr Trevn from the real attack.

Qoatch had passed all he'd learned to Jazlyn through the common Cherem, who had told him that his Great Lady had found the king's harvest of new root and was having it loaded on the ship. Qoatch hated being apart from her and hoped she took care with King Barthel's guards.

Abaqa spoke, and Harton translated. "This temple houses many spirits, including the male ancestors of our people." The giant pointed to the apex where the birds were perched.

Giants continued to stream inside and take seats wherever they could find a place. Before long the structure was packed with onlookers.

A hush fell over the crowd on Qoatch's right. A man had entered and was descending the steps toward the altar. He wore an ornate headdress and a heavy black cape made of feathers that swept over the steps behind him and sent up a trail of dust.

Master Harton translated Abaqa's whisper. "This is Duu Ovdog. He is the ... *kholoi*?" Harton grimaced. "The word translates as *voice*, but I suspect he's some kind of priest."

Duu Ovdog reached the bottom and began to circle the platform. His headdress was like a warrior's helmet, covered in shiny black feathers. A veil of black tassels across the brim cast his face into a murky shadow. He carried a scepter made of bone. The top had been decorated with black tassels tipped in feathers and bone shards. He removed a flask from his belt, drank from it, then spat into the nearest fire, sending up a cloud of flame and smoke.

Movement on the other side of the altar drew Qoatch's attention—the man's dark skin. What was one of King Barthel's men doing over there? Abaqa would surely rage if one of his guests were caught so near the altar.

Something about the man's face made Qoatch look more closely. He knew him, though not from King Barthel's guard. The familiarity continued to nag. Qoatch was staring hard when the man met his gaze. The face registered surprise, then vanished.

The act so startled Qoatch that he wanted to stand and see if the man had ducked behind the cistern. Ridiculous, of course, with such a shallow altar. Where had he gone? Had Qoatch been seeing things? Might they be burning some kind of hallucinogen in those fire pits?

Duu Ovdog approached the next fire, again drank from his flask, and spat into the flames, creating the same effect as before. The flask must contain some sort of alcohol.

Qoatch glanced down his row and caught sight of the familiar man. Only he wasn't fully there. He was transparent, nearly sitting on top of Filkin Yohtheh-reth, who did not seem to notice the invasion in the slightest.

The trespasser was fully inside the Veil. It could not be possible, though Qoatch, being a seer, knew the truth. The Veil made the man's skin look strange. Grayish.

As Duu Ovdog spat into the third fire, the answer came to Qoatch just as the familiarity in the man's face clicked into place. This must be the boy Grayson. He had aged a great deal since Qoatch had traveled with him back in Rurekau. Yes, he was positive he was looking at the same person.

Duu Ovdog spat into the fourth fire, then stretched his scepter toward one of the entrances and said, "*Beleg abja.*"

"He said to bring the sacrifice," Master Harton translated.

Murmurs in the crowd drew Qoatch's attention away from the boy turned man. Two giants dragged an elderly man down the steps. He was pale—one of the Puru people. The way his body sagged between the giants made Qoatch believe he was unconscious, but as they reached the platform, Qoatch saw that the old man's eyes were open, roving about in obvious terror. His wrists were bound before him, and he seemed incapable of movement. The giants laid him on his back in the cistern beside the shrouded, much larger body. Each giant drew a dagger, took one of the old man's hands, and slashed their blades across his wrists.

The old man's eyes continued to move—Qoatch thought he heard him moan—but still he did not struggle. In the Veil, the shadir swept up to the old man and circled him, crooning as his blood seeped onto the rock bottom of the cistern.

The giants climbed down, and Duu Ovdog positioned himself outside the cistern, by the feet of the two bodies.

"*Avakh beleg tsusny!*" he yelled, his voice rough and deep. He knelt, closed his eyes, and began swaying from side to side, chanting words Qoatch could not understand.

"Accept this blood gift," Master Harton whispered, translating the priest's words. "Great sky, open. Release to us the spirit of Nogoon mi Huj."

Duu Ovdog lifted his scepter over his head and shook it. The leather tassels, bits of bone, and feathers clicked together as the priest repeated the chant.

Qoatch glanced down the row. Grayson was still there, watching. Oddly, Qoatch saw no shadir in the Veil other than those loyal to Dendron. Whatever magic the Jiir-Yeke possessed, it did not involve shadir.

Duu Ovdog spoke and Master Harton said, "Nogoon mi Huj, come to me."

"What's happening?" King Barthel asked Abaqa.

"He speaks from this world into the next," Master Harton translated. "Soon the earth spirit will enter his body and conduct the soul trade."

Two birds swooped down and circled over the altar.

"The spirits are descending," Harton translated.

Duu Ovdog's chanting picked up speed, and while he remained on his knees, his swaying became a dance. He flung his staff out like a whip as if spurring on a horse. The drummers continued to pound and chant. Even the crowd joined in. The sound grew to a fevered pitch.

The atmosphere and temperature changed. Something flickered in the Veil where Duu Ovdog knelt. Something that exuded coldness. The priest seemed to glow with a dark and unworldly presence. The radiance existed only in the Veil, however. No one else could see it, except perhaps Grayson. A shadir, likely, but different from those Qoatch had seen.

The thick, cold presence drew energy to itself. Fear gripped Qoatch, and he knew that no hope existed in this horrible world. Whatever creature had been summoned had draped a shroud of darkness over everyone.

Duu Ovdog stood, and all at once the crowd fell silent.

"A spirit has entered him," Harton whispered.

The priest walked stiffly around the altar. His eyes appeared black, his breathing labored. As he stared out over the crowd, people averted their gaze. Abaqa studied the ground. The headman looked almost frightened as Duu Ovdog drew near their seat.

"It's forbidden to look a kholoi in the eyes when a spirit is inside him," Harton whispered. "Bad things can happen to you."

Before the priest reached them, however, he spun around and dropped to his knees. He began chanting, dipped his staff into the cistern, and swirled it around like stirring a kettle. When he raised it again, the feathers on the end were coated in blood that dripped back into the altar. He shook the staff,

319

sprinkling the old man's blood over the shrouded body and chanting. When this was done, he held his arm steady, parallel to the floor, and gave a single, guttural command.

A black bird gave a long screech and soared down from the beams. It perched on the priest's wrist. Qoatch had expected to see a gowzal, but this was a raven.

"Blood quenches the spirit's thirst," Harton said. "The spirit will help Duu Ovdog release the soul of the shrouded man."

"How?" the king asked.

"The spirit will accept a trade. It will catch the soul of the dying and use its life force to bring back the soul of the dead."

Qoatch shuddered. He had seen some deplorable things in all his years serving the priestesses in Tenma, but this . . . He wanted to flee.

Duu Ovdog shouted and Harton said, "Release to us the spirit of Nogoon mi Huj!"

The priest reached out with his free hand, grabbed the screeching raven's head, and jerked.

Qoatch and Master Harton both jumped.

The bird went silent. The priest released it, and it fell, dead, into the cistern.

Duu Ovdog tipped back his head and howled like some kind of animal. Then he cackled madly, began to gyrate, and flailed his arms. He dropped his scepter, eyes filled with fear—or maybe it was pain. His breathing grew rapid, and suddenly he collapsed.

The two giants who had carried in the old man ran forward and helped the priest stand. They brought him to the floor on Qoatch's right. There he sat down, cross-legged, eyes closed.

A squawk pulled Qoatch's attention back to the altar. Something in the bowl moved. Something black. The raven hopped up on the shrouded corpse and stretched its wings over the bodies. But it was no longer a raven. It was larger, had a fur body, feathered wings, and the head of a rat. A gowzal. Qoatch sensed a hint of that same darkness that he'd felt in Duu Ovdog when the spirit had entered him.

The gowzal flapped its wings and took flight. The crowd of giants cheered as the creature soared overhead and flew out one of the entrances.

Had they turned the raven into a gowzal? Trapped a spirit inside?

When Duu Ovdog had somewhat recovered, he retrieved his scepter from the ground, drank from his flask, and spat into the nearest fire pit. The crowd

JILL WILLIAMSON

grew silent as he repeated the steps he had done before, preparing for another sacrifice. A group of guards swarmed the cistern, carried away the bodies, and left a new shrouded form in their place.

When the guards returned, this time they led in a young woman with fiery orange hair. They were about halfway down when Grayson appeared in their path, three steps ahead. He was hidden in the Veil, but just as the guards reached him, he entered the physical realm.

The crowd gasped. Grayson grabbed the woman around the waist, and they both vanished, leaving the guards alone.

Cries of astonishment rang through the audience. On the floor, Duu Ovdog yelled at the giant guards, who looked around, dumbfounded.

"That man looked Kinsman," King Barthel said, standing.

"He was the one called Grayson," Qoatch told the king.

Dendron vanished, and the king turned to Qoatch. "*Grayson?* He is a child."

"Root children grow faster than normal," Qoatch said.

Duu Ovdog and his guards ascended the stairs, but before they reached the exit, three other guards ran inside. Everyone began yelling.

"The captives are gone," Harton translated.

Duu Ovdog left. Some of the guards followed. One ran down to Abaqa mi Niseh, who lifted his hands and yelled foreign words to the crowd.

"He's asking everyone to sit in silence," Harton translated.

When Abaqa mi Niseh finished talking to the audience, he stalked toward King Barthel. "The intruder stole our sacrifice," he said. "He also released the others, including the Puru you brought us. He looked like your people. Have you betrayed us?"

"That was not one of my men," the king said, "but I know of him. He's called Grayson, son of Jhorn. He is from Armania, those settled around the lake in the southeast."

"Your enemies," Abaqa said. "He is our enemy as well. Such crimes are an act of war."

"I would welcome your help in an attack against Armania," King Barthel said. "And I'm happy to send you twenty new Puru people to replace those he took away."

"That is good," Abaqa said. "I will consult the ancestors. For now, your presence has upset Duu Ovdog. You have seen one sacrifice. Now you must leave."

"I understand," the king said. "I thank you, Abaqa mi Niseh, for inviting us here. I will do all I can to bring Grayson to Justness for defiling your temple. I

321

look forward to partnering with you in an attack against his king." He bowed his head, pensive.

Abaqa returned King Barthel's head bow, then stalked away.

"Let's go," the king said. "I want some distance between us and this temple before we make camp."

GRAYSO∏

Grayson popped into the council chambers and instantly lost his grip on the woman he'd rescued. Sosovik rushed forward and took her in his arms.

"What is wrong with her?" the queen asked.

"They gave her something to drink so she couldn't move," Grayson said. "Someone call the healer." He thought better of that. "I'll go."

"Why not carry her straight to the infirmary?" the queen said.

That was a better idea. Grayson reached for the woman, but Sosovik turned away. "She must go to the physician," Grayson said in Puru. "She's sick."

"*Nu mokto,*" Sosovik said. "*Pam nu sewa.*"

His sister? Grayson drew in a deep breath, wearied by all his traveling. "I will take you both." He wrapped his arms around Sosovik, the woman between them. He popped to the infirmary and explained to the physician as best he could, then returned to the council chambers and fell into a chair at the table. Three of the young children were giggling as they chased one another around the table. The rest were playing on the floor. The Puru women were lined along one wall.

King Trevn pulled out the chair beside Grayson and sat down. "That last one took a while," the king said. "What happened?"

Grayson told the king how he had tracked the hunters to the village in hopes of finding the queen's missing Puru children. He described the temple pyramid, the Puru captives in the pit, the new ones in the wagon, how he'd brought them to Armanguard, then gone back to the pyramid and witnessed the sacrifice, how Barthel Rogedoth had been there, and how Grayson had rescued the orange-haired woman in the middle of the ceremony.

A vein in the king's neck pulsed. "Didn't I tell you not to carry anyone through the Veil until I gave you leave?"

Grayson cowered. "You had me carry Lady Islah, so I thought—"

"My wife asked you to find the Puru children when she first came to Armanguard? And you've been at it ever since? Working entirely on your own?"

"Yes, sir," Grayson said. "I report to the queen whenever I have new information."

"And when did you last report new information?"

Grayson winced, certain he was about to get the queen in more trouble. "Yesterday."

"Yesterday," the king said with a glance at his wife.

"I didn't mean to cause trouble," the queen said.

The king released a pent-up sigh. "I sensed you were hiding something," he said. "Perhaps I should re-crown you Queen Regent, and I will be *your* consort, since you seem to think yourself above me."

"I don't think that."

"I specifically forbade you from looking for the Puru children, and all this time you had Grayson looking, behind my back. House Hadar has a word for that type of behavior. Can you guess it?"

Mielle shook her head.

"Treason," the king said.

Grayson shrank back in his chair. He didn't like hearing the king and queen fight and wished they'd do it elsewhere. Some of the Puru children looked afraid.

"He was only to look on his free time," Mielle said. "And I planned to ask your advice once I knew something worthwhile."

"Even if I hadn't told you to drop the matter of the Puru orphans," the king said, "Grayson is the prophesied Deliverer. You put him at risk by sending him all over the continent."

"It's heroic, what he can do," the queen said. "He saved many lives today."

"I take no issue with his heroism, but you should have told me you'd already asked him to find the orphans. And you shouldn't have sent him into Jiir-Yeke territory. Barthel Rogedoth may have seen him!"

"How was I to know where the Jiir-Yeke territory is or where Rogedoth would be? Besides, the way Grayson moves, he's practically invincible. What could possibly happen to him?"

"That's just it. We don't know. For you to take his life into your own hands and decide for yourself how you would risk him—for you to ignore my order and break the agreement I made with the Puru people—it's completely irresponsible."

The queen folded her arms and said nothing. A tear rolled down her cheek.

The king looked at Grayson, his glare softening. "You're too important to risk. From now on you take orders from me alone. Is that clear?"

Grayson looked to his lap. "Yes, sir."

"Mielle, take these people to the great hall and see them fed," the king said. "You and I will discuss this later."

"Of course," she said, a little stiffly. "But I cannot communicate with them. Not without Grayson's help."

"Grayson," the king said, "explain to our Puru guests that they are to go with my wife to eat food. You will join them shortly."

Grayson quickly explained the king's wishes to the old woman, who eagerly urged the women and children to follow the queen out the door. When they were gone, the king leaned back in his chair and set one ankle over his opposite knee. Grayson braced himself to be punished.

"Anything else you've neglected to tell me?" the king asked.

Fear made Grayson talk very fast. He told the king about the ritual in detail. "They made those rat birds, sir. Made them from the sacrifice."

"That's why the Jiir-Yeke take the Puru," the king said. "But why was Rogedoth there, I wonder?"

"I can watch him. Try to find out."

"No," the king said. "Rogedoth wants you for himself, and you must stay away. Do not return to that pyramid again. Is that understood?"

"Yes, sir."

"I rather like that maid's idea that you have a room to travel in and out of. I cannot have you frightening the residents of this castle on a regular basis. I will find you a room, and you will use it. Is that understood?"

"Yes, Your Highness. Thank you."

"Now, I do need your help with something right away. Empress Inolah is in need of assistance. The Ahj-Yeke have taken many Rurekans to their mines. Think you might be able to free them? Tomorrow, of course. After you've rested."

Grayson thrilled at the idea of helping more people. "Yes, sir. I can help them."

"Good. Now off you go."

Grayson didn't need to be told twice. He popped to the great hall to help feed the Puru, eager to finish and be alone for a very long while.

Inolah

Inolah sat at a table with the Rurekan council, going over their list of concerns, the most crucial of which involved the abducted Rurekans.

"Master Grayson has located the majority of our missing people in an Ahj-Yeke mine to the northeast of here," she said. "He has already begun carrying people out. Some of the children have been separated from parents, and we're working on reuniting—"

The door burst inward, and a man entered, followed by a dozen others, Rosârah Thallah included. The Igote guards leapt to stop them, but some of the intruding party muttered words that knocked the guards to the floor.

"Forgive me, Your Eminence!" said an Igote guard from behind the intruders. "I told him you were in a meeting, but he would not listen."

Inolah stood and took a closer look at the man leading the pack. It had been nearly twenty years since she'd last seen Barthel Rogedoth, but she recognized his ridged brow and long braid immediately. "How can I help you, Master Rogedoth?"

"How dare you enter my camp and attack my men?" he spat. "I demand you return the prophetess to me immediately. And her rescuer too."

"Rescuer?"

"Sir Kalenek Veroth," Thallah said.

Well, if this wasn't an amusing chain of events. Inolah fought back a smile. She'd known all along that Kal had harbored feelings for the prophetess. "The order did not come from us, sir, but it pleases me."

"You celebrate the breach of my defenses, Empress?" Rogedoth asked.

"Not at all, but I had it on my list to speak with you about Miss Onika's unjust captivity. Do you honestly expect me to rage when an innocent woman has escaped wrongful imprisonment?"

"I had good reason for holding her," he said.

"Do enlighten me," Inolah said.

The man ran his hand over his mouth, clearly unprepared to answer. "I did not forget you and Sir Kalenek are friends," he said.

"We were childhood friends, yes," Inolah said, "though it's no secret Sir Kalenek has long been banished from Armania. He serves Chieftess Charlon now. If you have questions about him, I suggest you take them to her."

"You expect me to believe it mere coincidence that Sir Kalenek just so happened to break into my camp only days after you arrived?"

"I don't expect you to believe anything," Inolah said. "I have no interest at all in your affairs. I came here to assist my son in his transition to regent. I've not seen Sir Kalenek since we were aboard the *Seffynaw* on the voyage across the Northsea."

"You may not be aware, Empress, but New Rurekau and Barthia have a treaty," he said.

"Since my arrival I have been discovering new surprises by the minute, and, yes, I was made aware of the promises Rosârah Thallah and Empress Jazlyn made to you. I have no desire that New Rurekau would break such a treaty unless you asked us to betray any of our long-term alliances. Surely you wouldn't do that, would you?"

Rogedoth's hands squeezed into fists. "You will regret your interference here, Empress." He whipped around, his cloak flying out, and stomped toward the door.

"I doubt that very much, sir," she called out.

His entourage scurried after him, and the Igote guards chased them out.

Inolah waited until the last Igote kindly closed the door and she again had some privacy. Thallah had remained behind. "Sit, rosârah."

"Thank you, but I have no interest in this meeting," the queen said.

"You're not invited to this meeting," Inolah said, "but you will sit this instant and tell us what your game is."

Thallah sank onto a chair on the other side of Sir Iamot. "What do you mean?"

"It has come to my attention that when Barthel Rogedoth first arrived, you greeted each other as fast friends. I want an explanation. Are you one of his loyal followers?"

Father's third queen folded her arms, and for a moment Inolah believed she might not answer. Then she slouched in her chair. "My history with King Barthel is long and complicated. Everything I've done was for my son."

"How does greeting Barthel Rogedoth with a kiss help Trevn? Or calling the man king?"

Thallah wrung her hands. Gone was her self-assured mask, and beneath it lay the face of a mother in pain. "King Barthel commands the great shadir Dendron, who is terribly powerful and rules a swarm of lesser shadir."

"What does that matter?" Inolah asked. "Your son is king of Armania and is loyal to Arman, the One God, who made the earth and everything in it. A much greater ally than any shadir. Why do you collude with Trevn's enemy?"

Thallah furrowed her brow. "It's to save Trevn that I do this. King Barthel promised not only to spare my son, but to give him land and title if he gives up the throne willingly."

What mad logic was this? "And you believe him?"

"What choice have I? King Barthel is the most powerful mantic in the world."

Powerful liar, maybe. Lady Islah had exposed the truth about Rogedoth being a malleant, but that was Trevn's information to use. "While I understand the maddening desire to save your child, I cannot comprehend such lack of faith," Inolah said. "Trevn is a clever young man. He has surrounded himself with a host of wise advisors—the best there are, in my opinion. And as I've already said, he trusts in Arman. It matters not what kind of weapon or magic or number of fighting men or demons come against him. He will step aside for no one."

Thallah sneered. "I've never seen your god deliver anything but ridicule and failure to those who follow him. Your brother died, and so will my son if he carries on with this One God nonsense. There's power to be had in this world, but if Trevn continues to refuse it—it will be to his demise."

"I find your opinions dangerous," Inolah said. "General, would you please escort the rosârah to the dungeon?"

"Gladly, Your Eminence." General Balat stood, but before he could reach Thallah, she got up and jogged toward the exit. The guards at the doors stepped in her way and raised their pikes.

Thallah whirled back and glared at Inolah. "You can't arrest me! I've done nothing but help New Rurekau."

"I doubt that very much," Inolah said. "And while I uncover all you have done here, I will hold you until King Trevn decides whether or not he wishes to charge you with treason against Armania."

The general grasped Thallah's elbow. "If you'll come peacefully, rosârah, I won't ask the guards to bind you."

"After all I've done for your children, you would betray *me*?" Thallah fisted her hands, chest heaving. "'People who think they are wise when they are not are worse than fools.'"

"I completely agree, rosârah, which is why I am doing this," Inolah said.

Her face darkened. "You'll regret siding against King Barthel." And she stormed out of the chamber. The general and the guards followed.

Well, that was a lot of mischief made in the space of a few minutes. Inolah hoped that pointing out to Rogedoth that Kal served Chieftess Charlon would in no way put Ulrik at risk. She wanted her eldest son back home, but until she figured out how to make peace with Empress Jazlyn, he was safer dead.

QOATCH

King Barthel exited his tent with Sâr Shanek and Miss Amala. Qoatch followed. The sun had not yet set fully, creating a pale pink dusky sky overhead. Tonight the king had broached the topic of the boy's future rule of Armania and his desire to help.

"I might not have as many soldiers as Rosâr Trevn," the king said, "but they will fight for you, if you wish it. As will the giants I've made alliances with."

"You believe Sâr Shanek should be king?" Miss Amala asked.

"He is Sâr Janek's son, lady," King Barthel said. "The line of ascension should pass to Sâr Shanek before it goes to Sâr Trevn."

"But Rosâr Wilek declared Sâr Trevn to be his Heir," Miss Amala said.

"Wilek stole the position from his brother Janek," King Barthel said. "He was not a popular king, nor is Rosâr Trevn. The people need a king who will give them what they want. I believe Sâr Shanek is that man."

Miss Amala smiled at the prince. "I think so too."

"What has King Trevn done wrong?" Shanek asked.

"Besides accept a crown he doesn't deserve?" King Barthel asked. "He forces his people to renounce the gods and worship no deity but his own. He also refuses to assign his nobles the land their titles deserve."

Shanek's brow sank and he looked at Miss Amala.

"Nobles are distant relations of royalty, right?" Miss Amala asked.

The king frowned at the young lady. "Sometimes, though more often they are families of rank, distinguished by a title that has been passed down from generation to generation."

"Titles like duke or earl?" Miss Amala glanced at Shanek, who was listening attentively.

"That's correct," King Barthel said. "Such titles were created by the king to set apart a family as one of great importance. Though the way Rosâr Trevn has been treating his nobles, you'd think them no better than commoners."

"Who are everyday folk," Miss Amala said.

Shanek glared at Amala and whispered, "I know *that*."

The king quirked an eyebrow. "You are very astute, my sâr."

"So," Shanek said, "if I am king—"

"*When* you are king," the king said, smiling.

"When I am king," Shanek said, "I must let the people worship their gods and give land to the nobles? Then I will be a good king?"

Qoatch winced at how the prince dangled his ignorance before the great viper Barthel.

"That would be an excellent start, my prince," King Barthel said. "Now come. I'm eager to show you my camp."

The king led the young couple on a tour, introduced them to some of his officers, and showed them the horses, including one giant horse the king had received from the giants in a trade. They ended back in the king's tent, where a second throne had been set beside King Barthel's. It was made of freshly sanded pine, decorated with carved flowers and scrolls, and cushioned in green velvet.

"Do you like it?" the king asked Shanek. "I want you to have a seat worthy of your station when you visit."

"Oh, Shanek, it's beautiful!" Miss Amala said.

The boy traced his finger along a carved vine in the headboard. He seemed to be fighting a smile. "I like it."

"Sit, try it out," King Barthel said, eyes glittering as the boy sank onto the green cushions. "I'm sure you and the Chieftess have an excellent plan for infiltrating Armania, but might you be open to suggestions? I served Rosâr Echad loyally for many years. I well know the way things work within their government."

Shanek frowned. "We don't have a pl—"

"What would you suggest?" Miss Amala asked.

"Time is of the essence," the king said. "Rosâr Trevn struggles to earn the respect of his nobles, but he is known to be charming. Given time, he will worm his way into their hearts. He should be deposed before he gets that chance."

"How?" Shanek asked.

"There are many ways," the king said. "Our armies could combine, and we could march on Armanguard."

"I don't have an army," Shanek said.

"Ah, well, I've seen how you can carry people. If you were to abduct Rosâr Trevn and bring him here, I could kill him. Or you could, if you preferred."

The young prince gaped. "*Kill* him?"

"It would make a fine story for your ascent to the throne," the king said. "Or perhaps you could take his wife. If she were missing, he would be distracted and—"

"Queen Mielle is my sister," Miss Amala said.

Qoatch hadn't known that.

King Barthel drew back. "I had no idea, lady," he said. "Have you any other siblings?"

"None living. Sir Kalenek Veroth was married to our eldest sister and raised us after she died."

The man who killed Sâr Shanek's father? Warden to both the queen of Armania and the woman poised to take her place? Jazlyn would love this.

"Lady, I am grieved to hear of so much tragedy in such a young life," the king said. "That you and Sâr Shanek have become close in spite of the dark past between you shows strength of character and mercy. What a wonderful example of bringing peace out of violence."

"Amala is part of my family now," Sâr Shanek said, which made the girl smile.

"I'm glad of that," King Barthel said.

"I cannot condone kidnapping my sister or killing her husband," Miss Amala said. "Shanek, it's not right."

"I won't hurt Amala's family," Shanek said.

"Of course we don't have to kill anyone. I . . . If we tried . . ." The king paused, clearly flustered. "Taking the throne of Armania will not happen without incident."

"Maybe Shanek could relocate Rosâr Trevn and my sister," Miss Amala said. "Put them safely away where they can live quietly?"

"An excellent suggestion, lady," the king said. "That would be ideal."

"I can't do it," Sâr Shanek said.

Miss Amala blinked her large brown eyes at the young man. "Of course you could."

He shook his head. "I've never been to Armanguard."

"Kal is going there. Isn't that what Nwari said? That he helped Miss Onika escape from here and took her to Armanguard?"

King Barthel began to cough and took a sip of wine.

Sâr Shanek turned his dark brown eyes on the king. "If he is in Armania, I can go to his side."

"He can only travel to a place he has been or to a person he knows," Miss Amala explained. "Those are his limitations."

"How intriguing," King Barthel said. "Would you be willing to go to Sir Kalenek? Once you are inside the castle, you could carry Rosâr Trevn and his wife to a secure location."

Shanek grimaced. "I don't know what he looks like."

"I have allies there who could help you," King Barthel said.

"You could do it, Shanek, I know you could." Miss Amala took hold of his hand.

The prince gazed at the girl, then nodded once. "I will try it, but only if I have a sword and shield and learn better to use them."

"I can supply weapons now," the king said. "Father Lau, take our future king to the armory and let him pick out a sword and shield. Then introduce him to Captain Orbay and have the captain assess his skills thus far."

"Right this way, Your Highness," Father Lau said.

Shanek and Amala got up to leave, but King Barthel caught hold of the young woman's arm. "Miss Amala, might you be interested in meeting my tailor? If it would please you, I'd be happy to commission a few dresses on your behalf."

She smiled broadly. "I'd like that very much, Your Highness."

"Excellent. Lady Mattenelle and Qoatch will come with us. The rest of you stay with the future king."

The group parted. King Barthel offered Miss Amala his arm and led her toward the tailor's tent. Qoatch followed behind with Lady Mattenelle.

"My dear, I'm so glad to have gotten to know you both," the king said.

"It has been a pleasure," Miss Amala said.

"Sâr Shanek will be king of Armania," the king said, "but getting him there won't be easy. I confess my magic is not what it was. Someone stole most of my evenroot. It seems betrayal surrounds me. I don't want that for Sâr Shanek. He must have a staff he can fully trust."

"I agree," Miss Amala said.

"It does my heart good to know that he has your excellent guidance," the king said. "If you are willing to confide in me, I'll better be able to foresee potential hazards he might face. I will also supply him with what mantics I can, though as I've said, my root supply has greatly diminished. I will not have access to magic forever."

"Perhaps you could learn to use the new magic that Chieftess Charlon wields?"

Qoatch flinched, but before he could interject or change the subject, Barthel had jumped on the topic, and soon the silly girl Amala was sharing all she knew. Jazlyn would not be pleased.

"I am surrounded by betrayal," King Barthel said to Qoatch long after Prince Shanek and Amala had departed. "She left you here to spy on me, didn't she?"

Qoatch said nothing. He'd spent the evening in King Barthel's tent, listening to him rant about the horrible way Empress Jazlyn had tricked him.

"Silence from you. Silence from her," the king said. "That's all the proof I need. She knew about the new magic, knew I had a supply of new evenroot on Islah, and went to claim it. Deny it, eunuch. Tell me it is not so."

Qoatch could not, so he did not.

"I should have you killed."

Qoatch didn't even flinch.

"The empress told me you made a root garden from a plant Chieftess Charlon had given her. I want it. Zithel Lau and a squadron of ten soldiers will help you carry it here."

"There's very little," Qoatch said, knowing Jazlyn wouldn't like losing her garden.

"I care not. Miss Amala says Sâr Shanek will give me a lesson if I supply my own evenroot. The empress has helped herself to my stores. I intend to return the favor. Go. Now."

Qoatch started for the door, but before he could leave, Dendron appeared not two steps in front of him. Qoatch slowed to a stop.

Lady Islah is not in her tent, the great said.

King Barthel scowled at Dendron. "Her guard must have taken her to use the privy."

There is no guard, Dendron said. *Captain Orbay had no answer as to the man's whereabouts. It seems he has fled.*

King Barthel pushed off his throne. "This is Sir Kalenek's doing. He must have taken Islah and the prophetess."

Not Sir Kalenek. The Armanian root child carried her to Armanguard.

"That cannot be." The king began to look panicked. "Without her bond . . . everything is lost." He shoved past Qoatch and out of the tent. Qoatch had never seen the man move so quickly. He and the other acolytes followed. They arrived in time to see the king exit a small tent behind his own.

"She's gone," he told the great. "What can be done?"

We will continue our plan to make use of the root child Shanek, Dendron said, his dark eyes fixed upon the king. *He must give me Dominion, or you must. Otherwise, I will leave.*

King Barthel's lip curled. "Bond with Shanek." He stormed past the great shadir, back toward his tent.

Qoatch didn't know who Lady Islah was or what any of this meant. Could the shadir convince Shanek to bond? Qoatch hoped Jazlyn returned soon. He didn't want to be here when such a thing took place.

KALENEK

K al woke screaming, the reek of blood and death as thick as the flies feasting on the fallen. He swatted at the insects buzzing around his face. "I'm not dead, you scavengers!"

"Sir Kalenek?"

The voice made him shiver. Where was he? "Livy?"

"It's Onika. Are you well?"

A nightmare. And the buzzing, only mosquitoes. Kal breathed deeply of the chilled night air, of snow and bark and moss. He and Onika had made camp for the night. He wished he could see her face, but it was too dark. "Forgive me. I was dreaming."

"How did you feel?" Onika asked. "In the dream?"

"*Feel?*" Terror, helplessness, devastation, rage . . . "I don't know. Angry? That so many good men were dying." What was the opposite of anger? Delight? Happiness? Peace? "It won't do, Onika. I can find no good in the death of so many."

"They held the border, didn't they? Kept the enemy from your lands?"

Kal pictured Liviana and their child, dead in their beds. "Some still managed to cross. It's how my wife and son died."

"You blame yourself."

"She wanted to go to Everton. If I'd let her go, she would've been safe."

"You didn't kill them," Onika said, then inside his head, *"You're innocent of this."*

He was *not* innocent. "Someone has to pay for their deaths."

"Vengeance is Arman's, Kalenek. Trust the God to judge those who killed your wife and child. But know that forgiveness also belongs to him. Give your regrets to Arman, and he will not only pardon you, he will free you from the burden. You cannot atone for yourself. No amount of good deeds or punishment will ever be enough."

Her words buzzed in his mind like a wasp. It was true. Nothing he'd tried had been able to make up for his crimes. But Arman had let Livy and their son die. He'd let Wilek die. He'd allowed Shanek to come into this world and be used.

A god like that could not be trusted.

The castle was an impressive structure that had been built on an island on the northern end of a massive lake. The bargeman asked no questions as Kal and Onika boarded. Onika had sent word ahead to King Trevn. They were expected.

For the briefest of moments, Kal had thought about leaving Onika on the barge and riding away. The True Prophet needed to get back to her king, but Kal had no desire to see the man. Wilek had warned him not to return. Death was all that awaited him inside those stone walls.

They exited on the island and stopped at the gatehouse. And still he did not turn back.

"Sir Kalenek," a man called.

Kal scanned the crowd until his gaze met that of Master Hawley, Rosârah Brelenah's onesent. Kal had known Master Hawley since he and Wilek had been boys. Kal led Onika to the man and released her long enough to clasp hands with the onesent.

"The king is waiting for you in his office," Hawley said. "I'll take you there."

"You're working for the rosâr?" Kal asked.

"My mistress offered me as his onesent and His Highness accepted."

"Smart move." Kal doubted there had been many good options for the position.

A soldier, who was staring his way, nudged a comrade and whispered. Soon it seemed everyone they passed was gawking and muttering about the pale prophetess and the assassin.

Hawley led them over icy ground sprinkled with pine needles and slivers of wood. They passed under a second gate, through a smaller inner bailey, and into an open archway that served as the front entrance to the keep.

Inside, a round foyer circled a wide spiral staircase. Up they went to the third level, then around the circular landing to a door where two guards were posted. Kal recognized them as sailors from the *Seffynaw*. Both looked him over as he led Onika after Hawley into a wedge-shaped room. There, behind the desk Kal recognized from Rosâr Echad's office aboard the *Seffynaw*, sat Sâr Trevn—king now. No sign of Mielle, but Sir Cadoc was leaning against the wall. At the sight of Kal, he jumped to attention and edged closer to the king.

Trevn hadn't aged a day since Kal had last seen him aboard the *Rafayah*, except for the creases lining his forehead and a pathetic attempt at a beard. He might have a bit more muscle on his arms, though that could be an illusion from the fancy sleeves of his tunic. The top button was undone, as if he'd found the neck confining. He wore a sliver of a crown over hair worked into warrior's braids that ran just past his shoulders. Kal noted a single kill braid woven in. He also recognized the signet ring on his finger from having kissed it dozens of times over the years.

Trevn looked up from his desk and his glance flickered between Kal and Onika. He released a long breath, briefly closed his eyes, and muttered, "Thank Arman."

"We are here in King Trevn's office," Kal whispered to Onika.

He bowed. Onika curtsied.

Trevn stood and clapped his hands together. "Welcome to Armanguard, Sir Kalenek. Miss Onika, welcome home. I'm sorry I was unable to liberate you sooner."

"All was done in Arman's perfect timing," she said.

"I'm glad of that. Now, I'm afraid if we're to do this right, we must call in some witnesses. As we talked about, Miss Onika, it may get a bit ugly, but I've prepared them, and your testimony will help immensely."

"I will do my part, Your Highness," Onika said.

Trevn looked past Kal to the door behind him. "Hawley?"

The onesent nodded and left the room.

Kal didn't like being the only one without a notion of what was going on, but considering his crimes, he had no right to complain.

"You saw Rogedoth's camp, Sir Kalenek?" Trevn asked. "What's it like? How many men does he have?"

Well, he did get straight to the point, didn't he? Kal rather admired that. "It's a military camp in concentric formation, lowest rank on the outside circle. It had six rows around the command center. My guess is he's got about a thousand men, maybe a quarter of them Kinsman."

"Voluntary Kinsman soldiers?" the king asked. "Why, do you think?"

"Men are loyal for many reasons," Kal said. "My guess is they like Rogedoth's power. He might also have made them promises. Could be a few criminals in the bunch. I know I saw some pirates."

"And Chieftess Charlon and her . . . son? Tell me about them."

Kal's heart sank to think that Trevn saw Shanek as a threat. But of course he *was*. "Charlon believes Shanek should rule Armania. It's an old Magonian prophecy."

"I'm familiar with the prophecy," Trevn said, "though they've misinterpreted it. Go on."

"They have no plan—not that I'm aware of, anyway. Charlon has developed a new magic using gowzals."

"*Gowzal?* The ancient word for bird?" the king said. "What do you mean?"

"It's what Charlon named the birds native to this land. They're black. Look like rats."

The king frowned. "I know them."

"Yes, well, when fed evenroot, they can be commanded." And Kal went on to explain about the new evenroot and how the magic worked.

The door opened and Hawley returned with three men in tow: Barek Hadar, Danek Faluk, and Oli Agoros.

"Holy gods," Oli whispered, his gaze locked on Kal.

"So it's true," Barek said.

"You think me a liar, Your Grace?" the king asked the Duke of Odarka.

"I almost hoped you were," he mumbled.

Trevn chuckled darkly, clearly amused by something only he understood. "Miss Onika, I'm sure the gentlemen meant to welcome you back safely rather than criticize my rule."

All three fumbled with apologies.

"Miss Onika," Trevn said, "please tell these men how you came to be here."

She tipped her head toward the king. "Sir Kalenek rescued me from my prison in Barthel Rogedoth's camp just outside New Rurekau."

"This is excellent, Sir Kalenek," the king said. "You have done Armania a great honor in bringing back the God's prophet."

"I'd do anything for Miss Onika," Kal said. "And for House Hadar."

Barek snorted. Kal met his gaze, and the duke withdrew his handkerchief and wiped his nose.

"Sir Kalenek also rescued Master Grayson from the Magonian ship when we were still at sea," the king said. "I've decided to appoint him High Shield to the young man."

Kal froze.

"What!" Oli cried. "He cannot be trusted with someone so—"

"Important? Precious? Powerful?" The king raised his eyebrows at the Duke of Canden. "Sir Kalenek brought Miss Onika all this way, unharmed. Is not our prophetess all of those things and more?"

"Yes, *sir*," Oli said, a little more firmly than necessary.

Kal fell to his knees, needing to make it clear he asked for no favors. "If it's my life they want, Your Highness, I gladly give it. I owe it many times over to House Hadar."

"*I* want your life in service," King Trevn said, "as would have Wilek. I pardon you for the crimes of which you are accused."

Kal gaped. He couldn't believe it. A pardon?

"Your Highness, are you sure this is wise?" Barek asked.

"*I'm* not," Oli said.

"Fortunate for Sir Kalenek that I am king instead of either of you," Trevn said. "Unless Duke Highcliff also objects to my decision?"

"Not at all," Danek said. "You are Arman's chosen king, and I trust you to decide what's best for all of us."

Barek and Oli shot the man glares, but the king seemed appeased. "Well, I'm glad someone does."

"Perhaps the Wisean Council should discuss this further, Your Highness," Barek said.

"My decision is final," Trevn said. "Sir Kalenek is pardoned and will serve as Master Grayson's shield. Arise, Sir Kalenek. All is forgotten."

Kal could not rise. Not until he did right by his new, merciful king. "First I must pledge my service to you, Your Highness. You have my loyalty and my sword."

"I accept your pledge, Sir Kalenek," the king said.

"You honor me, Your Highness." Kal pushed to his feet.

"I'm sure you well know that Master Grayson is a challenge to keep up with," the king said, "but he's one of Armania's most valuable assets and must be protected. You've known him longer than anyone, save Master Jhorn and Miss Onika, and I think you'll do him some good. I know Duke Canden has been struggling to teach him swordplay."

Oli grunted and looked away.

Kal had no idea if he could teach anyone swordplay, let alone fight to protect a charge. He wanted to tell the king about his malady, but now, in front of these men, was not the time.

"Council members, you may go," the king said. "Hawley will have you sign a document stating you witnessed these testimonies. After that, Duke Canden, please see that Miss Onika's chambers are made ready, and notify Master Jhorn and Grayson of her return. They'll be eager to see her, I'm sure."

Oli bowed his head and departed, his cloak swirling behind him. Danek followed. Barek frowned at Trevn and Kal, then strode out the door.

"Take a chair, both of you," Trevn said, claiming his own seat.

Kal helped Onika into one of the two chairs across the desk from the young king.

Trevn waited until both were seated, then began anew. "Tell me more about this root child, Shanek. What's he like?"

It hurt to talk of the boy as an enemy. "Though I love him as my own child, he's always been difficult to control. At present he looks to be your age and fancies himself in love with Amala. She came to Magosia with Sir Kamran, who had maltreated her on the journey. Shanek killed the man to avenge her."

"I heard Sir Kamran was killed, but not how," Trevn said. "Was it a duel?"

Kal sighed deeply. "No, Your Highness. Shanek can kill with his magic. He's done it twice now, that I know of, and I don't understand it. The first victim was a young woman Chieftess Charlon had given him as a concubine."

"He can't be old enough to have a concubine!" Trevn said.

"He's not, really, but as I said, he has the body of a man. His mind has developed rather quickly, though for someone who looks twenty, his understanding of human interaction is quite limited—often to the point of ignorance. Anyway, Shanek and the concubine fought, and in his anger, he created green light with his hands. I don't know if the light killed her or his desire. He told me he grabbed her thoughts with the intention of making her say nice things and she died."

Trevn stared at Kal, his eyes wide with shock. "That's quite a skill."

"Grayson has this power too," Miss Onika said.

Kal recoiled. "What?"

"His demeanor is such that he rarely gets angry," she said, "and Jhorn trained him not to use his magic, so it doesn't come naturally to him. But he once killed a fang cat with light from his hands. It was attacking Dunmore, and Grayson struck it. Dunmore said Grayson's hands had been pulsing with green light. As far as I know, it only happened that one time."

Heavy silence stretched over the room.

Kal compared the two stories and found them different. "Shanek didn't touch the girl, nor did the light ever leave his hands. I didn't see him kill Sir Kamran."

"I don't pretend to understand how any of this works," Trevn said, "but is it possible that Shanek killed the girl with his voicing magic? Perhaps someone powerful enough could in fact use the voicing magic to compel someone to die."

Kal certainly hoped not. "If you're right, Your Highness, I doubt Shanek knows he can do such a thing."

"If I'm right, let's hope he never figures it out."

"Arman made mankind upright, but they seek out many evil schemes," Onika said.

The young king's eyes, wide and brown, shifted to the prophetess. His throat bobbed. "You're right, prophetess. This power the God has given us . . . it's a great and terrible responsibility. I wish he'd better taught us to use it."

"Do not blame Arman for your failures," Onika said, her crystal gaze fierce. "A man knows what is right, and when he chooses to act otherwise, he offends Arman. But the Father is forgiving, and he who confesses his mistakes and forsakes them will obtain mercy."

Trevn nodded. "I'm not proud of all the ways I have used my powers. I know I've crossed the line. I have forsaken such temptation, prophetess, I promise you."

"Make your promises to Arman," Onika said, "and may he hold you accountable."

Kal turned his attention back to the king and noticed for the first time that he was wearing his blacks. "Your Highness, I'm deeply grieved by Rosâr Wilek's death. Had I been with him, he would not have died alone."

"He didn't die alone," Trevn said. "Novan Heln was with him."

Kal's chest constricted. "Novan was killed too?"

"No," the king said, "but Master Heln did all he could to save my brother. I have pardoned him, and Captain Veralla too, and will hear no complaints about it. Wilek would not have wished them harm. Or you."

"That's a brave notion, Your Highness," Kal said, "one my neck very much appreciates."

Trevn chuckled. "Yes, well, Master Heln has struggled greatly with losing Wilek. Fonu Edekk set five giants upon them. It was an unwinnable situation, yet Master Heln managed to kill Fonu and escape with Wilek's body. Such a feat deserves honor, in my opinion, not ridicule and shame. Due to Master Heln's determination, Wilek's head was buried with his body instead of being carried all over Er'Rets on a pike. That's not nothing, Sir Kalenek. It's more than I could have done."

Kal couldn't imagine what he would have done had Wilek died in his arms. "I know much of failure. If it isn't an inconvenience, I'll take Novan as a backman."

"Thank you, Sir Kalenek," Trevn said. "But he is one of my guards, and I've grown rather fond of him. And I think if you took a tally, you would find more successes in your career to count than failures."

Kal grunted. "Can one tally lives and deaths with mere strokes of charcoal?"

"One *could*," Trevn said, "but I think it wiser to live life knowing that you are not a god. You are one fallible man. You do your best. And whether you live or die is up to Arman. Since you are here, he still has purpose for your life. So do your duty by the God. Forgive yourself, and live well."

Kal didn't know if he could ever forgive himself for all he'd done.

"My wife is eager to see you," Trevn said. "Hawley will show you to your room where you can bathe and change into fresh clothing. When you're done, send for him and he'll bring you to Mielle. Dismissed."

"Thank you, sir." Kal stood, then took Onika's hand and squeezed. "Good midday, Miss Onika. I hope it will not be long before we see each other again."

"We have never seen each other, Sir Kalenek, at least not at the same moment. Though I'm sure it won't be long until we meet again," she said. *"And if it is,"* she added with her voicing magic, *"then we will talk like this."*

For the sound of that voice, Kal would always be listening.

Trevn

Trevn had Grayson carry Sosovik and the Puru people to Conaw's village. Once they were settled, Grayson carried Ulagan the Uul-Yeke giant to Trevn's office to discuss the Jiir-Yeke, who, according to Princess Saria, had recently attacked two villages on the outskirts of New Sarikar.

"This is the first trouble any of the Kinsman villages have had from the Jiir-Yeke," Trevn said. "Any idea why they are attacking now?"

"Masaoo dishonored the Jiir when he stole their sacrifices," Ulagan said. "He endangered the chance for Jiir ancestors to become immortal."

Such a strange practice. Trevn didn't understand it. "But New Sarikar had nothing to do with that." Mielle and Grayson were to blame.

"Most Yeke think dirtmen are of the same tribe," Ulagan said.

Well, that was fairly insulting. "We have discovered another way to fight any who attack us, but it will take time to train our people." Miss Onika had promised to teach her new offensive magic to those with the mind-speak ability. Trevn hoped it worked on giants.

"The Uul-Yeke tire of the evil the Jiir and Ahj wreak on the Puru," Ulagan said. "We will stand with you against the Ahj and Jiir if war comes."

"Thank you, Ulagan," Trevn said.

After Grayson carried Ulagan away, Hawley brought in Trevn's next appointment: Captain Veralla's sons, Sir Keshton and Zanre.

"Thank you for coming, gentlemen," Trevn said. "I'd like you to look at this map." He motioned to his desk, where he'd anchored his map of South Er'Rets with weights. Veralla's sons stepped closer, while Cadoc and Nietz observed from the door.

"See this line?" Trevn traced his finger along it. "It's a river that branches off the Great River and runs all the way to the coast near Er'Rets Point. It's not large. Perhaps fifteen paces at its widest, but it makes a nice natural boundary. I want to build some border houses along this river. We have the watchtower at Er'Rets Point, and New Sarikar sits on the eastern arm of the Great River in the north. Three border houses in between would be ideal."

He tapped his finger over the map to show the locations he had in mind. "I've asked New Sarikar to build a border house in the ridgelands east of the river, just south of the fork. Armania will build the other two, and I'd like you to take charge of one. A basic fort surrounded by a palisade. Big enough to store supplies for our army. Should Rogedoth march upon us, these posts could stop his army from reaching the farms and the city, which will save a lot of lives. I know it's asking a lot to uproot you from your families in the middle of winter, but will you oversee the building of the central border house?"

"Yes, sir," Sir Keshton said, and his brother nodded his agreement.

The door opened and Hawley peeked inside. "Barek Hadar to see you, sir."

Trevn masked his annoyance. "Is Duke Canden out there?"

"Not yet," Hawley said.

"Tell Barek I have meetings scheduled all day. He may have five minutes." Hawley nodded and shut the door.

"Who have you asked to build the southern border house?" Sir Keshton asked.

"I'm still deciding," Trevn said. "I welcome any recommendations."

"Sir Ransen would be a good choice," Sir Keshton said of Lord Idez's eldest son.

"He's on my list." But the man didn't have his own army as Sir Keshton did. The only officers with personal armies were, unfortunately, from noble families Trevn didn't trust.

He worked out the details of the border house with the brothers, and when they left, Barek Hadar entered. The man took a seat before Trevn's desk and waited for Hawley to leave. Trevn could feel Barek's agitation. Once the door was closed and they were alone but for Cadoc and Nietz, Barek got right to his point.

"You're making a grave mistake with Sir Jarmyn Koll."

"Am I? Sir Jarmyn not only deserted his post, he directly defied General Ensley's order to attack the enemy commander. That's *two* orders disobeyed. The pole is the minimum penalty."

"You must release him at once. Sir Jarmyn claims he misheard the order, and his father's men are very loyal to him. They might all rise up against us."

"Let them," Trevn said. "Then I'll have reason to arrest Gunrik and his men too."

"Tace Edekk also supports him."

"Because Tace's daughter is Sir Jarmyn's wife," Trevn said. "Sir Jarmyn's charges are based on his actions. I cannot help what he did."

"But he claims to have misheard the order. Would we accuse him of lying, then flog him?"

"Whether or not he heard the order, he didn't turn back when I voiced him. Armanians died because of his choice. My sentence stands. He will face the pole tomorrow."

"This humiliation will only further divide the nobility against the throne."

Mention of the nobility further annoyed Trevn. "The nobility has no bearing on my decision."

"It should!" Barek yelled, and Trevn felt his anger flare. "Do you recall history, Your Highness? Under the reign of your ancestor King Nathek, who openly defied his peers, three noble families infiltrated the castle and deposed him. They mercilessly tortured and executed the king's closest friends and molested his wife."

"Yet the king overpowered them and had them all hanged. I know the story."

"So you know what you risk," Barek said.

"The throne is not a tool of the peerage," Trevn said.

"They'll rise up against you. I've seen this kind of division before in Sarikar."

"Let's leave the prophecies to Miss Onika and Father Wolbair, shall we?" Trevn said.

Barek banged his fist on the desk, and Cadoc and Nietz swept up to stand on either side of him. Barek's expression grew sheepish. "My pardons," he said.

"Your Grace," Trevn said, struggling to keep his own temper, "You serve on the council because I value your opinions, but do not forget which of us is king."

Barek stood and bowed. "Thank you for hearing me, Your Highness." And he stormed out, angrier, it seemed, than when he'd entered.

"Good day," Trevn said to the man's retreating back. He felt Mielle's concern reach for him but pushed her aside, then fingered the red imprint of the shell on his palm, the mark of their soul-binding. He still didn't know what to say to her—how they could fix what she had broken. He wanted to forgive her and be done with it, but it wasn't that simple. She continued to justify her actions. It didn't seem to matter that she'd broken his trust. And trust wasn't so easily mended.

Hawley peeked into the room. "Are you ready for Duke Canden?"

"Yes," Trevn said, clasping his hands on his desk. "Send him in."

Oli entered and sat across from Trevn, who relaxed. Here, at least, was a person he could trust fully—who had proven himself loyal.

"Your Grace, what news have you for me?" Trevn asked.

Oli used his hand to rest his wooden arm in his lap. "Rosârah Zeroah's mind-speak progress is a bit . . . uncomfortable." He explained how Zeroah had pulled forth one of his memories. "The end result is, well, she changed me."

"Changed you how?"

"That memory had plagued me for years, but now when I think about it, I feel . . . rehabilitated. She comforted me as a boy, and it forever softened the sting of that dark time. She exposed my shame for what it was. Unnecessary violence and cruelty on my father's part."

While Trevn could plainly see the raw emotion in the duke's face, he didn't understand. "What was this memory, Duke Canden?"

Trevn sensed the man's unease and sent Cadoc and Nietz out of the room. Once they were alone, he did his best to reassure the duke. "Whatever you share will stay between us, Your Grace. You have nothing to fear."

"I'm not afraid, I simply . . . Oh, very well." Oli sank back in the chair. "As you know, most boys become pages at seven, backmen by fifteen, soldiers by twenty. It's the way of things. My father wanted to prove to Rosâr Echad that I was special, so he had me serving as a page in his army by age four, and by the time I was seven, I was responsible for some tasks that today I would only assign a trusted officer. Most of my assignments involved spying. Father would dress me in rags and send me into enemy territory to see what I could learn."

The duke went on to tell a story about a time during the Centenary War that his father had ordered him to spy on a Magonian regiment, but he had fallen asleep. "Father felt that I deserved the same punishment a grown man would have received, so he sent me to the pole."

"Sands," Trevn said, aghast that any man would treat a child so, though unsurprised that his own father, King Echad, had allowed it.

"The point is, Your Highness," Oli said, "Rosârah Zeroah inserted herself into that memory without my permission, nor could I stop her. And now, when I recall the aftermath of that day, she's with me, comforting me as if she'd been there all along. I can no longer remember the incident any other way."

"That's most strange."

"It's remarkable. She has healed a small part of my soul. Such an ability could be a tremendous asset, but . . ."

"But?"

"If this magic can be used to alter a memory for one's healing, I fear it could also be used to alter a memory for one's detriment, especially as a war tactic. There might be a way we could use this to our advantage in battle."

"A fairly terrifying idea," Trevn said, thoughts spinning at the prospect. "You will continue to work with her, won't you? See if you can train her to use the gift better?"

"I'm honored to help her develop her gift and see what can be learned, though I'm certain she would never harm another human being—even our enemy. She has too much grace and compassion—sees us all as Arman's children. The woman actually longs for everyone to know how much they are loved by their creator and that nothing can separate us from him."

The words from the Book of Arman washed over Trevn. "I didn't know you had converted, Your Grace."

"I haven't, Your Highness. I'm simply repeating the dowager queen's words. I caught her proselytizing to a group of guards in the great hall last week, and yesterday she was telling my manservant about Arman's many gifts."

Trevn chuckled. "Yes, Mielle said that Zeroah is better at sermonizing than any priest."

"She would never let herself be used as a weapon. But if I can learn how she does it, perhaps I can teach others."

"Changing one's memories." Trevn fought the urge to shudder. The idea was rife with possibilities and danger. "How would we ever monitor such a thing?"

"It would be impossible," Oli said.

That's what Trevn was afraid of. "Thank you for your efforts in this regard, Your Grace. Continue to practice with Zeroah, but do not teach anyone else without my permission." He stood, Oli stood with him, and Trevn walked the duke toward the exit. "This reminds me. Hinck told me about something extraordinary your sister did." Trevn told the duke about how Eudora had given Hinck her memories. "I wonder if Rosârah Zeroah can do the same?"

"I'll look into it at once, Your Highness," Oli said.

"Excellent." Trevn opened the chamber to let Oli out. "Hawley, could you have a snack brought up, please? I'm famished."

"I'll send for one right away," Hawley said.

"Thank you." Trevn was about to go back inside when he saw Hinck leaning against the wall. "Hinck. Are you waiting for me? How long have you been out here?"

Hinck pushed off the wall. "Since the Veralla brothers left. I need to talk to you."

"You can talk to me anytime," Trevn said, tapping his temple.

"Yes, well, I know it might sound strange to one so busy as you, but I'd like to occasionally look upon your face when we speak. Especially when I have something important to discuss, which I do."

"I understand that desire. I've seen my face." Trevn re-entered his office. Hinck followed and closed the door behind them. Trevn sat on the front edge of his desk. "Well?"

"I want to go to Saria."

Trevn sighed. Why would nobody listen when he declared an issue decided? "You have new reasons, I'm sure."

"With the Jiir-Yeke attacks and her conniving council, well, as you said, she needs someone." Hinck shrugged. "As it turns out, I am that someone."

"That's the whole of your reasoning?"

"No, but . . . growing up in her home . . . and, well, she is our sister in the faith, if not from years of hair pulling and pranks. How can you ignore her plea?"

"Because I have no alternative," Trevn said. "I trust no one well enough to send."

Hinck held out his hands. "Yet here I stand."

"I need you here."

Hinck tapped his temple. "As you have just indicated, you truly do not. Besides, I am little to you anymore but a listening ear."

"You've always been far more than that, but I do rely upon your counsel like no other."

"I understand, Your Shortsightedness, but because of the voices, you will still be able to reach me at any time. Since I've returned, you and I have had a few moments together in which you tell me your woes, I listen and give what thoughts I have on the subject, then you leave to contend with all your very important duties of the crown, and I'm left alone, completely unengaged until you have woes to share again. I have no purpose, Trev, and I need one."

"I could set you up to train some bowmen. Though I would prefer my bowmen actually learn the skill from one who can properly loose an arrow."

Hinck did not even smile at Trevn's jest. "Ever since you've mentioned Saria's troubles, she has been on my mind. She has lost much. We cannot abandon her to those wolves in her council. With Finnel Wallington married to her aunt, I wouldn't doubt he's plotting to take the throne of Sarikar. It's in our best interest that he not become king of anywhere, don't you think? And with the giants attacking . . . we need Sarikar strong. Rogedoth will likely go there first."

"But what can you do about it that General Norcott cannot?" Trevn asked.

"I'll think of something. I've had over a year's training in the art of corruption under Barthel Rogedoth. I likely picked up some tips on treachery that Saria could put to good use."

"You haven't a treacherous bone in your body, Hinck. Any plans you come up with will undoubtedly involve some gentlemanly code of honor that traps you in Sarikar far longer than I wish to give you up, and I don't see how you'll get a council with Finnel Wallington at its head to hear anything you say."

"Please, Trev? You've replaced me here. You no longer need me as a backman or a onesent or even a council member. I find myself hovering outside your door each day, hoping you might devise some errand to occupy even a half hour of my time. I crave a greater purpose. Let me go to Sarikar and give aid. I know I would be of greater use to you there than here."

Trevn sighed again. "I do need New Sarikar to build that border house. Saria's council rejected my plan."

"I'll convince them," Hinck said.

Trevn hoped so. "You're the best man I know, Hinck. What shall I do without you?"

"Precisely what you have been doing. Rule the realm and keep Rogedoth from taking it." Hinck flashed his huge smile. "Thank you, Trevn. You won't regret this."

Trevn wasn't so sure.

After Hinck left, Trevn picked at the food on the tray Hawley had brought in and weighed the many things that were bothering him. The Jiir-Yeke. Rogedoth. Shanek. Sir Jarmyn. Tace Edekk. Barek Hadar. Hinck leaving. His fight with Mielle.

It was all too much. Though he continued to strive, he couldn't possibly handle it all on his own. He wasn't strong enough or wise enough. Something was going to get left behind, and he worried it would be Mielle—out of sight, out of mind. And that shouldn't be. He needed her. Yet he didn't know how to fix what she'd broken.

"Are you well, Your Highness?" Cadoc asked. "Can I get you anything?"

Trevn glanced up at the man, sensed his pity. "What I need cannot be given like a gift."

"Actually, it can."

Trevn narrowed his eyes. "How so?"

"Repairing broken trust does not lie with the one who broke it, nor does it depend upon that person proving they are once again worthy to be trusted. The power lies solely with the one who has decided not to trust. Your anger is justified, Your Highness. But as long as you hold tight to your anger, there's no hope of reconciliation."

"So I must take the high ground? Is that what you're saying?"

"You cannot hope for change if you don't do your part."

"I did my part, Cadoc. I do it every day. And I'm tired. What you're suggesting is too much. I won't allow myself to be manipulated. When Mielle is ready to make peace, she knows where to find me."

⊙Lİ

li cleared his mind as he waited for Rosârah Zeroah to show him one of her memories. They sat side by side on the edge of the same longchair in the training room, eyes closed, alone but for the two maids and three guardsmen congregated near the door.

"Begin at any time," he said.

"I've already done so!" Zeroah cried, her voice laced with frustration. She sighed and lowered her voice. "I've been trying."

She wasn't trying hard enough. "Concentrate on a single memory. See it in your mind."

"I have been doing just that for the past half hour."

Oli opened his eyes and found her staring at him, brows creased. "You must be weary. Let us take a short rest."

"I'm not tired, Your Grace. I'm simply incapable of what you are asking."

How could he convince her to believe in herself? "If you have the power to draw forth memories, surely you can plant them as well."

"Only your memories have passed between us. Perhaps you are the gifted one."

Now there was a ridiculous thought. As if he ever would have shown anyone the humiliating moments she'd pulled from the depths of his mind. "You have an incredible gift, rosârah. We simply must discover what triggers it."

"You are mistaken, sir. You pulled me into your mind. You showed me those things."

"I would never!" he yelled.

Her eyes widened. He'd frightened her.

"Forgive me, lady." Oli fought back his frustration, not wanting to upset her further. "Let us stop for today, but please focus on your memories whenever you can. Only by practicing will you discover the range of this gift."

"If you insist."

Oli got the distinct impression she would not practice at all. It annoyed him greatly that she seemed to have already given up, but what could he do?

He stood and helped her to her feet, but when he tried to release her, she squeezed his fingers. "May I ask you a question, Your Grace?"

"Certainly."

"I wish to take Miss Vivia as one of my lady's maids."

Mention of the kitchen maid left him abashed. "I'm sure that would please her."

"I had thought so too, but when I asked, she rejected me outright due to the fact that she was soon to be employed elsewhere."

Vivia was taking a new position? "Else*where*?" he asked.

Zeroah glanced away from his eyes. "As your concubine."

So surprised was Oli by this suggestion, he laughed, but the censure in Zeroah's golden stare quickly sobered him. "I assure you, lady, I've made no such offer of employment to Miss Vivia, nor will I. I seek no such companion in my life."

"She's under the impression that you love her."

He tugged his hand free, shocked that Zeroah Barta would dare broach such a topic. Perhaps if he ignored her, she would realize how very rude—

"Do you? Love her?"

"Your Highness, I will not discuss my personal life with you or anyone." He couldn't fathom why this conversation was taking place.

"Well, she loves you. And if she is locked in a misunderstanding with you, I cannot secure her employment. You must have said something to give her the impression—"

"I have never said such a thing to any woman. Vivia means nothing to me."

"Then you must tell her so," Zeroah said. "So that she might accept the position."

Oli did not see why any of this was his problem. "Is there no other lady in the castle who might fill this role?"

"I don't need another lady's maid, Your Grace. I wish to be Miss Vivia's friend."

"A queen and a kitchen maid? Friends?"

"According to the Book of Arman, the One God shows no partiality. To him a king and a servant are equals."

"What's your point, lady?"

She scowled, and emotions surged off her, anger and confusion and disappointment. "I don't know." She walked toward the door, then turned back to face him. "You have always treated me with the utmost respect and kindness. Why not treat Miss Vivia the same?"

Simple. "Because she is not a queen."

Zeroah pursed her lips, as if collecting her thoughts. "I see," she said finally, nodding once. "Then you are not the man I thought you were. Good day, Your Grace." She walked away, leaving him standing beside the longchair, completely bewildered.

Convinced that he might have lost Zeroah's good opinion, that night when Vivia came to Oli's chamber, he fully intended to send her away. She showed up with a bottle of wine, however, and baked apples wrapped in sugar-dusted pastry. He couldn't resist the aroma and invited her in.

They sat before the fire, and as they ate, he watched her closely, trying to discern what, if anything, he felt for the girl. Curse Zeroah Barta-Hadar to the Lowerworld. The woman had gotten into his head, and not with her mind-speak ability. Now he must rid himself of Vivia and be done with it.

"Rosârah Zeroah told me she's asked you to serve as a lady's maid," he said.

Vivia's eyes grew wide. "She spoke to you about me?"

"She *did*," he said slowly.

She lit up. Her eyes and smile—even her posture—seemed almost giddy. "She said you and I are equals in Arman's eyes. She also said I should chase after my dreams."

Off all the interfering . . . Two could play at this game. "Then you must take the position with her. It would be far more enjoyable, I'm sure, than working in the kitchens."

She cocked her head, like a puppy trying to understand. "But, Your Grace, it's not my dream to be a lady's maid. I . . ." She picked at the peel of her apple. "Why don't you have a concubine?"

This was her plan? To hedge her way to the point in the most roundabout way possible? Oli didn't have the patience. "I would think such a thing would displease you."

Her eyes glistened in the low candlelight, but she offered him a quivering smile. "Maybe I don't want to be a maid forever. I have dreams, you know."

"So you've mentioned. Vivia, if you dream of serving as a lady's maid, I'm happy to put in a good word with Rosârah Zeroah. But if you hope to become my concubine . . . don't."

Her smile faded. "Don't?"

"Woman, hear me well, because I will not have this conversation again. This was only ever going to be a dalliance. I have no aspirations beyond teaching boys to become men and serving this realm as best I can. I seek no name for myself, no fortune. I'm a cursed man and will not yoke myself to another with any permanence."

"Because you're cursed? Or because you don't want to?"

"Both. I am what I am. If you can't accept that, I understand. Few can. Because few live so low as I do. You seek a better life? I applaud you. Find someone who can give you what you want."

"But I want you."

"You can have my body all you want, my dear, but the rest of me belongs to Gâzar. I pledged it to him long ago, and I'm afraid he will not give me up."

She frowned. "The queen says we all belong to Arman—that you only need to make an honor pledge and the Father God will accept you."

Comprehension tingled up his spine. Zeroah had been preaching to Vivia about her god. "Yes, well, she's half right. A man can make a pledge to any god, but the gods don't like to share. And once they own a soul, they keep it."

"That's a terrible outlook." She rose from the chair, glaring. "You lost half an arm, but you live like you're dead. It's pathetic!"

"You think dead men teach children by day and serve at their king's command?"

"Oh, shut up!" She wiped tears from her cheek. "Don't speak to me again."

"If you wish."

She stomped her foot. "You know very well I don't!"

His heart sank. He'd let this go too far. He didn't like to make women cry. "Vivia, I'm sorry to be such a disappointment. You truly deserve better than this."

"No." She strode to him, her expression tortured. "You don't get to break my heart and be charming."

"I'm sorry I hurt you, lady."

"Stop it!" She hammered one fist against his chest, then the other, and suddenly she was pounding with both. He let her have it out, until she struck his shoulder, where his father had stabbed him. At the sharp pain, he wrapped his arm around her and pulled her against his chest.

"Calm down," he said.

"Let go!" She let loose a scream, so high-pitched and desperate, it jolted his heart.

"Stop that!" He had to calm her down before her hysteria brought the guards. He pushed into her mind. *"Vivia, calm yourself."*

She stilled.

At first he didn't trust her obedience. She was pretending. The moment he released her, she'd start screaming again. But she held still for so long, amber eyes watching him, he finally released her. She remained silent. Unmoving.

How strange. Concern crept upon him that he'd magicked her somehow. Woes! Could Zeroah have been right? Had he such power?

If so, perhaps he could make things right for Vivia, take away her heartbreak. He took hold of her hands and concentrated on her thoughts. *"You don't love me."*

Tears welled in her eyes, and she began to cry. Oddly enough, she didn't speak or move. Was it because he'd told her to stop?

Perhaps he could alter her memory. He closed his eyes and voiced her. *"Remember when we met."*

The memory played across his mind as if it were his own. He saw himself in the great hall. Vivia filled his goblet with wine, and he complimented her on her dress. They talked for several minutes. He knew what was coming. She would be called away, but when she returned with his meal, he would ask her to visit his room that night. He let the memory play out. And when the moment came, he focused on Vivia's mind.

"You cannot hear him. It's too loud in here. He's asking you to sit beside him, which of course you cannot do. Decline politely, then get back to work before you are seen talking to him. His kind like to make trouble."

To Oli's surprise, the Vivia in the memory did just as he suggested.

He tried another memory. *"Remember our first night together."* The scene ran through his head. She was in his chamber—had brought him a berry trifle. *"Go back,"* he voiced. *"When you were on the stairs."*

The memory shifted until Vivia was ascending the circular stairs. She stepped off on the fourth floor, and Oli placed himself in front of her.

"Good evening," he said. *"Where are you going with that stunning dessert?"*

"I was bringing it to you," she said.

"Were you? I am flattered. But I'm leaving this moment on an urgent errand. Perhaps you could bring me one at dinner tomorrow night?"

Her expression sank, but she curtsied, said, *"Yes, lord,"* and started back down the stairs.

Oli continued to bring forth memories of their encounters. He changed each one, growing steadily troubled by his power. Zeroah had been right. This had been his magic all along, and while Zeroah had used his magic to help him, here he stood using that same power to manipulate.

It couldn't be helped. Vivia would be better off having forgotten him. She could take a position as Zeroah's lady's maid and learn all about the One God. Lead a good, respectable life.

When he finished, Oli sent Vivia out the door with one last altered memory of having drunk two bottles of wine. He watched her stagger down the stairs and hated himself anew for the self-absorbed cur he was.

He closed the door and fell into bed. He lay flat on his back, sick with the realization of what he could do. He tried to sleep, but all he could think about was how angry he was that Zeroah had complicated his life.

What right had she to meddle in his private affairs? To tell Vivia about Arman's love? He supposed a woman that pious must go around proselytizing to any who would listen. What maid would dare deny the queen her ear? But to tell the maid that her dreams mattered and to chase after them . . . Fool, idealistic woman. This wasn't a world that granted dreams. Zeroah should know that more than most, considering every member of her family was dead. How she continued to go about her days smiling and believing Arman was good was beyond his comprehension.

He fetched the bottle of wine from the tray Vivia had left behind, drowned his woes in drink, and eventually fell asleep.

Oli's dreams that night took him back in time to the bowels of Castle Everton, where his father had inducted him into the Lahavôtesh at age ten. Moon Fang had branded him and forced him to bond with a shadir to keep from dying. Even when Paliki took away the pain, the creature still taunted him, called him a baby for crying.

As the little boy wept, a woman appeared before him. Goodness radiated from her, melted the coldness inside Oli, and made Paliki fly away.

She knelt at Oli's head and stroked his hair. She was all warmth and goodness and freedom. "Do not be afraid, child. Arman is greater than this evil. He will protect you."

Rosârah Zeroah.

Oli woke with a gasp. The heat of Zeroah's touch faded to a sweaty warmth. He pushed off his blankets and sat up, head pounding from too much wine.

She'd done it again. Inserted herself into his memories and—No. He recalled all that had happened with Vivia. The memory magic had been his all along. He must have pulled the rosârah into his dream.

Why her, of all people? And why show her his childhood humiliations?

The answer came quickly enough. He'd never known someone so kind. He was drawn to her compassion. And the fact that she'd healed some of his pain.

Woes, he must find a way to stop this. It was far from appropriate and—

"Your Grace? Are you hurt?"

Oli reeled, shocked to hear Zeroah's voice in his mind. *"Why would you think that, lady?"* And why had his addled brain answered at such an hour?

"I was dreaming," she said. *"You were a child, in some cultic ceremony. And when I awoke, I felt you in my mind. You seemed agitated."*

For some reason, he answered truthfully. *"My childhood was not an easy one."*

"Was it the Lahavôtesh? I didn't realize they inducted children so young."

"They didn't," he said. *"My father made a deal to induct me early."*

"Did your mother know?"

"She did." He pictured her then, beautiful, proud, and bitter that her children would never rule. *"She was a princess, one step from the throne. She liked Father's ambition."*

"I well understand living under a parent's ambition. It's not an easy childhood when so many expectations are laid out in rigid order."

Her words ministered to the life he'd lived, and he suddenly felt a surge of affection for this woman who had somehow managed, after all she had been through, to be kind and empathetic to someone as toxic as him. The feeling so surprised and disturbed him that he quickly tried to offend her.

"You'll be pleased to know that Miss Vivia and I have parted ways."

She did not answer at first, and Oli wondered if she'd fallen asleep. But then she said, *"I am never pleased by heartbreak, Your Grace, though I did enjoy the opportunity to speak with her again."*

Fear shot through Oli's chest that he might be found out. *"You saw her? When?"*

"Last evening in the kitchen. She was not herself. I'm worried she might be dependent upon opiates of some kind. Have you known her to partake of such things?"

Oli released a trembling breath. *"Too much wine, perhaps, but nothing more,"* he said, horrified that he might have somehow broken Vivia's mind. *"Forgive me, Your Highness, but I am weary and must wake early for school."*

"Good evening, Your Grace. May your dreams be pleasant."

"Yes. Yours as well." He drew up his shields and fortified them, but try as he might, he could not find sleep again that night.

Mielle

Mielle and her staff had transformed the great hall. The tables had been pushed against the exterior walls and filled with food and drink. Mielle had stationed the minstrels and the royal band in one corner of the great hall and had done her very best to make use of the decorations that once had hung on the walls of King Echad's reception room in Castle Everton. She'd draped the blue and gold fabric around the edges of the ceiling and brought in the thrones from the tiny receiving chamber that normally housed them. Mielle didn't think Trevn had sat on the soft blue velvet since the coronation. Perhaps today would be the day?

Considering he was barely speaking to her, perhaps not.

Ever since the fight he hadn't been sleeping in their chambers. Hawley confessed that Trevn had asked him to make up a pallet in the antechamber off the council room. The king of Armania sleeping in the equivalent of a closet. To avoid his traitorous wife.

"Mielle, it is time."

Zeroah, looking glorious and slender in a beaded black gown, nodded toward the entrance. A family had crossed the threshold of the great hall and was headed toward the dais.

Mielle fingered the shell on the soul-binding necklace and hurried toward the throne with Zeroah. "He's not going to come, is he?"

"You must always hope," Zeroah said. "You apologized, didn't you?"

"Of course." But she hadn't. Not really. The realization flustered her, and she stepped on the hem of her dress, nearly tripping herself. *Oh, tuhsh.* She forced herself to walk the rest of the way, slowly, to move like a queen. "*People wait for their queen,"* Brelenah continually told her, yet when Mielle sat on her throne beside Trevn's empty one, she didn't feel like royalty. All she felt was Trevn's emotions through the soul-binding—the combination of his concern and his trying to mask it. He still cared for her. She must find a way to prove to him she cared too.

"Here comes Joret Vohan, the Earl of Idez, and his wife, Countess Cabena," Zeroah voiced to Mielle as the first family headed their way. *"Lord Idez is on the Wisean Council. Their sons are Sir Ransen and Master Enko and—oh!"* A smile lit up Zeroah's face. *"They brought their daughter, Lady Madara, though it seems she left her son behind."*

Mielle eyed the young girl and thought, *"She's married? She looks so young."*

"She is unmarried," Zeroah voiced. *"Do you recall Lady Eudora telling us about how Sir Jarmyn Koll seduced Lady Madara and got her with child?"*

"Vaguely."

"That's her. Poor thing. She's as sweet as can be. Address them as Lord Idez, Countess, Sir Ransen, Master Enko, and Lady Madara. Give your condolences on the loss of their son, Sir Greth, who died in the Battle of Sarikar."

The family reached Mielle and genuflected, which made her even more nervous as she desperately tried to recall everything Zeroah had just said.

"Lord Idez, welcome," she told the gray-haired man. "Countess, Sir Ransen, Master Enko. And Lady Madara, how is your son?"

Lady Madara curtsied. "He is well, thank you, Your Highness. I didn't think it wise to bring him out in such weather."

"It's very cold," the countess said. "We have partitioned off a section of the sitting room, right around the fireplace, and little Rennik and his nurse spend most of the day trapped there, soaking up the warmth."

"Yes, well, we are holding up the line," Lord Idez said, glancing behind him. "We look forward to speaking with the king. He will be here, won't he?"

"I believe so," Mielle said, hoping Trevn would not let her down.

More polite farewells followed, and the Vohan family moved on. Mielle barely had time for a deep breath before the next family stepped forward. Thankfully, she knew them. Hinckdan's parents bowed and curtsied.

"Your Grace, Duchess Zura, good midday," Mielle said. "Are you missing your son already?"

"Yes, of course," Danek said, his smile as wide as ever, "but we are proud that he has gone to help Princess Saria. We won't stall the reception line except to say well done. There is a very encouraging turnout in the foyer."

Relieved to hear that, Mielle thanked him. They moved away and the next party advanced. Two young women about Mielle's age were escorted by a large, elderly woman with so many beads wrapped around her throat they resembled a scarf. She looked desperately familiar, though Mielle could not place her.

"You know Lady Durvah from the court of King Echad," Zeroah said aloud, which thankfully jogged Mielle's memory. "And these are her daughters, ladies Tarla and Nolli."

"Thank you immensely for inviting us," Lady Durvah said. "I see dirty looks flying my way already, but I don't care. My husband made his choice, and I and my girls had no part in it."

"I'm very glad you came," Mielle said, clueless what the woman was talking about.

As they walked away, Mielle shot Zeroah a questioning look.

"Lady Durvah was married to Avron Jervaid," Zeroah voiced. *"He was the Wisean Council member who ran off from Canden House with the pregnant Queen Ojeda."*

Oh yes. King Echad's fifth queen. *"More are coming. Quick! Who are they?"* She would never remember so many new faces.

"Well, this is a surprise. The older woman is Duchess Gitla," Zeroah voiced. *"She is Master Fonu's mother, Tace Edekk's wife."*

"The man accused of abducting Armanian children into his army," Mielle said.

"That's right. With her are her daughters, Imara and Dendrelle, the latter of which is married to Sir Jarmyn Koll. As you can see, Lady Koll is with child. Her first."

Mielle took note of the young woman's bulging stomach. *"Isn't Sir Jarmyn the one who . . . Lady Madara?"*

"Yes, Sir Jarmyn is the father of both children and the man Rosâr Trevn sent to the pole for his disobedience in the Battle of Armanguard. His parents are just behind him. The gray-haired man is Lord Blackpool, then his wife, Countess Sabin. The others are servants."

Mielle spotted the orphan boy Porvil standing with the servants, which knotted her thoughts so badly that she called one of the women by her first name only and addressed Lord Blackpool's wife as Duchess Sabin.

"My wife is a countess, Your Highness," Lord Blackpool said.

His correction flustered Mielle further. "Do forgive me." Though from the glares this group was giving her, none of them had any intention of doing so.

"Sorry to hear about the death of our king," Lord Blackpool said to Zeroah. "And now we have one even younger." He turned his dark eyes on Mielle. "How long will he last, I wonder?"

"Not very long if he insists upon flogging innocent officers," said young, pregnant Dendrelle.

Truth.

The word whispered in the back of Mielle's mind. A burst of rage seized her. Not only did they dare to slight Trevn, but one of this group was using magic. She felt Trevn's unease rise up, but she pushed it aside and answered these horrible people in kind.

"I was sorry to hear of the death of Master Fonu, your son," Mielle said to Duchess Gitla. "It's hard enough to lose a loved one, but when that loved one committed multiple acts of treason and was responsible for the death of our sovereign, well"—she shook her head slightly—"it's unfair how such a thing taints the whole family. I understand that from the scandals my warden and sister put themselves through. Please know that your family is in my prayers."

Now her guests looked as livid as she felt, but this time they wisely held their tongues, bowed or curtsied, and went on their way.

"Oh, tuhsh." Mielle stomped her foot. "That was awful, wasn't it?"

"I thought it was brilliant," Zeroah whispered. "I could think of nothing to say."

Mielle glanced after the group and found Lady Koll glaring her way. Simply horrible. All of them. "Is Porvil their servant?"

"I believe he is apprenticed to the Edekk family." Zeroah elbowed Mielle, pulling her attention back to the line, where Oli Agoros, Duke of Canden, stood alone.

"Your Grace, hello." Mielle could not help but glance at his fake arm, though with his long-sleeved tunic and gloves, it looked no different from the other.

"Rosârahs." Oli bowed and continued on without another word.

"How odd," Mielle said, watching him go. "Did something happen between you two?"

Zeroah's silence pulled Mielle's attention from the retreating duke to her friend, who was fidgeting with a strand of beads on her gown. "Ah, here is Rosârah Brelenah and the sârahs."

Mielle greeted them warmly, glad for someone she knew, but they too passed quickly by, and strangers continued to flood into the great hall. Zeroah helped with names, and Mielle continually apologized for Trevn's absence.

"Thank the gods!" Mielle said when all had been greeted. "I thought that would never end. What would I have done without you?"

"Called them all *sir* and *lady* and been teased for it, but most would have understood. The majority are good-hearted people, though their interests tend to make them pushy."

So many were wearing black. "Was I wrong to dress in color?"

"Not at all. The five-month mourning period does not apply to you as it does Trevn and me. And it is nearly at an end. Your color reminds everyone that a new season is coming."

Mielle liked that idea. "Is it going well, do you think? So many seemed disappointed not to see Trevn."

"They are testing this," Zeroah said. "They want to experience it. Then they will judge, many of them harshly, but if they find the day entertaining and the report is favorable, those nobles who did not come will come next time. Shall I send Abree to fetch you something to eat?"

"I'm not hungry. In fact, I'd like to step out. I just need a moment to breathe."

Mielle walked behind the curtain into the servants' antechamber, Lady Pia and Bero at her heels. When the area was clear, she asked Bero for a handkerchief and entered the secret passage. Safely hidden in the dark, she let herself cry, dabbing her eyes with the handkerchief, and tried not to lose herself for fear all would see her puffy eyes and know how weak she was.

Horrible people, anyway. They were impossible to please. How would Mielle ever succeed as a queen? She couldn't even—

"Mielle, what has happened?"

The sound of Trevn's voice in her mind was too much, and she lost what little control she'd been fighting to maintain. *"Oh, Trevn! These people are awful! The way they say things, insults guised in compliments and advice. It's terribly hard to bear. I never realized how hard your job is. I haven't given you enough credit for the difficult decisions you have to make and the pressures you face each day. I'm sorry I didn't tell you I had asked Grayson to look for the Puru children, and I'm desperately sorry I didn't tell him to stop once you'd told me what Conaw's people wanted. It was very wrong of me. Please, Trevn, I beg you to forgive me. I miss you so desperately."*

She sobbed then, alone in the dark passageway. That he didn't answer right away filled her with dread. What would become of her now? Would he cast her out? Take another wife?

"I forgive you, Mielle."

A little gasp. Had she heard him right? *"You do?"*

"Of course. I've been hoping you would ask."

Laughter bubbled up from deep within Mielle's heart. *"Oh, Trevn. Thank you!"* She sniffled and wiped the moisture from her cheeks with Bero's handkerchief. *"I'm so relieved."*

"Where are you, Mouse?" he asked. *"Who is hosting court?"*

Oh tuhsh. *"I left Zeroah for a moment, but I will return at once."* She pushed open the door, returned Bero's now-bedraggled handkerchief, and strode back toward the curtain that led to the great hall. She was the queen of Armania with a party to entertain.

Mielle returned to her throne happy, but Zeroah fussed over her so much Mielle sent her to fetch a goblet of wine and some cheese. One sip and Mielle realized she'd been famished. She ate and drank and felt a great deal better—mostly because Trevn had forgiven her.

Rosârah Brelenah came to the dais. "You are doing very well, Your Highness."

Mielle doubted that, but she was glad the worst of it was over. Everyone was mingling at present and seemed to be enjoying themselves.

"The food turned out excellent," Brelenah said. "I particularly like the—oh! Well, look there. Isn't he a sight?" She nodded across the room, which had fallen suddenly quiet.

Mielle glanced up. Everyone was focused on the entrance.

A bugle played Trevn's tune. "All rise for Rosâr Trevn Hadar, may he live forever," the herald at the door announced.

Sure enough, Trevn stood just inside the great hall with Cadoc and Nietz in tow.

"Oh, Trevn!" Mielle leapt from her throne, grabbed two fistfuls of her skirt so as not to trip, and ran toward her husband. As she neared, she caught his raised brow.

"Easy, Mouse," he said to her mind. *"A queen walks."*

She slowed for two paces but ran the last few steps and threw her arms around his neck. "Tuhsh," she said, putting her face but a breath from his. "This queen is exhausted." She kissed him on the lips, then saw that she had left a red mark. The crowd chuckled and began to whisper, which sent heat rushing to Mielle's cheeks.

"Happy to see me, are you?" Trevn asked, grinning.

"Desperately so. Have you a handkerchief? I'm afraid I have all but ruined Bero's."

He withdrew one from his pocket, and Mielle wiped away the red smudge. This drew another round of chuckles from the crowd.

"Thank you for coming." She lowered her voice to a whisper. "You were right about some of these people being vultures."

Trevn signaled with his eyes to someone behind her. "Let the fun begin."

The nobles crowded around Trevn, each waiting their turn for a chance to speak with him. He never made it more than the five or six steps he'd taken into the great hall. People paid him compliments and asked favors. Men brought up titles and asked when he might parcel out the land to the peerage. They were all of them eager to build new houses and plant fields in spring. Trevn gave each the same answer. He was looking into the matter.

He answered so much better than Mielle had, especially when Gunrik Koll asked how close Rogedoth's men were, as if he were eager for them to attack.

"He is still hiding and trying to coerce the giants to fight his battles for him," Trevn said.

Lady Durvah approached next. "Your Highness, I must know, when will you bring back the theater? Surely you enjoyed that part of your father's court. My daughter Nolli has an affinity for acting. Do you know she recites monologues for us nearly every night? She excels at . . ."

As Lady Durvah went on, a familiar face in the crowd behind Trevn caught Mielle's gaze. Porvil, edging closer to hear.

"He's got a knife!" a man yelled.

Porvil ducked out of sight. Trevn knocked into Mielle. The guards swarmed, separating them. Women screamed. Through the soul-binding, Mielle felt confusion, shock, fear, and searing pain in her arm—no, her side.

"Trevn!" She reached for him, but he was no longer there.

"This way, Your Highness." Lady Pia, tugging on her arm.

Mielle pulled away, searching the crowd for her husband. "Where is Trevn?"

"Everyone back!" a man yelled. Master Bonds. One of the King's Guards.

The crowd parted in a circle, creating a ring around Porvil, who lay on his stomach on the floor, a guard pinning him down with one knee. A hand's breadth from his head lay a dagger with a bloody blade. No sign of Trevn.

Mielle screamed.

A gust of calm filled her chest. *"I'm fine,"* Trevn voiced. *"Don't worry."*

His voice brought tears to her eyes. *"Where did they take you?"*

"Behind the curtain. Cadoc said the blade slipped between my side and arm, cut my tunic."

"Come with me, Your Highness," Pia said. "I'll take you to him."

This time Mielle allowed the woman to lead her away. *"The knife is bloodied, Trevn."*

"I'm fine."

The crowd began to talk. The chaos of so much noise fed Mielle's fear. Pia and Bero led her toward the dais, but Mielle rushed ahead, pushed past the curtain and into the antechamber. Two guards stepped in her way but quickly recognized her and let her pass. Trevn was on his feet, shirtless, surrounded by more of his guards. She shoved past them, found Cadoc kneeling at Trevn's side, rolling a bandage around his torso. The only blood she saw was a narrow line on the back of his arm, just above his elbow.

Trevn's attention fixed on her. "A mere scratch," he said, smiling.

Mielle came to stand toe to toe before him. She took hold of his face and gently kissed his lips. "I thought I lost you when I'd only just gotten you back."

"You never once lost me. Now, go let everyone know I am well."

She released his face and took hold of his hand. "I'm not leaving your side."

"Mielle, you must. I'll join you as soon as Ottee arrives with a fresh tunic."

Go back in there? "Trevn, it's not safe."

"If I don't return, think of the rumors that will spread. I am dead or horribly wounded. Or a coward. Please go back, Mouse. We must not lose all we gained here today."

She gazed into his eyes, saw the urgency there. Her efforts must not be wasted. "I'll go right away." She kissed him once more, then swept toward the curtain. "Pia? Bero? With me."

When she returned to the great hall, Porvil was gone. Mielle did her best to reassure the court that Trevn was well, and he soon joined her and did the job far better. The crowd asked about Porvil and speculated over his motives, but Trevn deftly shifted each query into a new topic. In a very short time, all seemed to have returned to normal, but for Mielle's quaking heart.

Porvil had tried to kill her husband.

Gozan

L ife in Magosia had been dull for Gozan ever since Charlon had stopped taking ahvenrood. The mantics and shadir were restless without magic, and Charlon was always on edge, anxious and cranky, fighting with her maidens and men, and especially with Shanek and Lady Amala, who grew bolder with each passing day.

The only interesting development had been the arrival of Emperor Ulrik. While his obnoxious pride, constant demands, and philandering disgusted Kateen and Roya, the rest of the Magosians were delighted by the unbridled festivity he brought to their monotony.

Gozan passed by Sir Kalenek's old tent, where the young emperor now lived, ignoring the music, the squeals of laughter, and the thick odor of wine on the air. Such baseness bored him, though he was surprised not to see more of his swarm here, taking pleasure from this display of unabashed decadence. He quested for his shadir. The nearest presence came from behind him, in the tent at the very bottom of the hill.

He knew instantly where they were.

Gozan drifted into Shanek's tent. The prince sat cross-legged before his pitfire, whittling a block of wood, Miss Amala beside him. Sure enough, the majority of Gozan's swarm were swooping around the root child or simply hovering at his feet. With the entire camp out of old ahvenrood, Shanek was the only human who could fully interact with shadir. Add to that fact that many had been his companions since birth and, well, it had created a unique situation.

Gozan wearied of seeing his swarm behave with such desperation. He should banish the lot of them to the Lowerworld. That would teach them to prostrate themselves before a human.

Today the boy ignored them—had found some method of blocking out their voices entirely. Something Sir Kalenek had taught him. It did not keep Shanek from seeing the shadir, which sometimes annoyed him to the point of losing his temper and ordering them to leave. And they obeyed, the stupid creatures. Gozan did not understand the hold the boy had over them.

Today Shanek seemed to be tolerating their presence while Miss Amala chattered. Gozan shifted into his slight form and drifted closer, curious what the girl was going on about.

"I heard that Dendron spoke to King Barthel about it, and it sounds amazing. If magic comes through a shadir that has taken Dominion over a bird, think what it might do inside someone as powerful as you."

"I have magic already," Shanek said. "And Mother says I must never let a shadir inside."

Amala stroked his arm. "I fear she is keeping the truth from you, just like she did about Sir Kalenek killing your father. Just like she did about the baby."

Shanek's ridged brow sank low over his eyes.

"Why does she want another son, do you think?" Amala asked.

Shanek shaved a deep swath of wood off the block, frowning. Gozan was impressed. The girl knew how to manipulate the boy better than Charlon did.

"Because she knows you will leave her and go to Armanguard to be king," Amala said. "She wants someone to stay here and rule Magosia. She's going to talk you out of taking your place in Armanguard. That's what King Barthel said, and I think he's right."

When had the girl spoken with King Barthel? And why would she think Shanek of all people could benefit from Dominion?

"Fine," Shanek said. "If it will stop you from talking about it." His eyes shifted toward the half-dozen shadir in a heap at his feet. He reached for Roov, a leafy green slight, and to Gozan's shock, the boy was able to take it by the throat.

Roov squealed like a trod-upon piglet. His eyes bulged and his leafy body trembled. He tried to pull away from Shanek's grip, to no avail.

"Come into me, slight," Shanek said, "so I can do this magic Mother is hiding from me."

Roov's eyes swelled even more. *Take Dominion over you?* he asked.

"Yes and hurry up," Shanek said, giving the creature a shake.

Gozan couldn't believe it. For years he had all but begged Jazlyn for Dominion, and here Roov had received an invitation without even having to ask. He forced himself to remain calm, curious what the slight would do with his new power.

Roov wrapped his leafy vines around Shanek's arm and slowly sank through the boy's dappled-gray skin. Amala and the swarm watched, wide-eyed.

When Roov had vanished, Shanek studied his fingers, made a fist, and flexed his arm. "I feel stronger," he said, "though I don't see how this will allow me to make a new kind of magic."

Amala's eyes sparkled with reverence and admiration. "Tell it to make you fly," she said.

Shanek put down his whittling. "Make me fly, shadir. Right now."

Roov was only a slight. He hadn't the power for such magic. But perhaps Dominion would change all that.

Yet Shanek didn't budge off the ground. He scowled. "What do you mean you can't?"

Gozan considered coming forward, explaining the process more fully, and presenting himself as a substitute for Roov, the lowly slight. Would Shanek listen? Or would Gozan's eagerness make him look desperate?

"Get out, then!" Shanek yelled, and the tangle of green vines that was Roov flew from the boy's chest and drifted across the tent.

Gozan stared. Shocked. Dominion was supposed to be permanent, unless the shadir left, was ordered out by a greater shadir, or the human died. Was Roov really so weak? Or was Shanek's power stronger than any had realized? The boy had touched a shadir—grabbed the creature by the throat. It was something no human had ever done, that Gozan knew of, anyway. The realization kindled fear in his chest.

Roov was now hovering near the ground in the corner of the tent, looking as pathetic as a real vine that had wilted in the sun. A crowd of shadir circled him, all talking at once.

What did it feel like?

Why did you leave?

Can you go back in?

Another group of shadir had gathered around Shanek, pushing and shoving and begging for a chance to do better than Roov had done.

Let me try, master.

I can make you fly if you take ahvenrood.

371

Me, me! Take me!

"Get out, all of you!" Shanek yelled. "I don't want to try that again."

The majority of the shadir departed. Only a few commons remained, watching the boy from a distance, as Gozan did.

"Why didn't you like it?" Amala asked.

"He didn't make me fly," Shanek said. "I wanted to fly."

"Maybe I should try it," Amala said.

"You can't!" Shanek fixed her with an angry stare. "It would hurt you."

Amala tilted her head and smirked. "How do you know?"

"Because you aren't like me. You couldn't live with one inside you, not without ahvenrood. The old kind."

"I have ahvenrood in me still," Amala said, "from when the Chieftess fed it to me. That's why I can hear them and see them."

"I can get you more root if you want," Shanek said. "I know where Mother hid it. But you have to promise not to let a shadir inside you. It's not safe. Promise?"

Amala pouted, as if considering two poor options. "Oh, very well."

"Mother will be angry if she knows I gave root to you, so don't tell her."

"I won't, Shanek."

"Good." Shanek went back to whittling.

Gozan would have to keep an eye on Amala. If Shanek supplied her with ahvenrood, she might quickly become the most powerful mantic in Magosia. Perhaps he should bond with her, though she was so erratic and moody, he wasn't sure he could put up with it.

A whimper pulled his attention back to Roov, and Gozan shot over to where the shadir were clustered around the slight. He took the form of Rurek, grabbed Roov around the throat, and shook him. "What happened?"

"I don't know, great one," Roov said, trembling. "It was unlike the legends say. I had no power. I was at his mercy. Entirely."

The words mingled with the dread that had been pulsing in Gozan's chest.

Shanek DanSâr, a human, had Dominion over shadir.

Hᴉɴᴄᴋ

Hinck arrived in Sarikar late in the evening. He and the four guards Trevn had given him rode through a city ravaged by war. Every structure had been patched up in some way, including the castle itself. Even at this late hour a mob of people rushed them, begging for food or coins. Hinck gave out everything he had, but still people grabbed at his cloak and saddlebags until his guards drew their swords and forced them back.

Hinck was ushered to a bedchamber on the third floor. He slept well past morning bells, which embarrassed him. What kind of impression did such lethargy cast upon one sent to give aid? He ordered a bath and dressed in a green tunic to honor Sarikar and show his support.

He then went looking for Saria. In all honesty, he was a little nervous about seeing her. Despite years of childhood teasing and their short-lived adolescent romance, he had always held her in high regard. She was smart, confident, and exceedingly clever. He hoped there was some way he could help that she would accept.

He and his guards stumbled onto a sitting room in which Princess Nolia sat with her nieces and a dozen or so maids and honor maidens, all knitting or doing needlepoint or some such feminine activity. They were dressed in black, as all had lost a husband or father or brother in the Battle of Sarikar.

A shadir circled a cat lying on a cushion by the window. A pale shade of yellow, the creature was fat like a toad and had three large black eyes that were fixed upon the cat, who kept hissing each time the shadir drew near. Only Hinck and the cat seemed aware of the shadir's existence.

The women hassled Hinck about how much he'd grown since he'd lived in Pixford and begged him to tell all he knew of Queen Mielle's beauty and the gowns she wore. Hinck asked where he might find Saria, and two honor maidens were dispatched to help. Hinck and his guards followed them down a narrow hallway and up a flight of stairs.

"Through there," a maiden said, pointing to a partially opened door.

One of the guards pushed in the door and Hinck followed. They stood in a room walled in shelves that held nothing but scrolls. Sure enough, Saria was inside, dressed in a black gown and standing on a chair, her back to the door. She was reaching for a scroll on a high shelf.

Hinck cleared his throat. "Hello, Saria."

A gasp. The chair wobbled. Saria grabbed for the shelf and knocked a pile of scrolls onto her head. She shrieked, lost her balance, and fell.

Hinck lunged toward her, one pace too late. He grabbed her arms with the intention of helping her stand. This induced a second shriek, and he let go, dropping her.

"Sorry," he said, wincing as he looked down upon the heap of scrolls, tangled braids, and black fabric. "Are you hurt?"

Saria crawled toward the wall at top speed. She pushed to her feet and spun to face him, knife gripped tightly in one fist, a scroll in her other.

The guards drew their swords. Hinck lifted both hands. "Peace, lady. It's only me, Hinckdan Faluk, at your service." He told his men, "Put away your weapons," took a large step back out of her reach, then swept into a courtly bow. When he straightened, he found her smiling.

"What?" Hinck asked.

"I've never heard you say anything so utterly ridiculous. '*Peace, lady. It's only me,*'" she said in a deep voice, then laughed. "Oh, you are droll, Hinck."

Droll? "You'd drawn a knife! Where are your guards, anyway?" Hinck glanced around the room. "Does the queen of New Sarikar inspire such fear with her knife wielding that no one dares threaten her life?"

"My guards are busy with General Norcott at the moment, and I don't trust the other soldiers. Too many are loyal to Finnel. As I told Trevn, I'm not yet queen. The men here have been against me from the start and most of their wives support them. Only Father Wolbair's prophecies have kept anyone from deposing me outright. They have gall enough to stand against me, but not against Arman."

"That's something, at least."

She raised an eyebrow. "*You* fear Arman, Hinck? Since when?"

"Since he saved my life when Rogedoth tried to take it."

"Well then." Her eyes flitted over his face, lingering a moment on his burn scars. "I'm glad to see Trevn has some sense. When he told me he was sending Stink Dan to help me, I admit I was more than a little concerned."

Hinck frowned. "I'm not the one calling childhood names."

She motioned to a chair near the window. "Take a seat while I clean this up."

"Wait outside," Hinck told his guards. When the last man closed the door behind him, Hinck set the chair upright. "I insist on helping. I'll climb, and you hand these up."

"No need, I must read them all, anyway. Hold this." She handed him the scroll, then placed one booted foot squarely in the center of the chair and pulled up her skirt, revealing a sheath strapped to her thigh. "Put that scroll in your pocket. I need to keep it safe."

Hinck obeyed, eyeing Saria's exposed leg while she resheathed her knife. He wondered if she ever thought about their time at the king's wedding to Lady Ojeda. He'd always gotten the impression that Saria had regretted the kisses they'd shared during and after the celebration.

Knife sheathed, her dress fell back into place as she scooped up two arm-fuls of scrolls and carried them to her desk.

Hinck helped her move the rest of the scrolls. "What are you looking for?" he asked.

"Finnel Wallington has claimed a distant connection to the Sarikarian throne. He says because no male heirs of my father or grandfather remain, and since I am unmarried, that he and my aunt should be declared king and queen," Saria said, grabbing another armful of scrolls. "I'm looking for gene-alogies of Sarikarian and Armanian nobility to find someone—anyone—who could help me stop this."

So Finnel *did* want the throne of Sarikar. "He cannot mind-speak, so his claim would be weak at best," Hinck said. "In fact, I have more of a claim on the throne of Sarikar than someone from the Nafni family. My great-grandmother was a Sarikarian princess."

Saria dropped the scrolls on her desk and fixed her golden eyes on his. "You?"

He shrugged. "My father used to threaten me with relocating to Sarikar whenever he got angry with Rosâr Echad, which was quite often. I'm ranked third or fourth in line behind the royal family."

"Behind the royal males, you mean?"

"I believe so, yes,"

"All of whom are dead now," Saria said. "This is exactly what I hope to prove."

A chill ran up Hinck's arms. "That I'm the heir to Sarikar?"

"No," she said, as if he were a fool for suggesting it. "I simply want to list as many males as I can who would fall between Finnel and me. That should stop him from stealing my throne." She dragged the chair to the desk and sat down. "Help me look. I really don't have time for this."

Hinck sat in the chair on the other side of the desk and reached for a scroll. "Trevn mentioned you had problems with food."

"I have problems with everything. Giants have been raiding our villages, stealing food and people for their mines. And now those other giants who take people for sacrifice. Many Sarikarians fled to Armanguard. Dozens more have camped outside the castle gates, wailing for food."

"I met them. Do you truly have so little?"

"Our farmland has been taken over by giants. Trevn sent carts of food, but they were taken by my own people before they reached the castle stronghold."

"Better that Sarikarians have them than giants," Hinck said.

"I suppose, though it does not bode well for the future of Sarikar when my own people steal from me."

"Because they are desperate, lady, not because they dislike you."

"If I cannot rule, I cannot help them."

"You'll rule," Hinck said. "You just have to be patient."

"I have been! While I was loved as princess, my nobles hate me for regent. They've grown superstitious in their trek across the sea. I'm bad luck. They want a man. Any man. They'd love for me to marry that man, which would happily negate Finnel as an option, if I could find someone."

That Saria fully intended to claim rule of Sarikar as a woman impressed Hinck, but overturning hundreds of years of tradition would not be easy. He'd hate to see her wed some ancient lord just to please her council. "There's a shadir in your sitting room." He told her about the one teasing the cat and how Oli Agoros had made him a seer.

"You think there's a mantic in the castle?"

"There could be."

"Father Wolbair will know what do to. He's the only one I trust fully."

"What did he prophesy?"

"My father always knew my sickly brother could not rule, but he'd been dragging his feet about naming his heir. Uncle Rosbert was pressuring him to name Kanzer, but Father didn't think Kanzer could handle the job."

"I'm sure he was right about that," Hinck said.

"Shortly after leaving Bakurah Island, Father Wolbair told my father that to find his heir he should look no further than his own daughter."

Confirmation from the God's prophet. "Arman wants you to rule New Sarikar."

Saria shrugged and looked at another scroll. "That's what my father believed."

"I bet Rosbert didn't like that."

"Threw a dozen fits the first week alone. Of course my father had no intention of dying for many years, so he wasn't as worried about the prospect as Uncle Rosbert was. Anyway . . ." She dropped the scroll and folded her arms. "Why'd you come here, Hinck? Trevn said you volunteered." Her golden eyes fixed on his, demanding an honest answer.

He would not refuse her. "Trevn has so many people around him. I didn't feel all that useful there. And when I heard you were in trouble, I . . . well . . . I wanted to help."

She leaned forward, elbows buried deep in the pile of scrolls, and propped her chin on her fists. "It was the truth, then? Trevn didn't make you come?"

"I told you as much already. It's common knowledge that you and Trevn are both bossy, controlling, selfish, and somewhat heartless . . . but I can stand up to you both, believe it or not."

"Oh, Hinck. Now you seek to flatter me. I suspect it's the blood ancestors Trevn and I share that make us so special."

"And now blood *voices* too." Hinck hoped Saria and Trevn wouldn't talk to each other about him.

"Blood voices," Saria said. "I like that. Well, we've work to do." She held out her hand. "Let's see what that scroll says, shall we?"

Hinck removed it from his pocket and passed it over. She unrolled it and her brows sank.

Hinck came around the desk and looked over her shoulder. "Finnel's father was Lady Oriyd's son," he read.

"She was the youngest of Lord Lorek Nafni of Armania and Princess Riddah of Sarikar's three children. We now know her brother Ander had no true children, having secretly adopted Laviel and Darlis. Still, he had no male heir and entailed his title to his sister's son, Finnel's father."

"I never realized that. I should have, though."

"Too much time chasing Trevn over the roofs, perhaps?"

"Undoubtedly."

She released the scroll and it rolled up. "Well, his claim is legitimate. So I'm back to marrying an exotic prince or finding an heir ranked higher."

An idea struck Hinck. It was quite rash—foolhardy, Trevn would say. He swallowed, suddenly nervous, and studied Saria, fully aware that she might laugh in his face. But he'd always liked her. And it *would* solve her problems.

"Would you marry me, lady?"

She flinched. "Hinckdan Faluk, are you mad?"

Very likely, but the idea had merit. "Unless you prefer an exotic prince?"

Her eyes pierced his. "You're serious?"

"Perfectly," he said, liking the idea more and more. "Call a council meeting and—"

"They will not assemble for me."

"Will you let me finish?" Hinck asked. "Call a meeting and lead everyone to believe that you're going to abdicate the throne. This will raise enough curiosity to quickly fill the room."

Her glare darkened. "So far I am unimpressed with this plan."

"Once your council has assembled, you inform them that, second only to Prince Mergest, I have the greatest claim on the throne of Sarikar through my grandfather, son of Princess Maqee."

"I will do no such thing."

"Hear me out. Due to treaties signed by your father and Rosâr Wilek, and due to Armania's assistance in the war that went so very badly for all our sakes, Rosâr Trevn has asked us to marry to strengthen the alliance between our two realms and to put an end to any rebellions on either side."

"You want my throne. That's why you came here."

"I truly don't. But your council doesn't know that. Finnel Wallington doesn't know that. To them I'm a newly titled war hero just returned from saving Armania from the evil queen. Trevn said your council wants you to marry. Use me as the man they need to appease their superstitions. I promise I won't take your rule from you."

Saria eyed him warily. "Why should I believe that?"

He shrugged. "Because you know me."

"Power corrupts the best of men, Hinck."

"I spent almost a year with Barthel Rogedoth. That I survived should be some proof of my integrity."

"Proof of insanity, maybe . . ."

"It would stop Finnel and your council from scheming against you. Then you and I could do some serious work in helping your people. And mine. We could build the border house Trevn asked you for."

"My council has already rejected that proposal," Saria said. "There's no money."

"Let Trevn fund the project, but use Sarikarian workers to build it. That's carpentry jobs for the heads of forty or fifty hungry Sarikarian families."

Saria stared at him so long that Hinck flushed at the scrutiny of those eyes, so gold they put the Painted Dune Sea to shame.

"What?" he finally asked.

"You were always the clever one, Hinck. Trevn had a lot of big ideas, but he always left you to figure out how to accomplish them. What will he do without you?"

Was she saying yes? They sat still, watching each other. Hinck should feel terrified, but he didn't. This felt right. "He's been doing fine without me for quite some time."

Saria broke their stare and started shuffling through the scrolls on her desk. "I need proof of your royal line. And I'd have to work out a betrothal agreement with Trevn. You'd be king consort only."

Hinck needed more than that. "I must have some responsibility," he said.

"The army would be yours." She glanced up. "And you'd sit on the council as a voting member."

He nodded. "Thank you." Though he had no idea how to manage an army.

They stared at one another until Hinck's eyes began to water. Then Saria reached across the desk and squeezed his hand. "Thank you, Hinck. I accept your offer on the condition the betrothal agreement is written to my satisfaction. And yours," she added. "With your help, we just might have a chance to save this realm. Now help me find that scroll."

Saria released his hand. His betrothed. Hinck flushed, recalling Trevn's prediction that he would undoubtedly do something honorable that would trap him in Sarikar far longer than Trevn wished to give him up.

What would Trevn say when he heard this development?

Trevn

Stop laughing, Trev," Hinck voiced.

"Oh, but I cannot," Trevn said. "It's simply too delightful. I predicted you'd save the day by nobly sacrificing yourself, but marriage, Hinck? I told you to remain here, but nooo . . . You were bored. Needed some excitement."

"Are you against this, Your Royal Pain?" Hinck asked.

Trevn tapered off his laughter with a happy sigh. "Not at all. This is a fine development for Armania. It unites our two realms in a way I'd never considered. As much as I disdained the way my father married off his children, I never realized how helpful such a practice could be."

"You mock me."

"A little, yes. If you wanted to marry her, why didn't you just say something?"

"I didn't come here to marry her."

"Hinck . . ." Trevn tried to sound serious. "Don't you want to find your own bride?"

"Who is there to marry who matches my rank? No one I want. I suppose I could wait for your sisters to grow up, but Saria and I have history. This makes sense."

In a very logical, boring way. "If you mean to follow through with this, know I will support you."

"Thank you."

"But I won't allow you to be a consort alone. You must be co-regent. Perhaps His Royal Highness, the Duke of Sarikar or something like that. If you are only a consort, even the Sarikarian council would have authority over you. I won't make you their puppet, Hinck. You must have a voice."

"What if Saria refuses?"

"She asked that of you to keep from being under your thumb, so it's only fair that she afford you the same courtesy. She'll agree."

"If you say so," Hinck said.

Trevn closed the connection and chuckled again. Hinck to marry Saria. Ah, if that wasn't the most amusing idea he'd ever—

A knock on the door, and Cadoc entered. "Your Highness, I have news."

"Did Porvil confess?" Trevn felt the stiffness of the scabs on his side and arm and shuddered at what might have been.

"No, but we did confirm the knife belonged to Tace Edekk."

That figured. "I'll talk to the boy myself after my meeting with Miss Onika."

"Yes, sir. There's another matter. Our men can no longer enter Nawhar Forest. The duke's men threatened to attack if they did not leave."

Tace Edekk continued to astound Trevn. "He can't do that."

"He did, sir."

"Then I'll ask him why." Trevn leaned back in his chair, found the duke's mind, and forced his way inside. It was rude, but since his magic was strong enough, he felt the need to remind Tace Edekk who was king. *"You threatened my soldiers, Your Grace?"*

He felt the duke's surprise, his raised heartbeat. *"You needlessly flogged Sir Jarmyn Koll,"* came the nasal voice in Trevn's head.

"Come now, Your Grace. Sir Jarmyn disobeyed my order. Men died because of it."

"So you say, but as you have no proof, I'll take the word of my son-in-law over yours."

"It's to be rebellion, then? For you alone? Or for Sir Jarmyn, Lord Blackpool, and all of your men as well?"

"I speak only for myself," Edekk said, *"but you are no king of mine."*

"Then I will count you among my enemies and have the executioner sharpen his axe." Trevn closed the connection, shaking slightly from fury and shattered pride. He'd nearly lost control, which was something he could not afford to do with the likes of Tace Edekk.

He sighed deeply. Barek had been right in his prediction that Trevn would lose some of the nobles and their armies if he punished Sir Jarmyn. Now Armania was divided, and just when Inolah had told him that Rogedoth had begun packing up camp. Trevn hoped the man took his time about it.

"Are you well, Your Highness?" Cadoc asked.

Trevn stood. "Tace Edekk has confessed his rebellion against me. I fear I've lost not only his army but the armies of Lord Blackpool and his son as well. I must go to Miss Onika and learn what I can of this Veil magic. Perhaps it will make up for the loss of so many soldiers." He started for the door, but a great nervousness slowed his steps. Mielle, nearby and anxious.

Nietz poked his head inside and whispered to Cadoc.

"Send her in," Trevn said, curious what his wife wanted. Things between them had been much better since she'd apologized. Why would she be nervous?

Cadoc opened the door farther and Mielle strode inside.

The sight of her lightened Trevn's heart. "Good midday," he said, taking her hands. They were cool and trembling. Apprehension thrummed out in waves. "What's wrong?"

She pulled away and curtsied, strangely formal. "Thank you for seeing me, Trevn. I would like your permission to have Master Grayson help me with a project."

Grayson's name instantly set Trevn on edge. Already she wanted to use him? "What kind of a project?"

"No progress has been made in finding the missing Armanian children whose parents accused Tace Edekk of conscripting them into the military. I wonder if Grayson and I visited each home, and if Grayson held something that belonged to a missing child, he might be able to—"

"—pop to their location. Mielle, that's brilliant."

She smiled, laughed a little, and her nervousness faded. "I have your permission, then?"

"Yes, of course, but I don't want you putting yourself in danger. If you discover something, let my guards make the arrests. Is that clear?"

She nodded and kissed his cheek. "I will. I promise."

Trevn watched her go, confident that if anyone could find those children, it was his wife.

Madam Kempe led Trevn and Cadoc into Miss Onika's chambers. The prophetess and Rosârah Zeroah lay on two longchairs that faced the hearth, eyes closed as if sleeping. Sir Kalenek stood leaning against the hearth, the dune cat Rustian curled up at his boots. Zeroah's guards, Doth and Ephec, sat on chairs near the window, unconcerned with their lady's state. When they saw their king, they stood and bowed, then went back to their seats.

Sir Kalenek touched Miss Onika's shoulder. "The king has come, lady."

Onika's eyes flickered open. "Your Highness, thank you for coming. It's my hope that all who can mind-speak can also enter the Veil to banish shadir and storm, as Sir Kalenek calls it."

"I would very much like to learn both," Trevn said, eager to try.

"You'll need your own longchair," Sir Kalenek said. "To try this standing will leave your body empty. You'll collapse and might be injured."

"Take my chair, Your Highness," Zeroah said, standing.

Trevn reclined on the longchair Zeroah had vacated and found the cushions warm. He listened carefully to Miss Onika's instructions, then made several failed attempts before he was finally able to sit up into an ethereal world and leave his body behind.

In this place—which Miss Onika claimed to be the Veil between worlds—everything looked somewhat the same, yet it was brighter and bigger somehow. He saw Zeroah, Onika, Sir Kalenek, Kempe, the guards, the apartment and all its furniture, but no one could see him. Even more impressive, Trevn could move like Grayson. He need only concentrate on a person or specific location, and he appeared there. Miss Onika, who astonishingly had her eyesight in this place, led him first with short movements, instructing him to concentrate on following her. They went from her sitting room to the great hall to the forest, then all the way to the roof in Er'Rets Point.

Trevn stood breathless at the parapet wall. "We can go anywhere?"

"So it seems," Miss Onika said. "You only need imagine the place you want to go or the person you want to see."

Trevn thought of the quarterdeck of the *Seffynaw* and appeared there. Captain Bussie was at the whipstaff, talking with a sailor Trevn didn't know. So this must be why Grayson called this movement *popping*. It was instantaneous.

Miss Onika appeared beside Trevn. "You are a quick learner, Your Highness."

Trevn thought of Bakurah Island, where they'd left a settlement. He appeared in a grassy field he recognized as the place Wilek had been attacked by rebels and Trevn had first killed. It was dusk here, and in the distance, a village of wooden houses covered the side of a hill.

Miss Onika arrived beside him. "What place is this?"

"Bakurah Island. I wanted to see how they fared. In fact . . ."

"Your Highness, please wait for—"

But Trevn had already gone. When he arrived at Castle Everton in the Five Realms, he appeared underwater. The coolness shocked him, though he had no trouble breathing. He rose to the surface and into a dark night—could see little despite the moon overhead. His eyes adjusted slowly, yet there was nothing here but ocean.

Miss Onika's voice flooded his mind. "Your Highness? I cannot see you."

"I wondered if some had survived. Perhaps at higher ground?" Trevn focused on the summit of Mount Radu and found himself standing under a copse of trees outside a stone wall lit by torchlight. His heart leapt with hope. He popped up to the sentry wall and looked upon a village of mud and thatch huts. He counted the nearest ten huts and multiplied them to estimate at least two hundred. And in the distance, a great house. Who resided there?

Miss Onika emerged beside him. "Where are we?"

"At the summit of Mount Radu in the Five Realms."

"Praise Arman! I never thought to come look for survivors. Why is it so dark?"

"It's night here. The sun cannot shine on both sides of the earth at the same time."

"How fascinating," Miss Onika said.

Trevn was much more interested in the survivors of the Five Realms than the workings of the sun, though he supposed now was not the time to explore his homeland. "I'm returning to your chambers," he said, concentrating on his physical body.

He opened his eyes and found Cadoc standing over him with Sir Kalenek. Trevn felt oddly weighted to the longchair. It took effort to push himself to sitting, not because he was weak. He simply found his own weight cumbersome.

"Well?" Cadoc asked.

"That such a thing is possible amazes me," Trevn said. "There's no scientific explanation for such a phenomenon."

"Did you see us?" Cadoc asked.

"I did. Then we went to the tower in Er'Rets Point, then to Bakurah Island, then to Everton, and finally Mount Radu. Everton is gone, but there is a settlement at the mountain's summit. Some survived the Woes."

"My mother might have survived?" Zeroah asked.

Trevn found her gaze in the crowd. "I suppose anything is possible."

"Did you see any shadir?" Sir Kalenek asked.

"I did not, though I wasn't looking. Miss Onika, you must train others to do this. Duke Canden and Hinck to start. As many as are willing, actually. I'll make you a list. Then we must make plans as to how we can use this ability to stop Rogedoth and his giants."

Trevn ducked through the narrow doorway after Nietz and entered the dark cell. Nietz held aloft a lantern, which cast spilling shadows over the tiny space. The boy, Porvil, sat cross-legged in the center of the cell. He glanced up, sullen.

"Have I harmed you in some way, boy?" Trevn asked. "Since you failed to kill me, you may as well air your grievances."

"You left my mother in Everton."

Ah. Trevn preferred acts of revenge over blatant treason. "Did I?"

"The soldiers wouldn't let us board. Then some man ran down the docks, calling for orphans. Mother said I'd be an orphan soon enough. So he took me. But he wouldn't take her."

"She was a brave woman to save your life."

Porvil's face twisted into a snarl. "There was room enough for her on the *Seffynaw*. Lord Edekk said it was your idea who got on board. He wanted everyone saved, but you said no."

So Edekk *was* involved here. Trevn would have to add sedition to the duke's growing list of crimes. "Lord Edekk, who took no more than one hundred aboard his gilded houseboat?"

The boy's brows sank.

Trevn leaned against the cold stone wall. "I won't pretend things were decided fairly during the Five Woes, because such a thing was impossible. Do you know the population of Armania when the Woes came upon us? Or how many lived in Everton?"

The boy merely glared.

"Allow me to illuminate, Master Porvil. The realm of Armania had, at the time of the last census, just over half a million people. Everton, and its surrounding areas, was by far the largest city in our realm with just shy of eighty-five thousand. We gathered one hundred forty-one ships in Everton and, regardless of what you or the Duke of Raine think of our methods, managed to board some seventy-three thousand souls. Now, the *Seffynaw* had a maximum capacity of five hundred, but a roster in my brother's journal lists seven hundred ninety-two names. Can you guess how many were on board when we made landfall at Er'Rets Point?"

"No, sir."

"Two hundred seventy-one. The numbers are similar across the fleet. Over half of those who boarded ships out of Everton died before reaching land."

The boy's emotions had shifted from anger to overwhelming sorrow.

"Why did you steal Lord Edekk's knife?" Trevn asked.

"I didn't. He gave it to me. As payment. 'Cause I done work for him."

"What kind of work?"

"Ran wine to those who bought it."

"To the castle as well?"

"Yes, sir."

"Why did you attack me?"

Porvil swallowed and met Trevn's gaze. "'Cause Mikreh said to."

Trevn made the leap. "The god of fate?"

"He spoke to me. Said I'd be a hero if I did it."

Trevn's heart sank. "That was a shadir, tricking you into doing its master's bidding."

The boy shook his head. "No, sir, it wasn't. I saw him. He came to me at night. Promised he'd rescue me himself if I succeeded. Said he'd send a man like Grayson to carry me away."

A tingle ran up Trevn's arms. He turned and ducked through the narrow doorway, leaving the cell. He paused beside Cadoc. "I need Sir Kalenek in my office at once. It seems that Barthel Rogedoth has allied with Shanek DanSâr."

⊙Lİ

Oli could not believe he was hovering in the air outside the castle—inside the Veil. And here he had two hands. How could such a thing be possible?

Also learning this skill were Danek Faluk, Master Grayson, Madam Kempe, Rosârahs Brelenah and Zeroah, Sârah Hrettah, Lady Brisa, and Hinckdan, whose body was in New Sarikar. King Trevn had made this sound like some kind of warfare. That Oli might be able to fight on a different kind of battlefield had piqued his curiosity.

The sun shone brightly over the white snow, but it didn't feel as cold as it should. Miss Onika led them around the castle, and they flew like streaks on the wind. They followed the prophetess down over the surface of the lake until she stopped, hovering over the icy waters.

"Concentrate on Er'Rets Point," she said. "We've all been there, so you should be able to travel at once. I'll be waiting for you at the top of the tower." And she vanished.

Oli watched the others disappear one at a time. He imagined the fortress, and in a blink he was standing on the tower roof, looking south to the Northsea. It was snowing here, yet he couldn't feel the flakes. A person flew up the wall from below and startled him. Hinckdan.

The Duke of Armanguard chuckled. "Got you good, didn't I?"

"This does take some getting used to."

Oli watched Hinckdan fly away, twisting like a fish in the ocean. He did not see Rosârah Zeroah. He'd been avoiding her ever since their discussion about

387

Vivia and Oli's realization that the memory magic had been his all along. What if she'd gotten lost somehow?

"Rosârah Zeroah?" he called.

When no answer came, he concentrated on her presence and appeared on the castle parapet. The dowager queen was sitting between two crenellations, staring out at the snowy landscape to the northwest.

"Wilek and I used to walk in that forest." She pointed, a pained look in her eyes.

Mention of the former king struck Oli like a shock of cold water. The black gown she wore was a continual reminder of her mourning, but in the past few weeks he'd forgotten all about Wilek Hadar.

"I'm sorry for your losses, Your Highness," he said. "They are great and terrible."

"Some days I ache so deeply for the life I had. For a very short time there was more joy and hope than I ever thought possible. Even when Chadek was sickly, he was still ours, and we could hold him and sing to him. He thrilled my soul every day of his short life." She turned her golden gaze on him and her eyes looked glossy, though he didn't think it possible to produce tears in this place. "Do you think my son is in Shamayim?"

"I . . . I suppose so," Oli said, though he didn't truly believe the place existed.

"I know he is. And so is Wilek." Zeroah smiled. Her eyes flicked down and widened. "You have both arms."

Oli again regarded the arm that the cheyvah had eaten. "I don't know why."

"Because in the Veil, you are whole, as Arman made you."

Could that be true? Oli had never given Arman much thought. His life had been filled with shadir and their masters, but if Gâzar was real, might Arman be real too?

"Your Grace," Zeroah said. "Do you know that—?"

"Please join me on the tower roof." Onika's voice in Oli's mind.

Zeroah smiled and lifted off the crenellation. "We will talk later." Then she disappeared.

Oli concentrated again on the tower roof and traveled there in an instant. Everyone else was present. Grayson and Hinckdan were swooping about like sparrows, while Rosârah Brelenah and Sârah Hrettah floated out past the edge of the roof, looking down as the skirts of their dresses dangled like bells.

Miss Onika told the story of how she had come upon shadir in the Veil, heard Arman's voice, and banished them to the Lowerworld. "You will all learn to do this," she said.

Impossible! Oli had never seen such a thing done, not even within the Lahavôtesh.

"To practice, we must travel near our enemies," Onika said. "Follow me."

And the next thing Oli knew, he was again chasing after the prophetess, this time headed toward an unknown place.

They arrived on a grassy hillside that was surprisingly green without a hint of the snow that blanketed Armanguard. Oli instantly felt the familiar coldness of shadir, like stepping into a shadow on a sunny day. It made him shiver.

"Why is it so cold if there is no snow?" Rosârah Brelenah asked.

"The coldness you feel is the presence of hundreds of shadir," Onika said. "Look there."

She pointed to a gully between two hills that was filled with movement and color. Oli shuddered at the sight of at least fifty shadir, caterwauling and reveling. It took him back to the many meetings of the Lahavôtesh he'd frequented over the years.

Miss Onika explained how they would banish the creatures. This Oli found ludicrous. The group began to move, and Oli followed, convinced that Miss Onika was about to make a fool of herself. As the humans sailed into the center of the swarm, the creatures parted like fish in a pond, hissing and taunting and screaming. Oli felt his hackles rise. He marveled over the irony that he had once worshiped these creatures, and here he was among those seeking to destroy them.

"Please watch while Rosârah Zeroah demonstrates this process," Onika said. "She and I have been practicing."

Zeroah had been speaking to shadir? The idea made Oli want to grab the woman and haul her to safety. She did not look afraid, however. She lifted her chin and spoke in a commanding voice to a pale gray shadir that looked like a duck with a fish's face.

"You who answer to Gâzar will answer to the one who made him. In the name of Arman, Creator of all things, be gone to the foot of your master in the Lowerworld. Now go!"

Oli's heart trembled at the ferocity of the young woman's voice. To his utter shock, the creature squealed and sank beneath the grass.

"Well done, Your Highness!" Miss Onika beamed like a proud mother. "You will each try this. Remember, it's not your power. Arman does this by your faith. Trust that he can and wants to."

What words! Could the woman not see how small they were compared to the scope around them—to the distance they had traveled across the North-sea? If the Creator of all things did exist, why would he bother listening to the likes of gnats?

Oli watched with interest as the others set about the task of banishing shadir. Though he had just witnessed the dowager queen accomplish the task, he expected the others would fail.

Yet they did not fail. Hinckdan banished a slimy green snake. Rosârah Brelenah's command sent a cat with pink and blue feathers underground. Danek Faluk ordered a fat brown slug covered in spines into the depths. And Grayson sent three all at once screeching away. Even Lady Brisa, Sârah Hret-tah, and Madam Kempe succeeded.

Arman truly did exist.

Oli's gaze wandered over the swarm until he saw a frog-like shadir that re-minded him of Paliki, his first bond, though this one was pink and yellow. He approached the creature, eagerness welling inside at the possibility that he could command these creatures that once controlled him—that they might fear *him.*

"Foul beast," he said to the frog, "I command you into the Lowerworld by Arman's power and might. Go!"

The frog did not go. It merely stared, bored, it seemed, despite the unrest the other humans had made within the swarm.

Doubt cowed Oli. What had he done wrong? He recalled Rosârah Zeroah's exact words and repeated them as best he could. "You who answer to Gâzar will answer to his maker. By Arman's name, the Creator of all things, be gone to your master in the Lowerworld. Go!"

The frog snickered. "Fool, human," it said. "You pretend to be something you're not. My master and yours are one and the same. You have no power over me."

The shadir's coldness enveloped Oli, dwarfing the confidence he'd so briefly grasped. He should have known better. He'd pledged his soul long ago. How foolish to think mere words could change that.

"The creature speaks the truth, Your Grace. You have no power." Miss Onika spoke from Oli's side. How long had she been there?

"My words were correct," Oli said, perplexed how his semantics had failed.

"The words are not as important as the heart. You trust yourself, Your Grace, which is why you fail. You must give your trust to Arman. This is his power, not your own."

Oli didn't understand. Trust Arman with what?

Grayson swooped over and yelled at the frog-like shadir. "Be gone to the Lowerworld by Arman's holy name!"

The frog fell away, shrieking.

Shame festered in Oli's chest. The boy had succeeded easily where Oli had twice failed.

Grayson reversed his direction and flew into the swarm, which began to flee like a herd of deer from a predator. Some of the others—Hinckdan, Madam Kempe, Sârah Hrettah, and Zeroah—gave chase, banishing as many shadir as they could while Oli and the others looked on.

"It's both exhilarating and exhausting," Rosârah Brelenah said.

"Yet we must banish them all if we are to diffuse the power of our enemies," Miss Onika said.

All of them? Oli stared after the retreating swarm, awed by the prophetess's goal. "There are thousands of shadir, prophetess," he said. "How can so few defeat so many?"

"One at a time, Your Grace," Miss Onika said. "We could use your help, but you must choose."

That she had singled him out in front of Rosârah Brelenah and Lady Brisa embarrassed him, yet he ached to understand. "Choose what?"

"Who will be your master? Arman or Gâzar?"

Understanding came with a heavy dose of humiliation. Oli had made his choice long ago. He couldn't banish the creatures because he was already one of their number. Nothing could change that.

At the end of the training, Miss Onika bade them return to their bodies. When Oli opened his eyes, he was back on the longchair with only one arm.

Enough fantasy. This was the world he lived in, and he must remember that.

Oli continued to train with Miss Onika's Veil warriors, though he had no ability to drive away the creatures. As the days went on, it grew more difficult to find shadir, until one day, after hours of searching, the group returned to their physical bodies without having banished a single one. The king joined them in the training room as they discussed ways they might lure the shadir close. Oli knew better.

"They might seem like dumb animals, but they're not," he said. "You've destroyed enough of them that they're frightened. So they'll hide where you cannot find them."

"Where?" King Trevn asked.

"Where we are not," Oli said.

"Then we've succeeded," Zeroah said.

"Forgive me," Oli said, "I was unclear. They're not afraid of the humans they rule. They'll stay close to home. If you want to find them, you must invade Rogedoth's camp."

"Not yet," Trevn said. "I don't want Rogedoth to know what we can do."

"He likely already knows," Oli said. "The shadir would have told their masters, who would have told their mantics, who would have told Rogedoth."

"But he hasn't tried to stop us, so maybe he doesn't know," Danek said.

"How could he stop us?" Brelenah asked. "We have Arman on our side."

"He has already stopped us by having the shadir hide," Oli said.

Understanding rendered the group silent.

"There must be some way of luring them to us," Hinckdan said.

"None that I know of," Miss Onika said.

Oli knew of two ways. Shadir flocked to immorality and to those who used evenroot. Oli had taken a vial of root off his mother when he'd arrested her. He should have turned it in, but it had been too tempting. If he mixed it with wine and ingested it all at once, he might be able to lure dozens of shadir, maybe more.

Trevn would never allow it, nor would Miss Onika, but they didn't have to know. These good, pure people had to keep their hearts clear of evil if they were to remain in Arman's favor. Since Oli could never enter that place—and since he was useless at banishing shadir—this was his best chance to make a contribution to the cause.

The next time Miss Onika called her Veil warriors together, it would be to wage war against the swarm Oli had summoned.

Mielle

Mielle took Bero's hand as she alighted from the carriage in the Crescent, the neighborhood that had formed around the top of Lake Arman, where many Armanian commoners had built homes.

Tonis had located the family dwelling of each child who had been falsely conscripted into Lord Edekk's army or had simply gone missing. What had originally been complaints from seventeen families had grown to thirty-seven.

Clusters of people stood outside their homes, watching Mielle and her entourage. It wasn't every day that royalty descended into the Crescent.

Lady Pia and Bero escorted Mielle toward one of the homes. She met Tonis and Grayson at a door that had been stained grass green to match the shutters on the front window.

"The family is expecting you, Your Highness," Tonis said. "Are you ready?"

"Very much," Mielle said, eager for Grayson to get started.

Tonis knocked, and the door opened instantly to a middle-aged man dressed in brown. He stepped back from the door and bowed.

Bero entered first. Mielle ducked her head and swept inside with Lady Pia. The odor of unwashed bodies, mildew, and chimney smoke reminded her of the homes in the sink back in Everton. This one-room dwelling had a table and fireplace on her right and two box beds on her left. Standing before the beds was a woman, hands clutched before her, eyes puffy. Behind her, three children sat silently on one of the beds, two boys and a girl, all younger than ten.

"What's your name?" she asked the woman.

The woman curtsied. "Hayva, Your Highness."

"And this is Master Orban, the father," Tonis said. "Boy's name is Kyal. He's eleven."

Mielle took hold of the mother's hands. "I'm sorry to hear about your son."

Tears leaked from the corners of Hayva's eyes. "Thank you, Your Highness."

"Some of the missing children were taken by Mett Lycor," Tonis said. "Does that name mean anything to you? Have you seen him?"

"People say he's recruiting for Lord Edekk's army," Master Orban said. "It's been weeks since I saw him around these parts."

"Can you describe him?" Mielle asked.

"Certainly. He's average height. Short hair. A bit thick around the middle. Wild eyes. Can't stand still."

"Does Kyal have a toy or perhaps a spare tunic?" Tonis asked.

"Something a hound could use to find him?" Master Orban asked.

Mielle met the father's worried gaze. "It will help in our search." She thought it best not to frighten anyone by discussing Grayson's magic. These families had suffered enough.

Hayva lunged between the boys on the bed behind her and grabbed a worn tunic. "This is Kyal's," she said, shoving it into Mielle's hands. "Please find him."

"We will do all we can," Mielle said.

She sat with Hayva, holding her hand as Tonis asked questions about the day Kyal had been taken. When they had gone and were all back inside the carriage, Mielle gave the tunic to Grayson, and he popped away.

"I do hope he finds him," Mielle said, wringing her hands.

But Grayson returned far too quickly and alone, still holding the tunic.

"What happened?" Mielle asked.

Grayson shrugged. "I came out in a desert valley and there was no one there."

Desert? Mielle took the tunic from Grayson and handed it to Tonis, disappointed not to have found the boy right off. "Label that, please. We must remember who it belongs to."

They rode to the home of another missing boy. The mother gave Mielle a carved bird, which later led Grayson back to the barren desert. After the third attempt resulted in the same location, Mielle decided to try something else.

"I thought it made sense to begin with the most recent missing children," she said, "but let's visit the family of the first missing boy and see if that brings forth a different result."

So they went to the home of Zoeb and Oba Winlin, who lived on the outermost ring of the Crescent. Master Zoeb had been there when his son, Nikz, was taken away.

"Did you know the man who took your son?" Mielle asked him.

"No, Your Highness, but he said he was a soldier in the Duke of Raine's army and that my son was needed for an effort to fortify our borders."

"Can you describe him?" Tonis asked.

"Tall and very strong," Master Winlin said. "He had a great mane of warrior twists. Looked like a mighty hero, so I easily believed his word."

"That sounds like Captain Korvoh," Lady Pia said.

Tonis nodded. "It certainly does."

"Who is Captain Korvoh?" Mielle asked.

"Captain of Tace Edekk's guard," Tonis said.

Mielle's pulse began to race at the possibility of catching Tace Edekk breaking the law. All they needed was one piece of irrefutable evidence. Could this be it?

Oba Winlin gave Mielle a worn blue tunic that belonged to her son. The moment they had all returned to the carriage, Mielle handed the tunic to Grayson, and he left.

Mielle and her entourage sat silent, glancing from one to another as they waited. She prayed this time might be different, that Grayson would come back with the boy. When he didn't return right away, hope grew stronger. Oh, how she wished she could mind-speak like Trevn could.

"This feels right," she said. "That it's taking so long."

"Patience, Your Highness," Tonis said. "We mustn't get our hopes up."

A noise grew outside the carriage. It sounded like a fight.

Tonis leaned out the window. "What's going on out there?"

"Two lads going at it," Bero said. "Sands alive, one of them is Grayson!"

The guard sprinted away from the carriage. Tonis clambered out, and Mielle followed. A crowd had formed around two young men who were thrashing in the muddy slush. Some of the onlookers shouted cheers of encouragement.

"Just listen!" Grayson yelled.

"Don't care what you say!" the young man replied. "I didn't want to come!"

Bero and Lady Pia reached the two young men and dragged them apart.

"What's going on?" Bero asked.

"I must go back," the young man said. "Make him take me back!"

"He didn't want to come," Grayson said, brushing slush off his trousers. "Said he had to stay in the mines."

"In the giant mines?" Mielle asked. "Why would you want to stay there?"

"Nikz!" Master Winlin rushed upon the scene and embraced the young man.

The young man's face crumpled. "Father, please. I must go back. It's important."

"Why do you say this, my son?"

Nikz pushed out of his father's embrace. "I can't tell you."

"You can and you will," Mielle said. "Thirty-six other children have been reported missing. They're counting on you for their freedom, so you will tell me what you know at once."

Nikz frowned at Mielle. Took in her attire.

Bero nudged Nikz's shoulder. "Bow before your queen, boy."

Nikz flushed and dropped to his knees, head bowed, uncertain.

"I see you are conflicted," Mielle said. "Can you tell me why you're afraid?"

A defiant scowl. "I'm not scared."

"You simply prefer the life of a slave over one with your family?" Mielle asked.

"Answer the queen, son," Master Winlin said.

Nikz sighed. "The men said they'd hurt our families if we tried to escape."

"You do this for *me*?" his father asked.

"For all of you," Nikz said, voice choked. "It was King Trevn's idea."

"What was?" Mielle asked.

"Selling boys to the mines. To keep the giants away from Armanguard."

Fury threatened to set Mielle off. That someone would not only abduct children for slavery but threaten to hurt their families? And pin it all on Trevn? It was unforgivable.

Mielle set her hands on her hips. "Your king would never do such a thing. Who said this?"

"Master Lycor."

"Again we find this name," Mielle said. "I'm beginning to think Mett Lycor a root child the way he continually evades capture."

"I'm not so certain it's magic we're dealing with, Your Highness," Tonis said. "What does Master Lycor look like, boy?"

"A soldier," Nikz said. "Wears more warrior tails than I've ever seen on one man."

Tonis narrowed his eyes. "How was he dressed? Any livery?"

"No livery, sir. He and his men wore blue and black."

"We've heard this description before," Mielle said.

"Yes, but it doesn't describe Mett Lycor," Lady Pia said. "Master Orban's description was correct. Mett is about my height and soft around the middle. Drinks too much ale."

"Someone is pretending to be Mett Lycor," Tonis said. "And I think we all know who this warrior is."

Mielle sighed deeply. "Captain Korvoh."

QOATCH

"A caravan approaches, Your Highness," Captain Orbay told King Barthel. "Empress Jazlyn returns."

Finally. Qoatch breathed out his relief. He had grown weary of serving King Barthel.

"Back with my harvest of new evenroot, and just in time," the king said, glaring at Qoatch. "When she arrives, bring her here, Captain. I want a word. Now, where is Paliki with our report on Armanguard? Sâr Shanek needs to know what he is facing." He nodded to the young man, who sat beside him. Sâr Shanek and Miss Amala had been spending part of every day in King Barthel's camp. Now that the king had started to move out his men, he would be asking the couple to leave with him. Unless Jazlyn could stop it, Qoatch suspected he would have his way.

Paliki appeared before the thrones, looking every bit like an oversized frog.

"Report," the king barked.

The slight passed on news about the failed assassination, that Sarikar was gaining aid from Hinckdan Faluk, and that Lady Zenobia had nearly replicated the tonic King Trevn was using to keep Queen Eudora silent. "And the prophetess continues to attack shadir."

"Then stay away from them!" the king roared. "How many times must I tell you? They cannot harm you if you are not near them. Now, we must increase Sâr Shanek's attacks on the people of Armanguard. Go with him." Then to Shanek he said, "Edekk's men will join you."

"Why keep attacking the commoners?" Shanek asked. "Shouldn't I attack the castle?"

"You must prepare the way, my sâr. The time to attack the castle is coming, I promise."

Timmons stepped into the tent. "Your Highness? Captain Orbay has brought Empress—"

Jazlyn pushed past the onesent, followed by three of her Protectors. "You dare have me brought before you like some renegade criminal?"

Qoatch smiled, relieved to see his Great Lady again.

"Isn't that what you are?" King Barthel asked. "You lied to me, Empress. You went to Islah in search of my harvest of new evenroot. Deny it."

"Why should I? You clearly didn't want it."

"I want it now."

"Well, I'm afraid I didn't bring it with me," Jazlyn said, smirking.

"Search the caravan and bring me my root," the king told Captain Orbay. "Until it is found, keep the empress in custody."

"Do you really think you can hold me?" Jazlyn asked. "King Barthel, I would hate to have to kill any of your men."

The king's face darkened. "We have a treaty, woman!"

"The treaty is between yourself and New Rurekau. If you have a problem, I suggest you bring it up with my husband. Emperor Ulrik will be home soon."

An awkward hush descended inside the king's tent. Qoatch did not know what to make of his Great Lady's words. It must be some trick.

"You promised to help me take Armania," the king said.

"I did no such thing," Jazlyn said. "I have never been interested in your war."

"Then you are against me," the king said. "You stole from me, and you left your eunuch here to spy. I should kill you where you stand."

Jazlyn frowned, as if feeling sorry for the man. "You could not, Your Highness. Not even with the help of your new puppet." She raised her eyebrows at Shanek. "I am too powerful."

The king's jaw flexed and his eyes burned toward Jazlyn, yet he did not deny her—he did not dare. "I want no fight with you, Empress."

"I'll be on my way, then. I am quite exhausted from my travels and have much to prepare for Ulrik's return. Qoatch, come."

This second mention of Emperor Ulrik set the mantics whispering.

"I am not finished with the eunuch," King Barthel said. "I'll send him back tomorrow."

Jazlyn glowered at the man. "Before morning bells. Not a moment longer."

King Barthel bowed his head in agreement, and Jazlyn swept away.

The king grabbed the goblet off the stand beside his throne and threw it across the tent. "Insolent woman! She's mad, talking about the emperor's return. This must be a trick."

"Emperor Ulrik is not dead," Shanek said. "He's with my mother in Magosia."

The king worked his mouth, as if trying and failing to find words. Before he could succeed, Dendron materialized before his throne.

The king snapped out of his stupor, tried and failed to hide a smile. "Yes?"

You have become disrespectful, Mergest, the great said. *You treat my shadir like slaves.*

His smile vanished. "That's what they are."

To me, perhaps, but not to you. Without Islah, you do not have the power you once had.

"We are so close! We can still take the throne of Armania. So long as no one else betrays me." He glanced at Shanek. "Betrays *us*, I mean."

You speak of betrayal, Mergest, yet you have betrayed me.

The king looked up, brow pinched. "How so?"

Iamos. Yobatha. Haroan. Daliza. Paliki. They are not your bonded. Yet you use them for your magical experiments. Apart from me.

"The shadir are free to go their own way if they'd rather."

Or I could destroy them. I might, actually, if that's what it will take to get your attention.

"But you have no interest in the new magic!"

You would have nothing if not for me, Dendron said, *yet it has not crossed your mind to have Shanek fetch Islah back, nor have you given an answer to my offer of Dominion.*

"*That's* what this is really about? I've left you out of things, and you're jealous. For the past thirty years you have been my only source of power and strength, but now I have another way. Sâr Shanek and I . . . we don't need you."

You are mistaken, Mergest. It is you who have underestimated me.

The king narrowed his eyes. "What does *that* mean?"

Come here, Great One, Dendron said.

Rogedoth tilted his head. "Come where?"

Not you, Mergest.

Shanek appeared beside the shadir, hands at his side, chin raised.

"What's this, my sâr?" The king pushed to his feet. "Has this creature been bothering you?"

"He says I must not trust you," Shanek said.

"He lies," the king said, glaring at the great.

We would be wise to work with King Barthel, Dendron said to Sâr Shanek, *but we must make sure he does not take the throne for himself in the end.*

"You dare manipulate the sâr?" the king yelled. "He has been through enough."

Dendron chuckled. *You see?* he said to Shanek. *It is as I said. You are wise, Great One, and can make your own decisions. I leave the choice to you.*

"What choice?" King Barthel asked. "Sâr Shanek, you must not trust this creature."

Shanek's eyes widened. "He told me you would say that." He turned to Dendron. "Very well, shadir. Come into me, if you want, and make me king of Armania."

As you wish, my king. Dendron's pale eyes fixed upon King Barthel one last time, then the shadir began to change. His brown tree trunk shape lengthened and became smooth gray skin. Twiggy branches became two arms and two legs. His waterfall of hair shortened into a thick, curly black mop. He looked just like the young prince, then floated toward the boy until their bodies became one.

King Barthel staggered back and fell into his chair. "No."

Qoatch could not believe it either. Sâr Shanek had given Dendron the Great Dominion over his soul.

Onika

Onika was on her knees praying when the Duke of Canden spoke
to her mind.

*"Miss Onika, can you hear me? There are shadir on the roof. Dozens of them.
I am engaged elsewhere but thought you should know."*

"I hear you, Your Grace." Onika's heart raced at the opportunity. "Kempe,
help me to my chair. We must enter the Veil at once."

"Yes, miss."

Onika pushed herself to standing and waited for Kempe's rough hands to
grasp her arm. The woman led her to her longchair, where Onika lay down
and concentrated on the roof. She left her body behind and reappeared in
the midst of a cloud of shadir. The presence of so many made it difficult to
see and very cold.

Why would so many be gathered here? Could Master Rogedoth finally be
attacking? *Arman, what shall I do?*

"Wait for the others and attack as one."

"Warriors of the Veil," she voiced. *"Our enemy has congregated on the castle
roof! Come to me."*

She drifted toward the parapet, trying to find a place that was not overcome with shadir. Kempe arrived next, then Grayson, in his physical body.
The shadir closed around him. One perched on his shoulder. Another coiled
around his arm.

"Sands alive! There are a lot of them," he said.

Rosârah Zeroah appeared beside Onika. "Why are there so many?" she
asked.

"I know not," Onika said. "We will attack together when the others arrive. Fighting one at a time will only scare the rest away."

"I don't like it when they touch me," Grayson said, pushing away those around him.

Danek Faluk arrived at the same time as Lady Brisa. Onika explained her plan, then repeated it when Rosârah Brelenah and Sârah Hrettah appeared.

"We will speak to Arman in unison." Then she recited the prayer she planned to say.

"Where is Duke Canden?" Rosârah Zeroah asked.

"He is likely drunk," Lady Brisa said. "Or with some serving woman."

"That is unkind," Sârah Hrettah said.

"He is occupied elsewhere," Onika said. *Arman, is it time?*

"ATTACK, AND I WILL GIVE YOU VICTORY."

"We must act," Onika said. "Let us join hands."

Her warriors obeyed, forming a large circle.

"All together," Onika said, then began reciting. "Arman, by your name we ask you to banish these unholy creatures from this world. Send them back where they belong."

Heat flowed into Onika through the hand of Rosârah Zeroah on her right and Sârah Hrettah on her left. Noise erupted around them. Scattered cries from the creatures.

"Again," Onika said. "Arman, by your name we ask you to banish these unholy creatures from this world. Send them back where they belong."

This time the flock above seemed to screech all at once.

"Again!" Onika yelled.

They chanted the prayer, and Arman's warmth pierced the chill of the shadir's presence.

The creatures went wild, thrashing into one another as if they had gone blind. Slowly the cloud sank through the castle roof. Onika continued her prayer until long after the last shadir had vanished, wanting to make sure the task was complete.

"Well done, all of you," she said finally. "Arman has granted us victory."

Grayson crowed. The women laughed and cheered. Zeroah embraced Onika, then Rosârah Brelenah. The celebration continued until Danek raised a question.

"Who is that?" He pointed across the roof to the stairwell enclosure.

A man lay slumped against the back of the enclosure, as if trying to hide from any who might use the door. Onika floated toward him. He wore the hooded cloak of a garrison soldier and clutched a bottle in his hand. "Grayson?" she called. "Can you pull back his hood?"

Grayson appeared beside the man and drew back the thick fabric. It was Oli Agoros, seemingly unconscious. A sheen of sweat glazed his face. The women gasped.

"Why is he dressed like a soldier?" Danek asked.

"As I said," came Lady Brisa's voice. "Drunk."

Grayson sniffed the mouth of the bottle. "He's not drunk. Not on wine, anyway. He's taken too much evenroot."

Another collective gasp.

"Surely he wouldn't have," Brelenah said. "It's illegal."

"And depleted," Danek said. "Where would he have gotten it?"

"Trevn will not be pleased," Princess Hrettah said.

"Why would he have done it?" Brelenah asked.

"To call shadir for us to banish," Zeroah said. "I'll fetch the physician." She disappeared.

A heavy silence fell over their group.

"I'll tell my father," Lady Brisa said. "If there is evenroot in the castle, the council should know." She faded away.

The situation troubled Onika. "You may return to your bodies," she said. "I'll wait here. Thank you for your help today, for your faith. Arman dealt our enemy a crippling blow."

The Veil warriors left her alone with Duke Canden.

Arman, what does this mean? This man sinned against you in an effort to help us. His sacrifice worked, yet what of his soul? What say you of all this?

"IT IS MINE TO JUDGE, MINE TO REPAY."

Of course it was. While Onika wanted to make sense of everything, some circumstances she must trust to Arman alone. Footsteps drew her attention to the stairwell door. Zeroah walked through, followed by Sir Kalenek, Rosâr Trevn, Sir Cadoc, and Master Nietz.

"Miss Onika?" the king said aloud as he circled the stairwell enclosure and stopped where Duke Canden lay. "Are you still here?"

"I am," she voiced him.

"Explain what has happened."

Onika told the king how Duke Canden had summoned her to the roof. *"He said he was busy elsewhere, but he must have taken the root, called the shadir, then voiced me."*

"And hidden himself here." King Trevn relayed their conversation to the others.

"Is he dead?" Sir Cadoc asked.

Sir Kalenek crouched beside the duke and felt his throat. "He's alive, but barely."

Onika prayed that Arman would grant the king wisdom in dealing with the duke.

King Trevn ripped the bottle from the duke's hand. He upended it but only a drizzle came out. He paced across the roof, and when he returned said, "Arrest him. Put him in the dungeon next to his sister. Maybe that will stop her ranting."

"Nietz, get his feet," Sir Kalenek said, grabbing the duke under the arms.

"You will not drag him away like a criminal," Zeroah said, stepping in Nietz's way. "Order a litter, Master Nietz, so that the duke can be carried."

The guardsman glanced at the king, who nodded his assent. As Master Nietz hurried away, Sir Kalenek released Duke Canden. Zeroah knelt at his side and ran an embroidered handkerchief over his brow.

Onika voiced the king. *"What he did was wrong, Your Highness, that I know for certain, but had he not done this, we would not have succeeded in banishing an entire swarm of shadir."*

The king frowned. *"How many?"*

"Close to one hundred," Onika said. *"When I inquired of Arman about the duke, he reminded me that it is his place to judge and repay, not mine."*

A deep sigh from the king. "Duke Canden knew he could die, didn't he?"

"He knew," Sir Kalenek said. "He still might die."

"Arman spared him," Zeroah said.

"And continues to, for some reason," the king said. "Well? Don't look at me like that. I didn't say I'd execute him, but I can't very well pin a medal to his breast either, can I? He goes to the dungeon. For now." The king stalked away, Sir Cadoc jogging after him.

Onika remained with Zeroah as they waited for the litter. They took turns praying that Arman would have mercy on the soul of this man and heal whatever wounds had gouged his heart.

CHARLON

Emperor Ulrik had regained his strength. He was obnoxious. Demanding. Prideful. Flirted with the maidens. Hosted endless revelries in his tent. He was everything. Everything Charlon hated about men. She could not harm him, though. Could not afford to offend Empress Inolah or Rosârah Thallah. So she kept her distance.

"If you won't put a stop to it, I will," Roya said, standing before Charlon's throne.

Fool woman. "And just how will you do that?" Charlon asked.

"If you would teach me your new magic . . ."

Figured. Charlon's maidens were growing desperate. "I asked you to find out what Amala and my son have been doing. In their visits to New Rurekau. Do you have answers?"

Roya's eyes flashed. "They dine with King Barthel. Shanek takes sword lessons from the king's captain and sits on a throne in the king's tent."

Heat rushed through Charlon. "He means to steal my son from me."

"Was that ever a doubt?"

"Of course not." But now Charlon had proof. Why had Shanek gone in the first place? She suspected Amala's influence. Did not trust the girl. "Leave me."

Roya gave one last nasty glare. Turned and stalked away. Charlon would not be surprised if she left. Left to join King Barthel. *Good riddance,* her heart said. Charlon had never liked her.

She missed Sir Kalenek desperately. Had despaired the day he'd ridden away. Rurek had said he would return. For a while, those words had given hope. Until Masi told her Sir Kalenek had gone to Rurekau. Not to help Shanek, as he had claimed. But to rescue his beloved prophetess. The thought made Charlon queasy. Without the compulsions, he must have remembered. His love for that woman.

Why did despair hurt so? When Torol had died, the pain had been severe. No choice but to grieve and heal. And heal she had. Because of Sir Kalenek's kindness and care.

But Sir Kalenek had not died. He lived. Out there in the world. Apart from her. Choosing to love another. The pain was too great. Charlon could not cope. She screamed, keening anguish that rivaled that of any widow.

Goddess, why?

There had never been any goddess to pray to. Magon had been a shadir. A creature of the Lowerworld that Charlon had sent back. Now she had Rurek. But he was loyal to himself alone.

So must Charlon be. As always.

The tribe was restless. Those who had not flocked to Emperor Ulrik's revels stewed in anger. Bored without magic. It left Charlon on edge. She longed for the days when she had been naïve and powerful. When she had eagerly worshiped Magon. Obeyed Mreegan's every word. As Chieftess, she had failed to inspire the same fervor within the people.

"Masi!" Charlon called. "Recite the prophecy."

The slight's voice came inside her head. *In those days the root of Arman will be destroyed and usher in the end of all things. There will be mourning and great weeping heard throughout the land. Brother will turn against brother, and their swords will dash each other to pieces. And Armania, the glory of realms, the beauty of the goddess's eye, will no longer be the head of all things.*

"All of it," Charlon said.

I will bring peace between Mother and Father, and the two will be reconciled. From the line of Arman and Magon will come a Deliverer who will be ruler over all. He will crush the foreheads of our enemies, the skulls of all who come against us.

"Those are the words that Chieftess Mreegan so lauded?"

Yes, Chieftess.

Charlon did not understand. The destruction of the Five Woes had humbled Armania. But Mother and Father had not been united. Nor did that last part fit. If Mother and Father were reconciled, what need was there for a Deliverer to crush the enemy?

Kateen entered and bowed low before the throne. "Dinner is ready, Chieftess," she said. "Will you join us tonight? Or do you prefer to eat here?"

Charlon had no desire for company. But she couldn't stomach another meal. Alone in this tent. "I will come," she said, rising from her throne.

Kateen helped her into her furs. Once dressed, Charlon strode from the red tent and into the cold night. Rone and Nuel followed. Carried her throne. Down the snowy hill to the altar. An altar dedicated to no god but the magic Charlon had discovered. There a bonfire blazed, lighting the twilight in a fiery glow. Dozens danced on the altar, worshiping . . . what? They once worshiped Magon. Did they believe in her still? Did they believe in anything?

Charlon felt small. She should have called forth all her men. To carry her on her throne, as Mreegan used to do. She often forgot. Forgot to demand the royal treatment she deserved.

She reached the revelers. Saw Emperor Ulrik in their midst. Dancing wildly, surrounded by a cluster of maidens. Breath clouding in steady puffs around his face. Charlon suddenly wished she had not come. She had no desire to spend her meal watching the emperor carouse.

She bade the men set her throne on the opposite side of the altar. Where the bonfire would block her view of Ulrik Orsona.

Her men were quick to serve. Brought food and drink. Extra furs. She huddled beneath them. Munched on roasted fowl. Being with child made her hungry always. By the time she had eaten half her meal, the revelry had circled into her view. The emperor ran out of the mob. Dragged a young woman with him. Both were laughing. Stopped to catch their breath.

"I told you, Your Eminence . . ." It was Amala, Charlon realized with a start. "I do not wish to dance."

"But you excel at it. You even know the Rurekan steps, though I can't imagine how."

"I learned to dance with the Armanian princesses under the tutelage of Rosârah Brelenah," she said.

"My grandmother," he said. "I've never met her."

"Well, she is a stunning woman," Amala said.

"So are you," he said, walking closer.

Charlon rolled her eyes.

Ulrik reached for the girl. Took her hand in his and drew his other around her waist. "Dance with me, Miss Amala. I won't be here much longer. Who knows when we might have the chance again?"

Green sparks flashed between them. Amala shrieked. Lunged away from the emperor.

Shanek stood where the pair once had. "Stop it." He shoved Ulrik with both hands.

Charlon straightened, startled by the sudden conflict.

"I beg your pardon," Ulrik said, hands on his hips. "Stop what?"

"How you talk to Amala," Shanek said. "And dance with her. I don't like it."

"I have been nothing but kind," Ulrik said. "Ask her yourself."

"He has been kind, Shanek," Amala said. "There is nothing to worry about."

"Stop being kind or I'll make you," Shanek said.

Ulrik chuckled. "And just how are you going to do that?"

Shanek stood nose to nose with Ulrik, glaring. "Say you'll leave Amala be."

Ulrik grinned, devilishly handsome. Despite his shorn scalp and arrogance. "Are we but ten years old, Your Highness? Must we play such games?"

Shanek grabbed Ulrik and they disappeared.

Amala screamed. Several in the crowd yelped or gasped.

Charlon gripped the sides of her throne. *Fool!* What was he doing?

"Shanek!" Amala yelled, spinning in a circle.

Did the girl honestly think he was within earshot?

Amala ran to Charlon's throne. Fell to her knees in the snow. "Where have they gone?"

How could anyone know? "We will find out when he returns," Charlon said, taking another bite of her fowl. Pretending she didn't care. But if Shanek harmed the emperor—he would regret it. They all would.

"If anything happens to the Rurekan emperor, it will mean war," Roya said.

"I am well aware of that," Charlon snapped.

She continued eating. Watched the revelers. Many didn't realize the emperor was missing. Charlon finished her meal and returned to the red tent.

Free from ahvenrood, she saw clearly now. The prophecy was madness. Why make Shanek king of Armania? The boy was a fool. Knew nothing about running a nation. His method of solving conflicts was to demand his way. Zap someone with a green spark. Carry them off. He, thankfully, had not killed again. But Charlon had no doubt. If he was crowned ruler, he would destroy any who dared defy him. Why had Mreegan ever thought this a good idea? Shanek would be a tyrant king. If someone didn't kill him first.

Shanek appeared before her. "You were looking for me?" he asked.

So much indifference. It wounded her. "Where is Emperor Ulrik?"

He grinned. "Where the giants make people hunt beetles."

Charlon fell back in her throne. "Oh, Shanek, you didn't!"

"I took him to a mine filled with angry Puru. You should have heard him yell when they told him to work."

Charlon could well imagine it. "This is not the behavior of a man ready to rule a nation, Shanek."

He frowned. "What do you mean?"

"A grown man would have ignored such taunts. At worst, you could have had him imprisoned. To do the act yourself . . . You behaved like a child."

Shanek's eyes narrowed.

"Your short temper makes you weak. You don't think before you act. Because of that you are continually making a fool of yourself."

"I am not a child or a fool!"

"I made a bargain with Rurekau. To protect that man's life. Yet that means nothing to *Sâr* Shanek. You have no respect. For anything but your own whims. Bring him back here. Now."

"No."

Rage filled Charlon. "You would disobey me?"

"I am to be king of Armania. King is higher than Chieftess. Besides, Empress Jazlyn already knows the emperor was here. Better we hide him in the mines."

Could that be true? It didn't matter. Charlon must not let him change the subject. "You are not king yet, Shanek. In fact, I have decided that you will not be. I have studied the prophecy. It is vague. I believe Chieftess Mreegan misinterpreted it."

"She didn't! I am meant to be king of Armania."

"If you don't learn to control your temper, you will be nothing but a disgrace."

"Take it back!"

Charlon pushed off her chair. Straightened to her full height. Unfortunately, she was still shorter than Shanek. "Will you kill your mother? Is that what you will do?"

"I will be king of Armania," he spat. "I have more power than anyone. I will take my supporters with me. And you will sit on your throne of sticks and boss whoever is left."

He raised his hands, and a wall of green light flew toward her, knocking her off her feet. She hit the floor and rolled over the furs, stopping against the tent wall. When she looked up, Shanek had gone.

Betrayal, her heart said. Tears flooded her eyes. But she was not sorry. She had spoken truth. Said what she must. It wasn't her fault. If Shanek couldn't understand. Charlon had made her choice. She would abandon the prophecy. Continue to practice her new magic. Focus on building Magosia's strengths. That way, should Barthel Rogedoth or Empress Jazlyn attack, she would be ready.

But first she must inform Rosârah Thallah. Of Shanek's betrayal. She would not take the blame. And if Shanek had truly abandoned Charlon—at least she had the child within. To be her heir. To love her.

Trevn

Trevn sat alone in the antechamber of the council room, clutching one of Wilek's journals. This had become his favorite place to sit and think without fear of being interrupted. People came to his office constantly, but now that all the secret passageways were complete, he could move about with ease.

So much was happening at once. Trevn had been unable to question Captain Korvoh about abducting the Armanian children. Tace Edekk and his soldiers had blocked off the Nawhar Forest, and Trevn didn't dare waste soldiers forcing the issue—not with Shanek DanSâr now wreaking havoc in the city. Trevn had been so worried about Rogedoth, he had forgotten Janek's son. Speaking with Sir Kalenek only raised his fears. The root child had unstoppable power.

Now Oli had gone and broken the law. Again. Trevn had read in his brother's journal about the day Oli had taken root to save Wilek from the mutiny aboard the *Seffynaw*. Wilek had pardoned him. Trevn wanted to punish him, but he needed his First Arm. And Oli—misguided as usual—had only meant to help. If only Trevn could get rid of all the evenroot in this land.

The secret door opened and Cadoc peeked inside. "Lord Blackpool to see you."

One of the traitorous nobles? Here in the castle? "Whatever for?"

"He didn't say, though he looks distraught."

Trevn sighed. "He has likely come to berate me for flogging his son."

"I asked him that, sir," Cadoc said. "He said it was about something else."

"A declaration of war, perhaps? I suppose I must see him." Trevn made his way through the secret passage to his office, wondering what tricks his noble enemies were plotting. Once he had shelved Wilek's journal and was seated behind his desk, he bade Cadoc let the man in.

Gunrik Koll, Earl of Blackpool, entered. His clothing was wrinkled, as if he'd been wearing it for days, and his haggard expression matched the worry pouring off him in waves.

"Lord," Trevn said. "You wish to speak with me?"

The man bowed deeply. His throat bobbed. Reddened eyes rose to meet Trevn's. "Your Highness . . ." His voice came shakily. "I come to beg use of your physician." Again he paused for a trembling breath. "My wife and daughter-in-law have fallen ill. My—" He swallowed. "My own physician is at a loss. It's a fever. And a rash. . . . I fear for their lives. And the baby."

Lady Dendrelle, Tace Edekk's daughter and Sir Jarmyn's wife. Her child was due soon, if Trevn recalled hearing Mielle correctly. "What says Duke Raine's physician?"

"I've sent a bird but have received no reply as yet. I imagine he is . . . pre-occupied."

"Hunting, I suppose?" Trevn smirked. "Or plotting an attack against me?"

Gunrik hung his head. "The latter is most likely the case."

Well, this was an interesting development. "Of course you may have use of my physician, lord. I insist he accompany you back to your manor at once. Nietz, go with them."

"Thank you, Your Highness," Gunrik said, bowing again. "You are most generous."

"I know what it must have cost you to come here," Trevn said. "I would like us to have peace, sir. Is that at all possible?"

The man was no longer trembling. He raised his chin and spoke with conviction. "My son was wrong to disobey you, Your Highness. He thinks too highly of himself. I'm afraid he—"

"Ulrik Orsona."

Ulrik? What could he want? The interruption had caused Trevn to miss the last of Gunrik's words about Sir Jarmyn.

"I am not asking to make peace with your son, lord," Trevn said. "I speak to you. Please think on it. For now, you must hurry back to your manor with my physician. Your wife and—"

"Ulrik Orsona."

"—daughter-in-law need you there."

Gunrik jerked his head in a quick bow. "You have my thanks, Your Highness." And he departed. Nietz followed him out.

Trevn leaned back in his chair, pondering this turn of events.

"Could it be a trap?" Cadoc asked.

Trevn met his shield's gaze. "To steal my physician? Why?"

"If you were to be poisoned and your physician was away . . ."

Trevn grimaced. "I've never known Gunrik Koll to be a good actor. I think he was sincere. I hope this might be an opportunity to strengthen the army."

"Ulrik Orsona."

"My nephew is voicing me, Cadoc." Trevn opened the connection. *"Yes?"*

"Prince Shanek carried me to the giant mines where I have been attacked by swarms of disgusting beetles."

"He took you to the mines? Why?"

"Because he is a barbaric recreant. Mother said you could send Master Grayson to transport me out of here."

Trevn supposed he could, though he didn't appreciate Ulrik's rude demands. *"What happened?"*

"I was having a pleasant conversation with Miss Amala Allard and he went mad with jealousy."

Trevn doubted the truth was so simple. *"Sir Kalenek said Prince Shanek dotes on Miss Amala."*

"That doesn't give him any right to act like a child. He is dimwitted and unstable. You will send Master Grayson? It's time I returned to Rurekau, anyway. I was weary of Magosia. Plus my wife has recently returned, and it's time she and I had a reunion."

Speaking of unstable . . . Trevn rubbed his face. *"I will speak with Master Grayson."*

"Do hurry. Those giant fiends promised to make me eat beetles if I didn't work hard enough. I'm currently hiding in a small cave, but I cannot stay here forever."

"I will speak with you soon." Trevn closed off Ulrik and reached for his sister. *"Your son is in trouble,"* he said.

"Yes, I told him to contact you," Inolah said. *"I didn't know what else to do. He's supposed to be in hiding. If Shanek knows he is alive, I have no doubt Rogedoth does too."*

"Ulrik doesn't seem to care about that. He said he's looking forward to seeing his wife."

"I know. What a mess. He could very well upset everything I've been working

toward. Ferro will be overjoyed, though, both to see his brother and to lose the responsibilities of regent."

"And you?"

"I love my son, but he is too much like his father. It makes things . . . difficult. It worries me that he wants to see Jazlyn. I hope he isn't planning to cause trouble."

Trevn didn't doubt that was exactly Ulrik's plan. *"Is Rogedoth still with you?"*

"He is, though the camp is much smaller. He is sending out his army in pieces."

Sneaking away? *"Perhaps Grayson can locate them."* Though it wouldn't be easy without someone in each group to travel to. *"I must go, Inolah. I do not envy you the task of keeping Ulrik out of mischief."* Trevn closed the connection and reached for Grayson. *"I need your help."*

"Yes, sir."

"Emperor Ulrik is trapped in the Ahj-Yeke mines and needs a rescue. If you can carry two, take Sir Kalenek with you. Ulrik said giants have threatened him, and I don't want anyone hurt. Take Ulrik to Empress Inolah in New Rurekau."

"Yes, Your Highness. We will go right away."

"When you are finished, report to my office. I have a second task for you and Sir Kalenek this day."

"Yes, Your Highness."

Trevn opened his eyes to find Mielle standing before his desk. Seeing her lightened his load, and he went to greet her with a kiss. "What is it?"

"Tonis and I stumbled onto a new development in our investigation of the missing children," she said. "Of those Grayson carried back from the mines, eighteen were Sarikarian children. When I interviewed them, they all described the same man who had been present when they were taken. Two named the man as Sir Malder."

"The name is familiar, but I don't recall why," Trevn said.

"According to Tonis, Sir Malder is Finnel Wallington's shield."

A chill ran down Trevn's arms. Princess Nolia's husband involved in these abductions? Why? "This would connect the Wallingtons with Edekk."

"It will be too time consuming for Grayson to take each child home," Mielle said. "I thought he might carry them to the castle in Sarikar and Hinck could figure out where they live."

"That's a fine plan. I will voice him about it."

"I'd also like to speak with Princess Saria."

"I can voice her as well."

"Thank you, Trevn, but you're very busy. Tonis, Grayson, and I are immersed in the investigation. It would be so helpful if we could speak to her in person, together."

"You want to go to Sarikar?"

"Just for a quick meeting. A half hour would be enough to get my questions answered."

Trevn didn't like the idea of sending Mielle away, yet he couldn't argue with her logic. "You cannot go for merely a half hour. Servants would see you and word would get out that you had a secret meeting with the princess. It would cause all kinds of rumors. You'll have to go on an official visit. Stay at least three days, maybe as long as a week."

"A week?"

"I'll send you there in my stead, to take a betrothal agreement to Hinck for him and Saria."

"What betrothal?"

"Hinck's idea. He is set on marrying Saria, so we will support him. Go and represent Armania. Meet with the council, go out into the city and greet their people . . . everything that goes along with an official visit. Grayson may meet you there and help as long as I have no need of him. I suggest you leave tomorrow. And I'll let Hinck and Saria know you are coming and that you wish to discuss your investigation while you are there."

Mielle embraced him. "Thank you, Trevn! I'll do my best to make you proud."

"Be yourself, Mouse, and you'll do fine. And please be careful."

"I will." She kissed him, then walked to the door. "I must go pack."

He watched his wife go, hoping he had done the right thing. He well knew how pretentious the Sarikarian nobility could be. He almost wished he could be there to witness the exchanges between them and his outspoken wife.

Instead he must go back to the dungeon, this time to speak with his First Arm.

⊙Lİ

Oli opened his eyes to darkness. He listened, curious where he was. He heard breathing, the sounds of something dripping, a moan from somewhere in the distance, the clink of chains. He lifted his arm to scratch his face and found a chain on his wrist. This startled him and he tried to sit up. His ankles were clapped in irons as well. Grief and fear swelled up in his throat and tried to choke him. He must have died. And now he was in the Lowerworld. He had well earned his fate and tried to comfort himself with that fact. It did not dispel his anxiety.

His body ached as if he'd been sick for months. Residual effects of the evenroot he had taken. He despaired when he realized he still had only one arm. But why should an evil man be given a restored body, as Zeroah believed all received in Shamayim? That would be a blessed reward. One Oli did not deserve in the least.

Time crept by and nothing changed. He felt around him, found a stone wall, shifted and dragged his leg chains until he was leaning against it.

Someone began to cry nearby. A woman. The moaning continued in the distance. More chains clanking. More dripping. And every once in a while, footsteps passing by.

It wasn't until a man yelled, "Back from the door if you want to eat!" that Oli realized with sudden horror that this was not the Lowerworld as he had assumed, but the dungeon in Armanguard. He had come here before to question his mother and sister.

His heart clenched at the realization that he had lived. And now he would have to answer for his crimes. Helplessness threatened tears, but he turned it to rage and screamed out his frustration to the surrounding darkness.

He felt better for a moment, but it was still dark, the chains were still attached to his wrist and ankles, and the man bringing the meal was getting closer. He eventually banged on Oli's door, slid a tray through the slot on the bottom, then walked on.

Oli did not eat. Did not care. He cursed the physician for helping him, and Trevn for putting him here. He pondered the ways he might end his life. Strangle himself with one of the chains? Bash his head against the wall? Use his mind-speak to compel himself to stop breathing?

It was these dark thoughts that finally sent him crawling toward the door to see if his meal had included some sort of instrument he might fashion into a weapon to fall upon. Nothing but a cold meat pie. He left it there and listened to the sounds outside his cell.

Voices in the distance, growing near. A man and a woman. The woman's familiar voice curled his gut. Oli did not want her here. He lay down on the sticky floor and rolled to his side, hoping she would think him asleep. A fist banged on the door of his cell.

"Back from the door," the guard said.

Oli did not move. The door scraped open.

"I will go in alone," Zeroah said.

"I think not, Your Highness." This from Ephec, her guard. Footsteps drew near. "Let me put down my cloak, at least."

"That is not necessary," Zeroah said.

Oli lay still as shuffling footsteps stopped behind him. He grit his teeth, hoping she would not stay long.

"I know you are awake, Your Grace, so do not pretend otherwise," Zeroah said. "The guard heard you yell a moment ago."

What a foolish notion. How could the guard know which prisoner had yelled?

"I didn't understand you, at first," Zeroah said. "Your memories grieved my heart, but it wasn't until I realized you had so little regard for your own life that it all made sense. You think yourself worthless. And how would you know better? You've been told you are worthless by those who should have loved you best. But I see you, Oli Agoros. You are a good man. A kind man. You think you deserve death, yet each time you try to take your life, you fight to destroy as much evil as you can on your way out. It is noble of you, but misguided."

She paused, and he could hear her breathing. He waited, wondering if she would say anything else, wanting her to say more, desperate for the sound of her voice.

"You deserve life," she said finally. "But you must learn to extend grace to that little boy whose father was so very cruel and whose mother did not care."

Not his fault.

Two steps clicked over the stone floor, fabric rustled, and a hand rested upon his shoulder. "I believe in you, Your Grace. Arman wants you to honor and serve him with your life."

Oli's heart seized, so overcome was he by her words. But she did not understand. There was no good in him. Not really. He had given his soul to Gâzar long ago. He had to make her see what kind of a man he really was.

"I compelled Vivia," he said. "I couldn't give her what she wanted, so I made her forget. I changed her memories. She remembers nothing of what passed between us." He choked on a breath but forged ahead, determined to say all he must and be done with it. "You were right, Your Highness. It was my memory magic all along. And I'm afraid I have broken Vivia's mind in my attempt to save her from myself. So do not hold me up a hero, for I am far from it."

"Miss Vivia's mind is not broken, Your Grace," Zeroah said. "She is perfectly well, until I ask of you. It makes sense now why she becomes confused, but you did not—"

The door opened again, and another set of footsteps strode inside. "Leave us, please."

Oli groaned inwardly. All hail the king.

"This magic is new and strange, Your Grace," Zeroah said. "I daresay generations will pass before it's fully understood." She squeezed his shoulder. "I will continue to pray for you. Every day." Her soft footsteps faded away, followed by the heavier steps of her guardsman.

"Explain what the dowager queen was talking about," Trevn said.

Oli sighed and rolled to his back. The light was so low, he could only see the silhouette of the king and his guards from the torchlight leaking through the open cell door. "All that I told you Zeroah had done to me with her unique voicing magic . . . entering my memories . . . well, it turns out it was my power all along. I pulled her into my mind, and once she was there, she changed my memories with her kindness. I guess, without realizing it, I was drawn to her."

"I see. And where did you get the evenroot this time?"

Ashamed, Oli told the truth. "My mother had it on her when I arrested her."

"How much more do you have?"

"None. I had hoped that taking it all would lure the greatest number of shadir."

"Here is the fact, Oli: I need you. So I cannot have you killing yourself, no matter how much you might wish to die. You will stay here a few more days and think about all the reasons you have to live. When I come back, I want a report of at least twenty. Then you will help me with the important business of defeating our enemy. Is that clear?"

Oli smirked. "Yes, Your Highness."

"Good day, Your Grace."

A chaos of footsteps shuffled and receded as the king and his guards departed. The door to Oli's cell shut, a key jangled in the lock, the guard's footsteps faded, and silence returned.

"What did you do, brother?" A woman's voice from the cell behind his.

A shock made Oli twist around, though he could see nothing. "Eudora?"

"What magic do you have that destroyed some woman?"

"The voices of blood. I can change people's memories."

She chuckled. "I see why the king is your friend."

"He did not know I could do that until I told him just now."

"And he pardoned you for it."

"He pardoned me because he has mercy."

"No one has mercy," Eudora said. "You wait, he will ask you to pay him back someday."

"That is a cynical view."

"It's the truth."

"Hinckdan told me what happened to you. For what it's worth, I'm sorry."

"Yes, well, I am safe now. Until I'm executed."

"If the king were going to execute you, you'd be dead."

"I am Rogedoth's wife."

"Not by your choosing. And if you could give any insight into his plans . . ."

"You changed some woman's memories?"

Oli winced. "I meant to help her."

"It sounds like you did."

Oli wasn't convinced.

"Would you help me?" his sister asked. "I want to forget."

"Forget what?" But he realized he already knew and cringed that his words had sounded harsh. "Forgive me. I didn't think."

"I don't want to forget all that happened," Eudora said. "But I'd like to forget some of it. End my torment. Is that so wrong?"

Oli did not think so, but was this something he wanted to try again? He had taken Vivia's memories without her consent to ease her pain and suffering. Eudora was asking for relief. Her need to forget seemed far more compelling than Oli's desire to *help* Vivia.

"Please, brother?" Her voice had a wretched tone.

He would not deny anyone sanity. "I've only done this once. I make no promises. And it might . . . change you."

"I am not afraid."

"Very well." In the darkness, he moved against the bars separating their cells, took hold of his sister's hand, then reached for her mind. *"Think about what you wish to forget."*

As the first scene of horror began to play through his mind, Oli wondered briefly who would help *him* forget what memories he let in.

KALEΠEK

After Kal and Grayson had carried Ulrik to Inolah in New Rurekau, Rosâr Trevn tasked them with stealing Charlon's stash of evenroot. Kal carried a shovel to Grayson's receiving room and found the young man sitting on the floor against one wall, waiting.

Grayson jumped to his feet. "We can't go directly to Charlon or she'll see us. You'll have to show me the way, and I'll carry you league by league."

Kal grimaced. He'd made many magical trips since the king had named him Grayson's Shield, but he didn't like the idea of doing it over and over. He strapped the shovel to his back, then took hold of Grayson's arms. "Let's go."

Then they were moving, like someone had jerked the world out from under their feet. Everything blurred, except their bodies, which seemed to remain in place as they passed through the air like a figurine someone had thrown.

They stopped in a field a great distance from the castle, feet deep in snow. A gust of cold shocked Kal.

"You'll have to direct me from here," Grayson said, breath fogging from his mouth.

Kal squinted to the west and panned his gaze southward, taking in the endless snowy hills. With no roads, he suddenly doubted his ability to get back to Magosia without Onika's help. Nothing to do but try. He supposed if they got lost Grayson could always take them back to the castle. He pointed to the southwest. "That way."

They grabbed hold of each other, and again they flew, though this time Kal was able to see the snowy ground moving beneath their feet. They landed on the edge of a steep hill. Kal's ankle twisted, and he stumbled. The shovel swung, pulling him down. He hit the ground and slid, flailing to try to stop himself, though there was nothing to grab on to.

He struck a solid object and was surprised to see Grayson looking down. The young man had planted himself on the side of the hill, and Kal had run up against his legs.

"How did you—? Never mind." What Kal wouldn't give to be able to move like that.

Grayson helped Kal to his feet. The young man had built up some muscle since Kal had helped him escape the *Vespara*.

"You've grown since I last saw you," Kal said, brushing snow off his tunic.

"I haven't tasted any root since the *Vespara*," Grayson said.

Kal tapped his temple. "I meant here." He thumped the backs of his fingers against Grayson's chest. "And here."

The young man beamed. It was hard for Kal not to see the boy under those masculine features. Back when they'd traveled through Magonia and Rurekau, Grayson had annoyed Kal with his endless questions, but he liked this older Grayson a great deal.

"I wish Shanek could have had a childhood like yours," he said. "Jhorn was wise to protect you from your magic. To keep you from root."

"Did you give root to Shanek?"

"Chieftess Mreegan did. Every day of his life until she died." Kal's throat tightened, and he gripped Grayson's arm. "Let's keep moving."

They jumped again, this time landing on the bank of a partly frozen river. Next they moved to a snowy valley, beside a copse of snow-laden trees, then to the other end of that same valley, at the bottom of a large hill.

"How big is Shanek now?" Grayson asked.

"He looks about King Trevn's age, but he's really just shy of two years old."

Grayson wrinkled his nose. "Does he act like a baby?"

"Sometimes," Kal said, chuckling, "though not how you're thinking. His mind and speech grew with his body, which slowed once Charlon forbade him from taking evenroot. The damage has been done, though. And not from root alone."

"What else happened?"

"Charlon spoiled him rotten with delusions of grandeur. Promised he'd be king of Armania." Kal tugged on Grayson's arm. "Let's head that way." He pointed. "Southwest."

And Grayson jumped.

They traveled the better part of the morning until Kal caught sight of a familiar rocky outcropping. He directed Grayson to take them north until he spied the blip of red in the distance.

"The red tent is Charlon's dwelling," he told Grayson. "The other tents are white, so it's hard to see them in the snow."

"Is the evenroot in the red tent?"

"No." This made Kal grin. "The Chieftess's paranoia has made our task a simple one." He told Grayson how Charlon had made him bury the evenroot in the field where no one could find it.

"She trusted you," Grayson said.

"Aye, that she did, to her great loss."

"Will she hate you very much?"

"Perhaps, though she might never learn I was the one to take it. Come on."

Kal combed the clearing until he located the spot, which had recently been dug up. A pang of fear shot through him. Had Charlon moved it?

"Someone beat us to it, looks like," Grayson said.

Kal shrugged off the shovel. "Only one way to find out. You watch in the Veil. I want to know if anyone or anything sees us."

Grayson vanished, and when he next spoke, his voice came from inside Kal's head. *"I don't see anyone. Should I come out and help dig?"*

"Stay there," Kal said. "Since it's been dug up recently, it won't take me long." And he would much rather have a set of eyes in the Veil.

So Kal dug. Grayson reported no shadir, but he did point out a gowzal that had fluttered to a nearby bush. Kal hoped the creature wasn't one of Charlon's pets.

Before long, the head of his shovel struck the crate. He dropped to his hands and knees to dig with gloved hands. He should pull it out and have Grayson carry them away before they were seen, but curiosity got the better of him, and he used a dagger from his belt to prise up the lid.

The sight of so much root filled him with relief. Some was missing—a couple sacks, if he remembered right. He blew out a long breath, thankful it wasn't more, and replaced the lid.

A gowzal fluttered to the ground beside him. Kal shooed it away and glanced at the tree. The first gowzal was still watching. This was a second.

He dragged the crate out of the hole, then filled in the space with dirt and snow. A third gowzal arrived, and the first flew over from the tree. Kal finished his work, strapped the shovel on his back, and hefted the crate in his arms.

One of the gowzals flew up to his shoulder. Kal yelled at the creature, but it stayed put.

"Grayson! Let's get out of here."

Grayson appeared in front of Kal.

"I won't be able to hold onto you and this crate at the same time," Kal said, wincing as the gowzal nipped his neck. Another bird landed on Grayson's head and pecked at his hair.

Grayson twirled away, and the bird dropped. A second gowzal perched on the crate and squawked, sending foul breath in Kal's face.

"We've got to get away from these birds," Kal said.

Grayson grabbed Kal's belt with both hands. "Hold tight."

He jumped. They were moving more slowly, heavily, as if someone had grabbed onto their ankles. Kal took in the detail of a tree and a snowcapped boulder. They landed on a snowy plain, but the gowzal was still there, its claws digging into Kal's shoulder.

"Get off!" He tried to knock the bird aside with his head but hadn't the leverage.

Grayson released Kal and punched the bird, which squawked and fluttered to the snow.

"There's one on your back," Kal said.

Grayson twisted, spotted the creature, then vanished. He reappeared a few paces away, lying on his back in the snow. The gowzal shrieked, and suddenly Grayson was before Kal again, grabbing hold of his belt.

"There was a spell on the crate. We're breaking it, which explains the pull," Grayson said. "Here we go." They jumped, this time leaving the gowzals behind.

They moved gradually, the sun sinking lower with each jump. They stopped by a river, and Kal put down the crate to rest. He sat on the lid and stretched his arms up over his head, then finished off the water in his jug.

"Mine's empty too," Grayson said. "I'll go fill them."

Kal handed over his water jug and Grayson jumped away.

Kal breathed in a deep, chilled breath and listened to the heavy silence. The moment took him back to the farm where he'd grown up. He and his brother used to stop by the creek on their way home from the training camp. Their father had been gone to the war for years by then, and it had been Kal's greatest dream to join him.

A distant wail pulled him back to the present. Grayson knelt on the riverbank, seemingly fine. That had been a child, hadn't it?

Kal surveyed the countryside. Across the river he spotted an unpainted carriage with bars on the windows being pulled by two horses. A prisoner transport? Out here?

Kal dragged the crate behind a nearby bush and heaped snow on it. He left his and Grayson's packs there, along with the shovel, then walked to the river.

"There's a carriage." Kal pointed it out. "Can you take a look? Without being seen?"

"Sure." Grayson handed the water jugs to Kal, then vanished.

Kal carried the water back to where he'd stashed the crate and kept his eye on the carriage. He took a long swig from his jug, then left both on the ground beside the crate.

A crunch in the snow behind Kal sent him spinning around. Grayson had returned, and by the look on his face, had seen something shocking.

"Two men riding up front. They've got six inside. Children tied and gagged. One of them is wailing. They all look pretty banged up."

Alarm shot through Kal. He had no patience for sadistic men who sold children. He touched his sword, hesitant only because his arm might fail him.

He'd been trying to make peace with his past, as Onika had said. Would it make any difference?

"We don't have to fight," Grayson said. "I could carry the captives to my receiving chamber."

That would be easier than a confrontation. "What about the men?" Kal asked.

"We could leave them. Or I could carry them to a cell?"

"You might be hurt."

"Not if you disarmed them first," Grayson said.

Kal narrowed his eyes at the distant carriage. He could likely do that much. "Drop me in front of it. I'll confront the men. You take the children to Armanguard."

"I could help you," Grayson said. "Then take the children once the men are captured."

Kal wasn't sure about that.

"I can disarm one of them easily," Grayson said.

The more Kal thought about it, the more he saw the asset of Grayson's abilities. "Carry me to the road, then take the sword of whichever man looks the strongest. If you can get swords off both men, do it. If not, come to my side, and we'll confront them together."

Grayson grabbed Kal, and the world spun. Before Kal had time to breathe, Grayson had left him alone in fresh snow, facing the oncoming carriage, which was moving slowly, its wooden wheels spinning uselessly in the snow each time the terrain dipped.

Two men on the driver's seat stared at Kal and exclaimed to each other. The driver jerked the reins and called to the horses. The second man stood, a steadying hand on his seat.

"What you doing out here, stranger?" the driver asked.

That voice sent a prickle of remembrance up Kal's spine. He took in the portly frame and balding head, the fringe of short warrior's tails attached like a mane. Kal knew him. Donn Flane, a soldier from the war. He'd fought in the second division out of Raine.

Tace Edekk's man.

Kal didn't know the companion. Strong and surly with a crooked nose, he was glaring at Kal when Grayson appeared, standing on the footboard, and drew the man's sword from his belt.

"Hey!" He grabbed for Grayson, who vanished, causing the man to fall forward. He just managed to grip the footboard before tumbling over. "Where'd he go?"

The driver dropped the reins and drew his blade, suddenly alert.

"Flane," Kal said, hoping to unnerve him. "What does Edekk have you doing for him these days? Abducting children?"

"I don't know you, stranger," Flane said, "but you best mind your business, lest you and your friend get yourselves hurt."

Kal drew his sword, and a tingle ran up his arm. "Don't you know me? After we fought side by side against the yeetta outside Lifton?"

Flane's face sank into a plain mask. "*Kal?*"

Kal started forward slowly. Grayson appeared on the seat behind Flane and pushed him. Flane fell off the side of the wagon, dropped his sword, and landed on his back in the snow.

His partner jumped down. Grayson appeared on the ground and reached for Flane's sword, but the stranger got there first. He swung the blade at Grayson, who vanished before the sword could find its mark.

"Mantics!" the stranger said.

"What do you want, Kal?" Flane was on his feet now. He'd pulled a dagger, which he held flush against his leg.

Kal stopped two paces away, eyes darting between the stranger's sword and Flane's dagger. "You've got some passengers who don't belong to you. I've come to take them back."

"They're none of your business," Flane said. "And since when do you serve Armania? Last I heard you'd turned traitor."

"The king pardoned me," Kal said. "I might be able to convince him to do the same for you if you come quietly and tell us who you're working for."

"We can take him," Flane said to his comrade.

"But he's got the mantic."

"Now!"

Both men lunged toward Kal. He raised his blade to meet the sword, then shoved off and deflected a stab from Flane. The stranger came at him again, but Grayson appeared and shouldered him aside. The stranger stumbled headfirst into the snow. Grayson vanished and reappeared, standing on the stranger's sword hand.

As Grayson disarmed the stranger, Kal swung his blade for Flane's head. Flane caught Kal's sword with the guard of his dagger and slid in tight where the blade couldn't hurt him. Kal grabbed Flane's tunic and yanked him close, twirling his sword into a reverse grip so he could stab from behind. Flane spun out of reach, then came back, stabbing the dagger toward Kal's face. Kal seized the opportunity, regretting what it would cost his old comrade. He sidestepped and sliced a hand's breath higher than the dagger, severing Flane's hand from his arm.

Flane howled and collapsed on his knees. Kal kicked his back, knocking him face-first into the snow. He looked for Grayson and the stranger but saw neither, so he sheathed his sword, which took him three tries—but not because his arm was numb. It pinched, like he had a sore muscle. Curious.

He checked Flane for more weapons, took two knives off him.

"You've killed me," Flane said, his voice broken.

"Only if I leave you here," Kal said.

"I've no life with only one hand."

"The Duke of Canden has managed just fine," Kal said.

Grayson appeared beside them, eyes wide as he took in the bloody snow. "I carried his friend to an empty cell in Armanguard."

"See if you can find something to stop the blood flow," Kal said.

Green light appeared on Grayson's hand, just like the kind Shanek could make.

Kal shied back, shielding his eyes with one arm. "What are you doing?"

"I helped the physician after the Battle of Armanguard," Grayson said, crouching at Flane's side.

"Keep back, mantic!" Flane rose onto his knees and one hand, clutching his stump to his chest. He tried to crawl away but fell onto his side.

Kal straddled the man's chest and pinned the bleeding stump to the ground. Flane bucked beneath him. "No!"

Kal held fast, trying not to look at the blood. "Hurry. He's making it worse."

Grayson popped to Flane's side and knelt in the bloody snow. He pushed the green light against the stump. Flane shrieked, then went limp. Fainted.

Kal sat back. "Take him, then inform the king about both men. Hurry back. I'll check on the children, but I'll need you to transport them. Then we must get that crate to the king."

When Grayson and Flane disappeared, Kal approached the carriage. He flipped the latch and opened the barred door. Two children fell back, squirming on feet and hind ends. Hands bound behind their backs, ankles bound, gags in their mouths. Someone was crying, but Kal couldn't tell who.

"You've been rescued," he said. "Will you let me untie you?"

Three of the dirty faces nodded.

"Who's first?" Kal asked.

A girl with golden eyes threw herself to her knees in the open doorway. Kal raised his dagger to the girl's ear. She tensed, head shrinking into her shoulders.

"I'm going to cut the fabric," Kal said, slowly sliding the metal between her skin and the hemp. His blade sliced through and he pulled the cord free from her mouth. "Who's next?"

While Kal cut away ropes, he struck up a conversation, speaking loudly over the wails of the crying child. "You know each other?" he asked.

"We're cousins," said a boy.

"What happened to you?"

"We were fetching cattails for flour when the men came," the golden-eyed girl said. "There were six of them, dressed in black with blue capes."

"Some of them had the snake and goblet on their tunics," a smaller girl added.

Tace Edekk's sigil.

Grayson came back and transported the children, one at a time. When he was done, he returned for Kal and Charlon's evenroot.

The king was overjoyed by their success and bade Grayson and Kal help him dispose of the magical substances. They burned dry root in the king's fireplace and dumped the contents of the bottles down the nearest privy hole. While they worked, they discussed the children.

"House Edekk's livery is evidence enough to convince me," the king said. "He must have been trading children to the giants for sacrifice, but why?"

"An alliance?" Kal guessed. "Or to keep the giants from attacking him."

The king looked weary. "I'll have to speak with Ulagan. If Edekk has giants willing to fight with him, that's trouble enough. But if he's also allied with Rogedoth, and I suspect he is . . ." He sighed. "Shanek has attacked in the village again, Sir Kalenek. Do you think he will come to the castle?"

"I know not, Your Highness." Kal couldn't fathom why Shanek would attack innocent families. "He likely will, and I fear he has allied with Rogedoth too."

"Arman help us," the king said. "Only the God knows what's to come."

Hınck

Hinck followed Saria into the meeting chambers of the Sarikarian Council. The chatter ceased as all eyes watched him. There were six men present, and only Father Wolbair greeted him with a smile. Hinck pretended not to notice and took a seat beside the old prophet. His nerves were on fire just thinking about how these men might react to Saria's announcement. She and Trevn had gone back and forth on every word of the betrothal agreement, and Trevn had been right. She'd given Hinck more than she had initially said she would.

Saria strode to the head of the table where Finnel Wallington was standing. Finnel was married to Princess Nolia, Saria's aunt, and was the son of the Duke of Everton—one of the suspected traitors in the Armanian nobility. He was in his late thirties, slender, and primped to perfection.

"Gentlemen, thank you for coming." Saria stopped so close to Finnel, the girth of her skirt forced him to step aside. "I believe you all know the Earl of Dacre, recently titled Duke of Armanguard. We owe immense gratitude to our Armanian brothers, who came to our aid in the Battle of New Sarikar. The duke comes to us as more than an ambassador, he—"

"We've no time for visitors, Princess," Finnel said, his voice throaty and smug as he took a seat across from Father Wolbair. "I know it's difficult for a woman to understand, but this council deals with important matters."

"Is this about building that border house at the river fork?" Duke Brixmead asked. He was a portly old man with a receding hairline and no teeth, that Hinck could see.

"We've discussed this already. Don't have the funds." This from Duke

431

Pixford, who had more wrinkles than Duke Brixmead but was tall and wiry enough to still wield a sword.

"We never finished discussing the border house," the Earl of Faynor said. He looked to be the age of Hinck's father and wore a long mustache that was braided into his beard. "We were interrupted when word came of the giants' attack on the northern village."

"The border house would be a great asset to our security," General Norcott said.

"I was told that this meeting was about your relinquishing your claim to the regency, Princess Saria," Finnel Wallington said.

"I heard the same," Duke Brixmead said, smacking his gums.

"If you'll give me a moment to explain, all will become clear," Saria said.

"A moment?" Duke Pixford said, his wrinkled cheeks stretching with his smile. "Girl, you talk more than my wife."

The men chuckled. The disrespect they showed their princess shocked Hinck, and he found Saria's restraint impressive.

She raised her chin and cast a regal gaze around the table. "A new claim to the throne of Sarikar has come forward."

Finnel Wallington jumped to his feet. "Who has made a claim?"

"Sit down, Wallington," Father Wolbair said, "and the princess will tell you."

Finnel lowered back to his seat, casting the prophet a dark glare.

Saria unrolled the scroll that proved Hinck's heritage. "Second only to my-self and Prince Mergest the usurper, Hinckdan Faluk has the greatest claim on the throne of Sarikar through his great-grandmother on his mother's side, Princess Maqee of Sarikar."

"Rubbish!" Finnel snatched the scroll from Saria's hand and inspected it himself.

"Speak now, Hinck, before Finnel tries to refute you," Saria bloodvoiced.

Hinck pushed back his chair and stood, holding the betrothal agreement Mielle had brought with her from Trevn. "At the blessing of my king, I offer this betrothal agreement between myself and Princess Saria. It is our wish to rule the realm of New Sarikar as co-regents."

"That is outrageous!" Finnel dropped Saria's scroll and snatched Hinck's.

The Earl of Faynor picked up Saria's scroll and inspected it. "Claim seems valid," he said. "I'd forgotten about Princess Maqee's line."

"Why should King Trevn have any say in who rules Sarikar?" Duke Pixford asked.

"Or whom our princess should marry, for that matter?" Duke Brixmead added.

"We led King Wilek and his army into a slaughter as they fought to defend us," General Norcott said. "That sacrifice alone has deeply indebted us."

"Add that we have continually asked Armania for aid since arriving in this land," Lord Faynor added. "They've sent us more food than we've grown ourselves."

"Precisely," Saria said.

"Know your history, men!" Duke Pixford said. "Armania has been in debt to our realm for over one hundred years. Do you know how many ships we built for Rosâr Echad?"

"Seventy-six," Duke Brixmead said, "and they still haven't paid them off."

"Immaterial," Lord Faynor said. "New Sarikar is a new realm."

"Whatever they owed us in the costs of ships, wood, and food, they have paid for threefold in blood," Saria said.

"The princess is right," Lord Faynor said, passing the scroll of Hinck's heritage to Duke Brixmead. "We are not in a position to deny the king of Armania anything."

"You don't honestly think we should go along with this?" Finnel asked.

"The claim is legitimate," Lord Faynor said. "Hinckdan Faluk is clearly next in line for the throne. I move that we accept this offer straightaway, with grace and gratitude, in hopes that King Trevn doesn't take over our realm entirely."

"I second that motion," General Norcott said.

"He's sent his man to rule us!" Finnel gestured to Hinck. "He *is* taking over our realm."

"It would take very little for King Trevn to absorb our nation into Armania," the general said. "We are in that much trouble, whether the rest of you will admit it or not."

"It's only by King Trevn's kindness and regard that he makes this offer," Lord Faynor said. "That he would marry his Second Arm to Saria is a great honor. And a co-regency at that. We still rule through our princess."

Saria quirked a brow at Hinck. *"Hear that?"* she bloodvoiced. *"They still rule."*

"Patience, lady," Hinck said. *"They're leaning toward acceptance. I can feel it."*

Duke Brixmead grunted. "What say you to this, Father Wolbair?"

"Arman is with Rosâr Trevn and his nation," the prophet said. "To align with them is to choose life over death."

"This is absurd," Finnel said. "We would be handing our nation over to two children. What do either of them know about ruling?"

"I spent nearly a year as a spy in Prince Mergest's camp," Hinck said. "I stopped Rosârah Laviel before she could attack Armanguard. No child could have survived such feats. As to your fears, I'm sure Princess Saria would agree that we shall need your wisdom to advise us as we seek to strengthen New Sarikar and defend against our enemies."

"Undoubtedly," Saria said.

"I'm in favor of this plan," Lord Faynor said, nudging the scroll on the table between him and Duke Brixmead. "This proves that Duke Armanguard has the blood right to Sarikar. He's a decorated war hero, just returned from saving his realm from the evil queen, and Wolbair supports him. I say we vote."

"Let me see that betrothal contract," Duke Pixford said. "You wrote this, I hope, Your Grace? Best not to sign anything contrived by a woman."

A full hour passed as the men debated, repeatedly inquiring of Father Wolbair and questioning Hinck as to his motives and plans for the realm. Hinck was almost certain they'd gotten their votes, until Finnel Wallington again raised the subject of the border house Trevn wanted New Sarikar to build. Then everything started anew, and Hinck had to convince them why the border house was ideal. When they finally did vote, it was split, Lord Faynor and Duke Pixford for the agreement, Finnel Wallington and Duke Brixmead against.

"The tie-breaking vote belongs to General Norcott," Lord Faynor said.

"Not in matters of regency," Finnel said.

"Why not?" Duke Pixford asked. "Because you want the title for yourself?"

"I vote to accept the betrothal and make Princess Saria and her husband co-regents," General Norcott said.

Lord Faynor clapped his hands. "Then it's settled. We must schedule a coronation."

"Not before a wedding," Duke Brixmead said.

"A swearing in of co-regents will do temporarily," Duke Pixford said.

"You're all fools!" Finnel strode to the exit, pausing to point his finger at Hinck's nose. "You will regret coming here, Your Grace." And he left.

Hinck had expected resistance from Finnel, but not a threat. The council then swore in Saria and him as co-regents, though it wouldn't be finalized until after the wedding—a wedding Hinck had no intention of celebrating until after they helped stop Rogedoth.

TREVN

"Rogedoth has left," Inolah said. *"I got word this morning, then went to see for myself. Every tent is gone. Worse, at last report, he took three hundred seventeen of our men with him. I knew many of our soldiers had befriended his, but not to the point of desertion. I sent scouts to follow his trail, but they found none. Magic, I suspect."*

"Surely he is coming here," Trevn said. *"I wish the border houses were complete. Sarikar just broke ground on theirs yesterday."*

"And Shanek?" Inolah asked. *"Is he still causing trouble?"*

Shanek DanSâr was the bane of Trevn's life at present. *"Plenty. He killed a field of sheep with his magic. Jhorn has heard over thirty eyewitness testimonies. He is terrifying my people."*

"Foolish if he seeks to rule them."

"Is it?" Trevn asked. *"I can't imagine anyone would dare stand against such power."*

"One cannot rule by fear for long," Inolah said.

"Father managed it for twenty-four years," Trevn said. *"At some point, Shanek is going to come into the castle and attack me. How will I stand against him?"*

"Let Arman stand against him. You simply stand with Arman."

That sounded good in theory, but such a plan hadn't kept Wilek alive.

A knock came on the outer door and Cadoc entered.

"I must go, Inolah." Trevn closed the connection. "What is it?" he asked Cadoc.

"Unexpected guests, Your Highness. Randmuir Khal and his daughter, Zahara."

435

The names brought a chill over Trevn. "What do *they* want?"

"To speak with you. Should I have them sent away?"

Trevn thought about it. "Bring them here—no. Take them to the council chambers. Allow no more than two of their guards to accompany them. I assume they brought men?"

Cadoc nodded. "No more than two, Your Highness."

His shield closed the door behind him, and Trevn said a quick prayer before seeking out the minds of Randmuir Khal and his daughter. He was surprised to find both well shielded, though he supposed that after Fonu's compulsion they had reason enough to take such precautions. That didn't keep Trevn from sensing their emotions, and while Zahara seemed driven and desperate, her father's temperament was a crucible of too many feelings to name.

As Cadoc had promised, when Trevn stepped out from the antechamber and into the council room, Hawley was waiting with four pirates. Of the two standing guard at the door, Trevn recognized one as Rand's son, Meelo, still missing his lips from a long-ago encounter with Charlon Sonber.

Zahara and her father had taken seats along one side of the table. The former looked healthy and intimidating. Dressed all in black like the rest of the pirates, her fitted tunic revealed an athletic body and muscled arms that could do serious damage with or without a weapon.

Her father, however, had aged ten years since Trevn had last seen him. His hands were clasped and resting on the table, wrists bound with thick, braided hemp. A collection of welts, fresh and scabbed over, ringed his arms from elbow to wrist. His eyes were bloodshot and creased, and his threadbare tunic had holes in both elbows and was frayed around the cuffs.

Those reddened eyes found Trevn's, looked him up and down. "I see you've benefitted from your brother's death," he said.

Heat flashed up Trevn's spine. "What do you want, Master Khal?"

"Father, hush." Zahara stood. "Thank you for seeing us, Your Highness. In honor of my grandmother, I hope you'll allow the Omatta to join you in your war against Barthel Rogedoth."

Interesting. "Why?" Trevn asked. "What do you get from this?"

"A mantic," Randmuir said. "To remove my compulsion."

Fonu Edekk had compelled Randmuir to capture Grayson and take him to Rogedoth. A compulsion sometimes ended when the mantic who cast the spell died, but it didn't in Randmuir's case—hence the way he had bound himself to keep from trying to obey the magic.

"I can't promise to capture a mantic," Trevn said. "And even if we could, had he or she any magic left, it would undoubtedly be used to try to escape, not to help you."

"Let us fight," Randmuir said. "I'll worry about catching my own mantic."

Trevn took a deep breath as he considered the request. "I cannot add men to my—"

Zahara cleared her throat.

"My pardon. I cannot add men *and women* to my army who might, when the moment arises, abandon my cause for their own."

"We have three hundred sixty-two trained warriors," Zahara said. "We dedicate three hundred fifty to your cause and will send the other twelve after a mantic."

Trevn considered the risk. Randmuir was compelled to abduct Grayson, and though he was fighting against it, what if he succeeded? Plus, these were pirates. Such a group would have no loyalty to Trevn's officers. They'd also have their own methods of warfare.

Yet he needed soldiers. Badly.

"I must consult my prophet," he said. "In the meantime, I'd like you to meet with my First Arm. He is gifted in the mind-speak magic. There may be something he can do to help."

⊙ Lİ

Shortly after lunch, guards escorted Oli from the dungeon to his chambers, where he was told to bathe, shave, dress, then report to the king's office. He obeyed, and Trevn gave him a rather odd assignment—to head to the council chambers to meet with pirates.

There he found a woman seated with three men. Upon Oli's entry, she jumped to her feet and grabbed the hilt of a short sword she wore at her waist. Oli recognized her instantly as the woman who had given Janek the scar on his nose.

He couldn't help his smile. "Good midday, Miss Zahara."

"*You* work for the king?" she asked. "Aren't you part of that cult?"

"I was, but no longer."

"Who is this person?" the man beside her asked. By his bound wrists, Oli guessed him to be Randmuir Khal of the Omatta.

"This is Oli Agoros, a duke," Zahara said. "He was a close friend of Sâr Janek's."

Randmuir scowled at Oli. "This is who the Armanian king sends to help me?"

"Janek and I parted ways several months before he died," Oli said. "I've come to assist with your compulsion. I have a unique blend of knowledge and skills that might be of use."

The pirate's eyes narrowed. "Say that again in plain language. I've wasted enough of my life trying to decode royal speak."

As much as Randmuir hated royals, the man sure did remind Oli of King Echad. "If you'll allow it, I would like to look into your memories so I can discover the type of compulsion placed upon you and the name of the shadir used to create the magic."

"Why would that help?" Zahara asked.

"It might not," Oli said. "But if the spell was temporary, we could try to track the shadir and destroy it."

"You can destroy a demon?" Randmuir asked.

"*I* cannot, sir, but the prophetess Onika can. I've seen her do it."

Randmuir's scowl faded. He looked at his daughter. "Well?"

"What do you have to lose, Father?"

"My mind." He gestured his bound hands at Oli. "He wants that I should lower my shields and let him dig around in my head."

"I don't want to do anything harmful to your mind, sir," Oli said. "My king has asked me to try to help you. It makes no difference to me whether you agree or refuse."

"Oh, cease your pompous babble and get on with it."

"Very well." Oli started around the table.

Zahara resumed her seat, which was on her father's right. Oli pulled out the chair on Randmuir Khal's left, which put his fake arm closest to the man, so he twisted and grabbed Randmuir's forearm with his left hand.

"Please recall the day the compulsion was placed upon you," Oli said.

"I don't know that," Randmuir said.

How unfortunate. "When did you first meet Master Fonu Edekk?"

"He was a sailor I picked up in Everton," Randmuir said.

"No." This from one of the guards at the table, a man whose lips had been cut off, baring his teeth. "He come aboard long after that. From one of the ships we pirated. A month or two before we found land."

Randmuir twisted in his seat. "That recent?"

"Master Fonu was aboard the *Seffynaw* out of Everton harbor," Oli said. "After the mutiny he jumped overboard to avoid arrest."

"And snuck aboard my ship, then worked his magic to make me Rogedoth's slave?" Randmuir followed this realization with a host of unsavory epithets as to what he really thought of Fonu Edekk, Rogedoth, nobility, and the world in general.

"Think back to the last time you remember being in full control of your mind," Oli suggested. "Or if there was a time you remember doing something out of character."

"Don't remember nothing like that," the pirate said.

"The decision to attack that pale's ship," the lipless man said. "Made no sense to me why you'd want that rickety outfit. That was the first time I thought you was out of your head."

"Recall that day, if you can," Oli said. "And lower the shields around your mind."

Randmuir growled but closed his eyes. Oli did as well. He connected with the man's mind, and images started to flash by.

The process moved tediously through the day, then all of a sudden, Oli saw Fonu join Randmuir at the stern. It felt strange to look on his old friend, knowing he was dead. Fonu complimented the size of the pirated fleet, and Randmuir snarled and sent him back to work. Yet the conversation had continued, which seemed out of character for the pirate captain.

Oli inserted himself into the memory and asked Randmuir to back up and retrace his steps before he had walked to the stern. Oli found Fonu, standing by the mizzenmast as Randmuir passed by. He followed as Fonu trailed Randmuir up the stairs to the stern deck and saw that he'd whispered a spell as they walked.

"Haroan *tsamad ani. Ten shel cheber tokef.* Randmuir Khal *yahal pelach ani.* Randmuir Khal *yahal shmah shel aymer.*"

"I've found it," Oli said. "It was a permanent compulsion using the common shadir Haroan, who takes the form of a brown wolf. Haroan likely went to Rogedoth once Fonu died."

"Can you kill him?" Randmuir asked.

"Not I, no. And even if Miss Onika manages to, it won't break the spell."

"Why not? I want that creature dead and my mind back!"

"Calm, Father," Zahara said. "The duke said it might not work."

"There must be something you can do," Randmuir said to Oli. "I'm mad to find that root boy and drag him to Rogedoth. It's all I think about. All I dream about. There must be a way to end my torment beyond taking my life."

The words "*end my torment*" reminded Oli of Eudora. He'd taken great pains to manipulate her memories. If he could help Randmuir forget he ever heard the compulsion, might that break its hold over him?

How thrilled would Eudora be if Oli could break the compulsion Rogedoth had placed upon her? She'd be able to tell King Trevn all she knew. In fact, if this worked, Oli might be able to break any compulsion, as long as he could get into the head of the one who'd heard it.

It was risky, though. Something could go wrong.

He released the pirate's arm. "I'm sorry. Compulsions are strong magic. I don't—"

Randmuir grabbed his tunic. "Don't keep things from me, royal. You hesitated. I deserve to know what you were thinking. Whatever it is should be my choice, not yours."

Oli drew in a deep breath and smoothed his tunic. "I do have an idea, but I've never tried it before."

"What's the idea?"

"I would attempt to convince you that you never heard the spell in the first place."

"I didn't hear it!"

"But you did," Oli said, "or I wouldn't have been able to see the memory. Fonu likely compelled you to forget."

Randmuir growled. "If I've forgotten, how can I forget again?"

Oli had confused him. "Forgive me," he said. "Fonu wouldn't have compelled you to forget the spell he placed upon you, but to forget that you'd heard him speak that spell. If you don't remember hearing those words, it might break the magic. Like I said, I've never tried it. And it might be years before we'd know if you had suffered any aftereffects."

The pirate glanced at his daughter, who shrugged. "It's your choice, Father."

Randmuir turned back to Oli. "All right, royal. Let's try it."

A thrill of excitement ran through Oli. He again took hold of the pirate's forearm. "Take me back to that same memory, and this time, I'll try to change it."

"This is remarkable," Trevn said. "By freeing Randmuir's mind, you removed a threat against Grayson and gave me a small but fiercely loyal group of allies. Randmuir Khal will forever be in our debt. He has already agreed to man our southern border house."

Oli smiled—couldn't help it. He had astounded even himself. "I never would have thought it possible to break a compulsion," he said.

"All things are possible with Arman," Trevn said. "And he works everything together for the good of his children. I wonder if you could search Tace Edekk's memories from afar?"

"I cannot search memories, Your Highness. I can only see what is shown me. The duke would have to recall enough that I could insert myself into a memory. Once I'm there, I can move about some, but I cannot get inside unless I'm invited and shown where to go."

"Don't be so certain," Trevn said. "It seems to me that if you can enter someone's memory and—how did you put it in regard to Randmuir? *Back through time?*—then you should be able to search as well. You need only practice."

Oli did not want to search through that much of anyone's memories. "It would be terribly invasive."

"I'll find you a practicing partner to see what you might discover."

"So I'm to become an experimental subject?" Oli asked.

"We have all been experimenting with the voicing magic. Even I found I can manipulate another's thoughts. You are the only one who has exhibited abilities involving memories."

"And Eudora," Oli added. "She showed Hinckdan her memories."

"That's right," Trevn said slowly. "Practice with your sister, then. Teach her what you can do and see if she can learn. I want you both able to break compulsions quickly."

"That's impossible, Your Highness," Oli said. "With Randmuir it took over an hour to find the right memory, and I couldn't have done it without his participation."

"And so you will practice," Trevn said. "Start by breaking the compulsions Rogedoth placed upon Lady Eudora. I'm hoping she knows something that could help us. And if Rogedoth still holds compulsions over Puru or Ahj-Yeke or even Kinsman people, you could break those as well."

"But I don't even speak the same language as those peoples! You expect the impossible, Your Highness."

"Everything seemed impossible once," the king said. "I expect you only to try your best."

İⴲ⊙LⴸH

U lrik had promised to meet with Inolah before the council meeting. The nation was still celebrating the return of their emperor, who had told everyone that Rurek, god of war, had brought him back from the dead, never mentioning Charlon's magic or that it had been Grayson who'd liberated him from the mine. Her eldest had swept in and resumed control of the realm. Contrary to Inolah's fears and his own pretension, he had taken things well in hand.

All but one.

The door opened, and her heart jolted at how much Ulrik resembled his father. Inolah got straight to business. "What have you done to Empress Jazlyn?"

His eyes seemed to laugh. "Why do you ask such a question?"

"At dinner last night she told me how proud she was to be married to such a wise man."

A smirk. "You find that strange?"

"Ulrik, how?"

"She loves me, Mother. As she should."

Inolah fought to control her temper. "This is no time for games, Ulrik. Barthel Rogedoth has gone. He is no doubt off to wage war against Sarikar or Armania. If they lose, we lose. We must do what we can to support them."

"My uncle saved me from the giant mines," Ulrik said. "Of course I will support Armania."

"*Ulrik.* What have you done to Jazlyn?"

He met her eyes. Grinned. "Oh, very well. I shall tell you. But you must promise to keep it secret. Otherwise people might fear me, and I don't want that."

"For pity's sake, just tell me."

"I grew terribly bored in Magosia. I did not get on well with those people. They are primitive and plain and very dull. But I discovered I could go into their heads with my mind-speak magic and change the way they thought. They all became so much more agreeable then."

Stunned, Inolah managed, "Ulrik. Tell me you did not manipulate them?"

"I simply told them the truth in a way they could not ignore. When I saw how well that worked, I thought I'd try the same technique on my troublesome wife." He waggled his eyebrows. "But when I learned what that woman was planning, well, I couldn't let her get away with it. So I taught her obedience and reverence for her husband. You see how well she dotes on me now. It's as it should have always been."

"Oh, Ulrik."

"Don't feign disappointment, Mother. I've used my magic to better this realm." He offered his arm. "The council is waiting. Shall we go?"

What else could she say? Inolah let Ulrik lead her to the council chambers. They arrived to find the men in a heated conversation.

"Your Eminence!" Taleeb said, rushing toward them. "Giants have attacked the village."

Inolah's heart raced. "Again? When did this happen?"

"But an hour ago, lady." General Balat stood, clutching a crumpled sheet of parchment in one hand. "They came upon the villagers just as before, but this time we did not have the assistance of King Barthel's army."

"We did not have the assistance of King Barthel during the first attack either," Taleeb said. "It was Empress Jazlyn who defeated them then. With her magic."

"Then she will do so again," Ulrik said. "I invited her to this meeting. She should be arriving shortly."

Ulrik invited Jazlyn to his council meeting? Inolah stifled her desire to rebuke him.

"It's more than that, Your Eminence," the general said. "King Barthel set them upon us." He shook the parchment. "This was affixed to the back of one of our soldiers by means of the arrow that killed him."

"But giants don't use arrows," Inolah said.

Ulrik snatched the parchment, and Inolah leaned close to read along.

Empress Inolah,

When first I came to New Rurekau, Empress Jazlyn and I forged an agreement of peace. When she deceived me and stole the crops from my own land, she blatantly violated that agreement.

I henceforth revoke any treaty made between our peoples and leave you to your fate.

> *Barthel Rogedoth*
> *King of Barthia, Armania,*
> *and Sarikar*

"What did the empress do now?" Kakeeo asked.

"She recently returned from the island of Islah," Inolah said. "Perhaps she made some mischief there."

"She laid claim to a resource King Barthel had abandoned there," Ulrik said. "Clearly he has discovered its worth and changed his mind."

"What did she take?" Inolah asked.

"His store of new evenroot," Ulrik said. "Turns out it has magical properties after all."

The implications of such a statement filled Inolah with dread.

A knock at the door, and an Igote soldier peeked in. "Empress Jazlyn is here. She said she is expected."

"Of course she is. Let her in, man," Ulrik said.

The Igote opened the door wide, and in came Empress Jazlyn, her eunuch, and a crowd of Tennish Protectors. Her gaze fell upon Ulrik and she lit up, beaming.

"Ulrik!" She hurried toward him, arms outstretched.

When she was but three steps from reaching him, he held up his hand. "Stop."

She obeyed.

"An empress has self-control and always remembers her rank."

She curtsied lower than Inolah had ever seen.

"Now greet your husband." Ulrik tapped his jaw.

Jazlyn lunged forward and kissed Ulrik's cheek, looking the part of a fully trained puppy.

"I have grave news," Ulrik told her. "We are again under attack by giants, and King Barthel has broken the treaty you made with him. I go now to the armory to dress for battle. You will stand beside me and fight for New Rurekau."

"Of course, my love. It would be my honor."

Ulrik turned his focus to the growing crowd. "We will fight this enemy and prevail. They will think hard before coming against us again."

The crowd cheered, then parted for Ulrik and Jazlyn as they left the room.

"What do you make of that?" Taleeb asked Inolah.

The whole scene had been so strange. She sighed heavily. "I don't like it, but we may very well perish without Jazlyn's help against the giants, so I will praise Arman for his provision and stop there."

But she did not stop. She continued to pray that whatever mischief Ulrik had waged upon his wife, when Jazlyn finally learned of it, she would not visit her wrath back upon him tenfold.

"And he signed it 'Barthel Rogedoth, King of Barthia, Armania, and Sarikar.'"

"Did he really?" Trevn asked. *"Perhaps he and Shanek will destroy each other in their quest for my throne. That would greatly help matters. Do you think he sent the giants to attack?"*

"I do, but I've yet to tell you the most surprising part of all this." And Inolah told Trevn how Jazlyn had fought off the giants herself. *"I did not see the battle, but the reports are astonishing."*

"More astonishing than the first time she used magic against them?"

"This wasn't the old magic. It was something else. I suspect it involves the new evenroot and those rat-faced creatures. General Balat says they changed at her command."

"Changed how?"

"Transformed into weapons. Fire, arrows, blades of light that flew through the air without the need for anyone to throw them."

"I want to say that such a thing cannot be, but I'm not so naïve anymore."

"Nor should you be. General Balat said he never unsheathed his sword. Empress Jazlyn used her magic to kill every giant that crossed her path. Now, to be fair, there weren't many. Twenty-six, I believe was the report. And they weren't all together. They had split up to herd our people into wagons. Planning to take them to the mines. Jazlyn might have had a more difficult time defeating them if they'd all come at her at once. Still. She has won the soldiers' favor. Many are calling her a goddess. Cetheria in the flesh."

"What does Ulrik say about that?"

"He's playing the proud husband, but it's all a ruse to get revenge upon her for trying to have him and Ferro killed. He's forcing her mind somehow. I don't know what to do."

"He must be careful. Master Jhorn says a broken mind can be a prison. It would not be wise to anger someone as powerful as Empress Jazlyn. 'The companion of fools will suffer harm.' Sands, I can't believe I just used one of my mother's proverbs."

"It was fitting, Trevn, and I agree wholeheartedly. By the way, your mother disappeared from the dungeon. I don't know how she could have escaped, but I suspect she left with Rogedoth."

"That is unsurprising," Trevn said. *"Put her out of your mind. You have more important matters to concern you."*

"Yes, well, I'll be looking for a way to end this peaceably." Before Jazlyn found a way to destroy them all.

KALEИEK

K al was eating his midday meal in the great hall with Onika when a guard approached with a summons from Jhorn. Kal made his apologies to Onika and went straight to Jhorn's office, where he found Oli Agoros sitting in the chair across from the Master of Requests.

"The duke and I are having a debate, Sir Kalenek," Jhorn said. "One I hope you can weigh in on. Have you heard what His Grace has accomplished in breaking the compulsions on his sister and Randmuir Khal of the Omatta?"

"I did," Kal said. "It was a most impressive use of the new magic. Wish we'd had something like that during the war."

"See?" Oli said, raising his eyebrows at Jhorn. "Most impressive."

Jhorn's expression remained passive. "The duke also used his magic to compel Lady Eudora to forget several traumatic memories. What is your opinion on that?"

"They weren't my memories," Kal said. "Why should I care?"

"My concern is only partly for Lady Eudora's welfare and partly how this magic might be used going forward. A person's personality is made up of a web of memories. To disrupt one risks disrupting them all."

"I touched very few memories," Oli said.

"Imagine a wall of bricks," Jhorn said. "If you pull too many from the middle, others will go with them because they are interlocked. So are memories. And while you have erased memories, you cannot erase the attached emotions. Your sister may find herself suddenly drowning in a sense of uneasiness with no idea why. Without her memories, she could be lost."

"She will not forget what happened to her, I assure you," Oli said, his voice rising. "To erase a memory, I must experience it myself. And while I did erase those experiences, I did not erase her knowledge that they happened."

"I simply feel this could be crossing an ethical line," Jhorn said.

"If someone lives through a deep horror," Oli said, "why shouldn't that person be able to do away with the memory—especially if the memory haunts them and forgetting could improve everyday life? If the process is safe, permission is given, and only certain memories are magicked? Sir Kalenek, what say you?"

Kal thought of Charlon's compulsions. He still felt as if some part of his mind was missing. "Memory informs who we are," he said. "It's also about survival. A warning system to prevent us from repeating unsafe actions. Could be dangerous to meddle with that."

Oli sighed. "Even when someone begs you?"

"Chieftess Charlon did much to me while I was living under her rule," Kal said. "I'm still uncertain how much of my memory was lost due to her compulsions. Might be that it all came back. But the uncertainty is unnerving."

"I don't want people to suffer needlessly," Jhorn said, "but learning to deal with fear—the process of seeing your experiences as a logical observer—that can produce strength and freedom. To simply erase a memory cheats a person of the empowering experience of healing."

"Some things cannot be remembered logically," Kal said.

Oli looked troubled. "I once pulled Rosârah Zeroah into a childhood memory. I had just faced the pole for failing my father. The memory had plagued me for years—until the rosârah comforted the child inside my memory. She told that boy the truth. I still remember the event, but it no longer brings shame."

Jhorn nodded, a small smile on his face. "That's what we must seek to duplicate. Use your power to heal memories, not to erase them. Doing so will make the weak grow strong rather than allow them to live as if such traumas never happened."

Kal's stomach churned at the idea that such a thing might be possible.

"I couldn't do it alone," Oli said. "I'm about as comforting as a dune cat in a cradle. I'd need the assistance of another, preferably one with the ability to mind-speak."

"Like Rosârah Zeroah?" Jhorn asked.

Hope kindled within Kal and prodded him to say, "Or Miss Onika?"

Oli shrugged. "Or someone like them. Someone empathetic."

Kal wanted to try this with Onika. To see if she could diffuse his nightmares and—

"Hello, Father. I have come to visit you." Shanek's voice.

Kal jerked his gaze around the room. "Are you here?"

"Is who here?" Oli asked.

"I am with you, but in the Veil," Shanek said.

Kal leaned against the desk, shocked to have heard the boy's voice after so long. *"Stay hidden, Shan,"* he thought. *"It's not safe at the moment. In fact, we should go to my room."*

"Who are these men?" Shanek asked.

Kal didn't want the boy here, listening to their discussion about how the mind-speak magic could be used. How much had he heard already? "Forgive me. I must go." He left the room and ran upstairs to his own bedchamber.

His heart thudded in his chest, and he leaned against the door, catching his breath. The room was dark with the curtain drawn over the narrow window.

Why had Shanek come here? To attack. There was no other explanation. He had come for King Trevn.

A green glow appeared at the foot of his bed, balanced in the center of a hand, floating by itself in the middle of the air. The eerie light grew, illuminating arm, torso, and just a hint of the face of the young man who held it.

"It's safe now," Kal said. "I'm alone." He crossed the small chamber and lit the candle on his sideboard, then sat on the edge of his bed and motioned for Shanek to join him.

Shanek came the rest of the way into view and let his light fade. "Why did you leave Magosia?"

"Because you left."

Shanek came to sit beside Kal. "But I came back and you were gone."

"I'm sorry, Shanek. I set out to find you, but I got distracted helping someone. It was never my plan to come here."

"You aren't here to help me?"

"Help you how?"

"Become king of Armania." Shanek scowled. "He said you wouldn't help, but I didn't believe him. Amala didn't either. We thought you would be for us and not—"

"Whoa." Kal help up his hands. "Who is *he?*"

"Dendron. He's my counselor now. King Barthel betrayed him, so he is helping me. He says I'll be king of Armania. He says I'm powerful enough to someday be a god."

Kal's heart sank. Shanek had taken up with a great shadir? "What did Charlon say?"

The boy's posture slumped and he glowered. "She doesn't want me to be king."

"That doesn't sound like her."

Shanek shrugged. "I don't need her anymore. Dendron and I have our own plans."

"Did Dendron tell you to come here?"

"I came to see you, so I could carry Rosâr Trevn to King Barthel."

Was Rogedoth behind all this? "Oh, Shan. You mustn't take Rosâr Trevn."

"I have to. I can't be king if he is king."

Kal wanted to say that Shanek could not be king at all, but he didn't dare challenge the boy, especially if Charlon had already rejected him and Dendron had filled his head with lies.

"That might be true, Shan, but this is the wrong way. If you take Rosâr Trevn to Barthel Rogedoth, know that the man will kill him."

Shanek shook his head. "Amala made him promise to give Rosâr Trevn and his wife a nice place to live."

"He is twisting the truth," Kal said. "Rogedoth wants King Trevn dead."

"Why should I believe you?"

"You don't have to believe me, Shanek, but I would hope I have your trust."

"Will you come home now? I can carry you."

"I can't go back to Magosia," Kal said. "Charlon and I have parted ways."

"So have we. Can I live here with you?"

Kal's heart hurt to see Shanek's confusion at being abandoned. "You're welcome to stay here, Shan. I always want you with me."

"But not as king."

Kal met the boy's dark gaze, saw the anger there, mixed with hope. "Not yet, Shanek. Not like this."

"Dendron was right about you." Shanek vanished, leaving an imprint in the mattress where he'd been sitting.

Kal jumped up and fled into the hallway. He needed to warn Rosâr Trevn to get out of the castle before Shanek carried him to the enemy.

Halfway up the stairs he thought better of it. What if Shanek had stayed in the Veil, following Kal and waiting to be led to the king? Kal's next idea was

451

to find Grayson, but he was in Sarikar with Mielle and Kal did not have the ability to mind-speak.

He returned to Jhorn's office. He and Oli were, thankfully, still there.

"Your Grace," Kal said, "would you voice the king and ask him to speak to my mind?"

"Whatever for?" Oli asked.

"I cannot explain, but it's an emergency," Kal said.

"Very well."

As the duke went silent, Kal paced the length of the room and back, trying not to worry.

"What has happened, Sir Kalenek?" Jhorn asked.

"I will explain in time," he said. "First I must speak with the—"

"Sir Kalenek?" King Trevn voiced.

"Yes, thank you, Your Highness. I have dire news." Kal told him what had transpired with Shanek. *"He could be with me now, waiting for me to lead him to you. Or he might be exploring the castle, seeking you out. You should leave at once. Hide until a way to keep you safe can be determined."*

"I will not go into hiding," Trevn said. *"My place is here."*

"But Shanek means to give you to Rogedoth."

"Then he and I can finally have it out. Besides, Grayson can always carry me back."

Sometimes King Trevn was a little too confident. *"Shanek would not have come for you if he didn't have a way to keep you or defeat you."*

"Your concerns are noted, Sir Kalenek. And I thank you for the warning. Be assured that I will have Mielle remain in Sarikar until it's safe to return, but I will not leave the castle."

"At least dress to conceal yourself. Don't wear a crown or eat in the great hall."

"Good ideas, Sir Kalenek. I thank you. Now I must voice Mielle."

Kal's mind grew quiet. He took a deep breath and looked up, met Duke Canden's eyes, then Jhorn's. "The king is in danger," he said. "And I fear it's my fault."

Gozan

I shouldn't have sent Sir Kalenek away." Charlon sat her throne, slumped to one side, chin perched on her fist. Forlorn. Despondent.

You didn't, Gozan said. *He left of his own choice.*

"I drove him away. With my compulsions. I thought if he was with me . . . I thought he would stay. Always."

Gozan grew weary of Charlon's moping. The thrill of her misery had worn off, and now she was simply tiring. He had chosen the woman for her power and ambition, but she was chained by human emotion. Craved companionship as she had once craved ahvenrood. He no longer believed she would lead him to a seat of power. It might be time for him to leave.

Humans never seem to learn that love cannot be forced, he said.

"I regret nothing. If I had acted otherwise, I would not have this child." She palmed her belly, looking upon it with a dreamy expression.

Then you must focus on the child and forget the man.

"I can't! I love him. So help me . . . I am a fool. Mreegan tried to warn me about men. She was right. They use us. Then leave."

Amusing how she had made herself the victim. *Did not you use him?* Gozan asked.

She scowled. "He was my One. My ears and eyes where I could not be. My voice of reason. Without him . . . How can I hold on to Magosia? Kateen no longer respects my power. Roya seeks to take my place. Amala has taken Shanek. There is no one I can trust!"

You can trust me, lady.

453

She hummed, as if considering this, but Gozan saw the wariness in her eyes. No, she did not trust him, no matter what she might say or do.

Take ahvenrood and show your people the power you wield.

"Not until my baby is born."

A bit of ahvenrood here and there will not create a child like Shanek. His was an extreme case. Look at Empress Jazlyn's daughter. Princess Jahleeah's skin marks her as a root child, but she is not growing like Shanek did.

Charlon's brow creased. Was she considering his idea? If she agreed to take even a taste of ahvenrood, he might be able to find where she had hidden the rest.

"Make me a seer," she said.

The request surprised him. *Why?*

"So I would know who seeks to betray me."

She was afraid of Empress Jazlyn and Barthel Rogedoth, as well she should be. *I can see shadir, lady, and I tell you I am the only one here at present.*

"I want to see for myself. Make me a seer. I'll take enough ahvenrood for the spell."

It was tempting, but her insults had wounded his pride. *You don't trust me.*

"I trust myself. I am the only one. Who will not betray me."

You betrayed yourself time and again. You compelled Sir Kalenek. You stopped taking ahvenrood when you conceived. You allowed Miss Amala to stay, then fed her ahvenrood. You taught Shanek your new magic when he had no need of it. And long before any of that, you cast a spell to force away your fear of human touch. You smothered your pain rather than face it.

She sat up straight. "How do you know that?"

Shadir talk, lady.

"You prove my point. I can't even trust my swarm. There is no one. No one." She began to rock forward and back on her throne, hands clutching her knees.

She was going mad. Gozan didn't want to leave until he found her ahvenrood stash. *Forgive my kind, lady. We have lived thousands of years. How can I make amends?*

She looked for him, fixing a serious glare on nothing. She could no longer see into the Veil, so her attempt at intimidation was comical. "Make me a seer."

Anything but that. With all respect and admiration, lady, I cannot.

She narrowed her eyes to slits. "Cannot or will not?"

I have never made a seer. That is one spell I will not do.

She slid off the throne and took two steps forward. "You have never outright refused me before," she said. "Yet you want me to trust you?"

I never make permanent spells.

"Rubbish," Charlon said, folding her arms. "Shadir make permanent spells all the time. They make seers too. Qoatch the eunuch is one."

High Queen Tahmina and her great made many seers, but I have not.

"You've healed people. That is permanent."

That is different. Healing repairs the body. Puts it back to its original state. Making a seer imparts permanent magic to a human. Our master does not appreciate such . . . generosity.

"Master? What master?"

Gâzar.

Arms fell to her sides. "God of the Lowerworld?"

The very one.

She wandered back to her throne and sat. "How stupid I've been. All this time. I thought I had power. That I was special. Chosen. But I'm not, am I? *You* use *me*. Without you, I'm only human."

He did not deny her, nor did he set her straight. It was true that humans had no power without shadir, but it was also true that some humans were predisposed to magic and had a natural ability to wield it. Jazlyn had been one. Charlon another. Not just any human could do with evenroot what those women could. But Gozan did not want Charlon to know that. He must keep the upper hand with her if he was going to find her ahvenrood supply. Perhaps a threat?

You are *special, Charlon. I choose my bonds carefully. I need someone intelligent. Ambitious. But I cannot wait months for your child to arrive. Unless you take ahvenrood, I will have to bond with another.*

"There are no others."

There are, he said. *Empress Jazlyn, for one.*

Her eyes blazed. "You wouldn't dare."

I was her shadir for years. Now that she has found ahvenrood again, I am sure she would appreciate a great over her common.

"You were *hers*?" Charlon looked pale, but her emotions were anything but. Gozan basked in her growing outrage.

"There must be another way for you to remain here. With me."

Ungrateful woman. *There is. It is called Dominion.*

At the mention of that word, she completely shut down. "Leave me," she said, walking toward her bed. "I must rest."

Very well, lady.

He wanted her to believe he'd gone, but her anger and sorrow pleased him. He stayed behind as she tossed and turned in her bed. He soaked in her rage, depression, fear. These emotions would be his only pleasure until he made new plans.

Rurek the Great.

He was being summoned by a human. He ignored the brazen fool.

If Charlon continued to refuse ahvenrood, Gozan would lose access to the Solid until her child came. Unless he found another human. This brought him back to the problem of talent and ahvenrood supply. He was not desperate enough to go groveling back to Jazlyn. And King Barthel had Dendron. There were truly no more options outside of Dominion.

Charlon eventually fell asleep, so Gozan left her tent and floated through the Magosian camp. He passed a flock of gowzals and felt the shadir inside them. There was mild pleasure in possessing the birds—it was one way to enter the Solid without ahvenrood—but it did not compare to the thrill of feeding off a human's spells and their worship and loyalty and purging, in using their power to enter the physical realm where his own skin could feel—

Rurek the Great.

Twice this stranger dared summon him? He concentrated on the source, let himself grow to his most intimidating height, and appeared beside the human.

It was Miss Amala. What did *she* want?

"Thank you for coming." Her voice trembled slightly. Gozan noticed that her eyes were light gray. She had taken a fresh dose of ahvenrood recently. His desire thrummed at the very idea of sponging off this girl.

Why do you summon me?

"I want to bond with you, great one," she said.

The audacity of such a request stunned him. Never in all his days had a human so recklessly tried to steal him from his bonded. *Why would I bond with you?*

"Because Chieftess Charlon is useless. She should lead her people instead of wallowing in her bad fortune. You deserve someone better."

What do you know of Charlon Sonber's life? Gozan asked. *She has done magic greater than you could imagine. If she knew you were trying to steal me away, she would kill you.*

The girl narrowed her eyes, and they glinted in the candlelight. "I'm not afraid of her. My fear is for Shanek. He has gone to Armania to fight for his throne, but King Barthel told him to leave me behind. I don't trust the king, and I cannot help Shanek on my own."

What do you wish to do for Shanek? Gozan asked.

"I want to make sure he's not being used for King Barthel's gain."

Of course he was, and Gozan had no desire to go up against a man bonded with Dendron.

"I know where the Chieftess has hidden her root stash," Amala said. "If you won't bond with me, I'll be forced to choose a lesser shadir."

Gozan fought the urge to smile. The one thing he wanted, second only to Dominion, and this fool girl was willing to hand it to him. *How do I know you are gifted enough to handle a great shadir?*

"Try me and find out," she said.

This time he did smile. *Show me the ahvenrood and we have a deal.*

She shook her head. "Not until you bond with me."

The girl was smarter than he thought. *Very well,* he said.

"*Rurek, ata yakhol bara hay ecâr rakas yahda shelno nehfesh,*" she said, her ancient speech choppy.

Gozan accepted her vow and forged a bond between them. She wasn't the strongest human he'd bonded, but she was far from weak. She had reserves inside her too. Gozan drew from them greedily, as if he'd been starved and was finally eating again.

The ahvenrood, then? he asked.

She extended her hand. "Carry me there."

Transport will weaken you in a hurry, Gozan said.

"Then I will purge and take more root."

It seemed almost wasteful, as rare as ahvenrood was these days, but Gozan did not deny himself a chance to enter the Solid. He transformed into his true self, complete with wings. Amala's eyes widened as he towered over her, a hideous beast to her human eyes. Her outstretched hand began to tremble.

Buoyed by her fear, he drew upon her magic to enter the Solid. The cold prickled his skin and made his coarse body hair stand on end. Her eyes grew even wider, and as he grabbed her around the waist, she yelped.

Show me the way, Miss Amala.

Breathing hard, she managed to point east. Gozan tipped his wings and soared that direction. She was like a child in his leathery arms.

They landed not all that far from the camp. Amala disentangled herself and set out at a good pace. Gozan took flight, blissful at the feel of air against his wings.

Amala stopped near a pile of dirty snow, frowning. "Someone has been here." She pointed at the pile. "We must dig."

I must dig, you mean?

"Yes."

If it meant a hoard of ahvenrood, Gozan didn't mind soiling his hands. He let his fingers grow longer, thick with claws, then scooped away piles of snowy dirt. He dug and dug, but found nothing. Soon the hole was so deep, he would have to crawl into it to continue.

How much deeper? He looked at his bond.

Tears streaked the girl's face. "We should have found it by now. Someone has taken it."

Gozan's hope shattered. Amala buried her face in her hands and wept.

While Gozan enjoyed her agony, he did not like being manipulated. Had the girl lied in order to trap him into a bond? If so, she would soon discover the folly of such a plan.

"I cannot keep up with Shanek if I am not a mantic," Amala said through her tears. "He's so much more powerful than me. If he becomes king, he will leave me behind, I know it."

Gozan wouldn't blame the boy for that. This girl was as emotional as Charlon.

She sniffled and wiped her nose with the back of her hand. Charming. Her eyes lit with an idea and shifted to meet his. "Unless . . ."

You have a plan, Miss Amala?

"You could take Dominion inside me."

Gozan didn't mean to, but he gasped. *You dare jest about such a thing?*

"I do not jest. Dominion is a way for you to share your power with me, isn't it?"

Oh, the delightful, foolish girl! *It is . . .* he said slowly, as if considering the idea carefully.

"Then I want it, if you think it will accomplish my goals."

I don't see why it wouldn't. Not that Gozan would promise the girl anything.

Miss Amala took a deep breath. "I don't know the ancient words for Dominion."

The Kinsman tongue will work well enough, Gozan said, trying not to appear eager.

She cleared her throat. "Come into me, Rurek, great shadir of the Five Realms. I give you Dominion over my body so that we might make magic together."

Rurek wasted no time, lest the girl have a sudden change of mind. He flapped his wings, hopped, and soared to her side. He picked her up in both hands and thrilled as he felt her body tense in his arms. Despite her fear, he felt no barrier between them, so he pulled her close and dissolved through her skin until he was fully inside her.

She was a great deal smaller than expected, but such warmth! He had never felt so alive! Not only could he feel the Solid on her skin, he felt whole inside this body.

Human.

No wonder Master Gâzar sought control of each precious soul. So much power in a human life. So much potential.

"Now I am just like Shanek," Amala said, somewhat giddy. Her voice sounded different from inside her head. "We are both bonded to greats."

A prickle of fear tangled Gozan's thoughts. *What do you mean?*

"Shanek has given Dominion to Dendron, the great that once served King Barthel. And now I have given Dominion to you. I like this plan better."

After all Gozan had done to keep his distance from Dendron, he was now bonded to the female companion of Dendron's human host. What to do? Now that he felt the ecstasy of Dominion, he would not give it up. The power he felt inside this body . . . it made him feel invincible. Dendron, however . . . Shanek had Dominion over shadir, so Dendron would be a slave to the boy's whims. The thought amused Gozan. Trapped inside that reckless young man, Dendron's power would be diminished. Not that Amala was vastly superior, but at least Gozan had the upper hand with the girl. He was her master. Shanek was Dendron's.

Gozan would just have to wait and see what happened when Miss Amala and Sâr Shanek came face to face.

"I cannot wait to tell Shanek I've bonded with a great shadir. He will be so surprised!"

Gozan snapped out of his stupor. He must put a stop to that line of thinking right away. *You must not tell Sâr Shanek that truth yet.*

"Why not?" she asked.

Because Dendron will see me as a threat. And you mustn't upset the future king at so perilous a time. He needs to focus on his plan.

"But we could help him," Amala said. "Two great shadir are more powerful than one."

Great shadir do not work together. One must rule over the other, and neither Dendron nor I will give up our freedom. No, Amala. We must help Shanek in secret for now.

He felt her reluctance. "I will think about it."

Amusing, how the fool girl didn't yet realize the truth. When she had accepted Dominion, she had given Gozan full power over her actions and speech, if he wanted to make use of them. She would do what Gozan wanted her to do. He doubted she would be pleased to learn this.

He couldn't wait.

HINCK

Hinck's day had been long and arduous. Trevn thought he had problems with the nobles in Armania. That was nothing compared to the daily condescension and ridicule Saria suffered. The council members seemed to like Hinck just fine—all except Finnel Wallington, who never passed up an opportunity to insult him and predict his ultimate doom.

Evening was upon them again, however, and Hinck was thankful for a private dinner with friends. Queen Mielle and her staff were still here. Trevn had sent her as his ambassador and to continue her investigation, but now that Shanek was looking for them, she would remain a while longer.

Six had been seated at the table tonight. Saria and Miss Abree, Mielle's honor maiden, sat on either side of Mielle. Hinck sat across from Saria, with Grayson on his left and Tonis, Mielle's onesent, beside Grayson. Outside the open door, Hinck's guards stood with Mielle's guards, Bero and Lady Pia—a more awkward visitor in Hinck's new world he could not have imagined.

"I like eating here," Mielle said. "It's much quieter than how we do dinner in Armanguard, and far less stressful."

"Hinck and I have not been crowned," Saria said, "so there is no point eating in the great hall, where so many would glare and whisper behind raised goblets."

"A great hall does tend to put one on display," Mielle said.

"That is part of ruling," Saria said, "but I have no stomach for it without the security of a crown."

"When will you marry?" Mielle asked.

"The coronation and wedding are in the planning stages," Hinck said, "but we are waiting to set a date until the threat of Barthel Rogedoth has passed."

"Sometimes I think that will never happen," Mielle said.

"It will happen," Hinck said. "His army is headed this way now."

"I'm sorry I haven't had a chance to meet with you until now, Your Highness," Saria said, changing the subject. "I thank you again for recovering those Sarikarian children. I'm ashamed that I didn't know any were missing."

"Finnel Wallington is involved in all this," Mielle said. "If only I could prove it."

"If I can help in any way, I am most willing," Saria said.

"As am I," Hinck said. "I would relish any reason to arrest that man."

"The Sarikarian children described Sir Malder as their captor," Mielle said. "Is their description enough to arrest Finnel's shield?"

"Not without adult witnesses," Hinck said. "If they'd taken a noble child, maybe."

"He's right," Saria said. "Our council is quite old fashioned. They would never take the word of common children over that of a nobleman. We must find stronger evidence."

"Or catch them in some other crime," Hinck said.

"Mett Lycor is the missing piece," Grayson said, drawing the attention of those at the table. "Every trail leads to him."

"Mett Lycor formerly of Raine?" Saria asked.

"He's an apparition," Mielle said. "We cannot find him anywhere."

"Well, no," Saria said. "Because he is dead."

Hinck hadn't heard that. "When did this happen?" he asked.

"In the Battle of New Sarikar," Saria said. "He fought alongside Fonu Edekk and was struck down by one of my father's guards. As he was minor nobility, his body was returned to his mother. She lives on the estate of Tace Edekk."

Mielle sat back in her chair. "Of course she does."

"All this time, Mett Lycor has been a diversion," Tonis said.

"Something still doesn't fit," Mielle said. "Everyone we spoke to described Captain Korvoh when asked to describe Master Lycor. Except Master Orban, the first father we visited. He described the real man—said he'd seen him weeks before."

"Which means he knew him," Hinck said.

"Which means he lied," Mielle said. "Lycor would have been dead when Orban claimed to have seen him. He has to know who is behind all this. They must be threatening him—perhaps holding his son captive." She pushed her chair back and stood.

Hinck rose to his feet, as did Tonis, and after a moment, Grayson.

"Are you leaving us, Your Highness?" Saria asked.

"Forgive me, but I must consult my papers." She started for the exit. "I might know what happened."

"Please let us know the moment you puzzle it out," Saria said.

"I will," Mielle said. "Abree, Tonis, I insist you stay and enjoy the meal. Grayson, I'd like your assistance."

The young man exhaled a deep breath. "Yes, Your Highness."

Mielle paused in the doorway to wait for Grayson, who pocketed two rolls on his way out. "Good evening," she said, then ushered Grayson from the room.

"I do hope she has made a discovery," Saria said.

"It will be such a relief to find out what happened to those children," Miss Abree said.

"The queen is a most tenacious woman," Hinck said. "I have no doubt she will succeed."

"How do you like working with the queen?" Saria asked Miss Abree.

"Oh, it is wonderful," the girl said.

"I do not have an honor maiden," Saria said. "It did cause me some trouble until my betrothal was announced. My dearest duke has solved so many of my problems."

Hinck grinned and bit into his chicken leg, watching as Saria engaged Miss Abree in a discussion about Queen Mielle's favorite pastimes. The princess was beautiful and brave and witty. Hinck had always admired her and could already feel his heart attaching. He was going to enjoy being married to Saria. The question was, how did Saria truly feel about him?

Hinck entered his chambers, eager for bed. He pulled off his belt and loosened the laces on his tunic. Mielle had not returned to dinner, and he wondered what, if anything, she had discovered.

The door to his chambers opened and Wix, Hinck's recently appointed onesent, entered. Wix was thin, with short hair cut like the top of a mushroom. He stood at Hinck's height, but his posture was so hunched that if he straightened he'd likely be two hands taller.

"Good evening, Your Grace," Wix said. "I thought I heard you come in. Are you hungry?" He walked to the hearth and stoked the fire.

"I just came from dinner," Hinck said. "I crave only my bed and a dream-less night."

Wix nodded, plucked the belt from Hinck, and draped it over his arm, then took over unlacing Hinck's tunic and helped him with his boots. For all Hinck's years as a young noble, working as a backman to Trevn had kept him living below his status. He still wasn't used to having servants of his own.

"I placed hot coals under your bed about half an hour ago," Wix said, "so it should be nice and warm. Is there anything else I can get you?"

"No, thank you, Wix. Have a good evening."

Wix departed. Hinck lifted a candlestick from a table near the fire and carried it into his bedchamber. Light danced over the walls until he set the candle on the bedside table and stilled the spinning shadows. He stretched his arms above his head, and while he held himself taut, a shadow moved on the wall.

Heat flashed over Hinck, but he remained calm and reached down toward his bed as if to pull back the blankets. Instead he grabbed the dagger he kept in a sheath attached to his shin. He drew it, then dove onto his bed, rolling to his feet on the uneven mattress, blade extended.

A man stood at his bedside, also clutching a dagger, though his was gleaming bronze. Finnel Wallington. He stabbed at Hinck, who jumped backward off the other side of the mattress. Finnel circled the foot of the bed, hemming Hinck against the wall. Behind him hovered the pale yellow, toad-like shadir Hinck had first seen in the sitting room with Princess Nolia. Its three bulging black eyes were fixed on Hinck.

"Now, this is a surprise," Hinck said, waving his dagger before him to act as a shield. "You seem the type to send a servant to do your killing."

"That's where you're wrong." Finnel lunged, grabbed Hinck's wrist that held his dagger, spun in a half circle, and elbowed him in the face. Pain spiked through Hinck's nose and he dropped his weapon.

"*Saria!*" he bloodvoiced. Her shields were up. "*Saria!*"

Finnel set his blade to Hinck's throat. "I expected more difficulty in disarm-ing the highly esteemed Duke of Armanguard."

Hinck scrunched his stinging nose. "I'm really more of a bowman."

"*Hinckdan?*" Saria said to his mind. "*Is something wrong?*"

"*I'm under attack! Send some guards to—*"

Something hard bashed against his head. Hinck slumped to his side, stunned. The shadir cackled.

"With you dead"—Finnel's voice came near Hinck's ear—"once I dispose of Princess Saria, the throne will be mine."

A blade slid into Hinck. Sharp waves of heat sharpened his focus to the pommel of Finnel's bronze dagger extending from the center of his chest. The shadir flew circles around him, laughing madly.

Saria's worry pressed against his fear. *"Hinckdan, where are you?"*

"I am dead." This was the end. He'd been murdered by Finnel Wallington.

"Stop joking at once and tell me where you are."

"Finnel . . . the shadir." He could think of nothing else but the pulsing throb in his chest. He must be bleeding. He should try to stop the blood.

"Drop him in the river," Finnel said from afar. "I don't want his body found."

Sir Malder's face overhead. A flash of fabric and darkness descended, shrouding Hinck in prickly burlap that smelled of onions.

Arman, he prayed. *Protect Saria.*

A shock of cold woke Hinck. He opened his eyes to a blur of swirling darkness. He briefly thought he was dead until he choked in a mouthful of burlap and frigid water. Finnel's men must have thrown him in the river, and he was sinking fast. He pinched his lips together and desperately tried to determine which way was up, but it was too dark. He kicked hard but the sack inhibited movement, plus there was something heavy in the bottom, dragging him down.

His lungs burned for air, and his whole body ached from the cold needling through him. Darkness clouded his vision. Death was going to take him now, and there was nothing he could do about it. After all of his adventures, he would end in a watery grave.

He panicked and wriggled wildly in the water, though his strength was quickly waning.

"Hinckdan!" Saria's voice in his head revived him. *"Hold still."*

"I'm drowning. Finnel had Sir Malder throw me in the river." Plus he'd been stabbed. Oddly he felt little pain from the wound to his heart. How could that be?

Something scraped across his back. There were likely rocks down here and submerged trees, maybe even some fish.

"I said hold still. I don't want to cut you."

A hand touched his side, slid down his legs to his feet. Saria was here? Underwater? A surge of affection for this woman distracted Hinck from death's call. The burlap tugged tightly over his face. He suddenly lost control and sucked water up his nose. This made his body writhe and his nose and throat burn. His vision faded just as a great weight fell away from his feet. He floated upward, turned. Hands gripped the sack, near his side and his shoulder.

He was rising.

He burst through the surface into the cold night and sucked in frigid air. Coughs wracked his body. Water ran down his face and spilled into his mouth, but the cold froze the moisture on his skin, making his cheeks and forehead stiff.

"Here!" Saria yelled. "Sir Oris! Help us!"

Voices called out, drew nearer. Water splashed. Multiple hands grabbed him, dragged him from the water. He was still coughing—his nose and throat stung—though breathing was getting easier. As air began to pass in and out of his lungs, he noticed the cold more. And the dull throbbing in his chest.

He'd been stabbed. He could still die.

Arman, please don't torture me any longer.

"Where's the litter?" Saria again.

"Behind you." A man's voice. Sir Oris.

"We need blankets here!" Saria yelled.

Hinck's feet found the ground, but when he tried to stand, his chest hurt too much and his knees buckled. Strong hands supported him as others dragged the burlap up over his head. The night was dark, filled with faceless shadows. Hands lifted him, set him on a firm surface, covered him in dry fabric. Then he was moving again, this time carried on the litter. A thousand pinpricks tingled his skin. He was getting warm. That was good, right?

"Where's the physician?" Saria asked.

"Here, Your Highness." Master Vento's voice. "Bring him into the rear sitting room."

Hinck watched the dark sky change to a dark ceiling as the litter entered the castle and twisted and turned through several rooms. He saw the toad-like shadir once, floating above him, but when he looked for it again, it was gone.

"You're going to be fine, Hinck." Saria brushed aside the hair matted to his forehead.

Hinck wanted to tell her about the shadir, but he couldn't find the strength to speak. Plus his body had begun to shake uncontrollably.

He didn't remember reaching the sitting room, but a sudden chill brought him back from sleep long enough to hear a man say, "There's a lot of blood here. Where's that coming from?"

"His shirt. Cut that off him. Carefully now."

As hands pawed at his chest, two others grabbed the sides of his head, and he found himself staring upside down into Saria's face. A wrinkled brow betrayed the falseness of her smile. "Hold on, Hinck. Please? I need you here. Stay with me."

But Hinck could not. Sudden pressure on his chest induced shocking pain, and he knew no more.

MIELLE

ielle and Grayson had read through all her notes and talked circles around how Master Orban might be involved in the abductions, but they'd found nothing. So she decided to have Grayson carry the man here, where Bero and Pia could question him.

Grayson left but didn't come back. The candle clock burned through an entire hour. Tonis and Abree returned from dinner, but still no word from Grayson.

Mielle paced the room, wringing her hands. "What if something happened to him?"

"He's lightning fast, Your Highness," Bero said. "No one could harm him."

Mielle wasn't so sure. The virtue of patience wasn't an easy one to strive for. She walked back to the fireplace, staring into the orange flames as they warmed her. She rubbed the shell on her soul-binding necklace and felt Trevn's curiosity rise over the distance.

"I wish I had the mind-speak magic." Then she'd know exactly what was happening with Grayson. And she could speak to Trevn whenever she wanted, rather than be forced to wait—

Cold air gusted behind her. "Found him!"

Mielle spun around. Grayson held not a man in his arms, but a girl of about ten or eleven. She wore a wool dress and leggings that were wet from the knee down and dusted in snow, as was the hem of Grayson's cloak. Both had pink cheeks and noses and were breathing heavily.

"This is not Master Orban, Grayson." Mielle pulled a blanket off her bed and draped it around the girl's shoulders. "What's your name?"

"Leean, ma'am," the girl said. "Is this Armanguard?"

"This is the castle in New Sarikar," Mielle said. "You've been rescued by Grayson, son of Jhorn, a hero with great magic. He can carry people from one place to another in an instant."

"The Deliverer," Leean said. "Will he rescue the others too?"

"There are more," Grayson said.

"Of course he will help them all," Mielle said, "but I must speak with him first. Sit here by the fire and warm yourself. Miss Abree will bring you some tea and food. Abree?"

The honor maiden nodded and rushed from the chamber.

"What happened, Grayson?" Mielle asked.

"There was no answer at Master Orban's house," he said, holding his hands out to the fire, "so I popped to his location. He was in a cabin in the forest with a woman. Not the wife we met before, but someone else. I snooped around and found a wagon on a trail that led to a shed in back, with more than a dozen children inside. I told them I'd be back soon and grabbed this girl."

Mielle fetched her cloak from the hook by the door. "Take me to the children. Now."

"Best wait until morning, Your Highness," Bero said.

She could not wait! "I won't leave those children alone another moment. They'll be brought here at once." *They must be freezing!* She went to her trunk to find more cloaks.

"Grayson can carry the children here, Your Highness," Lady Pia said. "No need to go."

"It'll take time for Grayson to move them all," Mielle said, draping a cloak over her arm. "I'll wait with the others until all have been rescued."

"I'll go first," Bero said. "Then Lady Pia. Then you."

Mielle supposed it was wise to bring her guards. She bade them fetch their cloaks and any extras they could find.

"How many will be coming, Grayson?"

"Around twenty," Grayson told her.

"Once you've freed them, Grayson, carry Master Orban and the woman to separate cells in the dungeon." When the guards returned, Mielle put on her own cloak and three extras, draped two more blankets over her arm, and removed the lantern from the sideboard hook. "I'm ready."

Grayson carried Bero away first, then came back for Lady Pia. By the time he took hold of Mielle, his clothing was cold again.

"Here we go, Your Highness," Grayson said.

Suddenly they were moving. Darkness swirled around them in the space of one deep breath, and they appeared between two buildings, knee-deep in snow. The lantern light revealed a cabin on Mielle's left and a shed on her right, the door cracked open.

Mielle pushed in the door. "Hello?" She held the lantern ahead, which created a void of blinding brightness. Beyond the light dozens of eyes reflected in the glow.

"I'm here, Your Highness," Lady Pia said.

"Where is Bero?" Mielle asked.

"Checking the cabin."

Mielle didn't like that he'd strayed from the plan, but the children needed her, so she put him out of her mind for the moment. "My name is Mielle. We've come to help you."

Movement caused her to step back.

"I'll take those, ma'am." A boy's voice, adolescent. He claimed the blankets.

"I'll carry this one next," Grayson said, hand on a little girl's shoulder. At Mielle's nod, they popped away. This made the children gasp.

"Don't be afraid," Mielle said. "My friend is the man known as The Deliverer. He's taking you to safety." The children whispered to one another, eyes wide. Mielle turned to the boy who'd taken the blankets. "What's your name?"

"Kyal Orban."

Master Orban's son! "How is your father involved in all this?"

The boy frowned. "My father died in the Five Woes," he said.

"Oh, I'm sorry." Then who was the man who had claimed to be Master Orban? And the woman who had posed as his wife? And the mystery woman in the cabin?

Grayson appeared, grabbed a boy, and vanished, this time making the children exclaim.

"How long have you been here, Kyal?" Mielle asked.

"It's different for all of us," he said. "Some have been here a few days. Some have been here weeks. I've been here longer than anyone, but I lost count how many—"

A woman's scream drew Mielle's attention to the house. Green light flashed in the shed's open doorway, followed by a blast of noise and heat. Wood splintered. The children screamed.

"Stay calm," Mielle said, despite her own fear. "Lady Pia?"

The woman was already outside. Mielle strode toward the door and peeked out. The cabin was on fire.

Kyal grabbed Mielle's arm. "You mustn't go outside. She's a mantic witch, and she'll punish any who leave."

A mantic? Someone was walking through the thick, white smoke. "Lady Pia?" Mielle called, suddenly terrified. "Is that you?"

A woman stepped out of the smoky haze, but it wasn't Pia. She was dressed as a peasant but held a regal posture. Mielle recognized her from a lifetime ago. She'd been part of Sâr Janek's retinue, but Mielle didn't recall her name. Gray eyes gave away her power.

Movement behind the woman turned out to be Lady Pia, rushing back. "Bero is dead. Master Orban too." She slowed to a stop, eyes locked on the mantic. "Mattenelle?"

Lady Mattenelle, that was it. She and Lady Pia had been Sâr Janek's concubines.

"What happened to your face?" Mattenelle asked.

"Sir Kamran," Pia said.

"That ingrate," Mattenelle said. "I'm not sorry he's dead. Why are you here?"

Pia gestured to Mielle. "I am High Shield to the queen."

Mattenelle looked from Pia to Mielle and back, a smile curling her lips. "Pia, that is wonderful! I'm so pleased for . . ." Her expression faltered. "I'm sorry, but I need her. The boy too. We've waited so long. I'm sorry." She thrust her hands at Pia and yelled, "*Yashen!*"

Lady Pia collapsed.

"No!" Mielle ran to kneel at Pia's side, shook her arm.

"Your Highness?" Grayson stepped out of the shed.

"Hide!" Mielle yelled at the same moment Mattenelle yelled, "*Âtsar!*" Grayson froze mid-step.

"Grayson!" Mielle pushed to her feet, saw Kyal and some of the other children huddled in the shed's doorway, watching the scene. Mattenelle moved her hand toward Mielle.

"Don't do this, lady," Mielle said, heart thudding.

Trevn's concern pressed against Mielle as the woman raised her hand and yelled, "*Hahsaw! Ba qol da rahyon.*"

Mielle stiffened and her mind went blank.

PART NINE

WARRIORS OF THE VEIL

Trevn

ielle? Answer me!"

Trevn searched with his mind for his wife, but it was as though she'd vanished, gone mute. He leapt off the longchair and reached for his shield's mind. *"Cadoc? Something has happened to Mielle."*

When his shield did not answer, Trevn flung open the antechamber door and ran into the council room. There stood Cadoc, leaning against the arrow loop window.

He pushed off the wall. "Your Highness, Master Hawley is—"

"Something happened to Mielle," Trevn said. "Why didn't you answer me?"

Cadoc frowned. "Forgive me. I didn't hear you. What happened to the queen?"

"And now? Can you hear me?" Trevn voiced.

Cadoc walked toward Trevn. "What has happened?"

Trevn tore out of the chamber and ran past Novan and Bonds, voicing people along the way. *"Hinck? . . . Saria? . . . Master Grayson? . . . Duke Canden? . . . Miss Onika?"*

He fled downstairs, desperately trying to understand what had happened. Shanek must have found Mielle, but how had he sabotaged the voicing magic? Trevn turned on the stairs. His King's Guards were right behind him. "Where might Duke Canden be at this hour?"

"The roof, likely, with his students," Novan said. "Or in the great hall."

That those locations were opposite one another made Trevn want to scream. "Find Duke Canden and Master Hawley and bring both to my office at once." He continued down the stairs, frantic to locate anyone with the ability to mind-speak.

"Master Hawley is in your office," Cadoc said from behind. "He asked to see you at your earliest convenience."

That turned Trevn around, and he jogged back up to the third floor. "Did he say why?"

"No, sir."

Trevn found Hawley sitting at his small desk behind Trevn's. "Something has happened to Mielle," he said. "She cannot seem to hear my voice."

Concern etched the man's face. "Both Miss Onika and Rosârah Zeroah complained this morning that they were unable to use their mind-speak magic. And Duke Canden was having trouble last night."

Others had lost their magic? "I spoke with Princess Saria not a half hour ago about the attack on Hinck, but now I can hear no one."

The men stared at Trevn. He paced to his desk, not sure he wanted to sit. "How is Duke Armanguard?" Cadoc asked.

Trevn met Cadoc's gaze across the room. "Saria said the wound is not fatal. I can feel Mielle to the northwest. There must be a way to find her." Grayson had been with her. Trevn reached for Hinck to ask about Grayson, then stopped his foolishness. If he had no magic, he could contact no one.

"Would the God take away this magic?" Hawley asked.

Trevn didn't know, but he suspected a different cause altogether. "I believe we have been silenced. Gather everyone who has the mind-speak magic in the council chambers as soon as possible. And bring Cook Labren to my office. I'll speak to him after I discern how many are affected."

Cadoc nodded to Novan, who set off at a run.

"The âleh tonic has been decreed highly confidential," Master Hawley said. "Only a select few should know about the substance."

"Which is why I want to speak with Cook Labren." The man had been tasked with creating âleh tonic for the prisoners in the dungeon. He'd know if any âleh was missing.

"And the queen?" Cadoc asked.

Trevn fell into his chair and ran his hands over his hair, tugging at the braids. "I sense her, but I cannot find her without the mind-speak magic or Grayson's help."

"Let's get you to the council chambers so you can question Master Grayson," Hawley said.

"Master Grayson is with the queen," Cadoc said.

Hawley instantly sobered.

Trevn could take no more. He rose and started for the door. "The âleh will wear off as long as we don't take any more. The sooner we discover how we ingested it, the sooner we can recover our voices and find my wife. I'll be in the Temple Arman."

Father Mathal made a burnt offering on behalf of Mielle, and led Trevn and Onika in prayers. When he finished, Trevn remained on his knees before the altar, Miss Onika at his side.

"Trust Arman to bring you through this, Your Highness," the prophetess said.

Trevn's anger flared. He wanted a prophetic word about Mielle's safe return, not vague lessons. "I never trust anyone fully, Miss Onika."

"People will let you down, Your Highness, because people make mistakes. But you still need people in your life."

"I *need* Mielle back safely."

"You need to trust Arman. He will fight for you. And he never makes mistakes."

"That's not a prophecy," Trevn said. He could feel it.

"No," Onika said. "It's a fact."

By the time everyone had assembled in the council chambers, the evening bells had chimed. Trevn stood behind his chair at the head of the table and gripped the back.

"I cannot mind-speak either," Hrettah was telling Lady Brisa.

"Nor I," Lady Brisa replied, picking at her fingernail.

"I didn't know that I couldn't until Trista told me she couldn't," Barek said.

"Vallah can," Trista said. "And Rashah too."

Hope filled Trevn. Perhaps not all had been compromised. "Please stand if you still have use of your mind-speak ability."

The two young princesses stood. No one else. Two of the thirteen present. "Voice each other right now, girls," Trevn said. "Confirm that you are still able."

Every eye on the room focused on the twosome.

"I heard her," Rashah said.

"Me too," Vallah said.

"Very good," Trevn said, somewhat relieved. "I want you each to voice Master Grayson and find out where he is. Do so now."

Another strained moment passed. Rashah's brow wrinkled in concentration. Trevn prayed the young man would reply with good news.

"He doesn't answer," Vallah said.

Rashah slouched. "Me either. Is he hurt?".

"I have no reason to think so, Rashah," Trevn said. "No one here is hurt, are we?"

The girl shook her head.

"I do need your help, though," Trevn said. "Will you help me?"

The girls nodded.

"Good," Trevn said. "Rashah, please voice Princess Saria and inquire as to the whereabouts of Queen Mielle and Master Grayson."

A collective gasp rose from those seated at the table. Rashah's bottom lip began to quiver and tears filled her eyes.

Perhaps Trevn should have worded that better. He seemed to have frightened his sister. "As I said, there's no cause to worry, Rashah. Please try to send those messages."

Rashah began to cry. Rosârah Brelenah, who was seated beside Trevn's littlest sister, scooted back her chair and pulled the girl onto her lap. "Perhaps Princess Vallah could voice Saria, Your Highness?"

Trevn nodded at Inolah's daughter. "Please do so, if you can, Princess."

Vallah curtsied. "Right away, Your Highness." She sat down, folded her hands in her lap, and closed her eyes.

"Is the queen in peril, Your Highness?" Zeroah asked.

"I don't know," Trevn said, sick to his stomach.

"Have we been poisoned?" Lady Brisa asked, now biting her thumbnail.

"Silenced, at least," Trevn said. "Until I find out what has happened, you will all eat and drink in this room. I'll make sure everything served here is uncompromised."

Vallah still had her eyes closed. Trevn couldn't stand here waiting for the girl. He had to speak with the cook. "Rosârah Brelenah, bring Princess Vallah to me when she has finished speaking with Saria. I'll be in my office."

Trevn returned to his office with Cadoc and Hawley, where they found Captain Veralla and Cook Labren waiting.

"Report," Trevn said.

"My âleh supply has not been tampered with, Your Highness," Cook Labren said, "nor have we recently employed any new servants."

A dead end there. "How long ago did you hire the newest?" he asked.

"Over two months, at least," Cook Labren said.

"The âleh must be coming from another place," Hawley said. "But where?"

Trevn sat down, frustrated. "I put a ban on imports from the houses Sârah Jemesha named as her allies. Could some have slipped by?"

"Not through the kitchens," the cook said. "I and my staff have been very careful."

If the silencer had come from one of the banned houses, they must have gotten it here another way. "Keep a sharp eye, Cook Labren. Dismissed."

The man bowed and departed.

"I'd like to be alone," Trevn said. "Inform me the moment there is any news."

Hawley and Cadoc bowed and left the room.

Trevn put his head in his hands and reached for his wife's mind.

"Mielle? Can you hear me?"

There was only silence.

GRAYSON

Grayson had failed. He'd led the queen into a trap and gotten them both captured. That mantic woman had placed a spell on him, just like Chieftess Mreegan had aboard the *Vespara* so long ago. As Grayson had stood frozen in the forest, he had tried to voice King Trevn but received no answer. Not from Onika, Oli, or Trista either. He'd even tried speaking to Kal and Jhorn. Maybe the spell had done something to his magic? Or something terrible had happened in Armanguard.

A strange young man had appeared in the forest with many shadir. Thin with dark eyes, long limbs, and dappled gray skin, just like Grayson's. It must have been Shanek DanSâr, the root child. There had been something powerful and cold inside him that had frightened Grayson.

Shanek had taken Queen Mielle first. He'd returned a few minutes later and popped away with Grayson.

"Everyone says we're the same," Shanek had said as they'd sped through the Veil. "But I'm better than you because I'm going to be king."

Grayson hadn't been able to think of a reply. Shanek had left him lying on a straw mattress in a tent and joined the two women who'd been waiting. Zenobia and Lilou, Grayson had known, from when he'd spied on Rogedoth. The women had forced him to drink âleh tonic.

Now he lay flat on his back, unable to speak *or* hear.

Trapped.

He watched Shanek and the women but couldn't hear their conversation. Moments later, Barthel Rogedoth entered, and Grayson came face-to-face with

480

his grandfather. Rogedoth motioned to a man behind him, who was carrying a stool. The man placed the stool beside Grayson's mattress, then scurried away.

"Well done, King Shanek," Rogedoth said. "And the queen?"

"She's in the tent you prepared," Shanek said.

"Bring Trevn here next," Rogedoth said. "Then Oli Agoros. Once both are detained, you will seize the castle and take your place on the throne."

Shanek nodded and popped away. Most of the shadir followed.

A chill ran over Grayson as the words of prophecy played back in his mind. *"The Deceiver will be deceived. He will break from his true family and be led astray by those he considers friends. He will stir up against Arman's remnant an army who care only for their own pleasure and have no delight in the truth."*

Shanek DanSâr was the Deceiver. And Grayson would have to face him. To fight him.

"Remove the spell that silences his speaking voice," Rogedoth said, sitting down.

One of the women mumbled something, and Grayson felt a catch in his throat.

"I'm pleased to finally meet you, Master Grayson," Rogedoth said. "Losing you was the biggest regret of my life."

Grayson tried his voice. "I don't want to talk to you," he whispered.

"I understand that," Rogedoth said. "Your father likely poisoned you against me."

"He didn't talk about you at all," he said, his voice stronger now. "I never knew you existed."

If that had bothered the man, his face didn't show it. "I shouldn't have sent you to Raine," he said. "Lord Edekk was not the most attentive man back then. I should have kept you in Everton. I was afraid, you see, that if someone found you out, I might lose you."

"You did lose me."

"I shouldn't have, is my point. You should have been my highest priority."

"No," Grayson said. "Your wife should have been, but you locked her away to get what you wanted. Whatever you want is your highest priority. And you don't want me. You want to use me. But you can't. Because I gave my allegiance to Arman and King Trevn. Since you're against them, we're enemies."

Rogedoth looked down his nose at Grayson. "You've thought this through."

"I have," Grayson said.

"But we're family. Family is stronger than anything."

"We share the same blood," Grayson said, "but that doesn't make us family. My family are the people who cared about me my whole life. I don't know you at all. Except that you took me prisoner. Not a very good start."

"What matters is that we're together now," Rogedoth said. "I will soon have rule of Armanguard, so you must decide how you will spend the rest of your life. Would you rather live like this, immobile and imprisoned? Or would you rather serve me?"

"Neither of those things will happen," Grayson said. "I grew up with Miss Onika, a True Prophet of Arman, so I know you'll fail."

Rogedoth smiled, but it looked more like a snarl. "You're wrong about that, my grandson. I realize I have asked a great deal of you, so I will give you some time to reconsider." He stood and walked toward the tent opening. "If your answer is the same by the time I return, know that you have chosen death."

MIELLE

Mielle awoke, lying on a hard leather mat inside a tent. She could tell from the yellowish glow coming through the canvas that it was morning. The chill made her guess she was in a place that had snow, not far from home, hopefully.

The horror of her capture came rushing back in fragmented images. Kyal's warning. The fire. Mattenelle the mantic, shrouded in smoke. Lady Pia saying Bero was dead. The spells on Lady Pia and Grayson. Trevn's concern. And now Mielle couldn't speak or move, just like when Sârah Jemesha had put a spell on her when she and Zeteo Agoros had tried to take Castle Armanguard.

Mielle didn't like being immobile. She wanted to fight and rage and buck like a horse, but all she could do was lie still and stare at the tent ceiling.

She figured this must be Rogedoth's camp. When she'd awakened briefly last night, two women had fed her a mug of bitter liquid. She'd recognized them as concubines from King Echad's court. Trevn hadn't spoken to her since the attack, so the mug must have contained âleh. That he couldn't reach her bathed Mielle in fear, though she could still sense him through the soulbinding. She fixed her thoughts on the leather cord around her neck and wished she could hold the shell. Touching it always made Trevn feel closer. She hoped he was safe.

As the hours passed, Mielle relived each moment that had led to her capture. Her biggest fear was for Grayson. She hoped he was still alive.

Footsteps approached. The door flap shifted, and a man ducked inside, holding a lit lantern. As he hung it on the center tent pole, a long line of people entered behind him, several that Mielle recognized. First came King Echad's former prophet, Filkin Yohthehreth, the one who had always annoyed Trevn back in Everton. Then came a younger man, followed by three women—the two who had fed her the âleh and Mattenelle—and finally, Barthel Rogedoth.

Mielle's heart sank into a pit of fear. This was Trevn's worst nightmare, come to life. *Arman, help him cope. Help us both.*

Rogedoth approached and loomed over her mat. His eyes were golden, where they'd been brown before. No reason to hide his heritage as Prince Mergest of Sarikar anymore.

"Your Highness," he said. "Welcome to my camp. I hope you are comfortable." He smiled, which looked sinister in the dimness. "I was surprised how long it took you to puzzle out the clues we left for the missing children. I thought you would have figured out Mett Lycor straightaway. And what about the desert? Master Grayson did lead you to the desert, didn't he? Did you wonder if his magic was failing?"

Under the spell, Mielle had no way to respond.

"Those children were there, Your Highness, but they were buried. That is the location the Jiir-Yeke take the bodies of their sacrifices after the ceremony. The Duke of Raine traded children to the Jiir-Yeke and the Ahj-Yeke, ensuring that the giants would side with us."

Mielle's fear turned to hate. This man had no honor.

"Shanek is fetching your husband for me as we speak. Not to this tent, of course. I'll keep him elsewhere until his army is defeated and Shanek has taken Armanguard. I just wanted you to know he will not be neglected. I would hate to have you worry."

She wanted to claw his eyes out, but she could only lie there like a stunned fish.

His golden eyes fixed upon her waist, and he crouched. What was he looking at? He reached out, his fingers—long and dark—like the legs of spiders. They brushed her stomach, and inside she cringed. Was he going to cast another spell? Trevn had said he couldn't do magic.

Something moved at the back of her neck, tickled. A bug? Her mind winced, overcome with the myriad of possible spells someone so depraved might impose. The tickle vanished as the press of the leather cord around her neck cut into her skin.

The soul-binding pendant.

No!

Rogedoth gripped the shell and tugged until the cord snapped. He stood and dangled the necklace over Mielle. "A soul-binding cast by Charlon Sonber is strong indeed. I'd be hesitant to meddle with it if not for the knowledge that the shadir who created the bond is no more."

Because Magon was dead. Could Rogedoth's mantics harm Trevn through their magical bond?

"Did you know discouragement is one of the most effective strategies a general can inflict upon his enemy? It seems to me that if Rosâr Trevn cannot mind-speak his wife, and if he also lost his unique soul-binding connection to her, he might be overcome with despair."

No doubt he would, but Mielle hoped he would first remember his place as king and do his duty to the realm. She tried to muster as much hatred and defiance in her eyes as possible.

Rogedoth handed the shell to the older of the three women. "Break this spell at once."

The woman stepped into the place Rogedoth had just vacated and lifted her arm over Mielle, holding the shell pendant in her fist.

Mielle wanted to scream. The soul-binding could be a frustration, but she needed it. The magical bond was the only thing that kept her and Trevn connected.

"*Kabada âthâh,*" the woman said, waving her hand over Mielle. "*Bâqa ze ecâr. Nêzer illek nephesh. Bara châphash netsach.*"

Mielle felt Trevn briefly. A surge of pain passed between them as if they'd been stitched together and were suddenly ripped apart. The incredible loss consumed Mielle in a rush of solitude and panic. She writhed inside. Tears flooded her eyes until she couldn't see. Sobs made her chest heave.

Lady Zenobia opened her hand. White powder sprinkled over Mielle like sugar on a cake. The cord hung loose and empty from the mantic's wrist. At the sight of the pendant destroyed, Mielle sobbed so hard she began to choke. She couldn't breathe and still couldn't move either.

Mattenelle knelt and rolled Mielle to her side, rubbed her back. "Let her breathe, at least. She does no one any good drowned in her own tears."

Rogedoth nodded to Zenobia, who, with a whispered word, returned movement and the use of Mielle's voice.

Her sobs intensified, and she found the sound so startling that it brought on a new bout of tears. She curled into a ball and wailed.

Rogedoth and his acolytes left, taking the lantern with them. Mielle continued to sob, alone in the cold. She reminded herself that Trevn was still alive. He still loved her. Just because she no longer felt him inside her didn't make that untrue. But with no way to warn him what was coming, she feared he might not be alive much longer.

TREVN

Trevn pushed aside his breakfast to hear more from Rosârah Brelenah and Princess Vallah. Before they could speak a word, however, a flash of terror from Mielle seized him so abruptly that he cried out. *"Mielle? What has happened? Can you hear—?"*

Searing pain shot through his chest and down his sides into his legs, yet it seemed to simultaneously run up his spine to his head. He released a ragged breath and clutched his heart, which seemed somehow dead. He took a deep breath, confused. It was still beating.

"Your Highness, are you ill?" Brelenah was at his side, touching his shoulder.

"Mielle," he whispered, terrified that he could no longer sense her. What had happened?

Brelenah's golden eyes met his. "Did she speak to you?"

"Gone," he managed.

She squeezed his shoulder. "She was taken, yes."

Tears pooled in his eyes and he shook his head. She didn't understand. Everything was warm. Why was it so warm? Why did he feel so strange? The ache. The emptiness. He turned up his palm. The imprint of the shell had disappeared. "No!" He bowed forward, head on his knees.

"Your Highness? Trevn?"

Sorrow fell heavily. Unimaginable, the weight of it. The intensity. He couldn't breathe. Emotions assailed him. So overcome by the combination of emptiness and pain, he wailed and slipped off the chair. He hit the floor. A woman called for help.

How long he lamented, he did not know. Voices surrounded him, but he ignored them, consumed by the knowledge that Mielle was dead.

At some point he felt a hand on his back, heard a woman mutter, "He will cover you and protect you in the shelter of his wings."

Zeroah?

Trevn opened his eyes. He lay on his side on the floor, knees drawn to his chest. The dowager queen sat near his head, praying. Father Mathal was present too, as well as Rosârah Brelenah, Vallah, his sister Hrettah, and Miss Onika—all crowded around him on the floor.

A cold wave of shame spilled over him. What was he doing? He sniffed to clear his head, but his nose was clogged. Sands alive, what a lamb he was, crying like a babe on the floor. His cheeks burned and he pushed himself up.

"Enough of this." His voice sounded odd in his ears, and his arms trembled. He was still borderline hysterical. He cleared his throat. "I am well." For now.

Cadoc lunged in and grabbed his arms, helped him stand.

"Is the queen alive?" Vallah asked.

"Hush," Brelenah scolded her.

Trevn shuddered. "I know not." He held out his hand for all to see. "The mark is gone."

"That doesn't mean she's dead." Oli pushed into the circle around him. How many were in his office, anyway? "I was with your brother when Harton removed the soul-binding Charlon had placed upon him. It could be they removed the spell to confuse you or to keep the two of you from communicating."

Hope kindled just as his nose cleared, and with it, his ears. He nodded at Oli. "Thank you." Took a deep breath. "Princess Vallah, what have you learned?" he asked his niece.

"Princess Saria didn't know Queen Mielle and Master Grayson left the castle," Vallah said. "She hasn't seen them since dinner last night. She said the queen had learned something about the missing children and left."

"Did she say what Mielle learned?" Trevn asked.

"That a man named Mett Lycor died in the Battle of Sarikar."

Lycor was dead? "What of Master Tonis, Lady Abree, Lady Pia, and Master Bero?"

"Master Tonis and Lady Abree are in Sarikar," Vallah said, "along with three orphan children that Master Grayson found in a cabin in a forest. Princess Saria said the queen's guards are also missing."

Well, at least Mielle had not gone off alone. Little comfort that gave him at the moment. Trevn sighed, terrified that his wife had stumbled onto a group of evildoers. He never should have allowed her to investigate the missing children on her own.

"If they have taken the queen," Oli said, "they will surely come for you soon."

"No doubt," Trevn said. "That is why we must find out how we were silenced and get our magic back. When Shanek does come, I want to be ready."

Living on the edge of despair made it difficult for Trevn to stay rational. He wanted to plan a rescue for Mielle, though he had no idea if she was alive or how he could find her until his mind-speak magic returned. While he would have rather eaten his midday meal alone—and while that might have been safer, considering the threat of Shanek DanSâr—he forced himself to dine in the council chambers with the others, hoping his presence might inspire hope.

At Cadoc's insistence, Trevn wore no crown. His signet ring was strung on a chain around his neck and tucked inside his tunic, out of sight. And he sat on the side of the table, two chairs from the throne at the end. No one would sit there, in case Shanek came looking.

Ottee set a platter of food before Trevn, then filled his goblet with wine. Trevn had little stomach and picked at his meal. While the table was by no means filled with people, those present spoke little. He had given Barek Hadar, his daughters, and Danek Faluk permission to stay in their own homes. They would not return until the source of the silencer had been discovered.

Trevn took a sip of wine, but the hint of cranberries made him spit the liquid back into his cup. "Don't drink the wine," he said, pushing back his chair. "We should have finished the duke's wine months ago. Give me the bottle."

Ottee scurried to the sideboard and returned with a brown glass bottle, his eyes like two round eggs. "Cook Labren sent up a fresh one. I uncorked it when you entered the room."

Trevn held it up to regard the seal and date. House Edekk's sigil, dated only a month ago. This bottle had not been part of those Edekk had given him after his visit to Nawhar House. Panic ran through him, though he calmed himself with the reminder that this must be the answer—and one that was not only fixable but again pointed to the traitor Tace Edekk.

"I strictly forbade deliveries from House Edekk. Hawley, how did this get here? Who signed off on the delivery?"

Hawley took the bottle in hand. "I will have to inquire in the kitchen."

"Go now."

Hawley departed.

"This fits," Enetta said. "Princesses Rashah and Vallah don't drink wine."

Trevn nodded, appeased that his theory made sense. "Please continue with your meal. Ottee, fetch some fresh goblets for those who were drinking wine and pour them water instead."

"Yes, sir." Ottee ran into the antechamber.

Trevn sat down and picked at the roast fowl. Waiting for Hawley to return nearly drove him mad. The convenience of the mind-speak magic had made him impatient.

"Cadoc, with me." He left the room and headed downstairs. He had just reached the ground floor when he met Hawley coming out of the kitchens. "Well?"

"Barek Hadar signed off on the delivery, six days ago."

Trevn fought to keep his composure. "I want to speak with him. Now."

"He's not here, Your Highness," Hawley said. "You granted him permission to—"

"Ready my horse, Cadoc. We are going to visit the duke."

A short ride later, Trevn and his guards dismounted in front of Barek's house, which sat on the lakefront on the inner rim of the Crescent. Servants scurried out of the way as Trevn and his men entered the house.

"Where is the duke?" he asked.

"In his office, Your Highness," a portly man said.

"Take me there at once."

Trevn followed the servant down a short passage and into an open sitting room. Duchess Arzah and Lady Trista stood, embroidery in hand, and curtsied. Mother and daughter looked to have been crying. A door on the back wall opened and Barek Hadar stepped out.

"Your Highness," he said, his expression startled. "To what do I owe the honor?"

"I require a private word, Your Grace," Trevn said, striding past the duke and into the office. He did not wait for Barek to ask him to sit. The moment Cadoc closed the door, Trevn spoke. "Six days ago you approved a delivery of wine from Lord Edekk, after I forbade the import of any goods from that manor. Hawley?"

Hawley rushed forward to show the duke his signature on the register.

"Explain why you did this," Trevn said.

Barek's demeanor shifted into one of confusion. "That's not my signature."

Trevn fought back a growl. "Everyone in the castle knows your face, Barek. How could someone forge your name? Hawley? Is this possible?"

"Only if the deliverer and the receiver were in league with one another," Hawley said.

"Who works receiving?" Trevn asked.

"Several people," Hawley said. "I would have to consult my ledger, which is—"

"The orphan boy, Porvil," Barek said, with a heavy sigh. "And Brisa."

"Lady Brisa, *your daughter?*" Trevn could not contain his shock.

"It's only a guess," Barek said, lowering himself to a longchair. "Brisa went to visit Lady Koll, only my wife discovered yesterday that Lady Koll is in town with her in-laws, gravely ill."

"I'm aware of that much," Trevn said.

"It turns out, Brisa went to . . ." The man's frown grew deeper. "I can hardly say it. She has taken up with Sir Jarmyn Koll. I'm convinced the man is a mantic, the way young women flock to him, no matter that he is married with a child on the way and heedless of the trail of broken hearts he always leaves behind."

"I am sorry, Your Grace," Trevn said, grieved by this news. "But simply forging your signature would not get the wine where it needed to be. It leaves too much to chance. And Porvil is still in the dungeon."

"That root child was helping her," Barek said, frowning. "My wife saw them talking in this very room three days ago. Not Master Grayson. The foreign one."

A chill ran over Trevn. "And you didn't tell me?"

"You already knew he was terrorizing the area. And I was worried for Brisa."

Trevn took a deep breath. He and Barek rarely saw eye to eye, and Trevn had sent Gunrik Koll's son to the pole, but he needed these men now—might fail without them. It was time to ask his nobles for help. To trust them, even though he would rather not. To trust Arman. "Our enemy has maneuvered us well, Your Grace," he said, "but it's not too late. I need your help. And Gunrik Koll's as well. I need soldiers. As many as I can get. Will you gather your men? Will you fight for Armania?"

"I will, Your Highness," Barek said. "As will Gunrik. I'll see to it."

The asking hadn't been difficult. Now Trevn would see if the armies actually turned out. "We must prepare for an attack. I feel it is coming, any moment."

Trevn had never felt so alone. The loss of his soul-binding with Mielle had killed something inside him. His work was the only thing keeping him from collapsing into another fit of despondency, so he spent every waking moment at his desk, refining defensive plans with Oli, General Ensley, and Marshal Winstone.

Trevn sent ravens with warnings to Randmuir and Sir Keshton at the border houses, annoyed that they would take hours to arrive. He felt impotent without his mind-speak magic—*bloodvoicing*, Hinck and Saria had been calling it. Without drinking any wine the âleh should wear off in a day or two. Until then he was handicapped.

Late that evening, he was in his office with Oli, Cadoc, and Hawley when Shanek DanSâr appeared on the left-hand side of Trevn's desk.

Startled, Trevn stood. Oli, Cadoc, and Hawley jumped to their feet as well. Cadoc drew his sword. "Back away now."

The intruder's eyes shifted from one man to the next. "I only want to talk with the king."

Trevn doubted that very much. The young man had Janek's eyes, nose, and hair, though he was rail thin. Trevn wanted to ask about Mielle, to grab the root child around his throat and strangle the truth from him, but he said nothing, not wanting to give himself away.

"Your Highness," Cadoc said to Oli. "Shall I escort our visitor out?"

Shanek's gaze fell on Oli. "You don't match the description of the king."

"Take this intruder to the dungeon at once!" Oli yelled.

Cadoc reached for Shanek, but the young man vanished.

Trevn twisted around, looking for him. "Where did he—?"

Shanek appeared on Trevn's right and grabbed him around the arms in a bear hug. Cadoc and Oli yelled. Trevn bashed his head against Shanek's, but they were suddenly whisked away.

The dark, snowy landscape sped by until they stopped inside a tent. The air was chilly, the ground covered in woven mats. Shanek released Trevn, then flashed to the other side of the tent, holding his head beside a woman and two men, all dressed in leather, furs, and foxtails. Trevn's forehead stung as well. He surveyed the tent but did not see his wife.

"Your Highness," the woman said. "Welcome to Magosia. My name is Kateen."

"Where is Mielle?" Trevn asked.

"With King Barthel," Shanek said. "Don't worry. Amala made him promise that you and your wife can live together. Somewhere far away."

Miss Amala was helping them? "You cannot trust Barthel Rogedoth."

"That's why I brought you here," Shanek said. "Now I can be king."

Trevn panicked at the idea of this strange person tormenting his people. "It takes more than wishing to be a king," he said.

"Make sure he stays here," Shanek said to Kateen, "and you will get more root."

He vanished just as the woman started speaking in an ancient language. Trevn's arms and legs went stiff. Distressed, he opened his mouth to speak and found he could not.

Kateen approached, a wicked grin on her face. "You look like your brother Wilek." She pushed two fingers against his chest. Such little force was enough to send him toppling backward like a felled statue. He slapped against a mat. The force knocked the air from his lungs.

"Make him drink this," Kateen said.

Trevn couldn't see her, but she had to mean âleh. Sure enough, the men converged on him, made him sit, and forced the bitter liquid down his throat. He wanted to fight them off, but the spell kept him immobile.

"Might as well sleep," Kateen said when the men were done. Then she left Trevn alone, trapped with his dark thoughts.

Gozan

Amala begged Gozan to take her to King Barthel's camp so she could check on Shanek, but he refused. This infuriated the girl, who claimed Gozan was holding her prisoner. He manipulated her mind, and she forgot her complaint until she had the idea anew to help Shanek. Round in circles they went, the girl complaining and Gozan continually making her forget.

Gozan had searched her mind, but Amala had not been included in the planning of Shanek's takeover of Armanguard. She knew only that the young man would, at some point, abduct Rosâr Trevn and carry him to Magosia—a side plan the two of them had made because they didn't trust King Barthel not to kill Rosâr Trevn.

Amala was sitting in her tent, cross-legged on a mat beside her pitfire, weaving bark into a basket when Shanek appeared out of nowhere.

The girl scrambled to her feet, and before Gozan could think to stop her, she threw herself into the young man's arms.

Gozan recoiled at the power within Shanek. There was so much magic there already, but Dendron's presence emanated in a thick, suffocating cloud. Gozan drew into himself—tried to hide deep inside Amala—but such a feat was impossible.

Shanek pushed back from the girl. "What have you done? I sense magic in you."

Do not tell him about me, Gozan reminded her.

Amala opened her mouth to do just that, but Gozan changed her words. "I am weaving a basket for you."

Shanek frowned. "What do I want with a basket?"

Amala's thoughts raced with confusion. She tried again. "Rone harvested the inner bark from one of the white trees and I . . . thought you'd like it."

"Have you taken more root from Mother's hideaway?" he asked. "Is that it?"

Her heart leapt as his words jogged her memory. "It's not there! Either she moved it, or it has been taken."

"That's unimportant at present," Shanek said. "I left the deposed king with Kateen. Come with me now to inform my mother."

Sense the changes in him? Gozan asked Amala. *His demeanor, his word choice? That is the great within him.*

Amala ignored Gozan and took hold of Shanek's hand. "What of Mielle?"

"She is safe with King Barthel."

"Is he treating her well? Did you see for yourself?"

"I've been in Armanguard, hunting the king."

Amala said no more, but panic thrummed through her at the thought that she might have put her sister in danger. Such negative emotions once thrilled Gozan, but now that he felt them as his own, he found them annoying.

He pressed calm upon Amala's fears. *We will check on Mielle ourselves once Shanek leaves. Only when we see with our own eyes will we be satisfied.*

This appeased the girl, though her sister lingered at the back of her mind, an ever-present concern that needed to be dealt with as soon as possible.

Amala and Shanek walked the length of the camp, holding hands. Gozan felt Dendron's curiosity within the young man, but the human bodies surrounding them kept Gozan's true strength hidden.

"Did you like the castle?" Amala asked Shanek.

"It is an impressive fortress," he said. "Much more so than the wooden one in New Rurekau. I shall like living there very much."

The girl wanted to live there too. "When will you go there to stay?"

"Directly after leaving here. The Duke of Everton's soldiers are moving into place. He has some in the castle already."

"Will you carry me with you?"

"We talked about this, Amala. I need you here, helping Mother watch Trevn."

Her heart ached at being left behind. "What about King Barthel?"

"He wanted to come to the castle, but I made him see his error. I need no assistance to take the fortress and hold it, and he must lead the army."

They reached the red tent, where Rone stood guard. He bowed his head and quickly pulled aside the door flap so they could enter. Charlon sat slouched on her throne, watching a half dozen gowzals meander about on the floor before her. Gozan felt the shadir inside them but could not identify them. Likely all were creatures of Magon's swarm. That Charlon had never fully trusted him had been their biggest obstacle.

At the sight of her son, she straightened. "Shanek, you've come home?"

"I am moving to take Armanguard," he said. "I have brought King Trevn here to Magosia and secured him in Kateen's tent. You must keep him safe. Once I am installed as King of Armania, I will convey him elsewhere."

Charlon pushed off her throne and walked through the clustered birds, which scurried out of the path of her bare feet. Turmoil played over her face as she struggled to respond to this news. She stopped two paces from her son.

"My sister, the queen, is being held in King Barthel's camp," Amala said. "When this is all over, she and her husband will live together in peace, somewhere far away from Shanek's kingdom."

Charlon's eyes fixed upon Amala, and Gozan reveled in the betrayal he saw within those dark orbs. "Will King Barthel allow that?"

"It is not his decision," Shanek said. "I do not trust that King Trevn would survive King Barthel's care at present. Promise me you will keep him here, secure but safe."

Charlon shifted her gaze back to Shanek. "I will care for him well, my son. But surely his men will come for him. He built a fort not far from here."

"Do not worry," Shanek said. "Roya is there already, holding the fort for me."

Charlon's eyes glittered. "You have thought this out fully, I see."

"I must claim my kingdom now." Shanek pulled Amala in to a crushing embrace.

Again Gozan did all he could to draw deep into the recesses of the girl's mind, where his power might not be so obvious. He could feel Dendron questing for the source of magic within the girl, but Shanek vanished, and the world seemed suddenly lighter.

Until Charlon seized Amala by the hair and jerked her close. "You dare betray me?"

Amala squealed. *Stop her, Rurek!*

Gozan did not want the girl to get used to ordering him around, but he relished the idea of toying with Charlon. He sent power to the girl's hands and shoved Charlon, who flew back and knocked against her throne. The chair tipped on its side and the tent jerked and trembled.

"Chieftess?" Rone rushed inside, shard club raised. "What is happening?"

Amala pushed Rone back out the doorway and walked slowly toward Charlon. "You have grown lax, Chieftess. Someone has stolen your hoard of evenroot."

"That's not possible," Charlon rasped from where she lay on the floor.

"It is, and now I have given your great shadir Dominion inside me. Rurek has abandoned you. I have his power now."

"Fool!" Charlon said. "He controls you, not the other way around."

"I am his master!" Amala yelled.

"No, you stupid girl. *He* has the power. You have nothing."

Amala screamed, mad with fear that Charlon might be right. *Kill her,* she thought to Gozan. *I want her dead.*

But Shanek wants her alive, Gozan said. *Are you ready to betray him so soon?* Amala quailed at this reminder.

The Chieftess is merely jealous, lady, Gozan told the girl. *She is angry that she refused my offer of Dominion. And she is envious of the love Shanek has for you.*

Yes, Amala thought. *I have taken her place now. So I must cast her down fully. I will become Chieftess of Magosia, and she will serve me.*

My, but this girl was an impulsive little creature. *A fine idea, lady,* Gozan replied, *but you must have patience. And you must decide what you want. You cannot live both here as Chieftess of Magosia and in Armanguard as Queen of Armania.*

This realization knotted the girl's thoughts, so Gozan spoke for her. "I hold Shanek's heart, Chieftess. I do not wish for strife between us, so if you want to know your son, you will show me respect." He forced Amala to stride away, leaving Charlon on the floor.

As Gozan made his way down the hill, he could feel the girl struggle. Fear and despair had silenced her, but her courage was growing. The moment they were back in Amala's tent, the girl's thoughts burst forth like fire from the mouth of a cheyvah.

It's true what she said, isn't it? You control me. You're my master.

They would get nowhere together if the girl felt herself a victim. She must believe she had power, even if she did not. *My power is mine alone, Amala, but our bodies are one. I will lend you my power if I wish to.*

But if I have no power, then what Charlon said is true. You are my master.

Not at all, lady. Don't you see? By hiding myself within you, who will know that I exist? You are the face they see. You are the one who will grow a name for yourself.

497

And if I want to use your power?

You only need ask.

She was still breathing rapidly, trying to calm herself. *I want to see Mielle. I don't trust that King Barthel is treating her well. Can you take me to her?*

It *would* be entertaining. Shanek and Dendron were likely in Armanguard now, so Gozan saw no reason why he couldn't infiltrate Dendron's swarm and cause a little mayhem.

Very well, he conceded. *If we leave at once, we will likely look upon your sister before this time tomorrow.*

This pleased the girl. *And if King Barthel does not immediately improve her situation, we will bring her back with us.*

Yes, Gozan agreed. *But not before we punish him for his negligence.*

CHARLON

Charlon slowed her horse. Already she could see. Brown soil mixed with snow. Dismay rose above her anger as she dismounted and fell to her knees. Dug until hands grew numb. Scraped rocks. Fingernails tore. Still she dug. Until she was sure. Sure it was gone.

It was. Someone had taken her root. Only Shanek knew this place. Shanek and Kalenek.

She rode back to camp. Tears blurred her vision. That Rurek had betrayed her so utterly. That Amala had foolishly accepted Dominion. That Shanek had been pulled into King Barthel's snare.

And Kateen and Roya, involved in this too? Charlon could not abide it. *Treachery,* her heart said. *They all must pay.*

She could not worry about her stolen evenroot at the moment. King Trevn being held prisoner in Magosia took priority. Charlon reached Kateen's tent. Dismounted. A gowzal fluttered to her shoulder. Others flew toward her or scurried downhill from the red tent like a brood of chickens.

Charlon went inside. Her first maiden lay on a pile of furs before her pitfire. She sat up, watching Charlon. A man lay on his back on Kateen's pallet. Charlon circled the pitfire. Looked down on Trevn Hadar, King of Armania. Her flock settled around her feet.

King Trevn's eyes were open. Rolled to fix upon hers. She had last seen him at his wedding. He had more hair on his face now. Looked older. Tired. She understood. Ruling a nation was no easy task.

"They told you?" This from Kateen, who approached Charlon, surging with power.

Charlon had been so angry. She had not noticed. Noticed the power in Kateen. "You have magic again," she said. "Where did you get it?" Had she taken Charlon's evenroot?

Her First tensed beside her. "I needed it in case someone should try to rescue the king."

"*Where* did you get it?"

"Does it matter?" Kateen spat. "You would not share yours. Did you really expect me to go without forever?"

Charlon turned her head slowly. Eyes locked with Kateen's. "I expected my First to obey me. Without question."

"You are mad. You have driven our once great nation to dust. Magic is to be shared, not hoarded. That is one of the tenets of Magonia."

"Magonia died with its goddess."

"Because you killed her! We were better off with Mreegan at our head," Kateen said. "She wasn't so afraid that she hoarded power for herself."

"You think I am afraid?"

"I know you are. Everything you do stems from fear. Because of what your brother made of you."

"*Hahsaw!*" Charlon yelled, thrusting out her hand.

Kateen's eyes widened, then she laughed. "Forgot you are dry, Chieftess? Well, I am not." She lifted her arms and spoke, "*Hali âthâh. Le hahkpi shel ôyeb.*"

Cold bathed Charlon's skin. Icy and fierce. A breath coated her nostrils and throat in ice. She choked. There was little time. She reached for the gowzal on her shoulder. It hopped to her fingers. Loyal. She threw it at Kateen. Managed a single, breathless word.

"*Puroh.*"

The creature transformed into a bolt of flame that engulfed Kateen. Charlon's First screamed. Threw herself to the floor. Rolled about. The mat beneath her began to smolder with thick white smoke.

Charlon shivered violently. The ice reached within. Fingers and toes numb. Frost coated her throat. She crouched and hugged her knees. Could find no warmth. Not until Kateen died. The gowzals roosted on Charlon. Fur and feathered bodies eased the cold. It was not enough.

Kateen stilled, her flesh smoldering. Yet a hand reached out, whispered. Too late. Few shadir would obey a dying master.

Fog shrouded Charlon's thoughts. Heartbeat slowed. She must hold on. A moment more.

A low, rattling groan came from Kateen. The cold began to fade. Charlon's throat watered. She coughed. Gasped in deep breaths of rank smoke.

"Hali." She took another gasp. Could not see the common who had served Kateen. It was likely still here. Feasting on the woman's death. On Charlon's fear. Hali would make a worthy addition to Charlon's army. "You are welcome in my flock."

Oh, that smell! Her stomach churned. Queasy from her pregnancy. She put her head on the mats and stilled. Tried to hold it in. She needed air. And soon.

Charlon pushed to her feet. Surprised to find King Trevn standing. Watching her warily. He had witnessed a great horror. Would he attack her?

"Let us depart, Your Highness," Charlon said. "I fear I will be sick if I stay." She fled Kateen's noxious tent. Outside the chilled air gripped her. Fresh. Clean. A crowd had formed. All watched her. Nuel held a bucket.

"Was there a fire?" he asked.

"Yes," Charlon said. "Dispose of Kateen's body. You might have to burn the tent. It's quite horrible. Your Highness, this way." She motioned the Armanian king to follow. Set out for the red tent.

King Trevn walked on her left. Their steps tapped over the packed snow. "I never thanked you for the wedding present you bestowed upon me and my wife."

Charlon tensed at the king's sarcasm. "I know not why Magon wanted me to do it. Did it burden you in some way?"

"At times, but it's gone now. I don't know if it was removed by one of Rogedoth's mantics or if my wife is dead."

"Queen Mielle is not dead. My son told me. She is being held in King Barthel's camp."

Relief eased the strain on the young king's face. "Thank you."

"I was only just made aware. Of my son's plot against you. I had no idea you were a prisoner here."

"You expect me to believe that? It has been your nation's goal from before you were Chieftess to put your child of prophecy on the throne of Armania."

"The Deliverer. That was Mreegan's goal. I came to see it as folly. Shanek disagreed. Now he is following King Barthel and his shadir. It will likely end in his death."

"You would let that happen?"

She set her jaw to hold back tears. "None can stand against my son. Sir

Kalenek promised me that I would lose the boy. If I tried to control him. He was right. As much as it pains me, Shanek must go his own way."

"The prophecy is real," the king said, "but the Magonians misinterpreted it."

Charlon sighed, weary of men and their arrogance. "And how do *you* interpret it?"

"The Puru people Grayson rescued from the Ahj-Yeke mines gave him the name Masaoo, which translates as *deliverer*. I'm afraid Shanek might be the Deceiver. Him or Rogedoth."

Apprehension tingled down Charlon's arms. All this time? Had she helped create a monster?

They reached the red tent, and Rone pulled aside the door flap. Charlon entered first. Motioned for the king to sit on the furs at the foot of her throne.

The king folded his arms. "I prefer to stand."

So like his brother Wilek. "Very well." Charlon sat on her throne. Rubbed the back of her neck. Her entire body felt sore. "How can I be of service, Rosâr Trevn?"

"You want to help me?"

"King Barthel will use my son. Shanek still believes that the man will let him rule. A testament to my failure as a mother. I'll do all I can. To stop him from destroying my boy. Though I am likely too late. So, I ask you again. How can I help?"

The king thought for a moment. "Your mantic fed me âleh to silence my mind-speak magic. It will be some time until it returns. Can you deliver a written message to someone in New Sarikar?"

"I can send one of my flock." She gestured to the gowzals.

The king eyed the birds warily. "I will need a pen and parchment and some sealing wax."

"You shall have it," Charlon said. "You should also know. Another of my maidens betrayed me. She rode for the fort you built southeast of here. Has taken it for King Barthel."

This sobered the king. "I must take it back. Would you loan me a horse?"

"I and my men will ride with you."

"I will not ask you to do magic for me, Chieftess."

"You don't have to. Roya is my problem. I will deal with her."

The king frowned, his suspicion plain. "What do you want in exchange for your assistance?"

"Nothing but your promise. Once your fort is safe, you will kill King Barthel."

"I am confident that my army will defeat his, but whether or not I strike the killing blow is not important to me."

"As long as he dies. I will be appeased."

The king folded his arms. "How can I be certain you won't turn against me once the Pretender is dead?"

"I tire of games, King Trevn. This I cannot prove. But I have no ambition beyond ruling my people. I seek only peace for myself and Magosia." And her coming child.

King Trevn swept into a courtly bow. "Then let us ride for my southern border house in the morning. Once it is secure, I will continue on to join my army. If King Barthel is on his way to attack, no one will have peace until the Pretender is defeated once and for all."

Hinck

Hinck opened his eyes to a bright day. His first thought was for Mielle and Grayson, lost while in his care, and how Trevn and all of Armanguard had been silenced by âleh. He could not worry about them at the moment, though. He had trouble enough to deal with here. He sat up, wincing at the strain on the stitches in his chest.

"You're not supposed to do that without assistance."

Hinck turned carefully to the window seat where Saria sat, embroidering. That she was here pleased him. "I thought you hated embroidery."

"I do, but I wanted to be here when you woke, and believe it or not, doing nothing but watch you sleep is even more tedious than embroidery."

"I'll have to take your word for it. I've never seen myself sleep."

She smirked. "Yes, well, I am eager to arrest Finnel Wallington. If I had my way, he would have died the night I pulled you from the river."

"You were wise to wait."

"I'm not so certain. Think of all they could have plotted in the past two days."

"Our plan is solid, Saria. Trust it."

Finnel Wallington's blade had stabbed Hinck at such a slight angle it had cut through his skin and scraped along the sternum. Once Master Vento had determined the wound was not fatal, General Norcott had stepped forward and suggested his plan. If Princess Nolia and her husband thought Hinck was incurable, they would wait for his death, then swoop in to claim the throne.

This plan had been impossible with the toad-like shadir roaming around, spying. Hinck had learned enough in his brief training with the Veil warriors

504

to banish the creature, so he'd left his body and entered the Veil. Once he'd sent it back to the Lowerworld, he'd returned to his body, knowing it was now safe for him and Saria to plot against Finnel and Nolia.

Saria had grossly exaggerated Hinck's prognosis as dire to the council and pretended not to know who had attacked him. All had gone as planned, and today Hinck, Saria, and General Norcott were going to enact the second part of their plan.

"Send for Wix," Hinck said. "Have him prepare me a bath. Once I am dressed, I will meet you in our office."

Saria jumped up from her window seat and started for the bedchamber door. "Your bath has been ready for the past hour. I'll have Wix add hot water, but bathe quickly, my husband-to-be. I am eager to arrest Finnel Wallington and blackmail my aunt into submission."

Since Finnel Wallington could not mind-speak, they waited until he was away from his wife to make their move. When he went with some companions to the stables for a ride, instead of finding horses saddled and ready, he met a contingent of guards. The moment Hinck got word that Finnel and Sir Malder were locked away in the dungeons, he and Saria set out for Princess Nolia's chambers. General Norcott and another contingent of guards met them there.

"How are you feeling today, Your Grace?" the general asked Hinck.

"A little sore, but eager to neutralize this threat."

The general nodded to one of his men. "Open the door."

The soldiers let themselves in to the apartment that Princess Nolia shared with her husband. Hinck heard the woman protesting before he crossed the threshold.

"What is the meaning of this? How dare you enter my rooms without permission?"

"Your husband gave us permission, Princess," the general said. "He insists you help us."

"What do you mean? Where is Finnel?"

Hinck walked inside and took his place on General Norcott's right. Princess Nolia was on her feet, arms folded. Her eyes locked onto his, and the panic Hinck saw there made him smile.

Saria came to stand on Hinck's other side. "Your husband has been arrested for attempting to murder the Duke of Armanguard," she said. "He has confessed and assured us that you have information about Barthel Rogedoth's uprising. As you can imagine, I am not eager to pardon a man who tried to kill my betrothed, but His Grace is a forgiving sort of person, and I will not begrudge him such a noble trait."

"I want to see Finnel," Nolia said.

"Voice him if you like," Saria said. "But you will not be together until this is all worked out. And, Aunt Nolia, he *will* be executed for his crimes, should you decide not to help us."

Nolia glared but sank slowly to a longchair. She closed her eyes and was silent a very long time. By the changing expressions on her face and the tears that leaked down her cheeks, she and her husband knew they had lost.

She finally opened her eyes. "King Barthel has allied with some of the giant tribes. They will attack this fortress when the king attacks Armania. If you want to live, you must leave."

Hinck's heart sank at the mention of giants. He supposed they might evacuate the castle, though that would mean handing it over to the enemy. There was nothing to do for the moment but carry on as planned. "If you want a pardon for your husband, you will help us," he said.

Nolia sighed and folded her arms again. "What will I have to do?"

"You will carry on your conversations with Rogedoth as if nothing has changed," Hinck said. "Tell him I died. Tell him to let the giants come as planned."

"That would be foolish," Nolia said. "The giants will kill us all."

Saria scowled at Hinck as if agreeing with her aunt, but Hinck saw no other way.

"Let me worry about the giants," he said. "Do we have an agreement?"

Nolia shot Hinck a fierce scowl, but said, "I will do as you say."

"Excellent," Hinck said. "Our guards will remain here at all times to see that you do not try to escape." He exited the room. The others followed, and once he was in the hallway, he turned to see Saria and the general behind him.

"That went well," the general said.

"It was a disaster!" Saria said. "Let us worry about the giants? Hinckdan, really? How will we do that?"

"Give me more than a minute to think about it, will you?"

"As long as you tell me you are in fact thinking of something," she said.

"I am," Hinck said, quickly turning it over in his mind. "The giants will attack us no matter what. If Rogedoth knows we have learned of his plan, he'll change it. This way we can at least prepare. New Rurekau has survived several Jiir-Yeke attacks. I will voice Empress Inolah and ask her advice. It could be she knows of a weakness of some kind."

"It could be she will pass on her condolences to the realm of New Sarikar," Saria said.

"Do not be so negative, Saria," Hinck said. "You are starting to sound like me."

Empress Inolah did not provide encouraging news. The Jiir-Yeke were a ruthless bunch. Yes, New Rurekau had twice defeated them, but only due to Empress Jazlyn's magic. Hinck was not about to ask a mantic to come and rescue them, so he voiced Ulagan of the Uul-Yeke and asked if he might send some giants to aid them. Ulagan said he would consult with others. Hinck would check back in a few hours and see what had been decided.

In the meantime, he went into the city to recruit more carpenters to finish the border house. While he was there, a rat bird accosted him. Hinck had always hated the wretched creatures but even more so now that he knew how the Jiir-Yeke created them. He and his throng of servants tried to shoo it away, until Wix yelled, "Wait! It's carrying a scroll."

Sure enough, a small tube had been attached to the creature's right foot. Wix caught the bird and quickly removed the scroll. "It bears Rosâr Trevn's seal!"

Hinck snatched it away, confirmed the imprint of the signet ring, and opened it.

Hinck,

I am alive and well in Magosia. Shanek DanSâr carried me here to keep me from Barthel Rogedoth, but Chieftess Charlon wants no part of this war and has decided to help me escape. By the time you receive this, I will have ridden for the southern border house, which one of Charlon's mantics has taken for Rogedoth. Hopefully once we reclaim the fort, my voicing magic will have returned. Please inform the Duke of Canden of my status and location. Also tell him that Barthel Rogedoth will likely reach our central border house by tomorrow. Do all you can to prepare.

Trevn Hadar
King of Armania

Trevn had gone missing? Could the message be a fake meant to lead the Sarikarian army into a trap? He tried reaching for Trevn's mind, just in case the âleh had now worn off, but his knocks still went unanswered. Hinck needed someone who hadn't been affected by the âleh. His mother had stopped attending dinner in the great hall when Hinck came to Sarikar and instead remained at their house in the city. Perhaps she could answer Hinck.

"Mother? This is Hinckdan. Can you hear me?"

"Yes, I hear you, my son."

Relief calmed him. *"What news from the castle? Have they learned what happened?"*

"Lady Brisa planted bottles of wine that contained âleh in the castle, so most who ate their meals there have been silenced. And the king, queen, and Master Grayson have been carried away by Shanek DanSâr. Your father remains in the castle with the Duke of Canden. They hope their magic will return soon. Can you speak with the king?"

"No," Hinck said, *"but I did receive a message from him. Will you transcribe it and take it to Oli Agoros at once?"*

"Certainly."

After Hinck had finished speaking to his mother, he stared again at the scroll. The news had sobered him, but he had no time to waste. Wix still held the bird. Hinck supposed he should send a reply to let Trevn know he'd received the message. He tore off a blank corner of the scroll. "Do you have any ink, Wix?"

"I have a wedge of charcoal in my pack," he said, nodding to the carriage. "Would someone take the bird?"

No one moved. "You stay put," Hinck said. "I'll fetch the charcoal." He found it and drew the Renegade *R* onto the slip of paper, then folded it and secured it to the bird's ankle.

"Take that back to my king," he said, clueless whether or not the bird could understand, but the creature ruffled its wings, leapt from Wix's grasp, and took flight to the south. "Continue on without me, Wix," Hinck said. "I must return to the castle right away."

"Rogedoth is advancing and we must prepare," Hinck told the council. "Half our army will stay here with Duke Pixford and guard the castle. I will take the other half to the Sarikarian border house."

"But it's not finished," Saria said.

"It's finished enough that we can make a stand there," Hinck said.

"You cannot leave us," Duke Pixford said. "You are our regent."

"Co-regent," Hinck said. "Princess Saria will remain here."

"I will not," she bloodvoiced. *"If you're going, so am I."*

"You wanted to rule," Hinck replied. *"Here is your chance."*

"I want to fight too," she said.

"This won't do at all, Your Grace," Duke Brixmead said. "I am very put out. We accepted you as our regent—"

"Co-regent," Hinck added again.

"—and we expect our regent to remain here and rule us."

"Your Prince Mergest has begun his march," Hinck said. "I have confirmation of it from Empress Inolah and now King Trevn."

"But what about the giants?" Duke Brixmead said.

"Ulagan of the Uul-Yeke is sending twenty giants to us to help," he said.

"Only twenty?" Duke Pixford asked.

"Send General Norcott to the border house," Saria said. "He can handle it."

"The general is coming with me," Hinck said.

"But you are injured!" Saria said. "You cannot possibly wield a sword."

"I am not too injured to sit in a command tent," Hinck said. "And if I must fight, pulling a bow is steady and slow, not like swinging a sword. I will be well, I assure you."

"Father Wolbair?" Saria asked. "What is Arman's will in this matter?"

Hinck's interest perked. Yes, he should have consulted the prophet himself.

"This is what the God says. 'You, House of Sarikar, in times long past, broke from Armania when that nation fell away from me. But time has brought everything full circle, and now it is Armania that clings to my promises while you plot ways to avoid my will. I no longer act for one nation, but for each heart that serves me. I will gather my people from all the nations where they have been scattered. Only when they stand together in my name will I give them success against the evil they have brought to this land.'"

Hinck shivered. The man's prophetic voice had felt like Onika's. Hinck knew the words had come from the mouth of Arman.

"Those who follow Arman will prosper," Hinck said. "We have that promise from the God himself. But he won't bring success to those who won't fight. So I will take our army south to hold our section of the border." Hinck glanced to each face around the table. When no one spoke, he stood and walked out the door.

"Hinck, wait." Saria rushed out into the hall after him. "I want to come with you."

"That won't do, Saria. You must stay here and guard your throne."

"But what if you don't return?" Her golden eyes were glossy.

Was she frightened to rule without him? Or worried that he might be killed? He tipped his head, trying to figure out what was bothering her. "I promise to return, Princess."

A sniffle. "That is not a promise you can make."

Hinck grinned. "I just did."

She grabbed his neck and kissed him. Hinck was so shocked he stood stiff as a tree, but Saria seemed intent on kissing him thoroughly, so he wrapped his arm around her waist and put in a little effort of his own.

Someone cleared his throat. Saria tried to pull away, but Hinck held her in place. Duke Brixmead was standing in the doorway, watching them.

"Ah, young love," he said. "It isn't always roses and singing birds, is it, Princess?"

Saria pinched Hinck's arm. He jumped, and she slipped out of his grasp, pushed past Duke Brixmead in the doorway, and disappeared inside the council room.

Amused, Hinck reached for her mind. *"Farewell, Saria. Until I return."*

"Make it soon, please, my husband-to-be."

"I live to serve, Princess."

☉ Lİ

Oli stood at the head of the table in the Wisean Council chambers. He had called together the war council and extra staff in hopes of quickly dealing with the catastrophe of their missing king. He had just read the message the Duchess of Highcliff had brought to him personally—her transcription of a message Trevn had sent to Hinckdan. Now everyone was talking at once.

"Silence, please," Oli said. "Let's have one at a time. Master Jhorn?"

"Chieftess Charlon cannot be trusted," Jhorn said. "She's a mantic."

"I agree that Charlon is unstable," Sir Kalenek said, "but she loves Shanek. I'm not surprised she would side with us against the man who deceived her son."

"You say the poison silencing you will soon wear off," Lord Idez said. "Once it has, you can speak to the king and find out if this message is real."

"If the message is a hoax and the king is still in custody," Captain Veralla said, "surely they will continue to silence him. Even when you can speak again, he will likely not hear you."

"But if the message was true," Danek said, "and the Chieftess is helping the king, then his magic should return with ours."

"Whether or not the king's magic is restored doesn't matter," Oli said. "Once our magic is restored, the Veil warriors can travel to him."

"Yes." Danek nodded to Oli. "Wisely said, Your Grace."

"We are living in the midst of a great battle," Miss Onika said.

"Indeed," Oli said. "And we must prepare for the coming attack."

"You are right, Your Grace, we must," Miss Onika said. "But I was not speaking of the war with your former pontiff. What I speak of is so much

511

bigger. Long ago Gâzar declared war on all who follow Arman. His minions are loose and wild in the Veil, creating havoc wherever they go. They must be stopped. Arman is raising his army. Those who ally with the God against this invasion of darkness share in his authority over it. We must rise up—speak up. Stand united with the God. His enemy has made his move. We must make ours."

Oli did not deny that the prophetess's words were true—he well knew Gâzar's ways of darkness—but he disliked her vagueness. "What do you recommend, prophetess?"

"We must pray," she said. "For our king and queen's safety, for Grayson and the missing guards, and for our magic to return."

"Pray all you like," Oli said. "I have no issue against it."

Miss Onika fixed him with a stern expression. "I meant that we should pray corporately for Arman's intervention. Our magic is his. He gave it to us, and he has the power to restore it."

Oli couldn't banish shadir, so he doubted his presence would help such an endeavor. He shrugged. "Miss Onika, by all means gather Arman's most faithful and pray."

"And the rest of us?" Lord Idez said. "What will we do?"

Oli fixed his attention on General Ensley. "Anything from the scouts?"

"A rider came last night from the central border house," the general said. "Rogedoth's army is but a day away. Marshal Winstone and our army have already left to position themselves to intercept him. They will be ready."

That much was good. "Sir Kalenek, what is Shanek DanSâr capable of?" Oli asked.

"Terrible magic," the knighten said. "If he comes here, we would all be wise to obey him, at least until your magic returns."

"What can our magic do against him?" Oli asked.

"Not enough, I'm guessing," Jhorn said.

"Veil warriors can destroy shadir," Sir Kalenek said. "That will help, since they are Shanek's friends and advise him. But only Grayson stands a chance against Shanek's magic."

"Where might Shanek have taken Master Grayson and our queen?" Oli asked.

"To Rogedoth," Sir Kalenek said, "since Shanek believes the man to be his ally. Shanek has no army of his own, and I can't imagine he would know how to—"

The door swung open and young Lady Trista entered, face gleaming from perspiration. Novan Heln followed behind.

"You must hide yourselves, quickly!" The girl curtsied, breathing hard. "Enemy soldiers are invading the castle this very moment."

"Calm yourself, lady, and explain," Oli said.

Trista took a deep breath and flopped onto a chair Novan pulled out for her. "I saw the betrayer, the one they call Sâr Shanek. He is carrying Duke Everton's soldiers inside the castle as I speak. One by one to the cellar, I believe. And Brisa told the duke you are likely meeting in this council room, and here is where they plan to come once they are all inside."

The room fell into chaos. Many began talking at once. Barek's voice rose above the din.

"Did you talk with Brisa?" he asked.

"No, Father," Lady Trista said. "Hirth Wallington came to our home this morning, looking for you. He gave me his message. He has long harbored feelings for Brisa. He could not accept that she chose Sir Jarmyn—a married man. Master Hirth said the Duke of Raine has a mantic and an army and has sided with Barthel Rogedoth. And he told me Sâr Shanck was carrying the enemy into the castle and where I might go to see for myself. The guards wouldn't let Master Hirth inside the castle—he is being held in the gatehouse. But I went down to the kitchens, and I saw the truth of his message. We must hurry!"

Oli couldn't believe the foolishness of Brisa Hadar. "We must begin to evacuate the castle," he said. "Women, children, servants. I want everyone out. Send them to Duke Highcliff's manor, if you don't mind, sir?"

"Not at all," Danek said. "I'll go at once to inform my wife and prepare."

"Captain Veralla, I want a vast majority of the soldiers disguised as servants," Oli said. "Wait. Make that any soldier who does not know someone within the armies of Tace Edekk or Finbar Wallington. Hopefully that will give us some hidden help, should we need it. Have those men stash extra weapons throughout the castle. And kill any trespassers. No mercy. But do so as stealthily as possible. I don't want to alert the enemy. And Kipp," he looked to his honor man, "take charge of finding serving uniforms for the soldiers. All of you, go now."

Captain Veralla and Kipp followed Danek out the door.

"We cannot all abandon the castle," Lord Idez said.

"We will not," Oli said. "We must hold it for the king's return. Let us move our meeting to the mind-speak classroom. It's not a place anyone would readily search."

"The castle is small enough that we will eventually be found," Lord Idez said.

"I only seek to afford us a little more time," Oli said. "Ladies, I will not ask you to remain in the castle should you wish to leave. In fact, I would feel better if you relocated to a safe haven within the city."

"My place is with the king," Miss Onika said. "I will wait for his return."

Sands, Oli forgot to inquire of Arman. "You are the king's prophet," he said to Onika. "Have you any word?"

"From Arman, you mean?"

"Yes."

"He has not spoken to me audibly today, but I have not spent much time in prayer. I would like to begin immediately."

"I will join her," Zeroah said. "We are Veil warriors and must stay close until our magic is restored."

"I will stay as well," Brelenah said, "though I would like Rashah and Vallah taken to safety first. Hrettah will stay with the Veil warriors."

"Send the girls and their staff to my home," Lord Idez said. "My wife would love to have them."

"Thank you, Joret," Oli said. "Where will you ladies be praying?"

"We can use my chamber," Brelenah said. "That way we will be close."

"I would come with you to pray," Master Jhorn said.

"We would welcome you, sir," Brelenah said.

"Go now," Oli said. "Leave in groups, and keep watch for anyone suspicious. I must question Hirth Wallington."

Oli entered the gatehouse. Though it was chilly in the castle these days, the gatehouse was as cold as being outdoors in the winter snow. Hirth Wallington sat across from two guards at a small, roughhewn table. All three men stood when they saw Oli.

"Your Grace, thank you for coming," one of the guards said.

Oli and Hirth had grown up together with Janek, trained side by side for years. "What do you know, Hirth?"

His eyes fixed upon Oli. "The Duke of Raine is leading a rebellion in conjunction with the pending invasion from Barthel Rogedoth," he said. "Yesterday his army set out for the fort New Sarikar has been building for Rosâr Trevn. They have with them a group of compelled Ahj-Yeke giants. Altogether they number two hundred seventy-some men."

Not more compelled giants. "Who compelled them?"

"Master Natod," Hirth said. "He is Tace Edekk's onesent."

"I know him," Oli said. "How many giants did he compel?"

"Eighty-two, if I heard correctly. I was meant to march with them." Hirth did not hang his head in shame or even look regretful. Rather he stared at Oli, jaw set, proud.

"So, why didn't you?" Oli asked.

The question deflated his posture some. "It didn't feel right to betray the king and all of Armanguard in such a way."

"Do you feel Barthel Rogedoth should be king of Armania?" Oli asked.

"No, sir. I did once. But not now."

Oli narrowed his eyes. "What changed your mind?"

"It started when I fought Rosâr Trevn that day on the practice field. He was brave, coming out there like that. Wasn't his fault he hadn't the skill. I began to wonder when I'd become so set against House Hadar. My brother, my father, my uncle, the other men . . . their negativity affected us all. We'd trained all our lives to support our king, to fight for him. I didn't think we should falter from the vows we'd taken. They mean to put King Barthel on the throne in Armanguard, while my brother, Finnel, acts as regent in New Sarikar. It's not right."

"Do you feel you made the wrong choice coming here?" Oli asked.

"No. But I . . . my father, the other men, Lady Brisa . . . they'll think I have."

"What has Lady Brisa to do with any of this?" Oli asked, curious where the woman was.

"She believes in their cause. She uses her mind-speak magic to spy for them, told the one called Shanek to carry enemy soldiers into the cellar."

Oli tensed at this news. "Aren't the two of you—?"

"We were, Your Grace, but no longer. She told me she loves Sir Jarmyn."

"He's a mantic too, you know," Oli said. "At least he was. He's never been good at anything but love spells. Janek taught him."

Hirth released a ragged breath. "Brisa is under a spell?"

The hope in his voice sickened Oli. "I couldn't say, but I would put her out of your mind, if I were you, Hirth. If she doesn't die in the coming battles, she will likely be executed for treason."

Oli pulled Miss Onika from her prayers and told her all Hirth had said. "The moment your magic returns, you must find Lord Edekk and his army.

And take care. Edekk has partnered with Rogedoth and has the mantic Natod at his disposal. As soon as you find them, count their numbers, determine how close they are to the Sarikarian border house, and inform the Duke of Armanguard to prepare for an ambush."

"Yes, Your Grace," Miss Onika said.

Oli returned to the mind-speak classroom and joined Captain Veralla at a table Master Hawley and some servants had set up. They began to coordinate defensive tactics for the castle. Those leaving the stronghold were being sent in small groups so as not to look suspicious. Oli sent Lord Idez and Sir Kalenek to the great hall. Lord Idez would remain there under the guise of being the highest-ranking noble on the premises. It would be his task to greet Shanek DanSâr if and when he arrived, to keep him from finding Oli, and to stall him. Oli wanted Sir Kalenek there as well in case Shanek traveled to his location again, and for his knowledge of the young man.

There were three stairwells leading from the lower levels to the first floor. Oli sent twenty soldiers to each—men in complete uniform—in hopes of intimidating enemy soldiers. One peek above the landing, he hoped, would be enough to send the enemy back for an alternative plan.

Oli was thankful Lady Brisa had no military wit and had told Sâr Shanek to carry the enemy to the cellar. They would have had greater success had he carried his army to the roof, from which they could have descended. "I want men on the roof as well," he told Captain Veralla. "That is the only other entrance we have neglected to—"

"Your Grace!" Sir Cadoc escorted Miss Onika inside the classroom.

"What is it?" Oli asked.

"My mind-speak magic has returned," Onika said. "You could not hear me, so I wanted to come in person."

Oli tried to reach for the prophetess, but his magic was still hindered. "Has anyone else's magic returned?"

"Not that I know of," she said. "The king still does not answer, nor does Grayson or the queen, but I would like to try to find them through the Veil."

"I insist you go to the king at once," Oli said, eager to find Trevn. "No, wait." He paused, frustrated. "Seek out Master Grayson instead. We need him to fight Sâr Shanek. Tell Brelenah and Zeroah to find the king and queen the moment their magic returns. And I still need you to find Lord Edekk and his army."

"Will you take the message to the rosârahs, Sir Cadoc?" Onika said. "I must lie down."

"Certainly, Miss Onika." Sir Cadoc led her toward the longchairs in the back of the room.

Relief gave Oli a moment to breathe calmly. He looked at the plans before him, trying to remember what they had been talking about before the interruption. The door opened again before he had the chance. This time it was Kipp who ran inside, face flushed.

"I bring a message from Sir Kalenek, Your Grace," Kipp said, breathing hard. "Sâr Shanek just left the great hall. He came alone, looking for you. Lord Idez told him you were in the city and invited him to dine while he waited for your return. He declined and said he would come back in two hours' time."

"Thank you, Kipp," Oli said. "Go back and tell Lord Idez and Sir Kalenek to hold their positions and keep me informed of anything new." Then to those in the room he said, "Our enemy has come. Miss Onika, you have two hours to find Master Grayson and get him back."

QOATCH

Ulrik is using his magic to manipulate me," Jazlyn said, pacing before the fireplace in her sitting room. The three gowzals she'd bonded with for the new magic hobbled on the floor, trying to trail along beside her, but they could not keep up with her long strides. "Every time I remind myself I hate him, something compels me against it." Her eyes found Qoatch, where he stood behind her empty longchair. "Speak, Qoatch. Advise me."

"I agree, Great Lady," he said. "You have behaved most strangely since returning here."

"I have never loved a man. Not once!" She resumed pacing. "I must leave to establish New Tenma as planned. The sooner I am away, the better. If I am to go mad for Ulrik Orsona, let it be at a safe distance where no harm can come of it. Where you can talk sense—remind me of the truth."

"The first Tennish delegation awaits your order," Qoatch said.

"I have given the order twice!" she yelled.

"And taken it back twice," Qoatch reminded her.

She groaned. "That odious man! If only I could kill him."

"*I* could," Qoatch said.

"No," Jazlyn said. "I do not understand the mind-speak magic enough to risk his wrath. I only wish to take the Tennish remnant to the land I've chosen. To start anew with no interference from false kings or controlling young emperors or giants or anyone! There must be a way."

"The answer is simple, Great Lady. Order me to ignore any commands from you which I know to be folly."

She raised her eyebrows. "Are you mad?"

518

"In all the years we have been together, have I not proven myself loyal? It is my greatest hope to see you installed as the High Queen of New Tenma, as you rightly deserve."

Jazlyn continued pacing. His Great Lady had listened. Qoatch could ask for nothing more.

She was still roving about the sitting room when a knock sounded on the door. Qoatch opened it and found a Rurekan servant waiting.

"A message for Empress Jazlyn, may she live forever," the man said, handing over a sealed scroll.

Qoatch accepted it with raised brows, surprised by the respect in the man's voice, though ever since Jazlyn had defeated the giants, many had changed their opinions toward her. He closed the door and carried the scroll to his Great Lady.

Jazlyn ripped it open and read quickly, her eyes trailing from left to right. She frowned and handed the message to Qoatch. "Read it and tell me your thoughts."

Qoatch drew open the scroll.

Empress Jazlyn,

I think we all can agree that the discord between us has moved beyond the normal quarreling of a husband and wife. I know you wish to leave and establish New Tenma, and I am prepared to let you have your way. It is my fervent hope that we also might put an end to all manipulation of mind or magic. I propose that you and I sit down for a formal negotiation of peace, with my mother and your loyal servant Master Qoatch as witnesses. If it is convenient for you, we could meet tomorrow at morning bells.

Ulrik Orsona
Emperor of Rurekau

"He means to trap me in some way," Jazlyn said. "Shape my thoughts to his liking."

"Forgive me, Great Lady, but I disagree. If he meant to take advantage of you, he would not have included Empress Inolah and myself as witnesses."

Jazlyn snatched the scroll from Qoatch and read it again. "But I do not trust the emperor. He will toy with my thoughts."

"If you sense him in your mind at all, you must say so. If the man will not respect you, we will not stay for the negotiations."

Jazlyn tapped the scroll against her palm, lips twisted in thought. "Very well," she said at last. "But in the meantime, you will send word to the first Tennish delegation. They must set sail for New Tenma and help those I left behind to build the fortress. Should I change my mind on this, I give you leave to ignore me. Do not tell me you're doing so. That will only raise my ire."

Qoatch bowed, fighting back a smile. After a life of service, he well knew how to deal with Jazlyn. "I will do as you say, Great Lady."

"Nothing is to be said of New Tenma during this negotiation. It is my wish that no others from the Five Realms will ever find it."

"I will do everything in my power to make your vision a reality," Qoatch said.

"Good. Now let us craft my reply to the emperor."

GRAYS⊖N

Rogedoth didn't speak with Grayson on the second day. Many shadir came and went from his tent. Gowzal birds too. The mantic women cast different spells on Grayson so he could eat and drink, but he couldn't pop away. It was like he had forgotten how.

The third day, Rogedoth came to see Grayson again. "Have you changed your mind, my grandson?" he asked.

"I'm not going to help you do evil," Grayson said.

"What one man says is evil, another man says is good."

"No," Grayson said. "Evil is the opposite of good. You can't tell the difference because you hate Arman, but if you followed him, you would know."

Voices outside the tent rose, and the women went out to see what was happening.

Rogedoth didn't move—acted like he didn't hear the noise at all. "You have quite a lot of strong opinions, don't you?"

"Yes, sir. And you should know something else. That other root child? Shanek? There are prophecies about the two of us. He's going to lose, and I'm going to help make that happen."

This made Rogedoth's eyes flash. "Others than Miss Onika make prophecies, boy. Just you remember that."

The man called Timmons entered. "My pardon, Your Highness."

Rogedoth spun around. "What is it?"

"Me, Your Highness."

A young woman strode inside. The few shadir still present flitted away from her, watching warily. Rogedoth's mantic women rushed in after the newcomer.

Lilou grabbed her arm but was thrown to the ground with a wave of the young woman's hand.

"Miss Amala," Rogedoth said, stepping away from Grayson.

This must be Queen Mielle's sister! Had she come to help?

Rogedoth frowned at the girl. "Did Shanek carry you here?"

"I came on my own," Amala said. "You broke your promise to me, Your Highness, and if you don't remedy the matter immediately, you'll forever regret it."

"What promise?"

"I've seen the disgusting tent you put my sister in. And she's bound by some horrible spell. It's disgraceful how quickly you have neglected the things Shanek and I asked of you. What else will you ignore, I wonder?"

Queen Mielle was here and alive? Grayson hoped he could rescue her.

"Miss Amala, this is war," Rogedoth said. "You should not be here wasting my time with your whining. Zenobia, get her out."

But the moment Lady Zenobia touched Amala, she too was thrown down. "You cannot defeat me, lady," Amala said. "My shadir is greater than yours."

"She has power, Your Highness," Zenobia said, rubbing her arm.

Rogedoth narrowed his eyes. "What shadir did you bond? Did Charlon give you root?"

"That's not your concern," Miss Amala said. "But if you don't immediately remedy my sister's accommodations, I will unleash upon you the full extent of my power."

Rogedoth lifted both hands, eyebrows raised. "That won't be necessary, my dear. If my servants have treated your sister poorly, you have my word it shall be remedied at once."

Amala stepped aside. "After you, Your Highness."

Rogedoth's nostrils flared, but he inclined his head and exited the tent. Amala, the mantic women, the shadir, and two gowzals all followed, leaving Grayson alone.

Grayson expected Rogedoth would return at some point and continue to harass him, but the first person to come back was Lady Zenobia.

"It's a shame you wouldn't obey your grandfather," she said. "A waste of great magic."

"A waste?" Grayson asked. "How?"

Sâr Shanek arrived then, standing in the open doorway. "Where is he?"

"We are here, Your Highness," Zenobia said. "He is under a spell. Shall I remove it?"

Shanek popped across the tent and stood over Grayson, glaring down. "No. This is better." He crouched and dragged Grayson to a sitting position.

"Where are you taking me?" Grayson asked.

"You angered the king," Zenobia said. "Since you will not help him, he will trade you to the Jiir-Yeke. They very much want the man who freed their captives. So you will go to them, and in exchange, they have agreed to join us in the coming battle."

Both facts filled Grayson with dread. "What will they do with me?" he asked.

"I imagine they will kill you in their temple sacrifice."

Before Grayson could object, Shanek carried him away.

Trevn

Trevn rode southeast with Chieftess Charlon and a group of three dozen Magosians toward his southern border house. The terrain was hilly, forested, and snow-covered, which slowed them immensely. He hoped to reach the fort before dark, reclaim it, and prepare Randmuir Khal for the enemy that would be coming from the west and north. Then he needed to go north himself.

The Magosians were joined by a flock of gowzals flying overhead. Occasionally one or two would perch upon Chieftess Charlon's shoulder or the rump of her horse and ride along.

Charlon had given Trevn furs to wear for the journey and a shard club as a weapon—something he had no idea how to use. Add to all this the fact that he'd lost his voicing magic, the soul-binding with Mielle was gone, and none of his guardsmen were with him, and the whole experience left Trevn feeling like he was living through a dream. He longed for anything familiar to anchor him and found that reciting from the Book of Arman gave both comfort and hope.

Trevn and Chieftess Charlon rode in the center of the group, yet no one spoke to them. He found it curious how little she communicated with her people. She gave commands when necessary but never made small talk. So when she spoke suddenly, it came as a surprise.

"I might," Charlon said.

"You might what?" he asked.

"Someone is speaking to my thoughts." She held up a finger, signaling for him to wait. "Tell me this message."

Hope rose within Trevn. Had the âleh worn off in Armanguard? Could this be someone trying to find him?

"What of Sir Kalenek?" Charlon asked.

That wasn't much of a clue. Charlon might have sent a shadir to spy on Sir Kalenek.

"That is very much like him. But Shanek will not like it." Charlon reined her horse and turned her attention to Trevn. "Your prophetess speaks to me, Your Highness."

Miss Onika. Was she here in the Veil now? "What does she say?"

"She wishes you to know that Queen Mielle and Master Grayson were being held in the camp of King Barthel. Though Grayson has been given to the Jiir-Yeke. Shanek carried him away moments ago. In exchange, the giants will fight alongside Rogedoth against you."

This was terrible! "Tell her we must do all we can to rescue Grayson. Has anyone else's mind-speak magic returned?"

"She said nothing about—" Charlon frowned. "Brelenah and Zeroah, she says."

Trevn hoped it would all return soon—to Oli, at least. They would need his help breaking whatever magic had been keeping Grayson prisoner. "What of Duke Canden? What goes on in Armanguard?"

"Your staff in Armanguard awaits Shanek's return," Charlon said. "Sir Kalenek hopes to convince Shanek that King Barthel is not to be trusted. That he should return to Magosia. Where he will be safe." Charlon frowned. "Shanek will not listen."

"Ask Miss Onika to go back to my wife and tell her I am well."

Charlon stared at her hands. "She promises to do so. And will continue to bring you updates. Until your magic returns."

"Thank you, Miss Onika," Trevn said.

Silence grew, and Trevn became aware that the Magosians had circled around them.

"She has left," Charlon said.

"Then we should continue on." Trevn spurred his horse forward.

Charlon continued alongside. "See? You just accepted my assistance. My assistance with *your* magic. Yet you disdain mine? Is not magic magic?"

"It's the shadir I want nothing to do with, Chieftess," Trevn said. "They are enemies of my god. They are also tricksters who seek to destroy all that is good."

Charlon seemed to think this over. "A mantic can use shadir magic for good."

"But there is still a cost," Trevn said. "You cannot control evil. The only way to stop it is to expose it for what it is. To stand against it. If you do not, the shadir will continue to use you."

"I am in control now," Charlon said. "I wasn't before. But the new magic is different."

"You think you are in control, Chieftess, but you still rely upon shadir. Needing them at all makes them your master, not the other way around."

"On that we will have to disagree," Charlon said.

That did not surprise Trevn in the least. They rode on. The ground leveled out, yet the forest thickened. Clouds filled the sky, so when the sun began to set, dusk fell swiftly. Bright lights appeared in the distance like twinkling stars. That had to be the border house, though it was difficult to see how far away it actually was. Chieftess Charlon sent her gowzals ahead to scout, and they returned shortly.

"My shadir tell me, once we pass this thicket, there is a vast clearing around the fort."

Trevn had designed it that way. "We will leave the horses here and go on foot," he said.

It felt good to get down and walk. The smell of torch smoke reached Trevn long before he caught sight of the distant palisade through a gap in the trees. Movement on his left halted his steps. He raised his hand to signal the others, but as the Magosians weren't his soldiers, they didn't understand. "Halt," he said, as loudly as he dared.

The man called Rone glanced back. His eyes fixed beyond Trevn and widened.

All around them, shadows emerged from the trees and seized upon the Magosians. Trevn reached for his shard club, but the cold point of a blade at the back of his neck stopped him.

"Identify yourselves," a woman said from behind him.

"I'm an Armanian," Trevn said. "I seek refuge in our border house."

"Then why leave your horses behind?"

Trevn knew that voice. It was too dark to see, so he asked another question. "Why are you out here? I wouldn't think Randmuir Khal's daughter would patrol like a common soldier."

"Who are you to make such assumptions about my identity?"

"I'm the one who asked Oli Agoros to break your father's compulsion," Trevn said.

"I'll be bludgeoned. King Trevn come to our rescue?" Snow crunched and branches snapped as Zahara Khal stepped around to Trevn's front. She looked harmless, shrouded as she was in a hooded black cape. Trevn knew better.

"How many are with the mantic who took the fort?" he asked.

Zahara was studying the Magosians with something like disgust. "Fifty or so compelled Puru. What are you doing with this group?"

"Shanek DanSâr carried me to Magosia, but some of them decided to help me."

"Lucky, that," Zahara said. "Can they help with their kinswoman?"

"I can," Charlon said.

"Is this all of you?" Trevn asked, wondering where the rest of the pirates were hiding.

"We've got three patrols," Zahara said. "Father and Meelo head up the other two. The mantic came yesterday. When Father wouldn't let her in, she blew open the gates with a wave of her hand. We lost so many that Father gave the order to flee out the back and make a perimeter in the woods. He figured if we couldn't keep her out of the fortress, we could at least keep others from joining her. Unless they're mantics too." She glared at Charlon.

It occurred to Trevn then that Charlon had killed Randmuir's mother. Keeping the two apart might be tricky. "If you'll lead the way, we'll follow," he said.

"Let's go, then." Zahara set off through the forest, and the Magosians followed.

Trevn grabbed Charlon's arm. "Try not to let them know your name," he said. "Randmuir Khal would enjoy killing the person responsible for his mother's death."

Charlon nodded gravely, then continued after the others. She whispered a word, and all but the gowzal perched on her shoulder transformed into a thick, white fog that hid their party as they left the cover of the forest and approached the border house. The magic unnerved Trevn.

"Mercy on me," Zahara said. "Father won't like that I've teamed up with mantics."

It was certainly a strange situation. Trevn gripped the shard club, ready to face whatever enemy came his way. Though he moved in the center of the pack, he was completely alone, a feeling he hadn't experienced in a long time. No Cadoc, no guards, no council, no Mielle.

The smack of a shard club. A man grunted. The front of the line had reached the gate. Being in the center kept Trevn five paces behind the action. He stepped over three dead Puru at the gate, then two more just inside it. The smell of fresh blood pulled his mind to another time, and dark memories from the Battle of Armanguard flashed in his mind's eye.

"Enough fog," Trevn yelled. "They know we're here, so let's see them."

The fog dissipated, and Trevn's hope sank to the pit of his stomach as he took in the number of Puru surrounding them, holding swords. Trevn's shard club suddenly felt inadequate.

The Puru screamed and charged. Trevn watched Rone use the weapon and mimicked his actions. He crouched, waited as the Puru closed in, aimed for one who was running toward Charlon, and . . . now!

He swung the club from side guard, keeping it even with the ground. The obsidian shards sliced through the man's leather armor and into the flesh of his stomach. He doubled over, which made it impossible for Trevn to pull free his club. He kicked the man to the ground, and the moment the Puru dropped his sword, Trevn scooped up the familiar weapon. He instantly felt more at ease and forged on, cutting down compelled Puru one after another.

A woman's scream pulled his attention to the cabin keep. Green light shot out from cracks between logs, and the western wall exploded. Trevn threw himself to the ground and covered his head with his arms as splintered wood rained around him. When the noise died down, he glanced up. In the wreckage, two women faced one another. Chieftess Charlon and another Magosian—Roya, he guessed. Charlon held a glowing green orb in each hand.

"You dare turn my people against me?" Charlon yelled. "Magosia wants no part in King Barthel's war against Armania. I made that clear when he tried to force me into a treaty."

"Those who aid me do so without my urging," Roya said.

Trevn crept toward the cabin. A Puru rushed around from the back. Trevn engaged him with the sword and lost track of the Chieftess's conversation.

The compelled Puru fell quickly against the Magosians, the pirates, and one Armanian king. Trevn soon found himself with no enemy to fight. He turned in a circle, scanning the courtyard for pale faces, but all lay in the snow, dead or dying. Shame fell heavily at the fate of so many innocents, turned into tools by his enemy.

"Shanek is a child!" Charlon yelled from the rubble. "He's not ready to rule anything."

"He's a powerful mantic," Roya said. "He has taken Dominion over Dendron the Great."

"Shanek would never give Dominion to a shadir. *Sabab bay êsh!*" Two gowzals perched on the broken wall shot toward Roya, morphing into balls of fire as they flew.

"*Mahgayn!*" Roya thrust out her hand, and the fire ricocheted off an invisible barrier. Charlon dove out of sight as one fireball struck the wall and the second hit the floor, sending great cracks as the fire broke through the wood.

"*Râbab teren* Charlon," came a small voice from the remains of the fort. And suddenly there were three of the Magosian Chieftess, rising up from the destruction.

"As usual, you do not listen," Roya said. "Shanek has Dominion. Not the other way around. The creatures are loyal to him. They are his *keliys.* They have no choice but to obey."

"*Puroh!*" the Charlons yelled.

A bolt of fire sizzled out from the hands of all three Charlons. Roya leapt aside and yelled something indiscernible that caused shards of wood to shoot up from the depths of the debris and toward Charlon. The Chieftess screamed, and the two illusions vanished.

The fight went on. Charlon continued to shoot fire at Roya, who in turn used her magic to pick up logs and debris and throw it at Charlon. A section of wall struck the Chieftess just as one of her firebolts seared through Roya's chest. Both women screamed and fell.

The pirates cheered and hooted. Was it over? Trevn scrambled into the rubble of the southern border house. "Give aid!" he yelled. "We must see to the Chieftess." He found Roya's dead body and pieces of gowzals, as if they'd been blown apart, but couldn't find Charlon.

"She's here!" a man yelled.

Trevn moved toward the voice, but before he could reach them, a familiar voice said, "Tell me that is not who I think it is."

Trevn winced as he came to face Randmuir Khal. "She is under my protection."

Randmuir's face twisted. "This is my roost, royal."

"You are here at my command," Trevn said. "Chieftess Charlon rescued me, and I will not see her harmed."

"Don't watch, then. She killed my mother, and I owe her for that."

"I know you two have a past," Trevn said. "And if you wish to seek your revenge once this war is over, I won't stand in your way. But it will not happen today. Not here."

The Magosian men lay the Chieftess on a plank of wood not far from where Trevn stood with Randmuir. The pirate leader stalked away, and Trevn approached Charlon.

"Is she alive?" he asked the men.

"What of Roya?" Charlon croaked.

Trevn knelt at Charlon's side and met her dark eyes. "She's dead," he said.

Charlon smiled and closed her eyes. "I thank you, Your Highness."

"No, Chieftess Charlon. I thank you." He stood and spoke to the nearest onlooker, a pirate. "Gather some wood and build a fire. And you," he said to a Magosian man, "come with me to see if any part of the fortress is still standing. We must find shelter. The night is going to be a cold one."

The men were quick to obey. Barracks were discovered along the eastern palisade wall, untouched by the magical duel.

"Build some pitfires in the barracks," Trevn said. "We will sleep there tonight."

The men set to work, and Trevn went looking for Randmuir Khal. He needed to make peace—make sure the man understood. They all must put aside personal wars if they were to have a chance of winning the larger one still looming.

KALENEK

Kal took in the scene from his place at the end of the high table in the great hall. Shanek had appeared on the dais moments ago, just to the right of Lord Idez's chair—Mielle's regular seat. The king's throne sat empty. Behind Shanek, dozens of soldiers dressed in red pushed past the curtain. Shanek must have carried them to the antechamber before appearing on the dais.

Kal counted six burly serving men, who were Armanian soldiers in disguise. Not enough.

"Has Oli Agoros returned to the castle?" Shanek asked Lord Idez.

"Not that I am aware of, sir," the earl replied.

"Did you send my message?" Shanek glared down like an angry parent.

Kal stood, eager to make himself known before the boy did something foolish. "Shanek, I'm glad you are here."

The boy's dark eyes shifted, lit up when recognition set in. "Father."

Kal pulled out the chair on his left. "Come sit. Tell me what you've been doing lately."

Shanek took two steps, then his eyes hardened and he drew up his posture, shoulders back, chest out. Regal. "I am not here to visit, Father. Did not this man tell you I came before?" He gestured to Lord Idez.

Shanek's vast improvement in language and bearing puzzled Kal. "The earl mentioned you're looking for Oli Agoros."

"He was supposed to be here by now," Shanek said, glaring at the earl.

"I'm sure he'll be along soon," Kal said.

"Did you or did you not send someone to fetch him?" Shanek asked Lord Idez.

"I saw no need," the earl said. "I did not expect him to be gone this long."

"You lie!" Shanek circled the back of Lord Idez's chair. "I am not a fool."

Lord Idez kept his gaze fixed on Shanek as long as he could, then quickly turned in his seat to catch sight of him on his other side. "I must say this is highly improper, young man," he said. "It is bad manners to barge into a castle and make demands. If you would sit and eat and wait patiently, I'm sure the duke will come."

Shanek sneered down on Lord Idez. "You dare lecture your king? You have not taken me seriously, so you have none but yourself to blame for the consequences."

"No need to get angry, Shan." Kal pulled out the king's throne. "Sit and eat. I'll find the Duke of Canden myself."

"It's too late for that, Father." Shanek extended his hand, and green light flamed up from his palm.

"Shanek, no," Kal said.

But the boy tossed the flame like one might a pebble, and it engulfed Lord Idez in fire. The earl screamed, stood, and stumbled back, knocking over Mielle's throne. Kal whipped off his cloak and wrapped it around the man, smothering most of the flames. A servant doused them both with a pitcher of cool water, and Kal helped the earl lie on the floor. By the time he drew back the charred cloak, what remained of Lord Idez was unrecognizable. At least he hadn't suffered long.

Kal shoved to his feet and rounded on Shanek. "Why did you do that? Lord Idez was a good man who meant you no harm."

"He lied to me." Shanek said this in a bored tone, as if his reasoning was perfectly fair.

"You can't go around killing people who don't do what you want, Shanek," Kal said. "Besides, Oli Agoros was Lord Idez's superior. The earl could not summon him at will. What you did was very wrong."

"Perhaps you don't remember why I'm here, Father. I am King of Armania now. A king makes the laws of his land and therefore is never wrong. So I will do what I want. Anyone who does not obey me"—he gestured to the body of Lord Idez—"will suffer the consequences."

What had Rogedoth done to the boy Kal had raised? "You would kill any who disobey you? Is that the kind of man you wish to be?"

"I am no ordinary man. I am king of all Armania. There is none more powerful than me."

"Who told you this, Shan? Was it Barthel Rogedoth?"

"I don't answer to you! If you want to live, bring me the Duke of Canden. Now."

Kal sighed deeply. "I don't know where he is, and it's growing late."

"Find him or you shall end up like this one." Shanek stepped over Lord Idez's body and sat down on the king's throne. "You have until morning, Father. You there!" He pointed to one of the soldiers dressed as a servant. "Bring me some food. I'm hungry."

Kal ran along the dais to the steps and down to the floor of the great hall. He would not find Oli Agoros because Shanek would kill the man or carry him away, but he could look like he was trying, which should buy them all a little more time. He hoped Onika found Grayson and brought him here before any more were killed.

Oꞁika

Onika found Grayson lying on his back on a table inside a hut in the Jiir-Yeke village. Two giants were there, sorting ceramic bowls and wooden utensils. Her first instinct had been to storm their souls to the Veil, but that would only alert the other giants that someone sought to rescue Grayson. Until Onika could free him, there was no point setting the giants on guard.

Rogedoth's people had fed Grayson âleh, just as they had Queen Mielle, but since his very nature enabled him to see into the Veil, Onika could speak to him, and he could answer aloud.

"What happened, Grayson?" she asked.

"Rogedoth realized I wasn't going to join him and had Shanek carry me here. Lady Zenobia said he traded me to the giants so they'd help him with the war. Did Shanek go back to the castle?"

"Namgum!" one of the giants said to Grayson. Both glared at him, likely wondering who he was talking to.

"Yes," Onika said, hoping to hurry her conversation before the giants got too angry. *"Sir Kalenek is trying to stall him, but he's growing impatient."*

"Shanek is the Deceiver," Grayson said. "He has a huge swarm of shadir. And he thinks Master Rogedoth is going to put him on the throne, but it's a lie. He's using Shanek to help him. Shanek is being led astray by friends, just like in the prophecy."

One of the giants shook Grayson's shoulder. *"Khuu, namgum!"*

Miss Onika took a deep breath. *"There is no time to waste. I must go for help. Stay strong, Grayson. Trust in Arman. I will come back as soon as I can."*

As Onika returned to the mind-speak classroom, she begged Arman to spare Grayson—felt near certain he would. Grayson was the Deliverer, after all. He must fight the Deceiver. He couldn't die in a barbaric sacrifice. He simply couldn't.

The Duke of Canden was still working at the table. Of those in Armanguard, all mind-speak magic had returned except for the duke and Kempe. The others were out looking for the rest of Tace Edekk's army. He had divided his men and giants into thirds. Danek had found a group of ninety in the foothills of the Uul-Yeke mountains. Hrettah had spotted a second group moving parallel along the southern side of the road from Armanguard to Sarikar, but there was still one group unaccounted for. Hinckdan Faluk had been warned, and was doing his best to prepare his army to fight.

Onika didn't want to waste time going back into her body to update Duke Canden. *"Sir Cadoc,"* she voiced. *"Will you speak to the duke for me?"*

"Certainly," the man said.

Onika relayed all she had learned regarding Grayson, Rogedoth's deal with the Jiir-Yeke, and Shanek.

"Can your Veil warriors look for Jiir-Yeke troops as well as Edekk's?" Oli asked after Sir Cadoc had passed on the message.

"I could divide them," Onika said through Cadoc, wondering if Brelenah would prefer to work with Hrettah or have the girl go with Danek.

"Warn Princess Saria to be on her guard," Oli said. "And keep watch over Master Grayson."

She might be able to do all those things had she more than five Veil warriors at present. Onika sent Brelenah and Hrettah to Sarikar in search of Jiir-Yeke warriors and bade Zeroah and Danek to keep looking for Edekk's army. Then she spoke with Princess Saria and returned to Rogedoth's camp to check on Queen Mielle, who was still under several spells but had been moved to a bigger tent. She now lay on a pallet covered in thick furs.

Onika then went to Grayson. She found him in the same place, though this time he was alone. She told him all she'd been doing, and asked how he fared.

"They didn't give me the black drink I saw them give Sosovik's sister," Grayson said. "Likely because Lady Zenobia put a spell on me to keep me from moving."

"I'm glad about that," Onika said. *"It might have been a permanent—"*

The giants returned with two others, the latter bigger and scarier than the first pair. The newcomers each took one of Grayson's arms and dragged him off the table.

"They're taking me in!" Grayson yelled.

"Duke Canden?" Onika voiced, hoping that this time he might answer. Nothing.

Onika watched in dismay as the giants dragged Grayson out of the hut and across the walkway that led to the temple. She called repeatedly to the duke and prayed Arman would let him hear her. Inside, hundreds of giants filled the rows of steps leading down to the altar. The giants paused at the top of the stairs and waited while a man below chanted in a foreign tongue.

"Miss Onika?"

The duke's voice. Onika nearly wept with relief. *"Your Grace! I hear you!"*

"I thought I heard someone calling my name from the hallway, but no one was—"

"You must come at once, Your Grace. They have taken Grayson into the temple."

"Call your Veil warriors to join us there," the duke said. *"And pray that Sir Kalenek can stall Shanek DanSâr."*

Onika broke her connection with Duke Canden, then called out to her warriors. *"All who are able, travel through the Veil to Grayson at once. We need your help to rescue him."*

By the time her Veil warriors had arrived, Grayson had been taken to the shallow pool on the altar and laid next to a giant's shrouded body. Duke Canden was kneeling inside the pool, at Grayson's side. Both Kempe and Hrettah were here now too.

Onika hovered over Grayson. *"Duke Canden is here,"* she said.

"I see him," Grayson said. "Tell him to hurry."

The giant shrouded in a black-feathered robe and headdress circled the altar. He carried a bone stick with bead tassels on the end. Two giants approached Grayson, knives in hand.

"Danek, storm the dark-haired one," Onika said. *"I'll take the other. The rest of you, pray."*

Onika flew at the giant, focused on his mind, and pushed his soul from his body. As it soared away, crying out for help, his body crumpled.

The crowd exclaimed. Moments later Danek's giant collapsed as well. Several giants leaped out of the stands and ran to assist the guards. The crowd began to stir.

Onika flashed to Duke Canden's side. *"How are you doing, Your Grace?"*

"Grayson has shown me the memory," he said, *"but it takes time."*

Zeroah appeared beside them. *"Do not fear, Grayson, for Arman is with you."*

An older giant barked orders at some guards, who approached the altar tentatively. Danek and Onika stormed them one by one. The crowd began to flee toward the exits.

The black-clad priest approached the side of the altar, opposite where Duke Canden knelt. He shook his bone stick, making the beads rattle. *"Avakh beleg tsusny!"* he yelled. He drew a dagger, reached for the guard Danek had felled, and sliced the blade over the man's wrist.

Onika recoiled. The man shook his stick again. A bird swooped down from the ceiling and circled over the altar. Surprisingly not a gowzal, but a raven.

It suddenly grew very cold. A shadow shimmered in the Veil. A thick darkness that exuded fear. Onika somehow knew it was an incarnation of evil from the Lowerworld—an evil she had never seen before. The shadow slithered into the priest, whose demeanor changed to something more sinister than that of an old man. He stood and circled the altar, his steps suddenly more sure than they had been before. Onika wanted to storm him, but the sinister shadow held her back.

"I've done it!" Duke Canden yelled.

Onika turned her attention to Grayson in time to see him pop away. *Praise you, Arman!*

The possessed priest yelled, *"Saikhan amraarai!"* and struck Duke Canden in the back of the head with his staff.

To Onika's shock, the duke disappeared.

"Your Grace!" she yelled.

The priest cackled, the sound seeming to come from the darkness within him.

"Back to the castle," Onika told her Veil warriors. They must not stay here another moment.

She focused on Grayson and appeared in the bedchamber he shared with Jhorn and Danno. He lay on his bed. Jhorn sat on the edge, Zeroah and Danek hovering behind him. Duke Canden was not here.

"The duke did not return?" Onika asked the queen.

Zeroah glided toward Onika. *"I have not seen him."*

"He left when the priest struck him with his staff," Onika said. *"I had hoped he had come back with Grayson."*

Zeroah's eyes widened. *"You don't think . . . Could he have gotten lost?"*

"I'll go look for him," Onika said. *"Perhaps he is simply in the mind-speak classroom."*

"Let me go," Zeroah said. *"Grayson needs you."*

Onika nodded. *"Be careful, Your Highness."*

"You as well." Rosârah Zeroah vanished.

"How do you feel, Grayson?" Onika asked.

"Tired," he said. "And I still can't voice anyone. But thank you for saving me."

"Thank Arman," Onika said. *"Do you feel well enough to jump with me to Barthel Rogedoth's camp and carry home Rosârah Mielle?"*

His eyelids drooped, but he said, "Sure. I can do that."

"Whenever you are ready," Onika said.

The boy popped away, and Onika followed, thankful they had saved Grayson and praying that the Duke of Canden was not lost forever.

TREVN

Trevn sat before a fire in one of the barracks at what remained of the southern border house. Most of the men were sleeping, but his thoughts were overcome. Tomorrow, if Onika's messages through Charlon had been right, they would face Rogedoth once and for all. Trevn wished he was in his office with Cadoc, Oli, and Hawley, where he could—

"Trevn, Trevn, Trevn, Trevn . . ." A child, saying his name over and over.

Trevn's heart leapt. Had the âleh finally worn off? *"I hear you. Who is this?"*

"Oh! Oh, Trevn, it's Rashah. Are you well?"

"Yes, actually. I'm at the southern border house with Randmuir Khal."

"I'm so glad! Yesterday, the Duke of Canden bade me try to voice you until I succeeded. So even though I have gone to bed, I kept at it. I must tell Enetta at once."

"Rashah?" But his sister had left him. Trevn instantly reached for Mielle but felt nothing. Not surprising, really. He tried Oli next, but when the duke did not answer, panic niggled at his heart. Had something happened to his First Arm? *"Miss Onika?"*

"Your Highness?"

Relieved to hear her voice, Trevn relaxed. *"Where are you? What is happening?"*

"We rescued Grayson from the Jiir-Yeke temple. And we have just returned from freeing Queen Mielle. She is well, though she cannot speak or move."

Joy rose within Trevn, but concern quickly overruled it. *"Can Duke Canden help her?"*

"We lost him, Your Highness," Onika said, then went on to tell the story of

how they had rescued Grayson and the duke had been struck by the priest. *"Rosârah Zeroah is searching the Veil, but it does not look good."*

Oli lost? That explained why he hadn't answered. *Arman, help Zeroah find him.* Knowing that Mielle was safe should be enough, but Trevn didn't like leaving her vulnerable. *"See if Lady Eudora is able to help Mielle,"* he said.

"Are you certain you trust her?" Onika asked.

No, Trevn wasn't. *"Oli does, and that's enough for me at present. Have Grayson carry her to my wife and bid her do what she can. What of Armanguard?"*

Onika told him how Shanek had returned to the great hall, killed Lord Idez, and claimed rule of Armania. *"He demands to speak with the Duke of Canden and gave Sir Kalenek until morning to find him."*

Grief for Lord Idez and his family pressed upon Trevn, but he brought up a new subject to make the most of this time. *"One of Chieftess Charlon's maidens said Shanek has Dominion over shadir. She used the ancient word keliy."*

"I do not know that word, but Dominion usually involves ownership of a human body."

"The word keliy means vessel or instrument—sometimes weapon. And she said Shanek has control over shadir, not the other way around. I wonder if Grayson has the ability too."

"Grayson knows better than to make bargains with shadir."

"Yes, but might this be something he could use to defeat them?"

Miss Onika did not answer for the length of several breaths. *"I will ponder that further, Your Highness."* She went on to update him about Hirth Wallington's confession and Tace Edekk's army closing in on the Sarikarian border house.

Trevn gave his own report to Miss Onika with instructions to pass the information to Captain Veralla, then repeated his request that she send Grayson for Lady Eudora. *"And keep me informed about Oli as well,"* he said.

"Yes, Your Highness. I will send Kempe to assist you in the morning. It would be good for you to have a set of eyes in the Veil while you are fighting."

"Thank you, Miss Onika." Trevn closed his mind to the prophetess, relieved that his magic had returned. He prayed that Zeroah and Eudora would both have success, but his mind was too worried to concentrate. He distracted himself by checking in on Hinck.

"Trevn, thank Arman!"

"The âleh wore off only moments ago," Trevn said. *"You got my message, I saw. And now you're preparing to face Edekk's army?"*

"They're coming in three groups, but they should all arrive fairly close, some-time tomorrow. Those Veil warriors also found a troop of Jiir-Yeke headed toward Castle Sarikar, just as Princess Nolia said." He explained how he and Saria had blackmailed the princess into divulging this information.

"Tomorrow is the day for battle, it looks like," Trevn said. *"How many men do you have?"*

"Seven hundred and twelve here. Another six hundred at Castle Sarikar. But hear this. When I first learned of the Jiir-Yeke, I voiced Ulagan for help. Turns out he brought more men than promised, but he took them to your central border house. Apparently he misunderstood me."

"Oh dear," Trevn said. *"Perhaps Onika and her warriors can storm the Jiir-Yeke?"*

"I forgot about that," Hinck said. *"I haven't had as much practice as the others, but I understand the concept well enough to give it a try."*

"Don't risk yourself unnecessarily, Hinck." Trevn told him how Oli was currently lost in the Veil.

"And I thought being stabbed was bad," Hinck said.

"How did you survive, anyway?" Trevn asked.

"The knife went in at an angle. Sliced into me well and good. Chipped my sternum, so says the physician. I was lucky."

"You're hard to kill," Trevn said. *"Are you certain Nolia will truly help us? There's no way to be certain she hasn't voiced Rogedoth."*

"Attempting to kill a co-regent of New Sarikar is punishable by death. Princess Nolia must truly love Finnel Wallington, because she's willing to do what she must to save his neck."

"How romantic," Trevn said.

Hinck chuckled. *"Saria didn't think so. She wanted to kill them both. She's quite intimidating when she is angry."*

"Can you blame her? The man dared try to kill her betrothed!"

"Where are you, anyway?"

"At the southern border house. I ride for the central one first thing in the morning." He told Hinck how Charlon had helped him escape, then helped take back the fort.

"Do you think that's wise, letting a mantic help you?"

"I didn't know what else to do, in all honesty. But it didn't feel wrong to let her stop her own mantic. We had no way to fight the woman."

"I suppose. But Charlon Sonber—she tried to kill Wilek!"

"I know it. And she did kill Randmuir's mother. The man is itching to have his revenge. The whole idea of working with her grated on me, but it's over now. Tomorrow morning I'll leave her behind."

"What will she say about that, I wonder?" Hinck asked.

Trevn didn't know.

Trevn left before dawn to avoid any awkwardness with Chieftess Charlon. He took with him as many of Rand's men as he could, leaving behind just enough to hold the fort. They reached the central border house before morning bells, and though Trevn had voiced Sir Keshton Veralla to let him know they'd be coming and knew all was well, he still felt relieved to see the structure safe with no sign of enemy soldiers.

Zanre Veralla and a troop of Kinsman soldiers were waiting at the edge of the clearing to escort them to the gate. Madam Kempe was there too, unbeknownst to the soldiers. She had arrived in the Veil while Trevn had been riding. Trevn thanked her for coming and sent her to check Rogedoth's location. Then he surveyed the lay of the land.

The fort had been built at the southern end of a gap between two woods, which someone had named Mishor Field. The gap looked to be about three furlongs wide and was the most convenient place for a large army to pass through when heading toward Lake Arman. A river ran out of the northern forest and into the southern one, where it bordered the western wall of the fort. The river made a nice boundary that, since it was so cold, would hopefully keep Rogedoth's army from crossing easily. Armanian soldiers peppered the snowy field, most of them dragging logs between them. Trevn could hear the chops of dozens of axes in the trees.

Madam Kempe returned and told Trevn that Rogedoth's army was packing up camp. She didn't know how many soldiers he had, but she hadn't seen any giants with him. She thought he might be two or three hours away.

This was the day. After all this time, today Trevn would fight his greatest enemy. Win or lose, it would be decided here.

Zanre led Trevn toward the border house. As this had been the first built, it was bigger and more complete than the southern one had been. A double log palisade enclosed a vast area that would allow for expansion and crossed over a creek on one end, so water could be gathered from within the safety of the walls. The keep was a three-story log structure with crude cutout windows covered with plank shutters. Stone and mortar fireplaces ran up all four sides and puffed smoke out into the sky. There were barracks here as well, though these too were more impressive, lining up like soldiers at attention along both sides of the keep. They passed through the palisade gate and stopped outside the fort. There, Sir Keshton met them.

"How fare you, Your Highness?" Sir Keshton asked as Trevn climbed down from his horse. "I hardly recognize you in that getup."

Trevn tore his gaze from the architecture and met Sir Keshton's amused expression. "I am perfectly well, considering," he said. "I require a private room and some breakfast." He needed to do some voicing to check on Mielle and to see if Grayson was well enough to carry Trevn's guardsmen here. He didn't want to fight without them.

"I've prepared a place for you, sir."

Sir Keshton led Trevn into the fort and down a short, cramped hallway with a low ceiling. A half dozen doorways shot off the hall. Sir Keshton opened a door on the left and nodded into a large room that held six tables.

"If your men are hungry, they can take turns eating here," he said. "My office is across the hall." He pushed through a door on the right and walked around to the back of a table covered in maps that instantly drew Trevn's interest. "I have a chamber prepared for you upstairs, Your Highness, but you can set up in here for meetings. I'll move myself elsewhere."

"Thank you," Trevn said. "Give me a report."

"Rogedoth was camped two hours west of here last night." Sir Keshton tapped a place on the map spread across his desk. "I've received word that their army is tearing down their camp already. They could be heading out any time."

Trevn had learned that much from Kempe. "How many men do they have?"

"Somewhere close to fifteen hundred," Sir Keshton said.

That was more than Trevn had expected. "Any giants?"

"None at present."

"And how many do we have?"

"My garrison has one hundred fifteen. With Lord Blackpool's army and the hundreds of volunteers from Armania—farmers and tradesmen, mostly—and Ulagan's giants, we number just under two thousand. Ulagan brought seventy giants under the command of one Moul Rog."

And left poor Saria defenseless. "Where has Marshal Winstone camped our men?"

"In a valley but ten minutes to the east of here. General Ensley is due to arrive today."

"Where does he plan to make his stand, do you know?"

"Right out on the field," Keshton said. "He likes the way the forests force the enemy to cross where we can keep an eye on them. My men have been felling trees for the past two days to make stakes and arrows. Plus they've been leaving some trees where they fell, uncut to make it difficult for anyone to sneak through the forest and come up behind us."

Trevn nodded. "Excellent work, Sir Keshton. Your preparation will undoubtedly make a huge difference. It seems we are well positioned to win this battle."

"But for the mantics," Sir Keshton said.

"Yes, well, we have our own magic now," Trevn said, thankful his mindspeak ability had been restored. "I think our Veil warriors will present a fair challenge for the Great Pretender."

CHARLON

King Trevn thought he had slipped away. Away without Charlon knowing. But she had been awake. Readying her people to depart. Before Randmuir Khal caused problems.

The king's warnings about shadir irritated her. For too long she had been trapped. Trapped by her own magic. Had used it to master her fear. But she was no longer afraid. The time had come to stop hiding within. She must choose. Choose what kind of a person she would be. What kind of Chieftess. Fear had not fostered loyalty. Nor had manipulation. Or magic. She could not control anyone. Anyone except herself.

Charlon disliked the woman who had used Sir Kalenck. Who had made him a victim. She did not want to be that kind of person. She wanted to use her magic for good. Not evil.

She should go home. But she was tired of hiding. Tired of worrying about the future.

Fight, her heart said. *Fight.*

Rogedoth had taken her son. Ruined what little good Sir Kalenek had fostered in the boy. Charlon could not allow him to prevail. What magic he had left, combined with Shanek's powers, would crush King Trevn. Charlon felt no allegiance to the narrow-minded Armanian king. But her desire to thwart Barthel Rogedoth drove her north. Toward the battle.

İΠΟLΔH

I *wish you would tell me what this meeting is about, Ulrik,"* Inolah voiced.
She and her eldest were sitting alone in the council chambers. He had
summoned her from breakfast to say he required her presence in a meeting
with his wife. Jazlyn and her eunuch had arrived together and now sat across
the table from Inolah and Ulrik.

"You think I don't listen to you, Mother, but you are wrong," Ulrik replied.
*"It's time I stopped toying with Jazlyn's mind. I know she wants to go, so I plan
to draft an agreement that will leave us happily parted forever. You and Qoatch
will act as witnesses."*

"That's a fine idea." Surprising to see maturity in her son after so much
of the opposite.

"Thank you for coming," Ulrik said to Jazlyn and Qoatch. "The purpose of
this meeting is to find a way for the two of us to part ways amicably."

"The answer is simple," Jazlyn said. "Stay out of my head."

"It's not as easy as that, and you know it," Ulrik said. "I would never have
gone into your head if you hadn't tried to kill me and my brother."

"I did no such thing!"

Ulrik laughed dryly. "You forget, my dearest, that I've been inside your
mind. You can hide nothing from me. Go ahead and tell my mother how you
ordered your eunuch to kill us, then ran off to visit Chieftess Charlon in—"

"This torment is unacceptable!" Qoatch said. "If the emperor is going to
treat my Great Lady with such disrespect, we will not take part in this negotiation."

"Ulrik has promised to behave," Inolah said, raising an eyebrow at her son.

"My apologies." Ulrik leaned back in his chair and folded his arms. Oh, yes. He looked very cooperative.

"I apologize as well." A tear rolled down Jazlyn's cheek. Inolah had never seen her look so fragile.

Qoatch handed Jazlyn a handkerchief. "Release her mind or we will leave, Your Eminence."

"I don't know what you mean," Ulrik said.

"This negotiation was your idea," Qoatch said. "What do you want from Empress Jazlyn?"

"To stop plotting against me," Ulrik said.

"I stopped plotting against you long ago," Jazlyn said.

"Lies!" Ulrik yelled. "Again you forget that I know your mind."

"Ulrik," Inolah said.

"You have been meeting regularly with the Tennish remnant for quite some time now," Ulrik said. "You promised them a New Tenma. And over half of your remnant set sail already."

"How do you know that?" Jazlyn asked.

"I won't stop you. In fact, I want you to leave and never come back," Ulrik said. "You want the same, so don't pretend otherwise."

"I do not deny it," Jazlyn said.

"Good," Ulrik said. "Resolving personal matters between us is only part of my goal here today. There is another matter to discuss that is far more urgent."

Inolah stiffened at this announcement. What could be more urgent?

"Go on," Qoatch said.

"You parted ways with King Barthel," Ulrik said.

"He and I did not agree on many things," Jazlyn said.

"No one agrees with you on many things," Ulrik muttered, "but that is beside the point."

Inolah gave her son another withering glare.

"What *is* your point?" Jazlyn asked.

"For months you harbored that villain here, made treaties with him, and pretended to be his dearest friend. Now he has gone to attack Armania and has sent the Jiir-Yeke to attack Sarikar."

"I don't see what that has to do with me," Jazlyn said.

"You helped him!" Ulrik said. "You let him hide here while he gathered his strength and made powerful allies with the giant tribes."

"So?" Jazlyn said.

"So, you owe it to us all to fix the trouble you caused. As I said, the Jiir-Yeke giants are marching on New Sarikar. You will use your magic to stop them."

Inolah stared at her son. "*Ulrik...*"

Jazlyn's shock came out in a breathy laugh. "I have no war with the Jiir-Yeke."

"You want your own nation again," Ulrik said, "but if Barthel Rogedoth takes control of the Father Realms, know that he will not stop there. He will come after all who wronged him, especially those who stole his harvest of new evenroot."

At this Jazlyn shot to her feet, her face a mask of rage. "You are spying on me? How?"

Ulrik's soft laughter broke the silence.

"Why are you laughing?" Jazlyn asked.

"I cannot believe I ever thought you a clever woman. This very day I gloated over knowing your mind, yet you do not seem to comprehend what that means. My magic allows me to know you fully, my dear. It allows me to *be* you, should I wish it. But... 'if you will defeat the Jiir-Yeke at New Sarikar, I will promise to stay out of your head."

"Your promises mean nothing," Jazlyn said.

"I know I can be trying, I do," Ulrik said, "but on this I swear to agree."

"That alone and I can go?" Jazlyn asked.

"No," Ulrik said. "If I'm to remove my compulsions and stay out of your mind, you must not only defeat the Jiir-Yeke, you must give me my children and swear to leave us in peace."

"The children are mine," Jazlyn snapped. "They will be raised in New Tenma."

Ulrik leaned forward. "I will not negotiate on the children."

"Nor will I," Jazlyn said.

"My love," Ulrik said, gazing longingly at Jazlyn. "I beg you be reasonable."

Again tears filled Jazlyn's eyes. "You're right." She nodded, dabbing her eyes with Qoatch's handkerchief. "Children need their father."

"He is manipulating my Great Lady," Qoatch said. "We will sign no contract if he continues in this manner."

"Ulrik, you promised," Inolah said, though she felt like things were already out of hand.

"What if," Qoatch suggested, "you each raise a child?"

Jazlyn glared at him. "Give up one of my children?"

"Out of the question," Ulrik said.

"I too would hate to see them separated," Inolah said.

"They are already separate," Qoatch said. "They each have their own nurse, and as they grow older, they will learn different things, based on their gender. My guess is that you would readily agree as to which child you each prefer."

"My son," Ulrik said at the same moment Jazlyn said, "Jahleeah."

Eventually they drafted a contract that both were willing to sign. Emperor Ulrik would keep Prince Jael, whom he called Adir, and Jazlyn would take Princess Jahleeah to New Tenma. The details of visitations would be worked out later. Ulrik would remove his compulsions only when the Jiir-Yeke had been defeated, Prince Adir was placed into his arms, and Jazlyn had left the area.

When Qoatch finally escorted Jazlyn to the door to leave, Ulrik called after her.

"If you betray me in any way, I will come after you with the full force of my magic. The slightest breach in this contract will be treated as an act of war. And I promise you, if I enter your head for such a reason, you will never know yourself again."

Jazlyn drew in a deep breath, but before she could reply, her eyes softened and her bottom lip trembled. "I would never betray you, Ulrik. You are my heart. To hurt you would be to hurt myself and our children. I promise you, that I will never do."

Qoatch glared at Ulrik and steered Jazlyn out the door. Ulrik's laughter chased them out.

"Well, Mother? How did you like that?" Ulrik asked. "I not only got rid of my wife, I employed her one last time to fight the giants."

"I am glad the two of you have made an agreement," Inolah said. "But, Ulrik, did you consult Princess Saria about this?"

"Why would I? She will know when I voice her the good news."

Oh, her son. Sometimes he was the most colossal fool. "My concern is that Sarikar is a pious realm. Their abhorrence of magic was the cause of the Great Parting and the very reason the mother realms came to exist in the first place."

"You think she will refuse Jazlyn's help? Mother, that's madness. Jazlyn is unstoppable. Without her aid, Sarikar will be decimated. That will put Saria in my debt, and now that I've gotten rid of my wife, I'll need a new one. And I can't marry just anyone."

"Nor can you marry Princess Saria, Ulrik. She is betrothed to Hinckdan Faluk."

Ulrik snorted. "She won't marry a duke when she could marry an emperor. And, like I said, New Sarikar will be in my debt. When their council receives my offer of marriage, they won't be able to turn it down."

GRAYSON

Grayson jolted awake. Queen Mielle was bent over him, touching his arm. "I'm sorry to wake you so early, but we need your assistance."

Grayson pushed himself up, gaping at the queen. "You're all right?" After he'd carried Lady Eudora up from the dungeon last night, he'd fallen asleep watching the woman try to help the queen.

"Yes, Lady Eudora was able to break the spells. She and her brother have become quite adept at the skill. I'm so glad to see you well, Grayson."

"Me too," he said. "I mean, I'm glad to see you."

She smiled, which made Grayson feel like a hero. "I know it's early, but Shanek DanSâr is going to return this morning, and there's much to do before you must face him."

Grayson swallowed, his throat dry. "I'm ready, Your Highness, but . . . Duke Canden?"

"Still missing in the Veil, I'm afraid."

Grayson glanced at the Duke's body, lying on a longchair not far from his. "Because he came for me?"

"According to Miss Onika, it was because a Jiir-Yeke priest possessed of a dark spirit struck him. Do not fret. I'm sure Rosârah Zeroah will find him soon. In the meantime, Trevn needs you to go to him at once. He has several tasks for you."

Grayson nodded and focused on King Trevn. He flew through the Veil to arrive in a small office beside a desk where the king sat alone, poring over maps.

He moved into the physical realm. "Good day, Your Highness."

The king jumped. "Ah, Master Grayson, good dawning. I'm relieved to see you alive and well. You are well, aren't you?"

551

"I think so, sir."

"Good, good. We have a hard day before us. Are you prepared?"

"I don't know, sir."

The king sighed. "It's daunting, I know. But if Arman is with us, who can stand against us?"

Grayson shrugged. "I guess so."

"Don't guess, Grayson. Believe it." The king stood and sat on the edge of the desk. "Now, I need you to carry Lady Eudora to Hinck, where she will be tasked with removing the compulsions placed upon the giants in Tace Edekk's army."

"Can she do that?" Grayson asked.

"She did well enough for my wife, and I have offered her a pardon, should she succeed. I hope that might increase her effort." He grinned. "I also need you to carry my King's Guards here along with my armor and sword and my personal copy of the Book of Arman. It's in a leather satchel in my chambers. Hawley will know where."

Why would the king need a book? "Is there something written that will help us?"

"Most certainly. And I want to carry the book into battle. Arman will take care of our enemies. He will triumph this day."

Grayson wished he had the king's confidence. "I can do that, sir."

"Excellent. And there's one more thing. Shanek DanSâr has killed Lord Idez and has demanded to see Oli Agoros at morning bells. Might you be able to lure Shanek out of the castle? I saw Chieftess Charlon throw green fire, like the kind you make. Have you ever tried to throw it?"

Grayson nodded. He'd played with it out over the lake before. "You want me to throw fire at Shanek?"

"To make him angry, yes. Then lead him on a chase. You might have to stall every so often and let him insult you or attempt an attack, just so that he thinks he is getting close. It will be your job to keep him busy—outside the castle, if you can—and away from the main battle at all costs." He winced. "I am sorry to put so much on you at once. Are you up to all these tasks?"

"Always, Your Highness." Though today, it was scary.

"It is like a dance, what you do," Lady Eudora said after Grayson carried her through the Veil to the New Sarikarian border house. As he led her into the newly constructed fort, she took hold of his arm, which both embarrassed him and made him feel like a hero.

Everything inside was freshly sanded wood. Nothing had been painted. The office door had only a fabric drape nailed over the entrance. It shifted aside, and several men exited, including Hinckdan Faluk. Since Grayson and Lady Eudora were blocking their path, the men slowed to a stop, taking them in. The duke seemed particularly surprised to see Lady Eudora, though Grayson knew King Trevn had spoken to his mind about this already.

The duke bowed his head. "Lady Eudora, welcome."

Those sparkling eyes fixed upon Hinckdan. "It's good to see you again, Your Grace."

"You must start right away, lady," he said. "I've prepared a place for you in my office."

"Are you certain that is proper?"

"This fort is our command center and will have people coming in and out constantly. The office will give you some privacy." He inclined his head to Grayson. "Thank you, Master Grayson, for bringing the lady." And the duke turned on his heel and beckoned for Lady Eudora to follow him inside.

"Well, he's all business today, isn't he?" the lady whispered to Grayson, eyebrows raised.

"We *are* at war, lady," Grayson said.

He then left and carried the King's Guards to the central border house along with the king's armor, weapons, and his Book of Arman. After that, Grayson returned to Armanguard and found Sir Kalenek and Lady Islah waiting in the mind-speak classroom. Shanek had not yet arrived, but his guards still held the great hall. Sir Kalenek told Grayson to go there and hide in the Veil. He and Grandmother would come in to have breakfast and to meet with Shanek. Grayson must remain hidden until Sir Kalenek told Shanek that Duke Canden was gone. Once Shanek lost patience, that would be Grayson's cue to come out of hiding and lead him away.

Grayson was ready, but he wasn't at all certain Shanek would follow.

The morning bells rang, and Grayson was still hiding in the Veil, watching people eat. His stomach growled. He'd been too busy to get himself any breakfast.

A few minutes later, Shanek appeared on the dais and sat in King Trevn's throne. His soldiers all jumped to attention. Since Shanek could see into the

Veil, Grayson popped into position where he might be better hidden, behind the soldiers disguised as servants who were clustered in the front corner of the hall, holding various trays and pitchers. He slipped his hand into the physical realm long enough to steal a slice of bacon from a servant's tray.

The double doors at the opposite end opened, and Sir Kalenek and Lady Islah entered. Though their hands were empty, they walked side by side, purposeful and confident—like warriors come to battle.

Shanek stood from King Trevn's chair. "What is *she* doing here?" he asked.

"Do you know me, Shanek?" Islah asked. "Because we have never met."

"I know who you are," he said.

"I have come to meet my great-grandson. And to speak with Dendron."

"We don't want to talk to you." Shanek looked away from Islah, turned his glare on Sir Kalenek. "Father, I have been more than patient. Where is the Duke of Canden?"

"I'm afraid he was struck down in battle," Sir Kalenek said.

Shanek narrowed his eyes. "What battle? Where?"

"Attempting to rescue Grayson, son of Jhorn, from a Jiir-Yeke temple sacrifice," Sir Kalenek said.

Shanek snarled. "The duke could not have traveled so far in such a short period of time."

"He traveled though the Veil," Sir Kalenek said. "And now he is lost."

Shanek lifted his hand between them. "I am finished with your lies, Father." Green light sparked between his fingers. "You leave me no choice."

That looked like Grayson's cue. He stepped into the physical realm and pushed through the crowd, taking another slice of bacon off the servant's tray. "I'll take you to his body."

Shanek's head turned as he located Grayson. "You! It's true, then? The Duke of Canden rescued you?"

Grayson stepped forward slowly, chewing his bacon and trying to look braver than he felt. "He did. But he was lost to the Veil. If you want to see his body, I can take you to it." He popped to the double doors.

"Where did he go?" Shanek yelled.

"I'm here!" Grayson yelled, watching him from down the aisle.

The moment Shanek vanished, Grayson popped to the foot of the spiral staircase in the foyer. He waited until Shanek appeared in the doorway of the great hall. "This way!"

Shanek thrust out his hands. Green fire sizzled from his palms like bolts of lightning. Grayson dropped to his stomach to avoid being hit, then popped into the Veil by the ceiling. The firebolts struck the front entrance, catching fire to the double doors.

"You missed!" Grayson yelled.

Shanek spotted him and let fly two more streams of green fire. Grayson popped behind him and felt a coldness in Shanek, similar to what had been inside the Jiir-Yeke priest.

Grayson watched the flames blacken the white stone ceiling and decided he'd better take Shanek out of the castle before he burned it down. "Well, that made a mess."

Shanek spun around, a sword of green fire arcing out. Grayson popped away, but not before the blade nicked him and fire blazed up his arm. He cried out and appeared in the bailey beside the sentry wall.

"Grayson?" Onika called. *"What is happening?"*

Shanek appeared, and Grayson fled through stone wall of the garrison house. Light vanished as he zipped through the tiny space, until another green flame lit the room. He fled through the outer wall, then popped to the distant practice field, which was empty today.

"The green fire burned my arm," Grayson voiced. *"But he's still chasing me."*

Bit by bit Grayson lured Shanek toward the field. Anything to keep the Deceiver distracted and away from the battle.

HINCK

Hinck and two dozen Sarikarian bowmen climbed to the parapet of the border house. The structure had only been built two levels high, and the parapet was still unfinished timber at this point, but even that much height afforded them a better view of the approaching enemy.

The bowmen spread out along the sentry walk of fresh, roughhewn planks. Hinck took position in the center, where he hoped all would be able to hear his orders. A look through his grow lens showed no sign of attackers.

"How close are the giants now, lady?" he voiced Eudora.

"They are just about to enter the clearing."

"And the compulsions? Have you broken any?"

"I have tried," she said, *"but I don't understand the giant's tongue."*

"Voice Master Grayson," Hinck said. *"If he shares your mind as you enter the giant, he will be able to translate."*

"I'll ask him," she said.

Movement directly east caught Hinck's eye. The bright red capes were unmistakable, but a more careful look through his grow lens revealed black uniforms emblazoned with House Edekk's snake and goblet sigil. This must be the group coming along the road south.

"Enemy due east," Hinck yelled. "Wait until they're in range."

The men grew silent as the enemy approached. Because of the unfinished palisade, the army had hammered hundreds of stakes into the ground, creating a fence of sharp points to skewer enemy cavalry. General Norcott had positioned the infantry behind the stakes, outside the partially built fort. Most carried swords, but the general had stationed pikemen in the front, as he believed the weapon more effective against cavalry and giants.

Among the advancing enemy, Hinck spied some brown uniforms in with the red and took another peek through his grow lens. Giants. Hinck shuddered. He hated to kill the giants, knowing they were compelled and might retaliate in a separate war, but he would not let his infantry fight them if he could help it.

"Master Grayson is dealing with Shanek DanSâr," Eudora voiced. *"He cannot help me."*

"Continue to try your best, lady," Hinck said, frustrated. Then to the archers, "Draw, but wait for my word." He raised his bow and set an arrow.

All across the parapet bows went up.

"Miss Onika," he voiced. *"We need Veil warriors to storm the giants. Can you help us?"*

"We will come at once, Your Grace."

"Ready your aim. Draw . . ." Hinck's stomach fluttered, but he otherwise felt quite healthy. It wasn't until he drew back that his chest wound twinged.

He watched the approaching riders—fixed the line of his arrow upon one near the front. His gaze flicked to the trees behind the riders. The wind was blowing softly to the south. He compensated for it, paused. "Fire!"

Hinck loosed his arrow, which flew with a volley of others through the air toward the riders. Shields were raised, though some not fast enough. Hinck's target fell. As arrows rained upon the enemy, four fell from their horses, two horses reared, and some riders left the line. The vast majority held course.

"Draw at will!" Hinck yelled, setting another arrow. He again struck down one of Edekk's men, and in this manner, he shot in a steady stream. The enemy neared the infantry line, and too many giants still rode in the charge. "Take out the giants!" If they reached his infantry, the men would be slaughtered.

Arrows flew again. Several giants did fall, but it was too late to stop them all. The first giants trampled the southern end of the stake fence and rode over the Sarikarian infantry line like grass.

"Fire! Fire! Aim for the giants," Hinck yelled, drawing as fast as he could. He missed as much as he hit, but he had no time to dwell on it.

Mercifully, giants began to fall from their horses as they were hit or stormed. In the end they felled all of the giants and over half of Edekk's cavalry. With the giants out of the way, the infantry bounced back and quickly defeated the remainder of Edekk's men. A few enemy soldiers rode for the trees, and Hinck and his bowmen managed to pick them off.

Then it was over. The bowmen cheered and embraced each other, jostling the unfinished parapet. Hinck scanned the snow for green-clad bodies, trying to guess the number of Sarikarian casualties. He voiced General Norcott. *"Have some of the infantry gather our arrows, if they can. We have enough for one more attack, but not two."*

"It will be done," the general said.

"How many lost?" Hinck asked.

"Too early to tell. It could have been much worse, though."

Agreed. Hinck voiced Trevn and explained Lady Eudora's language barrier.

"I speak a little Yeke," Trevn said. *"Perhaps I can find the memory of the spell."*

"Your Grace," Miss Onika voiced. *"A second group is coming from the north. Shall we storm those giants too?"*

Hinck looked north through his grow lens but saw no sign. *"Wait for my signal. King Trevn is trying to help Lady Eudora."*

"You're bleeding, Your Grace," the man beside him said.

Hinck glanced at a patch of blood in the center of his chest, then pulled out the neckline of his tunic. A little oozing, perhaps, but his stitches were still intact. "I am well," he said.

A cry at the end of the parapet drew his attention. He pushed through the men until he reached a group who were pointing to the northeast.

The second wave shot out of the tree line. Hinck hoped Trevn would hurry, because if they ran out of arrows and those giants reached the infantry line, the border house would fall.

⊙ L I

Oli's head spun. Whatever had hit him, it had done some damage. He was drifting through a thick, cold fog. It wasn't dark, exactly, nor was it light. A voice called his name. Then another. Then several all at once.

"Oli, Oli."

Men, women, and children. Friendly.

"There you are!"

"We've been waiting for you."

"Come with us."

But Oli could not see them through the fog. "I'm lost," he said. "I must get back to Armanguard."

"We can help you."

"Follow us."

"This way!"

Anxiety thrummed through Oli. Something about this place bothered him. Why wouldn't the people stop so he could catch up?

Shadows moved in the distance. Oli glided toward them, but they drifted away.

"Slow down," he said. "Wait for me."

But they did not. "You must hurry," one said. "We can help you."

Oli tried to hurry, but the nearer he came to the people, the faster they went. On and on they sailed, through the muted haze, which grew ever darker. Oli wearied of the chase. He was tired of begging them to wait. The voices grew more demanding—sometimes critical and angry.

"He's too slow."

"I'm not surprised."

"He whines."

"Because he's weak."

"Disappointing."

"Failure."

Enough of this! Oli stopped, overwhelmed by their rudeness and that his own efforts continued to fail so miserably. He would follow them no more.

He realized with a shock that he was now in utter blackness. Dread coiled in his stomach. How had he not noticed the loss of light?

Someone whispered behind him.

He turned his head. "Hello?"

Multiple whispers rose on all sides, but he saw no one.

"Who's there?"

A shrill giggle. Hands on his back shoved.

"Hey!" Oli spun around, searched for the source of that laughter, but saw no one.

A slap on his arm.

"Stop that!"

A hand grabbed his leg and pulled. Someone cackled like a madman.

Oli swung at his leg but struck only himself. "Let go this instant!"

The hand squeezed tighter. Again someone pushed his back and giggled, high-pitched, like a woman. A fist punched his arm. Suddenly hands were all over him, grabbing and shoving and punching and pulling.

Oli struggled against them, but even with two arms, every effort failed. "Leave me be! Get off! Stop it!"

Teeth dug into his arm. Hair tore from his scalp. The laughter grew lighter, jovial. They enjoyed tormenting him. What *was* this place?

The violence increased. The attackers multiplied. Terror bubbled up in his throat and cut off his air. Oli had no defense. He could never touch them, but he could feel their hands and feet and teeth. He curled in upon himself and tried to be small. If he stopped screaming and fighting, perhaps they would leave.

They did not. It was as if they sensed his fear and despair—fed off it. He wanted them to be shadir but knew they were humans like him, others who had been trapped in this dark place. If he stayed, he would become like them, preying on the fear and pain of newcomers.

The hopelessness of his circumstances made him scream. This only fueled his enemy. Oli tried not to feel or hear them. He found comfort in the form of a memory. Words spoken in another time and place. A promise of peace.

He said the words aloud: "He will cover you and protect you in the shelter of his wings."

Someone screamed.

"There is no one to protect you here!"

"No one, no one!"

"You are forgotten."

"It's what you deserve."

"Arman!" Oli cried.

His assailants reeled at the name of the One God. Some went away, but others increased the passion of their attacks.

"He's not real."

"A lie. Lie, lie, lie!"

"You're wrong!" Oli said. "I have seen the miracles of the One God, Arman. Known his people. Heard prophecies from the mouth of his prophet."

Like shadir banished to the Lowerworld, the people screeched and fled. They didn't want to hear about Arman, so Oli continued to speak about his goodness until he was alone.

"Oli?"

"Go away!" he cried. "Or Arman will deal with you."

"Oli Agoros?"

He was about to yell again, but something in this new voice gave him pause. It was different from the others. Softer. Kind.

"Oli?"

There it was again. A woman. Oli knew her. Didn't he? Or was this another trick?

"Your Grace?"

Zeroah Barta. Oli strained to see her. "Rosârah?" he called out, desperate to see her face. "I . . . I am lost."

"Concentrate on Castle Armanguard, Your Grace," she said.

Oli tried to picture it, but the darkness was too overwhelming. "I cannot."

"Are you moving?"

He thought about it. "Drifting, yes. It's cold here. I cannot see." Oli blinked multiple times, hoping to help his eyes acclimate to the darkness, but he could see nothing.

"Force yourself to wake."

"How? I can't seem to—someone touched me! Was that you? Did you touch me?"

"I did not. Try to hold still, Your Grace. Fight the movement. I will come to you."

"I don't want you to get hurt." If the people tried to harm Zeroah, Oli would fight for her. But how, if he could not touch them? Hopelessness threatened to choke him.

"Your Grace? Oli Agoros, answer me!"

So close, she sounded. Behind him. Oli whirled around. A light bloomed in the distance. Beautiful and warm. He tried to move toward it and found he could not. He reached for it instead, desperate to grab hold. To touch that golden glow.

The light grew larger and took form. It was Rosârah Zeroah. She soared toward him, glowing like a goddess, her eyes two gems of topaz.

She stopped before him and took his hand in hers. They were so warm it burned, but he clutched them tightly and let the heat flood him until he shivered all over.

"This is not Shamayim," he said, terrified to stay here a moment longer.

"No," she said. "Let us leave this place."

He nodded, speechless.

"You cannot know how very worried I was," she said.

"Whatever for?" Oli asked.

"Because you are my friend, Oli Agoros."

Such a thing seemed impossible, especially here, yet Oli clung to those words, thankful for them. Thankful to Arman for sending her. Thankful to Arman for his goodness.

For some time, Zeroah pulled Oli along by the hand through the murky void. While he felt uneasy, her presence was like a shield that kept him safe from the menacing darkness.

"I do not like it here," she said. "Let me try something."

"What?"

"Give me a moment, please."

Oli waited, impatient to leave, but completely at the mercy of this glorious, warm woman whose knowledge of Arman made her safe and strong.

She began mumbling to herself, and Oli strained to hear her words. She was praying. Praying for help.

They suddenly appeared in another place, this one gloriously warm and smelling of grapes and roses.

"Oh my." Zeroah's eyes sparkled in the light and she smiled so wide that her teeth showed. "Do you feel the pull?"

Oli did not. Not like he had in the darkness. In fact, he felt like he was trespassing. "I hear music."

"Yes, isn't that lovely?"

Realization struck him like a blow to the chest. "*This* is Shamayim, isn't it?"

"Only the gate."

"Why don't I feel the pull you speak of?"

"That is between you and Arman."

"Because of my past? That is why he rejects me?"

"Arman rejects no one. It is we who reject him."

"I bonded with shadir. I'm detestable to him. That is why the shadir are not afraid of me, like they are of all of you."

"I suppose that's a logical conclusion," Zeroah said. "But Arman is not always logical by our standards. He loves us even when we don't deserve it. He pardons the unpardonable. Haven't you been listening as Father Mathal reads from the book?"

"I have, but . . ." He felt ashamed to say what he must. "I gave my soul to Gâzar long ago. There is no hope for me."

"Ahh," she said. "So that is the lie that has so trapped you. Your Grace, Gâzar has no power that does not come from Arman."

Oli had heard Zeroah say such things before, but he hadn't believed it possible for him. "Tell me the way out."

"Ask the God, Your Grace. That is between you and him."

Oli didn't know. He had always been certain there was no hope for him. His father has always said as much. But maybe he had been wrong. Father had never been a man of integrity that Oli should give credit to his word. And even the shadir obeyed Arman above their own masters. Arman answered the prayers of his faithful—had healed Hinckdan. And Oli had been to the Lowerworld. It was not a place he wanted to visit again.

"How will I know if he accepts me?"

"He will. And you will know."

Oli fixed his eyes on the golden gates. "But how?"

"You must trust him."

Oli didn't trust anyone. Except maybe Rosârah Zeroah. She certainly believed in Arman. Trusted Arman. If she could, after everything she had been through, perhaps he could too.

TREVN

revn watched through the connection Cousin Eudora had made with one of the giants riding toward the Sarikarian border house. In the memory, the giant was in Zuzaan, sitting around a fire, laughing with friends. "*Too far back,*" he told Eudora. "*See if you can find the first day he met with any Kinsman people.*"

"*It's not like I can ask him to show me when it happened,*" Eudora said.

"*I can.*" Trevn recalled the Yeke word for the label *dirtman*, which was what the giants called the Kinsman people. "*Bagir-ji,*" he voiced to the giant. "*Bagir-ji bodoh.*" Remember.

A new scene rolled through the giant's memory. He and dozens more of his kind stood in a field, all staring at Agmado Harton. "*This is it!*" Trevn strained to hear Harton, who was speaking fluently in the Yeke tongue. "*How can he have learned the language so well?*"

"*He's a mantic,*" Eudora said. "*Not a good one, but his cunning makes up for his poor talent. I can break the compulsion now, Your Highness.*"

"*Then I will leave you to it.*" Trevn drew back to his body and opened his eyes. Cadoc paced by the foot of his cot, Nietz behind him. "Report," he said.

Cadoc jumped to attention. "Rogedoth's army approaches. General Ensley has arrived with Marshal Winstone and the army. They've assembled fifty paces back from the eastern riverbank. The general hopes Rogedoth's army will cross the river to reach us."

Which would be terribly unpleasant in this cold. Trevn sat up and swung his feet to the floor. "Call Ottee to fetch my armor. I must dress for battle."

564

Cadoc nodded to Nietz, who slipped out the door.

Trevn voiced Hinck for an update, then Saria. While Hinck had already fought through one attack, no giants had been spotted in New Sarikar as of yet, though Saria was livid about the arrival of Empress Jazlyn and a handful of her Tennish Protectors.

"Ulrik sent her to fight the giants," Saria said. *"My council doesn't want her here. Nor do I. But when I told her she's not to use magic here, she said it's not my decision to make!"*

"Ulrik was likely trying to help," Trevn said.

"I didn't ask for his help! And if that woman uses magic in front of my soldiers, they'll be as spellbound as the Rurekan soldiers, despite our laws. How am I to stand against such theatrics? Why would Arman allow this?"

"I cannot speak for Arman." Nor did Trevn have time to start a fight with Ulrik. *"Stay close to Father Wolbair and trust his counsel. I must go now."*

Trevn then checked in with Randmuir Khal, who reported no sight of any attackers approaching the southern border house. One less battle Trevn had to worry about, perhaps.

"Mielle? How fares Castle Armanguard?" he voiced.

"Grayson led Shanek DanSâr outside, and Kal and Captain Veralla are working with the garrison to capture the enemy soldiers Shanek carried into the fortress," she said.

"That is excellent news. Where are you?"

"In the mind-speak classroom with Master Jhorn and—oh! Trevn, Duke Canden is sitting up. And Zeroah too!"

Trevn's heart leapt. *"Tell him to voice—"*

"Oli Agoros," came a knock in Trevn's head.

"We thought you lost forever!" Trevn said.

"Yes, well, I still would be if Arman had not sent Rosârah Zeroah through the gates of the Lowerworld to bring me back."

The horror of such a thing knotted Trevn's thoughts.

"The queen says my sister needs assistance?" Oli said.

"Yes, she's trying to break compulsions placed upon the giants fighting alongside Edekk's men. Miss Onika and her Veil warriors had to storm some, but I would rather free their minds if possible."

"I will go at once."

"Your Grace," Trevn said. *"I'm pleased you are safe."*

"As am I, Your Highness. May the God be with you."

Indeed. Trevn opened his eyes and found Ottee removing his armor from its trunk.

"Are you ready, Your Highness?" the boy asked.

Trevn stood and stretched his arms. "Yes, Ottee. Let's get me out with the men." It was going to be a long day. A day, he prayed, that would end in victory.

Trevn and his King's Guards rode out the palisade gate and onto the snowy plain. To the east of the river, hundreds of soldiers were slowly forming into ranks. The day was bright and cool, the sun hidden behind a hazy sky. Wet snow packed hard under the horses' hooves.

Trevn checked in with Sir Keshton, whose scouts put Rogedoth's army less than an hour out. Madam Kempe's report from the Veil matched this. Trevn and his men rode along the line, greeting the soldiers and thanking them for their service, one of which was the bannerman who was carrying his Book of Arman in a pack on his back.

Trevn admired Armania's blue uniforms and banners, the latter of which had been remade to depict his new insignia—a circle of flying Nesher birds. That is what Armania would soon be: free.

Sharpened stakes had been driven into the ground along their side of the river, but Trevn couldn't imagine an army charging through that deep water. Recent snowfall and warmer temperatures had left the water swelling up the banks.

They reached the forest on the northern end of Mishor Field. Timber cracked as a huge barktree fell, whipping past evergreens, breaking their branches, and dropping out of sight. Silence reigned for a moment, and Trevn heard the distant chops of other axes. The general wanted more trees downed in the forest to stop the enemy sneaking through. The archers had pounded their own stakes into the ground around them, making a protective barrier to hinder mounted attacks against them.

Trumpets caught Trevn's attention, and he and his men rode back to the center of the field, where General Ensley had positioned himself.

"Our enemy comes," the general said, nodding across the river.

Already? Trevn turned his horse and could barely see movement in the distance. *"Madam Kempe?"* he voiced. *"What do you see?"*

"The front lines are mostly compelled Puru. Kinsman soldiers are positioned toward the rear. And there is a new section of mounted giants. Then a single line

of mounted riders, perhaps fifty, with Rogedoth at the center with his mantics. The back line is archers—again, mostly Puru. I think there are about three hundred of them. There are quite a few of the rat birds flying above them. The creatures seem drawn to Master Rogedoth. I've never seen anything like it."

Trevn had. Somehow Rogedoth had learned Charlon's magic.

GRAYSON

Grayson held a ball of green fire in his hand. He concentrated on Shanek and popped into the Veil, exiting on the roof of Castle Armanguard. He stayed very still, holding the fire ready and looking for Shanek. He didn't see him anywhere.

A spear of green fire shot past his arm, scorching his tunic. Grayson yelped and spun around, but Shanek vanished before he could throw his own fire. Grayson moved high into the sky where he could look down on the whole roof.

There. Shanek appeared on the roof of the stairwell house, surrounded by shadir.

Grayson jumped behind him and threw his fire. Shanek howled and cradled his arm. Grayson popped back to his place in the sky before Shanek could strike back. His heart raced at the idea of killing anyone. But this was war. And Grayson had to protect Armanguard from evil.

Shanek no longer stood on the roof of the stairwell house. His shadir were gone too. All those shadir explained how he was finding Grayson so quickly. He had many eyes to help him.

Well, Grayson could get help too.

"Onika?" he voiced. *"Shanek has so many shadir looking for me that it's hard to sneak up on him. Could you come and banish some? It might scare the others away."*

"Yes, at once," Onika said.

Grayson formed another ball of green fire, then shifted through the Veil to Shanek, trying to move slowly in an effort to see him before he was close enough to be hit.

He came upon Shanek at the lakeshore to the south of the castle. He was kneeling with his arm in the water, crying. Shadir clouded the Veil around him, a lot of them talking at once.

"But it hurts," Shanek said. "Don't say that! I'm not a baby . . ."

A pudgy gray shadir fixed its three eyes on Grayson. *Master! Your enemy watches.*

Shanek looked up and met Grayson's gaze. Grayson pitched his fireball, but before it could make contact, Shanek vanished.

Grayson popped to the sky above the lakeshore, terrified he might get struck from behind. He stayed in the Veil, hovering over the water, but there was no sign of Shanek or his flock of shadir.

Again Grayson concentrated on Shanek's presence, and he reappeared a few paces to his right. Panic leapt up his throat moments before green fire shot past his head, singeing his hair. His ear throbbed, and he popped back to the sky above the castle roof, heart racing.

"We are here, Grayson. Where are you?" Onika asked.

Grayson spotted Onika, Danek, Zeroah, Brelenah, and Hrettah floating in the Veil on the castle roof. *"Above you,"* he said. *"I'm going to pop to Shanek now."*

"We will follow," Onika said.

Grayson passed through the Veil slowly, spotted Shanek kneeling at the lakeshore again, arm submerged in the water. He must be hurt too. Shadir twirled and sailed around him, crowing at each other, reveling, it seemed, in Shanek's pain.

Grayson stopped a distance from the shore and watched the Veil warriors fly into the swarm and call upon Arman's name for the power to banish shadir.

Grayson threw another ball of fire at Shanek, who had been so distracted by the panicked shadir that he didn't see the coming fire, which sliced across the back of his shoulders. He screamed and dove into the lake, vanishing beneath the glassy water.

"I got one!" Sârah Hrettah yelled.

The Veil warriors had banished more than that. While many shadir had fled, Grayson quickly counted eight, no, nine shadir sinking into the lake.

He watched the area warily. Shadir still swarmed the sky, which meant Shanek was here. Didn't it? Unless Grayson had killed him? His heart pounded. He formed another ball of fire on his hand and glided slowly toward the lakeshore, waiting for Shanek to come up for air.

But Shanek didn't come.

GOZAN

Amala rode a horse alongside Lady Mattenelle at the end of the row of mounted mantics. When King Barthel had seen what she was capable of, he had begged her to join the battle. The girl had been flattered. Gozan knew the man only meant to use her, but he wanted to test the extent of his magic inside this body, and a battle would be an ideal environment.

Shanek appeared suddenly, standing in front of Amala's horse. "I'm hurt," he said. "Find someone to heal me."

"Shanek!" Amala dismounted and rushed to the young man, who collapsed on his knees in the trampled snow. His shirt was singed in two places. His left forearm and the top of his back and shoulders had been badly burned, and the raw flesh oozed.

Gozan could feel Dendron's fury within, pulsing frustration that had no release. The army continued on, edging around the couple, but for Mattenelle and Lilou, who had peeled away from the procession with Amala.

"You heard him!" Amala cried. "One of you heal him this instant!"

Neither moved.

"Why are you just sitting there?" Amala cried.

"King Barthel forbade his mantics to use magic for anything other than his decrees until this battle is over," Lady Mattenelle said.

"And I'm only a malleant," Lady Lilou said.

"Shanek is to be your king," Amala snapped. "Would you really forsake him?"

The women merely stared.

Gozan hoped the boy would die—then Dendron would lose his host and

570

Gozan would be the most powerful great alive. But to appease Amala, he pretended to help, in a way that would only waste time. *Send Lady Lilou for Lady Zenobia. She knows Shanek's value to the king.*

"Lady Lilou," Amala said, rising. "Fetch Lady Zenobia at once. She won't let the king's great-grandson die. He's the only family he has left. His only heir."

Lady Lilou shook her head. "Go yourself if you must, but I won't disobey my king."

Lady Mattenelle, however . . . She raised her hand and said, "*Râphâ zōt geveeyah.*"

Shanek fell back on the snowy ground and writhed. Frost grew over his skin and clothing, coating everything in soft white crystals that were brighter than the muddy, trampled snow around him. The army had completely passed by now and was marching farther away toward the river.

Amala ached with hope as she gazed upon the young man. What a fool the girl was. Love. This boy was too vain to love. Once he became king, he would not keep Amala for long. Then Gozan would be forced to wallow in the girl's despair when she was cast aside for another. Now that Gozan was part human, he disliked the feel of despair.

Before the spell had time to complete itself, Lady Mattenelle collapsed against the neck of her horse, mumbling a prayer of purging to a shadir called Hwuum.

Shanek's healing hadn't had time to finish, but no more raw skin was visible beneath the jagged scars on his arm and upper back. He would live.

Lady Mattenelle, however, did not improve. She panted in hitches of air, her face wrinkled and gray, her eyes sunken. The evenroot was taking her, and it seemed the shadir Hwuum did not care. Had it left? Or had it refused her? Gozan wished he could see into the Veil, but Amala's human eyes limited him.

Amala helped Shanek sit. "What's wrong with her?" he asked of Lady Mattenelle.

"She broke King Barthel's decree, so her shadir will not heal her," Lady Lilou said. "The only evenroot that remains, the mantics have consumed and held in reserve. King Barthel was very clear that there were to be no exceptions. His shadir know this as well."

"The king would have made an exception if he'd known Shanek was hurt," Amala said.

"One of the slights went to him and asked," Lady Lilou said. "I obeyed my king. Lady Mattenelle did not."

Shanek looked fondly upon Lady Mattenelle, whose breath had ceased coming from her shriveled lips. Dead. The woman's shadir had left her for dead. At King Barthel's command. Shanek's brow wrinkled as he pushed to his feet. "King Barthel said to let me die?"

"He said only that his original decree be obeyed."

"That's the same thing!" Shanek yelled. A pulse of green light flashed in Lady Lilou's eyes, and she fell off her horse. Dead.

Amala's heart pounded. "Shanek, your mother was right. King Barthel means to use you to make himself king."

The young man seethed, angry enough to do something completely reckless. Dendron, no doubt, was encouraging that very thing.

Gozan attempted some manipulating of his own. *He should go after King Barthel.*

"King Barthel has but four mantics left," Amala said, coming to stand beside Shanek. "If you kill them, he will have no power at all. Then you can rule Armanguard unchallenged."

"I can't kill them. Not yet," Shanek said. "Grayson the root child is still in Armanguard. He burned me twice. If he hurts me again, I will need another mantic to heal me."

"Then defeat Grayson first," Amala said. "When he is dead, you can finish off King Barthel and his mantics. I will stay and watch King Barthel's progress. Speak to my mind if you wish to know what is happening."

Shanek nodded. "I will return soon." He embraced Amala, and while Gozan hid deep within her, he sensed Dendron's aggravation.

Yes, they had both made poor choices in Dominion. Young, reckless hosts who were too foolish to harness any real power. Gozan might have to leave Amala, yet he had no better options at present, and he still wanted to test his magic.

Shanek vanished, leaving Amala alone with the two corpses. She mounted her horse and rode toward the army, intent on staying close to King Barthel.

Oʜɪᴋᴀ

Onika and her Veil warriors banished shadir at the lake until all the others had fled. She found Grayson sitting in the snow on the riverbank, a dazed look on his face.

"Why didn't you chase Shanek, Grayson?" she said. "Are you hurt?"

"My ear," he said. "I was waiting for Shanek to come out of the water when I felt it hurting again. I guess I forgot. Do you think Shanek is dead?"

"No," Onika said. "His body would have floated to the surface of the lake. Though he might have gone elsewhere and died. You'll have to find him to know for sure."

Grayson scooped a handful of snow and pressed it against his ear.

"Miss Onika?" King Trevn's voice. *"Is it possible for your Veil warriors to storm Rogedoth and his mantics?"*

Onika thought about it. *"I can think of no reason why not, though they'll be surrounded by shadir, who might see us and give warning that we are near."*

"Can the shadir attack you?"

"No, but a mantic perhaps could. We have not ventured near any mantics yet. Grayson and Shanek can harm each other in the Veil, so it stands to reason that we could be injured too."

"Inquire of Arman on this matter," the king said. *"Storming Rogedoth and his minions seems the quickest way to end this war. If the God is not opposed, attempt it at once."*

"I'll let you know what the God says."

✦　✦　✦

Onika bade Danek and Zeroah stay with Grayson, then led Brelenah, Hrettah, and Kempe to the sky above King Barthel's location. She could see both armies from this vantage point, spread out below, one wearing red, the other blue.

"The God's answer was somewhat vague," Onika told the others.

"What did he say?" Brelenah asked.

Onika repeated the words. "'THE ENEMY MUST BE DEFEATED. BEWARE OF THOSE WHO WORSHIP GÂZAR. THEY ARE NOT OF MY KINGDOM.'"

"So not a no, but not a definite yes either," Kempe said.

"King Trevn wants us to try," Onika said. "So we will try."

"How many mantics are there?" Brelenah asked.

"Six, I believe," Onika said. "Three women and three men. Lady Zenobia, Lady Mattenelle, and Lady Lilou. Then Master Harton, the false prophet, and the priest."

"Yohthehreth and Lau," Brelenah said.

"The Duke of Armanguard said Lady Lilou was only a malleant," Kempe said.

"That's right," Onika said. "Only five mantics, then. Unless Lilou has learned the art. Let us attempt to storm Lady Mattenelle first. I believe she is less powerful than Lady Zenobia."

"I hate to attack Lady Mattenelle," Brelenah said. "She has always been a sweet girl. It wasn't her fault she was given to Sâr Janek."

"Perhaps not," Onika said, "but she serves our enemy now, and that is all that matters. Exit in the sky above her, if you can. Otherwise we might be seen."

Onika concentrated on Lady Mattenelle and appeared above a muddied field. She saw the army in the distance, moving away from this place. A quick glance beneath her revealed two bodies, lying in the snow.

"It's Mattenelle and Lilou," Brelenah said. "Is Rogedoth killing his mantics?"

"There is no way to know what happened," Onika said. "Let us storm Zithel Lau. He is likely the next weakest."

This time they arrived above King Barthel's army. Hundreds of men marched below, accompanied in the Veil by a vast number of shadir.

"Is it safe to attack this close to the other mantics?" Brelenah asked. "While we are storming one, the others might attack."

"We will each storm a mantic," Onika said. "If we act together, we might destroy them all at once and allow no opportunity for a counterattack."

Onika made assignments. She would attack Lady Zenobia. Brelenah would attack Filkin Yohthehreth; Kempe, Master Harton; and Hrettah would storm Zithel Lau.

The women were silent as they took a moment to locate their targets. Onika was not overly concerned. They'd done well earlier today, storming the giants attacking the Sarikarian border house. She had complete confidence in each of her Veil warriors.

"After you attack," Onika said, "return immediately to your body in Castle Armanguard. On three. One . . . two . . ."

Green fire shot toward them from below.

A woman screamed.

". . . three!" Onika fixed her mind upon the soul inside Lady Zenobia and flew toward it, concerned by the fire she had seen and what might have happened to whomever had screamed. Before she could reach her target, a gowzal on Barthel Rogedoth's shoulder took flight and flapped into Onika's path. Its wings caught fire, and it transformed into a shooting ball of flame.

Onika swerved aside, but not so quickly that she didn't smell the fire singe the ends of her hair. She appeared behind Lady Zenobia, then noticed a body on the ground between two horses. Before she could storm, another burst of green fire shot toward her, and she went back to her body in Castle Armanguard.

She sat up, disoriented to again be without her eyesight. "Have we all returned? Rosârah? Sârah Hrettah? Madam Kempe?"

"Here," said a small voice.

"We are all here," Kempe said.

"Hrettah is hurt." This from Rosârah Brelenah.

Onika could not abide blindness at the moment. She lay down again, left her body, and appeared at Hrettah's side.

The princess lay writhing on her longchair, brow pinched. The right sleeve and part of the neckline and bodice of her dress had burned away, leaving behind pink flesh, raw in several places. She gasped and said, "It hurts."

"Go for the healer, Kempe," Brelenah said, gripping the princess's opposite hand. "Tell him it's a terrible burn."

Kempe ran from the room, and Onika stared helplessly at the girl. *I'm sorry, Sârah Hrettah,*" she voiced, then repeated her apology to Brelenah.

The former queen kept her gaze locked on the young princess. "We know now that we are not indestructible in the Veil. Our enemy can hurt us."

"*Yes.*" Onika sighed heavily. "*I saw one of the enemy fall. Do you know who it was?*"

"Filkin Yohthehreth," Brelenah said, stroking Hrettah's brow. "I stormed him. Carried his soul out to sea before returning here."

If the Veil warriors dared such a thing again, they would have to be very careful. Onika prayed for the young princess until the physician arrived, then she returned to her body and voiced the king.

"Filkin Yohthehreth has been stormed, Your Highness," she said. *"And Mattenelle and Lilou are both dead, though not by our doing. Sârah Hrettah was struck with fire and is badly burned. The physician is tending her now."*

"How did this happen?" the king asked.

"The mantics saw us and attacked. Their dark magic can harm us in the Veil. There is more. Barthel Rogedoth nearly struck me down by transforming a gowzal into fire."

A long moment of silence passed before the king answered. *"That is grievous news, Miss Onika,"* he said. *"I had hoped otherwise. Do not attempt to attack the mantics again unless I tell you differently. Perhaps there is another way."*

"Yes, Your Highness." But Onika doubted that very much.

QOATCH

"Your palace is exquisite," Jazlyn said. "Much grander than what Ulrik commissioned."

"Thank you," Princess Saria said, eyeing the two gowzals on Jazlyn's shoulders warily. The third of Jazlyn's loyal shadir rode within a gowzal on Qoatch's shoulder, and he still wasn't used to the way the creature's sharp talons pinched.

Princess Saria was a stunning young woman. Qoatch could tell by Jazlyn's demeanor that she disliked being in her presence. The feeling seemed mutual. The young princess and Jazlyn had fought about Jazlyn's purpose in coming here. Princess Saria wanted no magic done in her realm, yet Jazlyn had a job to do and would not be hindered.

Qoatch had suggested a tour simply to distract from further disagreement.

They exited the great hall and followed the princess across a pillared vestibule toward a grand staircase lined in thin, green carpet. A door on the outer wall opened and a guard ran inside.

"Your Highness," he said, bowing. "Giants approaching from the north on horseback."

Princess Saria stiffened. "How far out are they?" she asked.

"They came out of the forest on the western bank of the river. They've not yet crossed the water, but those beasts of theirs move three times as fast as ours. At the rate they're moving, they'll reach the back of the castle in a quarter of an hour. Our men are armed and ready."

Jazlyn swept past the guard. "Take me to the back of the castle at once," she told the man. "I want to get them in sight as soon as possible."

Saria chased after Jazlyn. "Empress, please. I insist you leave the giants to us."

Jazlyn swung around. "That I cannot do, Princess. To stand by and watch the Jiir-Yeke destroy this stronghold and its people is to fail the agreement I signed with Ulrik. There is more at stake than you know."

"I'm sorry Ulrik insists on making himself a nuisance, but neither he nor you have any authority in New Sarikar."

"Must I use my magic on you, Princess? I will if you make me."

"I wash my hands of this," Saria said, lifting her arms as she stalked away.

Jazlyn turned her gaze on the quavering soldier. "Well?" she snapped. "Take me to the back of the castle. Now!"

The man quickly led Jazlyn and Qoatch down a twist of hallways and out into a snow-covered garden. To Qoatch's relief, the gowzal on his shoulder took flight and perched on the roof of a small portico. One of the creatures on Jazlyn's shoulders flew away to join it. The black birds were stark against the snow-covered roof.

It was equally easy to spot the giants riding over the snow on the opposite side of the river—a line of more than twenty, at first glance.

"Ziyph, go and count them," Jazlyn said, and the bird on her shoulder took flight.

Jazlyn climbed the portico. "Have your soldiers take up residence along the back of the fortress in case any giants get past us," she told the guard who had escorted them outside. "Qoatch and I have killed them before. We are not likely to need any assistance, but one cannot be too careful when giants are involved."

"Arman be with you, Empress," the guard said, then scurried away.

"I need the help of no god," Jazlyn muttered, breath misting from her lips. "Especially not Arman, who Princess Saria informs me will be offended by my assistance."

"What can I do, Great Lady?" Qoatch asked.

"Draw your sword and keep me safe. I would like to kill as many as possible before I am discovered." She lifted her hands, gave a short whistle, and closed her eyes. Cherem and Izar fluttered down to her wrists, each claiming an arm.

"*Bahraq, halam!*"

The gowzals transformed into two bolts of lightning, shot away, and struck two giants. Thunder cracked in the sky overhead as the giants fell from their mounts, seemingly dead. One of the horses went down as well, while the other reared up on its hind legs. This caused the back half of the giant force to slow and become disoriented. Most of the giants were looking up at the sky.

"Do you see the birds?" Jazlyn asked.

Qoatch searched and found them circling over the giants. "There!" He pointed.

"*Bahraq, halam!*" Jazlyn yelled, and again lightning zapped two giants from their mounts and made the sky crack with thunder. This time both horses reared and ran off, slowing the approach even further.

Ziyph fluttered to perch on Jazlyn shoulder. "He counted twenty-five giants," she said.

"Four fewer now," Qoatch said.

The remaining giants slowed before the river. The first five steered their horses down into the frigid water.

Jazlyn took Ziyph onto her fingers. "*Bahraq, halam!*" The bird shot away as the others had and struck the giant in the middle of the five.

Water exploded, and energy zipped across the water's surface in all directions, knocking all five horses and riders beneath the waves. The sky boomed so loudly the sound deafened Qoatch and made the ground tremble. As the giants' bodies bobbed to the surface, the ripples from the blast continued to circle out, reaching both sides of the river and lapping against the shore, though Qoatch couldn't hear it. Jazlyn was speaking to him as well, but the sound was muffled, like someone speaking underwater.

Across the river, what was left of the Jiir-Yeke force turned their horses back from the water's edge and retreated toward the trees.

Jazlyn's hands shot forward, and lightning again hit the ground across the river. This time three giants fell and two of the horses. The resulting thunder cracked in the sky, a dull rumbling in Qoatch's pounding ears.

By the time Jazlyn's gowzals had resumed their original form again, the giants had reached the distant tree line. A faint chorus of cheering pulled Qoatch's gaze to the castle and the soldiers there, who were jumping and embracing one another at the sight of the retreating giants. Princess Saria watched from a balcony above, frowning with her arms folded, though the people beside her seemed amazed.

Of course they were. His Great Lady had saved them all.

Qoatch's ears popped then, like coming down from a great height. Sound flooded back in: people cheering, the waves licking the shore, the faint squawk of a gowzal.

All three birds returned to Jazlyn. The first two perched on her shoulders. The third floundered and landed near her feet. With the same command of "*Bahraq, halam!*" Jazlyn sent the first two out again, this time into the forest itself. Trees cracked, splitting from their bases and falling into those beside them. The sky thundered, and in the forest a flame sprouted up along with the distant screams of giants.

Jazlyn turned to Qoatch. "Ulrik did me a favor when he compelled me to fight these giants alone with my new magic. Do you know that?"

"How so?" Qoatch asked.

"I did not know all that the new magic was capable of. It is true that the magic is not as great as with the old ahvenrood. I cannot heal myself or fly or compel. But wielding this magic in battle makes me nearly invincible."

"You were incredible, as always, Great Lady," Qoatch said.

A squawk pulled his gaze to their feet, where the third gowzal lay floundering and had brushed the snow in streaks of blood.

Qoatch reached for the creature, which nipped at his fingers. "Careful, now," he said. "Let me help you."

It's too late, eunuch. This from Izar. The red-and-yellow shadir had left the bird and taken its regular form of a snake with the head of a cat.

"What happened?" Jazlyn demanded.

The magic was too much for the creature, Izar said. *Its body couldn't handle it.*

"We'll just have to find you a new bird," Jazlyn said. "Good thing it lasted until I had defeated the giants."

Qoatch climbed the steps to stand beside his Great Lady. It was then that he caught sight of a second horde of giants charging toward them from the east. "Great Lady," he yelled. "Look out!"

TREVN

R ogedoth had magic.

For so long Trevn had avoided the man because he feared his magic. When Lady Islah had revealed Rogedoth was a malleant, Trevn had reveled in that truth, perhaps relied too much upon it. Now he was right back where he started.

No matter. Arman was with them. That hadn't changed.

Rogedoth's army had stopped some two hundred paces back from the river, well within range of Trevn's archers. They were dressed in black or red, and Trevn caught sight of a half dozen red, black, and gold banners depicting the head of Barthos.

Trevn compared the men. Overall, he had superior fighters. Most of his soldiers had been training since childhood, and while Rogedoth had a handful of those, the majority of his were compelled Puru with little or no training. Trevn had some untrained men, as well—volunteer farmers and tradesmen, eager to end the oppression once and for all. They'd come armed with pikes, staves, and poleaxes, forester axes, or weighted mallets. General Ensley had spread them out among the infantry so as not to have any weak places in the ranks. The giants helping them he had placed on the right, where they could ride their oversized horses without trampling any Kinsman soldiers.

Trevn rode along the front line of the infantry, behind the mounted cavalry. "Arman is with us," he told the men. "Take courage! The God is on our side. Today we banish evil from Er'Rets." He repeated these phrases until he had circled the archers from behind and rode across the face of the cavalry. Most of the men cheered. However, one man yelled, "But he has magic!"

"So do I," Trevn said. "Arman gave me this magic as a means of standing against the mantics we brought to this land. That is what I will do here today. What *we* will do. Defeat their dark magic once and for all."

But Rogedoth's army did not advance.

Trevn voiced Mielle. *"How fares Armanguard?"*

"Shanek DanSâr and Grayson have not returned. We arrested many of his soldiers. Captain Veralla says there still may be some in the lower levels."

"Good. Pray for Grayson's safety. Have Father Mathal make an offering."

"I'll do so at once. I pray for you, as well."

"Pray for all of us, Mielle. This day will be long, and many will die, but hopefully Arman will give us victory over our enemy once and for all."

Trevn closed the connection with Mielle and sat quietly on his horse. Things were different between them. Voicing her now was like voicing anyone else. He could sense her emotions, even know her thoughts, but she could never again know his—not like the soul-binding had allowed. The thought brought a pang of loss, yet it occurred to him that he'd fallen in love with Mielle long before any magic had knit their hearts and minds. He smiled then, thankful to have things back to normal—to the way Arman had ordained them. All would be well. Once this day had passed.

Arman, protect us from those who seek to destroy us. Go before us and grant us victory.

A short while later, Princess Saria voiced Trevn to let him know that the Jiir-Yeke giants had attacked and Empress Jazlyn was still fighting them.

"She is absolutely terrifying—shot lightning down from the sky."

Inolah's reports had been similar. *"How is Father Wolbair taking it?"* Trevn asked.

"He has locked himself in the temple and is praying."

Praying was all any of them could do at the moment. The energy of Trevn's men had grown lax. The cavalry broke formation in turns, pacing their mounts up and down the line to keep the animals warm.

Trevn rode to General Ensley's side. "Why do they wait?"

"Why do *you*?" the general asked.

Trevn scowled across the river. "I won't make our men wade through that water. We have the fort. We can renew our supplies. They'll have to act at some point."

Yet the day wore on.

"Your Highness!" Sir Keshton rode up to Trevn and his men. "Chieftess

Charlon has arrived with fifty-some Magosians. She says they have come to fight alongside us."

Sands. "Where are they?"

"We've stopped them by the fort. She insists on talking with you."

Trevn steered his mount out of the line. "I'll speak with her." Saria might be helpless against the giants, but Ulagan had brought Moul Rog and his men, and Trevn also had the Veil warriors. He could not allow a mantic to fight for Armania.

The Magosians were all on horseback, clustered outside the palisade gate, surrounded by Armanian soldiers.

"Make way for the king!" Nietz called as he led the way through the parting soldiers.

Trevn rode behind him, with Cadoc on his right and Novan on his left. Magosians steered their mounts aside, and soon Trevn reached the center where the Chieftess was waiting.

"Chieftess Charlon," Trevn said. "What brings you to my border house?"

"Magosia wishes to fight, Your Highness," she said. "Fight alongside Armania."

"I well understand the desire, Chieftess," Trevn said. "But it presents a problem for me. The realm of Armania follows the decrees of the One God, Arman. His Holy Book specifically states that Arman's people are to have nothing to do with shadir, who are enemies to Arman."

"You told me this before," she said. "I am the only one who can do magic. My men and maidens will fight with shard clubs."

"I welcome your warriors, Chieftess," Trevn said, "if they will join my infantry and follow the commands given them, but I will not condone shadir magic on my side of this battle."

Charlon's lip curled. "I meant no offense in my offer, Your Highness. We ride!" She kicked her horse and steered it out of the cluster. The Magosians followed, several shooting Trevn dark looks as they went.

Clearly Trevn had offended the woman. That could not be helped. He had more important matters to attend to. He did not wait to see them go, but turned his horse and began cantering back toward his army. It might be time to bait Rogedoth by sending Armania's herald across with an offer of peace to insult his pride.

Hinck

The second wave of Tace Edekk's army charged. Hinck and his bowmen fired arrows at the enemy, picking them off one by one. Hinck aimed at a giant and was just about to release his arrow when the man reined his horse and stopped. The rest of the charge parted around him. Hinck instead took out one of the Kinsman men.

He drew another arrow and saw that a second giant had stopped by the first, clogging the enemy advance. One punched the other, who fell off his horse. That man jumped up and dragged his attacker off the horse and into the snow. Three more giants stopped and dismounted.

"We've broken the compulsion on several giants in this charge," Oli said.

"I see that," Hinck bloodvoiced. *"Well done."* Then to his men. "Focus on the charge! Show mercy to those who've stopped advancing."

He forced his attention away from the skirmish and fired upon a Kinsman traitor. As his arrow struck true, he set another to his bow. With the giants slowly falling apart, their counterattack efforts were far more effective. By the time the enemy charge reached the Sarikarian infantry, the few remaining were quickly defeated.

The giants who'd left the charge were now engaged in a brawl that would make any pirate proud. There were at least a dozen involved.

"Oli? How close is Edekk's final group?" Hinck bloodvoiced.

"Last I saw, they were half an hour out. I'll check again."

Half an hour wasn't long. "Well done, everyone," Hinck said to his archers. "Rest up. There is one more group coming."

He went inside the border house and down the stairs to where General Norcott was standing beside a map of the area that had been tacked to the wall.

"How did we do?" Hinck asked.

"As well as expected," he said. "I've got the infantry repounding the stakes that were trampled. According to Lady Eudora, the third wave will come from the east. I've asked my scouts to alert me the moment they are seen."

"Duke Canden is checking on their status now," Hinck said.

"They did well with that last group," the general said. "Did the giants turn back?"

"Last I saw they'd started a war with each other." Hinck sat on a chair near the fire. His shirt had a bigger patch of blood than before, but he had no time to worry about it now. He closed his eyes and reached for Saria's mind. *"Princess? How fares New Sarikar?"*

"Hinck! The empress's magic terrifies me. She shot lightning from the sky. Giants and horses alike fell dead. She is so adept, our soldiers are in awe like spectators at a tournament. I fear they will worship magic after this. Wolbair is beside himself, locked away in the temple. Yet I cannot deny she has saved hundreds of Sarikarian lives. How about you?"

Hinck told her about the first two attacks, how well his archers did, how Trevn had helped Eudora find the compulsion in the giants, and how Oli was helping her now.

"I'm relieved to hear that Duke Canden survived. I wish I could do something to help. I need to defend my home, Hinck, to avenge my father and brother and uncles. Yet here I stand, safe on this balcony, watching a mantic dazzle my army with her magic. It's not right."

"All that matters is that the job get done, not who does it."

"That should be true," Saria said, *"but you know it's not. I will be criticized for my inaction. And criticized again for allowing a mantic to fight for us."*

Oli's voice barged into Hinck's mind. *"Edekk's last group is coming now."*

"I must go, Saria. We're under attack." Hinck opened his eyes and stood. "Duke Canden says the third wave is coming," he told General Norcott as he carried his bow toward the stairs.

"I'll have Dahlo send word to Captain Arons," the general said.

Hinck reached the parapet and roused his men. "To arms! The third wave comes." He took position in the center of the wall and looked east. No sight of anyone yet. On the ground, word passed through the infantry ranks, bringing the relaxed men back into formation.

Hinck reached again for Oli's mind. *"Where are they? I cannot see them."*

"In the forest nearest you. There are more giants in this group than in the

*last two—perhaps thirty? I've broken only four compulsions so far. Eudora
has done two."*

"I am most grateful for any." Hinck saw them now, galloping out of the
forest like it was on fire. "Draw!" he yelled. "Ready your aim . . ." He did as he
instructed. "Fire!"

The speed and nearness of this attack forced the archers to work quickly.
Shots were missed, and too few giants fell.

"Take care!" Hinck yelled. "These are all the arrows we have. Make every
one count!"

After that the shots flew with greater accuracy. Hinck fired arrow after
arrow, ignoring the pain in his chest. He ran out of arrows moments before
the cavalry reached the shield wall. There were still a half dozen giants riding,
and those in the lead ran right over the stakes.

Hinck paced to the corner of the parapet, searching for an arrow someone
might have dropped. There were none, of course. He watched the melee below
in dismay, wishing there were something he could do. This battle would not
end as swiftly as the previous two.

"To the ground, men!" he yelled. "Grab a sword and defend this fort."

His men scrambled down the stairs. Hinck went after them and found
the last few archers pawing through a pile of weapons near the door. Hinck's
sword was in the office. He crossed the room and pushed past the curtain
at the door.

Eudora's cot was empty. She lay on the floor, a hooded soldier kneeling
over her. By the arcs of blood streaked over the sanded pine floor, someone
was bleeding badly.

Hinck fell upon the man, whose hands were clenched around Eudora's
throat. Eudora's eyes had rolled back in her head. Hinck ripped the man off
Eudora, pinned him to the floor, and pulled back his hood, which revealed
coils of soft braids.

"Lady Brisa?" In one of the Sarikarian uniforms.

"I hoped she would bleed out," she said. "The shadir said she might. But
she felt the knife on her wrists and returned to her body."

Hinck glanced back at Eudora, who lay unmoving, eyes glassy and staring.
Deep cuts across her wrists were still oozing blood. *Woes!*

"General!" he voiced. *"I need the physician and two guards in my office now!"*

✦   ✦   ✦

The guards locked up Lady Brisa with those who had surrendered. She claimed a shadir told her how to find Eudora's body and stop her from freeing the giants. Hinck bloodvoiced Trevn and Oli to tell them what had happened, warning them to guard well the bodies of any who had entered the Veil.

The physician declared Lady Eudora dead. This Hinck already knew, but he'd hoped he was wrong. He apologized profusely to Oli, who now had lost his entire family.

"This is war, Hinckdan," Oli voiced back, though his voice sounded strained. *"Casualties are to be expected. I am thankful she died a free woman and doing some good for once in her life."*

Hinck wondered when Duke Canden had become such an optimist.

"It's all but over now," a voice said. It was the general, stepping in through the door.

"What happened?" Hinck asked.

"We have won, though we lost too many in that last attack."

"Not enough arrows," Hinck said. "And Lady Eudora . . ."

"Very sad, Your Grace. I didn't see Lord Edekk or Sir Jarmyn among the dead or the prisoners. They're likely hiding somewhere or have gone south to join the larger battle. Now, I insist you lie down and let the physician look at your stitches."

Hinck reluctantly lay back on his longchair, wincing at the pull on his chest muscles. He bloodvoiced Saria and told her all that had happened. When the physician finally looked him over, Hinck was dizzy from blood loss. He had ripped out over half the stitches. The physician sewed him up and ordered him back to New Sarikar to rest. Nothing Hinck said would convince the man to change his mind.

"A physician's order outranks even a king. Or a queen," General Norcott said.

Hinck didn't bother to challenge that statement. He knew both Trevn and Saria would agree.

GRAYS⊙N

At Queen Zeroah's insistence, Grayson popped to the physician in the castle and let the man coat his ear in aloe, which was all he said could be done for a burn. After that, Grayson went to the great hall and was relieved not to see Shanek DanSâr. Queen Zeroah and Danek appeared in the Veil beside him.

"What are you doing?" Danek asked. *"You need to find Shanek DanSâr and kill him."*

Grayson looked away from the duke's accusing eyes to Queen Zeroah's kind ones. *"The king didn't tell me to kill him. Just to keep him distracted. And away from the battle, which hasn't started yet."*

"Ask the king," Danek said. *"I'm sure he means for you to kill him."*

Grayson squirmed at the idea of killing anyone. *"I want to see how the queen is doing."*

He thought about Queen Mielle and moved. She was leading two maids down from the third floor to the second. Sir Kalenek stood on the second-floor landing, waiting.

"See that these women are sent to Duke Highcliff's manor," she said.

Sir Kalenek gestured to a nearby soldier, who had been watching the exchange. "You heard the queen. Get these women to safety at once."

"Yes, sir," the soldier said, escorting the women down the next flight of stairs.

Kal's attention fell on Grayson. "Grayson! What news?"

"Shanek DanSâr is gone for now," he said.

"That's a relief," the queen said. "I wish Amala had never met him. Or that she could influence him for good. To stop this madness."

Kal embraced the queen. "Amala thinks Shanek would make a good king."

They held each other, and the queen cried for her sister. Grayson felt awkward and in the way. Thankfully the front doors opened, and a soldier walked in. A female soldier.

"Lady Pia!" Queen Mielle ran to her shield. "I thought you were dead."

"No, Your Highness. Lady Mattenelle spared me. Apparently, nearly ten years in such service together builds loyalty for one another."

"What of the children?" Mielle asked. "Did the mantic take them away?"

"She left them and a horse and cart, which I believe belonged to Master Orban, so I transported the children here. Some guards in the bailey took them to the Duke of Highcliff's manor."

"Oh, Pia, you're brilliant!" The queen threw her arms around the woman. "Thank you for taking care of those dear ones. I wish I could—"

A blast of green fire flew past Grayson's arm. He dove aside and into the Veil, twisting to his back as he might when swimming. Around him, people were screaming and running. Shanek DanSâr had returned. He was walking toward Grayson, had passed by the queen and her guardswoman, by Sir Kalenek and the soldiers, who had all pressed back against the walls. They looked scared.

Grayson was scared too, especially when he felt the coldness coming from Shanek and remembered King Trevn saying Shanek had a great shadir inside him. He popped three times across the second-floor landing, hoping to confuse Shanek, then threw a ball of green fire.

Shanek vanished before the fire reached him. It struck the wall and a tapestry caught fire. Before Grayson could think, a stream of fire flew past, and heat seared his left side. He howled and popped to the roof. Shanek arrived a moment later, but rather than attack, popped away. Grayson followed him to the great hall and found Shanek standing just inside the doorway.

Grayson threw a ball of fire. Shanek stretched a glimmer of green light between his hands. Grayson's fireball struck the light and faded.

How did he do that? Grayson zipped through the Veil, exiting in various places outdoors, hoping that Shanek would follow, but he did not. Grayson again found him in the great hall. This time he lobbed a fireball at Shanek's back, but Shanek disappeared and the green flames fizzled out into nothing.

Before Grayson could give chase, fire scorched his left arm. He yelped and popped up to the ceiling, floating near the carvings and looking down. Shanek stood by the doors again, head swiveling as he sought out his opponent.

"You cannot hide from me," came Shanek's voice in his mind.

That was true, but Grayson didn't need a shadir's help to win this fight. He had an army of warriors loyal to Arman.

"Onika," he voiced. *"I need you to banish the shadir inside of Shanek DanSâr."*

Oniκa

"*hanek DanSâr has a shadir inside him,*" Onika voiced her warriors. "*We must banish it if Grayson is to stand a chance at winning this fight. Follow me and pray.*"

She trailed Grayson as Shanek pursued him through the Veil, but keeping up proved challenging. She exited in the gatehouse barely in time to see Shanek disappear. She then went to the roof, then the stables, the training yard, and the throne room. Onika arrived at each stop moments before Shanek disappeared, only seconds behind Grayson.

Again and again she chased until she reached the great hall. A green surge of light pulled her attention to the center aisle. She jumped there in time to see Grayson lying on the floor, Shanek standing over him. Green flames shot out from Shanek's hand and struck Grayson, whose body flipped over. The fire singed his blue tunic.

He looked dead. He couldn't be. *Arman, help me!*

She soared toward Shanek, hoping to storm him, but rather than grasp his soul and pass through his body, she struck something solid. Something cold. The shadir inside.

Onika spun off toward the ceiling but managed to stop herself before she flew too far. She looked back on the scene. The prince was still there, but Grayson had gone. Onika concentrated on him. Jumped. Appeared at the front of the great hall.

How could that be? She did not see him. She crouched and found that Grayson had crawled underneath the front table. Her heart wrenched at the sight of blistered skin under the gaping burn holes in his tunic.

591

"Can you banish the shadir?" he whispered.

"We will try, but I need you to try something as well," Onika said. *"Remember what King Trevn said about you having power over shadir?"*

Grayson paled. *"I don't think that's true."*

"Then you must trap Shanek some other way. We cannot banish the shadir if Shanek doesn't hold still."

"If I talk to the shadir, I can't protect myself from Shanek or make fire to throw at him."

"That shouldn't matter if you're commanding the shadir to stay still."

Grayson looked ill. "If you distract him, I'll go behind and—"

The table flew up, knocked off its legs by a burst of green light. Grayson vanished.

Onika cowered. *Arman, we need your help!* She felt the God's heat kindle inside. He was going to speak. She stood and faced the enemy.

Shanek frowned at her. "You're the prophetess King Barthel wanted to sacrifice."

"Hear my words, Shanek DanSâr," Onika said, the God's voice flowing straight through her. *"By the pride of your heart you say, 'I am a king; I sit on the throne of a king, so therefore I am the highest in the land.' But you are a mere mortal, not a god, and you have aligned yourself with my enemies against my chosen people. How then will you say, 'I am a god,' in the presence of those who kill you? You will die a mortal, not a god, in the arms of the one who loves you."*

Shanek yelled and grasped his ears, troubled by the prophetic words. Or perhaps by whatever Grayson was saying to the shadir within him. Onika shuddered as Arman's warmth faded. Rosârahs Brelenah and Zeroah were both praying aloud, Zeroah on her knees with hands lifted high, and Brelenah singing a lament. Danek, Oli, and Kempe stood with the women, echoing Zeroah's prayers.

"Holy Arman, you arm us with strength," Zeroah was saying. *"Guide us and help us rid the land of this creature who defiles your name and seeks to destroy your creation."*

"Save us, Arman," Brelenah sang, *"for the waters have come up to our necks."*

Shanek cowered behind a table. "Stop talking!" he yelled.

Onika stepped between Zeroah and Brelenah. *"Dendron, I know you hide within this young man, but I cast you out, unclean one, along with every bit of power the enemy Gâzar has equipped you with. In the name of Arman, be gone and stay far from all creatures of light. For it is Arman who commands you, Arman who flung you headlong from the height of Shamayim and into the depths of the Lowerworld."*

Shanek clutched his ears. "Don't say that!"

"You are mighty," Zeroah prayed. *"Only you can carry this shadir where it belongs."*

"Those who seek to destroy us seek also to destroy you," Brelenah sang. *"Let it not be so!"*

"It is Arman who commands you, Dendron," Onika said. *"Listen and tremble in fear, you enemy of the God, you foe of his chosen people, you bringer of death, you robber of life."*

"Stop!" Shanek yelled. "He doesn't like it!"

"Deliver us from those who hate us," Brelenah sang, *"from the deep waters that threaten to drown us all."*

"Fear him," Onika yelled, *"who triumphs over the powers of your master in the Lowerworld, where all darkness lives. Fear him and tremble."*

Prince Shanek fell on his side. Onika saw Grayson behind him, on his knees, lips moving silently, brow scrunched in concentration.

"By Arman's name, leave this man and the world forever!" Onika yelled, and Oli, Danek, and Kempe repeated her decree. *"Return to whence you came."*

Prince Shanek writhed on the floor as the creature seeped out of him. It was pale and massive, all legs and arms and coiled horns.

"Be gone to the depths of the Lowerworld," Onika cried.

The shadir roared as it slipped through the floor, arms and legs flailing to grab hold.

"Defender of all creation," Onika prayed, *"take Dendron into the depths where he can cause no more evil."*

The shadir lost its grip and slipped away. Peace blanketed Onika. She fell to her knees. *"Thank you, Arman. You are our mighty hero."*

Green light brightened the floor behind her. Onika turned, squinted. The light was coming from Grayson, who stood a few steps from where Shanek lay. A sheen of green light stretched between his hands.

Grayson laughed. "I did it!"

A groan pulled Onika's gaze to Shanek. The Deceiver was moving. Arman had taken away the shadir. Now the root children could fight as equals.

KALENEK

Something seemed to have hurt Shanek, and from the snippets he'd heard Grayson say, Onika was somehow involved. He imagined the Veil warriors were here, working their magic, but he could only see Grayson, standing over Shanek and holding what looked like a pane of green glass between his hands.

"We're even now," he told Shanek, stretching his hands apart, which made the green glass bigger. "If you surrender, I'll let you live."

Kal winced. Ultimatums never worked on Shanek. They only fueled his ire.

In a blink Shanek moved from the floor to his feet, his face twisted into a snarl. "I don't need a shadir to defeat you."

He blurred toward Grayson, plowed into him so fast that Grayson didn't have a chance to move. They hit the floor and skidded, Shanek on top. Grayson wrapped his arms around Shanek, and the green light curled with them, enclosing Shanek in a transparent glow. The light exploded, and both boys disappeared, into the Veil, likely, where Kal couldn't see.

Shanek appeared up on the dais, standing between Trevn and Mielle's thrones, looking somewhat dazed as he scanned the great hall.

Give yourself up, boy, Kal thought, willing Shanek to do just that. But unlike root children, mind-speakers, or mantics, Kal had no magical abilities. He wanted to help, to stop Shanek, but he knew the boy wouldn't listen. And if Shanek kept on like this, he'd kill Grayson and Onika and anyone else who stood in his way.

Kal couldn't allow that to happen. Shanek was his responsibility, no one else's. Wilek had assigned him the task, and Kal would not fail.

Grayson came into view behind Shanek, green fireballs in both hands.

Shanek whirled around just as Grayson let fly. The first fireball struck Shanek's shoulder. He howled but caught the second fireball with his right hand, which was also glowing with green light.

The boys flashed around the great hall and threw fire at each other. Sometimes they managed to shield themselves. Sometimes they didn't. Neither seemed close to winning.

At one point Grayson appeared along the wall, a few paces down from where Kal was standing. "Arman, help me," he mumbled. "I don't know how to win."

A flash near the entry doors drew Kal's gaze. Shanek stood there, fire burning in both palms. "I don't have to kill you, you know," he said to Grayson. "We could help each other. The prophetess is wrong to say we aren't gods, because we are. No one alive can stand against us."

"Arman is alive," Grayson whispered. He popped away. Green flames shot down on Shanek from the ceiling, then Kal spotted Grayson in the center of the room, lobbing what looked like a spear made of fire. How could the boys hold the fire and still be burned by it?

Shanek popped behind Grayson and grabbed him around the waist, his arms and hands crackling like he was made of lightning.

Grayson yelped and they fell in a tangle of limbs. Grayson managed to turn and set his gleaming hands to Shanek's face.

With a yelp, Shanek disappeared, leaving Grayson alone on the floor. The boy looked badly hurt this time, and Kal worried that he'd let things go on too long.

A few paces away, Shanek appeared, hands glowing, and leapt into the air. He spread his arms and pulled the light into a glossy green ribbon. He vanished, but the light arched over Grayson's head like a rainbow. Shanek reappeared on Grayson's other side and pulled the glossy ribbon to the floor. A clap of his hands, and the sheen closed in on the sides, encircling Grayson like a giant bubble. Grayson, who still lay on his stomach, reached out and yanked his hand back. Tossed fire against the barrier, but the bubble absorbed it. He didn't pop away.

Kal figured he couldn't. Had Shanek won?

Shanek waved and the bubble shrank. Grayson had to curl in on himself to keep from touching the sides.

"See?" Shanek said to Grayson. "You said you'd rather die than serve me. So you'll die."

Kal could take this no longer. He pushed off the wall and started across the room. "Shan, stop this at once."

Shanek turned his attention to Kal. "Father! Look, I've caught the other root child."

"You're not a killer, Shan," Kal said.

"I'm king of Armania now. He's a threat. He must die so I can rule."

Kal heard Rogedoth's lies in Shanek's words. "You're better than that."

"You don't know me anymore, Father." Shanek turned back to his bubble, admiring it with a small smile. "I'm different now. I learned much from the shadir."

"Don't do this, Shan," Kal said. "I warn you. I won't let you harm him."

"You can't stop me." Shanek pressed his hands toward the floor and the bubble began to shrink.

Grayson was going to die.

Kal could not let that happen. He drew his sword, and his mind went back in time. A yeetta warrior was standing over Livy's bed. There was still time to save her!

A single stroke was all it took to end him.

A man screamed, pulling Kal back to the present. He had fallen to his knees and was holding Shanek in his arms, rocking him like a babe. The green bubble was gone. Grayson was standing, staring. Kal's sword lay on the floor between them, the tang slick with blood.

"Father?"

Kal looked down on Shanek's blistered face. "You're okay," he said, his voice a raspy whisper. "I've got you."

"What happened?" Shanek asked.

"You were struck down, Shan. That happens in battles sometimes, even to men who think they're invincible."

The boy's gaze shifted from Kal's right eye to his left. "I wasn't invincible?"

"No, Shan. You weren't."

A tear leaked down Shanek's cheek and his eyes filled with more. "It hurts."

"I'm sorry, Shanek. I've got you."

"You won't leave me again?"

Guilt flooded Kal at the idea that he might have avoided this had he stayed with Shanek like he'd promised. "I'm staying right here. I won't let you go."

A familiar tune rose above Shanek's labored breathing. It took Kal a moment to realize it was coming from inside his head. Onika, humming her song. The realization broke him for a moment, but he pulled himself together for Shanek and hummed along, rocking his boy to sleep.

Trevn

Trevn watched his herald ride a white horse across the river, up the bank of the other side, and across the snowy field toward Rogedoth's army. He hoped this would work.

Miss Onika and her Veil warriors came to the battlefield to storm and banish shadir. She told him that Shanek DanSâr was dead, killed by Sir Kalenek, of all people. Trevn barely recognized Grayson when he appeared on the ground beside Trevn's horse. The sight of his blistered skin under gaping burn holes in his tunic almost made Trevn dismount and knight him that very moment. Instead he sent him to the fort for fresh clothes and whatever armor Hawley could scrounge up.

The herald stopped halfway between the river and Rogedoth's front line and waited. Waited a very long time. Some of the soldiers began grumbling. Was the king mad? Why would he offer peace? They wanted the Pretender's head on a pike! But Trevn knew Rogedoth wouldn't accept peace. He hoped the man would be insulted enough to send his vanguard forward.

So much time passed, Trevn almost called back the herald. Finally a horse rode out from Rogedoth's infantry. Trevn held his breath, curious what the outcome would be.

Rogedoth's man took the scroll, then he drew his sword and stabbed Trevn's herald.

The entire Armanian army seemed to gasp. Trevn squeezed his reins, horrified that anyone would kill a messenger. He felt the force of his men's indignation. Their voices rose up in growls and shouts of outrage.

Rogedoth's man pushed the herald off the horse, held up Trevn's scroll where all could see, then ripped it in two. He tossed the pieces, grabbed up the reins of the herald's horse, and rode back through the Puru infantry, taking the animal with him.

Trevn had his answer, though unfortunately at the cost of a man's life. "That was first blood," he said to Cadoc. "The battle has begun."

Cadoc nodded. "I'm with you, sir."

"I can throw fire at them, sir," Grayson said. He was against standing on the ground beside Trevn's horse, this time dressed for battle.

"Do nothing until you hear from me, Master Grayson. Cadoc, I must speak with the men." Trevn steered his horse into the open and yelled, "Soldiers of Armania!"

The men fell silent and stared at their king. Those in the back pressed closer, and the sight of so many eyes fixed on Trevn made his throat tight. He walked his horse between the cavalry and infantry lines. "Our enemy draws first blood. It is time to fight."

The soldiers around him raised their weapons in the air and hollered their agreement. The energy bolstered Trevn's courage, and he raised his hand and waited for the voices to fade.

"We fight today because Arman commands it," he shouted. "For too long Barthel Rogedoth, the Pretender, the shamed prince of Sarikar, used magic to control my father. Now he seeks to destroy us entirely and make the nation of Armania his own. I will not let that happen. My crown does not belong to him, nor do my people. You are mine, by Arman's will, and I vow to keep you so. Our enemy believes he can use magic to win this battle, but Arman has given me and those of my blood a magic of our own. We *can* fight the mantics and defeat them."

Again the men cheered. Trevn had reached the end of the line, so he rode between the archers on the right flank and the right infantry unit. He met Gunrik Koll's gaze and nodded, thankful to have mended his relationship with the nobleman. "As you just witnessed," he yelled, "I have made an offer of peace. But the Pretender will not have it. Our enemy seeks to kill us today. He wants our blood. He would give rule of our great realm over to shadir. To minions of Gâzar." He paused to let this sink in. "Soldiers of Armania, this will not be!"

A ripple of cheers passed through the ranks. Trevn wove his horse through the men, hoping to draw near enough to all at some point so that everyone could hear at least some of what he said. He nodded to the giants, to Ulagan, and hoped he could translate.

"Barthel Rogedoth, the Pretender, has forgotten his maker. He has forsaken the will of Arman and so he is blind to all that is good and right in the world. Soldiers of Armania, we come together to stop this man. I am your king, but today I fight as your equal. Your brother."

The men bellowed and cheered and thrust their weapons in the air. The sudden noise sent Trevn's horse skipping to the side, and he calmed it. He had reached the left flank now and steered his horse back toward the front.

"Arman is not only watching over us. He is with us. But we must do our part. The duty to fight for our realm has fallen at our feet. Arman has chosen us and equipped us. He is in our weapons, our will, and in our hearts. He will give us strength, help, and he will give us victory!"

Like a thunderstorm the men erupted, cheering and stamping their feet in a clamor that surely had been heard by Rogedoth, waiting with his mantics and shadir.

"General Ensley," Trevn voiced. *"Let the archers fire one round."*

The general gave the order, and Trevn waited, watching eagerly for the first arrows to fly. A man's voice called out, muted and distant from the left flank, and suddenly the whispers of hundreds of feathers sang, and a volley of arrows streaked across the sky.

A ripple of something like wind shimmered before the Puru infantry line, and the Armanian arrows clattered against an invisible barrier like twigs hitting a brick wall.

Terror rendered Trevn speechless, as it must have the entire Armanian army. Silence hung over them like a cloud.

"General," Trevn voiced. *"'We cannot win without our archers.' Didn't you say that?"*

"Not exactly, Your Highness," the general replied. *"I said they would give us a great advantage."*

Yet this shield gave Rogedoth the advantage. What if it protected each of his soldiers? How could Trevn's army stand against such magic?

Trevn's men were murmuring. Lost was the momentum his speech had gained. *"Miss Onika?"* he voiced. *"I need a—"*

"Shields!" someone yelled, and the warning was repeated across the field.

A horde of arrows was streaking across the sky toward them. All around Trevn, men lifted their shields, though only a quarter of the Armanians had them.

"Your Highness!" Rzasa shoved a shield at Trevn.

He accepted it, but before he could lift it overhead, green light flashed across the sky, creating a semi-transparent wall, like colored glass. The arrows twanged as they bounced off this phenomenon, which was slowly fading away.

A great silence followed, then murmurs of confusion that grew to a raucous cheer.

"What was that?" Sir Cadoc asked.

Trevn had one guess. "Despite my insistence that she not, I believe Chieftess Charlon is going to help us."

⊙ΠΙΚΑ

The king wanted answers of Arman, but the God did not reply to mortal demands. So far he had been silent on this matter. Onika tried again.

Holy One, hear my prayer. The water has come up to our necks and we are sinking. There is no foothold here but your truth. Our enemy seeks to destroy us, and I ask now for your favor. Rescue us from this flood. Deliver us from our foes. And please speak to me about this mantic Charlon Sonber. Do not hide your face from your servant, but give a clear answer. Shall we trust her or scorn her? And what if she will not listen? Speak, Lord. Tell me your will.

She went on to make proclamations of Arman's authority, his dominion over the earth and beyond, over all living beings—spiritual and earthly. She praised him, stated lists of historic wonders, and asked to be filled with his power. She invoked Arman's authority over this battle, and again asked for a word as to the mantic woman who had put herself on their side.

When Arman didn't answer, Onika could only guess. *"His silence most often means he has answered already,"* she told the king.

"Meaning that Armania should have nothing to do with shadir," the king said. *"And therefore nothing to do with Chieftess Charlon. I told her this already."*

"I can easily see that the woman listens to no one," Onika said.

"Will Arman hold me accountable for her actions?"

Onika didn't know. *"Forgive me, Your Highness. I have no answer to give. But I can tell you that Grayson is capable of creating the same type of shield. He did so on a very small scale when fighting Shanek DanSâr. He is unpracticed but a quick learner."*

"I will put him to work at once," the king said. *"Perhaps we will have no need for Chieftess Charlon after all."*

That would match Arman's promise, but Onika needed Grayson as well. *"If you keep Grayson near you to make shields, we cannot use him to try to break through the barrier surrounding Rogedoth and his mantics,"* Onika said.

"One side will have to cross the river soon," the king said. *"Until then, banish any shadir you see. And if Chieftess Charlon refuses to depart, perhaps I can at least advise her what would be most helpful. That is General Ensley and Marshal Winstone's suggestion. Would that cross the line?"*

"I cannot say for certain, Your Highness, though it does seem a risky compromise."

"Combat is a risky endeavor, Miss Onika. I pray Arman's mercy is greater than any misstep I might make."

CHARLON

Charlon marveled at the size of King Barthel's barrier. Had one mantic conjured it? Or were all working together?

"Chieftess Charlon."

King Trevn's voice inside her head. Like Shanek's sometimes did. He must be using the mind-speak magic.

"I thought we had an understanding."

"My son is dead because of King Barthel, Your Highness," she said. "I will fight him. To avenge my son. Whether or not you want my help."

The king did not answer. Angry to have been disobeyed, perhaps. People likely fell at his feet. Well, Charlon would not. She had been prepared to give him his wish. Had been riding to Magosia when Nwari had brought word. Of Shanek's death. At Kalenek's hand. So angry, she had been. So grief-stricken. She had nearly joined King Barthel. Until she asked about Shanek's body. And Nwari told her. That Kalenek was holding it. Holding it and weeping.

Charlon's anger had washed away in an instant. How quickly she had forgotten her vow. To do good. To trust others. She should have known. Known that Kalenek would never have harmed Shanek. Unless the boy had given him no choice.

She did not blame Kalenek. This had been King Barthel's doing. He had riled and puffed up Shanek. With his lies. None of this would have happened. If he had left Shanek be.

So Charlon had turned back.

"Is your shield one way, Chieftess?" King Trevn's voice in her head again.

"Anything goes out, nothing comes in."

"I don't suppose you know how to destroy their shield?"

"Are you asking me now for help?"

"You say you will fight despite my wishes. So I might as well know what you're capable of. I need ten to fifteen minutes for my archers to complete their attack. Can you provide that?"

Charlon did not know. "Have your archers ready their arrows, Your Highness," she said. "I and my shadir will do our best."

The king said nothing. Had he changed his mind? Then, *"The archers will be ready."*

Charlon had been given a chance. "Nwari!" she called.

Yes, Chieftess? came the voice in her ear.

"Go and watch King Barthel and his mantics. I want to know what they are doing." Then she commanded her birds. "*Gowzal ba shel ayder. Daah!*"

Her swarm took flight, their black wings stark against the pale sky. She had nearly thirty now.

"*Sabab bara mahgayn!*" she yelled.

Feathers and fur changed to green light. Light that rose over the river. Formed a wall.

"*Rachab!*" she yelled, and the wall expanded.

"*Ruhm!*" And the wall stretched higher.

When it felt big enough, she yelled "*Âtsar!*" and the wall stopped growing. She thrust her hands forward and commanded it to move. "*Ahthak!*"

The shield drifted toward King Barthel's army. Until it struck his shield. Collided in a blinding flash of light.

"*Ahthak!*" Charlon yelled, thrusting her hands out again. The gowzals squawked from inside the shield. They were straining. Their bodies weak. Some would die. Still Charlon's shield pushed King Barthel's back.

The Armanian soldiers whooped and hollered. Charlon fought the urge to smile. Stayed intent. Focused. On feeding power to her magic.

A voice somewhere in the Armanian army yelled, "Draw!"

Charlon yelled "*Ahthak!*" again and pushed her shield toward King Barthel's army. Little by little both shields drifted back. Passed over the heads of the first soldiers. Exposing them. A ball of green flame shot out from the rear. Struck Charlon's shield and disintegrated. She felt her gowzals waver.

The Armanians cheered. The distant voice yelled, "Fire!"

A swarm of arrows sighed as they were launched into the sky. Charlon's shield had almost reached the line of horses. Two more green fireballs died against her shield. Then the patter. Of arrows hitting bodies, shields, and bronze armor. Strangled cries. Men falling.

King Barthel's shield collapsed. So Charlon released hers. Her flock scattered. Converged again as they flew back toward her. She saw two birds fall.

This enabled King Barthel's archers to launch arrows at the Armanian army. Green fireballs shot into the air too. Knocked several of Charlon's gowzals from the sky. Arrows continued to fly both ways. No longer as a unit. As quickly as each archer could draw and release. Soldiers began to fall. Far more on King Barthel's side, it seemed.

Suddenly the arrows were no more. Charlon took stock of the battle around her. Men groaned. Horses stamped their feet. It was otherwise silent. What now? If they were to fight, one side must cross the river. It would be bitterly cold. Unpleasant for whichever side went through.

Three balls of green fire launched from the back line. Aimed for the Armanian army.

"*Mahgayn!*" Charlon yelled to one of her birds. Repeated the command to two more. The three gowzals shot into the sky. But before they could reach their targets, tiny shields of green light appeared before each fireball. Extinguishing them in bursts of sparks. Sparks that drifted down and died in the river.

Who had done that? Did the Armanians have a mantic after all?

"Rone," Charlon said. "Carry a message to King Trevn. If he wishes to cross the river, I will freeze the water. So that his men can remain dry. Have him voice me his answer. And I want to know who his mantic is."

Rone steered his horse away.

Another fireball launched, this time toward Charlon. She shielded against it. Then shielded three more attacks. It seemed King Barthel wanted to destroy her. She had just conjured an additional shield when King Trevn's voice sounded inside her head.

"*Master Grayson learned from your example, Chieftess. It seems his magic is similar to yours.*"

Charlon supposed that made sense. Shanek's powers had been like her own.

"*But Grayson cannot freeze the river,*" the king said. "*If you would be so kind, we will be ready to move the moment we see it happen.*"

"As you say, Your Highness," Charlon said, lifting her hands to command her flock.

QΘATCH

The giants approached in two groups. The first half had come on foot, scattered and scampering across the snow-covered garden. The second half were on horseback in the distance, walking the animals slowly toward the castle and watching those they'd sent ahead.

Hesitant to use lightning on this side of the river, Jazlyn transformed her two remaining gowzals into spears that launched through the air and each stabbed a giant through the chest. The birds did not return. Either they were fatigued or they were wounded like Izar's bird. Jazlyn stood helplessly on the portico as the giants drew nearer. Qoatch would have to engage in hand-to-hand combat, this time without the benefit of invisibility.

Five of the giants closed in on Jazlyn, wielding battle-axes with blades as big as Qoatch's head. He took position in front of his Great Lady, ready to do his part to protect her. The Sarikarian guards stationed along the back wall of the stronghold drew their swords and lined up on either side of Qoatch.

"Go for the legs!" he yelled to the Sarikarians, dodging out of the path of one axe, and lunging to cut across the back of the giant's knees.

Ziyph's gowzal finally returned, and Jazlyn sent it out in a burst of flame that caused the giants to dive to the ground. Qoatch and the Sarikarian guards seized the moment and fell upon the giants, hacking their smaller blades over legs and arms. The cuts were not deadly, but by the time the giants were on their feet again, Cherem's gowzal had recovered its form. This time Jazlyn conjured the bird into a double-sided blade with no handle on either end. With old language commands, she sent it spinning out in an arc above the heads of Qoatch and the Sarikarians. The whirling blade cut off three heads

606

and nicked or maimed a half dozen others. This left only four giants standing, and they began to creep backward. The giants on horseback had reached the castle and stopped a fair distance behind the remaining four.

"Ready to flee so soon?" Jazlyn extended her arm as Ziyph's gowzal returned to its perch. "Ziyph, *sabab bay êsh!*" she yelled, and the bird shot away in a ball of fire. It struck one of the four on foot. The giant screamed and staggered about, his entire body engulfed in flame.

The remaining three giants turned and fled just as Cherem's gowzal fluttered to Jazlyn's feet.

"Cherem, *gawdare!*"

Cherem screeched and shot away in an orb of green light that spread out slowly like a beam and struck the remaining giants—those on foot and those on horseback—and knocked them into the snow.

The Sarikarians gave chase, killing the nearest downed giants with stabs to the back. Those giants on horseback spurred their mounts into a gallop for the distant tree line.

Jazlyn sent Ziyph in one last cloud of fire that chased the giants into the forest. The blast never made contact but sizzled into the snow, melting a large swath down to soggy dead grass.

Cherem appeared before Qoatch in his original fiery orange likeness. *My gowzal is dead,* he said.

"Nor do I see Ziyph's," Jazlyn said. "No matter. We did what we came to do. Do you think they will return, Qoatch?" She turned her deep brown eyes upon him.

"They would be fools to do so, Great Lady," he said. "They are terrified of you."

"As well they should be." She started for the castle. "Let us wait out the rest of this battle inside. Once it is over, we will finally be free."

Hinck

When Hinck's wagon reached the castle, Princess Saria and Master Vento were waiting—Saria wearing trousers and a coat of chain.

"Why are you dressed like that?" Hinck asked as Master Vento drew back the heap of blankets and furs and examined his wound.

"I'm taking your place at the border house," Saria said.

"You are not!"

"Empress Jazlyn has retired to her chambers," Saria said. "You're to let her know if more giants attack, though she lost all three of her birds in the fight, so I don't know how much help she'll be. How bad is it, Master Vento?"

"The army physician did a fine job," Master Vento said. "The scar will likely be worse now, though."

"One more scar will hardly be noticed at this point," Hinck said. "Saria, you're supposed to stay in Sarikar. We promised the council—"

"That one of us would remain," Saria said. "Now that you've returned, I can go."

"But you—"

She leaned down and pecked his lips. "Get well, my husband-to-be. I would hate to lose you." She patted his shoulder and stalked away. "Derroh! Is my escort ready?"

"Saria, come back here!" Hinck voiced.

"Arman has answered my prayers by bringing you back—in mostly one piece. Now it's my turn to fight for New Sarikar. So wish me the God's blessings and take care of my house."

Then Princess Saria of New Sarikar walked out the front doors and was gone.

"The God's blessing upon you, Saria," Hinck bloodvoiced, his gut churning with helplessness. *"I will take care of your house if you will take care of my wife-to-be."*

He felt her amusement. *"I live to serve."*

An hour later Hinck was back in his chambers, confined to his bed by Master Vento's order, but he could neither rest nor relax. Not with Saria away, fighting in the war without him. Hinck wanted to be there. To protect her. He knew of only one possible way to do that.

Hinck called his guards to keep watch over his body and entered the Veil. He concentrated on Saria and appeared at her side. She was riding a horse south along the snowy bank of the Great River, water on her right and a thick forest on her left. Behind her followed the Earl of Faynor and a contingent of Sarikarian soldiers, dressed in green livery. There must have been at least two hundred. Only the first twenty rode horses. The rest were on foot. Why wasn't she at the fort?

Hinck bloodvoiced Saria. *"What news, Princess?"*

"I'm riding south from the border house, trying to run down the survivors from Lord Edekk's army. Several dozen were spotted on their way to join the Pretender in battle."

"Have they much of a head start?"

"I don't think so," Saria said. *"They were spotted not a half hour ago. We've come across at least ten Puru, who look to have fled the battle, but no sign of any Kinsman soldiers."*

Hinck soared ahead, seeking out the enemy. Before too long, the Armanian battlefield came into view in the distance, so he turned back, thinking he must have missed them. He flew north over the snowy ground, looking for tracks. He saw the fleeing Puru, but no Kinsman traitors. It wasn't until he spotted Saria and her men in the distance that a flash of red drew him into the forest. He sailed into the dark wood, weaving around snow-covered trees, though he probably could have passed right through them.

He happened upon a cluster of warriors with red capes and black tunics that bore embroidered snake and goblet sigils. Tace Edekk himself was among them, standing beside his servant, Natod, who Trevn had learned was a mantic.

Hinck drifted back out of the forest, noting how close Saria and her men were. *"Saria!"* he voiced, moving up beside her. *"Edekk and his men are hiding in the trees just south of here. Send some of your men into the forest to come up behind them."*

"How do you know that?" she asked, frowning.

"I'm in the Veil," Hinck said.

"The Veil! I thought you'd given that up?"

"I'm not one of Miss Onika's warriors, no, but that doesn't mean I forgot what she taught me. Besides, I wanted to help you."

A wide smile curved her lips. "Well, I am glad you did. How close are they?"

"See those three large boulders in the river up ahead?" Hinck asked. "Edekk is in the woods straight across from them."

Saria slowed her horse and informed Lord Faynor and her guards about the pending ambush. "Sir Menel, take twenty men through the trees to attack them from behind. I'll call a rest to give you time to get there. Lord Faynor, ready your men to fight."

Saria drew her horse to a stop and announced a brief rest. Sir Menel peeled out of formation and headed for the back of the line, while the earl turned to face his men.

"Keep watch on them, Hinck," Saria said. "I don't want any surprises."

Hinck returned to the traitors in the forest and wished he'd practiced storming. He understood the concept well enough—and the dangers. He spent the time counting thirty-six traitors and deciding which he'd storm first, if he got the courage to try. The tall one with more warrior tails than hair of his own. Tace too, of course. And Natod. No Sir Jarmyn here. Where was he?

One of Edekk's men peeked out through the trees. "They're moving again, lord," he hissed. "It won't be long now."

Tace urged his men toward the clearing. Tree branches snapped and dumped snow to the ground as thirty-six men attempted to sneak through the forest.

"She's nearly here," the lookout said to Lord Edekk.

"Close enough," Edekk said. "Natod, with me." The tall, slender man strode out of the forest, his manservant beside him carrying a white flag.

"Princess!" Edekk called, his normally stern expression twisted into an odd smile. "I am relieved to meet you here. We've been trying to surrender but lost our way in the forest."

Saria reined her horse. "Did you just bloodvoice the word truth, Hinck?"

"No," Hinck said. "But don't forget his man Natod is a mantic."

"Just you and your *mantic* surrender?" Saria asked the duke. "Or all those men waiting in the forest too?"

"She knows!" Edekk yelled, drawing his sword. "Attack!"

Natod dropped the flag and yelled some foreign word that knocked Saria, her guards, and Lord Faynor off their horses. Tace's soldiers charged out from the cover of the trees, bellowing battle cries. They headed straight for where Saria had pushed to her feet, sword at the ready.

"Cut them down!" Saria hacked her blade at Edekk, who lunged aside and sliced his blade across the flank of Saria's horse. The animal reared, and Saria dove out of the way. She landed well and cut down the nearest traitor with a slash to his calves.

Sands. Hinck hadn't realized the woman could fight.

Natod fixed a savage gaze on Saria and started mumbling. Fairly certain mantics could see the Veil, Hinck moved in front of him. Sure enough, Natod's eyes widened and his speech trailed off.

"You're not the only one with magic here," Hinck said.

Shockingly, the man turned and ran like a coward. Hinck took the moment to check on Saria. She twirled out of the way of a strike, parried another, and stabbed a man in the gut.

Hinck spotted Lord Edekk and six others dart into the woods just in time to meet Sir Menel and his men coming out.

Sir Menel engaged the traitors, but Lord Edekk sprinted south through the trees. Saria gave chase, so Hinck flew ahead to see if he could find where Natod had hidden himself.

That's when he saw the second ambush.

TREVN

The Armanian arrows that had poured down upon Rogedoth's infantry had greatly damaged his numbers. Chieftess Charlon had released her shield in order to turn the river to ice. Trevn marveled at her skill, though he still felt uneasy accepting her help.

At the general's command, the mounted cavalry advanced stirrup to stirrup toward the river, spear-tipped lances out and ready. They started slowly, taking care over the ice, then, on the other side, began to trot. Grayson popped ahead, stopping any aerial fire attacks with small magical shields. Madam Kempe stayed with Trevn in the Veil.

Trevn and his guards rode in the third line, swords in one hand, shields in the other. Behind them, a thousand infantry marched on foot. Trevn's stomach roiled with his own anxiety and the impact of the combined emotions around him. His muscles ached from being tense for so long, and his heart pounded in his ears, keeping beat to the sounds of the advance muffled by his bronze helmet.

Trevn's line crossed over the frozen water. Once they reached the opposite bank, they nudged their horses into a trot, then a canter, chasing after the cavalry. Up ahead, the first line had lost their tight formation and broken into a gallop. They delivered an erratic shock attack to a somewhat lopsided shield wall. The wall broke in several places, and the cavalry fought their way through, cutting down any Puru in their path. The second line pushed forward to engage the remaining Puru with spears, swords, and maces.

"With me!" Trevn yelled, steering his horse toward a gap. The plan was for the cavalry to pierce deep into the enemy ranks and divide them in two. Trevn was to work his way up the middle, straight toward Rogedoth.

Up ahead, a horse reared. A second turned and bolted back toward the river. A third kicked the horse beside it.

"Shadir are entering the horses!" Kempe voiced, moments before Trevn's horse shrieked and jumped to the side.

"Then get them out!" Trevn reeled from the confusion he felt emanating from Seeker. "Whoa, boy!"

"Dismount, Your Highness!" Cadoc yelled, already on the ground. "The horses have gone mad!"

Trevn slid off Seeker, and Cadoc dragged Trevn away by the arm. Novan slapped Seeker's rear, sending him streaking back toward the river. All around them the animals were bucking, leaping, kicking, and rearing.

"Grayson! Onika!" Trevn reached for both at once. *"Get the shadir out of the horses!"*

Trevn and his men picked their way carefully past the nearest horses. He thrust his sword into the air, shouted, "For Arman!" and ran into the fray.

He slashed his sword out around his shield, cutting down one Puru, then another and another, trusting his guards to protect his back. A slice to the neck, a severed arm, a thrust to the abdomen. Men screamed, both with fervor and pain. The occasional horse charged through, though the Veil warriors seemed to have dealt with most of the animals. The staff of a poleaxe slammed against Trevn's sword arm and stung all the way to his shoulder. Novan ended the wielder, and Trevn pushed forward.

Moul Rog's giant horses charged past, their riders pulverizing the enemy with swings of their massive battle-axes. Shadir did not seem to have overtaken them. Enemy giants tore out from the depths of the Puru infantry, and the two groups collided in a cacophony of roaring battle cries, squealing horses, and axes hacking through leather and flesh.

The sky was filled with slashing weapons. Trevn's shield took the brunt of the blows. Noise and emotions bombarded him. Thunder of shield against shield. Shouts of rage and pain. He tried not to let it affect him. As he moved deeper into the fight, each man who fell created a swell of confusion among the still-standing enemy as they fought to defend themselves and keep their footing on ground littered with the dead and dying.

"Attack!" Trevn yelled.

Nietz was fighting with an axe. He chopped down a Kinsman traitor, who fell into the snow and tripped two Puru. Trevn and Cadoc struck them down, then lunged over the bodies to reach new opponents.

Trevn swept his shield left, taking a Puru man's pike thrust, then he jabbed his sword forward and ran the point into the Puru's chest. He twisted the weapon and ripped it free. Another man was on his right, swinging for Rzasa. Trevn sliced across the back of the man's neck, then moved forward again. A Kinsman traitor came at him with a spear. Trevn kicked him hard, smashed his face with the shield. The man fell screaming. Trevn took a half pace forward. A spear jabbed toward his face. He ducked, twisted away, lunged again.

The chaos did not allow Trevn time to anticipate the moves of any one opponent. The Puru pushed and shoved each other. Whether they were seeking more space in which to fight, pushing to the front for greater fame, or Oli had broken their compulsions and they were trying to flee, Trevn didn't know. All around them bronze and iron clanked and grated, and soldiers shouted war cries such as "For Arman!" "For the king!" or the more basic, "Kill them! Kill!" The Puru and giants yelled too, though Trevn didn't understand them.

The Armanian infantry continued to force the enemy back over fallen bodies. More Puru went down, wasting their blows on the air as they stumbled and fell. A pike took Bonds in the side of the head and he fell into the dead. Trevn had no time to mourn the man. A group of Kinsman soldiers in red livery surged up on his right, lunging and stabbing Armanians as they came. Leading the charge was Sir Jarmyn Koll, dressed in shiny bronze armor as fine as Trevn's and wielding a two-handed longsword.

"I promised Lord Edekk I'd bring back your head, King Lackbeard," he said. "So come here and let me chop it off."

Trevn slashed his sword at the traitor. Sir Jarmyn caught Trevn's cut with the flat of his blade, threw off the attack, then whipped his sword back toward Trevn's head. Trevn let his magic connect with Sir Jarmyn's mind. He anticipated and blocked the attack with his shield, then flung his blade around it, striking Sir Jarmyn's side. His blade glanced off the man's armor.

Hundreds of weapons clashed around them. Men cried out. Boots shuffled over slushy snow. Trevn stepped back, nearly tripped on a dead man, but managed to keep his feet. He raised his shield as Sir Jarmyn cut down toward his head and cleaved his sword deep into the wood.

Trevn jerked his shield to the left, and when Sir Jarmyn's arms and sword went with it, exposing him, Trevn stabbed his side, between the leather points holding his breastplate together.

Sir Jarmyn gasped and yanked his blade from Trevn's shield. He staggered, dragging Trevn's sword arm with him, so Trevn released the grip and pulled a dagger from his belt. He used his shield to plow the dying man to the ground, then stabbed his dagger through his visor.

Sir Jarmyn's body shuddered. Trevn set his knee against the man's breastplate and yanked out his sword. He thrust it above his head and stood.

"Who else wants to fight the king of Armania?" he yelled.

This foolhardy invitation brought forward three Puru and a bloodied Kinsman wielding a mace. The man swung his weapon, which struck one of the Puru in the back of the head. As the Puru man fell, Trevn slashed his sword over the bearded face of the Kinsman before he could again swing the mace. Nietz drove his axe into a Puru man's chest, and blood sprayed Trevn. He stabbed another Puru, ripped his sword free, and bellowed, "For Arman!"

An echoed reply rose up, and Trevn felt the heat of Arman pulse within him. A savage calm descended, banishing the bitterness in his gut and the tenseness of his muscles. They had reached the Kinsman traitors, and Trevn deftly cut down the red-uniformed men who had defied Arman and House Hadar. They were the worst kind of deserters, hiding at the back of a compelled army. Trevn screamed and fought and took Justness in every kill, sending each man to stand before Arman's bench, for Wilek, for Rystan and Dendrick, for little Chadek and the children sacrificed for dead giants, for Lord Idez, Eudora, and Bonds, for hundreds of Armanian soldiers, and the compelled Puru and giants whose free will had been stolen.

Trevn was Arman's chosen, and he fought like it, slicing and stabbing any who crossed his path until they lay in a tangled and bloody pile at his feet. A sword slammed against his back, but his armor stopped the blow. Nietz growled and split the man down like firewood. On they fought until suddenly there were no more ahead.

Trevn and his men had fought through ten ranks of Rogedoth's infantry and reached the other side, but they'd gotten off course. He turned back to look into the fray, his guards forming a wall between him and the battle. They stood on the southern end of the line, too far from the distant streaks of green fire. Somehow he and his men needed to cross to the other side of the fighting, over half a battlefield away.

"We need to get to the firelight," Trevn said. "That's where Rogedoth will be."

"That's a long way, Your Highness," Cadoc said.

"Grayson?" he voiced. *"I need you."*

A man appeared in front of Trevn, and he almost swung his sword in defense.

"It's me, Your Highness!" Grayson said, popping a few paces back.

Trevn relaxed. "I need you to carry me and my men to Rogedoth."

"He and Charlon are fighting each other," Grayson said.

"Carry us behind Charlon's men. Take Cadoc first, then me, then come back for the rest."

"And after that? Shall I fight beside you?"

"Take your orders from Miss Onika," Trevn said. "You must continue to banish shadir, especially those who are serving the mantics. You can command them better than anyone. They have to obey you. Take confidence from Arman. He has equipped you for this."

"Yes, sir."

Grayson carried Cadoc away, then returned for Trevn, leaving him with Cadoc in the center of the battle, directly behind Charlon's men, who were chopping down Puru with shard clubs.

Trevn and Cadoc were immediately engaged by Kinsman soldiers in Rogedoth's livery. Grayson brought the rest of Trevn's guard, and they fought hard, slowly drawing nearer the magical battle. A pause in the action gave Trevn a moment to glance past Charlon, who was creating shields as fast as the archers had loosed their arrows. Just past her, Trevn saw not one but four Barthel Rogedoths, all throwing fire toward the Chieftess.

Hinck

More of Edekk's men were waiting inside the woods downriver. Hinck recognized Captain Korvoh's wild mane of warrior twists and scarred cheek.

Hinck jumped back to Saria, who was still chasing Lord Edekk. *"He's leading you to a second ambush! Let him go."*

Saria slowed to a stop, sliding a little on the snow.

Lord Edekk glanced back and grinned. "Giving up so soon, Princess?"

Saria panted heavily. "You're too fast for me." Then to Hinck. *"Keep an eye on them. I'm going to help Lord Faynor."* And she turned back.

Well, this was vexing. Hinck wanted to keep an eye on Saria, not the second ambush, though she certainly could take care of herself. He drifted south until he came upon the traitors.

And two giants.

Hinck almost choked. *"Saria! There are two giants in the second group."*

"Find someone to break their compulsions or storm them," she said.

Hinck voiced Miss Onika and Oli, but both were preoccupied with the main battle. Hinck would have to deal with this problem on his own. He let his mind quest into the first massive man, seeking out anything that felt like a soul. Strangely, he found it right away, just like seeking a mind before bloodvoicing. He recalled Miss Onika's instructions: *"By concentrating and moving swiftly, a Veil warrior pushes a person's soul from their body."*

Hinck frowned at the giant, not liking the prospect of pushing any part of this colossal man. Best to get a running—er, flying—start.

He moved himself back, then flew at the giant as quickly as he could, concentrating fully on his soul. At the last second he shut his eyes and winced slightly, not knowing what to expect.

He hit something hard, momentarily stunning himself. He opened his eyes and found himself soaring over the river, hugging the giant around his waist. He recoiled and his arms passed right through the man, which confused him. Hinck told himself to stop, and he did. He was now hovering over a snowy plain on the other side of the river, watching a somewhat transparent image of the giant soar away, a look of fright on his oversized face.

Hinck had done it! Storming appeared to be the same act as leaving one's body to enter the Veil, just done surprisingly to someone who wasn't expecting it.

A chorus of battle cries made his heart leap. The second ambush was charging toward Saria, who was still battling some of the first attackers. Hinck appeared at her side just as Tace Edekk rushed toward her back, sword raised to stab.

"Behind you!" Hinck voiced.

Saria whirled and cut her blade across Edekk's middle, slicing open more than his leather armor. The man groaned, staring dumbly at his killer, then dropped to his knees.

"You should be wearing plate armor, Your Grace. It's more effective." Saria kicked him to his back and stabbed him in the throat.

"Sands, you astonish me," Hinck said. *"I've never seen a woman fight like you."*

She jerked her sword free. *"Are you appalled?"*

"No," Hinck said. *"Greatly impressed."*

Saria grinned. Another traitor lunged toward her. She parried the strike and was swept away in combat.

A call of "Giant!" turned Hinck's head. The second ambush had arrived. Hinck spotted the other giant—who could miss a man who stood two heads taller than everyone else? He lumbered in back of the Kinsman traitors, massive axe in hand. Hinck couldn't let anyone get hit with that weapon. He sped toward the giant, focused on the man's soul, and repeated what he'd done before. He passed over a greater distance this time before he made contact, and when he opened his eyes, instead of sailing along the riverbank south, they were somewhere else entirely. Gliding through a deep green forest in the height of summer.

Hinck released the giant and stopped his motion. A bright glow in the distance piqued his interest. He floated toward it, curious what could create so much glorious light.

"*Hinck?*" Saria bloodvoiced. "*Did you attack the giant?*"

"*Saria.*" In a blink he was again with her, back at the river. The snowy ground was cluttered with dead bodies and patches of blood. The fight was over already? "*How long was I gone?*"

"*I know not.*" Saria was crouched beside the body of the second giant. "*There are no marks on this man. He's breathing, but clearly incapacitated.*"

"*I stormed him,*" Hinck said. "*Stormed both giants.*"

"*You saved us, Hinck. Saved me from Edekk. Thank you.*"

Hinck beamed at Saria. "*Just doing my part for my queen.*"

She pressed her lips into a thin line as if fighting off laughter. "*Are you tired? I'd like to continue on to the main battle and do what we can to help.*"

"*I am wide awake, Your Highness,*" Hinck said. "*I'll be at your side the entire way.*"

GOZAN

I'll kill him!" Amala screamed. "He's no father to me." Hatred for Sir Kalenek grew in Amala's heart, blackening every thought. She sat on her horse, alone, far back from the battle—had left the charge the moment Masi had brought word of Shanek's death by Sir Kalenek's hand.

Amala glared across the snowy field to the battle, watching the green lights of magic, and her heart wrenched. "First we must kill King Barthel. He's to blame. He drew Shanek into his plans. Convinced him it was all for the best. Shanek would have obeyed Charlon otherwise. He would have waited until she felt it was time."

Gozan cared nothing for King Barthel or Sir Kalenek. He was far more interested in another detail of Masi's story. "Dendron is truly banished?" he made the girl ask. "Gone from the human realm for good?"

"Stop using my voice!" Amala yelled. "If you want me to speak, you need only ask."

Gozan had no patience for her theatrics and listened carefully for Masi's reply.

Dendron is gone, master, Masi said. *You are the last great in the whole land.*

The last great. This changed everything. Gozan no longer need keep Dominion over this ridiculous child. He was the last great shadir in all Er'Rets—maybe the world. Shadir would flock to him as their new master. He could find a better host—someone intelligent, who was not so wounded. He might even pay Empress Jazlyn a visit.

But first he would entertain himself by leading Amala to her death. *Let's kill a king.*

Amala nudged her horse into a walk. The girl was a poor rider. Gozan connected to the animal's mind, and soon they were cantering across the snowy field.

"He will be near his mantics," Amala said. "Near the lights."

Gozan was not so certain of that, but he longed to watch the magical fight, so he did not disagree.

At first glance, King Barthel appeared to be losing. The snowy ground was covered in the bodies of his soldiers. Gozan bet shadir were clouding the Veil, reveling in the misery and fear. Soon, he told himself. Once he was free of Amala, he would again see all.

They approached the nearest source of fire and magical light, but Gozan saw only one mantic in this place. Harton Sonber.

Amala, weak in her state of grief, was filled with hostility at the sight of the man who had dared use and mock her. *We will kill Master Harton first,* she thought.

Fool girl. *And how will we do that?*

She dismounted and her hands found a cold sword in the snow. *We will stab him in the back, like he did to me so many times.*

She carried the heavy weapon toward Harton. The man was killing Armanian soldiers with bolts of flame. His cheeks were sunken. His eyes ringed in circles. He had little magic left. If he did not purge soon, he would die. Gozan wished he knew what shadir the man served. With so few mantics left, it must be a common of some strength.

Amala's steps were precarious in the slushy snow. She took the sword in two hands and pulled it toward her, ready to thrust. Gozan gave strength to her arms, knowing she would need it, but before she could attack, Harton spun around.

"*Mahamahts!*" he yelled, shoving his hand toward her.

Amala screamed and fell flat on her back, dropping the weapon. Wet slush seeped into her clothes, and she gasped at the cold.

Harton sneered down. "You would kill *me*? After all we have been through?" He chuckled and formed a ball of fire in his hand, held it over her, grinning widely.

Help me! Amala thought to Gozan. *Save us!* She struggled to sit, to wriggle away, but Gozan forced her to stay put.

Harton dropped the fire, but before the flames could touch the girl, a blast of green light extinguished them and knocked Harton off his feet.

Gozan released his hold on Amala, made the girl sit up and twist around so he could see who had come to her rescue.

Charlon Sonber stood behind her. Six gowzals perched on her shoulders, arms, and head. Another five clustered at her feet, and three circled in the sky overhead.

"You saved me," Amala said. "Why?"

"Shanek loved you," Charlon said. "I spare you for his sake."

Amala's feeble mind spun with what all this meant. That Charlon, who hated her, would save her life? "You just wanted to kill your brother," she said. That, at least, made sense.

"Harton is not dead," Charlon said, jutting her chin to Amala's left.

Amala glanced over her shoulder and saw Harton squirming in the slushy snow. "Kill him!" she said. "Quickly! Before he gathers his strength."

A burst of flame drew Charlon's gaze away. A ball of fire was streaking through the sky toward them. "*Mahgayn!*" Charlon yelled, and one of her gowzals shot from her shoulder and formed a green circle of light that met the fire, disintegrating both.

Incredible, how much she had improved.

"I will not kill my brother," Charlon said to Amala. "For too long I have been a force of destruction. But there is no lasting satisfaction in killing for revenge."

A current of wild anger filled Amala with energy. "If you won't kill him, then I will!" She picked up the sword from the snow and stabbed it down toward Harton's chest.

The man said, "*Sabab bay êsh,*" and fire engulfed Amala.

The girl shrieked as the flames seared her skin and hair. She fell to the snow, but the damage had been done. So great was the pain that Gozan decided to leave. She sensed his choice, and her heart quailed within her. Gozan didn't linger long enough to hear what she thought about the situation. He threw himself out of the girl and into the Veil.

He instantly felt cold. Lighter too, and free now that he was not confined in so little a person. With a clear view of the Veil, he could see the shadir swirling around the dying girl, reveling in her fear and pain. Gozan felt it too, only this time it gave him great pleasure.

Dominion need not be permanent, he was glad to discover, and he enjoyed Amala's pain until her last hitched breath carried away her life.

"You're sick, Harton," Charlon said, frowning down upon the charred corpse.

"She was trying to kill me," he said, rising to his feet.

"She was a child. She didn't know what she was doing."

"I disagree, sister. I was a child when I killed our mother. I knew exactly what I was doing, and it gave me great satisfaction. As did killing Amala. As will killing you. *Romahk êsh!*" he yelled, and a dagger of fire streaked toward Charlon.

She cried, "*Mahgayn!*" and another gowzal transformed into a shield of green light that blocked Harton's fire.

"Surely you can do more than shield," Harton said. "Why won't you fight me?"

"I have nothing but pity for you," Charlon said.

"I don't want your pity," Harton said. "I want you to suffer. *Âtsar rûwach!*"

Clever man. It was just the right spell. Not at all difficult, but one for which Charlon had no defense. Her eyes bulged. Her mouth gaped, opening and closing like a fish, unable to command her birds, unable to breathe.

Harton walked within reach, shoved her into the snow, and cackled. Gozan should have liked it. He should have reveled in her terror like the other shadir cavorting around the dying woman, but Charlon was too great a mantic to be defeated by someone so unimaginative.

Gozan searched the Veil, looking for the shadir powering Harton Sonber's spell. He noticed a woman standing barefoot in the snow, dressed in a thin, sleeveless gown of red silk.

Yobatha, Gozan said, taking his natural form and swelling to his full size.

The common's gaze pulled away from Charlon's dying body. *Who are you?*

I am Gozan the Great, also called Rurek, god of war. I require the use of your human.

What for?

That is my business, common. Do you wish to fight me?

Yobatha cowered. *No, great one.*

Then release him to me.

Gozan felt the common drop the thin thread of old magic in the man. So out of practice was he at doing magic of this type, it took him three tries to harness it. The moment Harton was under his control, he stopped the spell that had taken Charlon's breath.

She gasped for air and called to her gowzals. Her voice was too raspy, though, and croaked indiscernibly. Gozan wanted her to see him—to know who had healed her and to feel indebted. He had only a moment until she recovered her voice enough to shield herself.

"*Bara* Charlon *chazah*," he forced Harton to say, and the man's face contorted in confusion and dismay.

The last spark of magic left Harton Sonber, and he fell to the ground, in need of purging. Gozan doubted any would help him.

Charlon's eyes widened as the shadir swarming above her became visible. She stopped struggling and sat up, locked her gaze with Gozan's. "What are you?" she asked.

You know me as Rurek, he said to Charlon. *You wanted to be a seer. I have decided to grant your request.*

Charlon scrambled to her feet, breath misting from blue lips. "Why do you do this?"

Because you are worthy.

"Will I see you again?" she asked.

The shriek of shadir drew his attention away from Charlon. In the distance the prophetess Onika and her Veil warriors were banishing slights and commons. Gozan had no desire to test the strength of Arman's chosen.

Someday, perhaps, he said to Charlon, then streaked into the sky, heading for safety and the possibility of reuniting with his former slave.

Charlon

Charlon was no longer blind.

The Veil was filled with moving colors. Shadir reveling. Drawn by fear and pain and death. Some sated. Many still feeding. A select few bound instead by service. To Rogedoth and his mantics. To her gowzals.

Feathers fell around her like snow. Too many of her gowzals had died. Bodies broken from overuse. Unable to transform any longer. She still had four. King Barthel had at least five. Three to maintain each illusion of himself. The other two fighting her. He had more help besides. Two mantics on either end of the four King Barthels. A small man in robes and a woman. Mantics attacking with the old magic. Superior in so many ways. But they were fading. Needed to purge. Take more root.

Masi had told her they had no more.

Then there were the others. The humans in the Veil. Charlon had heard of this. But hadn't understood until now. They moved like shadir. Transparent and flying as if weightless. Shadows of themselves, yet brighter somehow. Their words sent shadir shrieking beneath the snowy ground, never to return.

They had been unable to attack the shielded mantics. A shield Charlon had tried many times to destroy. She had been unable to maintain a strike against it. Every time she tried. She had to release the spell. To protect herself.

But now she could see. See which shadir maintained the shield. She sent word through Masi to the one called Grayson. To have King Trevn's Veil soldiers attack those shadir.

They were working at it now. Chanting commands in the name of their god. Those they spoke to became immobile. Other shadir went wild with fright.

Fire shot toward Charlon. Three plumes at once. She shielded all three with one gowzal. The bird screeched but held the spell. She created a second shield to stop a spear of light. The bird succeeded but did not return. Fell dead to the snow.

Panic chilled Charlon. Only three gowzals left. She would need the help of shadir to retreat. Had she done all she could in this battle? Should she flee? She hated to leave King Barthel alive. But without magic, she had no way to—

The shield around King Barthel and his mantics fell. The mantics attacked the humans floating in the Veil. They zipped aside. All but the pale leader, who streaked toward the small man. Passed through him. Carried his shimmering likeness away.

His body fell.

Charlon ignored her surprise. Sent out two gowzals. In the form of flaming green orbs. Against two of King Barthel's illusions of himself. Hoping to strike the real man. Both illusions vanished. And her gowzals fell into puddles of black mud in the snow. Leaving only two likenesses of the king.

Which one was real?

Charlon used her remaining gowzal to shield herself from an attack from the last mantic. The woman. Where were Charlon's other two shadir? She looked for them, waiting for them to return. Prayed to King Trevn's god they would. A foolish notion. But the god who made such magic must be mighty. And Charlon needed help.

She held the shield. Waiting. Where were those birds? One fluttered toward her. Losing feathers from each flap of its wings. It would not last much longer. She waited for the second. Wanting to give the first as much strength as she could.

There! The second was on the ground. Hopping this way. Charlon sent both out. Sent them to bring down King Barthel and his last illusion with fire.

She held the shield. Watched her attack unfold. Both kings vanished. Gowzals fell to mud. Confused, she tried to remember when King Barthel had cast his spell. He'd created three illusions. Not four. She was certain. Yet four illusions had fallen. And the king was not here.

Trevn

Trevn fought his way through a cluster of Puru, enraged by the message he'd received from Onika. He reached for Charlon's mind, eager to have her version of the story.

"What happened with Rogedoth, Chieftess?" he voiced.

"He tricked me!" Charlon said. *"Conjured illusions of himself. Sneaked away somehow. I sent Mast to find him. He has ridden back to his camp. Is packing to leave."*

The coward.

"Miss Onika," Trevn voiced. *"I need a Veil warrior to lead me and my men through this melee to some horses—some safe horses."*

"Right away, Your Highness."

"Rogedoth is trying to run," Trevn yelled to Cadoc. "We must stop him."

Onika came through, and Kempe led the way, voicing Trevn directions. Soon he and his guards were mounted and riding away from the battle. They recruited any mounted Armanian as they went, and by the time they were riding hard for Rogedoth's camp, they had rounded up another twenty-one soldiers to assist.

With Kempe's help, they wove quickly to the center of Rogedoth's camp. They found his tent being folded by a group of enemy soldiers. Rogedoth was sitting in a wagon, nestled beneath a pile of furs, while Natod, Tace Edekk's mantic servant, supervised the packing of a second wagon with supplies. Trevn counted maybe twenty-five enemy soldiers.

"Arrest these men!" Trevn yelled, dismounting.

Fights broke out all around. Trevn walked to Rogedoth's wagon, drew his sword, and held his shield ready. "Running away, are you? You need to answer for your crimes."

"I committed no crimes," he said.

Truth.

"You dare mock the man who holds your life in his hands?" Trevn asked. "Come out of that wagon this instant."

Nietz scaled the wagon's side and jumped into the bed. He set the point of his sword to Rogedoth's back. "That was an order from your king. I suggest you obey it." He leaned into the blade.

Rogedoth scrambled forward. "Patience, man! I'm going." He pushed to his feet and took careful steps to the end of the wagon. Trevn tried to connect with his mind, but it was shielded. Rogedoth jumped to the ground, hand resting on the wagon bed, thick eyebrows furrowed. He pulled a sword from under a pile of furs and swung it at Trevn.

Good. Trevn wanted to fight him. He parried and countered with short, fast jabs that drove Rogedoth back. Either the man knew little about swordplay, or he was decades out of practice. Trevn should feel elated that the match would end quickly, but the calm expression on Rogedoth's face and the triumphant glint in the man's eyes bothered him. What had he to be triumphant about? He had lost everything.

The fighting around them had died down. Trevn's men had subdued the enemy, and his guards gathered close, all ready and willing to rush in and subdue Rogedoth the moment Trevn asked, yet stilled by some unspoken agreement not to intervene until then. To allow their king this moment to defeat his enemy.

Trevn slashed his blade across Rogedoth's chest, slicing a gash through the front of his leather jerkin. He knocked his shield against the Pretender's face, and the man stumbled back from the blow. Trevn came at him again, thrust his sword at Rogedoth's middle. The man twisted, and the blade glanced off his leathers but managed to cut through the side and into a bit of skin.

Rogedoth howled and hacked his sword down like a club. Trevn caught the blow with his shield, but the blade sank into the battered wood and stuck, splitting a crack through to the center. Trevn dropped the shield, which still held Rogedoth's blade.

Rogedoth stepped on the wood and wrenched his sword free, leaving himself open long enough for Trevn to stab his thigh. The Pretender cried out and staggered a few steps to the left, a look of surprise on his face. He lunged back toward Trevn, who caught the blade with his cross guard. A flick of his wrist, and Rogedoth was disarmed.

"Surrender?" Trevn asked.

"I can't!" Rogedoth snarled through clenched teeth.

What did *that* mean? "Then we fight on," Trevn said.

Rogedoth was favoring his right leg, so Trevn employed one of Nietz's brawling tactics. He swung the flat of his blade against the wound in Rogedoth's leg, stepped on his right foot, and shouldered into him.

Rogedoth wailed and fell on his side, hands cradling his injured leg. Trevn used his boot to roll him to his back, then set the tip of his blade against the man's heart.

"Do you surrender now?" he asked again.

"Trevn!"

Mielle? Trevn glanced up, shocked to see his wife here of all places. Barthel Rogedoth held a dagger to her throat. Stunned, Trevn looked back to the man on the ground. There were two? Had he been fighting the real one? Or someone else?

"*Mahgayn bay zōt adamah!*" Mielle cried, hands outstretched. The Rogedoth beside her lowered his dagger and stood watching as a sheen of green light shot toward Trevn.

"That's not Mielle!" Trevn yelled. He threw himself to the ground, hoping to dodge the magic, but the light wrapped over him like a sheet of frosty glass. He couldn't see clearly through it but could hear the muted yells of his men, saw flashes of brighter light, silhouettes running.

Trevn had fallen into Rogedoth's trap.

He reached a gloved finger toward the light. The moment he touched it, a shock ran up his arm and he jerked back. A form appeared on his left and leaned over him. He could just make out Mielle's face, distorted by the green light. "Do *you* surrender, Your Highness?" she asked.

"Never!" Trevn said, then closed his eyes and entered the Veil.

GRAYSON

Grayson had worked hard since coming to the battlefield. He had banished shadir and carried dozens of compelled soldiers to Duke Canden for help. But what the king wanted him to do . . . He wasn't certain about that. Shadir had always flocked to him, seemed to like him for some reason. But could the king be right? Could Grayson really command them?

He caught sight of three shadir circling a dying man and popped closer, then winced at the sight of a Puru man whose stomach had been ripped open. He kept his gaze on the shadir. "Leave this man alone," he said.

The shadir stopped moving—all three. They stared at Grayson, eyes bulging.

"I want to talk to the shadir," Grayson said. "Find your friends, and bring them to me."

To Grayson's surprise, they flitted away. He watched them, quickly losing sight of all but the red, who had swooped over to a cluster of shadir who were feeding off a dying horse. See? They hadn't obeyed him.

The clank of swords pulled his gaze toward two Puru men who were fighting each other. One must still be compelled. Grayson drifted closer, watching the fight until he figured out which had no self-control. He popped behind the man, grabbed him around the waist, and carried him to Duke Canden. A long line of Puru were fleeing up the river from where the duke had positioned himself on the north edge of the battle.

"Here's another for you, sir." Grayson released the Puru man beside two others.

His quarry scrambled about in the snow, panicked by his strange ride through the air.

"He'll have to wait his turn," the duke said.

Before Grayson could comment, Rosârah Zeroah voiced him. *"Sir Keshton has been wounded and needs medical care. Would you carry him to the fort?"*

"Coming." Grayson popped to Sir Keshton, who was bleeding badly from a wound to his shoulder. Before he could even touch the man, Hinckdan Faluk voiced him.

"Master Grayson," the duke said. *"Princess Saria and her men have reached the central border house. She would like to enter, as they have some wounded, but there's no one at the gate. Has the fort been taken?"*

"I don't think so, sir," Grayson replied.

"Can you get word to someone inside to let us enter?"

"Yes. Give me a moment."

Grayson carried Sir Keshton to the physician inside the fort, then flitted through the building until he saw someone he knew: King Trevn's onesent, walking down the hall.

Grayson popped beside him and entered the physical realm, which made his shoulder and ear burns sting. "Master Hawley? Princess Saria is outside the gates with some wounded. Will you see that someone lets her in?"

The onesent glanced at Grayson. "Princess Saria at the gate?"

"Yes, sir," Grayson said.

"I'll see that it's opened right away, Master Grayson." And he hurried off.

Grayson jumped to Hinckdan Faluk and found the man in the Veil, hovering beside the princess outside the gate.

"Master Hawley is coming to let you in," he voiced.

Hinckdan turned his attention to Grayson and gasped, his eyes roving all around. *"Woes!"* he said. *"The shadir!"*

Grayson glanced behind him, shocked to see a thick cluster of shadir all staring at him—maybe a hundred.

They had obeyed his order. Somewhat.

He thought over the prophecies that were supposed to be about him, wondering how he might go about achieving what they'd foretold. Should he banish them now? They'd be angry that he'd tricked them. But why should he care? Shadir were the worst tricksters of all.

He flew into the sky. The shadir followed. From here he was able to get a good look at the battlefield. It was an awful sight, all those dead bodies, the bloody snow. But there were still a lot of shadir flying around—many more than were in the group behind him.

Grayson turned on the creatures. "This isn't everyone," he said. "Look down there!" He gestured to the battlefield. "See them? I want to talk to every shadir—all at once. Find the others and bring them back." Then, to see how far he could push it, he said, "Don't make me ask you again."

Like a sudden windstorm, the shadir soared past Grayson in a gust that spun him around. He couldn't believe how quickly they had listened. Perhaps the king was right. Perhaps he did have power over them.

☉Lɪ

The first Puru compulsion to break had been the most difficult, but once Oli had found the right memory, things had moved much more quickly. The vast majority of the Puru had been compelled by Lady Zenobia at the same time, standing on a beach. Every so often Oli came upon a man who didn't have that memory. When this happened, he moved on to someone else. With no time to waste, he was much more effective focusing on the Puru with that same memory. Once the battle ended, he could take his time with the survivors. Grayson had been helping by carrying the compelled enemy here. Puru, giant, and Kinsman alike, no one was too heavy for Grayson to transport through the Veil.

Oli worked tirelessly, despite the niggling that pressed against his mind, as if he'd forgotten something important. Eudora's death. Or his journey to the Lowerworld. Maybe both. He couldn't think about Lady Brisa killing his sister without losing control, so he thought instead about how Zeroah had saved him and how he'd sworn allegiance to Arman. He was a free man at last. The entire experience felt like a dream, yet so did his current reality.

How he had come to this place was truly miraculous.

To the south the battle still raged, both in the physical realm and in the Veil. Armania's blue banners waved high over the melee in dozens of places—higher even than the heads of the giants—displaying King Trevn's insignia. There were far fewer of Rogedoth's red.

They were winning this fight.

The Veil warriors were working to banish shadir to the Lowerworld, but there were still so many. Normally such a thing would have set Oli on edge

633

to the point of distraction. No more. He floated among the shadir, unafraid for the first time in his life.

Grayson appeared on the ground below with a Puru soldier. *"Here's another, Your Grace!"* he voiced.

Before Oli could answer, Grayson vanished. The Puru man looked around, completely bewildered. He couldn't see Oli. All he knew was that one moment he'd been in the battle, and now he was standing on the outskirts.

Oli got right to work. The moment he freed the Puru's mind, the man set off at a run toward the forest. There were no more compelled waiting, so Oli scanned the battlefield and moved to a Puru man, who stood worrying his hands on the staff of his poleaxe, staring into the melee as if he couldn't decide whether or not to enter. Oli found his mind easily and sought out the island memory. Yes, there it was. He focused on that moment and changed it. A sudden lightness in the man told Oli he'd succeeded. The Puru's eyes widened in horror at the sight of the battlefield, and he turned and ran upriver, following the path the previous Puru had taken moments before.

As Oli swooped toward yet another Puru soldier, a flash of orange fire sailed past, startling him. He turned his head, searching the crowd for the mantic who had attacked him. His eyes locked with a woman on horseback. Lady Zenobia, Sir Kamran's mother.

"Your Pretender is losing this battle, lady," Oli said to her mind. Then he jumped through the Veil and exited ten paces behind her.

"I think not, Your Grace!" she yelled. Her head turned slightly, tipped up, side to side. She didn't know where he'd gone.

"By the lay of the battlefield, lady, it seems quite obvious."

"It matters not which side has more casualties," Zenobia yelled. "As long as your king dies, we shall win."

"Your Grace!" Danek Faluk voiced him. *"If you will continue to distract Lady Zenobia, I think I can storm her."*

"Gladly." Oli moved back in front of Zenobia's horse. *"My king has Arman on his side, lady,"* he voiced her. *"He won't die."*

"You are a traitor to us all, Oli Agoros," Zenobia said. "You shamed your family. You betrayed Sâr Janek and Sir Kamran."

"Your son was the traitor," Oli said.

"You are a disgrace to the Lahavôtesh."

"Thank you," Oli said, drifting slowly away. *"I've tried to turn my life around. It's heartening to know that people have noticed."*

"Puroh!" Zenobia cried. Fire shot out from her fingertips.

Oli vanished, appearing behind her, where he'd just been, and caught sight of a blur shooting toward her from the side. Danek passed alone into Zenobia's right, but he exited on her left, soaring away with another person, the two of them struggling.

A person who didn't look at all like Lady Zenobia.

It had all happened quite fast, so perhaps Oli hadn't seen correctly. He concentrated on Danek and chased after him. Sure enough, Danek was locked in a fight of sorts with the soul of a man, who was screaming and swinging fists.

Oli recognized him at once. *"Mahat Wallington?"*

The former merchant met Oli's gaze. *"What did he do to me? Put me back in my body!"*

"That was your *body?"* Oli looked back across the field to what appeared to be the collapsed body of Lady Zenobia. *"I thought you were a malleant."*

"I learned enough to be a decoy. Now put me back!"

"You'll have to find your own way." Danek shoved Mahat and turned him at the same time. The man spun slowly away, yelling obscenities, clueless how to stop himself.

"That was well done, don't you think?" Danek asked.

"Yes," Oli said, *"but for one thing. Where is the real Lady Zenobia?"*

"You know her better than me, Your Grace," Danek said. *"Lead me to her, and we will finish her together."*

Oli could free Puru minds later. Stopping Lady Zenobia was more important at present. He concentrated on King Echad's oldest concubine and appeared in a somewhat deserted military camp. He did not see Zenobia, but Barthel Rogedoth stood beside a collapsed tent with Rosârah Mielle, whose arm was outstretched as she held Rosâr Trevn to the ground with a sheet of green light.

TREVn

Trevn hovered in the Veil, looking down on his body trapped under the magical light barrier. No one seemed to have realized he'd left himself empty.

Many of Trevn's soldiers, who moments before had subdued Rogedoth's men, surrendered without reason. Compelled, no doubt, but by whom? The Rogedoth he'd fought lay on the ground, bleeding from the wounds Trevn had inflicted. He appeared to be dead, yet strangely no one seemed to care. The second Rogedoth was circling the wagon, speaking in a soft voice to a shadir in the form of a golden bird. And the mantic—the one who looked like Mielle—was still standing over Trevn's body, hand stretched toward the magical barrier holding him down, and arguing with Natod, Tace Edekk's serving man. Trevn's first instinct was to try to storm someone, though it would be wiser to assign the task to those more practiced.

Oli Agoros appeared beside the golden bird. Danek Faluk came seconds later.

"Oli! Danek!" Trevn called and the two men flashed to his side.

"We are looking for Lady Zenobia," Oli said, frowning at the scene. "That's her shadir." He nodded to the golden bird. "Perhaps she has taken another form."

"As Mielle?" Trevn asked, pointing to the likeness of his wife.

Oli frowned. "I cannot tell without storming her."

"Kempe," Trevn voiced. "Can you storm the mantic who looks like Mielle?"

"There is no point," Kempe said. "See how she glows?"

"No," Trevn said, at the same time as Oli said, "Yes."

"It's very faint, Your Highness," Kempe said. "An outline of green light."

Trevn saw it now. He'd thought it a reflection from the light barrier holding him captive, but the living Rogedoth had it around him as well. *"What does it mean?"* he asked.

"That storming them will fail," Oli said. *"We saw this on the battlefield. The shield must be broken before we can storm them, but only Grayson can do that. Or Chieftess Charlon."*

"Grayson!" Trevn voiced. *"I need you!"* He also called the other Veil warriors, wanting all the help he could get. He spotted Cadoc, Nietz, Novan, and Rzasa crouched behind the wagon, swords drawn and creeping toward the end—toward the Mielle mantic and Trevn's trapped body.

"Cadoc, do not attack," Trevn voiced.

"Your Highness! Are you well?" Cadoc thought.

"I am uninjured," he said. *"The Veil warriors are coming to destroy the mantics—then you can free me. Wait for my word."*

Zeroah arrived first, followed by Grayson, who brought with him a cloud of shadir that not only chilled the air, they blocked the view of the ground. Trevn had never seen so many of the creatures in once place. It was fairly terrifying.

"Why so many shadir?" he asked Grayson.

"I've been calling them to me," Grayson replied. *"To see if they'd obey."*

Miss Onika appeared beside Trevn, and a great many of Grayson's shadir fled at the sight of her, which enabled them to see the mantics below. Mielle and Natod were still arguing.

"What is happening here?" Onika asked.

Trevn explained about Rogedoth's trap. *"That's not Mielle but a mantic wearing a mask. My body is trapped under the green glow."* He indicated the light barrier.

"Why haven't they killed you?" Onika asked.

A fair question. Killing Trevn would win Rogedoth the war. So what was he waiting for?

"Puroh!" Rogedoth had spotted Trevn in the Veil. A burst of flames shot out from each of his hands.

Before the fire reached them, Trevn moved to a new location, now hovering in the air above the wagon. Most of the Veil warriors had reappeared in the sky behind the mantic who had cast the spell. Zeroah, however, had come into view above the horses. Rogedoth shot a ball of orange fire toward her. She disappeared in time, but Trevn didn't see where she moved to.

"What is the name of that mantic's shadir?" Grayson asked Oli. *"Do you know?"*

"*Rogedoth only ever had Dendron, which we now know was a lie,*" Oli said. "*The golden heron that was here before. It is named Kabada, and it has always been bonded to Lady Zenobia, though I don't know how you will find it again in this swarm.*"

"*I will call her,*" Grayson said. "*Kabada! I wish to speak with you at once.*"

Little by little, shadir in the swarm drifted aside until only the great golden bird remained, suspended in the air over the Rogedoth mantic.

"*Incredible,*" Oli said.

"*Come to me, now, Kabada,*" Grayson said.

To Trevn's relief, the shadir obeyed.

"What's it doing?" Natod asked Rogedoth.

"I don't know," Rogedoth said. "Kabada!" But the creature was not listening. It flapped its wings and came to a stop before Grayson, black eyes watching him.

"*Those mantics are against me,*" Grayson said, motioning to Rogedoth, Natod, and Mielle. "*You will abandon them at once. Is that clear?*"

"*I have served them for many years,*" the creature said.

"*Did you not hear me?*" Grayson yelled so loudly that Trevn flinched. He'd never heard the young man use such a commanding tone.

Kabada shrank until she resembled a youngling version of herself. "*I heard you clearly, Master,*" she said, "*but I—*"

"*Obey me at once!*" Grayson said. "*Abandon the mantics. And use up all of their evenroot reserves, if they have any. Do this now.*"

"*Yes, Master.*"

Trevn stared at the light barrier, expecting it to vanish. It did not. But the green shields around the pacing Rogedoth, Natod, and Mielle faded. Rogedoth began to change. The skin on his face bubbled and stretched. His graying hair in its long braid shortened, and shiny black curls sprouted over his head. His body shrank, long limbs growing slender and feminine.

It was Lady Zenobia.

"*Your Highness, look!*" Oli said, pointing at the dead Rogedoth.

He too was changing, arms, chest, and legs shrinking into a slight figure. A trim black beard and moustache grew on his face.

"*That was Natod?*" No wonder the man had fought so poorly, but what about the Natod arguing with Mielle? Trevn drew his gaze to the other two mantics, who were changing too. Natod grew taller, hair shriveling on the sides but extending into a long braid, gray at the top, black at the bottom.

"He's the real Rogedoth," Oli said.

Mielle's long hair coils grew thicker and more ornate. Her frame shrank, but her limbs, torso, and face swelled, still feminine, but chubby and very familiar. Trevn gasped, and a chill washed over him. *"Mother?"*

"Trevn!" She still held the light barrier but pointed her free hand at Rogedoth, who was still transforming. "He wanted to kill you, but I stopped him."

Trevn had no mercy left for his mother. *"Oli, storm Zenobia,"* he said. *"Danek, storm my mother. Grayson, you must stop the one who looked like Natod and is turning into Rogedoth."*

"No!" Mother yelled. "Trevn, please!"

Trevn turned his attention to Grayson, who now stood on the ground. He shot green light from his hands. It gushed over the light barrier and knocked the real Rogedoth to the ground. He instantly started to stand again.

A scream pulled Trevn's gaze to his mother, whose body collapsed in the snow. He saw her likeness shrinking and spinning into the distance. Stormed.

The shield over Trevn's body vanished. He returned to his body, scrambled to his hands and knees, then to his feet. He sprinted toward the wagon, where his guards were waiting. He grabbed the end and slid around the corner to a stop, peeking back around the side.

Lady Zenobia's body lay on the ground, but the Pretender was back on his feet amid a flock of gowzals. Three circled overhead. Two had perched on his shoulders. Another handful roamed around his boots.

"Ragaz, Shama, Daliza," Rogedoth said. *"Sabab bay kef."* Three of the birds by his feet melted into stones the size of fists. *"Daah!"*

The stones shot toward Grayson, who stopped them with a gleam of green light that spread between his hands. The rocks fell to the snow and slowly turned back into gowzals.

"Mikray, *sabab bay eben,"* Rogedoth said. One of the flying shadir clumped to the ground and swelled into a boulder that rumbled toward Grayson.

The young man popped out of its path and threw more green fire back at Rogedoth. The Pretender lunged aside, but the fire singed his tunic and he frantically patted out the smoke.

"Onika," Trevn voiced. *"Can you banish the shadir inside the gowzals?"*

"Doesn't work," she said. *"They're able to ignore us somehow."*

"Iamos, *sabab bay kefay. Daah!"* Rogedoth shouted.

One of the shadir on his shoulders crumbled into dozens of embers that melted through the snow. Another word from Rogedoth and they whizzed at

Grayson. He shielded most without difficulty, though they were so small that several got past and pelted him, scorching burn marks onto his leather armor. Rogedoth sent a second group of embers, and this time Grayson popped out of the way.

"Grayson?" Trevn voiced. *"Can you command the shadir within those birds?"*

"I tried," he said. *"But they're bonded to the gowzals, and the gowzals want to obey Rogedoth."*

"Can you order the shadir out of them?"

"They don't want to leave," Grayson said. *"They like it there."* He appeared behind Rogedoth and threw what looked like a sheet of green glass at the man. Rogedoth turned in time to repel it with a cry of, "Seeosi, *sawkal,*" which turned the gowzal on his other shoulder into a spear that pierced Grayson's glass and shattered it. The bird did not return as the others had. It lay on the ground between Grayson and Rogedoth. Dead.

An idea struck Trevn. *"Grayson,"* he said. *"The gowzals die when used too long for this magic. What if you told the shadir that gowzals are weak? Suggest they find a stronger creature?"* Trevn scanned the area, but all he saw were the dozens of horses his men had dismounted. He recalled the cavalry charge. *"If you convinced them to go into the horses, could you then command them?"*

"I think so," Grayson voiced.

"Haroan, Bahji, *sabab bay kef,*" Rogedoth yelled.

Two gowzals transformed into fist-sized rocks that shot toward Grayson. He again protected himself with a wall of green light. When the rocks struck the surface, both gowzals shrieked and fell dead to the snow.

"Shadir inside the birds," Grayson yelled. "See how small your hosts are? Easily killed, as you just saw. Why not go into the horses instead? Horses are much stronger than gowzals."

The birds squawked. One flew over onto the back of a nearby horse.

"Iamos!" Rogedoth yelled. "Don't listen to him! He's trying to trick you!"

"I only want to give my friends the strength they deserve," Grayson said. "What do you want for the shadir, I wonder, Master Rogedoth? To control them, it seems to me."

The birds squawked again, and this time three more flew over to the horses.

"Go into the horses, if you want, shadir," Grayson said. "I promise you'll feel much stronger in such noble creatures than you do in those scrawny birds. Horses won't die so easily."

"Shama, *sawkal, daah!*" Rogedoth yelled.

A gowzal from the ground transformed into embers that pelted Grayson. He popped away and reappeared near the horses the gowzals had flown to.

"Go ahead, Seeosi," Grayson said, patting a black horse's nose. "Now that your bird is dead, you should try a horse. Go inside this rouncy." Next he stroked the neck of the white horse beside it. "Bahji, you too. Come and try this courser. It's very fast. I think you'll like it. And, Haroan"—Grayson popped to the other side of the white horse and motioned to a huge war-horse—"you should take this brown destrier. It's much more like a wolf, don't you think?"

"Don't listen to him!" Rogedoth yelled. "Mikray, Iamos, *sabab bay eben!*"

But this time, nothing happened. Trevn had no idea how Grayson knew the names of the creatures, but they appeared to have listened.

"There are more horses here!" Grayson yelled, popping across the clearing. "Iamos, Mikray, come. Ragaz, Daliza. Shama, you too. Over here."

"Isaro!" Rogedoth yelled. "*Sawkal, daah!* Muteeo, Paliki, *sabab bay kef!*"

The shadir seemed to be done listening to Rogedoth, however. Grayson popped around the clearing, guiding shadir into horses, animals that had not been born from a Jiir-Yeke temple sacrifice and therefore were not as susceptible to a mantic's bidding.

Rogedoth continued to yell at shadir, but it earned him no support. "I have given my life to serving you!" he yelled. "I demand you obey me this instant!"

"He *has* been loyal to you," Grayson said. "Go back to him now. In fact, run. Run to your master. Run!" He slapped the rear of the courser beside him.

The horse whinnied and took off at a trot. Grayson popped to the next horse and whacked its backside as well. He moved quickly, frightening the horses and commanding the shadir inside to run, until over two dozen were bolting toward Rogedoth at once.

The former pontiff stared in horror at the approaching animals. "Stop!" he yelled. "Slow down!" But when the horses did not, Rogedoth turned and ran.

He moved quickly for a man of his age, but war-horses—trained for cavalry—could easily outrun even the most terrified of men. The animals trampled Rogedoth, and his bellows of pain and terror made Trevn wince, despite the Justness of the moment.

The horses slowed down and eventually stopped. Trevn sent Grayson after them. "I want the shadir out and the animals back here where they can be of use."

"Yes, sir." Grayson disappeared.

"Soldiers of Armania!" Trevn yelled to the men who were picking themselves up off the ground. "When the horses return, they will be safe for you to ride. Mount one, and capture or kill any of the enemy you see fleeing this area."

Trevn walked with his guards toward the body and finally came to stand over the former pontiff—the Pretender—the man who had caused so much trouble for so many for so long.

No more.

Barthel Rogedoth, Prince Mergest III of Sarikar, was clearly dead, trampled by pounding hooves. Underneath the blood that marred the man's features, Trevn could see skin that was old and withered, a ridged brow, and a long black-and-gray braid. The features that had long haunted him.

"Arman, have mercy on his soul," Trevn said.

"Do you really mean that?" Novan asked.

Trevn thought about it. "Doesn't really matter what I think. Arman is merciful, and he will do what he will do. Of that I have no doubt."

The air and sky felt peaceful and quiet, despite the distant sounds of the occasional clash of swords or a man's cry of pain. Some were still fighting. Trevn should find a horse for himself and ride back to the battle.

A niggling thought tugged at his mind. Rogedoth was dead, but he had forgotten something.

The shadir.

Grayson might have forced them out of the horses, but they were still gathered in the Veil, whether or not Trevn could hear or see them. He suddenly needed to see. He jogged back to Rogedoth's wagon and climbed inside.

"I'm going into the Veil, Cadoc," he said. "Guard my body."

"Yes, sir."

Trevn lay down on the pile of furs and let his soul drift up. Sure enough, the shadir were still congregated in this place. The cloud was so thick, Trevn couldn't see the sky.

"Grayson?" he voiced.

The young man appeared beside him. *"Here, Your Highness."*

"It's time to deal with these creatures."

"There are so many."

"You did perfectly with Kabada. And making the horses charge Rogedoth was brilliant."

Grayson fought a smile.

"You obviously have power over them," Trevn said. *"Why don't you banish the lot of them and be done with it?"*

"Some of them will argue."

"I didn't say it would be easy. But they will obey you."

The young man nodded and blew out a long breath. *"Yes, sir."* He drifted a few paces from Trevn, studied the shadir, then glanced back, a look of reluctance on his face.

Trevn offered his most encouraging smile. Seconds passed by in silence, then suddenly Grayson began to speak.

"Minions of Gâzar," he yelled in that same commanding voice he'd used before. *"Come to me and listen!"*

The horde swept closer, pressing all around Grayson and Trevn in a circle. They were so different, yet so alike. Bright, textured colors in many shapes and sizes. Faces like animals, humans, plants, water, feathers—too many things to imagine. All had at least one eye, or two or three or more. All those eyes were fixed upon Grayson with expressions a mixture of curious, confused, startled, and annoyed.

"I am your master, and you will obey my command," Grayson said. *"Return to Gâzar's realm now. Go back into the arms of darkness where you belong."*

The shadir reacted like an angry mob. Screeched. Hissed. Yelled curses. A few merely glared.

"You will obey me," Grayson said. *"Arman, the One God, is my master, and he has given me the power to command you. By his name you will leave this place."*

For some, that was enough. They shot toward the earth like dropped rocks. Others wilted in size, looking as if their feelings were hurt. The larger ones stayed put, eyes burning with fiery anger.

"A trick!" said one who looked like an old woman.

"Betrayal!" a brown wolf said.

"Treachery!" the golden bird added.

"Do not be fooled," a tattooed man yelled to the smaller shadir. *"He is but a human."*

Many of the smaller shadir stopped moving, eyes fixed upon the larger ones.

"I'm not here to fool you," Grayson said. *"I'm here to send you all home. You are no longer welcome in this realm. Leave and return to your own."*

"Who do you think you are, human?" the old woman asked Grayson.

"I am Arman's chosen," he said. *"And he has given me Dominion over you."*

"Lies!" the old woman hissed.

"We are more powerful than you, little human," the tattooed man said.

"You cannot make us go." This from the golden bird.

"You are nothing," the wolf said, baring its teeth.

The old woman circled Grayson. *"Do you know how many years we have lived?"*

"We don't have to listen to him!" the tattooed man said, and the cloud of shadir crowed their agreement.

"It's not working," Grayson voiced to Trevn's mind. *"The commons are too strong, and they're making the slights brave."*

Trevn drifted behind Grayson and put his hands on the young man's shoulders. *"You can do this! Let me call everyone to pray. Will that help?"*

Grayson shrugged. *"Maybe."*

Trevn called the Veil warriors, who circled around Grayson and joined hands. The air was filled with the sounds of hundreds of shadir screeching, cackling, and goading Grayson. Some pushed up near his face. Others swooped and spun like feathers in the wind.

Onika prayed softly, and Zeroah joined in with her own words. Kempe voiced her agreement, and the rest of them remained silent. Trevn prayed silently that Arman would hear them—that the God would not only protect Grayson but grant him success.

"You will listen to me!" Grayson yelled at the shadir. *"Arman is your master, and by his name you will listen. Return to Gâzar's realm now. I command you!"*

The creatures howled. Some writhed. Some dropped toward the earth, some drifted. Others flew in circles. The mob became a cloud of blurred colors that keened and moaned and wailed. Of the few shadir that remained still enough that Trevn could see them, their eyes rolled back and forth. Some hissed. Others spat curses at the praying humans. Trevn heard one panicked shadir ask another what they should do, but he could not hear the response over the din.

Grayson repeated his command to the shadir. Onika joined in the banishing. Zeroah sang a temple hymn, and Trevn recognized the lyrics from the Book of Arman. Kempe whispered too softly to hear, and Danek and Oli remained silent. Trevn continued to pray, overwhelmed by the strangeness happening around him.

The shadir cloud began to descend. Some still argued and fought and cursed, but any who tried to flee disintegrated like mist. Grayson, Trevn, and the Veil warriors kept at it until the entire horde had fallen beneath the ground, out of sight. Gone.

✦ ✦ ✦

Trevn rode his horse along the southern edge of the battlefield. The setting sun cast a golden sheen over the field of dead and dying men and glimmered on the hundreds of abandoned weapons in their midst. Countless men lay as they had fallen, tangled and broken, some horses too. Trevn spotted three of Rogedoth's red standards lying on the field, rippling in the soft breeze. Horses and carts were being tugged through the carnage in search of those still alive who could be saved. *Very few,* Trevn thought. The carts held more recovered weapons than men.

It was a terrible thing, war.

Trevn steered his horse through the now thawed river and toward the fort. He dismounted near the entrance. His body felt clammy beneath his layers of linen, leather, and bronze. His bones ached. His fingers and toes felt numb. He hadn't realized how very tired he was until he began to walk. He passed through the front door, and the glint of setting sunlight faded away.

Ottee approached, took Trevn's helm and shield. "I have a bath ready, Your Highness."

"You're a good man, Ottee." Trevn patted the boy's back.

He walked slowly up the stairs to the second level, eager to strip off his armor. His bronze breastplate was dented and smudged in blood, the top of his shield had been split practically in two, and a wing on one of the gold Nesher birds from the crown on his helm had been shaved clean off. Still, Trevn's heart soared in his chest. Arman had given them victory over their enemy. Rogedoth was no more. The shadir had been banished from the land. Armania could make peace with the Puru and giants now. Build a future free from tyranny and fear.

The war was over.

CHARLON

That evening, Charlon set up camp near the Armanian soldiers. They celebrated together. Until the dawn hours. Armanian soldiers danced with Magosian maidens. And Charlon demonstrated her magic. For a captive and enthusiastic audience. The soldiers loved her. Lauded her. Worshiped her. This so pleased Charlon that she toasted a new unity. Between their peoples.

As she watched the reveling from her throne, she considered. Considered the old Magonian prophecy of the Deliverer in a new light. King Trevn believed Grayson the Deliverer. Charlon had believed him. At first. Now she was starting to think otherwise.

The prophecy said the child would come "after." After peace had been achieved. Perhaps the Deliverer was the child Charlon now carried. Her own flesh might rise up to rule over all. A pleasant thought. For now, though, the strife between Mother and Father was no more.

Until morning came. And a herald brought a scroll from King Trevn.

Chieftess Charlon,

I am grateful for your assistance in the Battle of Mishor Field. You are a fine warrior and a worthy ally and neighbor. I am glad our realms are at peace.

My soldiers appreciated your lively and vibrant celebration of our shared victory over the Pretender, but my views on shadir magic have not changed. While most of the shadir were banished, it has come to my attention that some remained with you and your birds. Your magic is quite alluring, and Arman's warnings are clear. I cannot risk the potential poisoning of my people and ask you to return to your lands at your earliest convenience. I know you lost many of your men in the battle, so I offer you a royal escort home, should you like, in case Randmuir Khal were to cause you any trouble. At your request I will send a contingent of men to you immediately.

In the future, please send word to me at Castle Armanguard if you have need to enter Armanian lands. With my permission, you will always be welcome.

Trevn Hadar

King of Armania

Leave his territory? Not come again without permission? As if so much of this land was his to claim. Charlon fumed. Staring at the words on the parchment. Heart pounding within. Urging her to respond with threats of her own. To show this king. That he could not command her in any way.

He insults you, her heart said. *Make him pay.*

Charlon wanted to do good in this world. But some people made that difficult. Narrow-minded kings. Kings who had never known the depths of loss That Charlon had suffered.

She crumpled the scroll in her fist. "Rone!" she yelled. "Pen a reply to King Trevn in my name. Thank him for his offer of a royal escort. Ask for twenty men. No, fifty. I want volunteers. Men eager to serve the mantic Chieftess. Have him send them at once."

Rone bowed and went for the parchment. Charlon smiled. She would keep peace with King Trevn. On parchment. But she would not keep her people separate from his. The Armanian soldiers adored her. So she would take her time on the journey home. And make as many as she could her loyal followers. She could not help it. If some refused to return to Armania. And they might. After they saw how enjoyable life was. In Magosia. A realm with freedom and pleasure and magic.

The king sent his men. So eager was he to be rid of her. The fool. Charlon took a long and winding exit. Rode her procession through the Armanian camp. Many soldiers asked questions. Why was she leaving so soon? Where was she going?

Charlon told the truth. King Trevn disdained her magic. Did not want it in Armania.

The soldiers didn't see the harm. Knew it had protected them. Saved them. Some asked if they could visit Magosia. Now that the war had ended. Charlon welcomed them. Anytime.

When asked if she would teach them her magic, she said, "Perhaps."

Once they were away from the camp, Charlon pondered the question. Should she keep the magic to herself? Or share it? Hoarding magic had divided her maidens. Made Roya and Kateen side against her.

She thought back to when she had first come to Magonia. When Roya had discovered she was a woman. And taken her to Mreegan. Mreegan had freed Charlon. Healed her. Given her a new life. In the end, Charlon had despised both Mreegan and Roya. But they had saved her. In the beginning.

Everyone deserved to be free. To find healing. To be made whole. Mreegan had done it for Charlon. And Charlon would do it for any who asked. And if they asked for magic, then she would teach them. This new power was not a limited resource. As evenroot had been. Gowzals bred on their own. Charlon had seen their nests in her village.

Yes. She would teach others magic. If they wanted to learn. She would teach Armanians. Then send them back to Armanguard to teach others. See what King Trevn thought of that.

She chuckled. Liked her plan very much.

QꙨATCH

Qoatch, eunuch slav to High Queen Jazlyn, First Great Lady of New Tenma, stood proudly beside her throne. He had always known her struggles would result in a crown. Now all she needed was to grow her population. Two of her shadir were present. Cherem, the common, and the slight Izar. The other slight, Ziyph, patrolled the harbor.

Qoatch still did not trust shadir, but these three had proved loyal—were all that were left, if he understood the reports of the battle Princess Saria had learned from King Trevn.

"I must choose carriers," Jazlyn said. "But I also must crown my Great Ladies. I dare not make either decision rashly. Speak, Qoatch. What are your thoughts?"

The Tennish remnant numbered only two hundred sixty-eight. Seventy-three of those were eunuch Protectors, twenty-six were children between the ages of six and thirteen—with the exception of Princess Jahleeah—fourteen were male breeders, and the rest were women—twenty-one of which were too old to be carriers.

"Do not force yourself to assign all noble titles right away," Qoatch said. "A Great Lady cannot be settled upon. Choose only those who are worthy and wait until others show themselves as such. This is *New* Tenma, after all. Perhaps you will never choose twelve."

"A wise suggestion," Jazlyn said. "And what of the carriers?"

"Use the same method. Only those you know without a doubt will never be worthy of the status of Great Lady should be made carriers immediately. Any you are unsure of can be assigned other tasks in the meantime—tasks that will reveal their wisdom, bearing, and character. Then you will know who should become a Great Lady, and who should not."

"Princess Nolia should be one," Jazlyn said. "I invited her to come live here, but she is too in love with her idiot husband. I need more women like her. Strong willed and brave. Plus I was hoping she would teach me to better shield my mind. While Ulrik can no longer manipulate my thoughts, I can still hear him. And he has not yet given up in trying to torment me."

The shunned Sarikarian princess had befriended Jazlyn while they were in the New Sarikarian stronghold. When she'd heard the reason Jazlyn had come to fight the giants, Princess Nolia had taught Jazlyn to shield her mind against the voicing magic—against Ulrik, especially.

"Perhaps she and her husband would come for a visit, once we are better established," Qoatch suggested.

Jazlyn frowned. "Perhaps. You were right that Ulrik would be angry about Jael. He has declared war against us to defend his son's honor. I do not think he will find us as long as my shadir remain vigilant lookouts. Do you think I was wrong?"

Qoatch had warned her not to—that such a thing could not be undone—but Jazlyn had not listened. "It is Tennish tradition, lady, to make eunuchs of most of our men. You could not have left your prince a lowly *breeder*. It is not your fault if the emperor doesn't understand our ways."

"You know well enough that I didn't do it for Tennish tradition," Jazlyn said. "I didn't want my son growing up and making heirs in New Rurekau. Now my bloodline will stay here, in New Tenma where it belongs. With me. And Jahleeah."

"You will allow the princess to breed?" Qoatch could not believe it. Great Ladies did not serve as carriers.

"If she wishes to," Jazlyn said. "It will be her choice. In fact, that is a law I might amend."

Qoatch pondered this. Jazlyn would give noblewomen freedom to choose, but not all women. And still no choices for men.

No choice for her son.

In times like this Qoatch thought back to his childhood training with the Kushaw—the Tennish rebels who had believed men worthy of equal rights with women. None of the Kushaw had survived the Five Woes, and Qoatch wasn't prepared to start a new rebellion on his—

A shadir appeared in the center of the throne room, and Qoatch gasped.

Gozan the Great, who had served Jazlyn since before his time. The creature stood on its rear legs, which made him twice as tall as an average man. He had a rat's face, a man's chest and arms, a beast's legs and feet, and black skin covered in coarse hairs.

"Gozan," Jazlyn said, looking bored. "What brings you to New Tenma?"

Qoatch didn't know how she could remain so calm.

Our history together sets you apart, Your Eminence, the creature said. *So I come here to honor you as I would no other human. I once offered you a better way to do magic. I come now to extend that offer one last time before I seek out an alternative.*

Jazlyn glared at the great. "You know better than to come here and offer Dominion."

You never wanted it before, but now that the old magic is dead, I thought perhaps . . .

"I have new magic now," Jazlyn said. "Powers you cannot imagine."

I know all about your new magic, Your Eminence, Gozan said. *I and Chieftess Charlon invented it after we killed Magon.*

"*You* bonded Charlon? The one she called Mitsar?"

Mitsar, Rurek . . . I have many names. He bowed. *At your service, High Queen.*

"I am not interested in your service," Jazlyn spat.

So you no longer wish to live forever?

Her demeanor softened. "What do you mean?"

The new magic can create powerful illusions, Your Eminence, the great said, *but it cannot create immortality. You were wise to have Cherem make permanent your beauty, but he could not have made permanent your age. Surely you have felt the aches and pains?*

Qoatch's heart raced, and he whipped his attention back to Jazlyn, hoping this was incorrect, but the expression on her face betrayed the truth.

"Do you have a point, Gozan?" she asked.

The creature's rat-like eyes fixed upon her, and Qoatch could have sworn he saw triumph there. *I am the only Great shadir still living. If you want immortality, I am the only way.*

Qoatch wanted to scream—to remind his High Queen of the dangers of Dominion. But Gozan had played Jazlyn well. He knew her as well as any being save Qoatch himself.

Jazlyn lifted her chin, and her crown gleamed in the sunlight pouring through the open window. "I suppose it is fitting that the First Great Lady should partner with the first and only Great shadir," she said. "Still, I would like a few days to consider this offer."

Gozan's mouth curled into a grin, baring his pointed teeth. *Take all the time you need, Your Eminence. The High Queen of Tenma must not be rushed.*

"This realm is called *New* Tenma," Jazlyn said.

I see. And what do you call this great city? New Yobatha?

"No," Jazlyn said. "I call it Jaelport, in honor of the son that was taken from me."

Jaelport, Gozan said. *A fine name for a city.*

Trevn

Three months had passed since the Battle of Mishor Field. Trevn and Mielle had gathered with friends in the great hall in New Sarikar. The room was smaller than the one in Castle Armanguard, but the timber walls gave it a luxurious feel that the stone walls back home lacked.

Trevn and Mielle stood in a group with Oli, Sir Kalenek, Miss Onika, and Master Jhorn, discussing the concerns of the father realms.

"Have you heard from Chieftess Charlon, Your Highness?" Sir Kalenek asked.

"I have not," Trevn said. "On parchment we are at peace, but she is still angry." He hadn't wanted magic lingering in Armania, but in spite of his asking Charlon to leave quickly, interest in magic had risen a great deal in his realm.

"Her actions during the battle made her a hero to many Armanians," Oli said.

"Just as High Queen Jazlyn's actions did in Sarikar," Jhorn added.

The soldiers who had witnessed these feats had gone home to family and friends with tales of the mantics who had saved the Father realms from utter destruction. And over half of those Trevn sent to escort the Chieftess home had not returned. "Fallen in love with Magosian women," was the report he'd gotten from those who had come back.

The whole matter frustrated Trevn. "Unfortunately," he said, "none of the soldiers who fought at Mishor Field witnessed the supernatural deeds of Sir Grayson, the prophetess Onika, or any of her Veil warriors."

"Or how Duke Canden and Lady Eudora broke so many compulsions," Mielle said.

Oli favored Mielle with a nod of respect, which pleased Trevn. Those two seemed to have mended their animosity toward one another. He had a feeling it had something to do with Rosârah Zeroah's growing friendship with the duke.

"Saria and I both hired minstrels to write songs of those stories," Trevn said, "some of which will be sung at the reception tonight. Given time, people will learn the truth."

"No offense, Your Highness," Sir Kalenek said, "but minstrels will only turn such stories into legends."

"That is all I can do at present," Trevn said.

"I've been speaking with the Earl of Faynor," Jhorn said. "There have been meetings of magical societies here in Sarikar as well. He is uncertain if it is the same one. I will question the Sarikarians who've been arrested."

A magical society had cropped up in Armania. People had been hunting gowzals as pets in hopes of figuring out how they might make the creatures do magic. No one had succeeded yet—as there were no more shadir in the realm. The society was harmless but for the way they fed the myth that gowzal magic was powerful and worth learning.

"The mantic sympathizers do not understand why I harbor such coldness toward the woman they believe saved Armania," Trevn said.

"That's because they don't know the truth," Oli said.

"We would have won the war without Chieftess Charlon's assistance," Trevn said. "The number of casualties would have been much higher, but Arman's magic would have brought us victory without the aid of shadir."

"I don't doubt you're correct, Your Highness," Jhorn said.

"Indeed, you should have obeyed the God," Onika said. "Then you would have defeated the shadir completely. But now that you have only defeated them partially, they will come again, and next time—like giants appearing as children—you will not recognize them."

Trevn fought back a sigh. This was not the first rebuke he'd received from Onika on this subject. It did not matter that he had asked her advice that day on the battlefield and Arman had been silent. Onika had warned him of the risks, and Trevn had made his decision. The blame for his people's fascination with magic was entirely his.

The doors opened in the back of the great hall, and the herald standing beside the door played a line of notes from the Sarikarian anthem. Trevn and his group parted ways, each moving to their proper places.

Two people entered the hall, and whispers tore through the crowd. Women dabbed handkerchiefs to their eyes. A piper began the "Ballad of the Beloved"—the traditional wedding march for Sarikar—and the pair proceeded up the aisle: the Duke of Pixford escorting Princess Saria, who wore an emerald and ivory gown.

Mielle sniffled beside Trevn, but his eyes were on his friend. Hinck stood at his seat in the front row. Father Wolbair chanted prayers in ancient Armanian, then called Hinck forward with his witnesses—he'd chosen only three: Trevn, Danek, and Oli. While Hinck recited the list of gifts he had offered Princess Saria as a bride-price, Trevn, Danek, and Oli raised a canopy of ivory and gold silk at the front of the aisle. The Duke of Pixford accepted Hinck's offer on behalf of the Sarikarian Council, then left the princess standing alone at the top of the aisle.

"Who wishes to marry this day?" Father Wolbair asked.

"I have come to marry Princess Saria Pitney," Hinck said, his gaze fixed upon her. "And she has come to marry me."

"Is that so, lady?" Father Wolbair asked.

"Yes," she said.

"Then come, both of you, and stand under the holy canopy," Father Wolbair said.

Hinck took Saria's hand, and together they stepped beneath the silk. Trevn did his best to hold still, but his breathing made the canopy tremble.

He watched the ceremony with great amusement. He had warned Hinck not to go to Sarikar. Had the man stayed in Armanguard as Trevn had suggested, he'd be a bachelor still. But these two truly seemed smitten, despite the formal way their betrothal had come about. Trevn was happy for them both.

In the midst of Father Wolbair leading Hinck and Saria in prayers, Trevn caught sight of the entry doors swinging open. He glanced toward them and saw that Ottee had entered.

He reached for the young man's mind. *"Are you looking for me?"* he voiced.

"Yes, sir," Ottee replied. *"I've just received a message from Captain Bussie that the* Seffynaw *has dropped anchor in the Port of Armania."*

Trevn's stomach zinged. Tomorrow morning he and Mielle were going on a trip. This land Wilek had named Er'Rets was vast. There was much to explore, and now that peace had been established, Trevn wanted to map it all.

They would not be gone long, of course, as it was unfair to leave Oli in charge of the kingdom for too long. Upon Arman's word Trevn had vowed to rule Armania. He would not let anything keep him from filling that role.

He put aside all thoughts of his trip and his realm and watched his closest friend pledge a promise of his own. Armania and Sarikar were safe, for now, and with Arman's blessing, they would stay that way for a very long time.

The End.

A Note
From the Author

Thanks for reading *King's War*, the third and final book in The Kinsman Chronicles, which includes the parts *The Reluctant King*, *A Deliverer Comes*, and *Warriors of the Veil*. If you liked the land of Er'Rets, be sure to check out my Blood of Kings trilogy, which takes place five hundred years later and follows the descendants of many characters in this series.

I toyed around with writing an origins prequel to my Blood of Kings trilogy for a long time. I started writing it in February of 2014, and rewrites took me through the end of 2017. It's strange to have an idea and not realize how long it will take to go from concept to final product, but this epic trilogy took four years to complete. I'm thankful to have led Trevn and his companions from the broken and lost Five Realms to a new home in the land of Er'Rets. We all go through dark seasons in our life. My purpose in writing this series was to show that no matter what darkness people might find themselves living in, those who rely on their creator will find their way back into the light (Isaiah 9:2).

I love to hear from my readers. You can email me through my website and sign up for my Sanctum newsletter to get updates on upcoming books and events. If you'd like to help make this series a success, tell people about it, loan your copy to a friend, give it as a present, or ask your library or bookstore to order it. Writing a book review for online stores is also very helpful.

Discussion questions for THE KINSMAN CHRONICLES series can be found online at www.jillwilliamson.com/discuss.

If you'd like to see a larger version of Trevn's map of Er'Rets, check out the book's Pinterest inspiration page. You can also discover a lot of fun extras by visiting my website at www.jillwilliamson.com/books/kinsman-chronicles.

Acknowledgments

To my husband, Brad, and my amazing editors, Dave and Elisa, thank you for all of your help, your patience, your questions, and clever insight on this book. The story was so much better, thanks to you three.

A special thanks to author John Otte for bringing out the moose antlers to talk me through magic and ethics and all kinds of random story troubles, to horse expert and author Gillian Bronte Adams for helping get my horse details right, and to Melanie Dickerson for helping me brainstorm political intrigue between royalty and their nobles.

I'd also like to thank the Readers of Jill Williamson Facebook group and my street team for all their continued support and for helping me brainstorm during the course of this series. Special thanks to Lisa Gefrides, Carissa Barrows, Jennie Webb, Dana Black, Jessica Casella Dowell, Mindy Chumbley, Elisabeth Wheatley, Jeff Schenker, Bethany Baldwin, and Alexandria K. Mintah.

To my family and friends who have been patiently waiting for me to finish these epic books and come up for air: I did it! This trilogy is done. Thanks for listening and praying and being there. I appreciate you all.

And thanks also to you, my faithful readers, for reading this epic adventure. Arman be with you all.

ABOUT THE AUTHOR

Jill Williamson writes fantasy and science fiction for teens and adults. Jill grew up in Alaska, staying up and reading by the summer daylight that wouldn't go away. This led to a love of books and writing, and her debut novel, *By Darkness Hid*, won several awards and was named a Best Science Fiction, Fantasy, and Horror novel of 2009 by *VOYA* magazine. She also has written several books on the craft of writing fiction and teaches writing in person and online at www.StoryworldFirst.com and at www.GoTeenWriters.com, which was named as one of *Writer's Digest*'s "101 Best Websites for Writers." She lives in the Pacific Northwest with her husband and two children. To learn more about her novels, visit her online at www.jillwilliamson.com.

Sign Up for Jill's Newsletter!

Keep up to date with Jill's news on book releases, signings, and other events by signing up for her email list at jillwilliamson.com.

Don't Miss Book One in This Series!

Prince Wilek's father believes the disasters plaguing their land signal impending doom, but he thinks this is superstitious nonsense—until he is sent to investigate a fresh calamity. What he discovers is more cataclysmic than he could've imagined. Wilek sets out on a desperate quest to save his people, but can he succeed before the entire land crumbles?

King's Folly, THE KINSMAN CHRONICLES #1

BETHANYHOUSE

More Fantasy from Bethany House

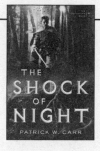

Reeve Willet Dura is called to investigate when a brutal attack leaves one man dead and a priest mortally wounded. As he begins questioning the priest, the man pulls him close, cries out in a foreign tongue—and dies. This strange encounter sets off a series of events that pull Willet into an epic conflict that threatens his entire world.

THE DARKWATER SAGA: *The Shock of Night, The Shattered Vigil, The Wounded Shadow*
by Patrick W. Carr
patrickwcarr.com

As a dynasty nears its end, an unlikely hero embarks upon a perilous quest to save his kingdom. Thrust into a world of dangerous political intrigue and church machinations, Errol Stone must leave behind his idle life, learn to fight, come to know his God—and discover his destiny.

THE STAFF AND THE SWORD: *A Cast of Stones, The Hero's Lot, A Draw of Kings*
by Patrick W. Carr
patrickwcarr.com

❖ BETHANYHOUSE